KU-311-415

ENGLEBY

It is the 1970s, and Mike Engleby is a university student, having survived a 'traditional' school. A man devoid of scruple or self-pity, Engleby provides a disarmingly frank account of English education. Yet beneath the disturbing surface of his observations lies an unfolding mystery of gripping power. When one of his contemporaries unaccountably disappears, the reader has to ask: is Engleby capable of telling the whole truth? *Engleby* can be read as a lament for a generation and the country it failed. It is also a poignant account of the frailty of human consciousness: heart-wrenching, funny — and written in the deepest shade of black.

Books by Sebastian Faulks
Published by The House of Ulverscroft:

THE GIRL AT THE LION D'OR
CHARLOTTE GRAY
ON GREEN DOLPHIN STREET

SEBASTIAN FAULKS

◆

ENGLEBY

Complete and Unabridged

CHARNWOOD
Leicester

First published in Great Britain in 2007 by
Hutchinson
The Random House Group Limited, London

First Charnwood Edition
published 2008
by arrangement with
The Random House Group Limited, London

British Library CIP Data

Faulks, Sebastian
    Engleby.—Large print ed.—
    Charnwood library series
    1. Great Britain—Social conditions—Fiction
    2. Large type books
    I. Title
    823.9'14 [F]

    ISBN 978-1-84782-042-6

Published by
F. A. Thorpe (Publishing)
Anstey, Leicestershire

Set by Words & Graphics Ltd.
Anstey, Leicestershire
Printed and bound in Great Britain by
T. J. International Ltd., Padstow, Cornwall

This book is printed on acid-free paper

For Gillon Aitken

'It is a small part of life we really live. Indeed, all the rest is not life but merely time.'

From *On the Shortness of Life*
by Seneca, AD49

1

My name is Mike Engleby, and I'm in my second year at an ancient university. My college was founded in 1662, which means it's viewed here as modern. Its chapel was designed by Hawksmoor, or possibly Wren; its gardens were laid out by someone else whose name is familiar. The choir stalls were carved by the only woodcarver you've ever heard of. The captain of the Boat Club won a gold medal at an international games last year. (I think he's studying physical education.) The captain of cricket has played for Pakistan, though he talks like the Prince of Wales. The teachers, or 'dons', include three university professors, one of whom was on the radio recently talking about lizards. He's known as the Iguanodon.

Tonight I won't study in my room because there's the weekly meeting of the Folk Club. Almost all the boys in my college go to this, not for the music, though it's normally quite good, but because lots of girl students come here for the evening. The only boys who don't go are those with a work compulsion, or the ones who think folk music died when Bob Dylan went electric.

*   *   *

There's someone I've seen a few times, called Jennifer Arkland. I discovered her name because

1

she stood for election to the committee of a society. On the posters, the candidates had small pictures of themselves and, under their names and colleges, a few personal details. Hers said: 'Second-year History exhibitioner. Previously educated at Lymington High School and Sorbonne. Hobbies: music, dance, film-making, cooking. Would like to make the society more democratic with more women members and have more outings.'

I'd seen her in the tea room of the University Library, where she was usually with two other girls from her college, a fat one called Molly and a severe dark one, whose name I hadn't caught. There was often Steve from Christ's or Dave from Jesus sniffing round them.

I think I'll join this society of hers. It doesn't matter what it's for because they're all the same. They're all called something Soc, short for Society. Lab Soc, Lit Soc, Geog Soc. There's probably a knitting group called Sock Soc.

I'll find out about Jen Soc, then go along so I can get to know her better.

* * *

I won a prize to come to my college and it pays my fees; my family's poor. I took a train from school one day after I'd sat the exams and had been called for interview. I must have stayed in London on the way, but I have no memory of it. My memory's odd like that. I'm big on detail, but there are holes in the fabric. I do remember that I took a bus from the station, though I didn't know then what my college looked like. I went round the whole city and ended up back at the station, having made the round trip. Then I took a taxi and had to borrow some money from the porter to pay for it. I still had a pound note in my wallet for emergencies.

They gave me a key to a bedroom; it was in a courtyard that I reached by a tunnel under the road. I imagined what kind of student lived there normally. I pictured someone called Tony with a beard and a duffel coat. I tried really hard to like the room and the college that was going to be mine. I imagined bicycling off to lectures in the early morning with my books balanced on a rack over the back wheel. I'd be shouting out to the other guys, 'See you there!' I'd probably smoke a pipe. I'd also probably have a girlfriend — some quite stern grammar school girl with glasses, who wouldn't be to everyone's taste.

In fact, I didn't like the room I was in that night. It was damp, it was small and it felt as though too many people had been through it. It didn't seem old enough; it didn't seem 17th century, or modern: it was more like 1955. Also, there was no bathroom. I found one up the stairs. It was very cold and I had to stay dressed until the bath was run. The water itself was very hot. Everything in the room and on the stairs smelled slightly of gas, and lino.

I slept fine, but I didn't want to have breakfast in the dining hall because of having to talk to the other candidates. I went along the street and found a café and had weak coffee and a sausage roll, which I paid for from my spare pound. I re-entered the college by the main gate. The porter was sullen in his damp lodge with a paraffin heater. 'G12, Dr Woodrow's rooms,' he said. I found it all right, and there was another boy waiting outside. He looked clever.

Eventually, the door opened and it was my turn. There were two of them in there: a big schoolmasterly man who showed me to a chair, then sat down at a desk; and a younger, thin man with a beard who didn't get up from his armchair. Teachers at my school didn't have beards.

'You wrote well on Shakespeare. Do you visit the theatre a good deal?' This was the big one talking. It sounded too much like an ordinary conversation to be an interview. I suspected a trap. I told him there wasn't a theatre where we lived, in Reading.

I was watching him all the time. How grand, to be a Doctor of whatever and to weigh up and decide people's future. I'd once seen a set of table mats in a shop which had pictures of men in different academic gowns: Doctor of Divinity, Master of Arts and so on. But this was the first real one I'd seen. He asked me a few more things, none of them interesting.

' . . . the poetry of Eliot. Would you care to make a comparison between Eliot and Lawrence?'

This was the younger one, and it was his first contribution. I thought he must be joking. An American banker interested in the rhythms of the Anglican liturgy and a pitman's son who wanted to escape from Nottingham, maybe via

4

sex, or by his crude paintings. Compare them? I looked at him carefully, but he showed no sign of humour so I gave an answer about their use of verse forms, trying to make it sound as though it had been a reasonable question. He nodded a few times and looked relieved. He didn't follow it up.

The big one leafed through my papers again. 'Your personal report,' he said at last, 'from your teacher . . . Did you have difficulties with him?'

I hadn't been aware of any, I said.

'Is there anything that you'd like to ask us about life in college? We try to make everyone feel welcome.'

It seemed wrong not to ask something; it might look as though I didn't care. But I couldn't ask any of the things I really wanted to know. In the silence we heard the college clock chime the half-hour. I felt them both looking at me. Then I felt a trickle of sweat on my spine. I hardly ever sweat normally, and it gave me an idea.

'What's the thing with laundry?'

'What?' said the big one, gruffly.

'Do you have . . . Well, like, washing machines? Is it done centrally or do I take it somewhere or what?'

'Gerald?'

'I'm not quite sure,' said the younger one.

'Each undergraduate is assigned a moral tutor,' said the schoolmasterly one. 'A Fellow of the college who can help you with all your personal and health questions.'

'So he'd be the one to ask?'

'Yes. Yes, I imagine so.'

I thought that now I'd broken the ice, it might be good to ask another question. 'What about money?' I said.

'What?'

'How much money will I need?'

'I imagine your local authority will provide a grant. It's up to you how you spend it. Do you have questions about the work?'

'No. I read the prospectus.'

'Do you find the idea of Chaucer daunting?'

'No, I like Chaucer.'

'Yes, yes, I can see that from your paper. Well, Mr Engle . . . er . . . '

'Engleby.'

'Englebury. You can go now, unless . . . Gerald?'

'No, no.'

'Good. So we'll look forward to seeing you next autumn.'

I didn't see how they could let me go without telling me how it had gone. 'Have I won a prize?' I said.

'We shall be writing to your school in due course. When we've completed the interview process. It's an exceptional year.'

I shook his offered hand, waved at the seated one and went out, down the oak stairs. What a pair of frauds.

★　★　★

In the evening I tear a ticket from a book and take it to the college dining hall, which was

6

designed by Robert Adam. You have to buy a book of thirty-five every term; you don't actually have to use them, but the cash you pay in advance keeps the kitchen going. I'm wearing a long black gown over my jeans and sweater and there are candles in sconces on the painted plaster walls. We stand up when a door behind the top table opens and the Fellows of the college come in to dine. The Master is an oceanographer, who once drew maps of undersea mountain ranges. He knows how Australia was once attached to China or how Ghana sweated in the foothills of the Andes. I think he imagines that New Zealand once broke free from Germany.

The crystal glasses glitter in the candlelight. They drink wine. We drink water, though you are allowed to ask for beer if you like. Stellings is the only man to do this.

'A pint of ale, please, Robinson,' he says to the stooping butler. 'Beer for you, Mike?'

I shake my head. Stellings brews his own beer in a plastic barrel. He calls it SG (short for student's gin: drunk for a penny, dead drunk for twopence) and once forced me to drink it, even though it made me sick, with its powerful taste of malt and raw alcohol, which he achieves by doubling the sugar input recommended on the side of the kit. There is no bathroom near his room, so I had to vomit into a plastic watering can on the landing.

I sometimes don't take dinner in the dining hall. I've found some places I like better. One of them is a pub, a walk of ten or fifteen minutes

7

away, over a green (there are a lot of greens or 'pieces' as they call them here), down a side street, up a back street. The beer there tastes much better than Stellings's homebrew. It's made by a brewery called Greene King. One of the King family, they say, is a famous novelist. The lights here are low, the floor is made of wooden boards; the other people are not from the university. They are what are called ordinary people, though each person is really too specific to be ordinary. It's quite dark, and people talk softly. Although the barman knows me, he doesn't intrude. I often have a baked potato, or a cheese and ham pie, which is messy to eat because the melted cheese is stringy and there's so much of it between the layers of filo pastry.

I also drink gin and vermouth, mixed. I like red vermouth better than white. When I've drunk two or three of these, I feel I understand the world better. At least, I don't mind so much that I don't understand it; I can be tolerant of my ignorance. After three or four, I feel that my ignorance is not only tolerable, but possibly in some way noble.

Other times, I go into the middle of the town. There's a bright Greek restaurant there, where it's embarrassing to be seen alone — but I like the food: they bring moussaka with rice and with chips and with Greek salad and pitta bread with olives and hummus, so if you're hungry it's a good place to go. Sometimes I don't eat for two or three days, so I need to load up. With this Greek food I drink white wine that tastes of toilet cleaner, and they go together well.

I also take drugs. I've tried most things. My favourite is opium, though I've had it only once. It's really hard to get hold of and involves a palaver with a flame and a pipe. I bought it from a boy who got it from a Modern History Fellow in Corpus Christi who had recently been to the Far East. The thing about opium is that it makes pain or difficulty unimaginable. If while you were under its influence someone were to tell you about Zyklon B and your parents dying and life in a dementia ward or Passchendaele, you might be able to understand what they meant — but only in a hypothetical sense. You might be interested by this idea of 'pain', but in a donnish way. I mean, I'm 'interested' in the special theory of relativity; the idea that there's a dimension in which space rolls up and time distorts and you come back from a journey younger than you left is certainly intriguing, but it doesn't have an impact on me, day by day. That's what opium does to suffering: makes it of hypothetical interest only.

I mostly smoke marijuana, which I buy from a boy called Glynn Powers. I don't know where Glynn buys it, but he has several kilos of it in the built-in bedside locker in his tiny room in the new Queen Elizabeth block, a short walk beyond Fellows' Pieces (i.e. grass area reserved to dons). The block was opened by a princess only three years ago and in the entrance hall of the building, next to the commemorative plaque, there's a picture of her standing in one of the little cells, smiling at the president, with the bedside locker in view behind them. The brickwork of the wall is exposed because they discovered when the building was completed that the size of each room was smaller than the minimum required for single human habitation by the Department of Housing. By removing the plasterboard they were able to add just enough volume to go legal.

In his bedside locker, Glynn keeps polished scales and brass imperial weights. *Mene, mene, tekel, upharsin*: you have been weighed in the scale, balanced and found wanting. Not that I'd argue with Glynn Powers or tell him he was wanting in any way at all. He wears a leather jacket with a thin fringe of tassels halfway down the back; he has a thick, trimmed beard and a motorbike. I have neither. He is studying Engineering. He doesn't smoke himself, which I find sinister.

And tonight is Folk Club, as I said. This happens in the college bar, because you can't have folk music without beer — in this case Double Diamond or gassy Worthington E. Brian, the professional barman who does the first two hours (after which the students take over), offers a free pint if you can drink one in less than five seconds. I have seen it done.

Bicycles start to arrive at about seven. There are striped scarves, coats; small, cheap cigarettes; most of the boys have hair to their shoulders, much of it grown out from a previous schoolboy style, so they still have a parting in the undergrowth. There are printed posters in the quads and linking passages. Hobgoblin, they announce. Avalon. With support: The Tim

10

Wills/Steve Murray Band. After the interval: Lyonesse. With special guests: Split Infinitive.

When there are enough people in the bar, I move in among them. It must once have been a cellar, I suppose. The walls are white brick. They start to sweat.

I've drunk some gin in my room and have taken a Nembutal, which makes you feel detached. I'm smoking a cigarette. I really love cigarettes. I like the moist fragrance of the ones you roll yourself and I like Rothman's King Size, advertised by a man's hand emerging from a sleeve with gold hoops to grasp a gear lever. (Why is the pilot or naval officer still wearing his uniform in his car? Is he trying to impress an unseen woman? Is the gear lever a symbol? In which case, shouldn't it be *her* hand on it?) I like the small piece of paper, like a miniature bookmark, that you pull up inside to arrange the fags in a little castle shape that makes it easier to extract the first one. (Now I come to think of it, this is one of the most courteous, customer-loving things any manufacturer has ever done. To go to the trouble of folding in this thin strip of paper, just so the smoker shouldn't be irritated by trying to fish the first one out of a tightly packed bunch and risk squashing the others . . . Ingenious, thoughtful and quite irrelevant after the first cigarette, whose absence leaves space for the remainder to be slipped out easily. One day an accountant will calculate that the infinitesimal saving of not including the strip, magnified by the huge number of packets sold, will enable the companies to make an extra one thousand pounds a year profit, and they'll stop doing it. For the sake of one thousand quid.) Another thing I like about smoking is allowing a small amount of smoke to escape from my lips then reeling it in again with a fast and deep inhalation. I like Gold Leaf, which used to be advertised on television by a man on a hillside with a red setter, or was it a spaniel? I like the mildness of Piccadilly. I like the toasted taste of Lucky Strike and Chesterfield and the way that French cigarettes hit the back of the throat like a blowtorch when you inhale. The best thing is the combined effect of nicotine with alcohol, greater than the sum of the two parts.

I change brands a lot. I'm smoking white-tipped Kent tonight and have a pleasant taste of tobacco and red vermouth, which I've bought from the bar. The boy on the bar doesn't know how much to pour, which is all right because he's given me a full wine glass, into which I have put ice. I'll try to make this last an hour.

On the sofas and armchairs there are piles of coats, and as the evening goes on and people dance, there are also sweaters, jackets, bags. I can see Jennifer and Molly and Anne, and I keep a close watch on them. Avalon have a violinist and a girl with very straight long hair in a crushed velvet dress who sings with a warble in her voice.

I imagine these folk songs go back many years, into some oral tradition. I make a note of some words. 'I have for to say,/My own true love,/Is gone far away/In the [inaudible] lights of noon./And weep shall I never/Keen no more/ 'Neath the mantle of the moon./So fare thee well

12

and fare thee well/Said the sailor to his lass/For the silvery light of the Hebden Down [?]/Has brought us to this pass, kind sir,/Has brought us to this pass.' It's hard to hear exactly what she sings because the drums are so loud. I don't think the first bard envisaged a mike with a grey blanket in the body of the bass drum.

I'm now propped up by a sweating pillar ... I'm watching. My body stays supported. ''Neath the mantle of the moon, kind sir . . . ' I shall return to Folk Club, to the present moment, loud and smoky, but for the moment I let myself go.

*　*　*

I have a car which I keep in the car park of the Queen Elizabeth building, which is reserved for the Fellows. Sometimes the porters glue pieces of paper with strong reminders (and a split infinitive as a matter of fact) to the windscreen to dissuade me from parking there. I peel them off.

Then I drive out to one of the villages. They have three-digit fingerposts dug into turf in the triangle where the roads meet. They have milestones leaning back a little by the hedgerows that in summer are heavy with hawthorn and cow parsley. They have war memorials (which I, perhaps alone, read) and brick-and-flint churches. They have pubs. Above all, they have pubs, and the beer in them doesn't come like the stuff in the college bar from a metal cask, pressurised by the addition of carbon dioxide, which makes it taste of chemical soda water. In these pubs the untreated beer is drawn by a hand pump from the cellar through a long thin tube and makes a whoosh as it swirls up the glass, chestnut-amber, then falls as the handle is returned to its upright; then surges again, sparkling to the rim as the handle is pulled a second time; stops with a thin white froth, then receives a final half-squirt; after which the base of the glass is wiped on the towelling mat where you leave it for a moment for the beer to catch the light from the false-antique light brackets of the Wheatsheaf, the Green Man, the Red Lion — a place where anyone can go, where social ties are cut, so you're frictionless, you're no one.

Does it sound as though I'm trying to keep something at bay here? Perhaps, but I don't know what.

Occasionally I stay the night, but not because I'm worried about driving. They normally have a room or two: damp, with a candlewick bedspread and a bathroom at the end of the landing. It's not an idyll. I don't bother with breakfast. I just want to be on the road. Undergraduates aren't allowed cars, but I joined a golf club called Royal Worlington (I never go there) and that was enough for them to make an exception. They encourage sport. My car's a bottle green Morris 1100, bought fourth-hand for £125, most of which I earned by working in a factory. It's never broken down, though once the exhaust pipe fell off

14

and I had to wire it back. I drive all over eastern England, in fact. Sandy, Potton, Biggleswade, Newport Pagnell, Huntingdon, Saffron Walden; even up to King's Lynn or Lincoln. There are houses on modern estates, houses by the side of the road, houses up drives with laurel hedges.

Who are these people? I ask myself. Who on earth are they? I carry golf clubs in the boot of the car and sometimes stop and play a few holes when I see a course. Usually, the club secretary is unfriendly and the green fee is expensive.

⋆ ⋆ ⋆

. . . And now, back live, we have special guests Split Infinitive. No one can hear themselves talk. I see Jennifer crane up to Nick, who bends his head to bellow in her ear, but she pulls away and smiles and shakes her head to say she still hasn't caught what he had to say, and he shrugs, as though to say it wasn't much anyway, which I can believe. Molly, Dave, Julia and several other people I don't know are dancing. When I try to move over to the bar to get another drink, I find my shoes have stuck. The rubber of the soles makes a sound like tearing paper as it pulls away from the soaked floor. The air smells of beer and sweat and No. 6.

It's cold outside where people in unironed tee shirts go to cool off and find the moisture dry on their faces. The breeze comes through the funnelling passage and makes your chest ache. Folk Club. It's the best night of the week.

* ★ ★

I went to a meeting of Jen Soc the other day. It was in Jesus, where I've never been before. There were queues to see a play called *The Crucible*. I think the charter of every college obliges it once a year to stage either *The Crucible*, *The Threepenny Opera,* or *The Good Person of Szechwan*. *The Crucible*'s about a group of American Puritans called Goody this and Goody that; it has self-righteousness and modern parallels. Students like it because it makes them feel enfranchised.

Jesus is unforgiving. Lose your bearings as you come in, and you're in trouble. Other colleges follow a pattern: a wooden door within a larger gate off the pavement by the street. But Jesus is unique; it's more like going to a school set in its own grounds. Next to one of the games pitches is a half-timbered pavilion.

By the time I found the room in a creeper-covered courtyard such as Billy Bunter might have lived in, the meeting was under way. I crept in to see a vote being taken on what our line was on Allende's Chile, whether we should vote aid to Nicaragua, if the sub should go up to fifty pence a time and if so whether this should include wine or only, as now, coffee and biscuits. I was for wine, perhaps from Chile, but didn't think I should say so at my first meeting, especially since on the way I'd drunk two pints of Abbot's Ale at the Footballers to wash down the blue ten-milligram pill I take each evening. Then there was the question of the summer

16

outing and where this should go. Managua, it seemed, was out of the question, but Paris was a possibility. Several boys complained that they didn't have enough money; they did this in such a way as to make Jennifer (who'd suggested Paris) sound like Marie Antoinette. The word 'working class' was used by one, of himself, and caused a warm ripple; I sensed at least two of the girls edge in their seats towards the boy who wouldn't go to Paris.

After the meeting we hung around and talked and worked through the coffee and the biscuits. Jennifer remained relaxed and indiscriminately friendly, despite the Paris thing. I wondered what her room was like. What was her life like? Lymington High School. Did her parents still live there? Where exactly was Lymington? She was wearing new flared jeans over leather boots and a grey polo neck in what might have been cashmere. In fact, it wasn't quite a polo neck; the collar fell away at the front, as part of the design, like a small hood in reverse. I don't know what that's called; but it showed the skin of her throat, which was slightly flushed. Her hair was fair and wavy, but quite fine; when she pushed it back behind her ear on one side I saw a couple of small moles beneath her ear, just above the grey cashmere. She was gathering papers into her bag and saying goodbye to people; her bag was of dark tan leather with a suggestion of the cartridge belt or Sam Browne.

★   ★   ★

17

Sometimes I imagine what it must be like to be in a young women's college. This is what I think it could be like:

It's teatime on Friday in November. Mist is coming off the river and is drifting up towards the Victorian buildings where the girl students live, a short distance out of town. The road is lit by the lamps of bicycles; cars pass at their peril, slowly, because the pedalling girls, some frizzy and stout, some slight and eager, the girls with their lights front and rear, are the queens of the highway.

In the college, the kettle's on and the curtains are drawn since there's no daylight left in the Fens. East of the town, there are no hills until you come to the Urals, so they say, which explains why it's so cold, because there's nothing to stop the wind from the Russian steppe. This is one of those things they tell you when you first arrive, and you're meant to pass it on or tell your family about it in a letter. It's like a shibboleth or password, to show you're local now.

Back from games, the girls are flushed; their faces are red from the Ural wind. Red Russian wind from communist mountains, from the giant Soviet factories. Some girls are returning on foot from town, where they've been to the University Library or to the shops. Jennifer is running down the corridor, lively with the sense of her good fortune. Her friend Anne's a Northern girl, dark. They're having tea now in Anne's room, which has a gas ring. Molly

18

comes in with cake she bought in town: a sponge cake with cherries. They sit on chairs and floors and beds. There isn't much room, but there's always music on Anne's cheap record player at this time of day: a balladeer, a minstrel, shock-haired with a guitar — afternoon songs for girls in jeans with coloured silk scarves knotted or held with silver woggles from Morocco. They wear little make-up; Anne has small round glasses. Cat Stevens is the singer. It's said the *Jewish Chronicle* had an article wondering if his real name was Steven Katz. He *looks* quite Jewish; he could be.

They ought to work, but they have to go to dinner in the dining hall at six-thirty and by the time they've finished tea it won't seem worth opening books for half an hour. So they talk instead. Jennifer's reading Carlos Castaneda, Anne has *Jonathan Livingston Seagull* hidden under a pillow. Anyway, they've already been to lectures today in History, Physics and Anthropology, and to supervisions with a don. They talk and talk over the music. Molly's family is from Portsmouth. She talks of her boyfriend and whether he'll come to visit; her breath is warm with tea and cherries. Will he at least come to the summer ball? The other two are sympathetic. Boys are difficult to understand, in their opinion. They're like stage flats: colourful, exciting. Flat.

Jennifer has enough friends in her girls' college not to mind about boyfriends. Anne sometimes tries to make her more interested in them because she finds Jennifer's detachment unconvincing. She doesn't want to admit how much she herself thinks about men, or more particularly, a man, *the* man — a being as yet so incompletely imagined that all aspects are provisional, except one: he's male.

There are noises in the corridor. Laughter, crockery, music suddenly through an open door, which is then banged shut.

The lives of these young women make a sort of harmony. Their goodwill towards one another sets a tone in which intimacy can flourish; they're happy.

Dinner bell rings. Lights fade . . .

That's what I think it might be like, but I don't really know.

Perhaps all that mist and goodwill, that music and cake . . . It's just *sentimental*.

The truth is probably more like this:

Anne, Molly and Jennifer are, like all women, weirdly obsessed by appearances — looks, colours, fashion, surfaces; they have no interest in ideas or deeper truths, only 'style' and status and the rapacious purchase of goods to underline them. Their cordiality conceals a sense of bitter rivalry that they'll carry to their deaths, without ever acknowledging it. Anne and Jennifer pretend to care about Barry or Gary or whatever Molly's boyfriend is called, but what they're really both intent on is finding a richer, handsomer and better man of their own.

They have no genuine interest in one another, because they are beings who live close to the ground. For all the lecture notes they've taken today, they're really machines for surviving in the competition for resources. Carrying the species in their wombs, they have to be.

Maybe that's little too much the other way, a bit severe. I wonder if we can ever know what it's like to be someone else. I doubt whether even Jennifer or Molly or Anne *really* know what it's like to be themselves. They probably take the crucial things for granted — because they've never known what it's like not to have them. What they talk about, or try to change, or think of as being important, are really trivial things, I expect. They're like a cat who wonders about its tail or eyes without knowing that the really distinctive thing about it is that it's feline.

I don't imagine they can help that. They can't see it any more than I can see what's peculiar about me. One thing I feel reasonably certain about, however, is this: that these girls are better adapted than we are. They have balance; they have a flair for living.

* * *

Most nights, I go out alone. There's this hotel called the Bradford where the barman's a transvestite. I quite often look in there for a drink. Come to think of it, the barman in the Waterfall is also a transvestite; at least, he has a

21

wig and make-up, though he does wear men's trousers. No one seems to comment on the fact that the barmaid in the Bradford is obviously a man, but I quite like it. There are a lot of pubs in this city. There's a tiny one called the Footballers just near the one I mentioned before, where I go for dinner. In the Footballers, the landlord sleeps on the floor behind the bar all afternoon and you have to wake him up at six o'clock when he's meant to reopen. His dog does a trick with bottle tops.

After the Bradford, I usually go to the Kestrel, where American aircrews burned their names into the ceiling while they were stationed nearby in the War. There are too many alcoholics in the Kestrel for my taste. What is an alcoholic? Someone who'll steal money from his only friend to buy a drink because the drink is more important and he'd rather lose the friend. I can't admire that.

A pair of goofy scientists came swaggering into the Kestrel at lunchtime one day many years ago to say that — just an hour earlier — they'd figured out the shape of human chemistry, of the molecule itself. I don't think the boozers in the Kestrel were impressed. I don't think this discovery was an answer to any of the top one hundred questions the Kestrel regulars would have liked an answer to — even if you allow for the fact that numbers one to fifteen were probably 'Whose round is it?'

That's part of the trouble with science. It doesn't always help. I don't find it useful to know that particles may appear in different places without having travelled the distance in between. I don't find it enlightening that the only truthful way of thinking of Herr Schrödinger's cat is as being simultaneously alive and dead. In fact, I don't believe it is the only truthful way of thinking of it. It may be the only logical way of thinking of it, but that's a different matter, isn't it? The real problem, though, is that I don't recall asking after the welfare of his cat in the first place.

'Here, this'll interest you . . . ' I used to dread what was to come when someone said that to me as a child. Or worse still, 'Have I told you my cat story?' 'Do you have a dog story?' I felt like countering. Or rather, 'I'll tell you what *would* interest me. Then you tell me if you have anything in that line.'

Heisenberg and Bohr and Einstein strike me as being like gifted retriever dogs. Off they go, not just for an afternoon, but for ten years; they come back exhausted and triumphant and drop at your feet . . . A vole. It's a remarkable thing in its way, a vole — intricate, beautiful really, marvellous. But does it . . . Does it help? Does it move the matter on?

When you ask a question that you'd actually like to know the answer to — what was there before the Big Bang, for instance, or what lies beyond the expanding universe, why does life have this inbuilt absurdity, this non sequitur of death — they say that your question can't be answered, because the terms in which you've put it are logically unsound. What you must do, you see, is ask vole questions. Vole is — as we have agreed — the answer; so it follows that your questions *must therefore all be vole-related.*

* * *

After the Kestrel, I sometimes drive out to one of the villages, it doesn't matter which one or what it's called — it might be Great, Little, Much or Long Standing. I listen to the car radio, which has been adapted by a garage to take audio cassettes, and I put the music up loud and think of Julie, my younger sister. She's keen on music, though of course we don't like the same things because she's only twelve. T. Rex, she likes. 'She's faster than most,/And she lives on the coast.' Get away, Jules. When she was very small, we used to put the record player on and make her dance. She used to like that. She wasn't much good at dancing, she just used to jump from one foot to the other in a short dress and you could see a big bulge of nappy under her navy blue woollen tights; but she had this look on her face, as though she was surprised at her good fortune in being alive at all.

I prefer not to think of it because it makes me feel bad.

I don't like staying in my room at night. I want to go out. There's nothing to do in my room. It has a poster for a concert by Quicksilver Messenger Service and a cork noticeboard on which I've stuck some pictures I pulled out of magazines. It has a sort of drinks cupboard in one corner, though I don't suppose it was intended for drinks. I keep some glasses and a bottle each of red and white vermouth in it. Plus gin if I can afford it. I have a plastic ice bucket I got from a petrol station and there's a fridge in the communal kitchen halfway up the stairs where I can get ice. The furniture is about twenty years old. It was worn out by people discussing Jean-Paul Sartre and the Korean War. I wouldn't say it has seen better days, because by all accounts that I've read, those days weren't better: the 1950s were like a tundra that they had to cross; but it's certainly past its best, the furniture.

On the other side of the sitting room, I have a bedroom. Just off it is a shower. It's in a glass cubicle, and the shower head is on a three-inch spout. Most students have to walk a long way to a bathroom block because their rooms were built before people understood about washing. To have your own shower is pretty much unheard of; I think it's a privilege that may be connected to the prize I won.

I tried it once. The nozzle of the shower head is about the diameter of a ten-pence piece. The water was very cold, then very hot. The degree of wetness I achieved was about what you might expect from the thing that squirts a car windscreen, but without the wipers to spread the water round.

There was something typical of my university in this, I thought. At some places, the senior dons go on television. They sit on panels and give opinions on the news, write columns in the papers or get paid to travel the world explaining the origins of language, minerals or cave paintings. They turn up at the Prime Minister's birthday party or at the opening of a new play at the National Theatre. They're pictured at the Ritz or driving down Piccadilly with a slightly intellectual actress. But the most famous philosopher from my university spent the last ten years of his life in his college room designing the lettering for his headstone.

I sleep late in the morning, and the woman who's meant to clean my room, the bedmaker as she's called, doesn't disturb me. I've only met her once. She looked like a female impersonator. Now I lock the outer door when I go to bed. This means that my room is not very clean, but then again the terms are quite short. And if I know I'm going to sleep out somewhere, I leave the outer door open, so this woman can come in occasionally and change the sheets.

★ ★ ★

When I was young, I used to worry a good deal. We lived in a redbrick terrace in a dingy part of town where the malt smell from the brewery hung over us. My father worked in a paper mill and suffered from asthma. He also had a heart murmur and we were afraid he might not be able to go on working. Disability pay, early retirement, chronic invalidity . . . These were the phrases I overheard; I didn't know what they meant, except for one thing: no money. My mother worked as a receptionist at a hotel called the Waverley on the Bath Road. She tried to be at home when I came back from school, but from the age of ten or eleven I was given a key and told to make my own tea. This was fine by me, as I could watch television without fear of being nagged to do homework. I also read books which I took out of the library on my way home, and there was no charge for them. This struck me as inexplicable, but good.

I knew we were poor, but I also knew there were people poorer than us. The Callaghans, for instance. There were twelve of them in a house smaller than ours, two streets away. It smelled damp and stale. They had an outside toilet — a double-seater, as I knew from having used it when my mother left me with Mrs Callaghan one afternoon. And all those places by the railway. You'd see the laundry flapping in the soot-grimed yard. How would it ever be clean?

There was a pretty young woman I used to see pegging out sheets and I was worried that she would grow old there and that no one would know how beautiful she was. And maybe she would die without ever having really lived.

I was concerned about West Germany as well. I'd seen newsreel pictures of how their cities had been bombed by our planes in the War and wasn't sure how they could manage to get going again. Then they were occupied by us and the Americans and this must be humiliating because it wasn't as though they were savages in far-off islands who knew no better. It was like being in permanent detention. It was like being forced to wear short trousers even when you were a man. I wondered how I'd feel if I was little Hans or Fritz in Düsseldorf or Hanover. I didn't think I'd like my life to be restricted by the consequences of what my parents had done.

I waited for my father's step on the path every night and the rattle of his key in the lock. I ran out from the kitchen to see how he looked in the light of the sixty-watt hall bulb. I became an expert in summing him up. By the time I'd reached him to say hello I knew by the movement of his ribs beneath his work shirt whether his breathing was constricted or relatively free.

It bothered me that people had so many children. There didn't seem to be enough food in the world for everyone even as it was, and we'd have to build more and more houses which meant that in England at any rate there would soon be no fields left. And then where could we grow the food?

Perhaps when the next world war started, all this would become irrelevant, because the next world war, which would be between us and the Russians, would be a nuclear one. I knew that my grandfather had fought in the first one, my father in the second, so it followed that my turn would come in the third.

Near the railway bridge was a large institutional building. I never knew what it was, but it made a big impression on me. Was it a hospital, or a poorhouse? Or a workhouse? What was the difference? In the winter, when the lights were on, you could see figures moving behind the uncurtained windows. There was something in the lights themselves that made me anxious. They can't really have been gaslight, but they looked like it; perhaps they'd wired up the old gas brackets and put low-wattage electric bulbs in them. That was probably it. Certainly it gave the building a look of something from another time, from the last century. The men I glimpsed through the windows were old. Perhaps they too belonged to that century; in fact, they must have been born in it.

I think I once saw a matron with a starched headdress. Because I could only see into it on winter afternoons, it seemed to me that it was always teatime in this place. This didn't mean nice food or cake or anything. It meant the beginning of a long institutional evening. And I always had this feeling that somehow the inmates of this place were immune to time, that they were somehow stuck at five o'clock in perpetuity.

I knew somehow what it was like inside. It's possible. Whether I dreamed it, whether my intuition just works well in this case or whether I have in some way lived before, I couldn't say. But almost every detail of it was known to me and I identified with these old men.

Something of the atmosphere of that place was universal, at least in England then. The clamp of institution. Gaslight, grey. Like the metal ache of an injection when it fills your arm. No colour, no home; no sister, daughter, lipstick, smile or music; only gaslight and vault, and arched corridor with tiled wall and stone floor for ever.

I feared to find myself in such a place. And I was always agitated for the men who were there. I wanted to look after them, put pipe tobacco wrapped in scarlet paper in their hands and lead them into colour.

For some reason, it was my responsibility.

★ ★ ★

It's going well with Jennifer. I see her at the Soc meetings and I've started going to history lectures with her. She's doing an interesting combination of topics, I must say, and it wouldn't surprise me if she did well in the exam coming up in the summer. The Unification of Germany is one of her strong suits. I don't think she's quite got to the bottom of Vichy France, but there isn't much material to work with, outside the archives. The German ones are hard to get at if you don't speak German (she only has O level) and the French have locked theirs up. (I know this because we covered this topic for A-level History at school.) She's pretty steady on the old schoolbook stuff — the Stewdors, the Frog Rev — but on Africa I think she's been misled by the Marxists. I mean misled about what actually took place, because as far as exams are concerned, of course, the Marxist *interpretation* will do fine. Most of the history dons are Marxist. They are careful to define whether they are 'pure' Marxist-Leninist, or Communist (which means Stalinist, in favour of the invasion of Hungary and Czechoslovakia because although those peoples didn't like being invaded or living under Communism, the Communists knew better and it was for their own good) or Trotskyist or Menshevik or

30

Gramsci-ist or Eurosocialist or Lukácsist or something even more refined. They do change, however, and they are hugely interested in their own small changes, like people in psychoanalysis. About once a year a rumour runs round that an important announcement is about to go out: Dr R — has moved position. There is a flutter in the faculty. After months of wakeful nights and self-questioning, after re-reading the key texts, Dr R — has made all the intellectual reconciliations necessary; he is ready to declare that he is now definitely a . . . Maoist. His students nod their heads. Mao. Of course. Some of the girls will want to sleep with Dr R — , to experience such rigour at first hand. By day, the Hist dons teach the dictatorship of the proletariat, and at night they read the Sits Vac column in the education supplements and apply to other universities where there's a better chance of tenure.

Yet from what I know of Mao he doesn't sound like a nice man at all. Doesn't that count for anything?

Incidentally, no one seems to mind my turning up to lectures with Jennifer, even though I'm reading Natural Sciences.

I should have mentioned that I switched out of English at the end of the first year. I went to see my Director of Studies to tell him and he spoke to his equivalent in Nat Sci, who then called me in to his rooms in New Court (which is the oldest court, but called new because it was once new, compared to the ruined priory in which the

31

college was first incorporated by seven Puritan divines in 1662).

The Sci don, whose name is Waynflete, made me do a catch-up exam of his own devising, but allowed me the summer vacation to prepare. It wasn't very difficult — rudiments of cell biology, physiology (including some neuroscience), biology of organisms, much of which I remembered from school — and he was then obliged to accept me. For the second year, or Part One B exams, I'll tackle animal and plant biology and biochemistry. I fancy genetics as a Part Two option. Although there was a bit of evolution in biology of organisms, I look for the human angle — the big picture rather than the molecular stuff — in Arch and Anth lectures given by a bearded Fellow from Melbourne known as the Australopithecine.

I don't miss English at all. No one explained what we were meant to do. They leave you to work it out for yourself. This is done in the name of respect for you; they call you Mr or Miss and treat you as equals, so it would be impertinent of them to tell you how to go about your studies. It may be a coincidence that this not-giving-guidance also gives them time to spend on their own work. Woodrow, the big schoolmasterly one, for instance, is writing a book on German engraving from Dürer to the Present Day (he doesn't seem to teach English at all), and the younger one, Dr Gerald Stanley, is writing a novel, I believe, set in a Cornish tin mine but written in the style of Firbank. (Can't wait.)

I did ask him — Stanley — once what the

purpose of our work was.

'Are we meant to offer new insights into these books or what?'

He looked appalled.

I went on: 'I mean, it's unlikely that I'll find something in *Urn Burial* or *Bartholomew Fair* that people before me haven't seen.'

'Yes, Mr Engleby. Very unlikely.'

'Or should we be trying to find out more about the life of the author or how the times in which he lived affected his work?'

'Good God, no. That's journalism.'

'So what are we doing?'

'Studying the text and reading round it.'

'To what end?'

'Scholarship.'

I felt: a) that he had outflanked me there; b) not really satisfied. Perhaps it was the old logic/truth separation again.

In fact, I did briefly see a way in which English could be studied. This was what they called 'Practical Criticism'. They gave you unidentified bits of poetry or prose and you had to deduce from the words alone when they had been written and by whom; then give reasons for your conclusions and a critical commentary. This was easy, but enjoyable; and it had a purpose — to demonstrate the range of your reading, and the subtlety of your ear for the rhythms of the 1780s, say, or the 1920s. You came to grief, though, if you picked up on some autobiographical clue that identified the author; that, too, was thought to be 'journalistic'. So when a religious sonnet in the language of the 1660s made reference to its author's loss of sight or an ode in 1820 high Romantic contained a bout of coughing, I made out that my oddly precise dating of the text relied on analysing the vocabulary alone. I came top of the college in this paper in the first-year exams, but it was really just a parlour game that I happened to be good at. It didn't seem like *scholarship*, which ought to have been harder.

I told Stellings this and he started calling me 'Groucho'. I liked this better than the nickname I had had at school.

Something else looked briefly promising. This was called 'Theory' and it was just coming in. The point about Theory was that it didn't matter if you read *Jane Eyre* or a fridge installation manual: what you were doing was studying how you studied them, and the important thing now was not the (anyway unquantifiable) 'value' of the original work but the effectiveness of the theory. *Vanity Fair* or Biggles was the guinea pig; the vaccine being tested was the -ism. Some of the theories came from the study of linguistics, which was partly based on neuroscience, and for a moment the poor English dons, so fed up with being looked down on by their scientific colleagues, could boast that they too had a 'real' subject with truths that could be tested in a lab.

The linguistics side of it hasn't been fruitful yet because the people writing about the basis of language don't seem to be able to write.

Other theories are coming in, but they're based on Marxism or psychoanalysis and other doctrines which haven't cut the mustard in their own world and now look as though they're just

34

trying their luck on defenceless Eng Lit — like soldiers cashiered from the regiment turning up as teachers at a struggling private school.

So for Gerald Stanley and the rest it looks like it's back to *Jane Eyre*.

You can see why, personally, I prefer to take my neuroscience straight, with options in genetics and pathology.

★ ★ ★

More to the point, however, than my academic work is this: an unexpected but very good thing has happened.

2

I'd better explain. It's October, the beginning of my final year. I left off this story all of a sudden because I had to do some work for exams. They didn't go as well as I'd hoped, but that doesn't matter.

This does matter, though.

In the summer vacation, I worked in my father's old paper mill for four weeks to make money. The work was boring (I pushed a rubber-wheeled wagon round the factory floor), but it wasn't hard. At some time the union had agreed that in return for deferring a pay rise, the workforce would have a ten-minute break each hour — excluding lunch and tea and the official tea breaks of fifteen minutes and the five-minute two-hourly toilet breaks. You could roll all the minutes up, if you liked, and leave an hour early. As a casual, I wasn't officially in the union, but I followed their rules and got paid in cash in a crinkly grey envelope on Friday afternoon.

Jennifer was going to Ireland to make a film with some people from Trinity. The director was called Stewart Forres and there were maybe thirty or so people, cast and crew and a few hangers-on, girlfriends, boyfriends, going to a large old country house near Tipperary.

There wasn't room for everyone in the main house, so some people put up tents in the grounds and some took rooms in the local village. I found one above the butcher's shop. The proprietor was called Michael Clohessy and we joked about having the same Christian name. His wife called me 'little Michael' and cooked breakfast of black pudding and bacon and sausage and soda bread. The rent was five pounds a week, and after Mrs Clohessy's breakfast I didn't have to eat again till the evening, when there'd be dinner on the lawn after the day's filming was over.

'You'll not be wanting rain on your fillum, will you?' said Mrs Clohessy every day as I left for the set. 'Let's hope you're lucky again.'

The odd thing is that we were. 'Tip', as they called the local town, has one of the highest annual rainfalls of any town in Europe, you half expect it to have gondolas, but we never saw a drop.

Day after day the sun shone. The lawn of the old country house began to look bare and brown. The owners worked in horse-breeding and they had stables with thoroughbreds, but they hadn't had much luck at the market or the races and they took in guests whenever they could. They were pleased to be full up, but after a week they said they wanted a day off, so we'd have to do dinner for ourselves.

In the morning I hitchhiked to Tip, where I found an off-licence. I'd noticed that the drinks stores were running down and I bought a dozen bottles of cider, some seven-pint tins of beer and half a dozen glass carafes of wine with sealed metal tops. The Clohessys' rent was so small that I still had plenty of cash left from the paper mill.

I bought a tray of cut-price chicken pieces from a supermarket and the ingredients for a barbecue sauce. I'd done a lot of cooking as a child because I got hungry waiting for my parents to come home. I had to feed Julie as well as myself and she was quite fussy about the way I did it.

It was tricky getting all this stuff to a point where I could hitch a lift back, but the man in the supermarket lent me a trolley. Everyone was off filming in a wood in the furthest part of the estate and there was no one around except a small girl called Jude, who had straight brown hair wrapped in something I think might be called a snood. She wasn't needed that day and had been told by Stewart to get a meal together. She was sulking about this; she said he'd picked on her because she was a woman and that he'd never have told a man to cook. I gave her a Glynn Powers roll-up and said I could look after the dinner.

At five, I put up a trestle on the gravel by the kitchen garden and laid out the drink with some paper cups I'd got from the village. I stuck the chicken under a marinade in a huge pan I found in the kitchen. With old bricks and bits of stone I picked up near the bonfire site I built a base for a barbecue with a good draught running under it, laid some wire netting over it, then gathered armfuls of wood from the parched grounds. By seven I had orange-grey embers, and by eight I was ready to offer marinated grilled chicken with barbecue sauce, baked potatoes and salad to thirty people.

I tried to pass it off as Jude's work, but

38

actually nobody seemed to care who'd cooked it; no one even asked who'd bought it or got it to the house. A guy called Andy said, 'Great sauce, man.' Maybe he thought I was a caterer.

I noticed that Jennifer enjoyed it too. I'd bought apple pies and cheese from the village to have afterwards. She laughed when some apple squeezed from the piece of pie she was holding and dropped into her lap.

Jennifer was playing one of the main parts in the film, as it happened. Stewart Forres gave a talk before the camera rolled. He had a thin brown beard and Christ-like hair parted in the middle. He said, 'You've all seen the script that Dave and I have developed. We started with this heavy concept — an acid *Twelfth Night*, if you will — but we've finished with something more unstructured. Most of the dialogue is going to be improvised, so you'll be work-shopping some of your scenes with me or Dave first. We're going to light some Tibetan candles now and sit in a ring. This is a good-luck ceremony. I'd like you to respect it.'

It looked really good with all the candles and everyone gathered round. The light from the flames shone up on their faces: Kathy and Dave and Amit from King's, and Hannah and Holly from Newnham, and Hannah's boyfriend Steve, and Stewart, of course, and Jennifer, who was sitting next to him, and all the others and the ones who did the lights and the sound and the runners and so on. I hadn't seen the script myself, but there was a feeling of relaxation and people seemed happy to go wherever it took them. The night was warm and someone had a guitar. Sitting there, they looked like Jesus and his disciples. They gave me a feeling I'd seldom had before, like sometimes when I'd watch Julie and one of her friends from school when she was five or six. I used to sit on the other side of the room and just observe them playing.

Most nights in Ireland were similar, but the night I cooked the chicken was the best. After I'd cleared up the plates and stuff, some of the people went off to their tents or their rooms, but most of us, about twenty, stayed round the fire.

Steve had a steel-string guitar, and he began to strum it gently, sitting with his legs crossed, pausing to suck on a joint and pass it on. He then began to pick at the strings instead of strumming. He didn't make a big thing of it; he played quietly, so if you wanted to listen you could, but it didn't matter if you carried on talking. In fact everyone did stop what they were doing, and edged into the circle, looking over to where Steve sat. They held their paper cups and cigarettes and waited in the darkness.

The notes picked by Steve's right hand began to form a melody. He played a Bob Dylan song, 'Girl From the North Country', which is like 'Scarborough Fair', but somehow full of concern. He wants a girl he once loved to be all right. He's worried that she's cold. 'Please see she has a coat so warm/To keep her from the howlin' winds.' (He's already spoken of the snow and ice, where 'the winds hit heavy on the borderline'.) I used to wonder if this was the border of Canada and America, maybe near the

Great Lakes, but now I don't think it matters. It could be any North Country. He isn't worried for his own loss or his own feelings — only for the girl he loved. He wants her still to have her hair long, and to be warm. I don't know why this is so sad.

We sat out there for hours and drank cider and wine and smoked more and listened to Steve's guitar. Then Holly played a little, but she wasn't such a good singer as Steve and she gave him the guitar back and he ended with a song called 'Fire and Rain'. As he was singing, I noticed Jennifer get up and stretch in the night and she walked right past me and laid a hand on my shoulder as she passed and said, 'Thanks for the dinner.'

I let myself in through the Clohessys' kitchen and went quietly up the stairs and pushed my window open and wondered if I could still hear any music, just faintly on a breeze. It was a very still night, though.

★ ★ ★

The boy in charge of the camera was called Nick, and they called him the DoP, which means director of photography, or chief cameraman. 'Ask the DoP,' Stewart said ten times a day. I think it was Nick's camera. It was quite large and could be mounted on a tripod, though for some shots Stewart used to put it under his arm and insist on walking around with it himself to give what he called a 'New Wave texture' (which is that thing where you feel seasick). Nick never seemed that keen on Stewart holding the camera and looked relieved to get it back on its tripod.

The other main female part was played by Hannah, who'd done a lot of stage plays earlier in the year, including *Hedda Gabler*, I think. She was confident and difficult to deal with; she often said things were 'getting too heavy' and she'd stop for a cigarette and Stewart had to be very gentle with her. Steve, her boyfriend, watched carefully.

There are lots of ways you can make yourself useful on a film set if you're good with your hands and if you're patient. When the sound man wants to go for a smoke, you can do the job for him. You put on the headphones and say, 'Just hold it there, everyone, there's a plane going over.' It's not that difficult.

I can also use a saw and a chisel and make things and paint them if I have to — not that Stewart required much extra scenery, what with it being a pastoral thing set mostly in the woods, except for the bits inside the 'castle', which was the house itself. If nothing else, there was always someone who'd like a cup of tea.

A few nights after the chicken evening, there was a shortage of dope and I had to go back to the Clohessys' and dip into the stash I had in my sponge bag. I had a brought a hell of a lot over on the ferry from Fishguard. Glynn Powers had told me, just before the end of term, 'Mike, you've been my best customer. I wonder if you'd like to do a bit of work for me. It's like I can't really handle it all.' He opened his locker and showed me these spherical lumps of hash the size of tennis balls. He had half a dozen and I took a

42

couple off him to dispose of and split the profit.

When I got back to the garden, I chopped some up into five-pound deals but sold it for a pound a go, credit accepted.

'Hey, man,' said Andy, 'Mike the cook's turned into Mike the pusher.'

The next morning, Stewart was serious when he called everyone together. 'Listen,' he said, 'we're having a closed set this morning. Just Geoff on lights, Tom on sound, DoP of course, me, and the actors — Alex, Jennifer and Hannah. No one else at all. Is that understood?'

'What's a closed set?' I heard Steve ask Hannah.

'It means Jenny has to take her clothes off.'

'Tom's not back from Tip,' said Dave. 'You know he and Bob went last night? He rang in to say he's got a migraine. He gets them.'

They needed someone to do the sound because they couldn't delay the scene. It was on the schedule for today and, who knows, it might rain tomorrow. I told Stewart I could do it.

'You happy with the machine — the cans and everything?'

I told him I'd done it before, which I had, when Tom was off one morning. Tom's heart wasn't really in sound; he wanted to act.

Stewart nodded. 'Everyone cool?' He looked at Jennifer and Alex and Hannah. Alex looked terrified. Jennifer seemed close to tears.

It was a rape scene of course, but it was feminist in the way Stewart filmed it so you were meant to share the rage of the woman character, played by Jennifer.

43

There were a lot of planes going over towards Dublin, so we had to keep redoing the bit where Alex's character pulled Jennifer to the ground and lifted up her dress. There was a problem with her underwear. It was difficult for Alex to rip it off without tearing it, and they didn't have enough spare pairs. Also, it took too long to get it off and it looked as though the camera was sort of dwelling on it.

Jennifer didn't seem to be enjoying any of this, but when Stewart asked if she wanted a break she made as if it was a test of her integrity not to complain.

Hannah suggested Jennifer should be naked under her dress because the pulling off the underwear was too much like a 'male fantasy', so it was agreed she shouldn't wear anything.

Then the lights weren't working so Stewart decided to start again using available light only and Hannah told him that's what he should have been doing all along anyway, and that made an even tenser feeling on the set.

Everything seemed to go wrong that morning. Hannah said she didn't think Jennifer should be naked if Alex wasn't because that would exploit the woman, but the trouble with having Alex naked was that he was always excited and that was exploitative, according to Hannah, because no one was meant to be enjoying this. Alex said that if he wasn't excited then there could be no rape and no point made, and presumably a rapist did enjoy it anyway, that was the point: he was sick.

Hannah told him not to give her any of that

44

Method shit, but Stewart persuaded Hannah that Alex's point was reasonable, but by this time Hannah had said so many disparaging things about Alex that he couldn't get excited any more. So then we couldn't film him naked because it was obvious that he couldn't rape someone, so we were back to having just Jennifer naked beneath her dress when he lifted it up. Stewart said it didn't matter in the long run if Alex was excited or not because these shots would be cut in the edit anyway.

Then Jennifer began to cry because . . . I don't know why Jennifer cried.

Perhaps it was because she felt Alex didn't desire her any more — even though it was only his character that was meant to desire her character, and even though he was a rapist and if you were a woman you wouldn't want him to want you in that way.

She seemed really upset, though, and she couldn't stop crying for about twenty minutes. Hannah told Alex he was a pig, and other things. Geoff the lighting man had been told to leave the set with his lights and the only person in the wood who seemed calm was the DoP, Nick. He had a pair of purple crushed velvet trousers.

I don't remember how it got resolved. I know there was a tender scene when Hannah's character came over from the big house to comfort the Jennifer character. Hannah said she should herself be naked for this, but Stewart would have none of it.

Then he and Hannah had another row about who was in charge and it was clear that Hannah knew more about acting, but it was Stewart's film, and it was Nick's camera.

Personally, I found it an interesting morning, but for fear of seeming voyeuristic and because I was only a stand-in for Tom, I never let my eyes leave Jennifer's face.

★ ★ ★

The shoot took three weeks in all. Towards the end, the evenings started to draw in. There was some rain at night. People seemed tired. I heard Jennifer say she really wanted a hot bath, though I'm sure there was hot water in the main house, where she had a room. Perhaps she was thinking of her parents' house in Lymington, or of a particular bathroom.

Stewart kept going well. He said he'd had inquiries from an 'independent distributor' and from the Student Film Council, who had partly funded the operation.

A week before the end, Steve discovered that Hannah had switched her affections to Nick, the DoP. Steve was angry. Hannah told him he was immature. He said he was sorry to get heavy about it, but he thought she'd been dishonest. She said he was possessive and she couldn't stand that. So he took his guitar and left in the night, like a thief, and it seemed to be his fault for not being cool about things.

I missed the music. Nick looked pleased but surprised, the new man in possession who has not sought greatness but had it thrust upon him. He was careful not to seem possessive, but

Hannah was always lighting a cigarette then putting it in his mouth or listening with intense respect when he talked to Stewart about a shot. These break-ups often happen in September, I think. The end-of-summer winds make people restless.

We had a party on the last night and Stewart told us all we'd be invited to the screening room at Film Soc to see a rough cut in due course. The party was a good one. Everybody seemed to be back at their best and all the differences were forgotten. I made some chocolate cakes with about an ounce of hash in them and bought a whole lot more cider from Tip. The people who owned the house seemed sorry to see us go and they made a big casserole of beef that they'd bought from Clohessy's, and rice with apple and raisins and red peppers for the vegetarians.

With the cider I took some Mandrax I'd been saving. Stewart did the thing with the Tibetan candles again and we all held hands — and this time I was in the circle, two away from Jennifer, and the light flickered up into her face.

★   ★   ★

And that was the really good thing that happened. I thought it would carry on, this communal feeling when the new term began in October.

We're now in the third week of it and final exams are still a long way away, next summer, but somehow people already seem preoccupied. I've been to Film Soc a couple of times, but not

47

many of the Irish people have been there: Nick (without Hannah, who was in *Uncle Vanya* at the ADC), Amit and Holly are the only ones who've looked in so far. Stewart's working with Dave on the edit. Apparently the rushes are promising.

But it's already cold outside, the leaves are wet on the pavements and it seems a long way from Tipperary.

I have a new room this year, in Clock Court. It's got its own pantry with a gas ring so I don't bother to go to the dining hall any more. There's no shower, but there's a bathroom I share with only five other people and few of them seem to use it. So I work the bath over with a cloth and some Vim from a saucer that the bedmaker replenishes, rinse off, fill up and listen to *The Archers* on my small transistor radio. There's a Northern Ireland barmaid called Norah who takes up too much story time, but I like the old man, Walter Somebody. He reminds me of the old men in the almshouse in the street where I was brought up. 'Heh, heh, me old beauty, me old darlin',' he says. Or something like that. I don't listen *that* carefully.

I've changed my routines a bit. For a start, I've almost given up drugs. This is partly due to the fact that my supplier has disappeared. I used to buy pills from a man in the Kestrel called Alan Greening. He had an executive metal briefcase that looked as though it might hold the secret plans of a Ukrainian nuclear reactor. All it had in fact were bottles of pills. He's been in and out of various hospitals and he's signed on with three

48

different GPs. He has a pharmaceutical directory and he looks up the drug he wants, then describes the symptoms it's prescribed for. He goes to different chemists to have them made up and no one checks up on the others. Tricyclics, monoamine oxidase inhibitors, benzodiazepines, all sorts of stuff — they make an awful rattle in his bag and most of them don't do anything at all for you. There's one called Nardil, an MAOI, that you have to take for weeks for any effect and if you eat cheese or Marmite or broad-bean pods it can give you a brain haemorrhage. Where's the fun in that? But Tuinal, Nembutal, Amytal, I quite like them; and Quaaludes go well with gin. It all depends. I've tried almost all the sleeping pills, even the banned ones, and they don't even make me feel tired. On the other hand, I'm susceptible to a patent hay-fever cure you can buy over the counter at Boots, which goes to show.

The only thing I wouldn't do is amphetamines — or LSD. They synthesised that stuff in a lab twenty-five years ago when they were trying to induce human madness in guinea pigs. Why take drugs specifically designed to send you insane? If you'd even glanced at neuroscience in Nat Sci Part One, then, believe me, you wouldn't go near those things.

The point is, I don't need any of this stuff any more. (Apart from marijuana and alcohol, but they don't really count, and anyway, I don't need them, they're just a habit, like cigarettes or going to the cinema.)

I don't need drugs because I can deal with

reality as it is. Reality is no problem for me. Poor old Eliot thought humans couldn't stand too much of it. But I can stand as much of it as you care to throw at me. As much as D.H. Lawrence anyway. I should have pointed that out to Dr Gerald Stanley in my original interview. (He looks at me sadly when I pass him in the cloister nowadays — though I greet him cordially enough. 'Ah, Dr Stanley, I presume. How's Jane Eyre? Married yet?')

I do keep some connection with Literature. I write poetry of my own in my room in Clock Court. With the proceeds of two of Glynn Powers's tennis balls I bought a record player and some records — Mahler mostly, and some Bruckner, Sibelius and Beethoven. I first heard Mahler's Fifth in the opening sequence of the film of *Death in Venice*, which came out in my first year. I liked it, but they shouldn't have changed von Aschenbach into a musician. To show how dry and intellectual he was as a writer (so his passion for the boy is all the more unruly), all they had to do was have the hotel manager pick up a couple of his books and wince at the titles. But to create that dry impression with a composer meant they had to have flashbacks to Germany with him arguing embarrassingly with a colleague about Art and Life, as though Visconti had yielded these scenes to Ken Russell, or worse. Why do film-makers make life so hard for themselves by assuming that the original writer has got it all wrong?

While I'm listening to Mahler, I write poetry — in pencil, so I can revise it as I go along. I've

50

completed a sonnet sequence (typewritten) and entered it for the university's poetry medal. If you can picture Mahler's Fifth, particularly the Adagio that plays over the opening shots of the film — that's the kind of feeling I'm after. It's not that easy to put into words because words have too many meanings that clutter everything up. Very blunt instruments, words — because of all those useless but unavoidable connotations. Though if you could find the words to go where Mahler went in that Adagio, I'm not sure you'd like it. A bit of the vagueness of music stops you going completely mad, I imagine.

⋆ ⋆ ⋆

Have you ever been lonely?

No, neither have I.

Solitary, yes. Alone, certainly. But lonely means minding about being on your own and I've never minded about it.

All right. I admit that before I knew Jennifer, I suppose there must have been times when I did mind a little. The times you might mind it are when your own company stops entertaining you. In your normal life that doesn't happen, because the routines you develop are ones you like — ones that help you through. So you don't get fed up. Another evening with Mike? Yes, that's fine. I like Mike. Good old Mike. There's also Gustav, there's poetry to write and if it gets bad, stick a coat on and go out for a drink in the Bradford with the transvestite barmaid.

My first summer vacation, I worked for a few

weeks in the paper mill to get money, then took a ferry to Le Havre. I thought I'd hitchhike somewhere interesting and do some reading on the way. I took big paperbacks I could tear the pages out of as I went along: *The Wings of the Dove*, *The Magic Mountain*, *Pamela* and *Anna Karenina*. I remember reading *Pamela* on a camping site near Tours and thinking I was glad I was becoming a scientist. I don't think it's famous because it's a good book; I think it's famous because hardly anyone else was writing novels in the eighteenth century. Posterity didn't tell Richardson he'd done a fine job; posterity told him he'd done an early job. You wouldn't want to fly in a Wright Brothers plane now.

There was something in those northern French towns, though, that did make me a bit lonely. I watched the widows with their raisin faces and young mothers with children. Red-faced old men in the cafés; young men absent, working. Those painters like Courbet and Millet, I think they'd seen something too: the peasant in the landscape, grey towns with shutters, churches — the solid-seeming apparatus of life that terrorised a generation of novelists with what Henry James called their 'puerile dread of the grocer', but which in reality was so fragile.

Homo erectus with his flint, *sapiens* with his empty church. Those speciating changes!

And the identical *boucheries* with their blood-smell and queues and the catechism of greeting and farewell that surrounds the purchase. Those cobbled squares and *tricolores* draped from the *hôtels de ville*. The red bulb in the window of the auberge with the typical cooking of the region with its period beams and clanking soup tureens, *potage du jour* with a half-bottle of Saint-Émilion.

The churches, above all. Their emptiness. God has been to Earth — and gone away. That did occasionally make me feel lonely.

The worst thing that can happen when you're away is that your mind tries too hard to make you feel at home. I remember this happening in a Turkish bus station, in Izmir. (Not much happened between Tours and Izmir, incidentally. Italy and Greece were fine.)

It was night and I was waiting for a bus. There were sodium lights over the grimy tarmac and the glass-sided shelter. There was that wailing Muslim music turned up louder than the cheap speakers wanted, so their tinny shuddering was added to the vibrato of the singer. For every would-be traveller, waiting for the overnight bus to Istanbul, there were two or three hangers-on, men with moustaches and worry beads, smoking cigarettes, approaching the waiting travellers and asking sly, brusque questions with their guttural voices and an aggressive jerk of the head, looking for . . . For what? Money? Sex? Something to pass the time? One came up to me and said something about 'yellow picture girls'. Was he offering to buy or sell? He plucked at my sleeve till I pushed him away.

It was one a.m. in the grey sodium light with the wailing music and the black ground with its spattered chewing gum and cigarette ends. I had started to pay too much attention to things. It

53

was almost as though I could see right through them into the molecules that made them. And that awful music. I suppose my mind was trying too hard to get a grip on this place, to anchor it for me, because I had the strong impression that I was really outside time or place, that the hostile otherness of my surroundings was such that my own personality was starting to disintegrate. I was vanishing. My character, my identity, had unravelled. I was a particle of fear.

I guess I was a little lonely then.

In general, in less extreme moments, lonely looks after itself. It helps you develop strategies that reinforce it. The comfort of the dark cinema and the company of the screen actors prevent you meeting anyone. Lonely's like any other organism: competitive and resourceful in the struggle to perpetuate itself.

I don't remember how I got to Istanbul.

★   ★   ★

There was a meeting of Jen Soc on Monday, and Jennifer, who is now officially the secretary, was of course present at the meeting of her own society. She has had her hair cut a little shorter and she was wearing a corduroy skirt, just above the knee, with cowboy boots and navy blue tights. I don't like the way people change over the long vacation. It's not as bad as schooldays, naturally, when a May child returns a man in September, but it's still unsettling.

Among the urgent matters we discussed were the mobilisation of American planes from the nearby airbase during the Yom Kippur War (I heard them thundering over Parker's Piece on my way back from dinner in the cheese-pie pub; it was pretty exciting; I hope the crews will come and sign the ceiling in the Kestrel on their return) and the CIA coup that deposed President Allende in Chile.

We will no longer contemplate Chilean wine, though I'm happy to say that under Jennifer's guidance we do now have bottles of something red called Hirondelle, on sale for ten pence a glass. I think 'hirondelle' means 'swallow' in French — the bird, that is, not the gulp, though gulp is what's best to do with it, so perhaps someone at Peter Dominic's had a sense of humour.

When we were clearing up, I noticed that a letter had fallen out of Jennifer's bag.

Without thinking, I slipped it into the pocket of my coat. Back in my room in Clock Court, I examined it beneath the fixed Anglepoise. It was addressed in her writing to Mr and Mrs R.P. Arkland at an address in Lymington. It had a second-class stamp on it.

I should have taken it back to Jennifer, but I thought I'd just post it for her the next day. Then, at about eleven, when I got up, I remembered that there was a photocopier in the porters' lodge. But those grey and surly men are nosey; they always read your stuff. There was also a copier in the issues section of the University Library, but that meant filling in forms. Then I remembered the general post office in St Andrew's Street.

First I went to my small pantry and boiled the kettle. Then I held Jennifer's letter in the steam and prised it open with a knife.

I took the letter to the post office and copied it on to slimy grey sheets that slid from the side of the machine. Then I returned to my room, refolded and reinserted the original and resealed the envelope, which was now dry, with the help of a trace of cow gum from a glass bottle. I tried to keep the glue light, to replicate the envelope's own flimsy closure. Then I walked back to the post office (I didn't want to stick it in the local box), posted it, returned — at last — to my room and sat down with a cup of Nescafé to read it. This is what it said:

Dear Mum and Dad,

Thank you for the letter and the tights and the cheque. All much appreciated.

It's really great living in a house. Anne and Molly are sharing a room at the moment because there was some sort of flood at the back and Nick refused to budge, even though he's got the best room by far. Typical man! Actually, it's best that they share as neither wants to share with Nick . . .

I've done what you suggested, Mum, and painted the kitchen, and that has certainly cheered it up a lot. I also found a nice old armchair in a junk shop for my room.

The only thing is that it's so cold! God knows what it's going to be like in January. The gas fire in the sitting room works on a meter and no one ever wants to fork out for it.

56

Nick always says he's going out, so he won't be using it.

As a result we don't use that room much and everyone goes to her own room to work, which is fair but a bit antisocial.

We have a rota for cooking and a kitty for shopping. Anne's the best cook but Nick complains she spends too much on food (meat especially) so we're going almost completely vegetarian. As Anne says, we can always be carnivorous at lunchtime. We each have a separate shelf in the fridge for our stuff, but even between four of us there never seems to be any milk.

The other problem is keys. It's just a single Yale lock, but Nick's is on semi-permanent loan to Hannah, who's meant to have one cut for herself but never seems to get round to it. So there's often a late-night banging at the door.

As well as a duvet and a rug, I sleep in my ski socks and don't turn the gas off in my room till the very last thing. Then I sprint across the floor and fly into bed.

But I love getting up in the morning. There's a tortoiseshell cat who lives opposite and he's half adopted us. I pull back the curtain and see him on the roof, stretching in the thin early sun. I love the jumble of small slate roofs on the brick terraced cottages. I lie watching for a few minutes while an 'inane disc jockey' (Dad) babbles on the radio. Then I put on socks, slippers, sweater and coat and go down to the kitchen, and, while the kettle's on, open the back door to the cat and call him in. He tumbles off the roof of the shed and comes shyly to the step where (if lucky) he gets a saucer of milk and a stroke.

I make tea and drop a mug off for Anne (not for Molly — no lecture till eleven) and go up and do my teeth (more toothpaste always appreciated: v exp). Do you really want to know all this?! Skip ahead if it's boring you, Mum . . .

Find suitable clothes (i.e. woolly, thick ones), make sure I have all the right books and go down for toast, quick Nescaff (if time) and wheel trusty bike out of hall on to street.

It's misty and cold, but bright as well, and the houses are so minute. They're like dolls' cottages. I bicycle slowly (beware Girton calves . . .) down the backstreets and many times see the same town people leaving home, walking to the bus stop, taking in milk bottles. I think this is my favourite time of day. Occasionally I see a furtive undergraduate (male) skulking back to his college after a night out. Naughty boy.

It's wonderful to watch the town come awake, the shops opening, the buses pushing down St Andrew's Street from the station. But I prefer the backstreets. I cut down Pembroke Street and Silver Street and over the river and I think of all the people who've gone before me — the men in the Cavendish Labs and the Nobel prize-winners and Milton and Darwin and Wordsworth, of course, but mostly of the generations of young men and women who

58

weren't famous but were so relieved to be here at last and to meet people like themselves, and didn't mind the freezing cold and no money for the meter and the greasy college breakfast. I think of the men in their tweed jackets with the elbow patches and the bluestockinged women in their clunky shoes and I feel glad for them still.

Incidentally (or 'incidently' as Sally would spell it), I am still seeing something of Rob, though I promise you I am not 'getting serious' and no, I haven't forgotten that I have all my life ahead of me, and no I haven't forgotten that at my age 'friendship is more important than romance' (copyright © 1968 by R.P. Arkland, MA; copyright renewed each year since . . .)

I get to the Sidgwick Site at 8.45 and meet up with friends, including Rob, Stewart (if he's not in London or Hollywood . . .) and various girls from college. The faculty has organised the lectures v well for poor third-years facing Finals Armageddon, so all courses over by lunch. Usu three lectures — say, nine, ten, twelve. From eleven till twelve I might be in the Faculty Library (provided roof not leaking: thank you, Mr James Stirling) or 'Advanced Research Centre' — i.e. tearoom. Best lectures from Dr Bivani (female: 19th century) or Mr Richardson (Mod. Europe); worst from horrid Dr Ditchley who is a monumental drag.

Often go back to coll for salad lunch in Upper Chamber (v good value) and in the afternoon I have volleyball on Tue and Thur, which I am really enjoying a lot. I always thought it was a bit of a joke at school, as you know, but in fact I really like it now. If not volleyball, often go to cinema (Arts or one of the mainstream ones) or coll library or to visit. Have met nice boy in Emmanuel (Charlie) reading English with amazing record collection and v amusing room-mate (Myles) from Leeds.

Early Fen darkness at five, sometimes tea in the Whim (known to Charlie and Myles by rude alternative name, I'm sorry to say), maybe go to bookshop or supermarket if I'm cooking. It's lovely getting back to the house, being the first in and getting it warmed up and cosy — as much as possible, at any rate. Listen to music on big sitting room stereo while kettle boils and make toast. Charlie lent me record by a group called Focus. Dutch, with keyboards, beautiful guitar — ah, but you wouldn't appreciate it!

On Monday, after supper, it's Society meeting in Jesus, which means a bit of preparation and homework. Not many people last week, which was disappointing — just the hard core, three or four freshers and that guy Mike I told you about(!).

Most evenings I work for a couple of hours, but I do go out a fair bit too. Rob takes me to various college jazz or folk clubs or sometimes just for a drink to one of the town pubs. The Mitre has a great jukebox. There's one called the Baron of Beef next door, which is also good fun. Best of all I like the ones in this part of town, away from the centre. Tiny backstreet rooms by the river with small coal fires. Don't worry, we don't get drunk.

I finally got to see a rough cut of the film we made in Ireland, and I must say I think it's really good. Stewart is a very talented guy. There's one scene I'm in which you're not going to like — I might as well warn you now. (Though you may never see it. It's not obligatory. It won't be on general release, so you'd need to go to a Film Soc special screening. But knowing you, you will. Like that rude book I warned you not to read and you went straight out and bought it.) Hannah is absolutely amazing and makes me look very inadequate. Even when someone else is speaking she seems to fill the screen. Alex is much better than I expected, though a bit eager in places.

There's so much going on and not enough time to do it all. I'm doing extra French Lang (to help with document research) with a little old lady off Lensfield Road and when I walk back I see the posters in the cottage windows: University String Ensemble, *'Tis Pity She's a Whore*, *Julius Caesar* at the ADC, Newnham Madrigal Society, *The Good Person of Szechwan* at St John's ... I know it's a cliché, but there aren't enough hours in the day.

Of course Finals are a worry, but I try not to think about it (them) too much. If I do get a youknowwhat (like the Scottish play, can't mention the word) it could cause more problems than it solves by more or less obliging me to go into what Rob calls 'research'. So might be better off with 'gentleman's' degree, Dad. Qué sera, sera, that's what I say. What an original daughter you have!

I'm glad you enjoyed Penny Martin's wedding. If you couldn't get an invite to Princess Anne and Mark Phillips's, I'm sure Brian and Gail's was the second best place to be. Did Gail do her special cheesy things? Did Brian make a speech? In which case, is he still going?

It's nearly midnight. Incidently (Sally again), I read in the paper that Grocer Heath is thinking of introducing a three-day week. I told Rob last night and he said, 'I'm not doing an extra day's work for anyone.' I thought you might like that.

Now I really must stop and go to bed. Before I turn the light off, maybe one final blast, Dad, of 'deafening popular music' . . .

Later: Ah, that's more like it. Long guitar solo by Jan Akkerman, max vol through the headphones. Now I can sleep easy.

Lots of love from your loving, very hard-working, rather poor and exceedingly cold (but happy) daughter,

Jen-Jen xxx

There was one bit in Jennifer's letter I really didn't like, and I expect you can guess what it was. What I really didn't like was: (!)

Not even a word. A single vertical line and a dot, parenthesised.

For the rest, I quite enjoyed it. Of course, like all students she was giving only an edited account of what was going on. No mention of drugs, or cigarettes, for instance — or sex.

Duplicitous, you might call her. Tactful would probably be her own word.

You couldn't help but warm to her father, though, could you? I pictured him a bit like Mr Bennett in *Pride and Prejudice*. ('Which reminds me, Dr Stanley, may I offer you four pages on 'Mixed Motives for Marriage in the Novels of Jane Austen'? No? Are you quite sure?')

I put Jen's letter away in the third drawer of my desk and locked it.

Yes, Mr Arkland sounded nice. Did Jen have sisters, then, I wondered? If he was really a Mr Bennett type, then she must have. And he was MA, which meant that he had either done postgraduate work at an ordinary university or been to one of the ancient ones and paid five guineas to convert his B to an M.

If the latter, he must be quite grand, because in his generation you got admitted not by competitive exam but only if you could pay the fees. They didn't have grants in those days. Their address sounded modest enough, but now I came to think of it, Jennifer is what you'd call 'well spoken' — not stuck-up, and with plenty of student 'yeah's and 'like's, but not common. Not like me. She's got a lovely voice, in fact. It

63

sounds as though she's always trying to suppress laughter out of consideration for the person she's talking to. You want to tell her it's all right, you don't have to be polite, you can let go and laugh.

The other striking thing about Mr Bennett, I mean Mr Arkland, the thing that really stirred me in the guts, is that he's alive — and probably only fifty-odd.

★   ★   ★

My own father died when I was twelve. I can't pretend we were surprised, obviously. I was looking after Julie one afternoon. She used to go to a free nursery in the morning, then my mother would drop her with the Callaghans or someone while she went back to the hotel and I'd pick Julie up on the way home from school.

I'd started at the grammar school, having done well in the elevenplus despite going to a desperate catch-all primary called St Bede's. The good thing about St B's was that no one bothered you. There was no homework to speak of and you could wander from one room to another and see what lesson you liked the look of. I think it was a county council 'initiative' or something. I went mostly to science or history, but one girl I knew spent five years in the craft room. (I believe she has her own design company in London now.) At St B's you never got asked home by anyone because most of their mothers worked and didn't want a stranger there. In my year at least five fathers were 'away' (i.e. inside) and the majority didn't live with the mother any more; we, the nuclear Englebys, were considered odd.

At the grammar school, though, there was a different kind of boy. All the parents were married. Some of the fathers did things like dentistry; one was a 'solicitor', according to his son. I found it difficult to find much in common with these boys, though I liked the look of their new satchels and their racing bikes.

My bus stop was only ten minutes' walk from the Callaghans' and I banged on the door, holding my breath against the stagnant, stuffy smell when one of the twins opened it. Why do poor people's houses always smell like that? Ours did, too, and I thought all houses did till I went to a reception for my year at the grammar school headmaster's house and it smelt of — I don't know, air and wood or something.

Julie came skipping out and took my hand and we set off down Trafalgar Terrace as we always did, past the sooty red brick and the small windows with china ornaments, brass pots and grey net curtains. I make it sound slummy, but actually I like weathered English red brick and it was all right. Take it from me, it was not too bad. Once we were home, I made a pot of tea and some toast and honey for both of us, then I sat Julie down in front of *Crackerjack* on the snowy monochrome Rediffusion TV and went to do my homework in the kitchen.

I heard the telephone ring and went to answer it.

'Mike. Thank God you're there. It's your dad. He's been taken poorly. He's in Battle hospital.

You'd better come over. Take some money from the pot on the kitchen mantelpiece. Ask for Lister Ward.'

'What about Julie?'

'You'll have to bring her.'

Everyone knew where Battle hospital was, it was famous, but it took two buses and a fifteen-minute hike to get there. I carried Julie on my shoulders for the last bit. The reception area had that grey aspect I'd seen through the windows of the old men's workhouse. We were directed down a long stone corridor, on which there were periodically signs to Lister, among the other notices — X-ray, Pathology, Mother and Child Unit, Rowntree Cancer Ward.

We found ourselves going through half-glassed swing doors and out into a courtyard with parked ambulances and dustbins. It was raining slightly and Julie was tugging at me, asking me to slow down. On the other side were more hospital buildings, low-built, more modern than the giant Victorian building we'd come through, but somehow already tinged with that same grey, as though prematurely aged by all the deaths they had housed and shipped on and forgotten.

Eventually we found Lister, an airless room with strip lights, full of screens and half-drawn curtains with old people lying flat, looking as though they were on their way out. There was a television showing an early evening news bulletin. I eventually made out my mother, sitting on the end of a bed near the window. She turned round when we approached, but didn't say anything. She was wearing a headscarf and still had her overcoat on. She raised a finger to her lips. My father was lying on his back with a tube up his nose and a drip attached to his arm. His eyes were closed and his jaw had fallen. His skin was ashy-grey and there was short white stubble showing on his chin; someone had taken out his false teeth. His pyjama jacket was open and there were wires attached with pads to his bony, hairless chest. I thought of his heart, a fat muscle that had always shirked the job.

I tried to think back to when he'd been younger — healthier. There must have been memories — of the seaside, or of him playing football with me in the park, or carrying me on his shoulders or helping to decorate the Christmas tree. There weren't. All I could remember was waiting for him at the side door of the paper mill on a Friday afternoon when he came out with his grey envelope. 'That's it then,' he said. 'Another week. Make sure you never end up here, Mike.'

I looked at him on the bed. He coughed once and a trail of brownish dead blood came out of his mouth and ran down the side of his chin. Then he stopped breathing. And I thought, I'll make sure I never end up here, either.

★ ★ ★

In one way, Dad's death was the making of me, and that way was the academic. At the funeral, the vicar took me strongly by the arms and looked me in the eye.

'You may feel alone, but you're not.'

I waited for the God-loves-you thing.

'Others have been where you are. I have stood where you stand today. You will survive, however stricken you now feel.'

I pulled my arm away because I didn't want to hear this. I actually needed to feel I was alone. Why did I need the grief of others? Wasn't mine enough? Why did I need to feel that this abandonment was plural, when it was heavy enough singular? The best way ahead that I could see was to drag this thing off and digest it on my own, like a python with an outsize kill.

Since we didn't have the kind of house you could ask people back to, the vicar invited the mourners to the rectory. There were some people from the paper mill, a supervisor, a manager, a couple of workmates, some aunts, uncles and neighbours, about three dozen in all, a respectable number. The vicar's charlady served fish paste and Sandwich Spread sandwiches and tea and fruit cake and sherry if you wanted it.

The vicar wouldn't leave me alone. 'I gather you're at the grammar school,' he said.

All the guests had now stopped being mournful and were making general chat, as though nothing had happened. I kept thinking of the damp earth on my father's coffin, wondering how soon he would decompose. Did they put an accelerator pack in there, a chemical to kick-start the process, as you might with a compost heap? Was he clothed in there?

'Have you thought of Chatfield?'

'What?'

'The naval school. I gather from the eulogy

that your father was in the Royal Navy in the War and served throughout. You might be eligible for a scholarship to Chatfield. I'm a visiting chaplain. It's worth considering, especially if you're not settled at the grammar school. I shall have a word with your mother.'

I didn't mind the grammar school, but nevertheless in March I did some exams in an unused room, invigilated by Miss Penrose, the art teacher. These were the scholarship papers for Chatfield, a 'public', i.e. private, school about an hour's drive away. It was a famous institution, founded by some naval bigwig for the sons of sailors killed in battle, which had grown to take in 'ordinary' boys as well; in fact, I had the impression it was pretty keen to find pupils of any description who could pay the hefty fees.

Which we couldn't. But the top award, the Romney Open, paid the lot for you. I had had a crash course in Latin, which I'd never done before, working evenings with Mr Briggs from the grammar school, who volunteered his services. I struggled with the prose paper, though the unseen translation from Latin into English was straightforward (a poem by Catullus and a bit of prose where I already knew the story). The other papers were easy. I was called for an interview with the headmaster, which we took to be a good sign.

It turned out my father had died just in time. They sent a letter to the grammar school and one to us at home saying they were offering me the Romney Open, the full fees, all expenses paid, to start in September, when I would be thirteen and a half. They sincerely hoped I would take up the place as the rest of the candidates had been retards.

No, they didn't say that, but behind all the posturing and telling us just how old and honourable and important they were — and how incredibly fortunate I was — I did sense a whiff of desperation.

Why should that be? I wondered.

3

I walked up from the station to the outer gates, which gave on to a tarmac drive about half a mile long, fringed with dripping evergreens. Eventually, I came to the main building and asked a man in the lodge where I was meant to go.

'Which house you in?'

'Collingham.'

'New man, are you?'

'Yes.'

'Go to the corner of the quad, through that door. It's new men's tea with the housemaster. You're late.'

I went where he pointed, and knocked. The door was opened by a grey-haired man in a black gown.

'You must be Engleby. You'd better meet the others.'

Three boys in tweed jackets and flannel trousers were hunched round a low table with teacups. I knew from a letter that the housemaster was called Talbot. There was a fair boy with glasses called Francis, a dark one called McCain and a third one with a black eye called Batley.

Mr Talbot explained that I'd lost my father and was on the Romney Open; the others looked at me fearfully. Batley lived on a farm in Yorkshire without electric light or running water;

71

Mr Talbot seemed to like the sound of this, though I couldn't see what was so great about it. Even in Trafalgar Terrace we had these things. I mean, even the Callaghans have electricity. Batley had scored 44 per cent in the entrance exam, though merely turning up and writing down your name got you thirty. Again, this didn't seem to be a problem for Mr Talbot — rather the opposite. Batley seemed to have what Chatfield wanted. (The other two boys, McCain and Francis, had no distinguishing features.)

We went out into the quad and over to a stone staircase with iron bannisters. Talbot led us up two floors to some tall, battered double doors and pushed them open. And there was Collingham, 'my' house.

It was a single wide corridor with cubicles. Metal shaded lights hung at intervals from the ceiling. The paintwork was battered and kicked, but predominantly green. We walked past maybe twentyfive doors on either side till we reached the end. Our names were printed on metal strips above the door. Mine was the last room on the left. Inside was an iron bedstead, a table, hard chair and a small chest of drawers. A window gave on to a flat roof, which led over other pitched roofs to the main bell tower. The partition with the next cubicle was wooden, but my other wall, being the end of the building, was just unpainted brick.

'Your fagmasters will come and see you and make sure you know the drill,' said Mr Talbot. 'Tea's at six in Troughton's. Any questions?'

'Yes, sir,' I said. 'Do you know where my stuff is? My clothes and things?'

'Didn't your people bring you? No, of course, you don't have a car, do you? If it came by train it'll be sent up from the station to the lodge. You'd better go and fetch it. Don't be late for tea.'

'Wouldn't the porter — '

'I'm afraid they're not *that* sort of porter.'

Francis and McCain laughed nervously along with Mr Talbot; Batley looked confused.

I lugged my trunk over the front quad and up the stairs; the boys going up and down swore at me for being in the way. When I pulled it into Collingham, an older boy, perhaps a 'prefect', told me to lift it up and not drag it on the wooden floor.

'It's too heavy.'

'Then you'll have to unpack it here and carry the stuff to your room till it's lighter, won't you?' He spoke as though explaining something obvious to an idiot.

As I carried down the corridor the armfuls of grey shirts, football socks and vests my mother had got from the school second-hand shop, some boys took them from my arms and threw them over the partitions into random cubicles.

My 'fagmaster' was a small, nervous boy called Ridgeway. 'If you hear a prefect call 'Fag',' he said, 'run like hell. The last one there does the job. There's a fag test in two weeks' time. You need to know all the initials of all the masters, all the school offices, like who's captain of fives, all the rules and all the school geography. Read these.' He put the rule book, the annual calendar and 'call list' on my table.

'Where's Troughton's?' I asked.

'Down Dock Walk, behind Greville.'

'Anything else?'

'Keep your head down. Don't speak. Don't be nervy.'

'Nervy?'

'Pushy. Don't show off. Be invisible.'

'Thank you, Ridgeway.'

I had spent a week in Bexhill once, but apart from that had never slept outside my parents' house, so I was interested to know how it would feel. I didn't know where I was meant to go to clean my teeth or what time I was meant to turn my light out, so I brushed them in the room and spat out of the window. I turned the light off early, wondering if Batley had yet figured out what the metal switch inside the door was for.

I can't remember much of the first few days. I think I expected that at some time someone would explain what it was all about, but gradually it became clear that *not* explaining was the Chatfield way. It was a sign of weakness to ask a question; 'initiative' was shown by not making a fuss. You were meant to know what to do. How? Instinct? Tarot? Sortilege? No, just by being a good crew member, by not making a fuss, by just *knowing*.

'Keep your head down.' It was Ridgeway's hunted look more than his actual words that stayed with me.

Being the holder of the Romney Open meant that I was placed in classes with boys a year or

74

two older. They responded to my impertinence by not talking to me — ever. Not in all the time I was at that school.

The lessons were given by masters who all looked alike. They wore black gowns over tweed jackets and baggy grey trousers; they had lace-up tan shoes with enormous welts, so they rolled along the cloisters as though on brown tyres. They all had flat grey hair and similar, one-word nicknames — 'Stalky' Read, 'Mug' Benson, 'Tubby' Lyneham, 'Bingo' Maxwell; it was hard to tell them apart, to feel anything for them or about them, and this indifference was reciprocated.

Stalky Read did have a particular phrase of his own, now I come to think of it: 'Take the first bus to the Prewett.' What the hell did that mean? Park Prewett, it was eventually explained to me, was a famous loony bin, near Basingstoke. If you made an elementary mistake in geography, Stalky's advice never varied: 'First bus to the Prewett. Leaves at two.'

When I was returning to my cubicle after lessons on perhaps my third day at Chatfield, I found that two-thirds of the way down the corridor, barring my path, stood a large boy, about seventeen, with his hands stuck in his belt. He glared at me as I got close, his face set in a sneer. I couldn't take cover in any of the rooms en route because I didn't know any of the boys in them. When eventually I reached him, he sidestepped to prevent me passing. I tried the other side, but he moved across to block the way. I looked up at him to see what he wanted. He was about two feet taller than me and had the features I'd already noticed were common at Chatfield: a mask of erupting spots and damp-looking hair. He didn't really seem to *have* hair, in fact, but something more like a pint of oil poured over his scalp and divided into shiny hanks; his complexion looked as though a carton of raspberry yoghurt had exploded in his face. Eventually he let me pass, kicking me in the coccyx as I went. His name, I was told, was Baynes, J.T.

He had two friends called Wingate and Hood. They told me they'd 'noticed' me. I was 'nervy', that was my trouble, wasn't it?

When I got back that afternoon after football, my sheets were soaking wet and all my clothes had been strewn round the room. I slept on the mattress that night, but the next day it, too, was soaked in water, so I lay down on the springs.

In the main corridor of Collingham there was a table where bread and margarine was sent up twice a day in plastic dustbins. The margarine was wholesale grade, stamped on the wrapper 'not for retail distribution', and often got smeared over the wall and floor, where it mixed with Marmite and golden syrup. A paper bag full of crystals was sent up in the dustbin with it; the idea was that if you mixed them with water, they made some sort of fizzy drink, though I never saw anyone try it. One of my jobs was to clean this area, and for this I was given a cloth that had been used to soak up milk. It was difficult to do more than smear the slick into new positions, while trying not to gag from the smell of the cloth.

My efforts were watched by a tall, pale prefect called Marlow, who looked as though the tightness of his starched collar was preventing the blood from reaching his face. It was to be done again, then again — not for the sake of cleanliness, but for some other, vaguer, reason. And then, said Marlow, looking at the floor, I could do it again.

Eventually, I was told to go and see the head of house, an unsmiling young man called Keys, with the grey face of someone who had eaten a hundredweight of bread and margarine in his five years, but had come to understand Chatfield. He told me that my 'attitude' was wrong and that he was going to beat me with the cane. I wasn't aware that I had an attitude, right or wrong. Alternatively, I could write out the whole school rules — about eight sides of single-spaced small print — three times by ten o'clock the next evening. Keys was short (he played scrum half), but he looked strong, and unstable; there was a deadness in his eyes. I opted for the rules. This meant writing by torchlight beneath the bedclothes and beneath the desk throughout lessons all the following day. Part of the punishment was the risk of being caught by the teacher and beaten anyway. Keys didn't seem gratified when I handed him the encyclopaedia-thick stack of curling sheets; he looked disappointed, and sent me off with a warning that next time it would be beating without the option.

I was told to get up half an hour early and take a cup of tea in bed to the boy in charge of our run of cubicles, who, it turned out, was Baynes. I had to shake him vigorously by the shoulder to rouse him, and when he had cursed me for a time and drunk some tea, he came to inspect my cubicle, running his finger along the glazing bars of the window to look for dust.

My days had a sort of rhythm. Breakfast, silent lessons, back to check on havoc in my room; clear up; more silent lessons, rugby; chores; bed . . . I had a tiny transistor radio, about the size of half a paperback, with an earpiece. I could sometimes manage to escape beneath the bedclothes.

God, I don't know.

★　★　★

The latrine block was some way from our house and no one had told me when we were allowed to go. One morning we were about ten minutes into Physics, when I put up my hand and said, 'Please, sir, can I go to the toilet?'

The teacher said No, I couldn't, I must wait. All the other boys started muttering 'toilet'. I thought I'd picked the wrong time to go, but no one had told me any better. Gradually, I began to see that it wasn't my choice of time but of word. Toilet was considered an outlaw word. I'd never heard the thing called by any other name at home, St B's or the grammar school, so what was I meant to call it? It took me a long time to establish. The big block was called the Jackson

Rears; the urinal halfway up the stairs, the one we shared with the house above, was called the Halfway House. The cubicle beneath the stairs was the Dump. There was no generic.

By the end of the day there was no one in Collingham who didn't refer to me as 'Toilet'. Toilet Engleby, that was my name. I had to suppress a flinch of recognition when someone called out 'Toilet!' in the corridor.

Baynes and Hood and Wingate weren't going to let me get away with that. 'Come here when I call you, Toilet. Don't you know your own name?' They took me to the Dump and held my head in the bowl, then flushed it.

'What's your name?'

'Engleby.'

They went on and on until finally when I came spluttering up, I answered, 'Toilet.' I thought that would satisfy them, but they seemed disappointed when they let me go.

* * *

It was surprising how quickly I got used to this. Every day I woke up with a feeling of low panic in my gut. My defences were on full alert by the time I went down to the bathroom to clean my teeth at seven-fifteen.

The other boys in my term, Francis, McCain and Batley, talked quietly amongst themselves. None of the boys in the year above would chance talking to me, especially the ones I went to lessons with. There was one boy called 'Spaso' Topley, who looked like a fish in specs — the

79

house joke, beneath even bullying — who occasionally gave me a sort of girlish simper but didn't risk speech.

I couldn't blame them. Batley was in some class so elementary that it didn't have even a year number attached to it, so I never saw him, except once, coming back from the rugby field, when he happened to walk past. He said, 'Bad luck, Toilet.' Batley was probably all right in a way.

I had surprisingly been picked for the second team rugby in my year. I played hooker, where the main job was, as Ridgeway might have put it, to 'keep your head down'. Then the First XV hooker got mumps and I was promoted. I didn't know any of the others, because although they were my age they were in different houses and a junior academic year. By some telepathy they'd picked up that it was dangerous to talk to me, though one or two did call me by my proper name, and one said 'Well played.' So I grew keen on rugby and stayed late practising — so much so that when the First XV hooker recovered he couldn't get back into the side. I became a tackler as well as a scrummager; I enjoyed driving my shoulder into someone's solar plexus to hear him gasp. I liked to run behind a pimpled little shit who'd 'toileted' me and throw myself at his ankles, risking the mouthful of studs for the pleasure of hearing him hit the ground; and then he might accidentally get trampled at the bottom of the ruck that followed. I swapped boots with McCain, who hated rugby but had metal studs; sometimes there was blood on my laces.

Afterwards, most people went to the small food shop and bought chips or sweets to supplement the swill doled out from metal troughs at mealtimes. For some reason — being broke, probably — my mother hadn't thought to give me any pocket money so I relied on the bread and margarine sent up to Collingham. One day, though, she sent a cake. When the post came, a young boy called out the name of anyone who had a letter. 'Parcel for Toilet!' called his unbroken voice, and a number of doors opened.

'I think we'd better have a look and see what's in there,' said Baynes, grabbing the parcel. It didn't take him long to tear off the brown paper. 'A cake! Who said you could have a cake, Toilet?'

'Look,' said Hood, 'it's home-made by Mrs Toilet. Can't she afford to go to a shop?'

'It's not a cake,' said Wingate. 'Feel how heavy it is. Catch.'

He threw it to to Hood, who caught it and tore a bit off. He put it in his mouth. 'Christ, it tastes of shit,' he said. 'It tastes of toilet shit.'

'Is that what you eat at home?' said Baynes. 'Toilet shit?'

They began to throw the cake around, sometimes dropping it on purpose, all the time keeping up a commentary, things like, 'What's for lunch today, Mrs Toilet? Let's have shit, shall we?'

I went to the table and picked up the wrapping from the floor and went back to my room, leaving them to do what they wanted with the cake. There was a note inside the brown paper

81

saying, 'Mike, Me and Julie baked this. Hope you like it! Love, Mum.'

It probably wasn't up to much, because neither of them were very good cooks and Julie was only five anyway.

A couple of days later I was doing the evening prep in my room, when Wingate opened the door without knocking. He was a troubled-looking boy who hung around the showers a lot. He didn't say anything, just walked round the cubicle, picking things up, looking at them closely, then putting them down again. He had fewer spots than Baynes, a blue, stubbly chin and dead-fish eyes.

I didn't say anything, and neither did he. He stood by the bed and looked at me. 'Get on with your work, Toilet,' he said eventually.

I looked down to the passage of Livy I was preparing for class the next day. I didn't dare to look at Wingate, but I became aware that he was doing something to himself as he stood over my bed. The Latin sentences swelled and dissolved. I couldn't make much of them. Wingate let out a small grunt. 'Better wash those blankets, Toilet,' he said, buttoning up his trousers.

★   ★   ★

Chatfield was in a straggling village that clung to the perimeter of the school grounds. Upper and Lower Rookley were bisected by the enormous college and its playing fields, its cross-country runs, its rifle ranges, its evergreen woods and assault courses. On top of the hill in Upper

82

Rookley was Longdale, a hospital for the criminally insane. The college and the hospital had been founded in the same year, 1855; the committee of the bin wanted the high ground for the views, the school governors wanted the flat playing fields below, so everyone was happy, if that's the word we're looking for.

Every Monday at nine-fifty, during our double Chemistry period, Longdale had an emergency escape practice, which meant sounding its siren. 'Sir, sir,' said twenty boys at once, 'Bograt's escaped, sir.' Bograt Duncan rolled his eyes and sighed. I tried joining in the communal joke once, but only once.

A patient did escape once, as a matter of fact, and the headmaster called an emergency assembly of the entire school. He warned us not to talk to any strangers in the grounds. I went for a walk in the woods that afternoon, half hoping I might bump into him.

What was odd about Chatfield was that it enjoyed a high reputation. It was expensive. It played rugby against other famous schools, like Harrow, and while a lot of its pupils went off to the navy, plenty went to universities, some even to the best ones.

I never thought of complaining to old Talbot about what was going on because it would have sounded feeble. 'They won't talk to me . . . ' Well, why should they? 'They wreck my room . . . ' Don't tell tales. 'Wingate . . . He . . . You know — on my bed.' Don't be disgusting.

Since the head of the house and the prefects

were all in on the deal, it was in any event semi-official. Why would Mr Talbot take the word of a new boy who said 'toilet' against that of the boys he had himself nurtured and promoted?

His report at half-term proved me right. 'Michael seems to be uncomfortably aware of his own precocity and must be careful not to ruffle feathers in the house.' My mother said, 'What's precocity?'

★　★　★

Sometimes I hid in the bathroom, where Sidney, the disreputable cleaner, took his tea break. Sidney threw a pile of tea leaves into the corridor each morning and swept up the dust with a moulting broom. He was about sixty, with muscular, tattooed forearms, a former corporal in some supply regiment, though evasive about how much 'action' he'd seen.

The problem was that by being there one became a captive audience for his foul stories. One day I found myself in an audience of two (Batley was the other, though I don't know why) sitting on the duckboards at his feet.

'This bird,' Sidney began, 'when I was on leave and we was gettin' on pretty well, and I rolls on top of 'er, see, and she says to me, 'Ooh, Sid, you mustn't do that,' and I says to 'er, 'I'll just put the end in, all right?' and she says, 'All right, Sid,' so I gives 'er a thorough good seein'-to and when I'm done, she says to me, 'Ooh, Sid, you said you'd only put the end in,' and I says, 'Yeah,

I know, but I didn't say *which* end.' '

He laughed until he made himself cough for a minute or so before resuming. 'Another thing. I'll tell you what. The average length of a woman's twat is nine 'n' a half inches. The average length of a man's prick is seven.'

'Really, Sid?'

'Yeah. That means that in Britain alone there's almost a hundred and fifty miles of spare layin' around, so — '

'Gosh, Sidney, that's an awful lot of spare t — '

'So make sure you gets your fair share.'

Batley and I were arranged like the figures in *The Boyhood of Raleigh*, but I don't suppose that this was quite what Millais's old salt was telling his boys. Though on second thoughts, I suppose with old sailors you never know.

In the holidays, I forgot about Chatfield. From the moment I got back into the house in Trafalgar Terrace, I put it from my mind. I've always been able to do that, to make as though things aren't really happening. When you look back at what you've been doing for the last half an hour, for how much of the time have you really been aware of it? When you drive a car, for instance, you're not aware of the functions that your brain and hand and eye are performing at eighty miles an hour, skilled movements that save you and others from death. You're thinking about something else altogether. The music on the radio. What you're doing next Tuesday. You're having an imaginary conversation with someone. We're not really conscious of what

85

we're doing most of the time.

As we entered the final week of the holidays, though, a dry taste came into my mouth. I couldn't sleep.

When I went back to Collingham, I wrote a lot of letters to my mother and some to Julie. My mother wasn't much of a correspondent. She was busy at the hotel and it became clear that writing to me was just one more chore in her busy day.

So, 'Dear Julie,' I might write instead, 'How's things? I've been doing Latin, which is the story of what the Romans did. They were early Italians who conquered other countries. Know the waiter in the Oasis Café near the cinema? He's a Roman. I'm having fun here. I have this game in my room with some socks rolled up in a ball. I try to kick them against a spot on the brick wall of my room. I have different teams, like the Animals against the Birds. You get points for how close you get. I write down the scores on a piece of paper. Starling is very good but Zebra is <u>no good at all</u>. Write to me, Jules. Tell me anything. Tell me about your friends at school and what you've been doing. Love, Mike.'

It was strange to see my name written down like that. It was weeks since I'd heard it. 'Mike.'

After about eight letters of mine, I got three pencil lines. 'dear mike, me and jane plad with her cosens. We had wimpey for tee, love juliexox.' I didn't even know she could write.

And at least I read it before it was intercepted. I gave the letter fag two shillings not to call out my name, so Baynes wouldn't be alerted. I stole

86

the two shillings from a jacket in the changing room, but I didn't know whose it was so I didn't feel bad about it.

I began to steal quite a bit after that. It was useful, and it had a good effect on my morale. I was extremely careful and never took notes, just coins that would be hard to trace, and only small sums, never more than five bob at a time. Once, when I was on changing room sweeping-up duty, I saw Baynes's brown tweed jacket unattended on its hook. I was the last one there and I knew Baynes was doing extra rugby practice until it was dark. There was a pound note in the inside pocket. It was very, very tempting, but I put it back. The one thing I had over Baynes was that I was cleverer than he was. That was an advantage I couldn't afford to blow. For all I knew, it was a plant and he'd noted the serial number.

Of course, it might have given him a dilemma if I'd been caught because I would have been expelled and that would have been a disappointment to him and Hood and Wingate, having no one to torment. But I guessed he would have found a way of not reporting it and of making my punishment more 'informal'.

One of Baynes's favourite tricks was to send me to do a rubbing from a brass engraving in a church a couple of miles away. You were given 25 minutes to change into sports clothes and get there and back, which was impossible, but meant that he could send you again. He only sent me in the first place if it was raining, so the piece of paper was always wet and spoiled and he could question whether I'd even got there.

I used to peer into the raspberry yoghurt, watching to see if any light of kindness might emerge. But there was only ever anger in Baynes's boiling red face — in his narrow, watery little eyes and pussy cheeks, which made him look like a crimson gargoyle.

'Do it again, Toilet. Go. Now.'

Sometimes at night, as I lay in the sopping sheets, I dreamed of killing him. I would show no compassion. Or I would show the same degree of compassion that he had shown to me. It would come to the same thing. Good night, Baynes, I'd say, looking hard into his watery, hating eyes. Good night, Baynes, you, you . . . I knew all the bad words, but none of them was strong enough for my hatred of Baynes. The f-word, the c-word, a lot of b-words . . . The c-word is probably the one I'd have picked. It had a good sound, but it referred to something else, which wasn't relevant; it was feeble, really: for power, it wasn't even close.

I never for a moment considered killing myself, because it wouldn't have achieved anything. Sometimes I had a fantasy of my body being found in the morning and the shock it would cause — how Baynes and Wingate and Hood would be chastened and remorseful; how it would be the making of them as men. They would become fine and philanthropic in their lives; they would spread so much happiness among men that the loss of unmourned Toilet Engleby long ago would in fact be a price worth paying.

But I knew it wouldn't really be like that. What

would actually happen would be that Mr Talbot would ask if anyone knew what the matter was. Keys, the head of house, would officially say I'd been 'nervy', but since he'd dosed me with the rules I'd appeared to be 'settling down'. Ridgeway, my little fag teacher, had got me through the exam and that was all he had to do, so he'd be in the clear. McCain and Francis would say, 'He seemed fine, sir.' Batley would scarcely understand the question. Hood and Wingate and Baynes would feel uneasy, but no more. 'Toilet couldn't handle it, then,' one of them would say, later, when Talbot had gone. 'Yeah, must've been trouble at home or something.' 'He seemed all right in the house.' The thing about those three was that they believed — or at least had convinced themselves — that what they were doing to me was part of the traditional experience that Collingham offered; on behalf of the school, themselves and even me, they were performing some semi-official service.

Mr Talbot himself wouldn't want to prolong the inquiry. Perhaps he'd ask the doctor if I'd been to see him.

The doctor was a nasty little man called Benbow, who specialised in looking at your groin. The first week at school, he had squeezed our genitals in the 'new boys' inspection'. At the start of each subsequent term he required us all to strip except for a dressing gown whose flaps we parted when we reached the chair where he sat, shining a torch to see if we had a fungal growth called TC, a sort of athlete's foot of the crotch. If so, the area was painted purple.

He'd be the last person I'd think of going to see.

Then Mr Talbot might ask the chaplain if I'd consulted him. The answer there would also be No. 'Spunky' Rollason was not consulted about anything, even by the under-chaplain.

My mother wouldn't make a fuss. She didn't understand how the world, let alone such an institution, worked. The headmaster could probably keep it from the newspapers. Within a few days it would be forgotten.

In the end, Baynes, Hood and Wingate would feel nothing, because in the end that's how everything that happens to you feels: it feels like nothing at all, really.

⋆ ⋆ ⋆

But I don't want to think any more about Chatfield now or about Baynes, J.T. It's long over.

It's now 6.30 on Monday 19 November, 1973 and I'm sitting in my room in Clock Court at my ancient university.

I like these details of time. 6.31 on Monday 19 November 1973 is the front edge of time. I live on the forward atoms of the wave of time. It's now 6.32. This is the present, yet it's turning to the past as I sit here. What was future when I started (6.31) is now already past. What is this present, then? It's an illusion; it's not reality if it can't be held. What therefore is there to fear in it? (I'm starting to sound like T.S. Eliot.)

Don't patronise me if you read this thirty years on, will you? Don't think of me as old-fashioned, wearing silly clothes or some nonsense like that. Don't talk crap about 'the seventies', will you, as we now do about 'the forties'. I breathe air like you. I feel food in my bowel and a lingering taste of tea in my mouth. I'm alive, as you are. I'm as modern as you are, in my way — I *couldn't be* more modern. My reality is as complex as yours; the atoms making me and this world in their random movement are as terrible and strange and beautiful as those that make your world. Yours are in fact my atoms, reused. And you too, on your front edge of breaking time, Mr 2003, will be the object of condescending curiosity to the future — to Ms 2033. So don't patronise me. (Unless of course you have completely overturned and improved my world, bringing peace and plenty, and a cure for cancer and schizophrenia, and a unified scientific explanation of the universe comprehensible to all, and a satisfactory answer to the philosophical and religious questions of our time. In which case you would be permitted to patronise primitive little 1973. Well, have you done those things? Got a cure for the common cold yet? Have you? Thought not. How's your 2003 world, then? A few wars? Some genocide? Some terrorism? Drugs? Abuse of children? High crime rate? Materialistic obsessions? More cars? Blah-blah pop music? Vulgar newspapers? Porn? Still wearing jeans? Thought so. Yet you've had an extra thirty years to sort it out!)

The important thing is that this is now: 6.38,

19 November, 1973. It's dark on Clock Court with its low box hedges and cobbled triangles. The lights are on in the dining hall where dinner will shortly be served.

Nothing in the future has yet happened. I find that a good thought.

As well as the Quicksilver Messenger Service poster, there is one for Procol Harum live at the Rainbow, Finsbury Park. I have on my cork board a picture of Princess Anne and Mark Phillips, taken from a magazine; one of David Bowie with Lou Reed and Iggy Pop, a rare monochrome poster showing them with their arms round one another's shoulders in some New York disco; one of Marc Bolan, because he reminds me of Julie; and one of Julie in her school straw hat with her sticking-out teeth.

I took a train to London from Reading to see Procol Harum when they premiered their new album, *Grand Hotel*, with an orchestra and choir. It was good, but I wasn't sure Mick Grabham was up to it as Robin Trower's replacement on guitar, particularly on 'Whaling Stories', a song of which I need only to hear the opening note to find my stomach tense and my saliva fill with the re-experienced taste of Glynn Powers's A-grade hashish. There's something essential in Trower's tone that Grabham didn't catch.

This being the case, I bought Trower's solo album whose first track, 'I Can't Wait Much Longer', bears a weight of melancholy that is unendurable — in my ears anyway. (Though I still quite like it. In the doom there's passion and booze and things to do with living. For a distillation of despair with *no* redeeming qualities, for a tincture of suicide in A minor, try 'Facelift' or 'Slightly All the Time' from Soft Machine's *Third*.)

I go to the corner cupboard and take out the white vermouth. It's that time of day: time for the small blue ten-milligram pill and Sainsbury's Chambéry with ice. I feel all right, within my limits. I've known much worse. Down the hatch.

I often think good music is too much to take. Think of Sibelius Five, when the earth's weight seems to shift on its axis in the closing moments. It's well made, as it recapitulates the main theme and finally lets it out; but it describes a place I don't want to look at, let alone inhabit.

I listened to Beethoven's late quartets yesterday. They're quite wintry, aren't they? But they have the feeling of a man thinking about death. And he can't keep out a slight sense of pleasure — of smugness. I'm old; I've won the right to fear no more the heat of the sun. Feel sorry for me and admire me. Indulge me. I've deserved it.

'Late work'. It's just another way of saying feeble work. I hate it. Monet's messy last water lilies, for instance — though I suppose his eyesight was shot. *The Tempest* only has about twelve good lines in it. Think about it. *The Mystery of Edwin Drood*. Hardly *Great Expectations*, is it? Or Matisse's paper cut-outs, like something from the craft room at St B's. Donne's *sermons*. Picasso's *ceramics*. Give me strength.

There's a lot of political activity at the moment to do with 'co-residence', which means boys and girls living in the same college, or not. At the moment there's only one, King's, which has both, and on Wednesday there's a torchlight march on (not to) St Cat's, whose Master is thought to be responsible for not letting girls, or women as we call them in this context, into men's colleges. I see I'm down for something called a 'co-residency lunch' in Trinity Parlour next week, too. I'll go because I think Jennifer's going to be there. She's not very political, Jen, though I think she'd like to be; she hasn't really got enough time, what with all those concerts and films and theatres and parties in those tiny cold terraces and writing for *Broadsheet*, the student mag, and studying for a first-class degree, and Jen Soc (which is a bit political admittedly) and cleaning the house for the others and dutifully writing home and volleyball — and sex.

But she's keen on co-res, I think, on the grounds that girls should have what boys have — viz., the best colleges, and not have to risk getting Girton calves bicycling out to their remote and defended buildings of no architectural interest.

I'll be there then for the warm quiche and oniony salad on paper plates and a glass of Hirondelle or maybe just white coffee. Something about milky coffee with food turns my stomach. The old Jews were on to something.

What do I think about co-res? I think the seven Puritan divines who founded my college

94

would be appalled at the thought of Goody Arkland and other witches in the rooms of New Court. Build your own colleges, you denimed jezebels, they'd be thinking. And it's true you can't bend with each fashionable wind — you can't be like the Church of England, constantly updating its eternal verities. Either Christ was God, in which case He knew what He was doing when He chose male apostles only; or, he was a hapless Galilean sexist now ripe for a rethink. Not both. That's what I think about co-res: a truth is either good for all time or it isn't true at all. (On the other hand, it would mean better bathrooms.)

★　★　★

Baths remind me of Chatfield. Now I'll tell you what happened next.

Yes. I can manage it. I'm not reliving it, I'm only describing it. I can deal with all my past experiences, I think. Here we go:

What I found trying was that Baynes, Hood and Wingate never seemed to take a day off. I felt that one day a week they might have games or work or something more important to do, but nothing, it seemed, took precedence over Engleby, T. (Even I thought of myself with this initial now.)

Hood sometimes paused when he saw me, as though for an hour or so his mind had been on something else; but the sight of me was enough to bring him back to earth. I studied their timetables and tried to make sure they never saw me. In the break between lessons, I didn't go back into Collingham. I stored my books in some open shelves at the foot of the staircase leading to another house. I wandered round the quads, reading the notices, but I grew very hungry and sometimes had to make a grab-and-run raid on the bread and margarine table.

Anyway, I was always visible at mealtimes and then, at six-thirty, there was a roll call, after which you had to go to your room to do prep — and from then on I was a tethered prey.

There was a break between preps of half an hour in which you could make cocoa or eat the bread and marge before prayers. Usually, Mr Talbot came up for this and read something improving by Albert Schweitzer or C.S. Lewis. Other times it was left to the head of house, dead-eyed Keys, to send us off to bed uplifted.

Second prep led into lights out and was strictly private. I was doing maths at this time one night, almost ready to call it a day, when Wingate came into my room. I was in pyjamas and dressing gown; he was in day clothes. He had hollow cheeks, floppy brown hair and never showed emotion. Unlike Baynes with his simmering violence and his explosive pustules, Wingate was neutral, as though everything was happening in a calm deep pool. His pointed Adam's apple dragged in his tight throat as he spoke.

'Time for a bath, Toilet.'

'No, my bath nights are Tuesday and Friday.'

'You heard me.'

He held the door open and I followed him

slowly out into the Collingham corridor. He led me down to the bathroom, on the floor below the Halfway House. There were two baths, a shower, a row of basins and some benches made of duckboards. On these were sitting Baynes, Hood and others — Marlow, I think, 'Plank' Robinson (said to be the dimmest boy at Chatfield, a title not easily won), 'Leper' Curran, Bograt Duncan and one or two more.

'Get in,' said Hood.

'Take your clothes off,' said Wingate.

I did what they said and climbed into the bath, which was cold.

'Get your head under,' said Baynes. And he held it under. He had huge hands. He was as strong as a man, stronger than my father had been. Eventually I got out from under his grasp.

He was laughing. Usually when they beat me up, I didn't resist enough for it to be fun for them — like when I undressed, I suppose I should have refused or struggled. But this time I fought back because you couldn't just let someone drown you.

I started to get out, but Wingate pushed me in again. It was very very cold.

'You get out when I say so,' said Baynes, snarling so much the words seemed to come out not through his mouth but through the pus of his cheeks.

I was shivering, in paroxysms, but managed to stay in. It was better to stay in than try to get out and have to fight, so they would have an 'excuse' to touch me.

I plunged my head under the water voluntarily. There were two reasons. One, I hoped it would give them sport or entertainment, so they'd let me go — they'd be satisfied.

Two, the physical shock took away the pain of being.

★   ★   ★

Still, I had that tiny radio beneath the bedclothes with its earphone like a deafie's. Radio Luxembourg, 208 metres in the medium wave. Terrible reception, but that dodgy signal was my connection to a better place. The Horace Batchelor Infradraw Method . . . Keynsham, K.E.Y.N.S.H.A.M, Bristol . . . But there was laughter, and, boy, I liked those songs. God. 'Penny Lane'. It wasn't a song, it was a book, it was a world. The Yardbirds, Sandie Shaw — and Dusty Springfield with that crack in her mid-range that sent a shiver up my back as I lay curled beneath the grey woollen blankets. Amen Corner. This was something to hang on to. Simon Dupree and the Big Sound, the Beach Boys, 'Wouldn't It Be Nice'. Oh yes, it certainly would. I'd read an article in a magazine about California and about the canyons above Los Angeles with their wooden A-frame houses (whatever *they* were), pet cats, dirt roads, girls with long hair and guitars, soft drugs and kindness and open house and everyone sleeping with everyone else in this heavenly soft climate and dreaming of it all on such a winter's d-a-a-ay . . .

'Toilet.'

I was so lost in 'California Dreamin'' that I almost had a heart attack when I heard Wingate's voice and felt a thump in the small of my back that had the hallmark of Baynes's superfluous violence. I pulled out the earphone and stuffed the radio down between my legs as I sat up in the iron bed.

'What is it?'

'Get out of bed.'

Wingate turned the light on.

'What's this?'

'It's a radio, Wingate.'

'Are you in Remove year?'

'No.'

'So why have you got a radio?'

'And why are you listening to it after lights out?'

'Let's have a look at it, Simon.'

'Whoops, John, you've dropped it.'

'Oh dear, I think it may be broken. Careful, Simon. Oh no, you've stepped on Toilet's radio. It's all broken now.'

'Maybe I could — oh dear, I've dropped it again.'

'Never mind, it wasn't much of a radio, was it? I expect Mrs Toilet got it from a cracker.'

'I expect she can get another one when Toilet gets into the Remove.'

★　★　★

The cold bath became a regular event. My genitals shrivelled when I heard the late-night

99

footfall outside my door.

It maybe doesn't sound so bad, but a cold bath on a winter night . . . Ever tried it? I don't know where Chatfield got its cold water from, but it felt as though they had a pipeline to the Baltic.

Sometimes it would just be Wingate on his own. But usually there'd be others. Bograt Duncan was keen.

They just stared. They lounged on the duckboard bench and stared. I wondered if they wanted to touch. Wingate liked to hold me under. Baynes liked a struggle, so I didn't offer one.

Hood merely gazed on, impassive. He smiled a bit. Hood was the only half-human one of the three; he was not grotesque to look at, but with his blue eyes and open smile, quite normal. He alone retained some pretence that this was all fair game, that it was part of normal life. For instance, it was Hood who told me that pouring a bucket of water over my bedclothes was an old Chatfield custom called 'splicing the mainbrace'. Was there a scintilla of comfort in thinking that we were all part of a great tradition?

Wingate and Baynes were in a different place. There was no pretence there. They had sold out, crossed over.

Hood's occasional smile wasn't reassuring, though. If, as it suggested, this was all just part of the way things were done, then it couldn't be resisted — or stopped.

I thought his smile showed it was costing him a bit, though. I think it was partly to square it with himself. He hadn't cut free like Wingate and Baynes. There was a twitch of stress or conscience there.

The strangest thing was that it never did seem to satisfy them. They always looked disappointed when they let me go. I wished I could have pleased them, so that then they might have relented.

★ ★ ★

There was a sweetshop in Lower Rookley that was run by an old woman. I asked her for a bag of sherbet lemons or some nonsense that meant she had to stand on some steps and reach up to a big glass jar. While her back was turned, I was able to take my pick of the chocolate bars spread out on the counter. There was no hurry, as her arthritic joints let her move only in slow motion. I pocketed a petrol lighter from a stand next to the cash till while I was at it.

I paid her for the sherbet lemons with a shilling I'd nicked from Plank Robinson's trousers.

'Thank you, dear.'

'No, thank you.'

In Upper Rookley, there was a similar shop, though the owner was a man, and quite a bit younger. He also sold cigarettes, but annoyingly he kept these behind the counter, out of my reach. One Saturday, I went round the back of his shop, which shared a delivery yard with the dry cleaners next door. I sat down beside the high wire fence and watched. At about five, there

101

was a delivery from a large van, and this was what I had been waiting for. If I couldn't get them retail, I'd go wholesale.

The security was hopeless. The delivery man left the back of the van open while he was inside the shop and he was never away for less than five minutes at a time. Tea, biscuit, chat, mustn't grumble.

The problem was that the back of the van was filled with large unopened cardboard boxes and I was only looking for a couple of cartons. It was not until the end of his visit, when the shop was fully restocked, that he'd return with some opened boxes. And he didn't hang around then, but banged up the tailgate and drove off.

On the third Saturday, I was lucky. I had moved a little closer and was crouched down behind a car. The driver went through the back corridor to get the retailer's signature on the docket, but in the meantime the shop phone had rung, so he had to wait. But I didn't. I moved swiftly and dipped my hand into an open cardboard box. Two cartons of . . . I was hoping for Benson & Hedges or Rothman's, but they turned out to be Embassy. Typical cheapskate Rookley. I was out of that gate and down the backstreet in two seconds with the cigarettes tucked into the duffel bag I lugged my books round in.

Back in Collingham, I Sellotaped them to the underside of my iron bedstead until I could think of a better place. The next thing I had to do was find a way of getting them into the

102

market. I knew who the likely takers were, but none of them spoke to me. Then I got lucky.

★ ★ ★

One day I was coming out of the Jackson Rears in the mid-morning break when I saw Spaso Topley leaning against a pillar by the quad. As I walked past, he muttered, 'Engleby?'

For a moment, I couldn't think who he was talking to. Then I stopped and turned and warily said, 'Yes?'

Spaso moved towards me. He had splayed feet and horn-rimmed glasses; although he had a deep voice there was something girlish about him. He said, in a rush, 'Would you like to go to the cinema on Sunday if you do we can get a chit from Talbot and I know where I can borrow you a bike.'

He was looking flustered and nervous. He kept glancing up and down the pillared colonnade.

'Well?'

I swallowed. 'OK.'

'See you by the bike racks at two but you've got to see Talbot first and bring your chit.'

He waddled off on his large feet before I could say anything.

Mr Talbot could be visited in his study after lunch, and when I told him what I wanted, he looked displeased. 'Topley? Isn't there someone in your own year you could go with?'

'It's just that Topley asked me, sir.'

He pulled a pad towards him, wrote on it and pulled off a small sheet. 'Bike Leave.' He handed it to me. 'Next time, Engleby, go with someone in your own year.'

Next time, Talbot, do your job and find out what's going on in your house. 'Yes, sir.'

When Sunday came, I got down to the bike racks at five to two.

I stood behind a hut, to stay out of sight, and kept looking at my watch. Eventually, Topley rounded the corner. He came up and handed me a key to a padlock.

He said, 'I've got Leper Curran's bike for you. He owes me a favour for saving him Tubby Lyneham's wrath. Electromagnetic fields. A Topley speciality. We toilers in the Collingham vineyard must stick together.'

He really was a prize ass.

We bicycled off together and found a cinema in the local town, about twenty minutes' ride away. It was showing quite a good film with Steve McQueen in it, though I can't remember the name.

Afterwards, we went to a café where I bought us poached eggs and beans on toast with tea and chocolate cake, courtesy of a ten-shilling note I'd taken from Marlow's rugby shorts. I'd broken my no-notes rule because I knew I'd be spending it off-radar.

'Do you smoke, Topley?'

'Good heavens no.'

'You must know people who do. In your year.'

'That would be telling.'

'I know. That's why I'm asking you. Tell me. I am buying the tea after all.'

It was hard work, but eventually I persuaded

him to act as go-between. He devised some rococo plan involving 'safe drops' in the Jackson Rears, which, since it was under a permanent fog of cigarette smoke, was one of the least safe places in Chatfield. But that was his problem. I left the goods, a packet at time, behind the cistern in the Dump; Spaso shipped them onwards. I never knew who the end-buyers were. It was a brilliant chain, with two natural cut-outs guaranteeing anonymity. We charged two-thirds shop retail price and split it down the middle. It was very good money. I think Topley spent his first pay packet on a second-hand rheostat.

★ ★ ★

What happened then? Oh God, I don't know.

Days. Days are what we live in.

Days came. Days went.

I reached puberty. No one threw raspberry yoghurt in my face; I didn't exude sebum through my follicles and pores; I didn't smell of feet or pits; my voice didn't do comic octave-jumps; my trousers didn't flap at mid-calf. All that happened was that my back grew about a foot in width one night; my feet looked suddenly remote (I bought new trousers — cash, no chit, to the manager's amazement — at the school shop); and one morning I awoke with evidence that I was capable of perpetuating the Engleby line. That was all.

I built the cigarette business and dabbled in marijuana, though it was risky and hard to come by. There were not that many takers at Chatfield either. I found an off-licence on the London road with a delivery arrangement as lax as the tobacconist's and was able to run bottles of vodka and whisky back in the saddlebag of a bicycle I'd stolen from outside the local girls' school. There was always a good market in drink, and I shipped it on through a Ghanaian boy in Greville whom I'd met in the Combined Cadet Force. Since he could hardly speak English he hadn't twigged that no one was meant to talk to me.

Hood and Wingate eventually left.

Baynes stayed another term (incredibly, he was not bad at work and was sitting the Oxford entrance exam in December). He had an accident, I was pleased to learn, coming back from late rugby practice in October. He was concussed, with a large contusion on the back of the head, and his leg was broken in three places; he appeared to have lost his footing going over the ditch at the edge of the wood by the practice ground, where he had been taking kicks at goal on his own in the twilight. He cracked his head on the concrete edge of the footbridge. He said he had no recollection of falling, but Dr Benbow put this down to the concussion (presumably after inspecting his groin by torchlight first).

Spaso Topley was discovered to have 400 Sobranie Virginia cigarettes in his tuck box and was expelled in the year of his A levels. I really don't know where they came from. Not from me. I think he'd become greedy and started operating on his own. It wasn't a clever place to keep them. I kept mine in a former ammunition box, with a lock, in the Armoury shed. As a midshipman I had been entrusted by Chief Petty Officer Dunstable with a number of keys during a CCF night operation, and a short delay in returning them had enabled me to have them copied at the shoe-repair shop in Upper Rookley. But keeping them in your tuck box in your room . . . Dear oh dear. I think with no A levels Spaso became a lab technician or something.

And what happened to me? Without Hood, Wingate and Baynes, my life became easier. The habit of not talking to me was hard to break. My classmates kept up their silence till the day they left. In the house, Francis and McCain occasionally asked for the salt or the tea, but I didn't bother to answer. I didn't need their belated acknowledgement. 'Pukey' Weldon in the year above asked me if I'd like to go see a football match and I told him where to put his ticket. He looked surprised. That was about it, until I turned my attention to the years that had succeeded us.

There was a boy called Stevens in the first year, who was outgoing and enthusiastic. He was in a school play and in a rugby team. People in his year seemed to like him. He was a small, fair child with smooth skin and laughing eyes. He was good at work, too, from what I gathered.

I saw his parents deliver him back at the beginning of his second term. The average Chatfield family group comprised a sexless crone of a mother with uncut greying hair in an embarrassing slide, like a small girl's; a repressed, bald father with a pipe; a bow-legged Labrador you could smell at twenty yards; and a dilapidated shooting brake of a discontinued kind.

Steven's father drove a new car, shiny, dogless; he looked alert and friendly. (Plus, he was alive.) The mother had glossy fair hair, newly set, and appeared to be about twenty-five. She had a figure. Both looked unashamedly fond of the smiling son, whom they saw off with embraces and jokes.

I noticed Stevens.

* * *

Significant things happen so slowly that it's seldom you can say: it was then — or then. It's only after the change is fully formed that you can see what's happened. We were doing World War Two in History at this time. To the occupied French in 1940, co-operating with the Germans was not only a practical but even a noble course of action, according to old 'Sapper' Hill — one that was enshrined in article two of the armistice and boasted of by the French government. Was there one fatal moment when co-operation went too far, so that they found they were doing the Occupier's dirty work for him? Was there a day — an hour — when in deporting Jews they stopped following the Nazis and began to lead them? Was it when they offered to fill the trains with Jews of French as well as other nationalities? Was it when they said the Jews could be taken from the Free as well as the Occupied zone? Was it when they offered the Jewish children — to fulfil the 'quotas'?

Yes, no, both, all. There was a day, there was a moment when something reasonable changed into something that would haunt them for ever. But it wasn't visible at the time, because at the time everything is only a tiny addition to what's already there.

Stevens had the room that I'd once had, the last one on the left. As you got older, you moved term by term gradually towards the middle of the corridor. I was coming out of my room one morning when Stevens brushed against me as he was running to a lesson. First-years were always rushed; they had no 'study' periods, no time off and hadn't yet been able to drop any subjects.

I called him back and told him to look where he was going. He smiled and apologised and shifted from foot to foot in a hurry to get going again.

It wasn't really good enough, was it?

A week or so later, during second prep, I found I was bored. I'd done all the work I needed to do. I'd written to Julie, not that she'd reply, and I was fed up with reading Mickey Spillane and Dryden.

I had no clear plan in mind as I left my room quietly and walked down to the end of the corridor. Stevens, T.J., said the strip above the door.

I was thinking of something completely different when I opened the door and found him bent over a book at his desk, in pyjamas and dressing gown.

My mind was elsewhere when I noticed the look of terror on his face.

'Time for a bath, Stevens,' I said.

4

The co-residency lunch in Trinity Parlour was what Chris from Selwyn called a 'real gas'. There were many more people than had been expected, so the quiche and Hirondelle ran out quickly. Jennifer said she'd go out and get some more food from a supermarket and I said I'd go with her. There was a whip-round of fifty-pence pieces and off we went to . . . God, I suppose it must have been Marks & Spencer. The shop opposite Boots at any rate. Quite a walk from Trinity. By the time we got back we discovered that someone had been to the college buttery and got bread and cheese as well.

Jen seemed a bit cross about missing the discussion, though her friend Molly assured her not much had happened. All the boys from places like Churchill and Fitz were understandably keen on the idea of having girls on their staircases, but even the ones from the older colleges like Christ's and Corpus were enthusiastic.

The girls were a bit more guarded. They wanted equality in all things and that meant equal numbers, but they felt attached to their bluestocking institutions. They didn't want *them* to go co-res. It wasn't what those fierce women founders had envisaged, was it, to have people like Chris from Selwyn in the corridors of female scholarship, in football clothes and leering.

Some boy from Trinity itself said shouldn't they suggest to the university a gradual change, so that the girls retained four colleges, boys had four and the others moved slowly towards co-res as their statutes permitted, aiming to have gone the whole way in about ten years' time.

This went down badly. He was called a 'Fabian' and worse.

Someone from Caius said there they needed a two-thirds majority of all Fellows past and present and that some footnote in the statutes implied that the wishes of the dead must also be consulted, or presumed.

The debate was fierce and long, but produced an odd atmosphere, something like a party. People came to know one another quickly and seemed to enjoy it. At three o'clock a porter came to close the room and demand the key. Most were in any case due at sport or experiments or lectures (I'd missed the Australopithecine at two).

Chris from Selwyn said we should carry on the discussion later, but his rooms weren't big enough. Simon from Pembroke said he knew a very switched-on Fellow of Sidney Sussex, a Classics don with a charming modern Greek wife, who should be asked along.

The grumpy porter kept asking for the key until Molly said in desperation, 'We can all meet back at my house. Seven o'clock. Everyone bring a bottle. And a supporter.'

Jennifer gave her an amazed look — 'My house?!' — as Molly slowly repeated the address a dozen times.

I dropped in on Stellings in his room that afternoon, but he was listening to the LP of *High Society* on his expensive headphones and didn't want to talk. I walked over Jesus's Bones or Christ's Pieces or Corpus Domini — some area of municipal green — and found myself in King Street. In my second year I did something called the King Street Run, a drinking challenge. You had to drink a pint of bitter in each of the street's eight pubs in less than two hours without going to the toilet for any reason. If you did, or if you vomited, you had to start that pint again. You had to be accompanied by a 'jockey' who'd done it before; mine was a friend of Stellings's called McCaffrey who, aptly, spent his life at Newmarket. He told me to eat a lot in the dining hall, to cover the food with salt and drink no water. Then we walked to the first pub. The boy next to me drank his pint so quickly he threw up straight away, was penalised with another and never made it out of that bar. I completed the course in an hour and a half, in the first group of finishers. It wasn't that hard. I had a slight sense of anticlimax when I got back to the college bar, where I had a couple of barley wines and a gin and tonic.

That afternoon, after the co-res lunch, since Stellings didn't want to see me, I went to the Footballers and helped myself to a pint of Adnams, leaving the money on the till, because the landlord was asleep in his usual place, on the floor behind the bar. I sat by the fire and had a few more, always being careful to leave what I owed.

113

At seven I set off for Jennifer's house and smoked a joint on the way. I rang the bell. The party had hardly started, but I felt surprisingly relaxed. Jen was in the kitchen, cooking a large rice dish, so I sat and talked to Anne for a bit while other people began to arrive.

By about nine there must have been seventy people or more in that tiny freezing house. It was almost impossible to get through to the kitchen, where the wine was. The corridor and the doorway were blocked by students, whose army greatcoats and sheepskin jerkins, beards and bushy hair took up all the space. I went to the off-licence on the next street and bought a bottle of wine for myself, which I kept in my coat pocket after I'd forced the cork in with the handle of a knife.

Music was playing — the Velvet Underground, the Eagles, Can and Roxy Music, I think. There were lots of people I knew there — Nick and Hannah and various others from Tipperary and people I'd met at the co-residency lunch. The rooms were what they call 'heaving', which is the right word when people are shoulder to shoulder and some are trying to dance, some to escape and some to manoeuvre a paper cup, a paper plate and a plastic fork in rice and chopped green pepper with occasional tiny flakes of tuna fish.

I went upstairs with my bottle to escape the crush and opened a door into a bedroom.

It was dark in there and it was cold. There was an unlit gas fire on one side of the room. The bed had a few coats thrown across it, over a

114

duvet with a pale blue, clean, just-ironed cover. This was the first duvet I'd seen in England, and it looked exotic in a drab, Scandinavian way.

I shut the door behind me.

The desk had history textbooks in three or four divided piles. I sat down at the desk. There were notebooks with her handwriting. There was a tiny piece of foil with about ten bob's worth of second-rate hash in it. (I licked some off my finger.) There was a photograph of a house with a man and a woman outside it, smiling. There was a birthday card with a boat on it and a half-used lipsalve.

Through the window in the darkness I could see the jumble of small slate roofs on the brick terraced cottages. I imagined a cat. I imagined a gas fire, ski socks (even though I wasn't quite sure what they were) and morning tea. I imagined humorous living parents, with enough money and jokes about toothpaste and boy-friends and tights and Brian Martin's endless speech.

I gently pulled open a desk drawer. Beneath some envelopes, a pad of paper and a new, unused blister-pack of contraceptive pills, I found a large diary, full of closely written entries.

I thought about my mother — for a second. Then I was able to put her out of my mind, along with much else.

* * *

There was a note in my pigeonhole this morning from Dr Woodrow, the fleshy one who interviewed me for the entrance award. 'Dear Mr Engleby, I would be most obliged if you could drop into my room (G12) for a brief informal chat one day. Would Tuesday at noon be convenient? Peter Woodrow.'

I stood outside, where I had stood that winter morning. I wondered what had happened to the clever-looking boy, my competitor; I'd never seen him again.

'Come in.'

Woodrow had glasses perched halfway down his thick nose; his grey hair needed cutting. He pointed me to the armchair where Gerald Stanley had sat to ask his asinine questions.

'How are you enjoying Natural Sciences? An unusual move for an English scholar.'

'I know. I didn't do that well in Part One B, but I think it's all right now.'

'Yes, so I gather. Have you thought what you might do when you go down?'

Woodrow was sitting at the table where he had sat before, leafing through my papers.

'No, I haven't.'

'I sometimes try to help out a bit. The university appointments board can place most people. But informally I sometimes . . . Would you like a glass of hock? Or sherry, perhaps?'

'No, I don't drink alcohol.'

'I see. Would you describe yourself as a loner?'

'No more than most. I have friends.' Stellings. Jen.

'Good, good, that's important. But self-sufficient?'

'I've learned to be.'

116

'Good, good. Equally good.'

Woodrow sounded as though he was choosing between the cheese soufflé and the orange posset at a college feast.

He lit a pipe. 'Do you speak any languages? German? French? Russian?'

'Not really. German and French O level.'

'So you have the basic grammar.'

'I suppose so.'

'And you're a quick learner.'

'Averagely.'

'More than averagely according to Dr Waynflete.'

'Maybe.'

'Have you ever thought of the Foreign Office?'

Not really. The idea of the Foreign Office scared me. I pictured it full of people from Oxford, or from schools like Eton and Winchester, Rugby and Wellington — bilingual, duplicitous. Debonair.

'Often,' I said.

'I could perhaps put in a word for you if you were interested.'

'That would be very kind.'

I had no intention of serving in the visa section of the Belgrade embassy, but I was intrigued by the interest shown in me. It was so . . . Unprecedented. I wondered if there was some gay aspect to it.

Woodrow coughed a couple of times. 'What are your politics? Are you much involved in that sort of thing?'

I thought of Jen Soc, Lib, Lab and Con Soc. I wanted people to be happy, but that wasn't much of a position. I didn't answer.

Woodrow looked at me. 'Will you vote in the general election?'

I shook my head. 'Who governs Britain?' That was the question. Who governs Britain? Heath or the miners? Heath or Wilson? What was the other guy called? Not him obviously.

'I understand you took part in the march on St Catharine's.'

'That wasn't political. It was about whether the colleges should have both sexes.'

'It acquired a political and ad hominem tone at one point, I understand.'

I didn't know what he was talking about. 'How did you know I was on that march?'

'I believe there's a march planned in protest against British troops in Northern Ireland. Will you be going on that?'

It depends if Jennifer Arkland's going on it. 'I haven't decided yet. When is it?'

'If you *are* interested in a career in the Foreign Office it would obviously be better not to be seen to be in open conflict with the government of the day. Obviously.'

Woodrow gave a small laugh. I nodded.

'In private of course you are entitled to whatever views you wish. Private is the key word here.'

'How would they ever know, anyway, if I'd been on some little student march?'

Woodrow breathed in noisily. 'On matters of national security, such as Northern Ireland, the security services are as vigilant as possible. They want information before not after the event.'

I felt my jaw loosen. 'You mean a photographer is — '

'I haven't the faintest idea how they proceed. I'm merely pointing out that if you are serious about the Foreign Office then you need to think carefully about such things.'

★ ★ ★

I left Woodrow's rooms and returned to my own in Clock Court, where I listened to some Mozart and *Rainbow in Curved Air* by Terry Riley.

I can't see the point of Mozart. Of Mozart I can't see the point. The point of Mozart I can't see. See I can't of Mozart the point. Can't I of Mozart point the see . . . I can't see the point of Mozart.

That's not a tune, that's an algorithm. An algorithm in a powdered wig.

Stellings has this idea that 'classical' music will die before Tamla Motown, because it has no tunes by which it can be remembered. (For the sake of his argument, you have to exclude opera, particularly Puccini.)

It still isn't true. Off the top of my head, I can think of at least ten great orchestral tunes. Elgar has three, Holst one, Schubert two, Brahms one, Tchaikovksy one, Handel two. Beethoven, er . . . Mozart, mmm . . . Hang on! Sibelius. The Intermezzo of the *Karelia* suite.

Not really a tune, according to Stellings, more of a brass-band march; or 'Sousa on a good day' as he put it. His point is that *My Fair Lady, South Pacific* or *Porgy and Bess* — let's say the work of Rodgers, Gershwin, Berlin — have more true melody, *and* of a better quality, than the whole 'classical' canon.

He jabs his finger in your face and barks out choices that you have to call at once. 'The main theme of the *Trout* quintet or 'This Nearly Was Mine'? *Fingal's Cave* or 'On the Street Where You Live'? Just pure melody, OK? Bach's 23rd Goldberg Variation or 'Stranger on the Shore' by Mr Acker Bilk? Piano Dirge for Wet Monday Afternoon in D Flat Minor by César Franck or 'All I See is You' by Dusty Springfield?'

Stellings is mad, though I suppose I see what he means.

Terry Riley isn't long on melody either, to be honest. You have to listen to it many, many times, and then you can begin to see how the patterns build up. He must have awfully quick hands on the keyboard.

The other thing you need to really appreciate T. Riley's music is to have smoked about ten quid's worth of premium marijuana. I'm pretty sure Riley had when he wrote the stuff.

That's what I did after I'd seen Woodrow. Although I find dope gives me some memory loss, I don't really mind about that. Quite apart from the effect of the chemical in the brain, the *taste* is so exquisite . . .

Perhaps it's obvious to you what old Woodrow was driving at.

If so, I must have misremembered or misrepresented what he said because it certainly wasn't obvious at the time.

* * *

All that seems a lifetime ago now. Why?

Because something truly terrible has happened. It's very hard for me to believe or think about it in any cogent way. I can't even believe that I'm sitting at my desk in Clock Court and I'm writing these words down, but it appears to be the case.

Nobody told me about it, as I feel they should have done. It was barely even 'news' by the time I heard it, having been known for almost twenty-four hours. And the first I find out is that I'm staring at a faculty noticeboard on Sidgwick Site and the lecture schedule is dwarfed by this large poster with a picture of a girl all too familiar. It takes me some time to register the full bleakness of what is being said. Third-year history student Jennifer Arkland has disappeared.

* * *

Notoriety is such a very odd thing. From the moment her face appeared on that poster, Jennifer has stopped being herself.

Vanished girl. Gone. Something pious has attached itself to her. It's no longer possible to think of her as the girl in the next seat at the lecture. It's impossible to think of her at all without a whiff of sanctimony.

People compete to express how well they knew her and what a great person she was — is. 'I refuse to speak of her in the past' has become a

121

self-righteous refrain in the tea room.

We all feel estranged from her. She's not herself any more.

For some days it was presumed, or hoped, that she had gone on a research trip or a holiday without telling her housemates, or her parents or her friends. This was in fact unlikely, bordering on impossible. She was an organised sort of person and aware of the anxieties of others. She could project herself into people's thoughts and imagine what they felt. It was a habit; she couldn't *not* show consideration for those near to her.

Still, on the grounds that the banal or simple is the answer to most mysteries, people keep saying there must be a straightforward explanation and that Jen will turn up fine and well in Harrogate or Paris or Lymington tomorrow.

She hasn't.

In the Kestrel and the Whim, among those who knew her less well or not at all, the consensus is similar, but for a different reason. These people back the anticlimactic resolution — she left a message with the porter and he forgot to pass it on; she left a note in her tutor's pigeonhole and it got lost in the other mail — for a different reason. They back the banal because they want the exciting; they would like her to have been abducted, tortured and disembowelled by a savage because that would be much more interesting than the missing-message explanation. They don't want to seem callous by speculating in the lurid, however; plus, it's tempting providence. If you're hoping for the premium-bond jackpot, you talk about the preponderance of £25 prizes.

What is clear, however, is that whatever the outcome, Jennifer has in fact been taken away from us. She could never be herself again, because even if she reappeared it would be difficult to think of her in the same way. That innocent girl who suggested the Soc trip to Paris, who cleared up the plates at the end of the meeting in her new jeans and grey sweater, pushing the hair back behind her ear . . . She isn't coming back.

★ ★ ★

The newspapers were slow to pick up what was going on — or not going on. It was round the university and in the local press for several days before one of the national papers ran a sizeable story on page five.

I know the page number because I have the story on the desk in front of me in my room in Clock Court now, as I write.

'Top girl student disappears' says the headline. 'Fears were growing last night over the safety of Jennifer Arklam, 20, a brilliant third-year geography undergraduate at . . . '

They did at least get the name of the university right.

'Popular and lively Jenny, oldest of four sisters from Lynmouth in Hampshire, was last seen walking back to her house from a party in Malcolm Street, near Jesus College. Her boyfriend, Robin Wilson, a third-year student reading history in Claire College, said, 'Jenny was very happy, she had no problems that I knew of. We are all very worried about where she is and I would beg her to get in touch if she reads this.' '

There's then a lot of stuff about her family. 'Richard Arklam, 52, an architect with local firm Boyd and Denning and housewife Lesley, 46, who hails originally from Newbury in Hampshire . . . Police found traces of the drug cannabis in Jenny's room . . . 'Brideshead' lifestyle . . . considering a re-enactment of her last walk . . . Police are anxious to talk to anyone who may have information about Jennifer's whereabouts. See page 19: Students: the Hamlet years.'

Other newspapers began to follow. I think they like being able to print pictures of Jenny, and they have found a nice one of her laughing, taken on the lawn of the house in Tipperary last year.

One of the popular papers (one which mysteriously thinks itself above the others) sent a star columnist to interview Jen's mother. 'Welcomes me in . . . Friendly, typical middle-class mum . . . Bottle green midi-skirt and court shoes . . . Lovely, candid blue eyes . . . Slight ladder in her tights . . . 'Jenny was always a star at school . . . so proud of her' . . . Childhood bedroom . . . soft toys and teddy bears . . . Quaver in her voice . . . Not giving up hope . . . Husband Richard puts his head round the door . . . Instant coffee, slightly soft Rich Tea biscuit . . . Talented draughtsman and pillar of local . . . Three younger sisters side by side on the G-plan couch, nudging and whispering . . . Have to have a heart of stone not to . . . Showed me to the door . . . Photo of missing Jenny . . . hall table . . . vase of tired tulips . . . But who can blame . . . '

I have gathered quite a file of cuttings from all the newspapers. I go through them with a blue pen and mark up the errors of fact and score them accordingly. I give one mark for getting wrong something they couldn't really have been expected to know better — e.g. that Robin Wilson was her boyfriend. I give two points for an error that would have taken only a phone call to check — Lynmouth instead of Lymington, for instance, Geog for Hist, 20 for 21. And I give three points for errors that didn't even need a phone call, things that are in reference books or are common knowledge — like Claire for Clare College or thinking Newbury is in Hampshire.

The most accurate, I was surprised to see, was the little pocket-sized *Sun*. Hardly anything it wrote was true in any significant sense of that word and there wasn't much of it anyway, but the 'facts' — spellings and so on — were fine.

I showed my scores to Stellings, who told me a weekend magazine had once done a long article on his father, who is something in the British film business. It had taken them three months to interview him and other people about him, write the piece, check it, and get the pictures.

'Well, it's different for magazines,' I said. 'They've got time.'

'Actually, there were quite a few mistakes,' said Stellings. 'My mother counted fifty-two.'

★ ★ ★

As the days go by, the story becomes an obsession. 'Jenny: Latest' say the news-stands and everyone knows what they mean — though the latest is always that they still don't know.

There is a character known as the 'ginger-headed man in the blue anorak' who has featured in the last 48 hours. A woman on her way home after doing some office cleaning saw this person in Jesus Lane at the right time, about one-fifteen. The sighting was confirmed by a college porter on his way home via Maid's Causeway at about one-thirty. This ginger man was seen to be behaving 'oddly'.

The rozzer in charge, Inspector Peck, has asked Robin Wilson to make a television broadcast on Saturday, after *Grandstand* and before *The Generation Game*. Nice to see her; to see her it would be nice. (I do like a good chiasmus with my tea on Saturday.)

In a separate development, as the news bulletins say, it's intended to re-enact Jennifer's walk home from the party to her house. I don't know who's going to play Jenny. There was a dumpy little WPC who clearly fancied the part, but she wouldn't be any good.

'Ginger Man: Hunt Intensifies', says the placard outside Bowes & Bowes.

Mr and Mrs Arkland are said to be 'distraught'. Mrs Arkland is on 'suicide watch' according to the *Daily Mirror*. Today the *Sun* had a picture of Jen in a bikini. The *Daily*

126

Express had an article headlined 'Secret sex life of missing brainbox', in which two undergraduates — one from King's, one from Downing 'neither of whom wished to be named' — were quoted as saying that they had (at different times) had sex with Jennifer and that she was a 'warm and liberated lover' (King's) with a 'fantastic body' (Downing). There was a cross-reference to: 'Page 22: The plague of student promiscuity by Jean Rook.'

She has become a different person.

              ★   ★   ★

Inspector Peck called a press conference this morning to say that his station had received an anonymous phone call which they were taking 'very seriously indeed'. He says his caller was able to give information 'that only someone who knew Jennifer well would be in a position to pass on. We are hopeful that he can help us further with our inquiries.'

Unfortunately he rang off before they could trace his call. He was said to have a strong Norfolk accent.

'Is Ginger from Norwich?' asks the placard for the evening paper outside Bradwell's Court this afternoon.

An advertisement in the window of W.H. Smith promises: 'Jenny: More Revelations in this weekend's *Sunday Times*'.

              ★   ★   ★

I've been to see my doctor. I'm suffering severe headaches. I don't feel well at all. I can't do any work. It's impossible to concentrate.

Dr Vaughan has a surgery on King's Parade, near the Copper Kettle. In his waiting room there are college oars mounted on the wall. On them are the names of the colleges whose boats he rammed or sank or something.

Vaughan is famous for the fact that the university's most renowned philosopher died in his arms. I think this is a strange thing for a doctor to be famous for. Saving him, maybe, or reviving him . . . But not showing him the door.

I have to wait a long time. Eventually the receptionist says I can go in. I think Vaughan went to the same med school as Dr Benbow from Chatfield. They have no bedside manner. I doubt whether either has ever been to a bedside, unless it was to issue a death certificate.

I once asked Vaughan for sleeping pills but he told me to take more exercise. That's why I started going to Alan Greening in the Kestrel.

A boy called Rough at Chatfield went to see Benbow and told him he thought he must be gay because he couldn't stop thinking about boys. Instead of passing him to a counsellor, Benbow sent him away and said that every time he had an impure thought he should go and play squash. It didn't help. (Though I'm told he won a squash blue in his second year at Oxford.)

Vaughan told me to sit down, then looked at me angrily.

'What sort of headaches? Whereabouts?' He seemed to be implying that I was making it up.

'Here . . . And here . . . And here. Intense.'

He shone a light in my eyes and ears and asked about my bowels.

'Have you had your eyes tested lately? Do you masturbate? Do you drink alcohol?'

'I think it may be that I'm worried about a friend of mine.'

'Stand up. Do you have adequate light in your room?'

'Could I have a prescription for some pills?'

'Certainly not. You can buy some aspirin with your own money if you want to. Don't drink beer. You can go now.'

★ ★ ★

But it's bad. I feel a sort of lassitude. As well as the pain. I also feel everything's my fault. It's like how I used to feel about the old men in the poorhouse. All this stuff is my responsibility.

I've started driving out to those villages again, like I did before I knew Jen. I take the 1100 out from the Queen Elizabeth car park and just drive. Grantchester, the Wilbrahams. Over Wrought. Middle Class. Nether World. It doesn't matter how much I drink or how much I smoke I just can't stop the pain in my temples.

Whoosh goes the chestnut-amber tide up the side of the straight glass as I tear the cellophane from a silver packet of Sobranie Virginia.

I sit at the bar and drink and smoke alone and I often think about my father for some reason. I wonder what it's like to be dead.

I didn't feel much when he died. I didn't cry,

129

though Julie and my mother both cried a lot. I didn't like him very much so it was hard to mourn him. Perhaps there's something wrong with me that I didn't cry.

What I felt was this: that his dying made a mockery of his life. The plans, the photographs, the 'future' — all the stuff they lived by. It was a delusion, wasn't it? See them in that black and white photo there, young and looking forward. What on earth was all that about, when this banal brutality was what all along lay in wait? When I look back on his life and what he thought he was up to, I feel . . . Embarrassed. Embarrassed by the extent of his self-delusion.

There was an interval after the funeral before the headstone arrived and my mother wanted me to mark the grave. People might otherwise think it was just a bit of builder's earth or a giant molehill or something. It might get washed away, like the grave of that girl in Hardy. In our small shed, I made a cross by breaking up a wooden apple crate. My father didn't have the tools for me to do a good job, but I managed two rough strips and wrote his name in ballpoint on the crosspiece, which I then hammered with an old nail onto the upright. It's pretty simple stuff, death. Say what you like about death, there's nothing fancy about it. I took the apple-box cross off to the graveyard and stuck it in the open earth a few inches above where my father's body was decomposing.

There was that poem by Catullus that we had

to translate for the scholarship to Chatfield. *Soles occidere et redire possunt.* The sun can set and rise again. But for us, once the short light is snuffed out, there is just one long night to be slept through. Catullus's response to this was to call for more sex while he was still alive to have it. That seems reasonable — and it sounds more profound in Latin. The other way of looking at it is that since the *lux*, the light, of our living is so *brevis*, short, compared to the *perpetua*, everlasting, *nox*, night, that is *dormienda*, to be slept through, then it's pointless to worry ourselves about what we do in it. What is a moment in eternity? Of no account. Of no account at all.

Time makes us pointless. If time is as we envisage it, our lives are not worth living. Time is probably not as we envisage it — sequential. But since we are incapable of viewing it in any other way, it might as well be.

If the colour green is *truly* red but to every living creature it is experienced as green, then green it might as well be.

And if the natural selection of mutations made by random errors in cell division has given us a conscious mind that cannot understand — no, cannot *conceive* — one of the dimensions it inhabits, we might just as well be dead.

I hope for reincarnation when we and our conscious mind have evolved a little more, say ten million years from now.

I do believe in reincarnation for the simple reason that I'm certain that I personally have lived before — and within the last century, which is worrying.

I don't want to come back again *that* soon. Christ.

★ ★ ★

Of course I think of Jennifer a lot too. I've been reading her diary and it's almost like having her back. You can hear her voice, that sense of her trying not to laugh out of politeness to the other person.

Oh yes . . . That diary. I only meant to borrow it then sneak it back, but of course now the house is crawling with policemen I can't do that and I'm stuck with it.

On Saturday I went down to the college television room to watch Robin Wilson's appeal for information. He sat behind a table, somewhere in London, I presume, with a bank of bright lights shining on him. He still had his Che Guevara moustache, but I noticed he had had his hair cut from shoulder-length to just covering the ears. I thought this was a pity, as though he was saying that long hair — other values, the counterculture — could be chucked out when the world got tough, when it got *real*.

He put on a grown-up voice, but still used a lot of undergrad terms, like 'notion' instead of idea.

'If by any chance you're watching this, Jenny, do please get in touch,' he said. 'If you could just get it together to make a phone call to your parents, that would be really amazing.'

132

At least he didn't go on too much about their 'relationship'.

He looked gravely intelligent, sensitive, compassionate in a manly way. The millions of people waiting to see Bruce Forsyth could barely have guessed that he was lying through his teeth. He was no more her boyfriend than Brucie was.

He concluded: 'If anyone can remember anything that might help police with their inquiries, I beg you to come forward. You can contact your local police station or ring the number on your screen in complete confidentiality. Thank you for your help and your concern. And Jenny, if you're watching, God bless you. Come back to us soon.'

He kept his still, unblinking gaze in the bullseye of the camera as the light faded.

What a silver-plated fraud. He'd even mastered all the professional stuff about 'the number on your screen', as though he'd spent his life in a studio, like Dickie Davies or Cliff Michelmore.

I couldn't help laughing as I got up from my leather armchair and prepared to leave the others to their Bruce Forsyth. As I did so, a boy in front looked up at the noise of my laughter with a puzzled and slightly accusing look. He appeared to have tears on his cheeks.

★   ★   ★

In the last few days there have been two developments. The first was a *Daily Mail* story headlined 'Varsity Jen was in blue film', which

133

insinuated that Jennifer was a more or less round-the-clock porn actress.

The second, more significant, is that Robin Wilson, Mr Telegenic Sincere, has become the principal suspect. Newspapers are running on the borderlines of libel as they reprint fuzzy photographs taken from his broadcast and ask questions about their 'relationship'. They innocently remark that the police are 'currently interviewing no other suspects'.

But Wilson: PC Plod has had him in four times to Mill Road station, and four times, after 'exhaustive' questioning, he's been released, though he can't go back to where he was living. They've sealed his staircase in Clare while they dismantle his room. They've chipped the plaster off the walls, they've raised the carpets and the floorboards, they've brought down the ceiling, they've taken it back to the medieval dust inhaled by Lady Elizabeth de Clare (Lady de Burgh) when she endowed the college shortly after its foundation in 1326. No dice.

Not yet. It's only a matter of time, I imagine. Everyone steers clear of Wilson when he comes to lectures; the women in particular look really scared. They have statistics by the yard. Eighty-five per cent of violent crimes against women are committed by a family member or by those closest to them. Rob looks fine, they're thinking, he was exemplary on television — modern, sensitive, non-sexist in his language — but he is for all that still a *man*. He can't be trusted.

Tomorrow night is the re-enactment of

Jennifer's walk home, or 'Jen's Last Walk: Latest' as it's known to the townspeople.

I have one question for the investigating team. Why was she not on her 'trusty' bike? Where, in fact, is that bike? Shouldn't Mr Plod be asking?

★   ★   ★

I suppose it was inevitable who would get the role of playing Jennifer. It's Hannah, of course.

It's a non-speaking role, it's a non-acting role if you ask me, it's a *walking* role — but Hannah has spent twelve hours a day immersing herself in the part, like some new girl at the Actors' Studio.

She's watched Jen in the Irish film about a thousand times, trying to capture the particular movement of her hips when she walked, the way she held herself and swung her arms. She's been to Lymington to go through old photograph albums, looking for a cock of the head, a dip of the shoulder, talking to the parents over soft Rich Tea — though they may have got in some fresh ones by now. (I noticed from a picture in the *Guardian* that they'd got rid of the tulips.)

Hannah sits in dancer's leg warmers, her uncombed hair tied up in a ragged ribbon (this is no time for vanity), smoking like a REME corporal, biting the ends of her fingers as she views the Forres movie one more time. Then she rises silently and walks back and forth across the bare boards of the Film Soc viewing room, tilting her pelvis a half-inch this way, a half-inch that.

135

She says it's tougher than Strindberg, more draining than Brecht. She frequently weeps while a bemused WPC Kettle looks on. Say what you like, she's giving it her all.

★ ★ ★

The Walk took place last night, two weeks to the day (important for it to be Friday, the same day of the week) after the Disappearance. We all wanted to go and watch, but weren't allowed to go beyond a barrier at the end of Malcolm Street. The only people allowed further were Hannah, WPC Kettle, Inspector Peck, Jennifer's parents, a camera crew from the BBC (camera, lights, sound, assistant, and same again in reserve, following recent ACCT union agreement with management, plus catering and transport, all on treble time apparently because it was after midnight), ditto from *Outlook East Anglia*.

In Jesus Lane, where it met Malcolm Street, there were about three dozen press photographers with hefty flashguns. They were held in a sort of extended low-level cage, such as you might find in a livestock market. They didn't seem to mind.

Hannah was standing outside the party house, about halfway up Malcom Street on the right going north. She was smoking furiously, wrapped in blankets, still in green-room character.

Molly, Anne and Nick, Jen's housemates, came briefly through the crowd to shake hands with Jen's parents and to wish Hannah luck, and were then ushered back behind the barrier. Hannah herself went up into the house and closed the door.

Peck spoke into the radio on his lapel. Watches were checked. Eventually, Peck held up his arm and waved to a colleague on Jesus Lane. He called out: 'Let's go.'

The door of the party house was opened, and a girl — presumably Hannah in a blonde wig, slightly wavy — tripped down the stairs on to the pavement and turned right. She pushed the hair back behind her ears; I wondered if they'd pencilled in a couple of tiny moles.

She dropped her cigarette (Jen hardly smoked), straightened up and began to walk.

As she came into the sodium light of the street lamp, I recognised the navy blue coat, a replica of Jen's own that had presumably vanished with her. She also wore a grey sweater, the polo neck that wasn't quite, blue flared jeans and boots.

She walked down the grey pavement, going away from us; her step was light and confident, and you felt all that Jenniferish excitement about being alive and it *was* her in all but fact: it was her again, you could smell her hair, her skin, and sense how much she was looking forward to the bump of the lit gas fire and the ski socks, as she quickened slightly in the cold, thinking of the cat tumbling from the roof in the morning and the day ahead.

She walked, this girl, with that slow stride suppressing gaiety, her love of living, the slight sway of her narrow hips as she moved onwards, away from us, turned right at the end of the street and vanished in the Fenland mist.

★   ★   ★

Jesus, Jesus, it's been tough.

At least I've started working again, which is a relief. The truth is that by going to so many of Jen's history lectures I'd missed out on a lot of my own course. Waynflete says my work is now 'back on track', though I don't know which track. Presumably the one that leads to a first-class degree, or a 'youknowwhat', as Jennifer called it. The problem with *that* is that it tilts you towards 'academe', which means no money, grant applications, no job, 'research' and studenthood extended into dotage; it means spending the rest of your life in digs in Lampeter.

However, the Foreign Office never sneered at a first, I imagine.

Increasingly, the FO's what I feel I'm going to do. I didn't search it out, it came to me. But I was impressed that Woodrow should think of me. And sometimes in life, I imagine, good things *do* happen. Most of the time, it's the opposite, obviously. But I don't think you should rule out the possibility that just occasionally chance might deal you a good card.

Then you should go with it. Go with the flow, as Stellings is fond of saying, often when he's opening a bottle of beer.

Engleby of the FO. It would be worth it just to see the faces of Wingate and Hood and Baynes.

No, not to see them; I never want to see them again. Just to picture them. (Incidentally, an old Chatfieldian weirdo in John's told me Baynes had to pull out of Oxford because he was getting migraines and petit mals. Such is life.)

Meanwhile: His Excellency Sir Michael Engleby KCMG, our man in Paris, at home in rue du Faubourg Saint-Honoré in the residence of the British embassy, a classic town house bought from Napoleon's sister, I read somewhere. Yes, yes, they'd say, HE's a natural scientist by training, would you believe? Always a high flier, Mike, but also a dogged individualist. For instance, he's the first ambassador to maintain that the smallest room in Napoleon's sister's old house is called a toilet.

★   ★   ★

Spring is coming. There are croci beneath the trees in Fellows' Pieces.

I had a note in my pigeonhole yesterday morning from Dr Townsend, the socialist geographer who is my 'moral tutor'. I saw him in the first week of my first year for a glass of sherry but haven't come across him since. I imagine that in the intervening two and a half years neither my morals nor my tutoring have given him cause for concern, or interest. His note asks me to come and see him at once in his rooms in the Queen Elizabeth building.

Knock, knock.

'Come in, Mike. Sit down. Thank you for coming so soon.'

'Mike', eh? I wonder if he had to look that up.

While he's talking to me, I'm also wondering how you get to be a socialist geographer. What articles and papers do you have to read? 'Oxbow Lakes and the non-Egalitarian Aquifer'; 'Andean Rainfall: the Case for Equal Precipitation'; 'Tectonic Plate Shift and the Command Economy'; 'Coastal Erosion: the Bias against Littoral Communities'; 'Soviet Flood Plains and the — '

'Mike?'

'*What?*'

'Did you hear what I said?'

'Yes, Inspector Peck wants to see me.'

'It's nothing to be worried about. They're talking to everyone who knew her, even just acquaintances.'

'That's fine. I knew her very well in fact.'

'Oh. Did you?'

'Do they want me to go the station or do they come to me?'

'They prefer to come to you. It's nicer for you that way. There's Peck, another detective and a student liaison officer. You can also have your moral tutor present if you like.'

I looked at Townsend's anxious face. He had twisted his fingers round and round and jammed his hands between his knees. It struck me that it had probably been a long time since he had had to deal with people, or reality.

'I don't think that'll be necessary.'

140

Townsend let out a whinny of relief and sprang to his feet.

The door was open and the spring breeze was gusting in from the Paddock.

'Let me know how you get on,' he may have called after me; but if so, I didn't hear it.

★　★　★

I went to the Buttery and bought some fresh tea and milk for my visitors, who were due at five, and some Rich Tea biscuits, very fresh, although I dislike them. I tidied up the rooms a bit, since my bedmaker hadn't been in for a couple of weeks. I put my hand up the flue of the fireplace in the bedroom and retrieved about eight ounces of hash in a polythene bag.

On the mantelpiece was my collection of pills, and although none were illegal as such, I had no prescriptions for them and Dr Vaughan was unlikely to come to my aid. I didn't think a backdated, beer-stained receipt from Alan Greening would count for much, so I gathered the dozen or so bottles together and put them in my old duffel bag — the same dark green one in which I'd stuck my first cigarette haul from Upper Rookley all that time ago. Great things, duffel bags — egalitarian, brilliant design.

I had a couple of magazines I didn't particularly want the plods to look at, so I stuffed those in too. Then I took the bag round to Stellings's room and asked if he'd take care of it.

'You can look in it if you like,' I said. 'But I don't recommend it.'

'Christ, Groucho, the last thing I want to do is know your filthy secrets. Do you want some Saint-Émilion, while you're here? La Dominique. I've just discovered it. The poor man's Pétrus.'

'No thanks.'

'Good luck with the cops. Can you lend me that Focus album one day? *Moving Waves*?'

'I haven't got it. I borrowed it.'

'Would I like it?'

'Bit riffy for you, Stellings. Quite a lot of yodelling.'

'Yodelling. Christ.'

'Yes. But two, maybe three, sublime moments.'

'Could be worth hearing.'

'I'll get it for you as a present for looking after my stuff.' (There was zero security in the old-fashioned HMV record shop in Sussex Street. I could nick a copy there.)

'Thank you, Groucho.'

Stellings put on his headphones again, which was my signal to leave. I think he was listening to *Gigi* — or 'the dry run for *My Fair Lady*' as he invariably called it.

One thing I couldn't risk with Stellings was Jen's diary. I stuffed the photocopy of her letter home inside it and went to the toilet on the half-landing of my staircase. By standing on the seat, I could reach round behind the back of the raised cistern. It was a perfect fit, with shades of the Topley run.

★ ★ ★

My room in Clock Court is on the top floor of an uncarpeted staircase, so it wasn't hard to hear the approach of three police officers.

I had candidly thrown back the outer door and had only to open the flimsy inner one when I heard the knock. I had bathed and shaved, trimmed my hair and put on my old Chatfield tweed jacket. I thought about a tie but didn't want to go too far. With jeans and an open shirt beneath the jacket, I imagined I looked normal.

I was looking forward to this interview. It was about time they came to see me, instead of messing about with that Wilson bloke.

Peck I recognised from Jen's Last Walk and from television. He was a genial type who smiled a lot. DC Cannon was about thirty-two with gingery sideburns, rather on edge. The 'student liaison officer' was a fat woman with a too-tight uniform and black lace-up shoes with rubber soles.

I got them arranged round the room and sat at the desk myself.

'So,' said Peck, 'I understand you knew Jennifer Arkland a little. Perhaps you could begin by telling us how well.'

'I knew her very well. I went to lectures with her most days. Although I'm doing Natural Sciences, I'm interested in history and I had spare time in my day, so I often went along.'

'I see. And what was her attitude?'

'What? To my being there?'

'Yes.'

143

'She was flattered, I think. Pleased. We were friends, so . . . It was, you know, fine.'

'And what about the lectures? Were they happy to have someone from another subject?'

'Oh, God, yes.' I laughed. 'In History they don't get much of an audience. They're delighted. More the merrier. It's not like Medicine or something where you have to go to all the practicals and sign in. It's not like school. In History, lectures are completely optional. Lots of people don't go at all.'

'I see.' Peck sounded a bit surprised. 'And it didn't interfere with your own studies.'

'Not at all. You can check with my supervisor, Dr Waynflete. He says I'm doing fine.'

'Thank you. We will.' That was said by Cannon. His first contribution.

Peck looked across at him. Cannon was sitting under the Procol Harum poster, with the photograph of Julie just behind his head. Their presence was quite intrusive really.

Cannon pulled a packet of Embassy out of his jacket pocket and lit one with a side-action Ronson Varaflame. I leaned over from the desk and pushed the ashtray across the low table towards him.

'Mr Engleby,' said Cannon, 'I'd like you to tell us more about Jennifer. How did you first meet her?'

I told him about Jen Soc, the meetings, getting to know her there, helping out with the clearing up, the film in Ireland and —

144

'Did she invite you to go on this trip to Ireland?'

'I can't remember.'

'Were you a member of the Film Society at that time?' said Peck.

'It wasn't a Film Soc project. It was a private thing. Nick had the camera. Nick, you know, her housemate as he became. Stewart Forres just borrowed some of the Film Soc facilities when he came back. For the edit and so on. The screening room.'

'I see.'

'Have you seen the film?' I asked.

'Yes. Several times.'

'Was it helpful?'

'Yes,' said Peck, 'it's very unusual in a missing persons inquiry to have such a clear and recent picture of what they're like.'

Cannon said, 'And what did you do on this film?'

'Some sound, some carpentry, some catering.'

'There's a rape scene, isn't there?' Cannon stubbed out his Embassy.

'Yes.' Something told me to keep the answers short at this point.

'Were you involved?'

It occurred to me that since it was now over two weeks since Jennifer's disappearance they must have talked to Stewart, Nick and Hannah — at least — of the Tipperary people.

'Yes, I did the sound that day.'

'How was Jennifer?'

'Fine.'

'Go on.'

I shrugged.

Cannon said, 'It's not every day a twenty-year-old girl pretends to be raped. In front of a camera crew.'

'No.'

'Come on, Michael,' said Peck in an avuncular way. 'Barry just wants to know if she seemed all right.'

I turned to face Peck again. 'Yes. She was an actress. It was a challenge.' I was thinking of her tears and wondering if anyone had mentioned them. 'I expect it was difficult but she was determined to get it right — because there was a political point to be made.'

'And what was that?' said Cannon.

'A feminist point about rape.'

Peck looked at Cannon as though asking him not to speak.

I also looked at Cannon and wondered what on earth he knew about feminism, rape or sex. I could tell what sort of family he came from. Slightly better than mine, but still working-class prudes. They don't do sex, those guys — the upper-lowers — except as a bargaining counter for marriage. I wondered how many girlfriends he'd had. Did they send him on a course to learn about the promiscuous middle classes and their soft ideas? 'Simone de Beauvoir for Plods'. 'Free love among the Posh: an introductory series of five lectures'. Don't get excited, Cannon. Keep your ginger hair on.

I found Peck was looking at me. 'And what was your reaction, Michael?'

'My reaction to what?'

'The rape scene. Were you upset?'

I bit my lips a little and looked at the policewoman. She looked down at her rubber-soled shoes. I looked over at Cannon, who was leaning forward in his chair, then back to Peck.

'Not at all,' I said. 'I was just doing a job. Trying to get a clean soundtrack without aeroplane noise.'

'And it didn't upset you at all to see this girl you were . . . very good friends with, as you say, it didn't upset you to see her being raped?'

I laughed. 'Not at all. It was fun. It was interesting. We were all acting. She didn't *really* get raped.'

'And when you saw the actor who played the rapist . . . Er . . . '

'Alex Tanner,' said Cannon.

'Yes,' said Peck, 'when you saw Alex pretend to rape Jennifer . . . You were . . . That was all right, was it?'

'I . . . Yes. That was all right. Stewart was very professional. Also, Hannah was there, the actress. You know, the girl who did the Walk. So she was like a chaperone.'

It was funny hearing them talk about all these people in that formal way — Alex Tanner, for instance — as though they were real grown-ups in a significant life. They were students, making things up as they went along. They didn't know what they were doing, right, wrong or neither. They had nothing to compare it with because it was all still being done for the first time.

'So you watched this young man,' said

Cannon, 'who was naked, I think, and this girl, your close friend, also naked . . . And how close did he actually go in his acting to raping her?'

'I don't know. I didn't look.'

I felt a tightening of interest from all three.

'Why not?' said Cannon.

'I was looking at her face to make sure she was all right. I told you. She was my friend.'

No one said anything for quite a long time. I could feel a headache starting, but didn't say so.

Eventually, Peck began again on the nature of my friendship with her. Had I been to her house? Yes. How many times? Not that often, we saw each other mostly at lectures. Did I know her parents? Certainly not! Most people don't admit to *having* parents . . .

I became quite bored with this after a while and offered to make tea. To my disappointment, they all said no.

'Now, Michael,' said Peck. 'I'm going to have to ask you a more difficult question. I want you to tell me what you were doing on the night of Jennifer's disappearance.'

I inhaled and turned round to look down at my desk. I heard the clock strike half-past five. I located my Heffer's ringbound desk diary.

'Let me see . . . Yes. I remember very well, in fact. I went to the party that Jennifer was at. It was in a house in Malcolm Street.'

'We know where it was,' said Cannon.

'And who did you talk to there?' said Peck.

'Jennifer, of course.'

'How was she?'

'Fine. Absolutely fine.'

'You didn't notice anything unusual. She didn't seem agitated or upset?'

'Not at all. She was always fine.'

'Who else did you talk to?'

'I can't remember. No one much. I didn't stay long. It wasn't my kind of party.'

'Can you remember the name of anyone at all that you spoke to?'

'The music was very loud, it was hard to hear. A guy called Steve. In Corpus, I think. Or maybe Christ's. Anne, maybe? Was she there?'

There was another silence. Then Peck said, 'Is there anyone who could corroborate your whereabouts on that night?'

'I called in at the Bradford hotel for a drink on the way.'

'The Bradford? Are you a regular there?'

'Fairly regular.'

'What's the barman's name?'

'I don't know. He's a transvestite.'

'Have you ever spoken to him?'

'Only to order a drink.'

'You're a regular but you've never spoken to the barman?'

'No, I . . . No.'

'Where were you between one and two a.m.?'

'In bed.'

'Can you prove that?'

'There was no one with me, if that's what you mean. I got back about twelve-fifteen. I rang the bell at the porters' lodge. The porter might remember letting me in.'

'So what time had you left the party then?'

'About twelve, I suppose.'

'So you did stay *quite* a long time at the party, then.'

'No, I got there late. After the pub. I really didn't hang around there.'

The pauses were now becoming more frequent and rather tense. There was a lot of body, a lot of clothes — a lot of cubic footage of police officer in my room.

Cannon fired his Ronson again. I noticed that although he was on his fourth cigarette, he still hadn't offered me one. I would have said no anyway, in case it made me look nervous.

'Do you have a girlfriend, Mr Engleby?' It was Cannon.

'Well, there was Jennifer.'

'I thought Robin Wilson was her boyfriend.'

'It depends what you mean by that word.'

Cannon began to speak, but Peck held up his hand. Another treacly silence.

Eventually, Peck said softly, 'Michael, are you being quite honest with us? We've talked to a lot of other people, you know.'

I said nothing.

'Do you have girlfriends at home?' said Peck.

'Some. No one special.'

'You see, what people have been telling us is that you prefer boys.'

I laughed. It was such a relief of tension. I couldn't stop laughing for about a minute, and I noticed them looking at one another and signalling.

'All right,' said Peck. 'I just want you to remember, Michael, that we're looking for a lovely girl, someone people were very fond of. If you remember anything — it doesn't matter how small — anything that might help us, I want you to ring this number.' He handed me a card.

'If there's anything you suddenly 'remember',' said Cannon. 'Anything you feel you'd like to share. Sometimes it's hard to bottle things up . . .'

'We're all on the same side,' said Peck. 'We're all trying to find Jennifer.'

'Sure,' I said.

I thought of saying 'Now if you'll excuse me', which is what the person in my position says in every detective story ever written for page, stage or screen. It's a law. They can't not.

But when I looked round their faces, I had a feeling that they wouldn't get the joke.

I just waited for them to gather up their stuff and thunder off downstairs.

Then I cleared up Cannon's mucky ashtray and threw the dog-ends in the pantry bin, where, after, a moment's thought, I threw the unopened Rich Tea as well.

I felt badly in need of a real smoke and thought of going to get my stuff back from Stellings. Then I thought I'd better leave it for a bit in case there was a sudden knock at the door and Peck stuck his head sound, saying, 'Sorry, just one more thing . . .'

But perhaps he hadn't seen that film either, because after an hour or so it was still quiet. Then I went to the drinks cupboard and opened a bottle of Johnnie Walker Black Label I had duffel-bagged from the Arthur Cooper's on

Sidney Street while the manager popped out the back for a moment.

I did it properly in a clean glass with ice from the fridge on the half-landing and a couple of inches of cold Malvern water. I lit a Dunhill King Size, drew the curtains and put on the first side of *Goodbye Yellow Brick Road* by Elton John.

I sat back in the armchair and watched the smoke rise up to the paper lantern-shade round the central bulb that hung from the ceiling. The instrumental 'Funeral for a Friend' gave way to 'Loves Lies Bleeding'.

I thought of Hannah/Jennifer walking off into the mist towards Maid's Causeway.

At the end of side one, I refilled my glass, flipped the record over, turned out all the lights, lit another cigarette and crashed back into the chair.

That sway of the hips — modest, not exaggerated, just necessitated by her frame. Slim, straight back, clean, fair hair pushed back, just touching the shoulders of the coat. Her step: light, but unafraid.

That flair for living.

Then into the darkness, the singer's voice: 'When are you gonna come down? When are you going to land?'

Sensational tune.

5

I was walking up Sidney Street yesterday and this beggar came towards me. He was only about twenty-five.

'All right,' he said, 'I'm talking to you and let's get that straight from the start. Don't let's do that thing where you pretend you haven't seen me, OK? Don't look the other way and hurry on as though you didn't hear. Is that clear?'

Dear God, a facetious beggar. A postgrad wino. I didn't feel like giving him money. I felt like *taking* his money — like elbowing him in the teeth, clearing out his pockets and selling off his dog for dog meat.

There's an alley down the side of Christ's Pieces. It's called Milton's Walk, after the poet, who presumably used it on his way to and from his college. 'The Lady of Christ's' is what the other boys in college called him at the time, though I don't know why; it's not as though they were even considering co-res in 1628. At the other end is King Street, which may have been more than a pub run in Milton's day. Cemented along the top of the wall on the right of the alley as you go down are bits of broken bottle to stop you climbing into Christ's garden (Gethsemane?). Below are graffiti. But they don't say 'Rovers For Ever', 'THFC Skins' or 'I love Tracy'; they say things like 'Life is not a Rehearsal' or 'All Things Must Pass'. Sometimes

153

it's wearing to live amid such banality.

I'm worried about my mother. She's had a hysterectomy and hasn't been able to go back to work at the Waverley hotel. Julie says she hasn't got out of bed for a week. I'm not sure what I'd do if she didn't have any income, as my father's pension from the paper mill barely keeps her in tea bags. I'm going to have to stop this life and get out to work.

We're nearly at the end of term, and that means I've got only one term left. Most people are anxious about their final exams, but I'm not. Waynflete has more or less told me I need only turn up to get a first and Woodrow has fixed me some sort of interview in the last week of April.

The situation with Jennifer Arkland has become clearer. Officially, the 'missing person' case remains open. The police files are still growing as, day by day, further interviews are made with people who knew her less well — with casual acquaintances, boys who met her once at tea, girls who twice played volleyball against her on a Tuesday afternoon. So the ripples spread further from the point of impact, until, presumably, they'll vanish.

Robin Wilson is under psychiatric supervision at the hospital in Fulbourn, formerly the county pauper lunatic asylum. The fifth time that Peck and Cannon did him over was apparently too much for him to take, and now he spends more time in group therapy than in lectures.

Unofficially, Jennifer's parents, friends and college have been told by police to assume that she's dead.

The college held a service yesterday in its 1880s chapel.

I have the printed order of service on my desk in front of me as I write. 'Jennifer Rose Arkland (b. 10 January, 1953): Service of Hope. 3 March, 1974.'

Although the organisers tried to keep the valedictory note out of it, there were two talks on Jennifer that inevitably sounded like eulogies. Anne talked about Jennifer the Student, and a girl from Lymington called Susan Something spoke about Jennifer the Schoolgirl.

This Susan person had what I took to be a New Forest accent. She was funny about Jen's sporting expertise at school. She was apparently quite good at hockey and lacrosse but didn't like the divided skirt, or the gymslips, or whatever. (Girls are always bitter about the frumpy games clothes they were made to wear at school, though it's not as if any boys were watching.) She was good at swimming, but hated being cold. So she ended up playing tennis because when she was eleven she admired Maria Bueno and liked her clothes. I'd always understood Miss Bueno was a lesbian, but this didn't seem to spoil people's appreciation of the joke, and I suppose there was something funny about the idea of this girl turning her back on the games she was good at so she could zoom about the tennis court in a white dress. Susan was also funny about Jennifer's attempts to sing in tune and her refusal to be excluded from the school choir. 'Singing was perhaps the only activity where her sense of humour failed her.'

Was. Though I think Susan would have defended her use of the word on the grounds that the school days were in the past.

Anne's picture of Jennifer was more austere. No gym skirts, no tennis. 'A clear-thinking and idealistic woman' was Anne's phrase. 'No doubt, she is destined for a serious career. She will do something where she can make a difference.'

No 'was' for Anne. She squarely inhabited the present tense. Anne's talk was also well delivered until she came towards the end and tried to address Jennifer personally. Then her voice wavered. Then it broke. She clung to the edge of the pulpit, sobbing, while the candles were reflected in the green Pugin tiles behind her.

The college chaplain, a birdlike man whose hands came out beneath his white surplice like claws, climbed up and half-guided, half-carried her back to earth.

I wondered how Anne had got to know Jen so well and care about her so much so quickly. I mean, they were just student pals, weren't they?

* * *

As I went past the National Westminster in St Andrew's Street this afternoon I remembered it was Friday. I looked at my watch: twenty past three. I'd forgotten to withdraw money and this meant I would be broke until the bank reopened on Monday at ten. This happens surprisingly often. Cashless weekends mean a blizzard of small debts (I owe Stellings 50p) unless you can persuade a barman to cash a cheque for you. I'm not on speaking, let alone money-lending, terms with the tranny in the Bradford. Since Stellings has anyway gone to London, I'll have to go into the jungle atmosphere of the cellar bar in Caius and help myself from a wallet in the heap of coats. I used to find cash flow easier to manage in the communal living of Chatfield with its open doors and empty changing rooms. I suppose I could just duffel some gin from Arthur Cooper's and use chits to eat in hall, but I still need cash for cigarettes. Also, Robin Trower's playing at the Tech on Saturday and I'll have to buy a ticket.

I've stopped going to History lectures. I've found that since Jen's disappearance I'm not that interested in the past.

And Waynflete was getting edgy about my low attendance rate at some obligatory experiments. I'm specialising in genetics for Part Two, but there are still some lab boxes to be ticked. Thank God I'm through with the 'Maths for Biologists' course, which was harder than it sounds and heavy on homework.

My final exams are going to be on 20–21 May and I'll have four weeks' vacation, starting 15 March, in which to revise. I suppose I'll have to go back to Reading because they've started using undergrad rooms for conferences when we're not here, so K. Jones, West Midlands Division (Sales) will be sleeping in my bed. I used to have a deal with the senior tutor that I could stay over the vac pretty much free, but they won't do that any more.

What am I going to do tonight? I've got to get out. I can feel a headache starting. I'll take the car and drive somewhere. Maybe that place the Tickell Arms with the crazy landlord and the Wagner tapes. He hates women so much he makes them pay for the paper at the bar before they use the toilet.

First, I'm going down to the half-landing for a read from my favourite book.

SATURDAY 12 JAN
Train drivers' strike meant had to come back by car. Term starts Tue, but Dad only free at weekend, so three days early. Love being early, can enjoy place with no work to do and time to sort things out, e.g. stock up on food and get <u>boiler</u> working. Had to be Sat as Sunday is Dad's tennis — over-forties doubles semi-finals day. Journey took ages as we could not exceed 50 mph speed limit (new E. Heath law to save petrol). But as usual Dad was v nice about it in the end. As we got nearer and nearer he became more and more solicitous. 'Now, Jen-Jen, have you got all you need? Do you want to stop at Boots?' Pretty sure 'Boots' is euphemism for Pill. 'Don't worry, Dad, everything's fine.' I don't know if he thinks am virg. int. Can't bear even to imagine how upset he would be. So do not think about it at all. (Almost.)

But did good stock-up at Sainsbury's, rice, spag, tea, tins, stock cubes, long-term stuff and dear Dad paid all. All seemed much better between him and M, which is a great relief. Tilly tells me she pretty sure he has dumped bitch at work. (T very knowing for 16-yr-old.)

Gail Martin still clearly has hots for D but he treats her with distance bordering on disdain. Clearly excites G even further.

Xmas was great in the end. Robin came down afterwards. We all went skating at Southampton rink. R very polite to M and D, though noticed quiet scrutiny from D. Not sure he really approves, but nothing I can do. Still keen on R and all going well. Don't know what will happen in June, but that still seems a long way off. Jill in Homerton apparently became engaged over Xmas! Will I ever feel that grown up?

Alone in house tonight. Slightly creepy atmosphere. For first time v much wish had TV. Went for drink alone in typical tiny pub with coal fire and jukebox. Had two halves beer and got kebab with mountain of raw onion later on Mill Road. Not v good start diet/healthwise, but bicycled vigorously home to compensate.

Had left gas fire on while out, so bedroom lovely and warm while rest of house arctic. V tempting to sleep late tmw, but lot to do so dutifully set alarm for 8. Hope Catty will drop in.

I am looking forwd to this term. Life v settled — viz. house, Robin, work (know what necessary), friends, projects — but also enough variables to keep gloss on it. Leaving aside June and End of Era, still so much unpredictable to be had from friends and their lives, and parties and meetings etc. Feel v lucky and not that cold. Goodnight Dad.

Thank you for everything. Sleep well back in Lym. x

MONDAY 14 JAN
Rang phone people to reconnect. First appntmt not for <u>three weeks</u> . . . Anne says have to pretend to be pregnant — ergo needing emergency line — to get anyone to help.

Train strike, coal strike, power strike. V hard to get anything done.

Catty no show at first but looked in later and I gave him milk. He a bit stand-offish. Perhaps punishing me for absence.

As I was crossing St Andrew's Street, saw Charlie from Emma. He invited me for tea. I like him, but he's very nervous. Wonder if gay? What wrong with all these boys that only fancy each other? Mind you, not sure about C. Many heteros wear eyeliner — Roxy/Bowie fashion thing. Some look good, though not as good as B. Ferry or B. Eno.

Went to Sidgwick, got full lecture schedule and borrowed books from fac lib. Didn't see anyone. Had cornish pasty and orange-and-lemonade at Mill for lunch. Mike (!) from Tipperary was at the bar. Never discovered what actual college he from, therefore known only as 'Mike from Tip' or 'Irish Mike' as though he not at uni at all but emerged from Emerald Isle. Robin unkindly calls him 'Prufrock'. Managed to finish lunch and slip out without being seen. M looked as though in for long Guinness afternoon. Where does he get his money from? Dope, I suppose, of which he always has a hell of a lot.

Beautiful day. River sparkling in cold winter sun. Wheeled bike through Queens' just for pleasure of looking at. Can't wait for everyone to be back. Went and bought food for welcome dinner tonight for Anne, Moll and Nick (I think). Also litre of Sainsbury's Moroccan red.

Had tea with Charlie in Emma Old Court overlooking paddock with ducks. He played some v heavy band on stereo. Offered to lend it to me. Declined. Nice rooms, though, large with two bedrooms. Myles came back from vac in Leeds. V funny about.

Something unstable and vulnerable about Charlie. Donnish joke about his room number involving Auden play title, *The Ascent of F6*. Sense he not happy at all, though smiles a lot.

What will happen to all these people? Previous generations did great things in politics, diplomacy, medicine, industry, 'the arts' — became great and good as though by natural progression, birthright.

All people I know resolute that they will do no such thing. No one will have 'nine to five' job. Can't imagine anyone I know here appearing on television in 20 years' time to offer expert view on — anything. Just not cut out for it.

I wonder why. Drugs? Partly, but we're not all out of it all the time. A generation thing, I suppose. We are a lost gen. (Rather than lost Jen, ha, ha.) Before us, the hippies; after us, perhaps keen people in suit and tie who will go straight to work in Con Party research and American banks. Poor us, lost souls. Maybe from ashes, one or two prophets or meteors? S. Forres in films? Him apart, wipeout. Hannah maybe, cd be head of Oxfam or something. Doubt she will make it as an actress — between you and me, dear D . . .

Here are my resolutions for 1974, a little late:

1. Work six hours each day in organised way. Not drive self stupidly. Not be downcast if don't get youknowwhat. Not end of w; in fact probably blessing in d.
2. Settle on subject of long essay for finals. Irish Q? By end of Jan latest.
3. Close watch on Robin situation.
4. No other men, no slip-ups.
5. Not lose temp with Nick for non-payment of rent, non-contrib to kitty etc.
6. Go at least four soc mtngs per term, even tho no longer sec.
7. Telephone home at least once a week, if line mended.
8. Give up smoking cigs completely. Dope only on Sat eves.
9. Volleyball or similar at least 2x per week.
10. Go to Well Woman drop-in clinic asap.

(Bit of a fraud, number ten, as already have appnt on Fri, but couldn't think of anything else, but fewer than ten looked too pleased with self).

Oh, I know. Get part in another film (pref without taking clothes off . . .) Apparently when Nick explained feminist political slant of rape scene to his father, he (father) said: 'For, or against?'

Now must go and cook dinner.

What can it be like to live like that?

In Jen's defence, I suppose you'd have to say that it was an unusually arid time of year and there was no one else about. The best diarists sound vacuous when nothing happens.

I put the diary back behind the cistern, safe from Mrs Lumbago's short reach. I had a bath and listened to *The Archers* (still too much of that Ulster barmaid) and then got in the car.

I drove fast in the Ely direction and followed signposts anywhere, thinking about Jennifer's father. My father never owned a car, but if he had I doubt whether he would have driven me back to university in it. He wasn't interested in education, perhaps because it had done nothing for him.

My father was in the North Atlantic convoys in the War. He never talked to me about it, except once, when he'd had too much to drink at the social club that served the paper mill. He wasn't much of a drinker, but his friend Ted Green had introduced him to a drink he liked called a 'mother-in-law' (stout and bitter) and he must have had half a dozen to judge by the state he was in. Six pints is a lot of beer if you're not used to it, not much if you are. He wasn't.

I was only about eight so I don't remember much of what he said, but I was left with a sort of overall impression. The ships were grey and everything was hard. Even in the place where you slept there was this steel bulkhead full of rivets just above your face. Though the waters of the sea were cold, it could be stuffy and imprisoning in your windowless quarters with the smell of the other able seamen and their feet. You heard the sound of the great engines turning and smelled the oil. The food was regular and hot but lacking taste, repetitive as the weeks went on at sea. The watches were interminably long and cold. You looked eternity in the eye, where time stopped moving on the waves. There was trade in polo necks and leather waistcoats. Much of the convoy was lost to sight in the mists so you often couldn't see the ships you were protecting. On the bridge they knew; by the ping of radar, the squawk of radio, they kept tabs on their charges — those vulnerable milch cows, the priceless laden females in the rolling herd. You longed for landfall, anywhere, somewhere there might be colour, something more than the grey of steel, the gunmetal grey of waves, the navy blue of uniform, the thin grey of mist.

A British merchantman was holed and sinking. My father's ship, *Peerless*, changed course to give chase to a German frigate they had no chance of catching. They were fearful of U-boats. The big guns fired and the noise was unearthly in the boundless mist. When they got back alongside the merchantman they found that many of the crew were in a blazing oil slick on the water, dying of cold, dying by fire.

My father shook his head when he came to this part, I remember. He seemed galvanised. I'd never seen him more alive. He was outraged by what he recalled, thinking the Germans had deliberately set the sea on fire to burn their enemy.

He stood in front of the fireplace in the sitting room, swaying a little on his feet, jabbing his finger at me.

Although I knew it had been a bad experience, I felt envious of him for what he'd seen. Maybe he was a little proud of it too, though he couldn't explain why. He couldn't share or offload any of that stuff. He didn't have the words for it, he just didn't know them or couldn't put them in the right order, and his failure seemed to make him angry.

It may have been that night that he first beat me. Just from a fury of frustration. I don't think he was 'damaged' — merely inarticulate. He had to get this thing off his back, he had to show people, show himself, how bad it had been. So breaking some taboo — beating a nearby child — was a simple way of showing that he knew what life was *like* beyond limits.

At least, that would be the smart 'psychological' explanation. In 'psychology', there is cause and effect. Everything is made to connect, as though there were Newtonian laws not only of celestial motion, but also of human motivation. For instance, Law One: All actions attract other actions in inverse proportion to the square of the distance between them.

Personally, I think my father was just a) not a very nice man; and b) drunk.

Then he got a taste for it. Not because the 'taste' was the inverse shape, therefore the natural expression of, the 'trauma'. No. But because he enjoyed it.

That's life. Christ, what else can you expect? The human being is genetically 98 per cent identical to the chimpanzee. The human being is genetically 50 per cent identical to the *banana*. Of the genes that make us up, the vast majority — 'junk' genes — do nothing at all. They're just hitching a ride.

Homo sapiens, according to current evolutionary theory, exists principally as a container for inactive bacteria which have been successful in the struggle for survival.

Laws of Newtonian elegance can't apply to human behaviour. Bananas aren't motivated by 'cause and effect'. Ask one.

★   ★   ★

I got up early and readied the 1100 for a drive: oil, water, air, expensive petrol from the garage in Jesus Lane. I was in Reading by late morning and went to see my mother at the Waverley. She was able to offer me something called an 'open sandwich' — a halved slice of French bread with shiny ham, cottage cheese and pineapple — on the house. We had it in the lounge bar, where self-conscious businessmen ordered gin and tonic and food whose name was given in French, which neither they nor the waitress understood, while ersatz music fizzed from a wall-mounted speaker. My mother ate nothing herself, though she drank a tomato juice. She looked thin and tired. I gave her ten pounds I'd taken from a coat

166

in the corridor outside the toilets, and I could tell it made a difference.

I needed some music to listen to in the car, so I went to the shopping centre and slipped a cassette of *Madman Across the Water* by Elton John into my coat pocket, then conscientiously bought a disc-cleaning cloth at the till. I couldn't face going back to Clock Court and all that, to a town without Jen, so I drove west on the M4, listening to 'Tiny Dancer', which Stellings had tipped me off about. He also rated 'Come Down in Time' from *Tumbleweed Connection*, but thought it spoiled by 'silly vocal phrasing'. 'Silly': not much of a critical term, is it? But it's only pop music.

I drove on through 'Levon' and 'Razor Face'. My direction? Anywhere. Because one is always nearer by not keeping still. At Newbury, I remembered Jen's mother, left the motorway and skirted the town, wondering which bit she had, in the newspaper's words, 'hailed from'. Is that hail as in stones, I wonder, or as in fellow-well-met? The ring road took me to the south, over the Hampshire border (Newbury was, to be fair to the reporter, pretty close to Hampshire — just not *in* it), where I followed signs for Winchester. I kept driving. In Romsey I bought a map which told me, as I was fairly certain anyway, that I was almost in Jennifer country.

Soon it was dark and I was in the high street of a town called Lyndhurst with a vast timbered hotel, the Crown, to my right. I drove beneath the arch into a car park. The desk girl was reluctant, puzzled by my lack of luggage, but could scarcely claim that such a barracks was full. They wouldn't bring dinner to the room, so I had to have the oxtail soup and some sort of meat pie with carrots at a solitary table in the dining room. The beer was keg fizz, so I got my reserve bottle of Johnnie Walker from the car and drank in my room till I fell asleep.

It was only a few miles to travel the next morning. In Brockenhurst I bought a toothbrush and paste and cleaned my teeth in the toilet of a café. The landscape became gorse-covered, the soil looked peaty and was dense with bracken. There was a hamlet called Goose Green. The wayside inns had facetious tourist come-ons. I went under a railway bridge and came into Lymington.

What did I expect? I hadn't pictured it clearly, except for one thing: it would be the town version of herself. The buildings would be Arkland-shaped, the streets would be redolent of Jennifer. It would breathe her presence.

I parked on the severely sloping high street. People greeted one another, stopped and talked. No one knew me. No one came up to me and said, 'This is Jentown. We're all so happy to live here.' I was invisible.

I saw it all through her eyes. The weathered red brick with the faded lettering of long-gone enterprises: 'Rand and Son, General Drapers, Ladies and Children's Outfitters', and next to it another clothes shop with union flags on poles at 45 degrees, like something from Victoria's jubilee. And halfway up the street a detached

168

Queen Anne building, fortnightly home of the Rotary Club, a solicitors' office. Doubtless her father had dealt many times with them as client or antagonist. On the railings in front was a poster for the Lymington Choral Society. Had what that girl Susan called her sense of humour limitation extended to Lym Chor Soc? Had she sung her off-contralto in the second row?

At the summit of the street was a bell tower with a clock, part of the church. I scanned the war memorial next to it. Almost one hundred Lymington men had died in 1914–18, mostly in the Hampshire Regiment, but no Arklands (the first name alphabetically was Backhurst, F. I remember such things easily).

I walked round the graveyard for a bit. The tombstones were lichened-over and illegible. Many were tilting or fallen. 'Remembered Always' they claimed, but it wasn't true. You can't recall someone whose name has worn away. In the far corner was a pile of chipped and broken headstones ready to be carted off. Newer burials were marked with small tablets flat in the grass, though you had to walk over the old graves to reach them. There was no escaping the arithmetic of the dead and the fact that the cemetery with its horse chestnuts and holly trees was unable keep up with them.

I couldn't sense Jen in any of this. I walked on, down an alley beside the cricket pitch and the town football club. There were obscene graffiti on the fence.

What is a town then? How should I know? Where did she live, where did she walk? Little

Jen, did you linger in the doorway of Fox & Sons estate agents, wondering, like me, how any grown-up ever found the money to buy even these poky bungalows? Did you hang around the Pick'n'Mix in Woolworths? Where was the action, where the clubs, the discos, pubs you went to with the girls from school? Where was your first kiss, grope and party?

Did you walk on Thomas Street and survey those Georgian brick buildings? What are they? Retirement homes, museums? Or were you like most kids indifferent to your surroundings — oblivious in your hurry to excitement?

I wandered on and on, expecting to see a schoolgirl in the derided games clothes or an undergraduate on holiday in corduroy skirt and boots. Then I was tired.

It was noon by this time and I was also hungry, having not been able to face a solo breakfast at the Crown. I found a tea shoppe on the high street and ordered a toasted cheese sandwich with bacon. The back of the menu said something about Lymington being the 'New Forest's most popular town'. Did I have to face the possibility that Jennifer's home town was not the paradigm of English Eden that I'd pictured, but a tourist resort? And if so, what on earth could people do here on their holidays? They couldn't just eat cream teas and walk up and down the high street all day.

The sandwich was brought by a waitress in a 'Victorian' white paper cap with trailing streamers and a short black skirt. I thought Jen might have had her Saturday job here. I could

170

picture local men ogling the skirt and the streamers — but then again they looked too old for that, the other customers. They talked loudly of their hospital appointments, their X-rays and their 'tables'. How could anyone seriously live in a place like this?

Something happened to this country, perhaps in the 1960s. We lost the past.

You've seen the pictures of the men queuing to enlist in 1915, their faces turned up in guileless hope beneath their hats. Those who came back found the same villages and towns, empty and with too many women, but still with a link that took them back through to the lives of their grandfathers and further — 200 years at least, to a life lived straight, sincere. Field, factory, office.

Even cars and buses didn't really change it. When my father returned from the North Atlantic in 1946 it was to a country cold and poor and short of food — vindicated, glorious, foggy, broke and miserable. Still, for all he knew of bodies burning in the sea, bodies burning in the ovens of Treblinka, children in flames in wood-and-paper houses in Japan, for all the millions unburned, unburied on the Eastern Front, it was still Reading. It hadn't changed (it had always been an unlovely town) and there was still a main line to the past.

How did we lose it? Now you walk those same streets and it seems as though it's all a sham, a play or a quotation. When I looked through the window of the shoppe, I didn't see people rooted in that town: I saw people floating through it,

171

disconnected. Field, factory and office have gone. The fields are mostly set aside, not worked; the factories have closed and the offices are let to national out-of-town concerns. The residents think most about Bournemouth, London, the Algarve and Coronation Street. These are people in a dream, of whom only the very old have some embarrassing idea of 'local history', though even they can only speak of it apologetically, knowing that the thread is broken and that while the past is real enough — the *only* true reality — the present has insufficient depth to register it.

I left the tea shoppe and bought a local street guide in the newsagent — because I did, of course, know where I was really going. After all, I had the address.

I drove down to the small quay to look at the boats. There was all the usual boat stuff — chandlery, sail shops — but I couldn't imagine Jennifer there. What would she do with her friends? There seemed nowhere for them to hang out.

No, there was nothing for me here. It was time to do what I had come for, though I felt for some reason reluctant.

I drove slowly along the side of the quay, past a private dock, to a public area with a green and a bandstand. I stopped again for a minute and looked at it.

The bandstand filled me with pain. I was half-remembering something — a day trip as a child, I suppose. I had gone to a seaside town, I had walked on the pier, I had been happy. There was a brass band. I had been lost, I had been beaten. I had been unhappy. I had felt the impotence and agony of childhood. I remembered, I did not remember. And the strange thing was, that, in the end, it came to exactly the same thing.

I drove round the end of the quay. Stanley Road, Westfield Road, a house called 'Mariner's Rest'. I looked at the street guide.

The roads went nowhere on the headland, but linked back onto themselves and into town. I was nearly there.

Was R.P. Arkland MA a sailing man, then? Why else live in this part of town? Maybe it was just the view he liked.

I was now in roads not quite suburban — outskirts is what you'd call them, I think. Detached houses of widely varying styles and sizes. Cheap post-War pebbledash, mock-Tudor with leaded lights, whitewashed villa. All had got their nameplates from the same supplier, whether wrought iron hammered into the wall by the drive or stencilled black-on-white with a single flower decoration. 'Woodpeckers'. 'Fairview'. It was the sort of area grand people would recoil from but if you came from Trafalgar Terrace you were daunted by.

Vitre Gardens, Rookes Lane. I checked the map. This was Jen country all right, this was the heart of it. Her road was a fraction grander than I'd expected. It had big views to one side over fields, and although some of the houses weren't up to much, they were all widely separated by gardens and gravel drives. I pulled over and walked the last hundred yards.

R.P.'s house bore the marks of his profession: picture windows, skylights, yellow frames, parts knocked through and tinkered with; a sort of lean-to folly on the garden side. But it still looked all right. Presumably the planners hadn't let him bugger it up completely. It still looked like a house where four girls could arrive home from school at slightly different times, throw down their bikes on the gravel and run inside.

I sat down on the grass bank opposite and looked at it. It was the house in the picture on her desk.

For a time I stared at the bedroom windows and tried to guess which one had been hers. I wished I'd had McCaffrey's binoculars. Without disturbing anyone, I could have looked through and seen her wardrobe, the hanging clothes, the soft toys that the journalist woman had commented on. How come she'd been allowed to go in and look, when I, Jen's real friend, had to sit on wet grass and imagine?

I sat with my head in my hands, looking. I thought of the passionate connections that a family like hers could make. I pictured family tea with four opinionated daughters. And old R.P . . . no longer tired from sleepless nights when they were babies, but no longer young either. How he must have missed grown-up Jen when she went off to university; and now he must be wanting time to stand still before the others all deserted him as well. These hot ties of affection and circumstance that seem eternal to you when you're young — he knew they weren't. He knew that all such bonds dissolve with death or time and that in the end you are alone. No wife, no Jen, no parents, no other children. Quite alone.

There must have been a shop somewhere in this area, probably in a short parade on one of the new estates — 'Oh, Jenny, just run and get some mint sauce, will you, before Dad gets home?' 'Why's it always me?' Because you're the most reliable, the best.

The thought of all that happiness was hard to bear. What's the point of happiness when all it does is throw the facts of dying into clear relief?

I went back to the car to get some Anadin, expecting to return and sit some more; but once I was inside the 1100, I couldn't bear the thought of it, so I started the engine and drove away.

★　★　★

It was growing dark near Newbury and I suddenly thought I'd like to see Julie, so I took the motorway to Reading and parked in Trafalgar Terrace. I got a Chinese takeaway for the three of us and slept like a child in my old room.

It was late morning the next day when I strolled in through the main gate of my college and made my way towards Clock Court. I stopped by one of the cobbled triangles and looked over to the foot of my staircase, which was barred by blue and white tape. Two police officers stood either side of the door into the building.

'What's going on?' I said.

'You can't go in. Police search. What's your name?'

'Engleby.'

'Wait here.'

One of the men went upstairs. I waited.

'What are they looking for?' I asked the remaining plod. I was thinking of the high-level cistern in the toilet.

'I'm not allowed to say. Just wait here.'

Eventually, the first officer came down again. 'Come with me,' he said.

I followed him to the top floor. Outside my room stood Inspector Peck and Dr Townsend.

'Ah, Mike. You've met Inspector Peck, haven't you?'

'Yes.' I nodded at Peck.

'He came to see me this morning. He has a warrant to search your room. It's in connection with Jennifer Arkland. I looked for you, but we couldn't find you. Where have you been?'

Jennifer's house.

No. 'I went to see my mother at home, in Reading. She hasn't been well. Can I look inside my room?'

Peck said, 'All right. Watch your step. We've taken up the boards.'

Inside was a man with rubber gloves and overalls — a pathologist, presumably — Cannon and another plain-clothes officer who was busy with screwdriver and scraper.

The carpet had been rolled up and was stacked on one end in a corner, next to some upended floorboards. I could see my floor joists and the ceiling of Dave Carling's room below.

176

The striped voids were full of dust. They'd gone into the wall behind the 'drinks' cupboard, through plasterboard, back to brick. You could see part of a timber diagonal behind the Chambéry and the gin from Arthur Cooper.

What were they expecting to find? The ghost of Jen? Bones? A bra?

Cannon came through from the bedroom. 'What are all these pills for?'

'I have difficulty sleeping.'

He looked at Peck meaningfully as he dropped them in a polythene bag. I suppose they were thinking that if the tablets made me sleep they could knock out someone else as well.

Since their last visit I'd got some old pill bottles that I'd had from the doctor in Reading (antibiotics, antihistamine) and transferred the Alan Greening stuff into them, so at least my name was on the labels.

The young officer was starting to lever up the floorboards in the small pantry.

'Do you have to do that?' I said to Peck. 'What are you expecting to find?'

Peck didn't say anything. He gave me a hard look as though to say things were serious now. There was no longer anything avuncular in his manner.

There was dust in the air from where Cannon had cut open the side of my mattress.

It was absurd.

I looked at Townsend, smiled and rolled my eyes. These plods, I seemed to say.

Townsend didn't smile back. He was twisting

his hands so violently he must have been burning the skin off them.

'Careful,' I said to Cannon, who was pulling down the Procol Harum poster. 'Let me do that for you.'

I put it carefully on the desk while Cannon unscrewed the corkboard and ran his hand over the flat plastered wall behind it. He knocked a few times, trying to look knowledgeable, like a Caius medic listening to his first chest.

I laid the corkboard also on top of the desk. Julie's funny little face grinned up at me from beneath her straw boater. She looked older than that now. She was thirteen. She had breasts, went to parties, listened to Queen — though I was pretty sure T. Rex were still her favourites. 'Metal Guru/I-is it true?' Oh, Jules.

Cannon was shining a torch onto the the ceiling — as though my idea of body disposal would be to bring all the plaster down, go up a ladder and stuff the jointed remains piece by piece between the beams, replaster, repaint and apply the right amount of dust so the cut sections blended in with the rest. Hope for no dropping bloodstains.

It's true that during their last visit I'd given them the impression that I was pretty handy on the film set, but there are limits to my ability with fretsaw and chisel.

The young one was going through my clothes, holding them up to the 60-watt overhead bulb, looking for stains, I imagined. He put some shirts and underclothes in a large bin liner. They included a Donny Osmond tee shirt Julie'd given me as a joke for Christmas.

I was thinking about the eight ounces of dope that I'd replaced up the chimney when I'd got it back from Stellings. You really had to know the chimney, and how to bend your hand round on itself to reach the inner ledge.

'I hope you're going to tidy up when you've finished,' I said.

'Don't take the piss out of me, you little shit,' said Peck, sticking his face suddenly into mine. This was about as unavuncular as you could get. 'We're going to get whoever did this. If not today, tomorrow. But don't you worry. We're going to solve this crime. Barry, look in the desk.'

Dr Townsend was twitching so much he had to go out of the room at this point, while Cannon went through my papers. The desk was fairly empty, in fact. I'd left most of my work in my locker outside the biology labs.

There weren't even any letters from girlfriends or from my mother in the drawers — though doubtless you could find even that absence suspicious if you were so minded.

'So you went to this, did you?' said Cannon. He was holding up the order of service from Jen's college chapel.

'Yes, of course.'

'Enjoy it, did you?' said Peck.

'It was a good service. But sad. Obviously.'

The other plain-clothes man was going through my books. I had wittily bought one called *The Grass Crop* from the ten pence secondhand shelf outside Galloway & Porter and cut a deep section from the middle pages to keep — well, grass obviously. I couldn't remember if there was any in it, but I thought not because it only held a little and I didn't deal in small quantities any more. It was the sort of title that might interest Townsend, I thought. *The Grass Corp: Uneven Distribution in Windborne Seeding.*

I had hoped that Townsend might intercede on my behalf, but he seemed hypnotised by the activity around us. When Peck addressed him, he was deferential.

'Very well, Inspector. Certainly.' Then he tried to establish his superiority with some donnish phrases: 'Do by all means proceed. I'm quite sure the means are proportionate to the end.'

Peck looked at him as though he was mad.

Eventually, after we'd stood around for about two hours, Peck called off the search and the officers all gathered at the door.

'Right,' said Peck to Townsend. 'This staircase is out of bounds until further notice. You'll have to find rooms for the other students until we've finished.'

'How long will that be?'

Peck looked at the pathologist. 'Two days at least.'

'I shall tell the Senior Tutor at once.'

We walked through Clock Court and on to the main gate.

'Goodbye, Inspector. Good luck with the investigation,' said Townsend, risking a light irony now that all seemed safe.

'We'll be back at seven in the morning,' said

Peck, not returning the winsome smile. 'Tell the porter.'

When they'd gone, we went to the domestic bursar's office and sorted out which college guest room I could live in till they'd finished with mine. Then we went back to the porters' lodge to sign a book and get the key.

Outside, looking over Front Court, I said to Townsend, 'I feel a bit anxious about all this. Could I ask you to — '

'I'm sure it'll be fine,' said Townsend tightly. He looked at his watch. 'Oh dear. Supervision.'

He ran away over the lawn in the middle of Front Court (only Fellows were allowed on the grass, but I'd never seen one run before); he cantered pretty quickly, as it happened, with a high-stepping action, till he vanished in the shadows of the Hawksmoor cloister.

★ ★ ★

That night I went to the Kestrel, but my headache was so bad I couldn't enjoy it, and I had to go back to my guest room, where I listened to the radio. I tried to do some work, but it was hard to concentrate. I looked in on the TV room, where I'd seen Robin Wilson's performance, but there was nothing worth watching. I ended up in the college bar, not a place I normally go outside Folk Club. I once worked a shift on the bar with Dave Carling when Brian, the professional, went home at nine. After we'd shut up at eleven, Dave and I stayed behind and drank a shot of every drink on sale. By midnight the only ones we hadn't got through were gin and Newcastle Brown. So we did them together in a half-pint mug, and that's not a mixture that I'd recommend.

The bar was full of amateur drinkers with halves of gassy keg bitter, playing table football and smoking No.6. It wasn't fun.

When I got back to my guest room, on the ground floor of Dr Woodrow's staircase, oddly enough, I felt detached from what was going on. I began to inspect the surfaces of the room closely, though I felt alienated by their texture. Wood, cloth, Formica, carpet, enamel.

It was a little like that time in Izmir. I felt I was beginning to unravel. It was as though all the molecules that made the entity known as 'Mike Engleby' had been kept in place by some weird centripetal force — which had unaccountably failed. Now those particles were flying outward into chaos.

I suppose all human 'personalities' are at some level makeshift or provisional, but it's unusual to feel oneself come apart in such a molecular way.

★   ★   ★

The next forty-eight hours were bad. I was taking four of those blue ten-milligram pills a day as well as some Tuinal I'd found in my sponge bag. Yet I'd still hardly slept.

Eventually, Peck and his men cleared out of my staircase. I didn't immediately return but stayed an extra night in the guest room so Mrs Lumbago could get in and tidy up the mess they'd left. She was indignant about this extra work, even though she'd had three days off completely.

Peck came to see me one last time before he left the college and moved his inquiry on to . . . To somewhere else. Hopeful Hall. Lucky Dip Alley. The lounge bar of the Bow at a Venture. Or even to Oxford, for all I know, home of lost maids' causeways.

'Did you find what you were looking for?' I asked.

He was standing in front of the restored Procol Harum poster. 'I've seen enough,' he said. 'This inquiry is not over, Mr Engleby. You never close a case like this.'

He was more disturbing now that he was being polite, oddly enough. When he shouted at me he had just reminded me of Chief Petty Officer Dunstable in a factitious rage on the Chatfield parade ground. This seemed sincere and powerful — and he was, after all, more than twice my age.

'We never give up. Jennifer was a young woman who was much loved by her parents. One day you might understand that, if you ever have kids of your own.' His voice suggested he thought this unlikely.

'To lose a life at that stage,' he went on, 'when she had it all before her. It's a very serious crime. The public and the police think the same way on this. It's as bad as they come.'

He looked round my room as though one final glance might yield a clue that four officers over three days had failed to dig up.

'One day,' said Peck, doing up his coat, 'we'll discover what happened to Jennifer Arkland. I promise you that.'

'So you do think she's dead.'

'Yes, I do. I'm sure of it.'

He looked so sad then that I had to look away. When I turned my eyes back to his face, he was staring at me.

I met his gaze, and for five or ten seconds we looked one another in the eye without speaking.

'If it's not me,' he said eventually, 'it'll be my successor. The files, the paperwork, the notes will all be left meticulous. Marked up, indexed, cross-indexed. And you, Mr Engleby, are going in the file marked 'Unhappy'.'

'*Tu quoque*,' I said.

'What?'

'You're going in my unhappy file, too.'

He didn't say anything else, he just brushed past me and went loudly down the wooden stairs.

★   ★   ★

I moved back completely into my room. They'd done a pretty good job of putting it all back together. The first thing I did was put my hand up the chimney and double it round on to the ledge. The dope was still there.

Next, I clattered downstairs to the bathroom on the half-landing and climbed on to the toilet seat. I was confident the diary was safe, because otherwise I would have heard about it. I dropped my hand over the top of the ironwork and down

184

into the dusty crack. I felt the the crinkled polythene and the book inside.

I ought really, I thought, to find a better hiding place, though in some ways where better than the obvious? Wasn't there some corny story about someone hiding a brooch by wearing it? Also, where better to hide it than a place that had just been done over for three days by the cops?

What I ought *really* to do, I thought, was return it to Jen's parents. But I didn't want to do that till the heat had died down a bit.

There was also a slight ethical problem. The book was private. It was bad enough that I'd given way to temptation, but it was clear she particularly didn't want her parents to read it. 'Can't bear even to imagine how upset he would be' she'd written at the thought of her father knowing about her private life.

So behind the cistern was the best place for the time being; then maybe I'd take it back to Reading in the vacation.

Over the next few days I began to feel a lot better. Although I knew Peck was free to come back any time (there was obviously no double-jeopardy rule in interviewing) there was something in his tone that made me think he'd got no questions left to ask.

Had he checked my movements? Did they find Steve in Christ's or Corpus — Steve I was supposed to have talked to at the party? 'And how did Mike Engleby seem that night?' Did they ask the porter what time I got in? Not that he'd have the slightest idea; he didn't keep a log or anything. I didn't care; it didn't matter. I was going to be left alone.

All the clothes the police had taken were returned, minus a couple of things, but I didn't chase them up. It was no worse than the average return from a service wash in the launderette.

Term ended, and during the vacation I saw a lot of Julie, whose work was 'showing promise' at school. My mother was only working three days a week at the Waverley; she'd got some sort of infection in the wound after the hysterectomy and it had taken a lot out of her. Jules said they thought at one time she had septicaemia and that she was going to die.

She looked old and worn down. I did a week's work in the paper mill and gave her most of the money. She found it hard to grasp what I was saying when I said I was going into the Foreign Office. 'Is that abroad then?' she asked. I think maybe she thought I'd still be working for the paper mill, but in its foreign office.

I did a fair bit of Nat Sci work. There wasn't much else to do in Trafalgar Terrace. Stellings, who lived in London, said he might be in Reading one day and if so he'd look me up, but mercifully he didn't.

★　★　★

I'm back in Clock Court and it's warm. The trees are in leaf. It's that time of year when you find you don't have the right clothes on so you're always peeling off, and then you're suddenly cold again.

People have forgotten about Jennifer Arkland. At the Sidgwick Site and all over town they've taken down the Missing posters.

It's worse than when they were up. At least her face was there before. She was, if not alive, present. Now you look at the plate glass of the gown shop on the corner of St Mary's Passage and King's Parade and where her eyes used to be it offers just a blank view on to college scarves and ties in different colours. Through the window of Fitzbillies cake shop you can now see sponges and éclairs. In my old Greek restaurant you can make out the potted palm and the greasy fan uninterrupted by a picture of that laughing girl in Tipperary.

The sight of ties and cakes and palms is bought at a price. Their presence is her absence, and it's ubiquitous.

The air on King's Parade is lighter. People are laughing at the outdoor tables by the river at the Anchor. She's gone.

In the warm spell, they've started punting on the river. Finals are coming, and she won't sit them. She'll never get her youknowwhat.

She's gone. Doesn't matter how many times you say it, because it never fully registers.

She's gone . . .

★　★　★

I went for my interview in London yesterday, in Carlton House Terrace, a big Nash building, scruffy and echoing inside. A secretary with fat legs and glasses made me wait. There were three others. We were told not to introduce ourselves; but to me they were Francis, Batley and McCain: nervous, dim, their own group. It was as though I was caught in a loop of time. Woodrow had told me to wear a suit and I'd bought one from the Oxfam shop near the University Arms.

I was interviewed in a room overlooking the Mall. It was completely bare except for a desk, two chairs and a man in a chalk-stripe suit. It seemed formulaic, barely more than checking my identity. You get used to this sort of thing as a student. You haven't yet done anything, so you just present and re-present your initials and your home address and your exam results and hope they please.

The man, who never told me his name, then gave me ten pounds for travel expenses. 'You can blow it all on taxis or go by bus and keep the change.' He gave me an address in Knightsbridge, where he said a doctor was waiting for me. I had a fair amount of cash on me from a Glynn Powers subcontract, so I took a cab in Pall Mall.

The doctor was not from the Benbow-Vaughan school. He had a gold watch chain, silver-blond hair and a smooth manner. He didn't examine my crotch by torchlight, squeeze my scrotum or tell me to stop drinking; he merely listened to my chest, looked in my eyes, ears and mouth and took a history. Diabetes? No. Tick. Heart disease? No. (I didn't want to drag my father into this.) Tick. He wrote on a pad with a shiny fountain pen. I couldn't think what his bill would be but felt sure it would be in guineas.

When I left, he handed me a piece of paper with another address on it, this time near Hyde Park. I hadn't done anything like this since Julie's tenth birthday treasure hunt.

This time there were four or five men at a table, again in an otherwise empty room. They looked like a convention of private school geography teachers. They asked me hypothetical questions.

'If you're on a train, do you always notice who's in the compartment with you?'

Depends if I'm sober. 'Yes,' I said.

'If you find yourself alone in a foreign city, what do you do?'

'I buy a map, walk around to orientate myself and go to a museum or a bar and try to make friends with some local people.'

Alternatively, I might score some high-grade hashish in the market square, find a hotel room, take back a litre of duty-free and watch television. When had I last been in a foreign city on my own anyway? Istanbul? And more on the way home. Split, Ljubljana, Venice, Geneva, Paris. I couldn't remember what I'd done in any of them. I do have these blanks.

An old-fashioned telephone on the table started to ring. The bald man answered it in a language I didn't recognise, then passed the receiver to me.

Someone was speaking to me in French. No one had done that since Mug Benson in the dry run for the O-level oral. (The board examiner

189

himself, in our one-to-one, had been happy to chat in English.) Had Woodrow overcooked my ability as a linguist? I said 'très bien' quite a bit and gave a short speech about who I was and where I came from that I still remembered, word-perfect, from Mug's revision group. Then, while I was still on the front foot, I put the receiver down and pushed the telephone back to the bald man.

They asked me for the names of two referees so that I could be 'positively vetted'. I offered Waynflete, my Nat Sci don, and, after some thought, the manager of the paper mill, John Symonds, who always seemed a bit shifty about my father's early death.

After a few more questions they seemed to lose interest and I was allowed to go. It wasn't the glorious opening to my ambassadorial career that I'd expected, but once I've sat the Foreign Office exams, which I do in early June, three weeks after finals, I presume the process will become less seedy. By the New Year I suppose I'll be a Washington insider, lunching in Foggy Bottom, dining in Georgetown.

★   ★   ★

It's 11 May, nine days before finals blast-off, and a strange tension hangs over the town. McCaffrey, my one-time King Street Run jockey, has returned from Newmarket and has been seen in the college library. (He's doing a four year vet's course.) Stewart Forres has come back early from the film festival at Cannes. Yesterday

Stellings walked down to the Sidgwick Site but was appalled to discover how far away it was and, before his revision lecture began, accepted my offer of a lift back to college in the Morris 1100. The only way he can get himself to look at his law notes is by spreading them on the floor, standing on the desk and reading them through McCaffrey's binoculars.

I finally lent him *Moving Waves* by Focus with a note telling him where the sublime moments were. 'Track Five ('Focus II') at 0.39 and at 1.35. Track Six ('Eruption') at 5.08, 6.14 and 9.17 — when he bends the note. Skip the rest.'

He read it. 'Christ, Groucho,' he said, 'you're even more bonkers than I am.'

Anne and Molly, compelled to cook since Jen's disappearance, have made two-gallon vats of brown rice and vegetarian stew to last them through the long barricaded days. They know they've left it too late to do all the work they should have done; they need more time — yet they also want the exams to come soon, to end the waiting.

I think we're all wondering in different ways how Jennifer would have managed the count-down crisis. Would her instinctive balance have deserted her? Would her moderation have failed her at the last? Would she have thrown up her hands a week early, shouted Qué sera, sera and dashed off to the Mitre to get drunk? Or would she have toiled all night on methedrine and jumbled up her head with unassimilated bilge?

I think not. I think she would have found that middle way, turning up the pressure on herself a

191

little (early nights and longer days) but retaining her perspective, the intuitive sense that never failed her: that always knowing the right thing to do. What a gift that is. Where does it come from? I don't think you can learn it. I sometimes think that she and I were polar opposites. My life has been marked by an instinct for the *wrong* thing to do: yes, in any given situation you can trust old Toilet to take the duff option.

Folk Club was a rather muted one. Even the second-years have Part One exams, so the crowd was mostly first-years — or 'schoolboys with a summer holiday' as Dr Gerald Stanley once described his freshmen, putting them at their ease as only Dr Gerald Stanley can.

I'm not going to miss all this, am I?

I think about that as I lean against the sweating pillar in the college bar, listening to the music with a glass of red vermouth in my hand.

What I'll miss least is the winsomeness, the use of citric humour as defence; the Maoist geographers, the smilers with the knives.

And yet I did warm to it. This town, it street names, its immanent past: the river mist in the beautiful courts of Queens'. What I liked about it was a version lived by others.

For instance, by Jennifer. I enjoyed her time here. I don't think her view was blinkered or deluded; she was in most ways unillusioned, almost as much as I am. No, I think that to see it as she saw it and play it as she played it was reasonable. It's a pity that it wasn't a way open to me.

I left Folk Club early, in the middle of Split

Infinitive (back by 'popular request'), and took my car out into the evening. Within twenty minutes I was in high hedgerows, in the warm darkness. I stopped at a Wheatsheaf and took a drink into the garden.

Then I walked into the lane. It was entirely silent and I tried to breathe its peace.

I've tried this in the past. You need the air to be warm, not hot, but balmy with a smell of grass or hawthorn. You need the black outline of branches against a sky that, while dark, still has a blue shade to it. What you're trying to do is get plugged into the depth of history going down through these villages, these houses, these lawns panting with their garden scent at evening.

And in that history you're trying to connect to something that once was yours — to something purer, better, something that you lost. Or something, maybe, that you never knew but that you *feel* you knew.

Inhale and hold the evening in your lungs. It needn't have been a 'perfect' afternoon (by which people usually just mean very hot); it doesn't have to be Midsummer's Day. Better if it's slightly early, slightly late, if the village has an ugly pylon, roadworks or a ruined telephone exchange. Sometimes you can get more easily to the universal through something that isn't typical. Something that's *too* representative can blind you with its own detail — like a painting by Canaletto — and stop you seeing through it.

I breathed and breathed and did feel some calmness enter in, though it was, as always, shot with a sense of loss. Loss and fear.

I found I'd wandered some way from the pub and was standing by a high brick wall, from the other side of which music was playing. A little further along was a wooden gate with an iron latch; the bottom of it scraped on the ground as I pushed it, but opened easily enough.

I was in a large garden with a well-lit marquee. With my pub glass still in hand I walked slowly towards the party that was spilling off the wooden flooring of the tent, over the stone terrace and into the house through two open doors. Most of the people seemed to be about my age and I imagined it was probably someone's twentyfirst. Inside the marquee, people were dancing to a discotheque, pretty standard stuff, 'Maggie May', 'Satisfaction'. Over to one side was a table with a man in a white tuxedo who was in charge of drinks. I held out my glass to a silver punchbowl and he ladled me out some reddish liquid with fruit in it. I lit a cigarette and stood to one side by a thin pillar wound about with paper streamers. The boys had dinner jackets, but most of them had taken them off to dance and were in white shirts with bow ties dangling. In the dim light I didn't particularly stand out.

The boys were boisterous as boys are on summer evenings, drunk. It was indeed someone's party and he made a speech, interrupted by his ribald friends to whom he brayed back happily, then thanking his parents with a sudden change of voice into a solemn key that must have made them gulp.

I had a few more drinks and danced a little,

not something I enjoy, but there was a sort of melee and I would have stood out too much if I hadn't jigged around a little. One of the girls, a dark-haired one in a strapless scarlet dress, smiled at me as she shook herself, like a dog emerging from water.

The boy whose birthday it was went past me, glass in hand, and said, 'Are you enjoying yourself?'

'Yes,' I said.

'Good.' He patted me lightly on the back. 'You're quite welcome here.'

I went back to the pub car park soon afterwards, disturbed. I don't like being rumbled, I like to be invisible.

6

Stellings has got a small first-floor flat in Arundel Gardens, Notting Hill, sandwiched between a bongo player and a junior anaesthetist. So if one makes too much noise at night he can apply to the other for relief, I pointed out. And so he does. The anaesthetist, who lives above, is a party man with an uncarpeted floor; the bongo player below, who bongoes only for an hour each day at noon, has an Alan Greening-like pharmacopoeia. If all else fails, Stellings puts on headphones and listens to Abba, by whom he has become obsessed. He goes on about 'Phil Spector wall-of-sound production' and 'lesbian Beach Boy harmonies'.

The street's a bit run-down and Stellings's flat's only a few yards off the smoky throughway of Ladbroke Grove, but he tells me Notting Hill's the coming place, next year's Bohemia but with bigger houses — 'the thinking man's Chelsea'. I suspect his father bought the flat for him. In return, Stellings has to study at the College of Law.

Me, I've got this room in Paddington from which I watch the toms get picked up by the men in cars. The toms are mostly girls who've been moved on from King's Cross, having arrived from some grimy Northern town where the mills have closed. They have swollen purple legs and dyed hair. Their skirts are too short and too tight because although they're starving and they give most of their money to the pimp, they're still fat. Sometimes, on my way home from the Tube, I give them cigarettes or drugs. I don't want what they offer in return. Imagine. That broth of germs.

For dinner, I sometimes go to the Ganges on Praed Street — small, dark, hot. Or the Bizarro, with its pasta in red sauce and its chicken in red sauce and red-and-white check tablecloths. The Concordia, further down, has better food, but you really need to be with someone or you feel conspicuous. For drinking, there's the Victoria in Sussex Place, but it has too many motor traders, so I go to the discreet White Hart at the end of a dark mews and drink Director's bitter. The local Unwin's is run by a lugubrious but watchful man from Stoke. I'm careful there.

I occasionally have dinner with Stellings at the Standard Indian Restaurant in Westbourne Grove. You can eat yourself to a standstill for £2.50, though it leaves you feeling rather stunned the next day.

It's eighteen months since we left university.

I'm not in the Foreign Office. Dr Woodrow called me in and said that in view of the attention paid to me by the police I was no longer considered a good 'security risk'. He gave me to understand that that was particularly important in the kind of work I'd been considered for. I asked him if that was with the Secret Intelligence Service and he didn't deny it. I felt glad to be out of it. I wouldn't have minded being a real diplomat, an ambassador, but I didn't want to spend the next twenty years pretending to be a visa officer while sniffing out details of Bulgarians' sex lives so I could entrap them and blackmail them over to 'our' side.

As a consolation, Woodrow referred me to the university appointments board, who referred me to Gabbitas Thring, an agency that finds teaching jobs for grads with no better ideas. They in turn sent me news of junior 'posts' at St Dunstan's in Croydon, or at Sycamore Trees in Guildford — which I, in turn, referred to the bin.

People drifted away after exams, many not bothering to finish the term. I went to say goodbye to Dr Townsend, my moral tutor, but he was out. I loaded up the 1100, checked the chimney and behind the toilet cistern, made sure I'd got everything and drove off.

I didn't get a youknowwhat in the end, and nor did anyone I knew; the very few they gave seemed to go to people no one had heard of, from colleges I'd never visited.

★   ★   ★

For the first year in London, I lived mostly by dealing (I used to meet Glynn Powers when he was in from Leicester). Then one night at the Standard, Stellings introduced someone he'd met at a party who worked for some studenty magazine — mostly just lists of what's on in the cinema, but with some reviews, interviews and conspiracy theory 'news' stories.

As I spooned out some lime pickle, I had a

sudden idea. I volunteered my services as science correspondent.

'Groucho's doubly qualified,' said Stellings, when he'd stopped choking on his poppadom. 'Literature and science. Two cultures are nothing to him. A man for both seasons.'

The journalist, a ferrety little bloke called Wyn Douglas, looked doubtful, and muttered about trade unions.

I thought he was wondering if I was left wing enough, so I talked soothingly for a bit about Chile and asbestos poisoning. Then I paid for his chicken korma and pulao rice and mushroom-peas and two pints of lager — and for Stellings as well, in case Douglas disapproved of bribery or payola or something. (I got the money from a coat on my way to the hideous downstairs toilet.)

He said he'd ask the editor. It was true they were light on science, but really they were looking to hire more women.

I told him I'd write under a female name if that helped.

To my surprise, I had a call about a week later. They wouldn't put me on the staff, but I was permitted to offer articles 'on spec'. I toyed with various noms de plume. Michèle Watt. Nellie Bohr. Betty Bunsen. They went with the first one, though they misprinted it with an 's' at the end, and so I became Michèle Watts.

It pleased me that my byline — my journalistic identity — was a misprint. Mike, Toilet, Groucho, Irish Mike, Mike (!), Prufrock, Michèle ... I sometimes saw it as that evolutionary drawing of the crouched ape who by stages turns into an upright human. (Completely fallacious, of course, that drawing, suggesting that *Homo sapiens* descended from an orang-utan. We are not descended from him any more than a gibbon is *descended* from us. All we did was share an ancestor, at some stage, before the human and ape paths diverged. For a metre or so in the hills of the Ardèche, the rainwaters of the Rhône and Garonne are one and the same trickle, as I learned on an interminable 'field trip' from Chatfield. Then you can see them split, on that pebble — there, *that* one — so one rivulet heads to Marseilles and the Med, the other to Bordeaux and the Atlantic. You put your hand in and lift out some water, rearrange it: no, it's the Med, thence Africa for you drops, after all, and you lot are off to New York City. Life, incidentally, is not like a watershed.)

Then I settled down to do the work. They wanted articles, so I had to give them articles.

How? Initially, I bought science and medical magazines and rewrote brief news stories from them in a more contentious way. If *Nature* reported developments in the chemistry of pollution and its consequences then it wasn't hard to deduce which multinational companies were most affected. Then I'd ring their press office to see what they thought about the article. Some were sniffy about my magazine, but some did call back with what they called a 'quote'. If the *British Medical Journal* said that money had run short for research into cervical cancer, it was easy to find out that the government body responsible for the grant allocation hadn't got a single woman on it, then ring some duffer and ask why not. I became familiar with that forlorn figure the 'press officer'. Soon the wire cage beneath my letter flap began to clog with press releases. Sometimes I merely rewrote them and passed them on to the magazine. With others, I could find a fault line or a nub — something that could be prised open. Then I rang the press office and kept on at them until they, or someone they had passed me on to, said something unwise. In the right mouth even 'no comment' looked like admitting they'd killed or maimed a hundred children with their procedures.

Then I started looking at the book-review sections of these journals and telephoned a couple of the publishers to see if their authors would like to be interviewed by a magazine they'd never heard of. They were so surprised to be asked that they sometimes said yes. I concluded that the market in scientific interviews was slack.

I bought a reconditioned typewriter from Globe Stationers on Praed Street and a *Teach Yourself to Type* manual, which involved covering all the keys with bits of paper till I could touch-type. I was able to check some facts in reference books in the Porchester library, which was in walking distance, but I had to spend a good deal on magazines and telephone calls. The cheques that stuttered in weeks later were at the union minimum rate (and this was one union that clearly hadn't flexed its muscles), but my work as Glynn Power's lieutenant made up the shortfall. Plus, since I had been at it for a decade now, I had developed the knack of helping myself if I liked the look of something. I read in the paper some lawyer offering mitigation for a klepto shoplifter on his fiftieth charge: 'My client, your honour, is unable to postpone the pleasure of acquisition.' Mine was more of a need than a pleasure, but I knew what he meant. I joined the National Union of Journalists, freelance branch, and they told me I could offset my subscription against tax. I didn't pay tax.

★ ★ ★

I kept the Morris 1100, and the Westminster parking wardens weren't officious, though eventually I did invest in a resident's permit. I bought a second-hand television from the Portobello Road, but there was hardly anything I wanted to watch on it, so in the evenings I tended to do what I'd always done: drink.

In London the distances are much greater, so I couldn't any longer stagger from the Kestrel to the Bradford to the Waterfall, from Bene't Street to Free School Lane. I could still drink, but now I was obliged to drink and drive. I started with some obvious Young's pubs in Hampstead and Chiswick and Mortlake and Battersea, and the Spread Eagle in Parkway. All Young's pubs are similar. You get a certain dependable effect from from four pints of Special: in the adenoids and the back of the cranium. Thunk. Then I winkled out dirtier places in Camden Town and Islington with wooden floors and men with odd tattoos. It

202

was only a few months before I was in the Isle of Dogs — in pubs sleepy, small and underlit, so you felt as though you'd crashed into someone's living room — and East Ham with its menacing camaraderie. The only area I avoided was the West End because all the pubs there were tourist-tormented and fake; also, even for an efficient smoker like me, it was like being in the beagle section of a Philip Morris research lab. Other districts? I wasn't an inverted snob. Chelsea had some pleasant bars in small streets going down to the river: men in polo neck sweaters with pet dogs and free bits of cheese and salt biscuits set out on the bar. Mayfair pubs are better than you'd think, and in Belgravia there are one or two — homely yet louche with tall, silent women — that I'd happily go back to.

Sometimes I went to the Hammersmith Odeon. I saw Ted Nugent there (Sunday 12 September, 1976; sorry, but I kept the ticket stub) and my ears rang for a week. I stood next to a tall girl in pink dungarees with long black curly hair; she was so beautiful I had to move away. Joan Armatrading. Thin Lizzy. Graham Parker & the Rumour. Or Dingwall's, Camden Lock, though there was something smug about that place. And the Stranglers. They seemed to be on everywhere, the Rock Garden, the Odeon. I could never get Stellings to go to these places ('Punk, Groucho? Got the wrong labial at the front of the word if you ask me'), so I went alone.

Overnight, everyone's stopped wearing flares after all these years and is suddenly back into drainpipes: jeans, needlecords, doesn't matter so long as they're straight. If you wear flares it's like saying you're into Barclay James Harvest or the Moody Blues.

There was a girl I noticed at a Graham Parker gig. She, too, stood alone, glass in hand. She didn't jump up and down, she didn't even tap her foot — she swung it, back and forth, so it grazed the ground, in time with the music, just. She had dark hair, cut to the shoulder, was about twenty-seven, with large brown eyes and an expression of resigned amusement. I tried to guess what she was on: detached but not spaced out, controlled but relaxed. Her clothes looked different from the other women's. She wore black woollen trousers and a quite long black jacket over a low cut white tee shirt with rows of silver necklaces.

I got another drink and moved into a position where I could watch her more carefully.

The gig ended with Parker singing 'Hold Back the Night'. This thin, rodent-like man with sleeveless tee shirt and bare arms — his snarling manner still seemed defiant even when admitting to emotion: 'Hold back the night,/Turn on the light/Don't wanna dream about you, baby,' he sang, but almost spat. According to *New Musical Express*, he used to be a petrol-pump attendant in Camberley, which is not that far from Reading. If only I'd had the 1100 in those days, GP could have filled her up.

The woman I was watching made her way slowly out of the building and walked towards Fulham Palace Road. I had nothing else to do, so

I followed, at a distance. What talent the Secret Intelligence Service had passed up, I thought, as I hung back momentarily in the doorway of the Kentucky Fried Chicken shop.

She turned down Lillie Road, then eventually went round the back of Nye Bevan House on the Clement Attlee Estate. I wonder what it's like to be remembered as a block with broken windows and urine lifts. Hugh Dalton the Man, I read once, was a pompous arse who went to Eton and Cambridge then got up the noses of his fellow leftist MPs; but Hugh Dalton the House . . . No games fields run down to the Thames at Windsor; no sound of college bells sends brainy boys hurrying to class. (Do you think clever boys like being all together, or does it sap their belief in their individual ability? Tell you one thing: I bet they have better jokes. I bet they aren't called 'Spaso' this and 'Toilet' that.)

But I wouldn't want to be remembered as a council block. 'The lift in Engleby's out of order again'; 'The council have refused to grant more money to clean up the graffiti on Engleby House.' No, no. 'The Engleby Choral Scholarship', that's more my line; 'The Engleby Foundation Award for International Peace' — though 'peace' marches and 'peace' committees have for so long been fronts for old Communists that perhaps I'll give that word a miss for another couple of decades.

In Tournay Road, my woman went into a house and banged the door behind her. I noted the number and lit a cigarette as I watched from across the street. Sure enough, a light went on in a first-floor window and I saw her come and spread her arms wide to pull the curtains. It was a fine gesture, maternal and inclusive.

Reluctantly, I began to make my way back to where I'd left the car. On Fulham Palace Road there was a small fags-and-paper shop still open. I went in to buy some B&H, and, while I was there, looked through the top-shelf magazines. Some specialise in short, dark-haired girls, some tend to have taller, leggier ones with fairer hair. (They don't advertise this, but you get to know them.) There's been a development in all of them lately, and it's not a subtle one. There used to be veiling, draping, covering — even baldness. Not any more. Now there is disclosure. The girls look a little surprised and some of it — pores, pimples, follicles — has been fogged, you can see, airbrushed and tidied up. But what on earth do they think they're doing, those girls, smiling as they display their clefts and folds? I suppose they're all toms and are paid a hundred pounds for it. Perhaps it's safer than getting in a car behind King's Cross. I feel for them, when I see their defiant smiles clinging to the centre of the lens, though it's not their eyes you stare back at. One or two look nice and I'd like to meet them; I'd like to push their knees together, throw them a rug, sit down and talk to them.

You can't browse for too long; you can't stand there, thumbing through a wide selection; there's an art in not embarrassing Mrs Patel at the till. Confidence is the key. There's no point in pretending that at midnight the magazines are incidental — an afterthought — and that your main reason for venturing into the shop was to buy this morning's *Daily Express*.

I placed two magazines frankly on the counter, then asked for cigarettes. I paid with a ten-pound note and Mrs P dropped the change from a safe height into my open palm.

She looked pale and sad, with her red shawl wrapped round her head and shoulders. She must have hated this country and her job, selling pictures of English girls with their legs apart. There were little patches of brown pigment round her tired brown eyes.

She also looked cold. In her mind, I suppose, she was hearing the warm winds of Uttar Pradesh.

Why are there so many Indians and Pakistanis in London? It doesn't seem to suit them at all. On Star Street, round the corner from my room, there's a grocer whose family got kicked out of Uganda by that tubby cannibal Amin. He's educated, this grocer man, went to university, but now has to sell raw ginger, woolly apples, chillies, UHT milk and canned lager for night workers who pay over the odds. He had no choice, I suppose, but to come here; and he's going to push his children hard in school. He goes to bed at one a.m. and gets up again at four to go to the markets; there aren't enough hours in the day for him. His family will be shopkeepers for one generation only, that's his vow. He also knows a hell of a lot about football and remembers every detail of England going out to Poland in the World Cup qualifier ('then Kevin Hector came on as sub') though he can't have been here long at the time. I'm pretty friendly with him; we've had a few chats.

I understand why these people came to England — because they had to. Also, it was good for us to have new blood, different customs, new music, revitalising cultures. (I'm trying to make it all not boil down to curry restaurants, though that's clearly been a potent aspect of it.)

A certain number would have been fine. But all those hundreds of thousands of Pakistanis who came just because they could — because their mother's cousin knew someone in Camberwell who had a spare room where they could sleep six more. Did you hear that, Saeed? There's a vacancy. So, forget the Khyber Pass; goodbye, Peshawar, farewell Karachi — come to Peckham.

I feel guilty about how disappointed they must be. There's nowhere near enough one-room shops in Tulse Hill for all these people to own. There's only so many raw chillies, Quavers and cans of Strongbow cider that Lewisham can stomach. Even for top-shelf mags and John Player Specials the appetite sometimes sleeps. You need a break. I think in Leicester and Nottingham these people work in factories; they've become the manufacturing labour force. But not in London, because there are hardly any factories here. And they don't do much on the buses or the Tubes or in the hospitals, either, because those jobs are mostly taken by West Indians.

And how miserable are *those* guys? What are they doing here? They look completely out of place. They'd been coming in small numbers since the War, but they say it was a Midlander with a thin moustache, a man called Powell, who urged them to come en masse and clean the hospitals when he was Minister for Health. But it was so cold when they got off the ships. It wasn't a change of town, it was a different world. Imagine arriving in Halesowen or Sutton Coldfield, shivering, looking like that — like someone whose forbears for millions of years had lived in the tropics — then having to cover your sensitive shivering skin with woollen hats and gloves. And sallow natives staring at you with their pink eyes. The only jobs on offer are shovelling human waste in dirty hospitals or driving trains in underground tunnels so tight they're like barrels round a bullet. So, from islands with big skies and the effects of sun you're imprisoned under windless locked grey cloud.

They don't like it, those people, they don't like it here and their children don't like it either. The kids don't play the game, though. They don't work or drive buses; they take drugs, play music and think of bright islands they've been ripped up from, but never seen. They're angry. Who can blame them?

The ferret on my magazine, Wyn Douglas, had a party in the Windsor Castle on Mayall Road in Brixton. He lives there. It's black council tenants and squatting white marginals: Trots, rad fems, primal screamers. The council's trying to pull the area down but they keep running out of money, so every other building's a dope centre or a speakeasy or an anarchist bookshop. They don't work, the West Indian boys, they hang out on the street with reggae music thumping all day. It hasn't happened yet, but they look like they're up for it, the black boys. The way they look at the police. The way the police look back. The cops seem oddly rural and old-fashioned — rather pale and bovine; they look well fed and scared. But the Rastas look fly. Even stoned, they look sharp.

The man who encouraged them, this Powell, soon disowned them and warned they'd kill us because they were breeding too many piccaninnies. Someone said you shouldn't use that word, and he said, No, no, it's an endearment, it's what my mother used to call me when she bounced me on her knee. Can that be right? Would you say 'Little doodums is going to grow up and kill us all with his machete'? Or: 'Darling possums is going to drown us in rivers of blood'? I don't think so, Mr Powell. Yet people were always saying how clever he was! Treble youknowwhat in Greek, Brigadier at age 19 . . .

Then he didn't say anything about West Indians at all any more. He seems instead — at the time of writing — to be devoting the rest of his life to a syntactical challenge: to speak on the radio for fifteen minutes twice a week without saying 'um' or 'er'. Same Wolves whine, same delusional content, but grammatically accurate, even when, as he gets bound up in his clauses, his self-imposed challenge involves adding convolution upon anfractuosity — 'pelion upon Ossa', as I've heard him put it — to bring the

210

sentence to a 'correct' conclusion. Weird. More than weird. Demented. Poor West Indians — poor, poor people, to have been answerable to that bloke.

They'd be much happier going home, don't you think? They're trying to have a street culture in the pouring rain. It's tragic. If we paid for them to come, why can't we pay for them to go back — those who want to? Expatriation, repatriation, why take offence at a prefix? Why worry, if you end up where you want to be and someone else has paid for the trip? Then we'd know that those who stayed preferred it here and we could stop feeling guilty about it — and they'd stop feeling sorry for themselves.

That's not considered an acceptable point of view, by the way. To whom is it not acceptable? To the *politicians*, oddly enough.

I was having all these thoughts as I walked back to the 1100, talking to myself. Then I drove home.

I pulled over just off Praed Street to listen to the end of Graham Parker singing 'Stick to Me' at max volume on the car stereo. I almost jumped through the roof when a hopeful tom rapped on my window and stuck her fat face against the glass. I had to drive round the block a couple of times till I reached the end of the tape.

             ★   ★   ★

There's been a development at work. The magazine, which is doing quite well considering half its contributors can't spell, has offered to take me onto the staff. This involves a salary — my first. They say they'll pay me £5,000 a year. This is £2,000 more than I grossed last year. That's an increase of 66 per cent, which even in Mr Callaghan's banana republic is somewhat above the rate of inflation.

Unfortunately, going on the payroll would mean paying tax at source, and although I haven't done the sums exactly, I think I'd only end up with roughly £3,500, so my raise in real terms would be only £500, from which I'd have to pay my fares to work in Covent Garden. I'd also have to spend time in the office talking to semiliterate Stalinists.

I don't know how I became a journalist. It's not something I ever set out to do, though now I've done it I can see that it suits me temperamentally quite well. The other thing about journalism is that although at the top end (not at my mag, obviously) it seems to attract well educated, even intelligent, people, it's basically quite unbelievably easy. You ask a question and write down the answer. You repeat the process a few times. Then you see what all the answers add up to, put them in sequential order with a simple linking narrative and go to the pub.

Even Batley could manage it, I should think. Even Plank Robinson could have done it. (Actually, maybe not Plank.)

Anyway, I went into the office, which is an old print works, suitably enough, off Endell Street and had a talk with the news editor, a woman called Jan Something. I suggested going out to

lunch, but she recoiled as though I'd proposi-
tioned her. Luckily I'd stopped en route for two
pints and a blue pill downstairs in the cellar bar
of the Oporto, on the corner of Shaftesbury
Avenue, where a table of what I took to be
military publishers were discussing print runs
(small).

The mag office was completely open-plan with
long trestle tables, piles of paper, typewriters and
posters for rock concerts stuck to the bare brick
walls. Unwashed mugs clustered on the top of
filing cabinets. I could imagine everyone being
too feminist or on their dignity to wash up. There
were clouds of fag smoke from young men who
were stuck to curly-wired phones. No sooner
were they off one call than they dialled another.
Flickwhizzgrind went the office pen as it turned
in the number hole; urrgrrrwhrr went the dial as
it countered back to zero. There was one office
separated by a glass partition — perhaps the
editor's den, though there was no one in it. The
wooden floorboards were stacked high with
newspapers, rival magazines, *Rolling Stone*,
Time Out, *Boulevard*; the work tables themselves were buried under typing paper, carbons,
cuttings snipped from other publications, stacks
of London phone books — the slim buff $A — D$,
the fat pink $E — K$ and so on. An air of
agreeable studenty endeavour hung over the
whole place.

I did a deal with the Jan person that I didn't
have to go into the office more than twice a
week: once on Thursday for 'conference', when
we discussed what would be in the next issue

213

and once on a Monday to deliver my 'copy' — i.e. articles — and catch up on anything that had come in. The rhythm of the week was good because it meant that I did all my writing at the weekend, which could otherwise be so difficult to fill. The phone calls and 'research' I did on Thursday and Friday. Tuesday and Wednesday I generally took off.

Jan also mentioned 'expenses'. This turned out not to mean a corner table at the White Tower, but reasonable reimbursement, on production of receipts, for directly work-related costs such as bus fares or photocopying. We haggled over the home phone bill and I won.

'Cheers,' she said as I left, 'and don't forget you're seeing Matt and I on Monday.'

I thought for a moment she'd said 'matineye', an East End pronunciation of 'matinee'. Was I meant to review it?

Then I remembered Matt was the production editor.

'Me won't forget,' me muttered as me went downstairs.

★   ★   ★

Wednesday afternoon is cinema time. It's usually the one at the top of Queensway, near the Porchester library, sometimes the Gate in Notting Hill, or occasionally I take the 1100 down to Fulham, have eggs florentine and a litre of house red in Picasso's on the King's Road then go to the Fulham Road ABC. I usually take a hip flask in to numb my critical faculty. (I'd drained it within the first half hour of *Julia*.)

I still like the cinema, however bad the films. Cowboy pictures I could never handle as a child, except *The Magnificent Seven*; for the rest, the costume and setting (dust, cacti, one-horse town) were too dull, and the older men looked silly in those hats, like bank managers dressed up. I really hated the identikit curly hairstyle of the obligatory woman in crinolines and the arch way she descended the steps to the bar, derailing the plot. For pulp, I preferred horror. I never failed to respond to moonlight — to hound dogs, long metal bell pulls, virgins in white dresses, blood on the teeth.

American cop thrillers are bad because you can't hear what they say, and often the story turns on a side-of-the-mouth remark, indecipherable, that the stand-in was a fake or that the plant was working for the others. And the trouble with almost all 'thrillers' is that they don't thrill; who but a child, who in their right mind, would care whether in the end they get the bullion out through Helsinki before the timer detonates the bomb in Berlin?

I still watch, though.

I engage with the story in my own way. I inhabit the sets. And I wear their clothes; I like the feel of them. I move house to the apartment in Santa Monica where Steve McQueen's girlfriend lives. I make out with her room-mate. I wear Steve's shoulder holster and drink with his buddy. I note the way he changes gear in the Ford Mustang GT-390 and feel the nub of the shift in my palm, long after I've ceased to follow or care which villain dumped which in the concrete overcoat and which one I'm waiting for at the airport, which one's going to feel my hand on his shoulder when he comes barrelling through off the Miami flight.

These are things that help me if not lose then leave behind, what else, my self.

I was immune to the recent big-deal film, *Saturday Night Fever*, though Stellings told me he thought there was 'something definitely going on' in the title song. I like the Curzon because the seats are lush and few other cinema-goers choose the afternoon to see foreign pictures. I saw *A Woman Under the Influence* there, a film by John Cassavetes. I admired the woman and I didn't see that she was as crazy as the others seemed to think. It was strong, repetitive, gripping — though there were moments when you could see the boom dropping in at the top of the shot! I never made that mistake, even as a stand-in sound man on Stewart Forres's film. How bad would that have been? If Jennifer's protests when she was being 'raped' by Alex Tanner had been made into a visible microphone just above her head?

I feel good when I leave the darkness of the cinema. It makes me feel my life is important. For a few minutes I stroll along the dark streets, thinking of myself as someone in a film — a man with a character, a destiny. I become aware of my clothes and my physical mass; of my quiddity, my value.

Gradually the feeling wears off, and I feel

swamped again by the inexplicable pettiness of being alive.

I feel my sense of who I am drowned out by static. On the street, in the world, there's too much extraneous filth and air and words.

I don't find life unbearably grave. I find it almost intolerably frivolous.

★   ★   ★

A lot of time has passed.

Is that good? I never know. I haven't stopped to reflect and write, and that suggests that I've been busy.

Busy *is* good, isn't it? Busy means we're hard at it, achieving our ends or 'goals'. Haven't had time to stop, or look around or think. That's considered the sign of a life well lived. Although people complain of it — another year gone, where did that one go? — tacitly, they're proud. Otherwise they wouldn't do it: you put your time where your priority is.

Suppose, though, you're not sure that what you're doing is at all worthwhile. Suppose you blundered into it over a spoonful of lime pickle. It's easy, it pays quite well. But really it's a distraction. It stops you thinking about what you ought to be doing.

Because what you really ought to be doing is weighing up the facts. If the history of *Homo sapiens* so far were represented as a single day, an average human lifespan would represent a little over half a second. That's your lot, that's all you have of living, then you return to the unconscious eternity that came before and will close back over you — over your half-second. If the *whole* history of the earth (not just the brief *Homo sap* era) were represented as one day then your existence would be too small to measure. No sufficiently imaginative chronometer exists.

So what you must do — being an intelligent, thinking creature — is make a very careful, well-informed judgement about how best you can spend your one and only half-second. You analyse yourself and your abilities; you match them to the world, its ways and possibilities, and you make a solemn decision to do what would most contribute to the well-being of the world and of yourself.

Except you've got a deadline, Friday at noon. And your lover coming round on Tuesday. And there's football on.

This 'busy' thing isn't a commitment, it's an evasion.

And what are we avoiding? Facing the problem of the one half-second. Because if that's really how it is, if that's time, then nothing is worthwhile and nothing makes sense.

If time is *not* really like that, then all might yet work out. And in fact — good news — we do believe time is not linear. The trouble is — bad news — that our brains can only *think* of it as linear, therefore we're doomed to see our lives as pointless.

It's funny, really. The most intelligent creature that's evolved so far (we think) has a design flaw at the heart of its superior intelligence. It can't grasp one of the dimensions it inhabits.

218

It's as though we had longitude, but no latitude. How then would we navigate or reckon our position on the earth?

We're deaf men working as musicians; we play the music but we can't hear it.

★   ★   ★

I see that a woman called Marguerite Walls has been found murdered in Leeds. It's almost a year since the death of the last of these women in Yorkshire and the feeling, or hope, was that the killer had packed it in. It's been a feature of life since I've lived in London: every three months or so another prostitute has been found dead in a redlight back alley in the merged badlands of Leeds and Bradford. Over the years, our magazine had done at least three long features on it.

This victim was found in a garden, half-hidden under grass cuttings and leaves. She'd been strangled, though, where the previous ones had been stabbed; she was in Farsley, not in itself a dodgy district; and, most important of all, she was not a prostitute. Ms Walls was a 47-year-old civil servant at the Department of Education and Science.

The police are therefore saying that this killing is unrelated to the long, squalid sequence that goes back to 1975. The modus operandi (as the, presumably Latin-speaking, West Yorkshire plods insist on calling it) is different; the area is one the killer hasn't been in before and the victim wasn't a pro. They are therefore looking for 'someone

219

other' than the serial killer — and since they don't know who he is yet, this new one's very 'other' indeed.

I wouldn't be so sure if I were them. This killer isn't as perfect as the papers make out. It's possible that as many as eight of his 20 intended victims so far have survived. That's not the work of someone who's exactly on top of things, is it? That's an assault-to-death conversion rate of only 60 per cent. Plus, Farsley, as any map will tell you, is very close to his centre of gravity. Suppose he was on his way to Chapeltown to find a prostitute to kill. Then maybe he saw this poor woman walking home — and he couldn't wait. If you're mad enough to have killed a dozen people you're mad enough to be a fraction impatient. Surely?

But the police 'psychologists' now have pride and money riding on their theories. They're so attached to their patterns that they've forgotten rule one of human behaviour: there are no patterns. People just do things. There's no such thing as a coherent and fully integrated human personality, let alone consistent motivation.

They know from footprints at several crime scenes that the guy's got a size seven shoe with severe uneven wear on the ball of the right foot, suggesting that he drives long-haul for a living. Every survivor says he has a dark beard. He left a new five-pound note, serial number AW51 121565, at the site of the murder of Jean Jordan, a prostitute whose head he had tried to cut off, in 1977. The new note went into payrolls in the heart of his area of operations on the day before the murder. The only way they think it can have crossed the Pennines within 24 hours, to Manchester, where Jean Jordan was killed, is if the man who had it in his pay packet took it with him.

The bank supplied the note in a payroll, though — surprisingly — it can't say which one. It might have gone to one of 30 companies in the area, and thence to one of 8,000 men.

But how many of those 30 firms are haulage companies, employing drivers? Maybe three? How many drivers in that total? Maybe a hundred? How many of those drivers are of medium height with black beards? Eight? Five? How many of those don't have bulletproof alibis for every night in question? Two? One?

Circumstantial evidence, eyewitness evidence, footprints, serial numbers . . . How much more do they want? How difficult *is* this?

★   ★   ★

Sometimes I don't do pubs in the evening, sometimes I go to wine bars. There are certain ones that have a reputation for being places you can pick up girls. For instance there's one called the Loose Box, which Stellings told me about. I'm not sure he's ever been there, I think he just liked the name. It's in Knightsbridge. I made the mistake of going there on a Thursday lunchtime. It had women all right, but they didn't want to sleep with you. They were people who'd come up for the day from Gloucestershire to go shopping; they'd come to look at curtain fabrics in

Harrods, to go to drapery and get the little men in shiny suits with shiny hair to haul down the heavy bolts of chintz. I listened to them as I stood at the bar. They had a 'light' lunch, but they talked one another into white wine, and it's cheaper by the bottle.

In the evening, it was different. No one sat down and no one ate. There wasn't room for tables because the floor space was jammed with groups of young women shouting and smoking round a bottle of searingly dry white wine. Men in ones and twos worked through them, occasionally managing to detach a single woman from her group. Some men carried bottles at the ready. They persevered, though few had much to offer at first sight: many were grey, had thick sideburns or wore ties with the designer's name printed on the front.

I was standing near two women in their thirties. One wore leopardskin-print trousers, the other a miniskirt. They appraised the men, while trying to seem absorbed by one another; occasionally they pointed or conferred.

You sensed a man's anxiety when he had to return to the bar and shove and wave folded banknotes at the keeper of the lacerating Muscadet; by the time he'd got wine and forced his way back to the woman he'd prised away, her group had recombined, made new unstable combinations and his girl was blocked: a man with a camel coat over his shoulders was dangling Jaguar keys and making her simper.

After an hour of standing next to the same two women, I knew that no one had yet spoken to them. I suppose I'd drunk a bottle and a half of the house red by then, and I said something to the one in the leopardskin trousers. She gave a single-word answer. I offered her and her friend a drink from my bottle and they backed off as though appalled — as though I'd suggested that they'd come to this seething, deafening room on Friday night to be — what was that expression — to be . . . *picked up!* They turned their backs on me. I left the remainder of the bottle on the corner of the bar and went back to the 1100. I thought of pulling over in Star Street, rolling down the window to a waiting tom and asking her to get inside. It might have been worth it just to see her face; it might have been worth it just to see if she'd say, 'What do you *take* me for?'

★   ★   ★

Last weekend Julie came up to stay for a couple of days. She's nineteen years old now and works in the brewery offices. The 'signs of promise' at school didn't come to much and my mother needed more money to help with the house. I met her at the station and walked her over to my room.

'It's nice, Mike,' she said, turning round in the small space, looking for somewhere to put her bag down.

'I'm getting somewhere bigger soon,' I said. 'With my big new salary.'

I made some tea while she sat on the bed.

'Where's the toilet?'

'At the end of the landing. Here. Take this.' I

threw her a roll of paper. At least I didn't, like the landlord of the Tickell Arms, make her pay for it.

She wanted to watch *Jim'll Fix It* on television, and I made some tea while a whey-faced lad from Bolton got to spend the day as a steward on a cruise ship going to the Norwegian fjords.

'Can I meet your friends, Mike?'

'I'm not sure if anyone's around this weekend,' I said. 'How's Mum?'

'Oh, you know. Up and down.'

Jules seemed a bit nervous. She was sipping tea from a Beecham's mug I'd been given at a press conference.

'When did you last come to London?' I said.

'I've only been the once. You know that, Mike. That time we all came up. When Dad was still alive. When we went to Madame Whatsits.'

'I remember.'

'And you bought me that model of a bus.'

'Did I?'

'Yes. You were always generous.'

I wondered where I'd got the money. 'You gave me nice presents, too.'

'Remember the Donny Osmond tee shirt? Mum was a bit shocked!'

She was wearing a cheap skirt that was tight across her knees as she perched on the edge of the bed.

I felt terribly sorry for her — with her funny little face and the wavy hair that she'd had cut like the dark one in Abba — too long and with too many layers. She had a velvet choker and a

224

tight sweater and clumpy shoes.

'Have you got a boyfriend, Jules?'

'I'm not telling you, Mr Nosey!'

She blushed at her own daring and I looked away, feeling I shouldn't have asked. What was her life like? All the junior execs and accountants at the brewery probably ogled her, made half-hearted passes. She wasn't anyone's dream girl, but at the Christmas party, after a few drinks, she'd probably do. Was she still what Jennifer would have called 'virg int'? I hoped she'd put the right value on it, so she could marry a notch or two above herself.

'And have you got a girlfriend, Mike?'

'Not at the moment.'

'I've never met any of your girlfriends.'

'I know.'

'There's a girl works at the brewery with me. I think you'd like her. She's clever — you know, like you. Uses long words, knows lots of things.'

'Useless information?'

'No, no! She's ever so nice, Mike, really, you'd like her. She's called Linda. She's head of accounts. She went to university and everything.'

'How old is she?'

'Twenty-seven, I think. Same sort of age as you. She just split up with her boyfriend.'

'So I could go in-off.'

'What?'

'Nothing. I'll look her up in when I'm next in Reading.'

Might be fun. We could talk screw-cap economies in the old light-ale market.

I offered Jules a Benson & Hedges, which she

accepted with an appreciative murmur. I couldn't think what on earth to do with her. We couldn't really drive round the pubs, though maybe . . .

'Would you like to see King's Road?' I said.

It was a winter evening, dark already. One thing I like about London is that when you step out into the night, it just swallows you. It's democratic, too. You can sweep past the palace, roar through the 'royal' parks, down the white pillared terraces of South Kensington, and no one stops you; no one stands in your way like Baynes and says, 'Where do you think you're going?'

We drove through the park, which I thought Jules would like, down to a pub I knew off Cheyne Walk. She drank gin and bitter lemon, thinking, I suppose, that that was what London girls drank. In fact, the London girls in Cheyne Walk drank cheap wine, vodka and tonic and draught Australian or American lager, made 'under licence' (as though there were a patent on water, flavouring and carbon dioxide) and transported in metal-barrelled mega-tankers that could barely squeeze down the narrow Chelsea streets, past Carlyle's old house, maybe shaking the very fireplace where Mill's maid had used the only manuscript copy of Carlyle's *History of the French Revolution* to get a good blaze going. (Interestingly, it was Carlyle, I read, who later had to comfort the distraught Mill.)

Jules swivelled her eyes round the pub as she kept the glass stuck to her top lip. I didn't think much of the place, but I suppose if your

226

movement is limited to Trafalgar Terrace, work, and back again, then anything else can look seductive. The yellowish light in the bar was good; some of the people were residents, they weren't all tourists or strangers, like me; you could feel, like Stellings with the title song of *Saturday Night Fever*, that there was something going on. Then we went to another place I knew, hidden in a square, but I sensed Julie was getting hazy with gin — or, given pub measures, more likely drunk on bitter lemon — and we went up to a bistro on King's Road, Dominic's perhaps, with a strong sense of people spending their week's money.

Julie wanted avocado with prawns, so I ordered it too and she looked happy.

'Do you remember Dad?' she said.

'Of course.'

'Do you miss him?'

'It's been so long.'

'I do,' she said, pushing a piece of buttered brown bread between her lips. She wouldn't have wine; I had to order a Coke for her. Coke with shellfish. God.

'Do you remember him?' I said. 'You were only — what — four when he died.'

'No, not really. Tell me about him, Mike.'

I poured some wine for myself. 'Dad was . . . I don't know, Jules, how do you ever know what it's like to be another person?'

'Oh, please, Mike. Do try.'

'I think Dad was someone who lived like an animal.'

'That's not very nice.'

227

'I mean, I don't think he could ever lift his eyes from the ground. Like a badger. Do you think a badger knows there's a sky? Do you think a mouse has seen the moon? Does a dog even know that it's a dog?'

Jules laughed, a little nervously. 'You are funny, Mike.'

'We all operate on different levels of awareness. Half the time I don't know what I'm doing.'

I could feel her looking at me.

'I don't think Dad ever reached a level much above a dog's. He'd been beaten and he beat. He was beaten by his life as a slum child, as a young man in the navy, then a worker in a factory. He was caught and he could never look up. He could never lift his eyes. He had no freedom of action. He didn't really miss anything because he never knew it was there.'

'What do you mean, 'he beat'?'

'Did he ever hit you?'

'No.'

'He beat me. Not that often, I suppose. The funny thing is, I can hardly remember it now. The first time was when he was angry. He hit me in the face with his hand open, like this. Then he hit me with a walking stick, like a schoolmaster.'

'Why was he always angry with you?'

'He wasn't. It became a habit. But I can hardly remember what it felt like. It's like everything that happens to you. It doesn't feel real.'

Julie didn't say anything for a long time as she worked through her steak, well done.

Then eventually she said, 'I miss him, Mike.

Now it's too late. I remember how he used to ruffle my hair and that. That's about all I remember really. And at the time I just thought . . . I just thought that's what life's like. Everyone has a dad. Then he wasn't there any more, and I felt like all my life had been just a dream. Then I'd woken up. But maybe I'll wake up again. Do you know what I mean, Mike? It's like I could be in a dream now. Still.'

'I know,' I said. 'I do know what you mean. It's what I meant with Dad. That he probably never woke up at all.'

I didn't want to talk about him any more. I said, 'Do you ever feel you've lived before?'

'Like reincarnation?'

Julie liked to give ideas a name familiar to her, and get them into boxes small enough to handle easily.

I smiled at her.

'Go on,' she said.

'It's my greatest fear,' I said.

'Why?'

'It's too bleak,' I said. 'I'll tell you another day. Have some sweet. Take another look at the menu.'

'Go on, Mike, tell me.'

I looked at her. 'Well . . . I see a child in the back of a car . . . A face behind glass . . . And it might be me again . . . All that I know now, I'd need to learn again . . . And I look at the child's parents and wonder if they're kind . . . I saw a mother slap her child in the supermarket, hit him round the head and scream at him . . . And that's the only world he knows . . . He's in a nest of boxes he can never, ever climb out of . . . '

I was rambling a bit. 'And, Jules, I feel it's my fault. When I used to see the old men in the institution and the lights come on in the grey corridor . . . I feel I'm trapped in some loop . . . Some loop of time . . . I can't face coming back and being one of them next time. Or that child.'

I don't think she understood what I was trying to say, and anyway it was difficult to put into words.

★　★　★

London's burning. You can hear the thudding of the helicopters in the night sky. South of the river you can see an orange stain of fire in the sky. I blame Wyn Douglas.

The police went to help a black boy who'd been stabbed by another black boy. A group of youths thought that instead of helping him to hospital they were beating him up. They broke police car windscreens. It stopped there, but stayed tense. Police saturated the area. I happened to be in the mag office, Friday, in the afternoon, and Wyn came on the phone to Jan.

He was very excited, I could hear. He kept saying, 'It's going to go off, it's going to go off.'

Jan said to me, 'If it happens, get down there.'

It didn't seem to me the right sort of story for Michèle Watts, who was currently doing a four-parter on tampon-related toxic shock syndrome, but Jan said she wanted all available staff to 'get their arses to the Frontline'.

I parked the car near Clapham Common Tube and walked down Clapham Park Road. It was quite a hike, but I didn't want the 1100 being overturned and torched. I'd seen police versus black activity before, during the Notting Hill carnival when I was sitting outside a pub in Talbot Road. A cop came and told us they were about to charge. He shepherded us all into the bar and slammed the door from outside. It's the first time I'd been to a police-sponsored lock-in.

There were signs of trouble in Acre Lane, before I even got to Railton Road. There was a look of joy on the faces of the young men, mostly black, who were kicking in windows and carrying stuff out. I got to Mayall Road and saw police vans on their backs, aflame. By the railway bridge another was burning under an ad for Golden Virginia tobacco that said: 'Get the economy rolling'. Good place to sell roll-up gear, Brixton.

I didn't take out my notebook or anything. I guessed I was meant to 'mingle', but I didn't look black enough. What I remember is a bit patchy . . .

There are bricks in the air and a white boy is hit. Black boys help him. I don't know whose side I'm on. There's fighting with truncheons and fists. Head wounds and bloodstreams. Stunned people sitting in the gutter, holding themselves with blood running through their grasp. I run away into Coldharbour Lane where a Special Patrol Group Vehicle is on its roof with black smoke rising. I see a young man break the window of the jeweller's shop. Then there are cheap earrings and necklaces all over the pavement. Next door is a 'consumer advice centre', whatever that is. My consumer advice to him is: help yourself.

Personally, I don't want any of this stuff. A bathroom shop is gaping, but I don't need any basins. A motor accessories shop is open house, but the 1100's been running fine lately. It's unbelievably loud, you can't concentrate. All the shop alarms have gone off. The shops are screaming. The car alarms are panicking and shrieking and the police are hammering their shields as they regroup on Railton Road. They're trying to seal off one end and make a charge, I think.

Black boys are shouting that someone's killed a cop, but I think it's just a rumour. A boy runs past me with a big stereo; the window's being kicked in by an old lady. It could be his gran. There's something in there she really wants, because she has to kick it several times before it gives. I can hear a police charge beginning in the next street. I can hear the thunder of the truncheons on their shields.

You get the feeling no one knows where this is going to end. We're in uncharted country. For several hundred young men this is the most exciting thing that's ever happened, ever will, ever could. It could be war, there could be a thousand dead.

I ought to go home, but I have this odd desire to do the story right, plus I really want to see what happens. But I might get killed. It's dark, it's smoky, choking rubber tyre, petrol and bitumen; it's night-time and it's going to hell. It's unbelievably exciting.

So I think what would make me feel better is a drink, and I have this idea I'll go to the Windsor Castle, where Wyn had that party, so I'm doubling back up Mervan Road to get to the Frontline. A policeman on a horse is chasing a black youth towards me and I step aside. I remember that the first British action in the Great War was on horseback, at Mons, with swords.

When I get to the Frontline there are three lines of cops with their shields up. It's raining bricks. They really should have pulled these buildings down, not left the job half-finished. A Molotov cocktail is thrown onto the shields and fizzles out. The other side of the road is a barricade of burning vehicles, a literal no-go area. Down Mayall Road, I finally push my way to get a view of the pub, but it's on fire. It's like newsreel of the Blitz, Victorian brickwork flaming, the skeleton of the building showing through.

I told you they didn't like it here.

Before my eyes the pub collapses, brought to its knees like a prehistoric animal too heavy to survive. It just falls.

The fire from the ruins is the only light because along Mayall Road the electricity has failed. The houses are in darkness. There's just the wah-wah howl of sirens and the beating sound of modern war.

7

I haven't thought about Jennifer Arkland for years. I've been preoccupied, and the idea of her hasn't been able to push itself into my mind — or at least not into the main auditorium there.

Your brain can only have one thought at any time. It's odd, that, isn't it? We accept it as normal because we're so used to it. But when you consider how many million memories our brains can store, and with what ease, it's rather surprising that we can only *think* one thing at any time. It's like a Maserati whose windscreen washer works fine — but not if the engine's running. What on earth are those gazillion unused synapses doing at any one time? Redecorating? Dozing? R and R?

That's what people believe, anyway. Personally, I'm not so sure. I think I'm capable of having two or more thoughts simultaneously. I'm not talking about 'beliefs' here. You can believe many things about one subject; you can even, as George Orwell had fun pointing out in *Ninety Eighty-Four*, believe two mutually contradictory things at the same time. But beliefs are what you 'hold'; they're like memories; and you only become aware of them when you explain, revise or put them into words. Everyone does that.

What I can do — and I gather this is rarer — is have two or more conscious thoughts at the same time. It's as though the auditorium of my

234

conscious brain has a split screen. Generally, of course, there's just one picture; but frequently there are two. Each has its own soundtrack; each runs happily at its own pace; they do not snipe at, quote or contradict each other.

Also, they don't depend for their existence on the relative point of view of the observer or any of that stuff. They just exist and run autonomously and I am equally conscious of each. Occasionally, my screen redivides and I can manage to be thinking three or four things at the same time. More than that, however, is troublesome. It's tiring, and there comes a moment when I ask myself what I'm doing. Then all the thoughts tumble, like the batons of a juggler who has become self-conscious.

Given that capability, it's a bit surprising that I haven't thought of Jen — especially when you consider all the nonsense — all the guff — I've given mental houseroom to.

What brought her back to mind was a small item I saw in the newspaper. 'Missing Girl's Father Dies', said the headline over a single column story, only an inch or so long, on an inside page. (It's what they call a 'nib', which stands for 'news in brief'.)

It said: 'Richard Arkland, father of Jennifer Arkland the university student who went missing in February 1974, has died at the age of 60. Despite a massive police hunt and a national television broadcast by her boyfriend, Jennifer was never found.

'Mr Arkland did not return to his architectural

235

practice in Lymington, Hants after the disappearance of his daughter. A neighbour said, 'He died of a broken heart.' Widow Mrs Lesley Arkland, 54, asked for the family's privacy to be respected. (See Page 24: Those Seventies: the Tasteless Decade.)'

My first response to this was that if his broken heart took eight years to conk out, then it must have been a doughtier muscle than my father's. But I did feel sorry for Mrs A and I wondered what I could do to help.

Grief is a peculiar emotion. I used to think that widows grieved in proportion to the love they felt for the husband. They *missed* him — like a temporary parting, an *angoisse desgares*, but magnified. I also thought the shape of the grief was that of the dead person: they mourned the absence of particular characteristics.

But from what I've seen — in my mother and a woman who used to live downstairs — it's not like that at all. The removal of the partner seems to precipitate a sort of top-to-bottom crisis in the way the survivor sees herself, her past and all her connections with the world. The long married life now appears to have been a species of delusion. She's not sure it really even happened: for all the evidence of children and photographs, she doubts its reality. She reverts in some ways to life before it, to girlhood. She becomes a dowager-child. For some reason, even going shopping or making a telephone call seems to require a confidence that's gone missing. She can no longer mediate with 'the world'. So, grief,

236

from what I've seen, doesn't look like a deep feeling that symmetrically mourns the absent shape; it looks like a disintegration of the acquired personality. It looks like going mad.

In these circumstances, what comfort can you offer?

Well, I thought I should maybe send back Jen's diary. That might be something.

I don't keep it behind the toilet cistern any more — even though I've got one of my own now.

I've just moved from the bedsit into a real one-bedroom flat. The sum I had to borrow from the bank sounded like enough to buy two sides of Eaton Square. Not so. (The deposit was also hard work to lay my hands on.)

Anyway, I'm just down the road in what they call Bayswater, though close enough to the old place that I still use most of the same shops. I have a living room, bedroom, bathroom, kitchen and a space known as 'Study/Bedroom 2'. I also have what the particulars called a 'TV Ariel Socket'. I half expect Ariel to dance out from it; he's always pretty much a t/v anyway, the way they play him capering round Prospero in a tunic. The main room also has a view of a 'garden square', in effect a grassless rectangle with a couple of horse chestnuts and some skeletal shrubs, where people track their dogs with polythene gloves, ready to swoop and grasp. Their failure rate is high enough to deter any non-dog-related traffic from entering the 'garden'.

One thing occurs to me. If I return Jennifer's

diary, I won't any longer be able to read it. I could photocopy it, but that won't be necessary. I've memorised the whole thing.

Don't believe me? Try me. Pick a date at random.
30 May, 1973?
OK. Easy.

Went with Anne this afternoon to look at a possible house for next year. A bit remote, the other side of the river, towards Cherry Hinton Road etc. and not very glamorous part of town. But therefore cheaper. Tiny house but can sleep four (one in ground floor back). I fell absurdly in love with it. Have already redecorated 'my' bedroom in my mind. I will sign the lease, if I can persuade Dad to stand surety, and will pay slightly more rent than the others in return for which Anne says I shd have first choice of room and who am I to argue with such a brilliant young woman, future leader etc.? V exciting prospect. Feel like putting on Crosby, Stills & Nash: 'Our house is a very, very fine house . . . ' Freedom, no porters, no gate hours.

Back in the real world, meanwhile: early college brek with Sue Jubb and Liz Burdene. Poor Sue's hair looks as though she has been electrocuted as in a Tom and Jerry cartoon. They just have tea and toast, but I get hungry later, so had to have the fried egg etc. The egg had been sitting for a long time so had to lever off hard little cap from the yolk. Underneath,

238

it was fine. At least, nothing that salt and pepper and a bit of tinned tomato couldn't disguise.

Check pigeonhole for possible letter from Simon (nothing: sob) and pedal furiously to Sidgwick. Arrive just in time for Dr Meadowes on the economic consequences of the Great War. I make notes dutifully, though do sometimes think it would be easier to read one of his numerous articles on the subject.

Fevered talk in the tea room about student politics. Find it hard to be that excited as all involved have identical 'broad left' views. Nice Jill Lewis likely to be elected to follow podgy garden gnome Charles Clarke as president. Jill v pretty. *Stop Press* has found brilliant non-sexist way of referring to this (and it would be bizarre not to) by referring to her always as 'Personable Jill Lewis'. Offence-proof word, but we all know what it means. Now known as PJL for short. (Tho' she not acidic like near-eponymous lemon juice. I like that word 'eponymous'. Must have caught it from Charlie in Emma. Now can't imagine how lived without . . .)

These men (i.e. not including PJL) do take themselves very seriously, even though the Broad Left is elected almost unopposed every time, like rotten borough Whigs and Tories. The national leader (called, unbelievably, Jack Straw, inev therefore known as Wat Tyler) clearly thinks he will automatically become (inherit!) PM or Foreign Sec one day. But why would anyone elect people with no exp.

239

outside committee rooms? Though, come to think of it, T. Heath, H. Wilson . . .

Back to coll for 'salad option' lunch. Reminds me that when it first started, teething problems meant that one day it was just the old rissole and boiled carrots. Malini Coomaraswamy at her bespectacled sternest asked chief steward why no option available, pointing to single dish of sweaty dumpling and gravy. 'Of course there's an option, miss. You can either 'ave it, or not 'ave it.' (Mal does brilliant E. Anglia accent. You had to be there . . .)

Worked in my room till four, then to volleyball. Was wearing purple Hendrix tee shirt and nice shorts I'd borrowed from Emma Mitchell and conveniently forgotten to return. Good practice for Friday match v Newnham. Still don't like way Ursula stands so close in shower. Anne convinced Ursula 'not as other women'. Hid self modestly as far as possible, but she solicitous with soap and shampoo loan. Had to <u>have</u> shower as meeting Rob in Whim for late tea.

Starving after 'healthy option' lunch and v'ball so had banana cake as well as toast and lovely fresh Darjeeling tea — much to Rob's delight. 'Mmm, you tuck in, Jen . . . What about a poached egg on that?' etc. He looking annoyingly gaunt and handsome as ever.

We went to see a friend of his, Tim, in Queens' and sat by the river, talking about Donne's poetry. I found this a bit awkward, as have barely read D, except the famous ones. R and T took very opposite views on D's concept of romantic love, whether based on sex, fear of dying, and general early 17th C darkness (R), or something more spiritual and 'corollary of the divine'(T).

It was a beautiful evening and the talk moved on, via Newton's obsession with alchemy and fear of God. This fear, according to Tim, held Newton back from outlining an ungodly theory of relativity 200+ yrs before Einstein. Then on to Watergate — Haldeman and Ehrlichmann (?sp) resignation — then to who had or had not been invited to some big party in Trinity on Sat. Not me. (Incidentally, didn't my O level German tell me Ehrlichmann means 'honest man'?)

Rob persuaded me to go and see a film at the Arts about sex psychologist Wilhelm Reich, called *W.R.: Mysteries of the Organism*. Funny because so earnest and so dull. Came alive only when Nancy Someone made plaster cast of a young man's *membrum virile*, as Miss Goff of the 5th Form might have called it. Prodigious size. R somewhat crestfallen afterwards. Told him man chosen for that reason only. After all, what other quals needed in castee? R somewhat reassured — don't know if he has anything to worry about in that dept!

We had kebab in Rose Crescent then I took him to the Baron of Beef for a drink to cheer him up. Worked wonders. Met Hannah (who had just done a performance of *The Three Sisters*), Amit, Nick and one or two others. I

241

made an excuse to go and do some work, but they wouldn't hear of it, and eleven o'clock found us in Amit's room in King's, listening to Neil Young *After the Gold Rush*, drinking wine and smoking mild grass.

Can do essay over the weekend as have nothing else on.

Got back OK through night gate just before lock-up at one. Felt a bit wobbly on the way, but bike steered itself, as Dad would say. Crept up to room. Teeth. Bed. Fell asleep at once.

Wonderful day.

I've always had what Jen might call a 'prodigious' memory, and it's not that difficult to recall her diary because the story provides a continual prompt. I know what happened next, so it's easy to be reminded. Also, she's a rather mannerly narrator, alternating splurge about her feelings with description of outside events and other people. Thus after some stuff about lack of self-esteem, bad haircut: 'In the forenoon, we did call upon Mrs Thrale . . . '

I suppose it would be easy to parody, but I try not to be too hard on her. Although diarists' motives are unclear, I really don't think she meant anyone else to read it.

I retrieved the book from its usual place, in the bottom drawer of my desk in study/bedroom two, actually a sort of alcove off the living room, though I suppose a double amputee might make a bed in it.

I held the diary in my hands for one last time.

242

It was a Letts day-per-page, A4 size, broken-spined, bulging with glued-in ticket stubs and snapshots among the packed blue handwriting. The burgundy cover was mostly obscured by a collage of small pictures: from mags she had cut round the heads of Martin Luther King, Grace Kelly, James Taylor and Steve Howe of Yes; there were snipped art postcards of a Leonardo madonna and a Vermeer milkmaid; and cropped photos of Mr and Mrs A, a boxer dog and a line of three passport snaps of Jen with Anne. There was also, bizarrely, a torn mag picture of a candlelit table with a Chianti bottle. What was that one about?

I wrapped it carefully in newspaper, then slid it into one of the padded book bags in which a scientific publisher had sent me a treatise on world food programmes that I had sold on to a book dealer in Fetter Lane. I thought of taking the parcel to the general post office on Praed Street, but something made me hesitate. I thought I'd wait till I was next out of town and post it there. I typed Mrs A's address onto a label, stuck it to the package and put the whole thing back in the desk drawer.

★   ★   ★

I get out of town a fair bit these days because I've got a new job. My report of the Brixton riot appeared under a three-way joint byline, but they pulled out a description of some of the worst fighting and ran it under my name alone. The new editor, who is obsessed by what he calls

243

'staff visibility,' entered it (without asking me) for some tacky press awards, along with the toxic-shock story and a background piece to the trial of Peter Sutcliffe at the Old Bailey in May last year. Our crime guy, Bob Nixon, did the trial itself, but I spent six days in Yorkshire, going over the territory. To cut a long (4,500 word) story short, I was commended in the mag features section and received a cheque for £100 at the award ceremony in a stuffy room in the Grosvenor House hotel where everyone was drunk.

This ended the career of Michèle Watts. She went up to collect the prize from David Owen, a big cheese in the new SDP, but it was Michael Watson who returned, cheque in hand, to the table. Since most of the staff is now female — from Jan (promoted to deputy ed), via Lyn Westmoreland, the ungrammatical fine-arts critic, to Shireen Nazawi, the EFL-speaking chief interviewer — Michèle had in any case outlived her usefulness.

A couple of weeks later I got a call from a Sunday newspaper, asking if I'd go to a meeting in the Howard hotel on the Thames. Here, the editor, a man in an expensive flannel suit with large blue-rimmed glasses, bought me gin and tonic and wondered if I would like to join the staff of his paper as a feature writer for a salary of £18,000 a year, plus traditional Fleet Street (i.e. bent) expenses.

The paper is 'upper-middle market'. It does have book reviews and two pages called 'Scrutiny' which purport to give the inside dope on the week's big event; but it also has a lot of stories that begin with what is known as a 'dropped intro', like this: 'When she clocked in to work on Friday at the Rusk-o-Slurry sausage works in Newark, Lincs., little could Mrs Betty Wigwam, 56, have known what a remarkable day lay in store for her . . . ' Presumably not, unless she was psychic. The paper also carries pictures of domestic pets.

My first response was to tell him to go whistle. I liked my life as it was because I didn't have to be in an office. Since Jan had been promoted, her replacement, a pathetic Trot called Keith Dale, wasn't able to compel my presence at 'conference' and I used to ring in later to ask if he had any ideas for me.

Why would I want to swap my life of solitary fulfilment to sit around an office with a lot of hacks with only one paper a week to fill? I told him I was happy where I was, but he persuaded me to meet someone called Tony Ball, the news editor, for further drinks.

This Ball I met in an underground room in Whitefriars Street where he drank three pints of cloudy Friary Meux bitter. I had gin and tonic again. (I don't drink vermouth so much these days.) I sensed he'd been told to clinch the deal, so I thought I'd see how far I could push him. I beat him up to £22,500, four days a week (Tue to Fri) and office attendance only on Tuesday (conference) and Friday (writing).

This left me no alternative but to take the job; and so Toilet Engleby became Michael Watson, newspaperman.

245

Newspapers tell you what happened yesterday. Sunday papers have one big problem: nothing happens on Saturday.

Therefore you have to invent stuff to fill them up.

I soon found out that the most valued people in the office were those who could 'come up with ideas'. Most of these came from other papers. If on Tuesday the *Telegraph*, say, did a short piece on something, then on Sunday we could do a longer one. My new colleagues spent the day with their noses in other publications, looking for things they could copy or expand. Others pored over the news agency wire services, whose bare reports could sometimes be fattened up with the addition of a few 'quotes' and passed off as one's own.

The sports people were happy because they were the exception; for them Saturday was the big action day. They knew exactly what time everything would happen and could make up the pages in advance; all they had to do was fill in the details. It was like painting by numbers, and their only problem was how to occupy the time from Monday to Friday without developing cirrhosis. On the foreign side, our six correspondents could do a digest of what their daily colleagues had written over five days and throw in a shorter 'funny' piece they'd pinched from the local press, safe in the knowledge that none of our readers would have seen it in the *Washington Post* or *Le Monde*. Their task was also straightforward.

For the rest of us, life was demandingly, agonisingly, 'creative'.

I had a desk with a phone in the newsroom, though I was seldom there. The sight of grown men, and some women, filling in expenses forms, going to the pub, reading newspapers and pretending they were working was absurd. The qualities needed to succeed at the job were patience, a flair for lateral thinking and the ability to write clearly — though none of these, slightly feminine, attributes was valued at all. What was admired in the newsroom was, in this order: belligerence, the knowing use of macho jargon and the ability to drink alcohol. The atmosphere that Tony Ball tried to create was that of a Royal Marines training school. And this, amazingly, was how it had always been.

Idle for four days out of five, the reporters hung out in the fiendish little pubs off Fleet Street, where they drank gassed-up Ind Coope or halitotic dry white and circulated rumours of imminent sackings and cutbacks. They spoke with envy of anyone who left for another paper, particularly the *Mail*, whose expenses arrangements were regarded with awe. The crime correspondent was better informed about the thinking of 'management' than on the briefings of Scotland Yard; twice a week, he drank with friends from the *Mirror*, keeping them warm for when the big chill would surely come our way.

They were vociferously loyal to Tony Ball when, periodically, word got round that management had finally rumbled him; yet they lived in

247

fear. Their hands shook, not just from nicotine and alcohol, but from the 'Bollockings' they took on Saturdays and from anxiety that the ambitious mortgages they'd taken out would become unpayable. Disaster was approaching, but for some capricious reason they didn't understand: a story wouldn't 'stand up'; it would get mangled by a casual Saturday sub-editor with previous convictions for butchery; it would get 'spiked' on the whim of a drunken night editor. Or maybe they'd been insufficiently pissed and collegiate at the Christmas party. Or they hadn't 'come up' with enough ideas. It was so unfair, this never-ending strain imposed by a fat four-section paper that gobbled up every half-thought they had, leaving them permanently empty-headed and hungover.

I always went home by four on Tuesday afternoon and told Ball to ring if he had something for me. He sent me out of town a bit, which I didn't mind, and once or twice asked me to interview people.

I didn't think this was my strong point.

I interviewed someone called Jeffrey Archer, who wrote books. The point of interest was . . . A new job, a new book, I forget. He'd been an MP, and wealthy, then lost all his money in a window-cleaning company but recouped it with adventure stories, childishly written but bought by adults. I was directed to a skyscraper on the south bank of the Thames, not far from Lambeth Bridge, and took the lift to the top.

As soon as I walked into Archer's office, he started to bark at me, like Chief Petty Officer

Dunstable on the parade ground at Chatfield. I suppose he thought it would unnerve me. He pretended to be angry, then stopped suddenly and gave a hard, brief smile.

He set me down on a sofa and pointed out some pictures by Andy Warhol (cans of soup, old film stars — first-year stude decor) of which he seemed proud. By this time he was yapping like a terrier. In answer to my bland questions he told me things he must have known weren't true and other things he must have known that *I* would know weren't true. He challenged me to disbelieve him. If you question any of this stuff, his drilling gaze seemed to say, then you'll really see my temper — not just glimpses, but the real thing.

Then, for no reason, he veered like a spring wind, sat down next to me, all smiles, and offered me champagne. He asked after my career, my family and where I'd been at school. He started to congratulate and flatter me.

Although he appears to be off his trolley, he's apparently very highly regarded in the Conservative Party. They keep offering him important positions.

At this point a blonde woman of a certain age (Mandy, Sandy?) came into the room (or 'penthouse' as Archer had two or three times called it) bringing the champagne and some smoked salmon sandwiches.

'Thank you, darling,' he barked at her departing back, as her black nylon calves crackled.

Then he winked at me.

I mean, really . . . I'd looked him up in the cuttings before I came out and seen that there was a Mrs A (some sort of chemistry gnome) and everything. But I'm ashamed to say that I smiled back conspiratorially.

I stayed and chatted to my new pal for hours, and in the end he took my home address and phone number and said he'd send me an invitation to his annual party, where, he mentioned two or three times, though I didn't understand why it was significant, we'd have cottage pie and champagne.

I must say I rather liked him.

★   ★   ★

This whole thing of meeting famous people was something I found intriguing. The news desk was always awash with invitations to launches, bashes, dos, promos, parties and functions; and since most of the reporters were too idle or too nervous to go, I sometimes taxied along to have a look. There was always free drink and it wasn't as if I had to write anything afterwards.

One of the ones I liked was the Foyle's Literary Lunch at the Dorchester. You could drink gin and tonic in the VIP room first, then as much wine as you liked with a perfectly nice lunch. This was usually smoked salmon messed up with cream cheese and stuff, then fillet steak with green beans and rather over-salted gravy — but it was fine. The white wine was some sort of hock, but the red was claret from a chateau you might even have heard of. (I was beginning

250

to notice these things by now. Was I getting posh? Don't know. I still said 'toilet' as a matter of principle; but did I now feather it with irony — with the ghost of an inverted comma?)

The only drawback to the lunch was that you had to listen to three or four authors stand up and talk about their new books. The thunder of false modesty was deafening.

'People often ask me how I first came up with the character of Horatio Beckwith, my famous detective. I think it was just one of those lucky coincidences. I was on a train, going to stay with my dear old friend P.J. Cowdrey in Somerset, when we stopped at a little station near Swindon. Rather an Adlestrop moment, I suppose! Anyway, a man got out of the carriage and made his way down the platform. I noticed that even though it was midsummer and hadn't rained for days, he carried a rolled umbrella with him. How very *English*, I thought! And, do you know, I think it was that umbrella that gave me the key — the way in, if you like, to the whole of Beckwith's character. I always carry a little notebook with me to jot down such observations, and by the time we reached Taunton I'd covered quite five pages with notes about Beckwith — the school he went to, which is not, as many critics have suggested, based on Eton — and no, I'm *not* going to tell you which school it *is* based on! — his nanny, his dear mother, his regiment, his unhappy time in Ceylon. To say nothing, of course, of his dear 'sidekick', Captain Trudge. As for the Captain . . . Well, he just sprang to life more or less fully formed, like

Aphrodite from the head of Zeus! I have learned from the great stylists to always try and keep my vocabulary simple. I'm always mindful of the other demands on the reader's time. I think of myself only as a privileged guest in the reader's life, and I try never to weary him — or her! — and never to outstay my welcome. Never use a three-syllable word where a two-syllable one will do.'

You'd think it was James Joyce up there. I mean, Christ, how many syllables are there in the words 'it', 'butler' and 'did'?

As I was leaving one day, I bumped into Sir Ralph Richardson at the cloakroom. He was retrieving a motorcycle helmet.

'Hello,' he said. 'Do you ride a motorcycle?'

'Yes,' I lied.

'What make?'

'Er . . . Yamaha. And you?'

'I ride a BMW. They're marvellous. I'm just going to look at a new one. Do you want to come?'

I looked at my watch. 'All right.'

We went into the BMW showroom, a short way up Park Lane.

'Don't you have goggles or a vizor?' I said.

'No, no, I just screw my eyes up like this.'

He climbed on top of a big bike in the window. He must have been nearly eighty. He lay flat down on the tank and twisted the accelerator in his right hand. 'Brmm, brmm. Like that,' he said.

A salesman stood by nervously. I think he'd recognised Richardson. I gave him a conniving smile. These actors . . .

Then Sir Ralph said, 'Go on. You have a go.'

I swung my leg over and gripped the handlebars. I'd never ridden a bike before, but I copied Sir Ralph's chest-to-the-tank riding position while he stood alongside going, 'Brmm, brmm, that's the stuff.'

When he had tried a couple more bikes, we wandered through the car section back to the front door. A car salesman with a severe limp opened the door for us.

As we went on to Park Lane, Sir Ralph said, 'I think perhaps he used to work in the motorcycle department.'

Then he called out, 'Goodbye' and walked off into Mayfair.

That's another nice thing about being a journalist. People are more or less compelled to talk to you, and this can be helpful if you don't have that many close friends. A bit odd that the last two people I had proper conversations with were Jeffrey Archer and Sir Ralph Richardson; but that's life.

★ ★ ★

Although I liked meeting these people, I didn't think I was a good interviewer. I wasn't good at summing people up. I said as much to Tony Ball (or 'Bollock' as he's known behind his back. You can tell the calibre of an institution by the quality of the nicknames it uses: compare, for instance, the brutal 'Spaso', 'Toilet', 'Leper' with the windy 'Iguanodon' and 'Australopithecine'.

253

The functional 'Bollock' tells you pretty much all you need to know about Fleet Street).

However, my Archer piece had gone down well and Ball was keen for me to do some more. He gave me a list of upcoming possibilities: Billy Graham, Ken Livingstone, Douglas Hurd, Naim Attallah . . . I barely knew who half these people were.

★ ★ ★

I think it's time to be a bit careful. And a bit frank.

I feel that my life is finally starting to fall into place. I like being a journalist. It's insanely easy and pretty well paid. There's a sub-editor on the woman's page called Margaret Hudson. She's a bit older than I am and she's not what you'd call glamorous, but she's not at all bad-looking. She wears rather old-fashioned clothes: knee-length skirts, thick-looking brown stockings, pleasant beige jumpers. She's no Jennifer Arkland, I admit; but she's busty and has a sparkle in the eye. What's more, she's nice to me. She says hello when we pass in the corridor; she never forgets to say, 'I liked your piece on Sunday'; she comments on the weather or says, 'We never see you in the canteen' — little things like that.

I ought to have lunch with her in that canteen one day, but the truth is I'd rather cut my tongue out than eat there. Imagine: queuing up with a tray, cutlery from a grey moulded bin, the glass of water, strip lights. It'd be like being back in Chatfield. The panic of the institution . . . God,

254

what are pubs and restaurants and cafés and bars *for*? They exist — to my mind — for the purpose of not being part of an institution. They are places you can be undiminished, unscrutinised and free. But the canteen . . . At the very thought my palms are wet, my armpits crawl.

Never mind. I'll find other ways of getting to know Margaret. The Features Christmas party, for instance — reputedly a day-long bacchanal, ending in a cellar under Fetter Lane.

My flat is working out well and I like the area. At night I lie in bed and hear the car tyres going over the wet streets towards Queensway and Westbourne Grove. I hardly ever have to take pills any more. Just the hiss of rubber on wet tarmac is enough to rock me off to sleep, with thoughts of others on their night-time journeys.

Careful, did I say? Yes. I want to be careful not to throw all this away. This happiness. I think this is what happiness is. I haven't got it yet, but I can sense it out there. I feel I'm close to it. Some days, I'm so close I can almost smell it.

To wake up and feel enlivened; to be in a hurry to get out of bed and into the day. To have friends you want to speak to, compare experiences with and be on the phone to . . . Well, to be honest, I'm still some way from *that*. But I do like the routine of my average day: the papers in bed while I listen to Timpson and Redhead on the radio with a pot of PG Tips; the coffee from the espresso bar near Chancery Lane Tube on Tuesday and Friday; the way the unshaved Sicilian whacks out the grounds on the wooden drawer and offers me a grunt of recognition.

And then there's my Sunday walk to Marble Arch, my weekly exercise. (Steady, Toilet, don't overdo it . . .) My lunch in the tratt off the foot of Edgware Road over the paper, where I see who got a piece in this week and who didn't. A small glass of Prosecco before the tonno fagioli, cannelloni and a litre of dense Etruscan red; then, their speciality: zabaglione, whisked in a copper pot, served with amaretti and a glass of vin santo before a snooze through the film on the big screen next door. Simple stuff, I admit, but hard to beat. Ciao, Mr Watson. Everyone calls me Watson, by the way, now; I even have an Access card in that name. I sign myself with virile candour pressing through the carbons: M.K. Watson. (Christ knows what the K stands for.) Ciao, Bernardo. See you next week. Ciao, ciao.

That's the careful bit, my advice to myself: Hang on. Don't take it for granted. Steady as you go.

Now the frank bit. Deep breath. Here it is.

One day in my first year at university I woke up in a psychiatric hospital.

This was (after Chatfield, obviously) the most unpleasant experience of my life up to that point. And this is how it happened.

It was during the vacation, and I'd got quite a well-paid job working for a plastic-seating factory in Basingstoke. My previous experience in the paper mill and some improvements to my CV meant I was in a semi-supervisory role. I had to get up early to drive the Morris 1100 down from Reading, but I liked the sense of escape, and it was only half an hour from the front door of Trafalgar Terrace. I was listening a lot at that time on the car stereo to *Time and a Word* by Yes (there was a song I liked called 'The Prophet' — all gluey organ intro, then zithery strings before the arrival of the ill-matched rhythm section, where the drums feather fast but the bone-rattling bass guitar clonks away right up front of the mix) and *The Low Spark of High-Heeled Boys* by Traffic, which ends with the longest saxophone belch in record history. I used to time it so the tape ended with its burp as I pulled up in the works car park — *Bleeeee-aaaeeeeeeeerrrrggggghhhhhhhhh.*

Wednesday afternoon was a half-day at the factory, and rather than go straight home I thought I'd do some shopping and look round a bit. The expanding town of Basingstoke seethed like Laocoön within its concentric ring roads. I followed the signs for the town centre, but, after I'd spent fifteen minutes negotiating round-abouts and obediently going where the signs told me, they had brought me back to where I'd begun. The end of all our exploring will be to arrive where we started and know the place for the first time. I didn't know that T.S. Eliot had been on the Basingstoke Urban District Council Highways (Ring Roads and Street Furniture) Committee.

I found myself angry, and this is something to which I should perhaps also confess at this point. Anger. I've found, at moments in my life, that this emotion can cut free from the thing that provoked it and become an independent force.

Just as grief, as I explained, seems to have a life of its own, away from the loss or the memory that caused it, there can come a moment in anger when, even if the source of irritation were removed, it would be too late.

This is perhaps important, so maybe I should try to explain.

Are you familiar with catastrophe theory? Think of a graph with two axes, the relationship between whose quantities is charted by a steady diagonal. On the vertical: Engleby's temperament; on the horizontal: the annoying thing; on the diagonal line you draw with your ruler and pencil: degree of anger. All goes steadily until a certain point: a camel-straw — or catastrophe. At this moment the relationship between the two axes stops being constant because a new element comes into being: rage.

To represent the relationship between the formerly two, but now three, quantities you need to make a three-dimensional graph, because rage, while related to Engleby's temperament and annoying factors, is in fact a separate entity.

What's frightening about this third dimension is that at some stage (and here we depart from the classic catastrophe theory model), the rage becomes not only separate, but independent and self-sufficient. Catastrophe indeed.

As I was circling in my car, I worked out that, just as the North Pole is always north, the town centre is always at a tangent from the ring roads and that it therefore didn't matter which

258

unsigned approach to it I took.

I was right — well, obviously — and ten minutes later parked the mildly overheating Morris 1100 in a new multi-storey car park and walked up the main shopping street. I was still angry, borderline enraged. What about? The factory work, the ring road, all that, yes, but other stuff as well. Stuff I couldn't put a name to even if I wanted. Deep; and unidentifiable, because I couldn't see it or name it. Fishy monsters at the mile-deep bottom of a loch, left over from some older evolution. Childhood or something; the dawn of awareness; the scramble to adapt — to mould what I was and what I felt into something the world could accept.

In the shops, which were virtually the same as the ones in Reading, I drifted round. I thought of buying a present for my mother or for Julie, but I didn't have much idea what they liked in the way of clothes, or of sizes. Size ten, for instance. Is that large or small? It sounded vast, but the dress didn't look that big.

Then I saw a record shop, on Church Street, and that looked a likely place to pass some time. For Jules I bought *Honky Château* by Elton John because I thought it might bridge the gap between the music I liked and the sort of crap she listened to.

The youth behind the counter (about my age, I suppose) said why didn't I get *Pictures from an Exhibition*.

'Because I want this,' I said, holding up the beige gatefold sleeve of *Honky Château*, 'and because I'm not paid till Friday so I can't afford two records.'

'Have you heard of *Pictures from an Exhibition*?'

'Of course. Everyone's heard of Mussorgsky.'

'Eh?'

'The composer. The man who wrote it.'

'No. I mean Emerson, Lake and Palmer,' said the youth, with a whinny of superiority. 'Have you heard of them?'

'Heard of them?' I could feel the catastrophe looming. 'I saw Keith Emerson and the Nice play the whole of *Ars Longa, Vita Brevis* at the Lyceum in '69. I got *In the Court of the Crimson King* by King Crimson with Greg Lake on bass and vocals from Virgin by post before it even hit the shops. I played 'Twenty-First Century Schizoid Man' and 'Epitaph, including 'March for No Reason' and 'Tomorrow and Tomorrow' ' so often I wore out the stylus. I hitch-hiked to Birmingham to see Atomic Rooster live, and, yes, they did have Carl Palmer on drums. *Heard* of them? I pretty much put them together. I first heard — '

'Keep your hair on, mate. Do you want a bag?'

No, I want to take you out back and beat your fucking head on the floor.

'Thank you,' I said, and took the bag out onto the street.

I had some blue pills in my pocket and I took two. I knew the symptoms, but I'd never had them this bad before.

Then I went to an off-licence and bought a half bottle of vodka. I drank it pretty much straight off, using the paper bag as cover.

The town centre was all coming down or going up. Earth movers and diggers and jackhammers were replacing parts of Hampshire with slabs of reinforced concrete, plate glass and shop names lettered in pink and turquoise corporate swirl. Their moving, digging and drilling was ploughing up the past and furrowing my brain.

I went into a large clothes shop. It might have been Debenhams or British Home Stores or Marks & Spencer, they all look the same to me. They all sell eight million *nighties*.

I walked slowly between the counters, and picked up many of the clothes in my hands. I felt nylon, wool, silk and cotton. I felt a lot of terylene and dacron. I let it run through my fingers because I wanted to reassure myself that it existed.

These molecules (polymers, I think) ran, slick and synthetic against the pores — the ever-so-organic, mammal pores of my skin, my *dermis*. The jackhammer in my temples, the enlarged molecules in my hand. It was like that time in Izmir when the centripetal force of Engleby had failed and I began to fly apart, into my atomic pieces.

I held on tight. Men's lambswool sweater. Woman's brushed nylon peignoir. Child's school socks (wool and polyester mix).

All reality about me now appeared to be in tatters, taken down and reduced to the civil war of its particles.

I held on very, very tight indeed.

Because in addition to that feeling, that disintegration, there was rage. I wanted to break something.

I could no longer move. I clung rigid to the edge of the counter. I could see my knuckles white. My finger was bleeding where my thumb nail had gouged it.

'Are you all right, sir?'

'No. Get me a doctor.'

I forget what happened, except that when a man came, I wept.

They brought a chair. This man put his arm round my shoulders. That's why I cried. That small kindness.

By the time an ambulance man came, the blue pills must have been flushed through me by the vodka. I drank a glass of water, which must in turn have released the loitering alcohol. I remember nothing more until I awoke in a cubicle.

I was lying on a bed in my clothes beneath a cellular blanket. I felt relaxed, though nagged at, worried by something. I felt I'd given vent to things I should have kept locked up. I'd let the cat out of the bottle, the genie out of the bag . . . I slept again. Some man asked me questions, offered me rest and I accepted.

Oh, the sweetness of giving in, of full surrender. It was dark, and two or three people were with me, speaking softly, with consideration.

I was obviously somewhere else now, but I didn't remember the journey. My disintegrating particles had become a wave. I had reappeared without apparently having travelled the intervening distance. Human beings, as atomic matter, must conform to the laws of quantum mechanics — even their thoughts, which are but electrical functions of brain. Perhaps I had thus solved the mysteries of human behaviour and motivation. God, how should I know?

I was offered hot milk and two white tablets. No injections, nothing sinister. Then a comfortable bed.

* * *

I awoke and it was day. I was in a dorm. There were five other beds in it, but no one in them. My clothes were folded over a chair at the foot of 'my' bed.

The first thing you do in such a situation is try to get normal. Do your teeth, have a cup of tea, find out where you are. I dressed and stuck my head into the corridor and saw a woman in ordinary clothes, not obviously a nurse.

'Excuse me, could you tell me where I am?'

'You're Michael, aren't you? We let you sleep in a bit. How do you feel?'

'Fine.' It was true. I'd slept deeply. I had no hangover. Good clean spirit, vodka, and I had an eighteen-year-old's resilience. 'But where am I?'

'You're in a hospital. You came in here last night. My name's Alison by the way.'

'Which hospital?'

'It's called Park Prewett. It's a psychiatric hospital. You were transferred from — '

'I want to get out of here.'

It appeared that I had finally followed Stalky Read's much-offered advice, albeit unconsciously: I'd taken if not the first bus, then some kind of ambulance to 'the Prewett'.

'Why don't you come and have some breakfast?'

I followed Alison reluctantly along a corridor, then down some stone stairs.

'I ought just to warn you,' she said, 'that we've got some visitors at the moment. One of the long-stay wards is having its kitchen renovated and their patients come to us for meals. Don't be alarmed. They're all nice people, just that some of them have got their funny ways.'

She led me into a stench of hospital food. I found my throat close tight. It was like the opposite of appetite; it made me feel that far from eating I could never eat again.

Maybe it wasn't just the smell, maybe it was the sight as well.

At two refectory tables were about fifty people, men and women of all ages but mostly much older than me. A man with a big shaved skull was banging a metal dish on the table and moaning. Women with funny, screwed-up faces were grabbing and gobbling.

Alison must have seen my expression. 'Come and sit down here. I'll find you a place. Come and sit next to Sandra here. Sandra, this is Michael.'

'Pleased to meet you.'

Bits of food were being thrown around. Some people ate with their hands. There was little speech — and no one actually conversed with anyone else — but there was a lot of noise. Shouting out; moaning, wailing. The whole thing seemed barely under control.

I pushed my food away and tried to raise the cup of tea in front of me, but my hand shook. I got some into my mouth but couldn't swallow it. It felt as though some mechanism was preventing me from letting anything from this crazed world enter me, over the membranes of mouth and throat. My body alarm was on, the doors were jammed. I let the tea dribble back into the cup.

I got up from the table and walked out of the bedlam, down the corridor. A nurse in uniform asked where I was going, not unkindly. I said I wanted to go outside and get some air.

'The doors are closed for the time being, until after breakfast is cleared and the C-block patients have gone back. Then of course you can go for a little walk. Which doctor are you under?'

'I don't know. I don't live here. I just want to go home.' The *smell*.

I suddenly thought of the 1100 in the town centre car park. It was going to cost me a packet.

The nurse took me to an office, a glassed-in place, where a man assigned me an appointment for the following day.

'You don't understand,' I said. 'I want to go home. I want to discharge myself.'

The registrar, if that was what he was, found my admission note.

'You were sent from the general hospital,' he said. 'A Dr Andrew Brown was on duty there. You're now under the care of Dr Leftrook, but she's not in today. You can see her tomorrow, and she can make an assessment.'

'There must be other doctors. I need to get out today. I've got a job. I need to get back to it or I'll lose it.'

After a lot of dim questions, he conceded that the Prewett had more than one shrink and I was given an appointment to see a Dr Greenhough that afternoon. The registrar wanted to know who my normal GP was, and fortunately I could give him the name of Dr Ray, on whose list I'd been at the grammar school. Since I hadn't consulted him for at least three years he'd give me a clean slate. (I wouldn't have wanted him to get the opinion of old Vaughan in King's Parade.)

Later, I saw an open door and went out into the grounds. My block was clearly low risk, which was reassuring. I walked about, being careful to steer clear of any mutterers in overcoats. The main building was gabled brick with creeper; there was a bell tower and a colonnade whose cloister was held up on steel pins rather than on plastered columns. In other respects, it was the twin of Chatfield, down to the distant games pavilion and the gravy smell. Hello, Batley, hello, Francis. I knew we'd meet again.

As I walked about I could taste the fear in my mouth. I thought of the old men's poorhouse that I used to see at twilight as a child. All these places were versions of the same thing. One could never finally escape, one was destined always to return.

Through a hole in the fabric of time, through a gate in the wall, through the moment in the arbour where the rain beat.

I sat on a bench in the garden and bit back tears.

I remember little of the day. I kept apart from the others, especially at lunchtime, until my appointment was due. Dr Greenhough was reasonable. He wanted to know my age and medical history, about my parents and if there was someone to take care of me.

I lied about my mother's capabilities as a parent.

He talked to me about the 'incident' in the shop and asked me to describe what I'd felt. I gave an edited version.

He nodded.

'Can I go now? I want to go home.'

He said the words I wanted to hear. 'I'm not inclined to keep you here against your will. In fact, I'm not allowed to. I would prefer it if you stayed. I think it would be better for you. But unless two psychiatrists decide that you are a danger to yourself or others, then — '

'Of course not. I've never hurt a fly. Still less myself.'

'But you should seek help when you get home. The panic attack that you experienced is a warning that something's wrong. I shall write a letter to your GP and I suggest that he refers you to your local hospital for treatment as an outpatient.'

'What would that involve?'

'Just talking to someone about your thoughts

and feelings. Some minor medication if he sees fit. Nothing very dramatic.'

'All right.'

'And you should do the same when you return to college. You're registered with a doctor there, I presume?'

'Yes.' I could just picture Vaughan as a psychotherapist. The return of the cold shower and the straitwaistcoat.

'I'm going to prescribe some pills. Only take them if you feel a repeat attack coming on,' said Greenhough.

I nodded. I was quite happy with the term 'panic attack'. Panic had indeed attacked me. I was also glad that it was not the whole truth: it made no reference to the rage — which I had quelled. Panic had overcome me and led me to the loony bin, but there was a reason: I'd been too overstretched to deal with it because I'd been capping off the rage and that had taken all my strength. No wonder I'd been vulnerable.

'How are you going to get home?'

'I can take a bus, can't I? Then I'll pick up my car and drive.'

He nodded sadly. 'Don't take any pills before driving. Ever.'

He was manifestly reluctant to see me go, whereas I felt my spirits rising by the moment.

I decided not to be mad any more; I was never going back to a place like that again.

* * *

And that was it. I got a bus, eventually, got my car out of the multi-storey which, to my relief, was a flat-fee-on-exit rather than a by-the-hour one, and drove home. I don't think my mother ever knew I'd not been back on Wednesday night. Julie was out at a friend's.

I rang the factory to apologise for missing a day and said my mother had been ill. They said they'd overlook it this time.

Tra-la. On we went. No more the madhouse.

Back to work, then back to university and the 19th century novel (I was still doing English at this time) the entirety of which we were required to study in one week. I calculated that even if I read for 24 hours for seven days I still wouldn't have got through Trollope.

'And where does that leave Dickens?' I asked Dr Gerald Stanley, who told me I should have done the reading in the vacation. Yeah, but I had to work. I gave the money to my mother for Christ's sake. It wasn't just dope and booze money. It paid the electricity bill.

★   ★   ★

OK, back live in '85, as they say on the radio. I'm off to interview Ken Livingstone and so I'm reading up on him. He seems very distrustful of the press, so I'll try to surprise him. I've worked out this thing with journalism, a way to do it. The pop papers talk about Red Ken, Loony Left, Newt-Fancier. One-Legged Lesbians, blah, blah. The 'serious' papers talk about 'the way he is 'perceived' ' (I presume they mean *mis*-perceived); they talk about the 'image' — but then go over the same ground as the tabloids in the same terms. The only difference between broadsheet and tabloid papers is that broadsheets put inverted commas round the received ideas.

Suppose, though, you neither regurgitated the cliché nor let the truth or otherwise of the cliché be the master of your trot round the block. Suppose you didn't mention it all. Suppose you asked Ken about what books he's read, what football team he likes, which politicians from history he admires, if he believes in God, whether he likes sex or cookery or going to the cinema, bath or shower, tea or coffee, where he takes his holidays, who his best friends are and how he spends his day. That could conceivably be almost *interesting*, couldn't it? Why has no one thought of this before? Is Michael Watson a newspaperman of Genius? See next week's paper.

★   ★   ★

I posted the diary to Jennifer's mum a few weeks ago, when I was on a story in Birmingham. I didn't think she'd try to track the sender in such a big city. I didn't put a note in it with it, so I've no way of knowing if it reached her safely, but I assume it did.

I miss the book itself. I miss the eruptive blue ballpointed handwriting squeezed in so tight between the red feint rules. I kept one of the

270

photobooth snaps of her and Anne, though. I couldn't resist. I have no other photographs of her, except some blurred ones from the newspaper articles which I keep in a box file. She doesn't look so good in those. It's hard to look your best amid columns of type describing your sudden disappearance and presumed death. They cast a shadow. But in the one I kept, while Anne has crossed her eyes beneath her bobble hat, Jen has been caught between silly poses and is staring naturally, with that slight smile, suppressing laughter, and looks quite beautiful.

As for the content, it's all safely memorised. I don't recite it to myself that often, just occasionally — as a way of paying my respects.

On Sunday night I was feeling nostalgic, and I decided to pick a day at random. With closed eyes I swirled a pencil round over a calendar of 1974 and stabbed. The date I landed on turned out to be one of the very last entries.

I paused, collected my thoughts, and pressed the recall button.

Interesting post. Molly had a conciliatory letter from Gary. Anne and I told her she better off out of it. I had a letter from Tilly saying she thought D's office affair had started again because she had found M crying for no reason. Bit of an assumption. Shall tell Tilly. Maybe M had just read sad book or something. Or seen Tilly's school report!

Lectures a bit uninspiring this morning, though Dr Bivani quite lively on Hapsburgs. Saw Rob for 'serious talk' in the Mill at lunch (had received note in pigeonhole by univ mail yesterday requesting 'summit'). He unhappy about course of 'our relationship'. I presumed this had something to do with sex, lack of, but unfortunately didn't get to bottom of it, as first Irish Mike (!) came in and sat rather close, then Malini Coomaraswamy with two girlfriends. V bad luck. Mal doesn't even drink and this probably her first pub lunch in three years!

R. exasperated by presence of Malini Coomaretcetera as he calls her. But we agreed to 'reconvene' at the Free Press tomorrow. Don't know why all top-level negs have to take place in what Dad would call 'licensed premises'. Rather dreading it.

Called in on Charlie in Emma on way back. Surprise! He seemed v pleased to see me but rather out of it. He has discovered Benylin. 'You go to the college nurse, Jen, and say you have a cough. She gives you this mixture. You drink the whole bottle straight off and you're zonked for hours. It's really amazing.' We listened to *Focus III* and drank tea by the gas fire. He told me some funny stories, then asked in a roundabout way whether he could sleep with me.

So I guess despite mascara he not gay after all! Just nervous maybe. Don't know what else in addn to bottle of Benylin he had consumed to force self to this point. I explained that things complicated at moment etc. He very understanding: just a long shot, no hassle, if things change, always here . . .

272

Actually, would rather like to. He has beautiful skin and torso, all waxy and sculpted and firm — saw him shirtless in gardens once. Thin studenty tummy and long hair but large shoulders as though rower, tho' he swears not. And gentle soul, too. Troubled, anxious, can be overpowering and a bit annoying and too self-deprecating, but you sense a true gentleness beneath. Trouble is, might be too nervous . . . Wouldn't matter, would be long-term thing, wd get better. But do I want long-term thing at this stage? Deep waters . . .

When I went out on to St Andrew's Street, I found someone had nicked my bloody bike! Asked porter if he'd seen anything. No chance. It's not insured. How am I meant to get to lectures in the morning? Miles away. Will have to ring home and ask for money to get new one. Hate to do. Will have to call it loan from Dad and work it off in vac. I'm so *bloody* annoyed abt this.

Normally when I've had a diary session, I feel immensely tranquil. I go and have a bath, lie back with the light off and feel myself re-inhabit those days a dozen years ago. It's as close to time travel as you can get. I'm in the cold rooms of those tiny backstreet terraces; I can picture Catty tumbling off the roof, I can taste the Abbot ale.

This time when I'd finished, however, I felt as though I'd unwittingly jammed my finger into an electric socket.

I was in the armchair in my sitting room and I stood up, staring at the blank wall. I had had a memory.

Was it false or true?

I didn't know.

All I wanted to do was force it out of my thoughts. I couldn't rest, I could never sleep again, I couldn't *think* until I'd got rid of this vile picture.

I paced up and down the room, I poured a huge drink of Johnnie Walker and swilled it down. Then another. But I couldn't shift it.

This is what the 'memory', true or false, consisted of.

After lunch in the pub, I walked up Mill Lane, then up Pembroke Street. Outside Emmanuel, I happened to see Jennifer leave her bicycle in the rack and enter the college. I hung around for a couple of minutes, studying the menu in the window of the Varsity, the little Greek restaurant. Then I crossed the road, pulled her unlocked bike from the rack and rode off on it.

8

I bumped into Stellings the other day in Chancery Lane. I hadn't seen him for a long time, and he looked sleek and optimistic. His clothes were obviously expensive.

I have this odd feeling that, not far from where I work, there are people suddenly making huge sums of money — I mean, preposterous, dizzying, comical amounts. They are doing it legally, every day, and getting home late. No wonder they look . . . Glazed. Honey-glazed. Money-glazed.

I don't know how this happened. When I grew up in Reading, there were rich people, I suppose. The man who owned the paper mill, for instance. He had a new Jaguar and a house with remote-control gates. There were toffs who lived in the countryside nearby who'd inherited money. Then there were prosperous people who worked in industry or business and maybe at the top of the professions.

But there weren't millionaires. Above all, there weren't vacant-looking gonks in their twenties who had to keep opening new accounts in different banks to stop their inflow from flooding the pavements; there weren't young men who, by making a few stabs in the dark about pig-iron prices found themselves grossing more than Portugal.

Do you know what? I think I missed a trick.

Most Chatfield leavers went into the navy; some went to university; plenty went off to train as accountants. No one really contemplated 'the City'. It was considered a last resort, appropriate only for boys who, even by Chatfield standards, were desperate. Bograt Duncan, for instance, became a stockbroker. I believe 'Backward' Page surfaced in the reinsurance business. Even Plank Robinson eventually found a berth playing housey-housey with futures prices in some sort of on-screen gambling outfit.

What I want to know is: when did these guys stop being charity cases and become arterial cash explosions? I made an error of judgement there, didn't I? I didn't find out enough about 'the City'; I was sniffy about it, just because of the people I knew who tried it. Is it too late for me now to broke some futures, plant a hedge fund or take a few positions in derivatives? If it all went belly-up I could blame the 'market'.

If only I could have my time again.

As for Stellings, he's just a solicitor, for crying out loud; the father of a boy I knew at the grammar school was one of those and they used to live in a semi in Tilehurst. Stellings qualified as a barrister, but he didn't like it; now he's in the litigation department of Oswald Payne and he seems to like that very much indeed. He's married to someone called Clarissa and they already have a child — a boy called Alexander. He mentioned twice in the space of our short talk on the pavement what a small wedding it had been — presumably so I wouldn't feel put out at not having been invited. We arranged to meet for lunch at an upmarket curry house on the far side of St Paul's the following Tuesday — after 'conference', by which time I would have drawn my expenses, for which modest weekly writing exercise we are reimbursed with rolls of new cash.

'Great place, this,' said Stellings, sitting down. 'They have Puligny-Montrachet for ten quid a bottle. When it changed hands five years ago, they forgot to update the wine list. You often find great deals in ethnic restaurants.'

'I've heard of Montrachet. It's famous, isn't it?'

'Not Mon-*trash*-ay, Groucho. The 't' is silent. Think of it like Mont Blanc. Mont Rachet.'

'I've only heard it said the other way.'

'A common error. In both senses. I'm having Chicken Madras.'

I didn't mind Stellings correcting my pronunciation. Fine wines was not an area Mug Benson took us into during preparation for O-level oral, though come to think of it, he did provide that natty phrase *angoisse des gares*. Perhaps it was his translation that stuck in my mind: 'It's that moment when your parents put you on the train at the age of eight and as you puff out of the station you think that you might never see them again.'

Stellings poured the wine, whatever it was called, and banged on euphorically. He seemed to be high on something. 'Things are changing, Mike. Faster than they've ever changed in our lives. Take Gorbachev, for instance. I think he's going to bring the Cold War to an end.'

'But he's a KGB man, isn't he? Andropov's protégé?'

'Yes, but he's seen the writing on the wall. Do you know how many heart clinics there are in Moscow? One. It's on the eighth floor of an old building. And there's no lift. Do you know what the most common form of birth control is in the Soviet Union?'

'No.'

'Abortion. The average Soviet woman has six abortions in her life. It's cheaper than the Pill. Gorby knows they have to have more money. They have to open up to trade.'

'I feel a bit nostalgic at the thought of that era coming to an end,' I said. 'I grew up expecting to die in a nuclear war.'

'Me too. For the first time in my life, I don't think it's going to happen. The fax machine is also partly responsible. And the proliferation of telephones. You can only run a totalitarian society if you keep your citizens in the dark. But the means of information have now overrun their defences. Your average Joe in Irkutsk knows about what's on offer in the West. He wants colour television, Coca-Cola, Scotch whisky and a choice of candidates. Plus if they don't make more money they won't even be able to manufacture tanks.'

Lunch with Stellings brought home to me how little the world had changed in the 30-plus years I'd lived in it. It seemed to me that the divide between West and East was exactly as it had been since 1946, but more deeply entrenched. The Terrors and Gulags and invasions, and all the lies and oppression needed to deny or enforce them, had only made it more difficult for the Eastern Bloc to compromise. They reminded me a little of the police psychologists in the Sutcliffe case. The more you're challenged, the more rigidly you assert your beliefs. You have nothing to lose because without your beliefs you're nothing anyway: they make you what you are. It's shit or bust.

I thought Stellings was mad to think that the Cold War could just come to an end — snap your fingers and it's over. Say what you like about totalitarian communism, it's been in Darwinian terms quite a 'successful' organism. Because it's a closed system, it's to some extent immune to reasoned criticism. Like Christianity or Freudianism, its core beliefs are self-verifying. This may make it 'unscientific', but it also makes it formidable.

Future generations may be surprised to know that growing up in a world that you expected to explode at any time was not as frightening as it sounds. But in order to manage the background fear, you had to put it to one side of your mind. And by making that manoeuvre you tacitly admitted that you had — with whatever reservations — accepted the status quo. I found the prospect of it all changing, as outlined by Stellings over a second bottle of Puligny-Montrachet, rather unnerving. A free world? How on earth would the Russkies manage that? No imminent Armageddon? How were any of us meant to live with *that*?

'And apartheid,' I said. 'I suppose you're going

to tell me that'll soon be all over, too.'

'Shouldn't wonder,' said Stellings, sticking a shard of poppadom into the mint sauce.

'You mean Botha's just going to say, Sorry, Kaffirs, it's all been a big mistake. Let's have elections. And while I'm at it, Mandela can come out of prison. For a start, all the Nelson Mandela student union bars in Britain would have to rename themselves.'

'I promise you it'll happen within ten years. Botha won't last forever. There's this guy de Klerk coming up. He's a realist.'

'I bet you a hundred pounds it doesn't happen in the next ten years.'

We shook hands.

'All right, Stellings, here's one last test before we send for the straitjacket. Women.'

'What about them?'

'You know what it's like at the moment. How we have to pretend that they're the same as men in every respect. Otherwise you're a sexist.'

'You mean the feminism thing.'

'Yes. We make out that they think, act and feel identically to men. Not just that they deserve equal opportunities and equal pay but that they are at all levels already indistinguishable from men. We know it's not true. But that's not the point. What's required is to pretend that we're identical. They also know it's not true. We know they know it's not true. And they know we know they know we know they know it's not true. Yet every occasion at which women are present is a test of your orthodoxy. One deviation — and it's all over. The whole room turns on you and you might as well — '

'Christ, you must know some real schnauzers out there in Bayswater, Groucho. You should meet Clarissa. Come to dinner one day. After all — '

'But you know what I mean.'

'It's called politics, Groucho. That's how politics work. You overstate the case. You brook no compromise, take no prisoners, till you've got what you want. Equal pay, equal everything. Then you relax.'

'And when's that great volte-face due? Friday?'

'We have to live through this. It could be worse, Mike. If we'd been born in the 1890s we'd have been killed in the first weeks of the Great War. Or twenty years later, on the Normandy beaches. If all our generation has to endure is a bit of flak from grumpy feminists, then — '

'But what about the whole generation of men who — '

'It's better than the Somme.'

'And do you think that when it's over we'll forget the lies we all subscribed to?'

'Of course! Because it'll be so much fun we won't want to bring up the past, we'll want to forget it asap. By the end of the century it'll all be forgotten. You'll have women writing books about their own girlishness. Female chief execs of public companies admitting they can't read a map. They'll take pleasure in it. Because they'll have won the war, they'll be generous in the

281

peace. There'll be a boom in pink lipstick and lacy underwear.'

I had to laugh. 'And will they let us call them 'girls' again?'

'My dear boy, they'll call *themselves* 'girls' again. They'll call their own films 'chick-pics'.'

'Are you on drugs, Stellings?'

'Curry leaves and Puligny.'

'You're on a different planet.'

'Though sometimes I do have a tiny sniff of charlie at this time of day. It gets me through the afternoon. Want to join me in the Gents? The manager doesn't give a stuff.'

I looked at Stellings through the remains of the disembowelled paratha and the empty green Perrier bottle. I hadn't got much on that afternoon, so I followed him into the toilet.

★ ★ ★

Things have been going well with Margaret, the woman's page subeditor. Since I couldn't face the canteen, I decided to ask her out to lunch with me. Most journalists don't eat at lunchtime, they only drink, so it's quite a palaver proposing a real lunch with knife and fork: people think you're odd. I already knew Margaret wasn't a big boozer and that she did eat sometimes (that half-invite to the canteen), so I was hopeful of a yes. First I had to steel myself to ask. I didn't want to go to the usual place in case I was seen, so I took a blue pill, had a couple of pints of cloudy Burton and large vodka chaser in a fiendish little slit of a pub called the King and

Keys, which was full of red-faced men from the *Telegraph* with grey hair and ash on their suits, haranguing one another, already drunk by five past twelve. When I got back, I took the lift to the woman's-page office on the fourth floor, put my head round the door and popped the question. Margaret looked a bit embarrassed to be asked in front of all her colleagues, but agreed to meet me at the front door at ten to one, by which time she was looking slightly more made-up and coiffed.

We went to a Chinese called City Friends, near the Old Bailey. She told me she'd been married and divorced. He was a crime reporter for the *Sunday Express* and they'd met when both were working briefly for some regional paper. I gathered he was a big drinker and used to knock her about. She had custody of a girl, now ten years old, called Charlotte; they lived in a flat in Holloway. Derek, the husband, no longer visited, though his standing order towards maintenance had so far been honoured.

Margaret squeezed some rice between her chopsticks. 'I always look at the *Sunday Express* first and make sure he's got a piece in. That way he'll be happy and won't drink so much and he'll keep his job.'

Like me, she'd stumbled into newspapers. She came from Hertfordshire somewhere and, reading between the lines, I gathered that her family were a bit smarter than the Englebys (hard not to be). Local high school, some sort of further ed at the tech. Then, after spells as a secretary and a job in 'marketing', she met someone who suggested she train at Hemel Hempstead with a newspaper group. Thence to the regional rag where she met boozer Derek: a bit of news, some feature writing, but she had no ambitions in that direction, she preferred editing and layout. Couple of jobs with IPC (*Woman's Realm, Woman's Work, Woman's Trouble*), and then on to the Sunday paper, where she liked it very much indeed. She was six years older than I was, though she could have passed for a bit more. Marriage, children, the uncertainty of Derek . . . I don't know; but while she wasn't exactly motherly, she seemed experienced. What was nice about her was that she didn't come over as embittered. She was candid, optimistic and polite. She offered to pay for lunch, but I didn't let her.

I hadn't a clue how to move on to the next stage, whether she wanted there to be a next stage, or in fact whether *I* wanted there to be one. I hoped, perhaps, that with her greater worldliness she might take charge.

★ ★ ★

The interview with Ken Livingstone didn't go quite as well as I'd expected.

I did try to be something completely new — disarming, liberating, original — but he treated me with world-weariness, as though he'd dealt with my type a million times before.

We met in the Greater London Council offices at 10.30 on 29 May, 1985. It's always rather odd when you meet someone who's been so much

284

written about. I couldn't help but expect a bloody-handed ogre of the tumbrils; instead, I saw a tall, knock-kneed figure emerge from the humdrum twilight of a local government committee room, at the end of a long wood-panelled corridor. I wasn't sure if it was Robespierre or the borough surveyor of Dudley.

We had some milky coffee from a trolley brought in by a tea lady. Mrs Thatcher doesn't like Ken's policies, but he keeps getting elected, so she's had to close down the whole GLC. It was the only thing she could do. Short of having him rubbed out, I suppose. He's off to be an MP now for Brent East, wherever that is. It's a parliamentary invention rather than a real place; there was nowhere called Brent in the *A to Z* when I looked. I think it may take in the area round Harlesden and Dollis Hill. I remember taking the Harlesden night bus once and I was the only white man on it. (Ken must know where it is, though, because the very last thing he did as GLC leader was to give Brent, his future base, a 'stress grant' of two million pounds.)

He had no qualms about leaving his fellow-travellers in the scuppered GLC. He was quite perky about the whole thing, in a sour, corner-of-the-mouth way. 'The orthodox Trots have never taken on board minority groups, like blacks and gays,' he said. 'But we can now make a permanent new governing majority in Britain.'

I tried to picture the kind of cabinet this grouping might throw up.

'By the 'orthodox Trots', do you mean people

285

like . . . Like what's his name. The leader of Lambeth Council.'

'Ted Knight. Yeah, those people live in a workerist laager.'

Wow. I hadn't heard anyone speak like that since I was a student. Anyway, I quickly got the boring stuff out of the way, and began to ask from my list of 'interesting' questions.

'What are your favourite books?'

'I never went to college so I never got into reading much.'

'You must have gone to school?'

'Yeah, but I was useless at school.'

'Isn't it a problem being badly educated?' (I was thinking how I could be working in the paper mill.)

'No. It teaches you to trust gut prejudices. You mustn't allow facts to divert your instincts.'

'But you must have read *something*?'

'Yeah, well I suppose about seventy per cent of what I've read's been science fiction.'

I forced my fallen jaw back up. 'And the rest? The other thirty per cent?'

'Politics. Do you know the work of the early Jewish philosopher Hillel? He was a contemporary of Christ, only *much* more popular.'

His eyelids flickered with shy pride as he dangled this name for me.

(I hadn't heard of Hillel, unfortunately, so the next day I looked him up in the British Library catalogue. There was a book *about* him by Glatzer, Nahum Norbet, called *Hillel the Elder: the Emergence of Classical Judaism* (1957) and a lot of books about soil mechanics by someone

286

with a similar name; but the man himself seemed, like Jesus, to have written nothing, so it was hard to see how Ken had 'read' him.)

Anyway: back in Ken's office, I returned to my prepared list of questions.

'Where do you take your holidays?' I asked.

'I can't afford to take holidays.'

'How much money have you got?'

'None. I haven't had a job since 1970, when I stopped working at the Royal Marsden hospital.'

'Were you a nurse?'

'I was an auxiliary.'

'So what do you live off?'

'Off the councillor's attendance allowances that were introduced by Michael Heseltine and Peter Walker when they were the Tory environment secretaries.' He crossed his legs. 'I suppose I've got a lot to thank Michael and Peter for.'

'Do you have a girlfriend?'

'I can't discuss that.'

'Are you gay?'

'Private life. I never talk about that to the Press.'

'Do you believe in God?'

'No.'

I looked back down to my list of questions, and as I did so I noticed something odd about Ken's ankles. He was wearing flared trousers. I didn't know you could still buy them.

I asked if he liked cooking, but he quickly turned his answer, via kitchen work, into a lecture about sex and oppression. 'I don't believe in traditional gender roles in any case. The best men exploit women. Even the best whites exploit blacks.'

I guessed he wasn't much of a cook.

'Are you patriotic?'

'It's impossible not to feel some sort of crude stirring when you hear 'Land of Hope and Glory', but you have to set that against the systematic slaughter of the Tasmanian Aborigines.'

I looked down at my reporter's notebook. I'd covered about five sides of it, but that was nothing like enough for a 1,500-word article.

In the end, I had to resort to talking politics; he'd left me no alternative.

His round Chinese laundryman's face at last became animated. 'Oh yeah, I'm the most powerful left-winger ever to hold office in this country. Michael Foot and Tony Benn never had ministries in which they could really influence people's lives like I've done.'

Scribble, scribble. When I'd covered ten more pages, I called a halt. I'd been outflanked by someone determined not to let me let him be interesting. I felt doomed to write about the received ideas after all. Loony this . . . Newt that . . . I'd have to wear out the inverted-comma key on my typewriter.

As I left and walked back down that dingy corridor with its numbered doors, Ken called after me to point out that the very last thing he'd done as GLC leader — even after the Brent handout — was to twin London with Managua.

'Thank you,' I called back.

I left with a smile. I felt that Jen Soc, at least, would have liked that twinning. They'd have voted for it, eight to five with two abstentions. Then a glass of Hirondelle to celebrate.

★ ★ ★

The Chatfield Old Boys' Society contains some dogged sleuths. I'm flabbergasted by their persistence. Each year since I left I've dropped their pathetic entreaties for information into the bin; every time I changed address, I failed to tell them. Yet in the morning yesterday I found a copy of the *Chatfield Year Book* on the doormat. How on earth do they *do* that? It was addressed to me as M. Engleby, though in the Old Boys' News section, I was appalled to read: 'M. Engleby (Collingham, 1966–70) is reportedly working as a journalist in London under the nom de plume Michael Watson. Further sightings, please!'

The only thing that cheered me up was an entry in the *Valete* column. 'J.T. Baynes (Collingham 1963–68) died from a stroke in Stoke Mandeville hospital. He had suffered gradual paralysis over many years. Our sympathies to his widow Jane and their two children.'

'Gradual paralysis'. Was that a bona fide medical term? It was good enough for Lt Commander S.R. Sidway, RN, retd, editor of the *Year Book*. And good enough to have finished old Baynes.

As I climbed out of the underground at Chancery Lane and looked in the clothes shop with the Tudor half-timbering, I puzzled over one thing: how 'Jane' allowed that faceful of pus to rub on her skin while he impregnated her. I also felt slightly disappointed that he'd managed to find a wife at all — though Christ knows what sort of swamp-dweller he'd bagged.

For the rest, of course, the news was unalloyed delight, and at lunchtime I took Margaret to Langan's Brasserie to celebrate. We both had the spinach soufflé with anchovy sauce to start, and a bottle of the house champagne to wash it down. Then another bottle with the main course. Afterwards we walked over to the Ritz, took a room and had it off.

★ ★ ★

There was a message on my desk last Friday. The handwriting was that of Felicity Maddox, the sarcastic newsroom secretary. 'James Stellings's office rang. Would you go to dinner Thursday the 11th. 8.30, 152 Elgin Crescent, W11.'

I found the word 'dinner' a bit intimidating. Would it be just me and Stellings and his wife and child or was it a 'dinner party'? I'd never been to one of those, though I'd seen them in plays and films. (In *Accident*, by Joseph Losey, for instance.) Christ. I pictured this Clarissa in some sort of ball gown saying to the other guests, 'James has asked his funny little friend Toilet Engleby. He's known him since college, apparently. What a scream! Do be kind to him, won't you?'

Shit. I was actually out of London on the day in question, in Birmingham, and didn't get back till about seven. I had a bath and put Steely Dan on the record player. I ought to explain that I don't like new pop music any more. I'd always liked the latest thing, sequentially: rock 'n' roll, pop, soul, psychedelia, hard rock, progressive, glamour, punk, then: whooaaah! I remember the day I suddenly stopped. A deejay played a song that started 'I was working as a waitress in a cocktail bar,/That much is true . . . ' When it finished, he banged on about how brilliant it was, how it was the future and everything. And I thought *that* pathetic sound, those gutless hairdressers with a toy kazoo — *that* is the inheritor of Hendrix and Dylan and Stevie Wonder and the Beatles and Cream and . . . Dear God. I lowered the top half of the sash window, took careful aim and hurled the small radio out as hard as I could: over the street and into the grassless 'garden square', where it landed noiselessly. I liked to think of them warbling on till the batteries died, face down in the dog mess.

So for five years or more I've just listened to old stuff. I always liked Steely Dan. They must be two of the strangest men ever to imagine they were pop stars. You'd have had them down for maths professors or computer programmers. 'Dr Donald Fagen at nine on Statistical Analysis; Professor Walter Becker at ten on Boolean Algebra.' Except they were rockers, and so were the others in the picture: Jeff 'Skunk' Baxter, responsible, I gathered, for the fret-shattering guitar solo on 'Bodhisattva', Jeff Porcaro and the others.

That night, before Stellings's do, I was

listening to the melodious, early *Can't Buy a Thrill*. I thought its sweetness of nature would put me in the mood. I must have heard it a thousand times, but there's always something new there. I was humming along to 'Brooklyn (Owes the Charmer Under Me)' when I noticed with a jolt that I must always have misheard the lyrics. For a decade or more I'd had it as 'A race of angels/Bound with one another,/A dish of dollars/Laid out for all to see,/A tower room at Eden Roc/His golf at noon for three:/Brooklyn owes the charmer under me.'

Now this had always bothered me because in my limited experience of golf, a three-ball is frowned on. Some clubs you even have to get the secretary's written permission. But here was Donald Fagen, and maybe some girl he's singing to, or possibly Walter Becker — anyway, that makes two: but who was the third, and how were they going to swing it with the caddymaster? Maybe Don had the secretary's ear, and with a back catalogue like that, who's complaining? But it bothered me. Christ knows what Jeff 'Skunk' Baxter's short game was like.

Then, as I lay in the steaming water, it struck me that the words in fact were 'A tower room at Eden Roc/His golf at noon for *free*' and it all made sense. I got out of the bath, laughing with relief.

Why was I having these peculiar thoughts and chuckling to myself? My mental processes, I believed, could sometimes include humour, but they weren't normally facetious. What was going on?

I suppose I was nervous.

I'd bought a suit some time ago for going to Fleet Street, but it wasn't very new or very fashionable or very clean. I didn't have much else apart from jeans. It took me only a minute to glance through my 'wardrobe'. I picked a tan seersucker jacket that Margaret had once said she liked, some fairly new straight-leg trousers and a clean shirt (there was only one: it was a sort of maroon colour. It didn't quite go with the jacket, perhaps, but there was no time to wash and iron another one). I wasn't sure about ties. Most of mine were a bit on the kipper side. Then I remembered I still had a cowboy bootlace thing that Julie had given me one Christmas (it was one up on the Donny Osmond tee shirt. Where the hell did that go, by the way?). I put the tie on and I thought it did a job. If they were all wearing ties, well, so was I; if not, mine was a joke. My newest shoes were a pair of rubber-soled caramel-brown lace-ups, so on they went.

At the weekend I'd bought a pricey bottle of Montrachet to amuse Stellings and I got some flowers (dahlias, I think; I'm not good on flowers — orange jobs anyway) at 8.22 from the garage on Westbourne Grove for 'Clarissa'. I was keeping a tight watch on the time because I didn't want to be late. I walked on briskly.

When I first came to London, Notting Hill was full of squatters, potters and banjoists; but the tide seems to be turning. Many rooms have gone to flats, the flats back into houses and the houses have been bought by people in American

293

banks who wouldn't know a Bacon from a xylophone.

At 8.29 I punched the front doorbell in Elgin Crescent. It was opened by a small oriental woman in a white apron. She showed me into a large, empty sitting room with an open fire and a couple of huge oil paintings. One was of an old bloke in Gainsborough style (a Stellings or Clarissa ancestor, perhaps) and the other a more or less random splosh-and-twirl in grey and tangerine that seemed designed to trigger a sequence of sophomore thoughts about 'art'.

I was still shuddering at the banality of my own responses when Stellings breezed in.

'Christ, Groucho, you're punctual. Or Gaucho, we'll have to call you with that tie. Have a drink. Champagne? Wine? Scotch?'

'Yeah, Scotch.' I thought it would sit better on the three Johnnie Walkers and the blue pill I'd already had in my flat.

'Clarissa's just saying goodnight to Alexander. How's things? Any good scoops lately?'

I told Stellings a bit about the work I'd done. He was wearing jeans with an open-necked white shirt, espadrilles and no socks. He hadn't made much of an effort, I thought.

My drink was brought to me by the Thai or Filipina in the white apron.

A woman appeared in the doorway: tall, fair-haired, dressed all in black, so I wondered if she'd been to a funeral, down to the thin black tights on her long legs. She had rather more mascara than you'd expect for a wake, though, and reddish-pink lipstick. Also, she didn't look tear-stained or sad. I felt her eyes flicker over me, pausing for a moment at my feet.

'Darling, this is Mike Engleby. Mike, this is Clarissa — the old trouble and strife.'

Clarissa's soft hand entered mine and withdrew almost before it had made contact; it was more of a stroke than a shake. 'James has told me so much about you. Come and sit down. James, you're not looking after Mike properly. Have an olive.'

'Is it all right if I smoke?'

'Of course it is. Letitia, would you mind getting an ashtray?'

Clarissa's large blue eyes fixed on my face as she perched next to me on the sofa, shifting away only a few inches when some of my smoke seemed go up her nose. I felt swaddled by the intensity of her interest.

'And tell me more about your family,' she was saying. 'Are they still in . . . Reading? I had a friend who lived not far from there once. In Stratfield Saye. Do you know it?'

Her expression had the life-and-death curiosity of someone needing only one more score-draw for the pools jackpot.

'No. My mother's in the hotel business.'

'How interesting. I believe it's awfully hard work.'

'Yes. Yes. And . . . Er, my sister's in brewing.'

'Which side of it?'

'Accounts.'

'It's such a volatile market, isn't it, wines and spirits? There are so many conglomerates, aren't

295

there, but I believe many of the independent breweries have done well recently.'

'Yeah, well I think the real ale thing's helped a bit. And you know — '

'Of course. How clever of your sister. And is she married, did you say?'

'Not yet. She — '

'Sensible girl. Career first. And are you a Berkshire family on both sides?'

I did my best to make Mum and Julie's life worthy of this apocalyptic degree of interest. After a while, I half began to believe it myself, as the Englebys, in my account, emerged as yeomen of Mercia, devoted to their victualling heritage. Still, I was relieved when at about nine-fifteen some more people arrived.

I didn't catch many names, but there were I think four more couples, making eleven people in all, with only Engleby unpartnered. The men all had the same haircuts: shorter than mine, with straight edges, dark gloss and burnish. They had suntans and made candid eye contact with one another. Most wore suits and apologised for having come straight from work; they loosened their ties and showily threw the first drink down their necks — presumably to prove they were at home chez Stellings and no longer in the office. They talked mostly about sport and cars. The women were without exception good-looking. All were thin; most were in dazzling colours — puce and amber and lilac — as though they were stating some primal confidence. Their hair, too, smelled of salons and looked brittle and dry, though gleaming. They all had slim legs covered with some fabric I'd never seen before: like nylon, but finer. I orbited round with a B&H on the go, and occasionally got a word in.

For dinner, we went downstairs to a long table with a floor-length white cloth, candles and bowls of tall hellebores at intervals. I know they were hellebores because I heard Clarissa say so when one of the women asked.

I was put between someone called Laura and someone called Cecilia. The layout of the table meant that I couldn't really see through the flowers to anyone opposite and in any event they would have had to shout. So I talked to Laura for about twenty minutes, then to Cecilia for about twenty. Then when I swivelled back to give Laura her ration, she'd turned to her left. I switched back to Cecilia, but she too had turned the other way. So I stared straight ahead while the first course and the main course came and went and the maid filled and refilled my glass with white burgundy, then claret.

Then I had another right-and-left stint.

What did they say?

One had three children and told me about the schools they attended and the schools they hoped to send them to after that. She asked if I had any children and I said no. Then she told me which of her children were good at which subjects and which were having extra tuition. One of her daughters was also good at the violin, whereas her son was mad about football. Then she talked of the reputations of various schools that her children were not going to but which friends of hers had children at. She also talked of a new school that had just been started — somewhat too late for her elder children, and her youngest couldn't be moved because he was happy where he was — and how she thought it might be a great success because there would always be a need for good schools.

I agreed with her emphatically — as though she'd been only half-hearted in her own belief — that there would *always* be a need for good schools.

Something odd was happening in my head. Although I was receiving a large amount of random information, I didn't feel I knew any more about anything. On the contrary, I felt that, as far as data in the brain were concerned, I had suffered a net loss.

'And where did you go to school yourself?' she said.

'What?'

'Where did you go to school?'

'Eton.'

'Really? My brother was there. What years were you?'

'Sixty-six to seventy.'

'Which house?'

'Collingham.'

'I mean, who was your housemaster?'

'You wouldn't have heard of him. Which house was your brother in?'

'H.R.T.'s.'

'Right. I didn't know anyone in that one.'

'No one! Gosh, I thought only the scholars didn't mix.'

'Well, I was a scholar, you see.'

'So why weren't you in College?'

'I . . .' I took a long pull of white burgundy.

'*I* know. You were an OS, weren't you?'

'Yeah, that's right. An OS.' I had a brainwave. 'And I met Stellings — James, I mean, at university. We were in the same college.'

I thought I'd got away with it. I don't know why I told a lie. Maybe I couldn't face talking about Chatfield. Or perhaps my brain had just been scrambled by the occasion. As soon as I could, I turned to the other side.

This neighbour, she told me, had only one child, but had had six au pairs. She herself had returned to work at a bank — which was where she'd first met Clarissa, as it happened, when she was working in the mergers and acquisitions department — and so it was very important that the au pair should be a good one, since neither she nor her husband (who was sitting next to Clarissa and talking far too loudly as usual, she was sorry to say) was at home very often. He (the husband) had taken a bath, by all accounts, over some long term financial guesswork that hadn't come off, but had turned it all around in the last six months to the extent that he'd been head-hunted and was now on 'gardening leave'. In his new job, he was going to be remunerated on an 'eat what you kill' basis.

So, I ventured to suggest, the au pair crisis must have eased off a bit.

Far from it. Things had gone from bad to worse. The Latvian was lazy, the Czech was greedy and the Pole took money from Laura's (possibly Cecilia's) purse. We tried a bit of a

Czech/cheque/ check thing here, but it didn't really catch fire, possibly because it was the Pole who'd been the tea leaf. So we quickly got back to the child, who was now at a nursery school, which was a blessing.

Was it the new place, I wondered, the one that had just started?

It turned out that it was indeed the new one, and it was every bit as good as they'd hoped. They took such a lot of interest in the children. And it gave them a head start at big school. Talking of which, there were any number of possibilities for the little fellow — possibilities which we went on at some length to review.

My head cranked from side to side, ten minutes here, ten minutes there, like watching Wimbledon in slow motion. I began to feel that I was no longer making sense. The more I heard, the less I knew. Someone had put their fingers in my brain and uncoupled the trucks.

When the au pair one came back for a fourth knock I could see the dumb pain in her eyes.

I had imagined that at a 'dinner party' you talked to your friend, the one who'd invited you, and maybe his wife, and who knows, a couple of others and the whole thing became a sort of convivial, pooled chat. Like a pub or a café.

I hadn't thought it through.

It had never crossed my mind that I'd spend three hours talking to the wives of people I'd never met. It was like being stuck in a stalled Tube train, trying to make common cause with the strangers in the next seat, but without the *Evening Standard* for respite.

Coffee arrived at one o'clock. By then, I was no longer capable of thought. All that once I'd known, I had forgotten.

At one-thirty, I stumbled upstairs. I must have drunk at least a bottle of Stellings's Meursault and a bottle and a half of La Dominique (I noticed he was still keen on the 'poor man's Pétrus', or whatever he'd christened it). I was well into a second packet of B&H.

A couple of men were standing in front of the fireplace.

'Ah, hello, er . . . '

'Mike,' I said.

'Mike. Of course. We were just talking about this new school that's started in Cambridge Gardens. Do you know it?'

I felt a curious rage begin to swell in me . . . But I was tired and drunk and the blue pill swirled the last of its gentle magic through my veins as I sucked in deep on good Virginia tobacco.

'You bet,' I said. 'I gather it's fantastic.'

★ ★ ★

Back home that night, I restored some sense of sanity with a diary session. I lay in bed in the darkness and selected a special date, one of my favourites: the first ever.

THURSDAY 25 MAY, 1972
I've decided to keep a diary. My name is Jennifer Arkland and I'm 19 years old. I'm a

301

first-year history student and I've just done my preliminary exams, or 'prelims'. They don't give you grades, but they tell you your marks and I did better than I expected.

I've never kept a diary before, so I feel a bit odd writing this. Should I introduce myself? Why?! I'm not going to show it to anyone. And to herself, Jennifer surely needs no introduction.

If not to show it, then why write it? Do I have a 'deep subconscious' desire to be read — to reveal and be shamed? Doubt it.

I'm writing it for two reasons — or two that I'm aware of. One, so I can read it in old age, or middle age. Always regret so few photos of us as children. You think: what's the point, today like any other day, nothing special, not worth recording. But it is, it was. Why? Because it's all there is.

Don't mean that to sound morbid, like typical first-year: 'birth, copulation and death, that's all there is when you come down to it . . . ' No. Key word is 'all'. And that 'all' is plenty.

What I mean is that I don't have teleological view (great new word from Dr Abraham seminar on Puritans. They v definitely did have tel. view). I believe that the living and the breathing and the being with people you are fond of and the friendly exchange with them of ideas and stories and encouragement and love is the totality of what we are and of what we can do. Don't believe those exps can be forced into

302

meaningful 'shape' or 'journey', as per tel. view.

Do believe that the richness available in those exchanges is definitely enough.

Enough for what? you may ask, Hypothetical Reader. Without tel. view there is no framework, no criteria by which the experience of being alive can be deemed 'sufficient' or 'insufficient'. So: illogical question, dear HR!

I suppose I just mean 'enough to make me happy, curious and full of excitement'. That's the way I feel. Agnostic but happy. (I sound like a puppy. Do believe am a fraction deeper than that . . .)

How so? Well, maybe the love generated between people who behave well and kindly adds somehow to the available pool of existing good feeling in the world, and lives on after them. (Now sound like drippy hippy, but actually it's true and easy to prove.) Without good example such as preserved in literature, there would be nothing to live up to, no sense of transcendence or of our lives beyond the Hobbesian. So these feelings do endure and I believe they also survive through memory, orally and in families as much as in written word. So while living may have no meaning in any teleological sense, it does have practical purpose in the way that how we live can improve the experience of others alive and yet to be born; and thus, a bit more contentiously (because harder to define scale on which it's measured), it also has value. This seems so obvious to me as to be almost axiomatic.

But brings me to second reason for starting diary. First is for future reading pleasure, period quaintness, as described above. Second is because I feel so happy. Haven't always been this happy and know I won't always be so in future; so wanted to pickle and preserve, not just for historical interest but as possible future store to draw on in leaner years. Contentment as chutney or sauerkraut.

Why so happy? What so great, Jen? Live in rather horrid modern room in college. Small metal-framed window overlooks back delivery yard with bicycle rack, kitchens and rubbish bins. Bedcum-sofa, window seat, desk, chair. Pantry and bath down landing. Bathroom always occupied. Not nearly as nice as my room at home.

Friends . . . Yes, but no one as close as family or Susan and Becky from school. Molly down corridor v nice and think Anne cd become friend. Emma M? That Indian-looking girl — Malini, is it? Bit scary. So not exhilaration of fab friendships making me so happy.

Work is interesting, but, despite what Mum and Dad think, have never really been a swot. True, did well at school, but not hard, not v brainy school so not much competition — yet good teachers. In final term three of them teaching three of us univ candidates. What staff/pupil ratio!

Anyway, work here is fine, though I don't think that in the appointment of dons to college or university positions the ability to teach was considered at any stage. Most v ungifted in that dept, and manifestly more into their own work than ours.

I like work, but not carried away by it, not like some people.

Am not 'in love' either. Don't have boyfriend. Am rather freaked out by sex ratio imbalance. You feel quite self-conscious in lectures being one of sometimes four girls among 50 boys. Also, many of the academic girls — or women as we call ourselves — are not that glamorous, to be frank, and attract zero interest from boys — so others of us feel need to show solidarity with them rather than flirt vacuously.

Boyfriend thing is certainly one to take very slowly. Unless bolt from blue. Am romantic enough to hope a tiny bit for such a thing. Also realist enough to know that I couldn't feel much happier anyhow, so to some extent: what wd be point of Prince Charming? (Listening to Miles Davis at Jazz Club last week, earnest boy from St John's said that most touching part of 'Someday My Prince Will Come' was 'slight illiteracy' of first word of title, suggesting uneducated girl in Harlem standing on tenement balcony looking wistfully over broken neighbourhood . . . Could be.)

So where's it coming from, this feeling, this funny low euphoria? A little bit from the town, I think. I do love the dirty brick of the miniature terraces and the mist from the river and the cold mornings, even now in May. And then the sudden huge vista of a great courtyard of King's or Trin or Queens', when everything that's been pinched, and puritanical and cold and grudging and sixpence-in-the-gas-meter is suddenly swept away by the power and scale of those buildings, with their towers and crenellations and squandered empty spaces, built by men who knew that they'd calculated the mechanical laws of time and distance and that there was therefore no need whatever to build small.

Also . . . What? As Dad often says, I'm a 'lucky girl' — by which he means I have a good 'temperament'. By this Jane Austeny word, he means that I am 'naturally at home in the world' while some people are 'all across it'. Don't know how scientific that is, but perhaps something in it.

I think I could put it more simply. I like being 19. I wasn't that keen on being a child because I always felt I was missing out on things; and I know I'll be no good at all at being 35 or 40 or — God help us — 50! But 19, 20 and so on seems to me wonderful. There's nothing 'they' won't let me do, and I occasionally think there's almost nothing I couldn't do.

Sometimes in my cramped room am so excited when I turn the light out by prospect of coming days and weeks that I can't sleep. Must be careful. Pride before fall, Johnny Head in Air and so on. But can't *help* being happy and am b**ed if will pretend to fashionable gloom.

That's my girl. Interesting how she started off with all that showoffy stude stuff — 'teleological', 'Hobbesian' etc. — but her later entries were much more about sex and drugs. You grow up fast over those years.

But as Jen's writing got cruder, I can't help noticing, when I look back, that my own style has poshed up a bit. 'I miss the eruptive blue ballpointed handwriting squeezed in so tight between the red feint rules.' 'The expanding town of Basingstoke seethed like Laocoön within its concentric ring roads.'

Bloody hell.

I see the blue pencil of Dr Gerald Stanley making a sarcastic wavy line under those sentences . . . Actually, come to think of it, he didn't use blue pencil or red ballpoint, but black ink indistinguishable from that used by me and three-quarters of his students. A small thing, that lack of consideration and common sense, but in fact unbelievably irritating. It looked as though you'd scrawled graffiti on your own stuff.

The reason that my style has become less cramped, more expansive is pretty obvious, I imagine.

I'm happier. It took me a long time to recognise that that was the name of this feeling — happiness. It, as they say, 'crept up'. By this I mean that when I first acknowledged to myself that there was a fundamental change — in the way I viewed the day ahead, the way I looked at myself and my life, the mood that had become established as my default — I simultaneously admitted that the change had been in place for some time. That's what's meant by 'creeping up', I think.

Margaret and I had a party last week to celebrate our officially moving in together. It was her idea. She wanted to make some sort of 'statement', I think; she wanted to be respectable and show her friends that she wasn't a discard.

I thought it was a bad idea. For a start, I'm keeping my flat in Bayswater; I'm only moving a few shirts and a toothbrush up to Holloway. Second, I thought that if husband Derek gets wind of it, he'll stop the payments for his daughter.

I pointed this out to Margaret and it went down very badly indeed. The sincerity of my interest in her was called into question. She more or less implied that if I ended up footing the bill for someone else's kid — so what? That's what you did if you were 'serious about a relationship'.

It was our first argument, but obviously a big one. I went off and thought about it for a few days (the paper had sent me to Manchester anyway). One of the things about never having any money as a child is that you really want to hang on to it when you do finally get some. I didn't think I was particularly mean as a rule, but paying for wife-beater Derek's kid . . . That just didn't seem right to me.

On the other hand, I was happy with Margaret and I did like Charlotte. She reminded me of Julie at that age — obviously — though, to be brutal, she was not quite so gormless. She had a variety of friends from the local comprehensive whom I also — Christ, I must be 'mellowing' or something — rather liked. They tore through the flat, stripped out the fridge, took my cigarettes, misfired round the toilet, 'borrowed' Margaret's videos, grabbed tins of beer and left. But I felt there was no harm in them. I admired their rush.

As for Charlotte . . . I think I liked her clothes as much as anything. The effort she put in to looking good each day: the ribbons and the torn jeans, the lace mittens, the combat gear from Lawrence Corner at the foot of Hampstead Road, the black-rimmed eyes, the puffed-out nylon skirts and coloured basketball boots . . . And she was fun to talk to, when she could be bothered. She was very forthright, swore like a hooker and was experimenting with some sort of consonant-free London dialect. I went for her in quite a big way.

So I said yes to Margaret: yes, I'd take the consequences of a move and yes, let's have a party. We cleared most of the stuff out of the living room into Charlotte's bedroom and set up the record player. Margaret bought food from the large supermarket near Highbury Corner and got to work: sausages, paté, French bread, stodgy stuff to soak up the cases of Spanish wine I got from Oddbins.

Margaret asked about fifty people, many from the office. Tony Bollock, of course; the woman's page staff en masse; her sister Brenda and her obese husband from Little Chalfont. Lots of people I knew by sight from various pubs and bars in Fleet Street.

We had invitations printed with some embarrassing words devised by Margaret.

309

Something about 'shared life' or 'new beginning'. I honestly forget.

I invited a few people from my old mag: Jan, Wyn Douglas, Bob Nixon the crime reporter; Shireen Nazawi, the EFL-speaking interviewer. I thought about asking Stellings and Clarissa, but I knew they'd hate it.

Then I wrote off to some of the friends I'd made through interviewing. Naim Attallah, for instance. (I did find out who he was in the end. He was a Palestinian steeplejack who'd chanced into a jewellery business called Asprey, then bought a run-down publishing house.) He wasn't free to come, but he sent a card and a gift voucher to Margaret from his shop for £100.

I really wanted to ask Ralph Richardson, but alas he had died. In 1983, I think it was. I remember hearing the news on the radio while I was in the bath. At the time we met, he was pretty much the first person who'd spoken to me in a month.

I asked Ken Livingstone, but he didn't reply; he must get a hell of a lot of invites. Of course I asked Jeffrey Archer. And not only did he come, he also brought a magnum of champagne and made a short speech in our honour. I recognised one of the jokes from a Foyle's lunch, but he'd worked on the delivery since then.

The whole thing was more than just the usual pub bores on free booze and a change of venue. It felt like an event and it went on till three in the morning.

It certainly felt like an event when I was woken at seven by one of Charlotte's friends blundering in. Margaret brought me aspirin and tea in bed. (I'm very much in her good books now.)

I had an uneasy feeling when I read the *Daily Telegraph*, though. Police in Fulham had discovered the badly decomposed body (well, skeleton, I imagine, really) of a woman in a ditch by a District Line railway cutting where the Tube goes overground somewhere in the West Brompton area. They think the body may be as much as eight years old, but they have established that it is that of a missing 29-year-old German called Gudrun Abendroth. She worked in the A&R department of a Frankfurt record company, but had at the time of her disappearance been lodging in London, in Tournay Road, SW6.

Although the photograph was blurred, there was something in her face that looked familiar.

I was, mercifully, too hungover to be able to place it and too busy to brood on it.

9

One of our Victorian Linotype machines broke down last week and we urgently needed a new part before Saturday. They eventually found what they needed in a printing museum in Burnley and bribed the curator to let them have it for a week or two while we looked for an iron foundry to cast a replacement.

There's a secret room on the top floor where they keep half a dozen examples of a machine called a Tandy. These are small electric typewriters which, instead of paper, have a screen where you can read back what you've written; they also, amazingly, have a jack you can stick in a phone socket. Press 'Go' and the machine then transmits what you've written down the line into a computer in the office, from which it can be retrieved, messed up by the sub-editors, and printed.

We're not officially allowed to use a Tandy, because if they found out what we were doing, the union of upmakers, stonehands and Luddites would shut the paper for good. Steven Stringer, a foreign-desk sub, once changed the light bulb on his desk lamp and we lost that Sunday's paper in the resulting wildcat strike. It was a job for a member of the relevant union — Cosanostra or Natsopa — and the senior light-bulb changer is paid £75,000 a year, which is £2,500 more than the editor of the newspaper.

I know one of the compositors quite well. Terry, he's called. We've been to Upton Park a couple of times to see the Hammers. You'd think he'd be working on a Saturday, what with it being a Sunday paper. Sixty of them are paid, but only forty exist and only twenty need to turn up. Terry, being a senior guy, also gets one of the twenty 'ghost' pay packets, which he takes under the name of Billy Bonds, the West Ham captain. So he's paid double. For not turning up. And they're on double time anyway, because it's a weekend — even though it's the only day of the week a Sunday printer works, and it was always, by definition, going to be on a Saturday. So he's actually paid quadruple. The meat pies and the programmes and the Carling at the Boleyn Ground are therefore on him. He can't believe how little I'm paid (£26,800); he won't let me buy anything. He puts his big soft hand over mine when I go to get my wallet out and says, 'You're 'avin' a laugh, Mick. On your wages?'

We have to get back sharpish to Fleet Street after the game, because that's when Terry makes his real money.

As the bundles of printed newspapers come out on the conveyor belts, a fair number go into unmarked vans belonging to Terry and his brother-in-law Ray. These then go off to a depot on the Essex marshes where they're put in smaller vans and delivered to newsagents. Ray is a builder, but also draws a wage from my paper as a compositor — under the name of Trevor Brooking.

Terry becomes quite anxious at this time of

day on a Saturday and I tend to leave him to it. He invited me to 'Sunday dinner' once at his home near Epping. I calculate that he must be earning £120,000 a year from the paper alone, but his house, though well equipped, wasn't much bigger than our place in Trafalgar Terrace. 'You gotta be a bit discreet, Mick,' he said. 'People don't don't want you to wave it under their noses. Bloke opposite, see that little 'ouse there, 'e's a barristers' clerk. Same difference.' After lunch, Terry drew the curtains and showed me some slides of his place in Spain, with its underground car ports, heated pool and uniformed staff of four. He has them wear the old claret and blue, though I don't think they have any idea that it's the West Ham strip; they think it's the eccentricity of the English milord.''Ere, Mick, this one, she's called Manuela or some bloody silly name. Looks a bit like Ronnie Boyce, don't you fink?'

In fact, I do secretly use a Tandy on some stories. Like last week, when I had to go back to my old university. Tony Ball sent me off to the top floor to be inducted into the secrets of the machine. I had to carry it home in a Tesco bag so as not to excite suspicion and was warned never to bring it within a mile of Fleet Street. If it broke, I was just to chuck it away.

As for the story, there was a row in some grand college about its new Master, who was thought to have been foisted on the reluctant Fellows via the vice chancellor as some sort of political favour to the prime minister.

'Yeah, it's a sort of Maggie's Mafia/Trouble in

Paradise piece,' said Tony Ball over a cup of office coffee and an Embassy King. 'Maybe twelve, fourteen hundred words. Could be a page lead. Ever been there?'

'Yes, as a matter of fact, I spent three — '

'Town versus Gown. The old farts choking on their port. Our readers love this kind of thing.'

'Couldn't I just go and find out what happened, then write it down?'

'We might run a trail on the front. Dreaming Spires and — '

'Technically, I think that's Oxf — '

'Establishment Blues.'

'Might it be possible to just go and — '

'Why are you making such heavy weather of this, Mike? It's a bloody Corridors of Power story. Bog standard. Two Bloody Cultures. Twelve hundred words by five o'clock Friday. All right?'

★   ★   ★

It was almost twelve years since I'd been there and I was not prepared for its impact on me.

I walked down from the station, past a road I'd always thought was called Tension but now revealed itself to be called Tension Avenue. Bloody silly spelling, as I think Tony Ball might have agreed.

I checked into the University Arms hotel and looked over Parker's Piece. In the middle was the lamp post on which was written 'Reality Checkpoint' — scrawled, presumably, by some tripping third-year on his way back to Emma.

We knew nothing of drugs. I wondered how many of the bright-eyed boys — their parents' treasures, the comets of their hope — were now in Fulbourn and Park Prewett, fat and trembling on the side effects of chlorpromazine: an entire life, fifty indistinguishable years, in the airless urine wards of mental institutions because one fine May morning in the high spirits and skinny health of their twentieth year they'd taken a pill they didn't understand, for fun.

I had an interview arranged with one of the Fellows of the college in question at three, but nothing before then, so I went for a walk.

What was I hoping to find? The core, the truth. In any city I've always hoped to find the essence in some square or on some street corner; then I could stop walking and searching. The Marais, the Seizième, the Bastille, Pigalle, Les Halles . . . Make up your mind, I want to say, just let one of you be It.

I walked for an hour. Garret Hostel Lane, Tennis Court Road, Free School Lane . . . One of them must hold the key. Every few yards, there were churches. Yet I'd no recollection of that. How could I have missed them all? It was early March, but cold: not sharp, eartip-frostbite cold, but grey into-the-bone sepulchral cold. Many faces I passed in Pembroke Street were crimson, raw and watery-eyed; it looked as though almost everyone was crying.

I had lunch in the Mill, at the corner table overlooking Scudamore's Boatyard, sitting on the very bench where my closeness had irritated Jennifer and Robin. I wondered what had taken

316

place between them at the 'reconvened summit' at the Free Press.

My ordered sausage and mash arrived, the single sausage coiled on top, the potato an island in a sea of gravy. It didn't matter. I wasn't even living in the present. I was pushing, with all my might, at the thin door into the past.

It was so flimsy, so transparent. Why couldn't I just go through it? Christ, how much willpower would it take? I could picture my brain cells groaning with the effort. Compared to all the things we can and do achieve, how difficult can this really be? To do what we know is possible: to be in time as it truly is — non-linear.

I saw Rob lean forward at the table, his cord Wrangler jacket riding up a little, showing two or three lower vertebrae of his thin student back. I saw Jenny's bare legs, with their sharp knees beneath a floral print skirt. I reached over and put my hand on the bench, on the same place, on the same molecules of wood that her thigh had rested on. I felt them on the skin of my hand. Please, please, let me go back . . . Dear God, is it really so much to ask?

★ ★ ★

I was on time for my interview, and the don in question, a History Fellow, was helpful. He recommended other people for me to go and see; one of them, who knew the existing Master well but had no personal interest in the matter, was in my old college.

He even telephoned this man (Lightfoot: I

317

remembered the name) to ask if I could go and see him. 'Yes, that's right. He's called Michael . . . ?'

'Watson,' I said.

'Watson, yes. About five o'clock? Yes, he says that would be ideal.'

I arrived at the college half an hour early and walked briskly past the porters' lodge. I felt like an impostor. I expected to be arrested.

I kept a lookout for anyone who might remember me. Waynflete, Woodrow. Dr Gerald Stanley. Dr Townsend (fat chance). My feet took me to the staircase where I'd first been lodged. Nothing had changed. It had the same smell of overheated concrete and lino. The students' names were painted white on black, with some of the signwriter's guideline horizontals still visible. I went up to my room, but when I got there, couldn't remember whether it had been on the first or second floor.

I felt encouraged by this, as though I was not utterly the captive of a temporal malfunction, and turned to go down. A girl in a duffel coat brushed past me and let herself into what might have been my room. Co-res. Of course. Right on.

I thought she would report me, sound her rape alarm, blind me with Mace. But she appeared not to have seen me. She didn't even register my presence.

* * *

Back in my hotel room, I got on the phone and set up some interviews. Next day, I hit the dons: I dragged the rubicund fox-hunters from their cloistered wassails, marched them at gunpoint down the corridors of Tory power and landmined the shady groves of their academe. It was Town vs Gown, all right, and, boy, was I Town.

So I told Tony Ball.

In fact, all the dons I met were dyspraxic teetotallers with beards and a variety of uncompromising regional accents, like mine. All were helpful, off the record.

By noon, the story had fallen into place. You can tell when this has happened because you stop writing. The first person you interview, you can't move the pen fast enough, because it's all new to you. Gradually, returns diminish. When your pen is still, and you can pause to help the interviewee out with the names of his own colleagues he's momentarily forgotten, you're there. The blank page is the story done.

So I set off to lunch at the Free Press, and on the way I found myself in Prospect Row, a narrow terrace. I didn't remember this street much, but something made me stop. Had Stellings lived here one year? I had a memory of a door opening and a plain girl standing in the entrance.

The past was suddenly rushing in on me in a way I found hard to fight.

I was starting to bleed.

It wasn't me going back into the past and then reliving, doing better. It was the past that had broken through and was now enacting itself exactly as before, but doing it on me in my most reluctant present.

There was a small old-fashioned grocer's shop, John Cook & Bros, with a pyramid of baked-bean tins in the windows. I found I was back not to my student days but to my childhood when England was full of such places, in every high street, grocers with slightly different specialities, this one for cooked ham, that one for dry goods. From the shop there stepped out a man in a white apron with shiny hair and — I blinked and checked, and it was true — a centre parting. He might have been Edwardian.

I moved on rapidly, abandoning the idea of going to the Free Press. I hoped to clear my mind by walking fast: Parkside, then Drummer Street and the bus station where I'd once seen off Julie when she'd been to visit me. I cut right, up Milton's Walk, and emerged in King Street.

I paused. There was famously a choice of eight pubs in King Street. I picked the nearest one and drank two large whiskies, quickly. Then another.

It was important not to become too drunk. In order to open up the past, go back, relive and do better, one needed to be relatively sober.

I walked a short way and stood at the foot of Malcolm Street, where the press photographers had been coralled into their metal cage for the start of Jen's Last Walk.

It was unchanged. I could see how the unexpected width of it where it met King Street had made an ideal base for the police.

Once more, I saw Peck talking confidentially

to his lapel, raising his hand to a distant colleague on Jesus Lane.

I saw DC Cannon, all gingery self-importance, holding his arms out to the throng to keep them back.

Little WPC Kettle in her funny hat and plump black calves was walking up to the door from which Hannah, as Jennifer, would emerge.

With my eyes shut, I saw the evening mist, I felt the Fen cold, I smelled the smoke of student No. 6.

I pressed with all my mind's imagining force against the transparent portal of time.

As I stood with my eyes closed in the afternoon, the door gave way and I was through . . .

But it wasn't that night, the night of Jen's Last Walk, the reconstruction, that came back to me.

It was a night exactly two weeks before, at exactly the same hour. For the first time since the day itself I seemed to have a clear picture of what had happened. I don't know if it was a memory of fact; but it was certainly a coherent version of events.

I had parked the Morris 1100 — where else — on Park Street, opposite the ADC theatre. Having left the party, I got in and drove quietly round the corner into Jesus Lane, pulling over near a fine Georgian or perhaps Queen Anne building on the left, at the head of Malcolm Street. I turned off the lights, killed the engine and waited.

Occasional students — alone, in chatting twos and threes — drifted up onto Jesus Lane, laughing, separating, going home. The majority went the other way, left, from the party house, down towards King Street, the greater number of colleges lying in that direction.

Eventually, I saw a blonde head behind a cloud of vaporous breath, moving smartly towards me. I fired the engine, turned on the lights. She watched and waited, to see if it was safe to cross in front of me or if I was about to move off. Unsure, she stayed on the right-hand side of Jesus Lane and headed east.

She was opposite the main gate to Jesus, alongside yet another church, when I drew level and called out across the road through my rolled-down window.

'Jennifer. It's Mike. Can I give you a lift?'

She peered over the misty street, her eyes narrowing.

'Who? Oh, Mike. Yes.'

She hesitated.

'Go on,' I said. 'It's on my way. It looks freezing out there.'

She smiled in the light of the street lamp. I knew what she was thinking. She was thinking: it would look rude to say no. I'm quite happy to walk, but it would look as though I was snubbing Mike.

Turning her head to see if there were any other cars coming, she crossed the road, went round and climbed into the passenger seat next to me.

She closed the door with a bang. The car was filled with her scent and her clothes and her hair and the visible cloud of her wine and cigarettes and the breath of her living.

'This is very kind of you, Mike. Are you sure it's not out of your way?' And her voice: contralto, as though suppressing laughter.

'No, really. I've got to drop an essay off for my supervisor in De Freville Avenue.'

'That's just round the corner from us.'

'I know. I was meant to hand it in today. I thought if I stuck it through his letter box he wouldn't know what time it'd actually got there.'

Jennifer laughed as we swung up Victoria Avenue. 'What a treat,' she said. 'A real car, with heating. I normally bicycle, but some bastard nicked my bike from outside Emma.'

'Bastard.'

'I'm getting a new one tomorrow. My dad's coughed up.'

'Brilliant.'

I couldn't believe how fast the journey had gone. I drove as slowly as I could but we were already almost there. We went past the Fort St George to the right, the boathouses to the left, onto the bridge and all too soon we were at the junction with Chesterton Road. I had her all to myself. It was the best two minutes of my life.

Then Jennifer began to search in her bag, presumably for her front-door key. Although we were not yet in her street, she obviously didn't want to linger in the car, outside her house, while she looked for it. She wanted to be ready to leap out. I found this irritating.

Then . . . And then I had no further memory — if memory is what it was.

The recollection — no, I can't call it that — the narrative, the sequence of events that had come into my mind, was all quite clear up to the point we crossed the Cam. I could play it and replay it and it never varied. I remembered every word she said, the inflection of her voice, the super-friendly relaxation with which she overlaid her slight anxiety.

But at the moment the front wheels of the 1100 were north of the water — nothing.

★ ★ ★

I opened my eyes. It was two o'clock in the afternoon on King Street; the taste of Bell's whisky was in my mouth. The present was back with me in all its inescapable banality. 'The present'. God, I hate it. It has no depth of field; no context.

I walked back to the University Arms, took the lift, forged my way through the Trust House fug, heaved back the series of sprung fire doors and went at last into my room. I took two blue ten-milligram pills and drank deep from my emergency Johnnie Walker.

What are you going to do, Mike?

Well, nothing. Obviously. Wait for the drugs to take a grip.

Then write my piece for the paper on the Tandy.

I can't go into the past. *I* can't get back there. So why would anyone else want to?

And if they managed — somehow — to get there, how would they know what was true?

It's my dearest, most passionate wish to revisit, re-experience and do better.

With every atom of my being I long to be nineteen again.

Who in the whole world, if they were given a single wish, would not choose for the dead to live? Those you have known to breathe again and you to walk among them.

Who wouldn't give all they own to be that age again, living in those days of hope but knowing what you later learned. To meet once more those bright-eyed girls and boys, to use them with the kindness of age but the vigour of nineteen.

But if I can't manage this simple manoeuvre through the dimension of time that we poor, incompletely evolved homo saps can't fathom or bend to our will, why should anyone else?

And even if they did, why should we listen to what they claimed to find?

I opened up my notebook, folded the pages over, and began to type on the plastic keyboard.

★ ★ ★

Tony Ball didn't like the piece much; he thought it was 'a bit pipe-sucking. A bit too much on-the-one-hand-on-the-other.'

Margaret liked it, though.

'You're so funny, Mike. And that piece with Jeffrey Archer was hilarious.'

'It wasn't meant to be.'

'And Ken Livingstone.'

'That was meant to be serious, too.'

Margaret gave me the look of exasperated affection that was starting to get on my nerves. You're a funny boy, but I don't mind, it seemed

325

to say: you can't fool me, because I understand you.

Anyway, I stuck the piece, along with three others, in for some more press awards, and I got another commendation, which meant another lunch, this time at the Savoy, where someone from the *Mirror* threw up at our table.

I was sufficiently pissed off by Tony Ball, though, that when I read in the *Observer* that three journalists from the *Telegraph* were starting a new daily newspaper, I rang them up and arranged to go along and see them.

To be honest, I also felt that working on the same paper as Margaret as well as living with her, some of the time, was becoming too much. I'd never chosen to be alone, but that was the way things had turned out, and I'd grown used to it.

The new paper's offices were in a modernish block in City Road, near Finsbury Square. I would have thought it impossible for an architect to have designed a building so completely lacking character or distinction. But it had an advantage: it wasn't in Wapping or the Isle of Dogs, where the other newspapers were all fleeing from the trade unions.

Three men in suits were waiting at the end of a long open-plan room on the fourth floor. They explained that they were exasperated by the criminal practices of the print workers and the incompetence of management. A fresh venture could use new (in fact pretty old, but new to England) technology to produce a high-quality paper which the journalists could effectively typeset for themselves, on screen. Press a button and — bingo, out it rolled on fresh newsprint at four or five regional centres, ready for distribution to the hungry public — readers who were tired of the Murdoch-Maxwell tat.

I could imagine Terry's indignation. No on-site printing? No hot metal? No back-alley vans? You're'aving a laugh, Mick. Next thing you'll be telling me we've sold Tony Cottee . . .

The three men told me how they'd blagged millions from banks and pension funds to get the paper under starter's orders. Then they told me all the distinguished journalists who'd agreed to write for it. I'd heard of some of them.

'Who's going to be your features editor?' I asked.

They hadn't got one yet.

'What's the paper going to be called?'

They didn't know, but possibly. *The Nation*.

'Who's going to be the editor?' I asked.

'I am,' said the oldest of the three. He'd previously edited the *Investors Chronicle*. 'And what do you think you could offer us?'

'What I do now, I suppose. What other feature writers have you hired?'

'None yet,' said one of the younger two, a solemn, dark-haired man of about my age. He looked like an archdeacon after lunch; in fact, he looked as though he was struggling to stay awake. Despite having it written down in front of him, he couldn't get the hang of my name and ended up triple-barrelling me: 'Mr Ingle-Engle-Anglebury.' This wasn't promising.

'We may not have feature writers as such. All

327

our reporters and specialists will contribute to the features pages.' This was the third man, a zippier proposition with an explosive vocal style and narrowed eyes.

It was a bloody odd triumvirate. They seemed to have nothing in common with one another, for a start. Also, no one had heard of any of them — except maybe the older one, a little, if you read the City pages. Having tried once, I never did. The articles weren't real journalism, they read as though the reporter had gone along for lunch then taken dictation from the company's PR office.

I couldn't imagine anyone with a proper job on an existing newspaper throwing it in to take a chance with these jokers, unless . . .

'How much are you paying?' I said.

'We recognise we have to pay at the top end of the market, or above,' said the boss. 'How much are you paid at the moment?'

I was so surprised by the question that I told him.

'We could do better,' he said. 'To give you an idea, the head of a small department would get thirty-five thousand and a car.'

Well, I don't know. There hadn't been a newspaper started from scratch for more than sixty years, and the financial, technical and talent problems were surely insurmountable. But I was tickled, I admit, by the Three Stooges — by their posh voices and expensive grey suits; by the money they'd already raised and by the way they seemed to be making it up as they went along — trying to convince themselves as much as me that what they were saying was more than make-believe.

What it came down to was this. The old 'can't do' sub-Soviet Britain, where you waited three weeks to get your phone mended, was dead. That was their belief and their proposition. The country had changed, and the change was somehow connected to people like Plank Robinson grossing half a mill. From now on: forget early closing, go-slows, strikes and demarcation — you can do what you want. We've become America. Enjoy!

We left it that I'd write a job description for myself, along with an analysis of how the other dailies handled features and how a new paper could do better. Then I'd send it to them, with a note on what I wanted to be paid and so on.

On the way down, in the lift, I met a bearded man with large blue-rimmed glasses who told me he'd be working on the listings pages — the 'what's on' bit they planned for the back. If I came to work at the new paper, he said, I should perhaps come and stay the weekend with him in Suffolk. He and his wife had lots of guests and they were very 'easy-going'. Blimey. I couldn't wait to get through the swing doors and onto City Road again.

I never got round to sending in my application. The listings bloke had put me off. Also, the more I thought about it, the more ridiculous the whole thing seemed. I didn't give it better than one chance in ten of getting through to launch.

Word got out, though, that I'd been to see

them. I was called in by the managing editor of my rag, a ravaged trembly old hack called David Terry, known as DT's, who raised my pay to £32,000 and gave me sole use of a Peugeot 405.

It was the first car I'd had since the 1100 had finally conked out, so my trip to City Road hadn't been wasted.

★ ★ ★

It's General-Election time again. Midsummer Folly has taken the country in a gentle grip, and Tony Ball has sent me on the road. I had a day with Bryan Gould and Peter Mandelson, the Labour campaign organisers, who spent most of the time trying to neutralise wild remarks made to the press by Ken Livingstone. Now that Ken's an MP he seems to feel licensed to foul the nest at will and even the hardest heart (mine) grew weary of laughing at Bryan and Peter's anguish. 'Oh God. What now?' Peter would say to Bryan as the hotline rang once more. They were good to me, though, P and B, and let me into all their meetings.

'What are you going to do if you lose?' I asked Gould.

'Go into the country and find out what people want, then develop our policies to meet their aspirations,' he said.

I'd never thought of politics like that. I thought you stood for what you believed — and if the voters didn't like it, then tough luck. But I could see the attraction of doing it the other way round: like looking at the football league and seeing who was most likely to win, then becoming their supporter.

I don't really understand British politics, I must say. It's a bit silly for me to be writing about it. You'd have thought that nowadays most people would want some sort of market economy to get the motor turning vigorously, then buckets of free health care from the resulting tax take. Not so. Anyone who prescribes *that* mixture is viewed as pathetic, 'not having any policies' and not really being part of our island history. No. As of May 1987, a true Brit wants either a) socialism with as few deviations as possible from a command economy (Kinnock); or b) a Malthusian free-for-all, in which survival of the fittest takes on a quasi-moral dimension (Thatcher).

What a very odd people we are. Do you think we've read a book between us? Looked abroad? Learned anything at all? You have to wonder.

Off I go on the 'Battle Bus' with Mr Steel and Dr Owen. To general derision, they preach a middle way. They're considered to have ducked the question. Another problem is that they don't convince as a twosome. It's a *mariage blanc*. There's no heat, just a winsome cordiality. (Bet they have separate bedrooms.) Back home, Steel stays up drinking cider with the beardies; Owen's on the phone to orotund Roy Jenkins — who I think is going to lose his seat and concentrate on building up his stocks of Pomerol.

The other day I was with Margaret Thatcher. She's a rum one. I think she may be a natural scientist, like me. Or did she read Chemistry?

331

Actually, that would explain it.

To prepare myself, to fill in the background, I had lunch with a man called Alan Clark, whom I'd rung a couple of times for his opinion of other politicians I was writing 'profiles' of. Most of it was unprintable, but I'd used the odd 'quote', always off the record. So for instance, in my article on an incoming minister, it might go: 'For all his high reputation as an organiser in Whitehall, the new Minister for X is not without his critics. As one colleague put it: 'He's a pushy little Israelite who had to go out and buy the family silver.' '

Mr Clark had accepted my invitation to a swanky French restaurant near the Opera House in Covent Garden.

'What's so great about Mrs Thatcher?' I said. 'Is she very clever or what?'

'Not particularly, no. She intimidates people.'

'Who?'

'Howe, Baker, Channon. Fe-owler.' He pronounced the name in imitation of the way the man himself said it.

'What about you?'

'What about me?'

'Are you frightened of her?'

'I don't like this food. Waiter. Take this away.'

'Monsieur does not like the sea bass?'

'No. It died in the water.'

'Would Monsieur like something else to — '

'No. Just take it away, will you.' He lifted the plate up and thrust it at the waiter.

'I'm sorry about that,' I said. 'This restaurant's supposed to be — '

'Do you honestly like French food?' said Clark.

'No, not at all. But I thought you would.'

'I like it in France. Not this chi-chi nonsense.'

I breathed in deeply. I wanted to go to the toilet. 'Mrs Thatcher, then. Do you . . . Do you like her?'

'*Like* her? Christ.' He probed at an interdental cavity with a restaurant toothpick. Then his face relaxed a little. 'She has a certain provincial sexuality, I suppose. Women of her type often do — from that Nonconformist background. Sex for them is a way to bettering themselves, certainly not a pleasure. Yet there's something . . . Something there, and she seems to know it.'

'But are you frightened of her?'

'Yes, I suppose I am.'

'Though you're cleverer than she is.'

'God, yes. It's hard to explain. She has a peculiar force.'

'Who else is any good in your party? Geoffrey Howe?'

'Howe? Christ, no. I'd let him tie up the codicil to my auntie's will in Swansea, that's about all.'

So it went on ('Wykehamist arse-licker', 'poor man's Enoch', 'tub of kosher lard' and so on), but by allowing him to choose the wine, I managed to stretch out our meeting to the respectable time of two-fifteen before he rose abruptly from the table and strode off down Bow Street.

I waited for my first sight of Mrs Thatcher in the flesh with several other journalists on a

Midlands factory floor. I honestly forget what it produced. Pins and needles, pottery, brake linings. Something that entailed a fair amount of clanking, anyway.

I've always liked factories. The paper mill held no fears for me.

Factories are good for friendship. One of the hardest things about being alive is being with other people.

Take Alan Clark. His face was deeply lined, but his hair, while greying, was thick, like a young man's. And his suit, though presumably expensive (I can't judge these things; I'm not a clothes man) was . . . Well, there was too much flannel and pinstripe, just too much *suiting*. And I didn't want to see his teeth and his uvula. And his hand with the hairs on the back of the fingers wrapping round the glass . . . He was physically over-present. His molecules extended too far.

In factories, all being well, you don't hear that much. To be heard, people have to call out. You're alone, but it's companionable. I like the floors of factories, the pocked cement slab with pools of oil and small puddles of water; I like the stained tea mugs and the low grade paper towels. I like the way it's all stripped back, undecorated and it doesn't matter if you make a mess.

I don't suppose many of the journalists there that day had ever worked in a factory. They didn't know, like me, the secrets of the brew-room and the toilet break and stores where Fat Teddy used to have a twice-weekly knee-trembler with Mrs Beasley from the back office. Through a side window on the factory floor, you could see her emerge from the stores, all flushed, smoothing down her skirt, checking things off on her clipboard in a pathetic dumbshow of normality.

Mrs Thatcher's entourage consisted of about a dozen men in dark suits with carnations, blue rosettes or both. They talked to one another behind their hands as they waited; perhaps they were checking for halitosis or remarking on each other's ties. Should they all have gone for yes-man's Tory blue, or did a splash of daffodil show greater self-confidence? They stifled laughter. Each time one of them gave way, he immediately coughed and straightened up: his tie, his face, his spine. Even the older ones made repeated attempts at looking more dignified as they waited; then a whisper would start, and a giggle passed through them, making them look like ushers at a gay wedding.

From the machine room, the procession entered. There was a factory foreman in a brown coat, a couple of pinstriped youths and the sixty-year-old local MP — the undersecretary for postal orders or similar, who looked grey, shattered, as though he hadn't slept for weeks, padding in on rubber-soled shoes, gesturing and talking to his leader.

She herself wore a check woollen suit and moved with a purposeful bustle from the hips, head slightly to one side — the combination of forward momentum and strained patience that had struck fear into the chancelleries of Europe and the barracks of Buenos Aires.

Standing well apart from the others, she

335

addressed the gathered press about the qualities of the local candidate, the postal-order chap. Then she moved on to Europe and the economy and her desire for low taxes. When she spoke of the Labour Party, her voice hit a different frequency. It stopped modulating like normal speech and seemed to lock on to some short wavelength, perhaps favourable to dogs but hard on the human otic nerve. It was bad luck that she stood beneath a sign that said 'Ear defenders must be worn'.

When she'd finished her address, the supporters applauded showily, and it seemed surly of the press to keep their hands in their pockets, as their tradition of impartiality required.

Some of the local hacks then asked her trick questions about the town's hospital and schools and so on, but she swatted them in the direction of the MP, whom she once more endorsed. She said he was sure to win. Or else, you felt.

I managed a few moments alone with her later on.

'And this is Michael Watson,' said the grinning young minder, pointing me towards the Prime Minister, who was sitting on a sofa with her knees together in the office of the factory manager.

I sat down on a hard chair opposite.

'Do you read a lot of books?' I said.

Her eyes shot up to the minder. Her hair was like fine wire wool at the front, lacquered, though thin. There was a trace of orange in the colouring that I hadn't expected.

She smiled slightly and inhaled, tilting her

head again fractionally, like a cardinal who had decided, on balance, to grant an indulgence to a pilgrim. In private, her voice was gentle and low, an excellent thing in woman.

'I like to read biographies. I recently read one of Disraeli. One doesn't have as much time to read as one would like.'

'Do you believe in God?'

'We are a Christian family. We go to church.'

'Can you forgive the IRA men who tried to kill you in Brighton?'

'It's our job as the Government to help the police to bring the terrorists to justice.'

'Would you like to see them hanged?'

'There is no capital punishment in this country, as you know.'

'But for terrorists?'

She didn't answer, she merely looked at me, her blue eyes filled with pity and menace. I saw what Mr Clark had meant.

'When you closed the pits in South Yorkshire, might you not have helped the miners to find new work?'

' 'Helped'? 'Helped'? What do you mean?'

'By putting money into starting new projects or — '

'Whose money?'

'Money from the relevant department. The Department of Trade and — '

'That money would have come from the taxpayer. From you and me. It's not the role of government to start up businesses. It's our job to create a climate in which people can do that for themselves.'

'Talking of money, are you personally well off? How much money do you have?'

'Do you have any more questions about politics?' said the minder.

I thought for a moment. 'Not really. Yes. All right. Who do you think will win the election?'

'We shall of course!' The sun came out on Mrs Thatcher's face again. 'The Conservative Party. People trust us and know that we have done a marvellous job for Britain.' She had a slight wobble in the middle of the 'r': Brwritain. 'Though there is work still to do. In those inner cities, for instance, where we — '

'Sure, but . . . '

'What?' The face was plump and powdered, like a rich aunt's, but the nose was sharp. I could see the tiny blood vessels inside her nostrils.

'Sorry.' I'd lost my place for a moment. 'Yes. I know what I wanted to ask. When you look back at the riots in Brixton and Liverpool and places, the miners' strike and the Falklands War, the rate of unemployment and so on, I wonder if you had any regrets, if you would — '

'Of course not. Britain is a far stronger country, far better equipped to face the future than when we came to power in 1979. Inflation is at a quarter of what it was, our competitiveness has — '

'But surely you must have some regrets. It's only human to — '

'Let me tell you something . . . Michael,' said Mrs Thatcher, leaning forward so that her face was closer to mine. 'Let me give you a piece of advice. 'Too much looking back is a weariness to

338

the soul.'' She wagged her finger. 'It was St Francis who said that. If you want to make something of your life, you must keep your eyes on the horizon. Never be deflected. Don't look down, or you may stumble. Above all, don't look back.'

'Like Orpheus, you mean.'

She didn't answer, but she smiled in my direction and nodded graciously as the minder showed me to the door.

★ ★ ★

When I read through my notebook later, there wasn't much I could use. My article was thus made up chiefly of a description of the factory visit and of her entourage; for quotation I used some of the answers she'd given in public.

But in private, over the weeks and months, I did occasionally think about what Mrs Thatcher'd said to me.

I thought about it particularly when I was at an old church in Muswell Hill watching an amateur production of The Birthday Party by Harold Pinter. Margaret (Hudson, not Thatcher) was keen to go because a friend of hers had helped design the sets. I'm not interested in the theatre because I can't deal with the level of nonreality it offers, but with Pinter it's all right because he's not pretending to be realistic. It couldn't matter less whether you 'believe' in it or not.

I'd seen the play before, of course, in an undergraduate production. For students, it's right up there with *The Good Person* and *The Crucible*; it's nasty, brutish and not overlong. Posturing potential: limitless.

The other good thing about an old church is that it's not, like a West End theatre, heated to sauna point. You don't have to clap when the star comes on. You don't have to gasp if someone uses the word 'bloody'. You can stretch your legs and have a drink beside your seat; you can enjoy it.

And so I did. To begin with, at least. I'd forgotten how funny it was, the low-rent exchanges in the boarding house — like Steptoe or Hancock. And the way they can't get over the fact that two strangers actually want to come and *board* in their dingy house. I'd also forgotten how early the landlord flags up the fact that he's met these two men.

When Goldberg and McCann appeared, I presumed that whatever Stanley was meant to have done wrong had been invented by them. They were thugs, bad guys, so Stanley had to be OK. Anyway, how wicked could a failed pianist have been? Then there came a moment when I felt, with a lurch, that even if Goldberg and McCann are genuine villains, which they are, Stanley might still be guilty of something forgotten. That was not good.

It's impossible to deal with a world in which the polarities aren't mutually opposite.

When they turned the lights off to play blind man's buff, I had to leave the church hall. I stumbled down the row of chairs, kicking over drinks and ran to the back of the hall.

Outside, I kept running, across to the main road, where the lorries were thundering down towards Archway. I thought of throwing myself beneath one.

It was like the attack I'd had in Basingstoke. I didn't know what the hell was happening. But I crunched two blue pills in my dry mouth and got into a pub where I poured vodka down me.

It occurred to me as I stood there, waiting for the effect, that at such moments of extreme panic and anguish you do manage that trick with time: you are at last free from the illusion that time is linear.

In panic, time stops: past, present and future exist as a single overwhelming force. You then, perversely, *want* time to appear to run forwards because the 'future' is the only place you can see an escape from this intolerable overload of feeling. But at such moments time doesn't move. And if time isn't running, then all events that we think of as past or future are actually happening simultaneously. That is the really terrifying thing. And you are subsumed. You're buried, as beneath an avalanche, by the weight of simultaneous events.

★   ★   ★

I have no memory of what happened then. The next thing I can recall with any clarity is the following day, being in Margaret's flat.

I was in bed and the alarm clock showed a time of ten past twelve. I was wearing only my underclothes. I put on a dressing gown and went

341

to the bathroom, then through to the living room, where Margaret was reading the paper.

She looked up and smiled. 'Are you all right, love?'

I rubbed my head. 'Yes, I'm fine. What happened?'

'What happened? You tell me! One minute we're watching the play, the next thing I know you've run out and disappeared.'

'Yeah, I know, I remember that, but I don't know what happened next. I think I went to a pub. What did you do when I ran out?'

'Well, nothing. I thought maybe you'd just gone to the toilet or something. The speed you went, I thought maybe you were going to be sick.'

'So what did you do?'

'I left you to it. I thought if you were being sick you didn't want me fussing over you. Plus I didn't want to disturb the other people, or the actors. It was quite a small place and you'd already made an almighty racket going out.'

'I see.'

'Anyway, after about ten minutes, there was a short break and I crept out to see if you were all right. I expected to find you sitting in the churchyard, but you weren't there. I decided to have a look in the street, but you weren't there either.'

'Were you worried?'

'A bit, but not really. You're a big boy, Mike. I knew you could find your own way home. To be honest I was just a bit cross that you hadn't let me know.'

'Know what?'

'What you were doing. I mean, you might have said something, or left a note for me — to say you were going straight home, or whatever it was you were doing.'

'Yes.'

'So, anyway, what were you doing?'

'I don't know. I felt . . . I felt ill in the play. I went out and then I went to a pub. But I don't know what happened after that. What time did I get in?'

'Not very late. About twelve. The play finished at ten, I had a drink with Carol and Tom. I was back here soon after eleven and I'd just fallen asleep when you got in. You seemed a bit the worse for wear.'

'What? Drunk?'

'Yes. And your hand was bleeding. You seemed . . . Woozy.'

'How had I got back from Muswell Hill?'

'I suppose you took a cab. You didn't say.'

'I didn't say?'

'No.'

'But it must have been nearly three hours since I left the play. Didn't you want to know?'

'Yes, but you weren't very chatty. You went to the bathroom then just crashed on the bed. I helped you take your clothes off and you were asleep inside a minute.'

The timings all made sense. The narcotic effect of the blue pills and the alcohol must have taken hold eventually. But as to what I had been doing between, say, nine-fifteen, when I felt subsumed by panic, and, say, eleven-thirty when I had found a taxi, I hadn't the smallest idea.

★ ★ ★

I was in the Peugeot 405, on the M4, on my way
to Wales, listening to *The World at One* on
Radio 4. I suppose I was somewhere near
Hungerford and I was calculating whether I had
time to leave the motorway and find a pub with
reasonable food, or whether I should try and
hold down whatever Membury Services had to
offer.

On long drives I usually talk to myself and try
to sort things out. I rehearse what I'm going to
say to Margaret or to old DT's, when I go to ask
for a rise; or to the people at the *Independent* (in
the end they opted for that name over the
Nation) when I submit my tardy job application.
Sometimes I make a short political speech or
argue the case for re-evaluating Emerson, Lake
& Palmer's *Tarkus*. What I'm trying to say is that
although I have the radio or the cassette player
on, I don't listen carefully. I'm in my own world.

So it was with some difficulty that I tried to
rewind mentally and remember what I'd not
been listening to. The first words to penetrate my
private thoughts were these:

' . . . reports that police in East Anglia have
discovered the body of a young woman.'

Perhaps there weren't any important words
before that for me to have missed.

At any rate, my car swerved, the lorry behind
blasted me with his horn, I straightened up,
regained the centre of the middle lane, switched
to the inside, after indicating, and turned up the
volume on the radio.

344

'Yes, Brian, that's right. The police are expecting to hold a televised press conference at five o'clock this afternoon in which they'll be giving details of their discovery. At this stage they won't confirm or deny that the body is that of the student Jennifer Arkland, who disappeared in 1974. Her disappearance caused a great public outcry at the time.'

'Can you tell us any more at this juncture, Sally?'

'Not a great deal. I understand the discovery was initially made by a man walking his dog yesterday evening, near the village of Rampton. The police are unwilling to give any more details at the moment, though the secrecy with which they've surrounded it does suggest that they have a major announcement to make.'

'What would the identification process consist of?'

'Well it depends of course on how long the person has been dead. But if it really is Jennifer Arkland and she died at the time of her disappearance, then they are probably looking at dental records.'

'And that would be straightforward?'

'As I understand it. Yes, Brain.'

'And have her parents made any comment?'

'Well, her father died some years ago and her mother is unavailable at the moment.'

'Thank you, Sally. You can hear more about that story on the *P.M.* programme at five.'

★   ★   ★

345

I pulled off the motorway at Membury Services and followed the signs into the car park, where I pulled up and turned off the engine.

I didn't quite know what to do. I felt drained of energy. I leaned forward and rested my head on the steering wheel. Poor Jen. So she really was dead.

The sensation of immense fatigue climbed slowly through me, from the foot well, through the seat and up into my shoulders. I felt as though I might never move again.

10

I was in a hotel room in Cardiff at five o'clock. I had both the radio and the television on.

The press conference was about to start. There was a long table with a white floor-length cloth and blue screens behind it, on the central one of which was the coat of arms of the local constabulary, slightly skew-whiff. There were five seats with name cards in front of them, illegible at this distance, jugs of water, a bouquet of microphones pointing at the central chair and a single one in front of all the others. The orange, blue and black electrical leads trailed off the front of the trestle. Various technicians and town-hall clerks came in and adjusted seats, straightened mikes and disappeared again. The television camera briefly turned to show the rows of assembled journalists on foldaway council chairs. Bright overhead lights and spots were creating a circus atmosphere. The journalists chatted excitedly.

I thought of the child Jennifer in her first year, in a college scarf.

The TV reporter was beginning to struggle with the delay. There were only so many ways he could say that he didn't know what to expect. We were taken briefly back to the studio.

I stood up and poured some whisky. I went to the bathroom for water, and looked at myself in the mirror as I ran the cold tap.

347

The face that looked back was nearly 35 years old. My hair was receding on either side and had vanished from the crown of my head. My student days had been in another life. My current life was fine.

I sat down in the armchair and waited. There was a rustle and a sense that it was all finally happening. Figures emerged from behind the screens and took their places. They seemed burly and diffident as they clambered through the cables, trying not to trip up on the gathered tablecloth. The men stood back to allow a woman in plain clothes to pass in front of them, which created further awkwardness as each searched for the correct place, twisting the name cards round to check.

Eventually, they were settled. The central figure, a grey-haired policeman with silver braiding and a chestful of medals, leaned into the microphones and spoke. A caption identified him as Deputy Chief Constable Adrian Bolton, OBE.

'Ladies and gentlemen, first of all, thank you for coming along this afternoon, and thank you for your patience.'

He then introduced his colleagues: a ruddy superintendent; the bobby who'd been first on the scene; a female pathologist called Hedgecoe; and, finally, the third of the cops who was none other than DC — now Chief Inspector — Cannon: baldish, but still gingery, still pent-up and smirking.

'Let me come straight to the point,' said Bolton. 'At approximately five o'clock on Sunday afternoon a member of the public walking his dog near the village of Rampton discovered what appeared to be human remains. They were in a ditch, between the railway line and a watercourse at the edge of an area known as Westwick Field. This is open country, not close to any habitation. At the north side of the area is the end of Cuckoo Lane, an unmade road that leads into Rampton, and on the south side is the Oakington Road, though no lane or path leads up from it. It thus took some time for us to get the personnel and the equipment we needed to the site, which we approached from the Rampton end.'

I wondered how much more Fen geography this Bolton was intending to give. He was certainly in no hurry. He spoke with grave emphasis, enjoying his moment beneath the lights, unable to keep a tremor of self-congratulation from his voice.

'The body appeared to have been carefully buried, and covered not only with earth but also with pieces of concrete which were further weighed down with an old railway sleeper. Presumably this was in order to prevent the body being discovered or unearthed by wildlife or by dogs. Preliminary inspection established that it was the body of a young female, approximately twenty years of age. It was removed from the site on Monday evening and taken to a police laboratory. Tests carried out in the course of Tuesday and Wednesday established that the cause of death appears to have been a blow or blows to the skull which caused a fracture of the cranium and — presumably — internal head injuries. One of the legs was also broken. The extent of the decomposition of the body means that it is impossible to discover what further injuries, if any, to the soft tissues may have contributed to the death of the individual.

'I am not proposing at the moment to give further details about the young woman's body and this is for reasons of consideration for her family, and I know you will understand that.'

Bolton paused hammily and poured himself a glass of water. There was utter silence in the room and in the broadcast.

He coughed and resumed. 'I am further able to tell you that tests carried out yesterday evening and comparisons with existing dental records enable us to announce that the young woman has been identified as Jennifer Arkland, a 21-year-old student from Lymington in Hampshire, who went missing in February, 1974.

'I can further confirm that we will be pursuing our inquiries into this case with the utmost urgency. The case has never been closed, though it has been reclassified from one of 'Missing' to one of 'Murder' as of today. We have been in touch with the deceased's family, and I understand that it is her mother's intention to make a statement in the near future. In the meantime, I would ask all of you to respect their privacy at what must be a very difficult time for them.

'I would like to end by congratulating my colleagues on the extremely swift and professional way that they reacted to this discovery. I know that this exceedingly sad case of a young person disappearing on the threshold of adult life was not only the cause of much public sympathy at the time, but also has long been something that my colleagues were determined to bring to a satisfactory conclusion one day. I know that Chief Inspector Cannon is one of many officers who consider the pride and reputation of their force to depend on a successful outcome to this case and I want to stress that I have every confidence in them.

'If you have any questions you would like to ask me or my colleagues, then this is the moment. We have a time limit of fifteen minutes here, so I'm afraid you can ask only one question each. The gentleman in the blue blazer will bring the microphone to you and I'd be grateful if you could wait for him to reach you before you begin your question. Yes. We'll start with you. The gentleman in the front with the grey anorak.'

'Have you been able to date the time of death? I mean, how soon was it after she disappeared?'

Bolton nodded to the pathologist, Hedgecoe. 'We can't be certain,' she said. 'But soon afterwards. Certainly within months, I should say.'

'So it's possible she was alive for some time?'

'On the scientific evidence, yes.'

'But on the circumstantial evidence,' said Bolton, 'it seems unlikely.'

'Have you completely ruled out natural causes?'

'Yes,' said Hedgecoe. 'In our view it's

351

impossible for the head injury to have been accidental.'

'There's also the question of the interment,' said Bolton. 'Unless you're suggesting that she died in an accident and then someone buried her. Which would anyway be a serious crime.'

'Can I ask Chief Inspector Cannon if he'll be re-interviewing old suspects or starting from fresh. Is he in charge and what's his line of inquiry going to be?'

'I think that's four questions,' said Bolton.

Cannon leant forward eagerly. 'First of all, I'd like to stress that this file has never been closed. So all our records are up to date and accessible. It's not a question of 'reopening' anything, merely of continuing with an ongoing inquiry.'

'Does the discovery of the body give you new forensic evidence?'

'You mean scientific evidence?'

'Yes.'

'It's possible. It's too early to say.'

'Do the recent techniques used in clearing the suspect in the double murder in Narborough in Leicestershire — the so-called DNA testing — have any bearing on — '

I fired the 'Off' button on the remote control and the screen flashed away into darkness.

★ ★ ★

Over the next few days, the national papers disinterred, as it were, the whole story and printed many heart-stopping pictures of Jennifer. There were at least three interviews with

Anne, now head of a neighbourhood law centre in south London, and two with Molly, a GP in Staffordshire with plump twin girls — though none with the unfortunate Robin Wilson who, although he presumably long ago dispensed with the National Health psychiatric services, lives 'quietly' somewhere in Wales, where he teaches at the local college. There was also a 'quote' from Malini Coomaretcetera, a New York paediatric consultant; from Stewart Forres ('director of the edgy 1982 cult British film *Sheet Lightning*') and from his 'ex-wife Hannah Waters, who played Jennifer in the police reconstruction of her last night alive and is currently with the Bristol Old Vic theatre company'.

That 'ex' shook me up a bit. How fast other people had moved onward in their lives. I hadn't been to see the Forres film because the word 'edgy' put me off. It's code for 'the men all swear a lot'. ('Feisty' means the women all swear a lot.) I hardly ever swear myself and find it irritating. Perhaps I was also jealous of Stewart.

Eventually, I stopped reading the coverage. I couldn't stand another article about 1970s fashions, Abba or tank tops. This kind of decade-drivel used to be the territory of *Chick's Own* or *Bunty* but has now run through whole sections of once-serious newspapers.

On the following Monday I was telephoned by Tony Ball at home, and this was unusual, in fact unprecedented. He was ringing to suggest I do a big 'background' piece on Jennifer for the following Sunday.

'But you didn't like the thing I did about the new Master.'

'This is different, though. It's more your line of country. I remember that great piece you did on the Ripper. All that footwork in Bradford.'

'This isn't a serial killer, Tony.'

'How do we know?'

'Because there aren't any other bodies.'

'Could be linked to other unsolved crimes. Just that they haven't made the connection yet.'

'It looks like a straightforward domestic. It's bound to have been the boyfriend.'

I talked my way out of it, and for a time all went quiet. Ball still had no idea I'd been to the same university, let alone that I'd known Jen; and I certainly wasn't going to tell him now.

★　★　★

Then, a little over a week after Jen's body was discovered, Mrs Arkland made a statement for the television cameras. She read it in a comfortable-looking lounge, dimly lit by a couple of table lamps in front of drawn curtains. She had grown plumper over the years and her hair was grey.

You could still see in her face the happy housewife who had sent her eldest daughter off to university before turning her attention back to the three still at home, but her eyes were glaucous and bulky with pain.

'My eldest daughter Jennifer would have been thirty-five,' she said in a pitiless, accusing voice. 'No day has passed since her disappearance without my first thought on waking being of her. Not a single day. I have felt her presence in everything I have done. I have heard her voice in all my thoughts. I have taken her back inside myself.'

She looked down at her paper through the bottom of her bifocals. 'My husband died some years ago. He never recovered from the shock of losing Jennifer, from the agony of not knowing where she was. I thank God he did not live to see this dreadful day and to know the worst. My other daughters have suffered too. They have lost a sister and a father and I have not been the mother to them that I should have been.'

She looked down again and breathed in deeply. It was difficult to watch. I pictured people all over the country crying.

'I shall not be giving any interviews to the press or making any further comment. I ask all of you to leave me and my family alone. You will get nothing from us.

'We shall shortly be able to give Jennifer the funeral that has for so long been denied her. It will be a private ceremony at a private location. So we will bring this terrible story to a close. That much at least is a relief for us, and I would like to thank the police for their help and understanding both at the time of Jennifer's disappearance and over the last ten days.'

It seemed as though she could hardly bear the weight of her own head. Although she read from a prepared script, her voice didn't run smoothly; it seemed to have silted up with age, with the gravel of her fourteen years' wait.

355

'I would like finally to appeal to anyone who may know anything that might help us bring to justice the person or people who killed my daughter. I ask this not for revenge. It's too late for that. But I hope that any parent listening will understand why it is important that whoever was responsible for this terrible deed should be apprehended. If only so that no other family may suffer what we have been through.'

She took off her glasses and stared into the camera. 'I never stopped hoping. I never, ever gave up hope that one day Jennifer would walk up the drive, alive and well, with some explanation of where she'd been. Now I have finally despaired. I know that now we can be reunited only at my death. Good night.'

★ ★ ★

For several days I didn't see anyone, even Margaret.

I felt that my life was on two paths. There was the one I knew about and understood: Margaret, the paper, Charlotte and her friends, work, people, drinks and all the stuff of living in London — Saturday afternoon, the football crowds on their way to Highbury, the kettle on, a film in the evening, Chinese dinner, having enough money. All this had grown slowly better. I'd become more adept at being with other people; I'd lowered my expectations of them and learned to let my mind drift into neutral when they spoke. That sense of happiness just out beyond my reach — I'm not sure I'd grasped that exactly, but I'd got something close to it, contentment maybe, or at least a functioning routine with regular rewards.

But then there was the second path or strand, which I didn't understand at all, and I felt this was principally because I couldn't remember parts of it. Here I was with a memory that others assured me was freakish in its recall of facts and dates and long passages of writing; yet actions and events in my own past that really should have been able to remember themselves without prompting from even a workaday, let alone a Rolls-Royce, memory — they weren't there. They were not only unstored, unregistered, not indexed; it was as if these things had never happened.

So perhaps they hadn't.

About two weeks after the police press conference, on a Sunday afternoon, I began to feel uneasy.

Then I started to have symptoms of panic, such as I had had in the course of *The Birthday Party*. I paced up and down my Bayswater flat. I put some music on, then took it off again.

I felt that events which should have been attached to given dates — however artificial and downright wrong it was to think of time in that way — had shaken themselves loose and were happening again, as for the first time. What we childishly called 'the past' was somehow present. And, as at that moment when I had run outside the old church, everything seemed to be happening at once — now.

I did what I always did: took pills and alcohol

357

and tried to hold on. I went to sit on the bed, wrapping my arms tight round my ribs.

I'd had lunch at the Mill. I did know that. That much was sure. I went in there on my way back from the Sidgwick Site, where I'd been to a history lecture on Garibaldi and the unification of Italy. The lecturer was a woman called Dr Elizabeth Stich. I generally preferred the Anchor for its views and thought the Mill overrated, but for some reason, perhaps just for a change, I went in and sat at a table. I had a pint of bitter and ordered from the 'baked potato with various fillings' part of the menu. Probably with cheese. Good value. Jennifer was at the adjacent table with Robin Wilson. He leant forward to talk to her; they were having a conversation of the kind known as 'heavy' and didn't want others to hear. I noticed his jacket and tee shirt ride up at the back. Jennifer sat back against the wooden settle in a slightly defensive posture; she wore a floral print skirt. I could see her bare legs. She had a sharp patella that gave a fetching inverted-triangle shape to the knee. She was smoking a cigarette and trying not to laugh, but her eyes looked concerned and vulnerable as Robin's low voice went urgently on.

I have that picture of her with utter clarity. They talk of memories being 'etched' in the mind and you think of acid on a steel plate. That's how fixed that image is for me. Yet it's more living than the etching metaphor suggests. There's blood and breath and movement and fleeting colour. She is alive, God damn it, she is alive. She looks so poised, with that womanly concern beginning to override the girlish humour. I will always remember that balanced, beautiful woman/girl expression in her face. She was twenty-one.

They left. She was so absorbed by what Robin was saying that she forgot to say goodbye either to me or to her friend Malini who was at the other end of the room. She went through the door, hoisting her brown leather shoulder bag up, the hem of the skirt fluttering for a second as she tripped down the step onto the cobbles. I went outside and stood for a moment opposite the end of Laundress Lane.

I had drunk three pints of beer by now and had taken a blue pill, but I didn't feel good. I felt angry. I began to walk up the grey passage of Mill Lane with its high buildings. I felt trapped in a world that I couldn't mould to my own desires. Others were in sunlight; I was in darkness.

I kept walking north up Pembroke, then Downing Street, past the Museum of Archaeology and Anthropology, which made me wonder yet again at the nature of the anthropoid *Homo sapiens*, this functional ape with the curse of consciousness — that useless gift that allows him, unlike other animals, to be aware of his own futility. The story of Adam and Eve put it with childish but brilliant clarity: Paradise until the moment of self-awareness and then . . . Cursed. For ever cursed. (Christians called it 'fallen', but it was the same thing: the Fall was the acquisition of consciousness.) As I walked past Downing Place, I remembered reading, on Dr

Woodrow's recommendation, I think, Miguel de Unamuno, the Catholic philosopher from Spain, and finding the same thought there: 'Man, because he is a man, because he possesses consciousness, is already, in comparison to the jackass or the crab, a sick animal. Consciousness is a disease.'

Then in the wider light of St Andrew's Street, I saw Jennifer, arriving from the west, pushing her bike up on the pavement and sticking its front wheel through the railings outside Emmanuel. I stopped and watched her go in. I decided to steal her bicycle because if she was on foot she would be less independent.

I looked down at the menu in the window of Varsity, the Greek restaurant: dolmades, kleftiko, moussaka, the usual stuff, keenly priced for students. When I was sure she would have crossed the front court and be well out of sight I went over and pulled the bike out. She hadn't locked it, the silly girl. She was trusting like that. I rode it quickly away towards the station, then doubled round and took it back to the sheds at my own college. I put it in the furthest corner, in an unnumbered rack. Where better to hide a bicycle?

This much I remembered.

Then . . . Then . . .

Malcolm Street wasn't a street you went to very often, since it was merely a cut between King Street and Jesus Lane, two other places you had no reason to go. In fact, when I heard Jen mention its name to someone after a lecture, I had to look it up in the map on the front of my Heffer's diary. Then I went to inspect. It was a street which appeared to be subject to various planning restrictions because all the houses were painted the same colour. They were of that Georgian design much admired by conservationists, though despite their value they were subdivided and let to students; you could tell by the many bells and entryphones.

Jen had mentioned a house number and the name of the people whose party it was. It was only two days after I'd taken her bike and I doubted whether she'd have got a new one already. I decided to crash the party. This was always easy enough to do, particularly if you took drink. I bought two bottles of wine from Arthur Cooper and went to the Bradford hotel to get drunk. I calculated that by eleven the little house would be so full that the door would be opened by a guest not a host and that two bottles and a confident attitude would get me in.

Why did I go to the party at all? Why didn't I just wait for Jennifer to emerge? I don't know. I had no conscious plans. The party was crowded, jostling, shouting, loud, difficult to tolerate. There was dancing in one room. It was pointless unless you were an anthropologist. A jackass or a crab might have had enjoyed working out what function the gathering performed in the social behaviour of the species. I stayed as long as I could stick it, then went back to the Morris 1100 in Park Street.

I drove it round into Jesus Lane and waited, listening to the radio. When the car was fuggily hot, I turned off the engine and the heating. I watched a few students coming up Malcolm Street towards me from the party house; I saw others go the opposite way, back into town. I watched to see if I recognised them.

I feared that Jennifer would be accompanied, though I hadn't seen Robin at the party and anyway there were difficulties between them. But surely in his absence some opportunistic youth would have tried his luck . . . Or failing that, one of her many female friends would emerge with her.

But no. Eventually I saw that familiar walk — familiar to me, at least, from so much study. She turned and waved to someone going the other way, paused, and for a moment made as if to change direction; then she continued north towards me, running for a few paces to re-establish her course. She settled to a brisk and cloudy walk. I started the engine. She looked over the street, expecting to cross to my side, but was unsure if my car was going to move off. To be safe, she stayed on her own side of Jesus Lane and started to walk quickly eastward.

I pulled up opposite and wound down the window. I called out her name and she looked suspiciously across the road to see who I was. I offered her a lift and she glanced both ways up and down the street. She didn't really want to get into the car with me, but she did so *for fear of seeming rude.*

Once in the passenger seat, she made the best of it, saying how grateful she was and what a lucky coincidence it had been.

I was overwhelmed by her presence.

And in a minute, maybe two, it was over — as we crossed the river bridge. The ridiculous shortness of our journey together summed up everything that I hated about time and living.

It enraged me. When we came to the junction with Chesterton Road, I turned left in order to loop round the short one-way system, back eastward for a bit, then right and down into the quiet terrace where she lived.

But I didn't loop round. I was too angry. I went left up Victoria Road, then swung right at random, by a church — where else — and drove hard through a modern estate, then left and right and onto Histon Road, going north. It was late and the road was clear and I put my right foot down hard.

Jennifer began protesting, asking me to stop. Her charm was gone. By taking the wrong road then accelerating hard I'd forfeited the intimacy we'd had for that wonderful two minutes. The only reason I'd not taken her home was because I wanted to keep her with me; I didn't mean any harm. But the more I drove, the more it became impossible to return: she was backing me into a corner, and I didn't know how to deal with her.

She'd become a whiny, frightened, selfish child — though you could tell she didn't know quite how frightened to be. Sometimes she'd stop saying things like, 'For Christ's sake, you lunatic. Just stop', and try to be reasonable or what she thought of as charming. 'Listen, Mike. I don't know what you're playing at, but, look, let's just stop and talk about it.'

But she wasn't charming any more. Not to me. She was no more charming than the man behind the counter in the Basingstoke record shop.

Then she tried being silently sulky for a bit as I drove through Histon. It's extraordinary the faith that women place in sulking. Someone should tell them that far from impressing people, filling them with remorse or changing their minds, this routine merely makes them — the sulkers — look ridiculous.

It wasn't a road I knew. It wasn't one of those that led to Over Wrought or Nether World or any of those villages with their Wheatsheafs and Red Lions. It was a flat Fenland strip and the large villages were stuck to it like settlements on a trade route, though with gnomes in their lamplit gardens.

In one of them — Cottingham, Cotham? — I swung off the main road down a village street with a signpost bearing two names I couldn't read. As we left the village, the road was narrower, with higher hedgerows, a proper country lane at last, dark and uninhabited.

Then we came too soon to the outskirts of another village, Rampton, and I was furious that nowhere was there open country, fields and fens and trees. Everywhere there seemed to be cheap buildings, low shelters for people who would never raise their eyes.

By this time, Jennifer had started screaming and swearing at me, hammering my arms on the steering wheel. She was trying to impress on me how desperate she was, how serious this was, that she was prepared to risk making us crash. I pushed her away.

In the village there were no lights on, but I saw a fork ahead. The upper road led straight out again, presumably, and on to the second named village I'd seen on the previous signpost. The lower road was marked 'Dead end' or 'No through road' — or something that suggested it went nowhere. So I swung down it. A dead end was what I wanted. I had to shut her up. I couldn't go on driving all night, and her hysterical behaviour had left me no escape back into normality.

The road bent at right angles to the left. It stopped being made up and became concrete. I switched the headlights on to full beam and about a hundred yards ahead I could see that it stopped altogether and became a farm track. This really was the end.

★ ★ ★

I lay on the bed in my Bayswater flat, panting and sweating under the assault of memory.

Presumably it was the word 'Rampton', the name of the village, which I'd heard when Deputy Chief Constable Bolton mentioned it, that had slowly worked its way through my mind's defences and precipitated the recall.

What I didn't know for sure was whether the sequence of events it had eventually unlocked in my memory was a true or false

365

account of what had taken place.

I drank more whisky and eventually I slept.

* * *

Two months passed and the story went cold. There were no arrests and no developments.

Then I went into work one Friday, roughly ten weeks after the police press conference, to find a message on my desk from Felicity Maddox, the sarcastic newsroom secretary.

'Please ring Chief Inspector Cannon. Urgent.' There was a number, and then, still in Felicity's writing, 'He says 'confidentiality guaranteed' !? F.'

I could feel her eyes on me as I picked the message slip up off the desk, but I showed no emotion.

'When did this guy ring?' I called over.

'It says on the paper,' said Felicity. 'Under 'Date and Time of Call', oddly enough.'

'Right.' It was the day before. 'I'm going out now, I've got to go and see someone, so — '

'Aren't you going to ring your policeman?'

'No, no, that's just about a story I'm working on, a long-term project. There's no rush. I'll call him later.'

'Can't think why you bothered coming in.'

'It's for the banter, Felicity. I can't resist it.' Her own coin, I thought, but it didn't seem to register.

My heart was squeezed every time I thought of the word 'Urgent'. There was something about it. I couldn't pretend to myself that Cannon just wanted a chat for old times' sake.

I took the Central Line home and tried to put my flat in order. I wrote cheques for a couple of utility bills; I turned off the boiler and made sure all the windows were double-locked. I took the photobooth picture of Jennifer with Anne out from my desk drawer, took it over to the window overlooking the garden square and looked at it.

There she was: my fate, my self. I kissed her face. Or rather, I kissed the cheap photopaper that had been squeezed damp from the side of the machine. I felt no remorse or sadness.

Then I took my file of newspaper cuttings about Jen's disappearance and put a match to them in the fireplace.

After a moment's hesitation, I threw the picture in as well. Now she was gone. The edge didn't curl up as it's meant to; but I did see Jen's eyes look into mine one last time. I felt as though someone was prising my ribs apart with their bare hands.

When everything was quite burned, I swept the ashes out and emptied the pan down the toilet, which I flushed until every speck was gone.

I wondered what to do about Margaret. Best to find out what Cannon wanted first. I dialled the number and after being put on hold for a minute, got through to a young woman.

'Can I speak to Chief Inspector Cannon, please?'

'Who's speaking, please?'

'Michael Watson.'

'Will he know what it's in regard to?'

I breathed in hard. 'I'm not able to predict that.'

'Pardon?'

'I'm returning his call.'

There was a pause, then suddenly Cannon was on the line.

'Mr Engleby. Thank you for calling back.' He sounded exhilarated. 'We've had the devil's own job tracking you down. Thank goodness for your old school. They pointed us in the right direction.'

Cannon had become more confident with age; he'd also acquired a bit of bogus golf-club polish to his voice.

'Good,' I said.

'I expect you know what I'm calling in connection with.'

'Not really.'

'The case of Jennifer Arkland. I'm sure you remember.'

'Yes. Of course.'

'One or two things have come to light. I'd very much like to talk to you again. I'd like you to come up here and see me.'

'I can't come today.'

'Yes, you can, Mr Engleby. I'm sending a car for you. Are you at home?'

'Yes.'

'My man will be with you in a few minutes. I didn't come to your newspaper because I didn't want to make a scene in front of your colleagues. I have been requested by the family to play this very low key for reasons of press and publicity. In return for that, I'd appreciate your full co-operation. Please don't leave your house. Otherwise I shall issue a warrant for your arrest. I can play it rough if you prefer.'

'I understand.'

I put the phone down. I felt all right. He wasn't arresting me; it was all quite amicable. If they really thought I'd killed Jennifer, if they really had hard evidence, they'd have marched in and grabbed me. They'd have taken no chances. That's how the plods operate.

I called Margaret at work and told her I was going to Edinburgh and that I'd ring the next day. She received this news coolly, but things were not that good between us since I'd been spending less time in Holloway. I was relieved that she wasn't too inquisitive.

The bell rang and two reasonable policemen took me away to a tactfully unmarked maroon Volvo. We stopped for a sandwich and fizzy orange drink at a garage in East Finchley before we hit the North Circular. By two o'clock I was seated in the interview room in Mill Road police station.

★ ★ ★

A constable in shirtsleeves sat with me, saying nothing. I had a cup of tea in a styrofoam cup. I asked if I could smoke and he nodded, so I lit up a Rothman's, knocking the ash into a little tin ashtray on the table. One wall was clouded glass and I presumed it was a one-way, though that seemed a bit hi-tech for Mill Road. There was a cassette recorder on the table, housed in an odd, non-commercial wooden box.

What was I thinking as I waited? I don't know. Does one ever really think? I seemed just to drift through it. In order to keep itself functioning under pressure, the brain releases chemicals that make the bizarre and the frightening seem normal. The Nat Sci Tripos taught me that homo saps who did not have this brain function were unsuccessful in reproduction, presumably because they couldn't handle stress and got themselves killed a lot by animals or other saps. So we who were chosen, we survivors, have it in spades.

Oddly enough, it can work too well. It can sometimes render crises not just normal or dealable-with, but strangely flat. I had to keep on reminding myself to stay alert — that I was in danger.

Cannon came in, all beer belly and bluster. He shook my hand, sat down and lit up with orange fingers.

'See you haven't stopped either,' he said with a grin. This was a false note because he didn't know I smoked; I hadn't had one when he came to my room in college. He hadn't offered me one.

He swung his feet up onto the table. He was wearing brown suede shoes with uneven wear to the soles.

'So let's have a chat about Jennifer, shall we, Mike? Hang about. Better turn the old squawkbox on, hadn't we? Is there a tape in,

370

John? Jolly good. Here we go then. Date, 19 June, 1988. Time 14.24 hours. Those present . . . '

'What happened to Peck?' I said.

'I beg your pardon?'

'Peck. The policeman who was in charge before.'

'He took early retirement on health grounds. He lives in Huntingdon. Follows the case, though. Anyway, Mike, I've been having a little think about you. Why did you change your name to Watson?'

'I got a job for a magazine, but they wanted to hire women. So I took the name Michèle Watt. It was a joke. It was a mixture between my own first name and the surname of a famous scientist.' I paused. 'James Watt. But the magazine misprinted it as 'Watts'. Then eventually it wasn't necessary to pretend to be a woman any more. And I moved to another paper, where I wanted to be a man again, but my professional identity was sort of bound up with this Michèle Watts, so I just changed it as little as I could to make a clean start.'

Cannon looked at me, then at the tape machine, as though to make sure it had got all that down OK. He raised an eyebrow.

'So you pretended to be a girl, then there was a misprint, then you pretended to be someone else again. Have I got that right?'

'More or less.'

'I see. It wasn't because you were trying to disguise who you really were?'

'Why would I do that?'

371

'Did you change your name by deed poll?'

'No.'

'But you have credit cards in the name of M.K. Watson.'

'Yes.'

'That's fraud, Mike, isn't it?'

'It's harmless.'

'Ever been in trouble with the police — under either of your names?'

'No.'

'Never caught, were you? I asked around the shops a bit. At the time Jennifer disappeared. I showed your picture to a few people. Off-licences and that. I noticed the booze in your room — vermouth and gin — and I wasn't sure how a boy on a full grant could afford it.'

'I worked in the holidays.'

'Some of the shopkeepers weren't happy with you.'

I didn't say anything. I thought carefully. I could say, 'I don't have a record'; but I didn't see how that would help. So I stayed silent.

'I've done a lot of checking, in fact,' said Cannon. 'You became a bit of a hobby of mine, to tell the truth, Mike. I've had my eye on you off and on for all these years. You know, it's like blokes you were at school with. You're not in touch all the time, but out of the corner of your eye, you're sort of aware of what they're up to. Know what I mean?'

I nodded.

'Now let's talk about Jennifer, shall we?'

'OK.'

'Were you her boyfriend?'

'In a way.'

'What way? Were you having sex with her?'

'That's none of your business.'

'Quite a few boys did have sex with her, didn't they?'

'I don't think so.'

'According to what I read in the papers.'

'I wouldn't believe that stuff.'

'Well, you should know! Anyway, I didn't necessarily believe it either. So I went to check it out for myself.'

I could see that Cannon was trying to rile me.

'Oh yes,' he said, lighting up another Embassy, 'quite a hot little number, our Jennifer.'

I didn't rise to it. It wasn't true. One problem with her and Robin had been what she called 'sex, lack of'. Of course Cannon couldn't know this, because he hadn't read her diary.

I smiled, confident in my superior knowledge.

'A boy in King's and a boy in Downing both said — '

'Both lying,' I said. 'Just schoolboy braggarts. Perhaps they kissed her at a party and they wished they'd gone the whole way.'

Cannon stood up and went to a drawer in a desk in the corner of the room. From it, he took a plastic bag containing a large padded envelope, addressed to Jennifer's mother in Lymington.

'Do you recognise this?' he said.

I shook my head.

'Someone sent it to Jennifer's mother. It

contained her diary.'

I nodded. It was not a time to speak.

'There aren't any fingerprints on it,' said Cannon. 'Maybe whoever sent it wore gloves.'

'Have you read the diary?'

'Oh yes.'

'And was it helpful to you?'

'Very much so, thank you, Michael. Now I wonder why whoever sent this diary to Mrs Arkland did send it. Do you think he was suffering from a bad conscience?'

I shrugged.

'Anyway, there are just traces of possible prints on the diary itself.'

'Won't they be Jennifer's?'

'Could be. Hard to tell. She hasn't got any fingers left. Just bones.'

There was a pause.

'So,' I said, 'had this diary been with her flatmates or what?'

Cannon laughed. 'You're a bit late with that, aren't you, Mike? It's as though you *knew* it had been missing.'

'No, I didn't. I· didn't even know she kept a diary.'

'You were her boyfriend and you didn't know she kept a diary?'

'I didn't see her every day.'

'Listen, Mike, I'm going to give you a chance. I'm going to let you make a clean breast of the whole thing. It'll be in your best interests. It'll play really well in court. Remorse, regret. You can talk about the strain of exams and student life and all that. You'll get life, you could be out in ten, twelve years. You'll only be about my age. It's nothing.'

'I don't know what you're talking about. Well, I do, but I mean I can't confess to something I didn't do.'

'You might even end up in the loony bin. Broadmoor or Rampton. That would be appropriate, wouldn't it? Rampton. Like the village where you killed her.' He smiled. 'Of course, you've been there before, haven't you?'

'Rampton?'

'No. The loony bin.'

'What do you mean?'

'Basingstoke, wasn't it?'

I felt the air go out of my lungs, and I slumped in the chair — but only for a moment. Then I bit my lip and pulled myself up. Cannon came round and put his face so close to mine that I could smell him.

'Mike, I've pretty much got you. You had a car. You have a history of mental instability. You were obsessed by the girl. My chaps are in your flat in London at the moment seeing if they can match a typewriter to the address label on this envelope. In a moment you're going to give me some prints and we'll see if we can get something off the diary. You had no alibi for the crucial time on the night of the party.'

'That's all circumstantial crap and — '

'Circumstantial's OK, Mike. Circumstantial gets convictions. People like you journalists, you don't understand that. You don't often get eyewitness evidence. And people don't often confess. I wish they would. It would make our life ever so much easier. And it would make it much better for you too.'

My mind had suddenly gone empty. I looked inside and there seemed to be nothing. I had the impression that my brain was actually emitting a sound, like that of a clean saucepan being scoured with wire wool, or perhaps of a wine glass being made to ring with the note that any moment would shatter it.

'Please let it be recorded that I am giving the suspect one last chance to confess.'

I couldn't confess because I couldn't think.

There was a long pause. I heard the cassette revolving.

Cannon bit his lip. 'Right. There's another kind of evidence we didn't mention just now.'

'Is there?'

'Yes. It's called forensic, by which we mean scientific. Ever heard of DNA?'

'Of course I have.' Part Two of Nat Sci had been full of it.

Cannon nodded to the constable, who left the room.

'DNA was first used in a case in Leicester-shire. Just recently. It got a man off. A man called Pitchfork, oddly enough. But it could equally convict a man. I do wish you'd confessed. I really do, Mike.'

While we waited for the constable to return I asked myself what I was feeling. Not guilt, not fear, not apprehension. By far my strongest feeling was of curiosity. I really wanted to see what they'd come up with and whether it would prove that I'd done something wrong.

The constable eventually came back in with what looked like a glass museum display case. Suspended inside on a coathanger was an orange tee shirt. On it was the face of Donny Osmond.

'The suspect is being shown a tee shirt. Have you seen this before, Mike?'

'It rings a bell.'

'We took it from your room when we came to see you in college all those years ago. When we gave you your clothes back, we kept this along with a couple of other things. We looked after it well and kept it dry. Do you know why?'

'No.'

'See there's some of it missing down here?'

A square of about two inches across had been cut from the tee shirt just below Donny's chin.

'It had a bloodstain on it. Not a big one, but big enough. That's why it's taken me so long to get in touch with you these last few weeks. We were having a DNA match done in Leicester. It takes them ages. But we got the results yesterday. The bloodstain on your tee shirt is a match with the DNA from Jennifer's bones.'

I said nothing. I felt nothing. I was thinking of those two chemists who burst into the Kestrel that lunchtime to tell the uninterested boozers that they'd cracked the human code.

Cannon drew himself up and spoke clearly. 'We believe you picked her up after that party, drove her out to the place where she was found, or very near it, killed her with a blow to the head with a piece of brick or a lump of concrete, and in a fit of rage you also broke her leg. You buried her either then or when you returned with a spade. You buried her in such a way that you hoped she'd never be found. You showed no pity, no remorse. You little shit.'

Cannon turned to face the cassette recorder and said solemnly, 'Michael Engleby, I am arresting you for the murder of Jennifer Rose Arkland on or about . . . '

To be honest, I wasn't really listening. It was hard to take it all in, the bad turn of events, the famous formula of 'anything you say may be taken down'. I wasn't thinking about Jennifer at all. I was wondering whether this would be a good moment to own up to having killed old Baynes as well.

11

I rang Stellings from Cannon's office to ask his advice. He was appalled. He said it wasn't his line of work, but he'd find someone and they'd be in touch. The odd thing was, he didn't ask me whether I'd done it.

Next, I was allowed to go to the toilet where I crammed in two blue pills before the constable who'd been sent with me saw what I was doing and stopped me.

Then they took me to a cell. I had to hand over the contents of my pockets, including pills, and I was anxious about how I was going to manage without them. There was a bed and a grey blanket in the cell. I lay down and curled up beneath it, but time had stopped and everything was crowding in on me. When a constable came with some food later I asked if I could see a doctor and he said he'd ask. I couldn't eat. The pills began to work and time realigned itself a little.

In the morning, I appeared in court, represented by a local solicitor provided by the police. I was remanded in custody for two weeks, and that night, when no one could see, was put in a van and driven to a prison. I was alone in my new cell, and I was relieved about that. The spyhole in the door opened at twenty-minute intervals through the night. I suppose they thought I might try to kill myself, though I had nothing to do it with. I just lay there and thought of Jennifer. The trouble was, I found it hard to picture her. It was all so long ago and she didn't seem real any more. I couldn't see or touch her. I had no real way of knowing whether she or I existed.

Some lag asked me the next day what I was 'in for'; I told him and he warned me not to tell my lawyer I was guilty — if I was. 'If you tell him you've done it, then you have to plead guilty in court. You can't confess to your brief, then ask him to run a not-guilty defence.'

'What if I do?'

'He has to turn down the case.'

'And is he bound to pass on what I've told him?'

'Who to? If he turns you down then he's not in a case and there's no judge for him to tell. And there's client confidentiality.'

'But you're saying I can't have it both ways.'

'No. Make up your mind before you get a brief. Work your story out first.'

I was grateful for this unsolicited good advice but worried that an old lags' code meant that I now had to pay for it in some unspeakable way.

That afternoon, I had a visit from a Mr Davies, the solicitor that Stellings had found for me. I didn't know what to say to him, so I asked him to tell me what might happen. He looked young, maybe only thirty, but he seemed to know what he was doing.

'If you're charged with murder, you can plead not guilty. That's fine, then your barrister will do his best to overturn the evidence against you, which I gather is largely forensic, with some circumstantial.'

'That's right.'

'Or you plead guilty and we look for all the mitigation we can find. Just by pleading guilty you reduce the sentence. You show remorse and contrition. We look for circumstances in your past that would have had a bearing. We call character witnesses. That way we can perhaps get the minimum term recommended before parole is considered down to something like fifteen years.'

The chief reporter on one of the tabloids, it was well known, had done time for murdering his wife. He behaved well, got out early and went back to reporting salacious stories for Rupert Murdoch.

'And?' I said. 'Any other possibility?'

'Yes, there's the hybrid, by which you plead guilty to manslaughter but not guilty to murder by reason of diminished responsibility.'

'The loony defence.'

'If it's accepted, you go to an establishment that's more of a hospital than a prison. But no picnic. And it's not easy to get released. In any event, whatever you plead, I shall have to brief counsel. I have one or two very good barristers in mind.'

I thought for a minute. 'If I'd killed more than one person, would the diminished responsibility plea have a better chance?'

He looked at me a little strangely. 'I really couldn't say at this stage. I advise caution. You certainly shouldn't admit to anything you haven't done. Best to say not guilty at this stage.'

'I see. Then what happens?'

'We wait for a date for the trial. It'll be weeks, maybe months. It's a big case for the Crown and they'll need time to prepare.'

'And meanwhile I stay here.'

'Yes. They won't grant bail in murder cases.'

'This DNA stuff,' I said. 'Will they accept it?'

'It's too soon to say. It's only been used by the defence in this country so far, though it's been used by the prosecution to convict in America — in Washington, I think. But it's new and untried and it's something the defence could certainly attack vigorously.'

'But if I plead not guilty and the jury accepts the DNA evidence and finds me guilty, then I'll go down for murder with the maximum time in a standard prison.'

'Correct. Though your mental condition can be reviewed later.'

I felt I needed time to think. Time was what I had. Time to think, time to do.

★   ★   ★

In my cell, I had a lot of diary sessions. I wished that Jen had written more because I knew them all too well by now. In that respect — only — they were like Vermeer's paintings.

The sole consolation was that there were one or two special entries — revealing, surprising — that I didn't allow myself to go over. I kept them back even from myself.

My barrister came up from London to see me.

He was a fleshy man in a suit with grey curly hair and a high colour. His name was Nigel Harvey, QC, and he was accompanied by a 'junior' (who looked older than Harvey, though thinner and more anxious) and by Davies, the solicitor. We met in a stuffy little room set aside for such visits.

'Very well, Mr Engleby,' said Harvey, unscrewing the top from a fountain pen and opening a blue foolscap exercise book, 'I've seen what you said to Mr Davies, but if you don't mind, I'd like you to go over it again for me. In your own words.' He had a rich brown voice that reminded me of Tubby Lyneham.

My own words? Who else's words could my mouth frame?

I told him about the party in Malcolm Street and how I left early and returned to my car in Park Street, how I drove round the corner into Jesus Lane to wait for Jennifer.

'Let's leave you there for a moment,' he said. 'I'd like to know more about this girl. How well you knew her, your feelings for her. Anything you think might help us.'

I thought very carefully. I was inhibited by the warnings I'd received about how I mustn't confess or say anything that incriminated me and still expect to be defended. This florid man was the closest I had to an ally and I didn't want him to walk out of the door; so it was a bit like being on trial already.

The trouble was, I only knew how to tell the truth.

I chose my words — my very own — with

precision. 'She was attracted to me. Though perhaps she didn't know or admit how much. I felt I had to make her see how much she needed me. She wasn't right with the boy she was with and I didn't want her to go off with someone else, as a kind of second best, or rebound. I was the right man for her.'

'What were your feelings for her?'

'Profound.'

I told him a lot about my family and my father and mother and childhood. He kept nodding. He made a few notes. It was surprisingly enjoyable. I must have wanted to get some of this stuff out of me.

'Let's go back to your car.'

'I saw her coming up the street. She hesitated, then turned into Jesus Lane. She saw my car. She recognised me. I think she wanted to get in with me. But then she must have changed her mind. But I stopped alongside, and she sort of bowed to the inevitable.

'She was in my car and I was happy. It was as though everything had come right. We were happy together. She was laughing and it was easy, there was something right about it. I wanted it to last. For ever, maybe. I didn't want to have to let her out and go back to everything being all wrong again. But it ended too soon. And I couldn't face it ending. So at the moment I should have turned right, I went left — just to prolong it. To prolong my time with her.

'Then I was worried that she'd jump out if I stopped, so I had to drive fast, very fast, through this sort of housing estate, then once I'd got out onto the Histon Road — the main road — I had to put my foot down.'

'Why?' said Harvey.

I thought for a long time. 'Because I felt a fool.'

'Go on.'

'The trouble was that she was reacting badly. She was behaving like a child and I didn't like that at all. It made me feel as though I was some kind of freak. She was screaming and shouting and banging at my arms. I felt she'd backed me into a corner.'

'What were your feelings towards her then?'

'I didn't like her any more. I wanted her to be like the girl I'd known before, not like this. She'd humiliated me and I wanted her to shut up. Yes, I wanted her to shut up.'

'All right. Gently does it, Mr Engleby. Carry on.'

I tried to remember. 'I thought I'd find somewhere quiet and let her out of the car and then drive off. That was bad, but not that bad. I could apologise, I could make it up. I wouldn't have harmed her. But I couldn't *find* anywhere quiet. It was all villages, you know, like ribbon developments almost. Then finally I got to this place, Rampton. There was a dead end.'

'And?'

I looked at him.

He coughed. 'I'm sorry. I understand. Please take your time.'

The road called Cuckoo Lane wasn't tarmac, it was made of concrete, what's called hardstanding, I think. At the end was a cart track into the Fens. I turned off the headlights. I didn't want Jennifer to get out and run. There were houses not far away. I didn't want her to make a noise. I squeezed her wrist very hard till she screamed; then I said, 'Stay there while I come round.'

I got out and went round to her side. I pulled her out. I couldn't see much in the darkness, but she was quiet. She wasn't screaming.

I said, 'Keep quiet and it'll be all right.'

She whispered, 'What do you want? I'll do what you want.'

She meant sex, I suppose, but that wasn't what I wanted. What I wanted was for her to say something that would make it all right, that would turn time backwards, that would turn her back into the old Jennifer and would give me a way out.

I was gripping both her wrists very tightly.

I said, 'Say something.'

'I thought you wanted me to be quiet.'

'Say something quietly. Say my name.'

She struggled in my grip.

'Say: 'Please, Mike.' '

I don't remember how, but I became aware that she had wet herself. Was there a smell? Did I hear it? I don't know, but she'd made herself disgusting.

And she wouldn't say my name.

'Say it, Jennifer.'

Her face was ugly with sobbing. She couldn't speak. I felt naked and humiliated by what I'd done.

My memory of what happened next is patchy.

386

There are only flashes.

One thing I knew: I couldn't go back, and I couldn't let her go back. There was a piece of loose concrete at the end of the hard-standing, where it met the earth of the field. Holding one of Jennifer's wrists, I bent down and picked it up. Then I swung it down on the back of her head. She cried out and fell to her knees. I hit her harder the second time and I heard her skull crack.

I went on hitting her. I think. I don't remember.

I think I went on hitting her because I had no choice. Then I carried her for as long as I could manage and threw her in a ditch beside the field. I covered her as best I could. I listened to her to make sure she wasn't breathing. She was dead. I lay on top of her with my face in her hair and I cried. I didn't know how she'd died, but I was filled with fury at her, for what she'd made me do. I was furious with her for being dead, for making me do this thing. There was another piece of concrete not far away, on the side of a sort of small canal or watercourse. I smashed it into the back of her head once more to be sure, then I broke her leg with it. I was intensely relieved that it was over. I felt more like myself again.

It was what I'd done with Baynes, except with him I'd planned it better. I'd planned it for weeks, lain in wait by the bridge, and I didn't kill him. Not at first.

The day after I killed Jennifer, I drove back to the place at three in the morning, parked my car in the village and walked down the lane, then the track, to where I'd left her. I had a spade with me that I'd taken from the gardener's hut near Jesus Ditch on Midsummer Common.

I dug for two hours or more, then dragged her body in. It was stiff and ugly and her fine hair was clogged. I didn't consider raping her, or even looking at her body. Then I covered her with earth, then with lumps of concrete that I fetched from the ragged end of the hardstanding, then with an old railway sleeper from the side of the track, then with more earth that I compounded hard. Finally, I roughed it up with the edge of the spade to make it look natural.

I felt relieved. Dawn was beginning to seep into the Fen horizon as I turned and left.

★　★　★

I told this — or a version of it, at least — to Harvey. It took a very long time, because I had to give him all the Chatfield stuff, all the background, as well.

When I'd finished there was a long silence in the small room. I could hear the rain outside in the prison yard.

Then I said, 'I think there may have been a third person I killed. A German woman called Gudrun Abendroth.'

He nodded.

I said, 'Do you think we could run the diminished responsibility plea?'

He said, 'I think we could.'

I said, 'Will I have to see a lot of shrinks?'

388

He said, 'Yes, you will.'
I said, 'That's fine.'
Then a warder came in with some tea.

★ ★ ★

The preparation of the case has taken several weeks. It's been very hot in my cell through the summer, but luckily I've been alone. With all the overcrowding, you'd expect that I'd be doubled up by now, but I think the nature of my case and the publicity around it has made them want to keep me apart.

I was also told by a doctor that it was for my own protection as 'people like me' were not good at 'reading the intentions of others' and could therefore be victimised. I exercise alone and don't join in group work activities.

I'm not on the nonces' wing or anything, it's just that I have very limited contact with the other prisoners — just at meals, really, or occasionally in the library. Fine by me.

★ ★ ★

I have done numerous psychological tests, including the Rorschach ink-blot tests, which were ridiculous. One was a squashed cat, one was a bat in flight, one was a three-legged abominable snowman, but most were not suggestive at all. The psychologist sat behind me taking notes, presumably thinking I was unaware of what she was up to. I think she wanted me to say that various splodges resembled reproductive parts of the anatomy, but they didn't; they looked like ink blots.

I've seen four psychiatrists, including the prison medical officer. Although I gather he'll be for the prosecution, he endeared himself to me by prescribing some blue pills at our first meeting; I was allowed one at midday and one at night — by which I really mean nine o'clock, which for some incalculable reason is when they put the murderers to sleep, or anyway turn their lights off.

The shrink I've seen most of is called Julian Exley, who's instructed by the defence. I told him I'd kept a sort of journal, off and on, and he encouraged me to bring it up to date. (Some plods brought the papers from my flat in Bayswater.) It's been a good exercise for me; it's given me something to do. I haven't changed anything in it, I've just tidied it up and smoothed it over a bit. I sometimes work in the library and sometimes in my cell. The early parts are handwritten; between the typed lines of the later sections I write corrections with a ballpoint pen. I'm aware that there are long gaps, but it didn't seem worth padding them out just for the sake of it.

This, of course — what you're reading now — is it. Or rather, the preceding pages are. As I sat in the library on Monday, looking back, I noticed how much my style had changed — how much less crabbed and self-defensive it became, how much more rhetorical — and I thought perhaps I ought to try to homogenise it for art's sake; but then I thought maybe Dr Exley could read something into the changes — some significant psychological development, or lack of. (Because obviously they all pored over it after it had arrived from London, and photocopied it, before they gave it back to me.)

And anyway, who knows or cares about unity or harmony of style these days? I read book reviews where the journalist doesn't even know the distinction between 'tone' and 'style' — something even Plank Robinson had more or less mastered by O level. Ah, the treason of the clerks — the 1970s schoolteachers who decided, for some perverse political reason, to withhold knowledge from our schoolchildren. The first generation thus deprived are now themselves the teachers, so it's less treasonous for them: they don't have the knowledge to hold back. We were bound to see the results of this anti-teaching before long. Stellings tells me the graduates who apply to Oswald Payne with firsts from Oxford and Cambridge can't spell or write grammatically; they have to send them on a basic six-week course before they can write a literate internal memo.

Anyway, when Dr Exley predictably asked if he could see the latest instalments of my journal/narrative, I said, 'Why don't we do a deal? I'll show you my evidence if you let me see yours.'

'What do you mean?' he said.

'Show me what else you've gathered. Show me my test results, your diagnosis, any character references from other people. All the stuff you're using.'

He stroked his chin, something he did quite a lot, and smiled. 'I can't do that at the moment. In due course, though, I don't see why you shouldn't know what's being said about you. I've always believed in patients having access to their records as far as possible, so far as the law allows. The idea that the men in white coats keep your own secrets from you is very Big Brotherish, I think.'

I should have mentioned that this Exley character is not quite what the phrase 'forensic psychiatrist' suggests — which I take to be someone like the old film actor Richard Wattis: severe, horn-rimmed. Exley wears floral ties and a corduroy jacket; he smokes roll-up cigarettes; he looks like a slightly left-wing publisher.

'Are you worried about what other people may have said about you?' he said.

I guessed this was preliminary question one in the Paranoia Profile, so I just shrugged.

In the course of one of our sessions he had to leave the room for about five minutes, and I read some of the papers in his folder. The one on top was this:

R v *Engleby*. Witness Statement.
James Stellings, Partner,
Litigation Department, Oswald Payne,
75 Finsbury Pavement,
London EC4 7JB.

Is this thing working? Testing . . . Testing. Right. OK.

I suppose the first er the first word you'd

use if you were describing Mike is that you'd say he was a loner. He . . . er . . . at college he was always on his own, he never seemed to be with other people. In the dining hall for instance he'd quite often sit apart. He'd get his tray if it was the self-service thing and go to the end of the table and if it was formal dinner, when it was laid and you sort of had to sit next to someone, then he'd sort of take his place. But he wouldn't try to engage anyone in conversation.

He . . . he didn't really seem to have any friends that I was aware of either in college or out. Though I know that he used to go out quite a bit in the evening but I don't know where he went to.

I first met him I think probably on the very first day we were there. I just happened to find myself sitting next to him at er at dinner and I thought it was friendly to introduce myself and we had a chat and I wouldn't say it was a very easy conversation, I mean, he wasn't er . . . the sort of person who was very at ease in company at all. He was awkward, he was physically awkward, and he was er, er . . . ill at ease, it wasn't, he wasn't a man who appeared to be well in his own skin as it were.

But . . . er, he was, he had opinions, he had views, and he had extremely strong views in fact [laughs] on pretty well everything. I mean, I think if you had to sum up Mike you'd say he was an interesting man but he just wasn't much fun to be with. I mean, unlike a lot of people where completely the reverse is true.

They haven't got anything interesting or worthwhile to say, but they're actually quite easy or amusing to be with.

Of course one of the first things you notice about Mike is his appearance. Um . . . you know, he's incredibly badly dressed and I remember him coming to dinner once at our house in London and turning up in some sort of bootlace cowboy tie and hideous sort of caramel-coloured slacks. I mean, you know, just the whole thing was . . . appalling. And his hair which was sort of wiry and always needed cutting but it wasn't long in the sort of student style, it just looked as if it hadn't been cut. And his thick glasses which were defiantly . . . Everyone in those days wore John Lennon-style round glasses but Mike had these er . . . thick sort of I suppose horn-rimmed at the top then rimless at the bottom. And physically he was he was pretty, to be crude, he was pretty unprepossessing. He was . . . Quite short, he wore these horrible clothes, I mean I seem to remember he'd occasionally have on a tee shirt of . . . with something rather inappropriate on the front of it. That was about his only concession to, you know, fashion at all. He grunted quite a lot, he made a lot of noise breathing.

And of course he was also . . . physically very strong. He had heavy shoulders and this big chest. I mean . . . He could have been a fantastic rower. He was a bit short I suppose, but er you know, he was, he gave the impression that, of being a very powerful

394

young man, though as I say I don't know if he actually took any exercise.

God, what else can you say? I kept in touch with him because I felt that . . . I . . . I saw something in him that I quite liked — but also I suppose out of a sense of kindness. He . . . er, I felt this was a guy who perhaps needed the odd friend. He certainly didn't have any other friends, so far as I knew.

As far as Jennifer Arkland is concerned, er I think I knew that Mike had met her because he sort of er . . . gatecrashed one summer when they were making a film in Ireland, I remember him telling me about it at the beginning of it must have been our last year I think. Mike just sort of invited himself along and then . . . um, made himself useful. So I knew that he would have met her then and he did mention her to me I think once. He said something about that she was a friend of his. He didn't say that it was anything more than that and I certainly never saw them together.

I knew almost nothing about his family. I knew that his father had died when he was young and that he'd . . . and that his mother went out to work but I couldn't tell you, I haven't the faintest idea what she did. Was there a sister? Did he have a sister or a younger brother? Er . . . I knew also that Mike came from a er . . . pretty er . . . simple background. He, you know, made no bones about that. He had quite a marked accent from wherever it was he came from . . . Reading, I think. Er . . . He didn't make any attempt to sort of make himself sound more posh or anything like that as I think quite a lot of boys and girls did when they first went to university.

I don't think he ever mentioned where he'd been to school. I assumed he'd been to the local grammar school. I mean that's what, that's where most people had been. There's a sort of misconception that all the undergraduates are terribly posh and drink champagne, but it wasn't like that at all. Most of them were from grammar schools. A lot of them were teetotal scientists who just scurried from their rooms to the lecture hall and back again.

What else? The other thing is that he was very clever. But again, so what? So were most of the young men and women there, and I've really no idea whether Mike had a higher IQ, more firepower intellectually than anyone else. But he certainly had a phenomenal memory. I mean, if you, if he, if you wanted to, you could test him on dates and lists and you know which record had been in the top ten when, but you know to his credit [laughs] he didn't show off that too much but he certainly had a superior memory.

When I hear this you know, this . . . development, the trouble that Mike's now in I'm . . . I'm surprised. Because I knew that Mike was a bit of an oddball, as I say — but I am surprised that anything . . . On the other hand, er, you have to say there was kind of concealed violence in a lot of his conversation, in the extreme positions he took on even little things, like music . . . And er politics and all sorts of things . . . He was extremely critical, I mean brutally critical of a lot of political thought and political belief. So there was a kind of maybe undischarged anger in the way that he saw the world.

The truth is I guess now I think about it, that you know that maybe I didn't really know him at all. People are always mysterious, aren't they? You know you find out that one of your best friends has been having an affair for years and you never knew anything about it. And I suppose in that way nothing should ever really surprise us because people are like icebergs, you only see the little bit on top.

On the particular questions that you . . . you mentioned in your letter, the particular points. Did Mike appear remote, unengaged, distant from others? Yes, I think I would say that. Next, did he have a 'loner' view of life? Yes, I'd definitely say yes to that, in fact it was the first word I used about him. Did he avoid social situations? Yes, I suppose probably he did. Perhaps because he was shy, but also perhaps because he thought he'd be bored, I think. Did he have low sexual desire? I know absolutely nothing about his sexual life at all. What's the next one? 'Interpersonal skills', whatever that means. Yeah, they were poor, I mean really [laughs] . . . poor old Mike, I think of him at that dinner party, I mean, it was, it was very funny in a way, in a cruel way, watching him floundering and trying to talk to these people, but yeah he wasn't able to handle that.

Next. His response to praise and criticism. Was he unresponsive? Yes. Indeed. I would say he was unresponsive to praise. For instance he did very well in the first-year exams and I said, 'Well done, Mike, that's fantastic,' and he then had a very good reason for why anyone could do it, and it wasn't any sort of achievement at all on his part. And that's when he acquired the nickname of Groucho as in Groucho Marx who said I wouldn't want to belong to any club that would have me as a member.

Now, 'difficulty in expressing anger' . . . That's also tricky. Yes and no. Um. I suppose it was bottled up, as I said earlier on, I certainly never saw him express anger. So . . . Of those six points I suppose I am answering in the affirmative to pretty well all of them. Sexual desire — except that one. I can't really say.

What else can I say about Mike? Well of course, he was a terrible pedant. He was always correcting you if you said 'between you and I'. And what was the other one that used to drive him up the wall? I forget. 'Internecine' maybe. Yes, I think I heard him go off on quite a rant about that. You know when people think it's just a posh word for 'internal'? I forget what it really does mean now. Better ask Mike.

But of course none of these things made him very popular. People don't like being ticked off for their grammar especially when they're just trying to be friendly and thinking maybe Mike could have used a friend.

I did like him, though. Why am I talking in the past, as though he's dead? I'd like to end

398

by saying that I did like him, though I may have sounded a bit lukewarm in this tape. And I will stick by him even if it turns out for the worst.

So what do I like about him? Mike . . . God. [*laughs*] Not his clothes, that's for sure. I liked his manner. I think. Although it was awkward, direct, embarrassing . . . It was embarrassing, it was painful to be around sometimes. But there was something deeply er . . . uncompromising about him. He told it exactly how he saw it. It made me laugh. Mike made me laugh a lot, though I often thought he didn't really get the joke himself. Yes, that's weird now I come to think of it. He could be very funny, but he hardly ever laughed. He very seldom laughed or showed any emotion at all.

I'll definitely keep in touch. I've certainly never met anyone else quite like him. I'll send him cards or go and see him. I think that's all. I'm going to stop this thing now.

I confirm that this is a true and accurate transcript of the tape I made. Signed: James Stellings, 24 July, 1988

Who would have thought old Stellings to have quite such pedestrian thought processes? And to be quite so radically inarticulate? I'd always thought of him with his Montrachet and his Rodgers and Hammerstein as rather debonair. But then as he himself remarked — with such shining originality — perhaps you never really know people.

Oh well.

Yesterday, Dr Exley — deliberately, I think — left some more papers on the table in the room where we do our interviews while he went out to talk to one of the officers. I wasn't sure whether the scrawly notes were intended to go to the lawyers or to his fellow defence shrink. Or perhaps they were just a memo to himself. Anyway, he was gone for ten minutes, so I read them.

Dr Julian Exley MD, FRCPsych

Preparatory notes for report on patient
M. Engleby in case of
R V Engleby.

(Philippa: please leave or fill gaps where indicated. I shall have to redraft in more formal way later. More typing . . . Sorry! J)

I recommend a plea of guilty to manslaughter but not guilty to murder on the grounds of diminished responsibility. I expect that expert opinion for the prosecution will agree with the diagnosis and accept the plea. However, in view of the notoriety of the case, it's possible that the judge will want to put it before a jury, so I have roughed out a report in more detail on the grounds that I may have to give evidence in person.

I.
Michael Engleby is a 35-year-old male of Anglo-Saxon/Caucasian descent.

He was brought up in a normal working-class family, he is unusually well educated (grammar school, public school, Cambridge University) and has a high IQ (see test results, to be appended). He has managed to retain a well paid and respectable job in journalism. He is financially solvent, has some savings and owns the leasehold (less outstanding mortgage) of a small flat in London.

He has a mild cardiac arrhythmia, and lung function test results (using Youlten peak-flow meter) are slightly below average for his age. This may be caused by excessive smoking. He has a borderline alcohol dependency problem and has been a heavy drug user in the past. Neither condition appears to be acute, however. In prison, he has been prescribed ten mg diazepam twice daily and this seems to be all that is necessary.

Throughout his life, however, he has had difficulty in forming even rudimentary attachments to others. He disliked his father, who, he says, abused him as a child by beating him regularly. His mother appears to have been the dominant figure at home, yet emotionally distant. He had little respect for her and minimal attachment. He claims to have been 'close' to a younger sister, but has hardly seen her in the last ten years. He had no close friends at school, university or work. He says that the resulting solitude has not bothered him, that in fact he prefers it.

His preference has been for solitary activities, such as reading or listening to music. In journalism, he made it a condition of his joining the staff of a newspaper that he need not go to the office more than once or twice a week, thus maintaining his solitude. As he put it to me, 'I'd rather be abandoned than engulfed.'

He exhibits a degree of anhedonia — viz., he takes little pleasure in life, even in the activities that he chooses. He evinces little emotion of a positive or negative kind. He exhibits a consistent flatness of response. He responds little to the facial expressions of others.

He declines to discuss his libido, but appears to have had only one sexual relationship of any kind. According to him, it was coming to an end at the time of his arrest. His partner/ex-partner has declined to be interviewed.

He admits to having been indifferent to the praise or criticism of colleagues, teachers or friends at any stage in his life. He has admitted that this was because he did not value their opinions.

Some of the defining symptoms of this disorder (e.g. anhedonia, flatness of affect) are associated with the so-called 'negative' symptoms of schizophrenia. However, the subject exhibits no positive symptoms of schizophrenia or psychosis in any form and I do not find that he is suffering from mental illness.

The subject has had a firm grasp of reality at most stages of his life. The exceptions are twofold. First, in the occurrence of occasional acute panic attacks, which are considered below. Second, there appears to have been occasional partial memory loss. These lapses in my view can be explained in simple psychological terms of defence mechanisms, stress and so on. It is ironic that they occur in someone whose memory is generally of an almost 'savant' or autistic order — but no more than ironic, and not in my view suggestive of psychotic illness or indeed of any neurological problem, such as local brain damage.

In my view, he suffers from a personality disorder, which amounts to abnormality of mind for the purposes of Section 2 of the 1957 Homicide Act. If pressed to answer, I would say that this disorder substantially impaired his responsibility for his offence, although I am mindful that this is properly a question for the jury.

Personality disorder diagnoses can cause problems because in many cases the crime is the first evidence we have of serious abnormality. However, in the case of Engleby we have the extraordinary advantage of his own written account of the formative years of his life.

2.
The following is a list of some notes I made while reading the journal.

Chapter One. His vanity while being inter-viewed for a university place. Contempt for his

403

superiors. Fetishistic attitude to brands of drink and cigarettes. Persistent alcohol abuse. Drug abuse. (It is interesting that the 'blue ten-milligram pill' he takes is almost certainly diazepam, or Valium, whose tranquillising effect may have been helpful in the long term, but may also have distorted the diagnostic picture by removing a degree of anxiety that might otherwise have been present.)

He 'does not like to think' about his younger sister. I believe this is not because he dislikes her, but because he has a fear of emotional closeness. Significantly, she is the only person he can feel sorry for (when she comes to visit him in London later) or empathise with at all.

Chapter Two. Explicit preferences for solitude, particularly in his student travelling. Note also his reluctance to name either his university or his college. Also, the pub he calls the Kestrel is clearly the Eagle. Etc. This may not be significant, but is consonant with a fear of being 'engulfed' by a social context which he found intimidating.

Chapter Three. Schooldays. One notes that he is abused and becomes an abuser. Systematic thieving. Disregard of social norms. Fantasises about killing his tormentor.

Chapter Four. Memory loss could be attributed to marijuana abuse, but more likely to the selective repression necessary in his building of a pathological defence system.

There is almost no sexual content in his descriptions of the girl Jennifer, very unusual in a man of 20/21 years old. He appears more concerned about whether she has sex with her boyfriend than whether she has sex with him.

Chapter Five. His only friend or acquaintance, James Stellings (see witness statement), does not look him up in the vacation. 'Mercifully' is how M.E. describes this omission.

Chapter Six. His only friend in London appears to be the shopkeeper, a refugee from Amin's Uganda. His account of buying pornographic magazines shows little libido. He is more interested in the imagined lives of the models and the homeland of the shopkeeper. His attempt to meet women in a wine bar is halfhearted and inept; his account of it is misogynistic. Note: his account of his father's abuse. Lacks detail. Detail suppressed? Or gravity of episode(s) exaggerated?

Chapter Seven. He recoils from Jeffrey Archer's mistress, or perhaps from the thought of sex when confronted with physical presence of two lovers. Although he doubtless interviewed people for his newspaper, the stories of his meetings with famous people are not always convincing. Creative fantasy?

His admission here to periodic rages, on the other hand, is extremely compelling. I think it is significant that it comes at a time when he feels his life is generally 'improving'. He feels more confident and is able to look at himself with detachment and recall these episodes.

Elsewhere he typically sees no problem with himself, only with others — the teachers, colleagues, would-be friends, acquaintances and even shopkeepers. This is characteristic of personality disorders.

Chapter Eight. His vagueness about how to proceed with Margaret suggests sexual inexperience, perhaps even virginity. His description of sex with her — 'We took a room and had it off' — is, even allowing for natural modesty, rather unconvincing.

Chapter Nine. He is unable to deal with the intimacy of living with Margaret and is moving back to his preferred state of solitude.

Narcissism is continually present in the Engleby journal. It is evident in all his accounts of the intellectual processes of others, which he views with contempt. Any failings of his own, on the other hand, are attributed to the poor judgement or misinterpretation of others. He is dismissive of all politicians, of all scientists, of playwrights, of almost all cinema and most music, with only bizarre and partial exceptions.

His own intellectual processes, by contrast, pass unchallenged. His social inadequacies and embarrassments are blamed on others. It never occurs to him that he is unattractive in any way or that his behaviour could be adjusted. His problems do not appear to him as problems because they are so deeply entrenched that they are ego-syntonic — i.e. they seem normal to him.

My belief is that he suffers from schizoid personality disorder (following criteria of DSM III-R) with elements of narcissism and antisocial personality disorder. This is a complicated picture for the court, however, and I note that in the latest figures we have from one Special Hospital (Broadmoor) only two per cent of personality disorder patients have schizoid PD as their primary diagnosis.

However, more than 80 per cent of these non-psychotics have psychopathic or unspecified PD as their main diagnosis. The worse the crime, the vaguer the diagnosis, on the latest figures; and I can therefore see no problem with Engleby being put in this looser category.

Although he has suggested otherwise, I am not convinced that the patient is responsible either for an assault on a schoolmate that may have led, indirectly, to his premature death many years later, or the murder of a German woman in London, in which case no forensic evidence survives, the victim's body having been flown home and cremated.

I suspect that the patient believes that a diminished responsibility plea stands a better chance of succeeding if there is more than one crime.

(Philippa: this next bit is technical. You can

407

leave it till later if you don't have time now, as I may need to revise it anyway.)

Winnicott (1965) characterises extreme aggression as arising at the moment at which a 'deprived' character tries catastrophically to revert to the instant before deprivation led him to erect morbid defence systems. It is a moment of hope: of asserting that, despite entrenched patterns, he can still *take* something from his environment.

Well, there were six more pages of this baloney and I will spare you the details. Old Exley really liked to beef up his argument by referring to previous shrinks, mostly American, as though they gave his own amateur meanderings some heft and authority.

In the fog of his prose, there were just a few moments of light. (Even a stopped clock is right twice a day.)

Here are the brighter bits.

Consensus in the literature is that rage is closely linked to fear of exposure, shame and damage to the narcissistic self. It is essentially defensive. The feared annihilator must be annihilated (Kohut, 1972); though it is not the object him/herself that is to be eliminated, but the danger he/she poses to the very existence of the fabricated self.

Violence in defence of a coherent sense of identity under intolerable threat must include gender and sexuality issues, most commonly fear of the exposure of sexual inadequacy (argued in US by Bromberg, Abrahamsen and other).

Perhaps also relevant is the notion of 'dissociative murder', which entails an altered state of consciousness in which there is no knowledge of motive. The murder in fact takes place at a moment of total 'ego disintegration'.

This is a frightening and difficult concept to grasp. But Engleby gives us two or three previous descriptions of something similar happening when he is under extreme pressure, e.g. something like: 'It is unusual to feel oneself come apart in such a molecular way.'

Engleby claims partial or 'snapshot' memory of the deed, which is consistent with dissociation. (Total amnesia is a highly suspect defence, unless there is evidence of brain damage or neurological deficits, which there is not in Engleby.)

The patient's behaviour after the crime is also consistent with this kind of dissociation. He feels no remorse because his emotion of relief at having eliminated the threat to himself and thus being able to reorganise his defence systems is so great that it leaves no room for other emotions.

This goes right back to Freud's 'constancy principle', which argues that the mind tends always to bring itself back to minimal stimulation by ridding itself of emotions that threaten its equilibrium. Great is the relief when stasis is restored — though remorse may follow.

The American psychologist Bromberg (1961) argues that explosive murders are usually connected to fears of being exposed as sexually inadequate. It is not hard to see how this may have been the catastrophic moment in Engleby's narcissism. Arkland's offer to 'do what [Engleby] wanted' may indirectly have cost her her life. It seems bizarre, but Ruotolo (1968) argued: 'Some personalised value was found to take precedence over the ultimate crime of murder . . . This unique image of oneself had to be maintained at any price.'

4. Conclusion
I don't suppose that the detail above will be necessary, but court/ counsel may need background on idea of personality disorders.

In lay terms, they arise as a result of an adverse reaction at the meeting place between, on the one hand, a child's temperament and character and, on the other, its family and social environment.
    This meeting brings us close to the key moment of human life: the moment at which a child becomes self-aware. The Adam and Eve myth dramatises it plainly. Few people find this extraordinary moment and all that it subsequently entails to be frictionless.
    'Temperament' may be defined as a person's innate disposition, and this has a biological

410

substrate in the chemistry of the brain. Sensitivity to light or noise, for instance, ability to relate to others, even 'adventurousness' may well have a molecular and/or genetic base. (In his important work *The Mask of Sanity*, H. Cleckley (1976) even found a possible neurological site for basis of psychopathy in the temporal lobe.)

If 'personality' is then defined as the sum of attitudes, responses and behaviours acquired by the developing child as it struggles to adapt to its environment, then a disorder may result if the child's temperament forces it to develop a 'personality' which, while successfully surviving in the short term, is chronically maladapted.

In adult life, there are then the further normal psychological pressures of life events on the individual which will affect his behaviour.

As I understand it, a plea of diminished responsibility can succeed only if the court takes the view that the accused is or was suffering from such abnormality of mind as substantially impaired his mental responsibility for his actions at the time of the killing (Section 2, Homicide Act, 1957).

The 'abnormality' must arise from arrested or retarded development (no); disease (e.g. schizophrenia; no); injury (no); or inherent causes. It's this loose category that M.E. fits, and his own narrative shows us how.

The crux is that there seems little doubt on

411

the basis of what he has told us that Engleby was indeed suffering from an extreme abnormality of mind, and that this abnormality did substantially impair his responsibility. If necessary, I can go further into the extent to which his personality disorder was shaped by biological factors it was beyond his reasonable capacity to modify.

I respectfully recommend that, if the defendant's guilty plea is accepted, the court consider making a hospital order under Section 37 of the Mental Health Act 1983. A requirement of the Act is that hospital treatment is 'likely to alleviate or prevent the deterioration of the condition'. Although medication and psychotherapy are generally of v limited use with such patients, I believe M.E. could easily benefit from both, particularly the latter. I have communicated with the relevant authorities at Longdale hospital.

I put the sheaf of papers back on the desk.

'Personality disorder'. I didn't know whether to laugh or cry. If instead of 'schizoid' he'd gone for 'borderline' personality disorder as his main diagnosis but had been equally unsure about that one too, might he have ended up describing me as having borderline borderline personality disorder?

What a way to spend your life.

But then again, if the court can be made to see it Exley's way I'll get to pass my time being scrutinised in a hospital — albeit with razor wire

412

and maximum security — rather than being banged up in a 'normal' prison.

I was also shocked to find so much Freud in his report (there was plenty more I've spared you). It was rather as if in a paper written by a Treasury economist you found continual reliance on Marxist economics.

Marx and Freud. Blimey. Say what you like about that pair of flat-earthers, they are nothing if not durable. Long after their train has gone, they are still kicking their heels in the station waiting room, grabbing the wrist of any poor traveller with half an ear to listen.

Freud dreamed up the Oedipus theory on the basis of *not* having seen his mother naked on one occasion as a child; and on further supposing that *if* he had, then he *might* have been aroused. And from that triple non-event, he extrapolated a universal 'truth'. Ah . . . Where would we be without the hard men of science and their rigour?

'I sometimes seem to myself to have been more of a short-story writer than a scientist,' he wrote, as though warning his apostles that Anna and Emmy and Lucy and all the other 'hysterical' women were merely characters in a book. But he claimed his fictions were true — even when it became clear that there was no such thing as 'hysteria', or not as he understood it; even when it was shown that these famous girls whose cures were to form the basis of a human panacea had not been cured at all, but carried on their spastic clacking and paralyses — even when it was

413

clear that they in fact had epilepsy or, in one shameful case, Tourette's syndrome — named after a former colleague in Paris, a man he'd worked with!

On the other hand . . .

I suppose we don't really believe that Jesus Christ was literally and actually the son of God. I mean, a few fundamentalists do, but no one else can seriously believe that he was God — 'son', avatar or incarnation.

But that doesn't mean his teaching is all worthless. Surely there's wisdom in much of what he said; and surely we wouldn't want to throw that ethical baby out with the superstitious bathwater.

And so with Freud. The edifice may have a foundation of guesswork and opportunism; but over the years, as he practised, the old short-story writer — the O. Henry of medicine — may have had moments of psychological insight, may he not? I mean, he was quite a clever man and he spent many years in practice.

And in the search for human happiness, are we really so well off and so pure that we can afford to ignore any such offerings, however tainted their parentage?

Especially if, as now, they seem to be working to my advantage by steering me towards a semi-civilised hospital with 'medication', therapy and craft rooms — rather than a Category A, round-the-clock fisting.

Or so I argued as I lay in my cell last night; so I reasoned — so I weaselled with myself.

12

My name is Mike Engleby and I'm in my eighteenth year at an ancient institution. Ring a bell? This one isn't a university, though; this one is Longdale Special Hospital (formerly Asylum for the Criminally Insane), in the village of Upper Rookley.

It's 7 March, 2006 and I understand that a film about gay cowboys has just won an Oscar. I'm only 52, but I feel a bit cut off from the world, as you would if you'd spent so much time in here.

But although I feel detached, I think that recently there's been an improvement in my memory of the past. With this in mind, I think it's time to bring my account of events up to date. I don't have access to what I wrote earlier, though I know it's kept on file here and is frequently referred to by the people who 'treat' me. I daresay I could have a look at it if I asked nicely, but I don't really need to since I can remember everything in it.

My improved recall is frankly a mixed blessing. But the fact is that, after a few hazy years, probably affected by 'medication', my memory has not only recovered its encyclopaedic range, it now has fewer gaps and a really tight focus on detail.

Take the day I arrived here, seventeen years ago.

The irritating thing was that I could see very little of Upper Rookley from the back of the van in which I was being driven. When you're going to be placed in an institution for an 'indefinite' length of time, one of the things you must worry about is the view. Odd, this, because I'd never thought of myself as visually alert, but I'd grown mighty tired of the sight of my prison cell during nine months on remand and I was desperate for some longer vista.

The van had a window, but I could only see out if I stood up, and the two prison officers with me were uneasy about that. Nevertheless, I could sense the topography as we turned into the high street, and through the barred, one-way glass of the window I caught a glimpse of the front of the cigarette shop whose backyard had supplied me with goods for Spaso Topley to ship onwards via the Jackson Rears.

I was reassured to see it. I don't know why.

Another odd thing was that in the five years I'd spent at Chatfield, with all the Monday morning siren practices and 'Sir, sir, Bograt's escaped', I'd never had a clear idea of where Longdale actually was. There were no signs to it from the village, and the teenage boy seldom lifts his eyes from the pavement. If Raquel Welch and John Lennon had moved into the cubicles on either side of mine in Collingham, I would have greeted the news with little more than a grunt as I toiled off to Mug Benson's double French. This is how most people live: alive, but not conscious; conscious but not aware; aware, but intermittently.

416

What was I thinking in those days? What *was* I thinking? Most of my life has been like that, like a woodlouse under a stone — while, as Newton put it, the great ocean of truth lay all undiscovered before me.

The van swung left not far from the back gates into Chatfield and began to climb. I was feeling carsick, as you do with no view out, and had vomited twice into a bucket, which the screws had stopped the van to empty by the road. Carsickness is one of the most underrated of trivial ailments; you'd rather die than have it carry on. So when the van finally stopped, the door opened and I was deposited outside my indefinite future home, a maximum security institution with thirty-feet-high walls crowned with twists of barbed wire, I viewed it with intense relief.

The handover from prison to hospital was a category shift (in the Ryle not the Home Office sense of category). Longdale itself was like Chatfield with higher walls: Victorian brickwork drenched with institutional indifference, its towers and windows of abandoned hope; but at the front there was a bright new block, something like a go-ahead primary school. This was the reception area, into which I was led by the prison officers, to one of whom I was still handcuffed. Two ordinary-looking women sat behind a long whitewood counter on bright red office chairs.

Forms were filled. I waited, wondering when I would next see any room like this, something that passed for normal.

Eventually, I was taken forward to a glass door. The screw removed my handcuffs. My shoulder was taken by a hospital employee, a burly young man with a beard, accompanied by an older man in spectacles, who smiled at me.

I was led into a glassed-in area where I was scanned by metal detectors and body-searched. Then they took me to a cubicle where I had to strip. The young man peered beneath my lifted scrotum, then asked me to bend over while he shone a torch up me. Then he peered into my mouth, pointing the light beneath my tongue, and I tried not to breathe on him, having not drunk even water since I'd vomited. They gave me a blanket to wrap round me while my clothes were passed through an airport scanner before being returned. Dressed again, I went through a short glass corridor under closed-circuit cameras that twitched their necks like birds.

After three more doors, one electronic, two worked by keys, I found myself in open air.

I glanced back through the modern transit building to see if I could still make out the prison officers on the other side; but I couldn't. They were gone, they hadn't said goodbye.

But I was no longer a prisoner or a criminal; they'd taken off my handcuffs; I was a patient now. My identity was changed, from an object of vilest hatred to something broken that must be cured. The transformation was too much for me to take in; it literally took my breath away, and I gasped.

I asked the men with me if we could stop for a moment. They let go of my arms.

I looked up all round me at the English sky. It was a grey March afternoon: cold, cloudy, any day.

The large asylum buildings loomed in front of me, with their battered doors and original cast iron drainpipes still in place from 1855.

Here was my indeterminate future, my home, and it was no more or less than I deserved: it was merely inevitable and familiar.

I put my head back and sniffed the wind.

I thought I could smell rain.

★   ★   ★

To begin with, I was pleased to be there. I was no longer 'Egghead Jen's Crazed Killer'. They couldn't call me the 'Fen Beast' or 'Schizo Scribbler' any more.

No. I was an object of concern and care; I was to be scrutinised, medicated, cured — released!

I was compliant with all this up to a point. I was put in a new building, where I had a room of my own with a bed, chair, table and so on. The window, however, was too high to see through. It was barred and sealed. If I stood on the chair I could see a bit of distant green and some buildings, but it wasn't up to much. I was locked in, and the door of my room, which was made of steel, had a low-level square of reinforced glass through which they could shine a torch at night. It had a rectangular slit through which they could pass newspapers, books, a plastic mug and 'medication' without opening the door.

So in fact it was like a cell, and at the start,

while I was being 'stabilised', I was locked up for long periods of the day. This was 'for my own safety' and was a 'temporary measure'. Eventually, I was given to understand that, if all went well, I would spend the day in various occupational therapy and day rooms, moving about with a degree of freedom. I would then graduate to a dormitory.

They gave me drugs, though I think only because it made them feel they were doing something medical. Some of these drugs made my tongue swell up. Some gave me blurred vision and a shaking hand. Most of them made me feel disorientated and afraid. All of them made me feel thirsty.

Inside my room, I was allowed newspapers, books and a radio. After a good deal of paperwork and letters to my bank, I had access to money of my own with which to buy these things. In general, the experience was better than being on remand in prison, because I did get to leave the room for three or four hours a day; I could go to the toilet, use the showers, walk to the dining room and so on. The staff were not dressed as gaolers but as nurses, though I was told that for some reason they belonged to the Prison Officers' Association. I didn't get beaten up, though there were plenty of extremely unstable-looking men that I stayed clear of.

I didn't like the dormitory (noises from the psychotics, smells, bad hygiene), but on balance I'd say Longdale was also better than Chatfield, down there in the valley. No

Baynes, Wingate or Hood. The only thing that nagged at me, even at the start, was the question of how long I'd be there. While a prison term was daunting, it was finite; but the doctors at Longdale were free to review and renew my detention indefinitely.

They say that if we knew the hour and place of our death, we could not go on living. Not knowing when my release might be, if ever, posed similar questions. Or to be precise, just one question: Why bother to go on?

The trial, incidentally, was something of a triumph for my team. Because I'd pleaded guilty to manslaughter, there was no identification issue and the DNA match wasn't questioned. Two shrinks for the defence and two for the Crown asserted that I was bonkers, but the judge, as Exley predicted, would not accept their opinion without putting it to a jury. Exley let me see the report of the prison medical officer, for the prosecution. It was written — scribbled, actually, in blue ballpoint — on a standard form available from Her Majesty's Stationery Office. This is what it said.

1. *Information to establish a persistent disorder or disability of mind.*
   His father died young and abused him. He was abused at school and abused others. He is a long term drug user and thief.

2. *Information to establish that the disorder or disability of mind results in abnormally aggressive or seriously irresponsible conduct on the part of the patient.*
He killed a young woman and claims to have killed a youth. He may have killed another woman. He shows no remorse and does not understand the seriousness of his actions.

3. *Information to establish that the disorder or disability of mind requires or is susceptible to medical treatment.*
He is a loner and introvert, cannot establish relationships with females and has contempt for other males in an antisocial and rather dangerous way. There is a likelihood he may respond to therapy in a structured situation.

4. *Reasons for the conclusion that the disorder or disability of mind is of a nature or degree which warrants the detention of the patient in hospital for medical treatment.*
He suffers from personality disorder and does not express remorse about his offences. In my view he is a potentially dangerous man and I shall recommend a Restriction Order under the Mental Health Act be ordered by the court.

That's it! Exley told me that many of them are even shorter. As for the pathetic circularity of the

422

argument — he's mad because he sinned, he may get better because he's mad — that too, Julian told me, is standard.

Ah, what a piece of work is a Man . . . The glory that was Engleby, the incomparable complexity of the human mind in all its glittering and bewildering beauty reduced to half a dozen non sequiturs in blue Bic on an HMSO form . . .

The trial itself, on the other hand, was entirely thrilling.

Although the prosecution made much of the fact that I'd lived a 'normal' life and had managed to function in a well-paid job, Harvey called an embarrassing number of witnesses to attest to how weird I was. He also put me on the stand and made me go through what had happened. I didn't try to appear deranged, but it was difficult to make the truth sound less than odd.

When his turn came, Julian Exley fluently outlined his position under Harvey's prompting, but didn't take well to being bullied by the prosecution counsel, a nasty piece of work called Tindall. I sensed that what Tindall wanted to get over was that anything short of locking me up in Parkhurst *sine die* would show improper regard for the gravity of the crime and insufficient sympathy for Jennifer and her family. He made several references to something called 'Section 47' — a sort of safety net that means the prisoner can later be transferred from prison to hospital if the shrinks so decide. He offered this as an ideal solution: show your revulsion for the crime by refusing the plea and get him sent to

Parkhurst; don't get bogged down in dodgy psychiatry, just let the experts sort it out later. This, I think, was what they did with Sutcliffe, and it looked like a worryingly attractive compromise.

The technicality of the plea, however, meant that for the most part Tindall was obliged to attack Exley's evidence, which he did on two flanks: both that the diagnosis itself was woolly nonsense (one saw his point) and, second, that even if — which was not admitted — there was something to it, then it still would not have *substantially* (he liked that word) diminished my responsibility.

We all agreed that the key issue was the degree to which my judgement had been impaired by my mental condition. Tindall argued that the measure of this was as much moral as medical and that psychiatrists had no special expertise here — any more than his lordship or the jury. It was a matter of common sense and 'gut' feeling. Exley ceded some ground but maintained his profession had 'a contribution' to make.

Harvey counter-attacked with a tremendous quote he'd dug up from the Court of Appeal where the senior judge had spoken of 'a state of mind so different from that of ordinary human beings that the reasonable man would term it abnormal . . . [affecting] the ability to exercise willpower to control physical acts, in accordance with rational judgement'. He made great play of the jury being 'reasonable men and women'; though of course this was essentially a completely non-technical point of the old circular variety: he must have been out of his mind to have done such a thing.

But it went well for him. His style was collegiate and constructive; he enlisted the assistance of his lordship and the jury — and me — as though solving a tricky cryptic crossword, all help gratefully received.

But Tindall was not finished. He returned to attack the whole 'personality disorder' category. Schizophrenics are mad all the time; but people not suffering from mental illness — e.g. me — only get into Special Hospitals if they do something terrible. The murder is the thing that allows admission to take place. Then he found his logic leading to something really terrifying: if psychopathy was really a mental abnormality, why were there no psychopaths being treated in normal NHS hospitals?

There was a nasty silence while we all let this sink in. 'Well, Dr Exley, I put it to you. How many psychopaths receive treatment *before* they commit a crime? Is psychopathy in effect no more than a fancy term for wickedness?'

Exley didn't have the figures, naturally enough, for non-criminal psychopaths in the civil NHS (bugger all, one suspected) and he floundered for a bit.

The judge, however, seemed to be of the view that this line of questioning had come too late in the day; we had moved on from categories into degree of impairment. Harvey made some more commonsense appeals to the 'reasonable' man and recalled Exley, who had recovered sufficiently to marshal his arguments in such a way as

425

to suggest that they were too subtle for Tindall to understand, but were well within the grasp of the jury and of his lordship. He was good; after a wobble, he was really good. So was Harvey, who was very alert — a bulky man fast on his feet — and quick to see which way the judge was leaning. Exley offered to go into the biochemistry of personality formation, including genetics, but the judge looked appalled at the idea. He'd had enough. And where he directed, the jury followed.

* * *

I was shocked by how quickly I adapted to the institution. I learned to build my day round small highlights. The cup of tea at seven: strong, hot and fresh because my dormitory was near the kitchen block. If I drank it quickly and timed my call properly, the auxiliary would stop on her way out and refill my cup. The sense of triumph lasted most of the morning. Or the Nescafé at nine. I used to be fussy about espresso and filter and cappuccino and all that. But the single spoon of standard Nescaff from a catering tin dissolved in hot-ish water was something for which I began to salivate from eight-thirty onwards.

The food, unfortunately, smelt of death and madness, that hospital reek I remembered from breakfast at Park Prewett. NHS hospitals are perhaps the last places in England where they think people eat boiled carrots, gravy and steamed pudding every day for lunch. Tinned pears with custard? Where do they even find this stuff? Perhaps the menu was set down by Mr Beveridge in 1948 and has yet to be reviewed. Luckily you can buy other things from the food shop; together with the pills, they made me put on weight. I gained almost two stone in my first year.

I was under the charge of a bluff psychiatrist called Braithwaite, who'd been to visit me in prison to see whether I'd be 'suitable' for transfer to Longdale. He believed in active intervention in his patients' lives. He didn't want a legion of the lost — of pale, violent men adrift in time; he wanted to make them better and move them on, preferably back into the world in which they had transgressed.

This was a laudable aim, I thought, consistent with the function of a hospital. In practice, what it meant was trying lots of different drugs — pink pills, blue pills, white pills — even for patients like me whose condition responded little to chemicals.

It also meant, about once a week, talking to Braithwaite or one of his assistants, generally a woman called Turner, about how I felt.

Not that great, usually: suffering from the side effects of the 'medication'. I wish they wouldn't rely on that genteel term, incidentally; I wish they'd call them drugs or pills.

Generally, I must say, they didn't go in for euphemism. Dr Turner (first name Jennifer, alas) was typical. She didn't blush or blink when she used the word 'murder' to me in our private consultations. There was something of the schoolmarm in her that made me feel as though I'd been caught for nothing more than smoking in the bushes; she was also quite pretty, though when I asked about her husband and/or home life I received a severely frosty response. She was going to treat me, but she didn't want or have to like me, that was what she implied, and I thought that that was fair enough.

I really did like her, though. She was an excellent person, so direct and practical. It's just a pity that the instruments she had at her disposal — drugs and chat — were so blunt. What Dr Turner needed was a way of reshaping the geography of my mind. She needed to shift the tectonic plates, reform the rifts and flood the valley. To do this, she needed to master time so that she and I could move about in it, not be the slaves of the homo sap delusion that it runs in a straight line.

She couldn't do this, unfortunately, so we were left with pills and talk and occupational therapy — viz., gardening, 'crafts' and painting. There were other things to do, but I wasn't 'ready' for them yet.

I was also sent to see psychologists, and this was preferable because one wasn't always being brought up against the evidence of how pointless it all was. Your psychologist likes nothing more than a 'test', and in the early days I was forever answering questions, ticking boxes, Y or N, or on a scale of one to . . .

One day I was asked to sit in a chair with an electrode attached to me for a test called 'penile plethysmography'. A nervous young woman in a white coat, possibly a student or trainee, then showed me photographs of women with no clothes on from various top-shelf magazines. The idea was to measure the degree of arousal and from that deduce . . . Deduce what? Whether I preferred blondes to brunettes, white girls to black, *Men Only to Mayfair*? They could have just asked.

I was anxious not to give the wrong impression, not to feel a flicker for the wrong picture — a flicker maybe delayed from a previous one. I didn't want to find myself paired up at some grim hospital social with Lizzie 'The Hatchet' Rockwell from the women's wing because I'd inadvertently twitched at the picture that most resembled her.

From what I know, it's true to say that in real life people frequently desire and have vigorous affairs with someone who is not at all their usual type. And what does a psychologist deduce from that?

In the event, the presence of the young woman in the white coat with the clipboard was so inhibiting that I pretty much flatlined.

★　★　★

In those early days, sex was very far from my mind. I think that lust is to some extent an expression of optimism: breed because life's good, let's have more of it.

That was really not my attitude when I first came inside Longdale. After seventeen years, I have regained a certain spark and pugnacity, I

429

think. But it took me time, and I must admit that I felt pretty low for the first . . . Well, perhaps two or three years.

To be confronted with what sane society made of me: it took some digesting. I dragged it off to my lair and tried to swallow it, slowly, over a long period. (My lair eventually became a private room, rather than a dormitory, a little like my cubicle at Chatfield. I also in due course acquired what was called a 'parole card', which allowed me to wander pretty much where I wanted in the grounds.)

I was helped in the digestion process by a couple of the other patients. Gerry was about twenty years older than I was and came from a farming family in Somerset. He had cropped whiteish hair and a practical, muscular air to the way he went about his business. I didn't in any way think of him as a 'father' figure, but I saw that he had managed to make a reasonable life for himself in this place (he'd been here for ten years already) by treating it as normal, something like school or national service — which he had in fact done, fighting briefly in Korea. Gerry was well informed about British history, albeit in a patchy, autodidactic way. Every morning he read the *Daily Telegraph* right through, smoothing each page out neatly on the table. He was good with his hands and made intricate though useless gadgets (pipe racks and so on) in the woodwork room. He sought me out quite early on and it was only after a bit that I understood, slightly to my embarrassment, that

430

he was hoping to learn from me. He had been at the local grammar school, but he hadn't been to university after national service because he was needed on the farm. We began each day by discussing what was in the papers over a cigarette in the day room, and I began to know what kind of thing made him laugh and to search it out.

Mark was younger and not, on the surface, as well sorted out as Gerry. He wore clothes that were a little too smart, and his hair was always neat. His intelligence was tightly wound and his views were expressed in syntactically flawless sentences (which is not, whatever Enoch Powell may have thought, the same thing as being eloquent). Mark was handsome, I'd suppose you'd say, and his clear brown eyes seldom blinked. What I grew to like about him (and it took time) was that he viewed life as a colossal, cosmic joke. Although he had periods of depression which took him out of circulation for a while, he made me laugh more than anyone I've ever known, more than Stellings or Jen or Julie or Ralph Richardson or Jeffrey Archer. I pined for Mark when he was off the ward in a black-dog spell and I think I helped him when he came back.

I knew what Mark had 'done' out there, why he was in Longdale, because he told me. It was serious and inexplicable, but not barbaric. I never knew what crime Gerry had committed and it didn't seem to be important to our friendship. Does that sound pious? Maybe. I admit that I was not above a little frisson when I

431

sat next to a celebrated disemboweller. I'm only human.

★ ★ ★

People think that men like me can only be released by the Home Secretary. In fact, the power resides with a mental health tribunal, which reviews my case every three years, or every year if I ask it to. The politicians can't legally overrule the tribunal.

In spring 2001, with the backing of Dr Turner, I applied for a conditional discharge. It was thought that with some support, I could, without endangering others, live a reasonably normal life in what is termed 'the community' — i.e. non-community, or world at large.

What windy joy, as Milton might have put it, had I that day conceived, hopeful of my delivery . . .

The judge at the tribunal looked set to give me the green light until at the last minute the Home Office expert witness came up with some particularly compelling and ghoulish evidence in my case, backed by some general statistics about reoffending. The judge, visibly appalled, decided that discretion was the better part . . .

Jennifer Turner had the difficult task of breaking the news to me.

'They aren't required to go into the detail behind the decision, Michael.'

'But we know what the reasons are.'

'Believe me, I find this as vexing — almost as vexing as you do.'

'I'm a patient in a hospital who is better but can't go home because the public wouldn't like it.'

'Public opinion may well be a factor. It was a famous case.'

'I know. I remember.'

'I'm sorry.'

'But,' I said, 'it looks as though the Home Office is now arguing that a hospital shall be deemed a prison. Why did we go through all that diminished responsibility nonsense?'

Dr Turner looked as though she might explode. Then she did. 'Dear God, how do you think it makes me feel?'

I ended up consoling her, like Carlyle with Mill. 'It's all right, Jennifer, I know it's not your fault . . . '

But the whole experience set me back a bit. They put me on a high dose of antidepressants and I gained a lot more weight. For the best part of two years I didn't really get out of my room. I just sat there watching a small television that Stellings had sent me. Thank God for television, for *Countdown* and the regional news.

★ ★ ★

Julie came to see me once when I was in prison on remand. She told me how our mother had died of cancer.

We were in the prison visiting room, either side of a table, under the eyes of the warders and a couple of social workers.

'She said to send you her love, Mike.'

'Thanks. Was it painful at the end?'

'Not too bad. She had the drugs. She was in the Sunset Room in the end. In the hospital.'

I nodded. 'Do you feel all right, Jules? Do you feel lonely?'

'I'm all right.'

'It's just you and me now. Of the old gang. And since they may never let me out, it's really just you.'

Julie looked down at her hands, which she was clenching on the table.

'Did Mum know I was pleading guilty?'

'Yes.'

'And what did she think?'

'She said she didn't know you any more. She said that once she felt you were a part of her. When you were a baby and that. That you were her own flesh and blood. Like you know, really, her own flesh, like — '

'I know what she meant.'

'But she said she thought that little boy had died, or got lost somewhere on the way.'

I was holding the edge of the table.

'She said if she was to meet you now she wouldn't know you.'

I swallowed. 'I understand. She's right, of course. She's right in more ways than she could understand.'

'I'm sorry, Mike.'

'You're not to blame.'

I thought for a bit. 'Julie, I don't think you should come and see me any more, wherever they send me. Send me a card on my birthday, that's all. To show you do still remember. For the rest of the time, you should put me out of your mind.'

I hoped she wouldn't remember the card. A kitty in a basket every April from here to the crack of doom. God.

She was biting her lip, still looking down.

I smiled. 'Got a boyfriend, Jules?'

'Yup.'

'Marry him. Be happy. Have babies.'

She kept nodding, dumbly.

'You'll be all right, Julie.'

'Oh, Mike.'

★   ★   ★

After I'd got over the disappointment of not being released, I felt that I'd gained a new perspective on my life and its events. Having not written a word in the 1990s, I began to pick up my pen again and jot down the odd thought. I found that I had a certain clarity.

Baynes, for instance. I had clear recall and a consistent point of view on all that. I didn't plan to kill him, but I did plan to hurt him badly; I wanted to break his legs. I knew he spent hours practising his goal-kicking on a distant pitch. In his final term he had no lesson to rush back to (he had a 'private study' period) so could carry on till it was dark. I simply doubled back from the food shop where I'd gone after my own rugby game and waited for him. The bridge over the stream that divided two large areas of playing fields was concrete with scaffolding poles for handrails. Nearby, I'd noticed lumps of loose

435

concrete, roughly mixed, full of pebbles, and a length of rusted broken pole. I hid beneath the bridge until I heard his studs clattering towards me. I caught him from behind with the pole and he went down. I lifted the pole and brought it down with all my might across his tibia. I heard it crack. I dragged him to the edge of the bridge and rubbed the wound on the back of his head into the rough edge of the concrete. Then I chucked the weapons into the stream and jogged back to the main school. He was groaning as I left and I knew it wouldn't be long till he was found. Dr Benbow would have examined him in his usual perfunctory manner when he was brought in, implying that he was wasting everyone's time. The leg was cleanly broken and he was well enough to take his Oxford exams a few weeks later. What I didn't know at the time was how hard I had hit his head. In fact, I hit it more than once, and it gave me pleasure to do so. I didn't mention it at the time in what Dr Exley called my 'journal/narrative' in case it was seen by someone.

The case of Gudrun Abendroth is more complicated. My time in Longdale has enabled me, as I said, to recall the Baynes incident clearly. I even feel a degree of remorse for his orphaned children, even though in my view they're better off without him. Fräulein Abendroth, though, is a different matter.

To put it simply: I still don't know if I killed her or not; and that single fact, that not-knowing, is what persuades me — more than Baynes, more even than Jen — that Longdale is

436

the right place for me. I followed a woman who looked like her from a Graham Parker gig to a house in Tournay Road. That much I wrote at the time. I have subsequently remembered for sure that I went back there on at least one occasion. I followed her. She went to a pub called the Cock on North End Road and I lurked at the other end of the bar, watching her. But why would I want to kill her when I didn't even know her?

If I did, I must be like Peter Sutcliffe or someone, but I don't think I am. Or perhaps I did get to know her, albeit briefly. And in that space of time, perhaps she posed a threat to the 'integrity' of my 'narcissistic self' so great that violence was my only self-defence.

The Exley theory, however, can't really be stretched to include amnesia on my part: he was rather strict on that point. 'Snapshot' memory, including partial forgetfulness, he could live with, but a complete blank he thought suspect. I suppose the only way Exley could be brought onside is if we beefed up the theory of 'pathological defences' so much that they annexed the memory function. It seems a bit far-fetched, though, doesn't it?

So, I'm inclined to acquit myself.

On the other hand, it smells a bit. Who else might have killed her? And the killer had what the Roman plods of Fulham called a modus operandi similar to mine: several blows to cranium; no sexual interference; deep grave.

But if I did kill her, yet can't remember doing so (compare Sutcliffe's detailed recall of his victims in court), how many more might there be?

At this time, I just don't know; and there are some things in the past that may have happened and some that may not have happened. But the reality of their happening or not happening *then* has no weight *now*.

Until we can navigate in time, I'm not sure that we can prove that what happened is real.

★ ★ ★

Back live, as they still say.

I remember that conversation with Stellings in the Indian restaurant in which he — insanely, I thought — predicted the imminent end of the Cold War, the sex war, apartheid and so on.

He was right, though, wasn't he? He might have added architecture too, which was then embedded in a desperate impasse. Either you built 'modern' — witless rectangular towers with metal-framed windows in which people rushed to kill themselves — or you built mock-Palladian (itself a classical pastiche). The two camps detested one another with pitiless venom. Now I look in the papers and I see buildings of light and air, glass and steel and uncovered brick. They look really nice. (I wonder if I'll ever be free to go inside one.)

Suggesting, back then, that using strong materials and good design might be a way forward would have earned you contempt from both the Legomen and the Pasticheurs. Like the way all British politicians are Social Democrats

438

now, but back then holding such beliefs was derided as 'having no policies'.

(Don't you love politicians? I think what I like best is their sublimely self-serving insistence that their 'private life' is nothing whatever to do with their 'public life'. So that the decision to shaft their secretary over the conference table five minutes before the cabinet meeting or to spend the night face down in a bathhouse cubicle taking on all comers is reached by a different person, or a different brain, from the one who, a few minutes later, decides to vote for family tax credits or the death penalty. God, if only!)

Anyway, these changes in society look all right to me, though of course in most ways things haven't changed at all. I remember my student questions.

'Got a cure for the common cold yet? Have you? Thought not. How's your 2003 world, then? A few wars? Some genocide? Some terrorism? Drugs? Abuse of children? High crime rate? Materialistic obsessions? More cars? Blah-blah pop music? Vulgar newspapers? Porn? Still wearing jeans?'

Stelling's specific optimism was right, but so was my less hopeful overview.

And other things are worse than even I foresaw.

For instance: my country recently invaded another country.

That's not something anyone could have foreseen. Invading other countries was what Hitler or Kaiser Wilhelm or the kamikaze Japanese did.

Not invading other countries: that was our thing. It more or less defined who we were. America likewise. Obviously there were those CIA things (Guatemala, Iran and so on) but they were unofficial: when we begged the American government to join us in our European World War Two, prim Mr Roosevelt said No: the US has not been attacked, so it wouldn't be proper. Then the Japanese bombed them at Pearl Harbor and it was OK.

This Blair guy, though. My age, Oxford-educated, looks and sounds quite reasonable. You'd have thought that he'd understand his own country's recent past, wouldn't you? Apparently not. They sent inspectors to find weapons and the inspectors came back empty-handed; they sent spies, and the spies returned with nothing.

Never mind, said Mr Blair, I don't care: if we can't find the weapons then he must be hiding them, and in half an hour or so he could attack us. We must get him first.

My old friend Peter Mandelson came on the radio. 'Oh yes,' he said, 'Saddam's got a supermarket.' He pronounced it 'shoopermarket'. 'Saddam's got a shoopermarket selling deadly weapons. We must invade.' Peter had seemed rather a sophisticated man, I thought, when I'd met him during that General Election. Why was he now talking this crap about a giant Asda in Tikrit?

The funny thing was that almost no one outside Westminster believed it. For instance, no one in Longdale believed it.

'Paranoid' Pete Smith on my corridor never thought we'd find hidden weapons, yet Paranoid is someone who rolls an orange under his bed each night to check there's no one there.

Johnnie Johnston wouldn't give the time of day to that 'intelligence' dossier, and Johnnie is a man who believes his own thoughts are controlled by the BBC Radio 4 long-wave transmitter at Redruth.

★ ★ ★

Not much has happened in Longdale in the last seventeen years. There have been some improvements in the kitchen — twice a week you can hold it down — and in the gardens and the workshops.

I am no longer under the control of Dr Braithwaite (retired) or Dr Turner (moved on, alas). My 'case officer' (sounds like MI6, but it isn't) is now Dr Vidushi Sen, a severe young woman in her first senior appointment in the exciting world of Special Hospitals. She has more than her fair share of old lags like me, poor thing; the senior doctors bag the newer patients because there's more hope of an outcome.

They stopped giving me drugs because everyone could see they did no good. Take drugs away from a patient and he may improve; at least he'll stop experiencing the side effects. But take drugs away from a shrink and all she has left is chat.

Dr Vidushi Sen is a very poor chatter. She sits opposite me with her shiny black hair tightly drawn back and pinned, in her pretty cotton shift worn over trousers that taper and button at the ankle. She blinks over her shallow black-framed glasses, clipboard in hand, and waits for me to spout.

I don't think Dr Sen subscribes to the Exley theory of 'personality disorder'. There's a nasty mix there of nature and nurture, of a 'biological substrate' and plain bad behaviour. All a bit murky for her, I think. Am I meant to be mad or bad? The Exley answer, which essentially says 'a bit of both' is not to Dr Sen's taste. And since I don't really fit into any category of mental illness in either the American or European handbooks, of which there have been several new editions since I've been in Longdale, all of which she's studied dutifully, Dr Sen is left with the conclusion that I am bad.

She thinks I am a very nasty man indeed and should really be banged up in Strangeways or Winson Green with the robbers and the 'sane' killers and the nonces. She believes I'm far too lucid, too well controlled and too reasonable to be mad. She'd like to say too well educated, too, but, in a way so convoluted one can barely follow it, that would be incorrect, politically.

Dr Sen would never actually say that I am bad. She's very hot on 'blame' and 'guilt': absence of need for, destructive effects of.

Another thing she's very hot on is me being gay. She hasn't said as much, because it's not her way to suggest things; but she's always leaving the pink door ajar, hoping that one day I'll sidle through. I'm dreading that in desperation she'll order up another 'penile seismograph' or whatever the thing's called, but instead of looking at some forlorn toms with their legs apart, I'll be staring at Master Meat the Butcher's Boy.

She's a keen student of my journal and reveals a good deal about herself by the passages she chooses for our delectation. Those concerning Margaret and my relationship with her are of particular interest.

'You called her 'candid, optimistic and polite'.'

'So?'

She says nothing, merely raises a shaped eyebrow. I know what she means: that these are the terms in which you might describe your chartered accountant, not your lover. I don't say so; I just give her rather boring justifications of each adjective in turn.

She echoes Exley's comment on my restrained description of the first time Margaret and I had it off together; I point out that I wasn't writing to titillate. She also draws attention to my repeated references to sodomy and fisting in Her Majesty's prisons, presumably wishing to imply that my obvious distaste is — oh, toiling paradox! — a concealed desire. I hear her big feet coming from the next valley.

'And this boy 'Rough', the one who became so good at squash because he had gay desires . . . '

'What about him?'

Again the raised eyebrow. She is at the very least implying that his name, as in Trade, is another throttled longing on my part.

'Dr Sen, as you probably know, there is a huge

amount of homosexual activity in this hospital. Two men in my block are virtually married, with the blessing of the supervising psychiatrist. They share a room. They have a standing order for condoms and KY from the hospital shop. Their relationship is said to have helped them both to earthly joy and the prospect of an early release. What's to hide? Being gay would only make things better for me.'

Dr Sen seldom pushes things. She's young, maybe thirty-two, and it's against her training to suggest. You must also remember that Longdale is a maximum-security institution. Although we have confidentiality for our tête-à-têtes, the door of the consulting room is unlockable and I sit nearer to it, so that if a rescue has to be made I am easy to get at. The wall behind me is half glass and gives onto the corridor where a male nurse patrols, never more than a few paces away. There can suddenly be an undertow of danger. I see her sense it. Sometimes I see fear in her wide dark eyes: the dilating black pupils almost cover the brown iris.

Her view — I know, because she is transparent, so much better at self-disclosure than I am — is that I am a furious misogynist whose hatred of women springs from a violently suppressed homosexuality.

She also thinks I am a racist, and this is delicate because even though she's as English as I am, with a similar regional accent, her family is originally from southern India. (Her first name, Vidushi, incidentally, means 'Learned' in Hindi, which tells you about her pushy parents in

444

Maidenhead. I looked it up in hinduism.about-.com on the Internet on the heavily firewalled computer in the day room.)

When she asked me about a passage I wrote many years ago on immigration, I repeated that I merely felt pity for the West Indians who were given a false prospectus and found Britain cold and inhospitable, and sorry that for the many people from the Asian subcontintent who traded in their beautiful country for the grey rain of Catford and Lewisham.

She didn't look convinced. She also brought up my description of Shireen Nazawi as 'EFL-speaking'.

I conceded that it was ungallant — but true: English wasn't Shireen's first language, and she struggled with it, as, consequently, did the readers of her articles.

Dr Sen didn't push too hard here, I must admit, because although racism was an important part of her view of Engleby as Utter Shit, it wasn't central to her assessment of why I killed Jennifer Arkland.

For misogyny, she relied on my description of the wine bar in Knightsbridge, suggesting I implied that all women were basically prostitutes, and on my 'fascination' for the street tarts in Paddington.

Obviously, I had no difficulty batting those two away.

More difficult was a sort of experimental undergrad riff that went: 'Anne, Molly and Jennifer are, like all women, weirdly obsessed by appearances — looks, colours, fashion, surfaces;

445

they have no interest in ideas or deeper truths, only 'style' and status and the rapacious purchase of goods to underline them. Their cordiality conceals a sense of bitter rivalry that they'll carry to their death, without ever acknowledging it. They're really machines for surviving in the competition for resources. Carrying the species in their wombs, they have to be.'

She didn't remember the exact words, but I was able to fill her in.

I then explained, as in a Dr Gerald Stanley supervision, that context is all. This wasn't necessarily 'my' view; it was a view that had been offered as a corrective to a romanticised depiction of the girl students' lives that had preceded it. It was a squirt of lemon in the eye to defuse the charge of 'sentimentality'.

Dr Sen did have one powerful argument for misogyny in my case, and we both knew what it was. To her credit, it was six months or more before, under provocation from me, she brought it up.

As I recall, I was irritated by her refusal ever to pass judgement on me for what I'd done. She never seemed able to express even so much as a mild disapproval.

'You're like Bill Clinton,' I said, knowing the comparison would appal her. 'He took the intern as his girlfriend, then denied it. He screwed her and he lied and lied and lied. But in the end when he coughed up he couldn't say that he'd done wrong, he'd only say what he'd done was 'inappropriate'.'

'I don't believe the idea of blame is helpful,' said Dr Sen, as always.

'With no blame there's no shame. A human society can't exist without shame. Shame is like handedness or walking upright. It's a central human attribute. In fact, it's the first human quality ever recorded.'

'Where?'

'Genesis, Chapter Three. The covering of nakedness. The acquisition of shame was the first consequence of consciousness, of the speciating moment. Take shame from me and you are calling me pre-human.'

Dr Sen coughed and rearranged her notes. 'I was merely thinking it might be worthwhile for you to think again about your attitude to women.'

'Why again? I've thought about it so many times. You seem to think that everything can be explained by it. You see significance even in the fact that I once stole a girl's bike when I was at school. It wasn't an insult to worldwide womanhood. It was because I needed transport for the gin and whisky I was stealing, so I could make money. It was about cash, not women. If there'd been a boy's bike to hand, I'd have stolen that instead.'

She stopped looking down at her notes and met my exasperated gaze, quite calmly.

'But you stole a woman's bike again, in Cambridge, didn't you?'

'What have bicycles got to do with misogyny?'

'That's your word, not mine. I've never said you are misogynistic. But if anyone wanted to

447

find evidence for that in your character, they needn't look far, need they? After all, by your own admission, you violently killed a young woman.'

She'd gone too far, and she knew it. She blushed a little, which gave her cheek a most beautiful colour, of rose under gold.

And in her shame was her humanity.

I don't think that's a misogynistic remark.

13

I had a visit from Stellings today. Yes, you can have visits here. I told you: it's a hospital.

Like you, I'd imagined iron-barred cells with famous Panthers and Rippers served food by armed yet windy guards through hatches using lengthy tongs while the men inside went more and more insane down the years, beating their brains against the damp brick walls.

In fact there are only a handful of people kept locked up and it's mostly for their own safety. But all the famous guys — you can bump into them over the seed boxes in the garden stores, or doing some fiddly work with a bradawl in the carpentry shop.

I met Stellings in the overheated day room where Johnnie Johnston and a couple of others were watching *Neighbours* on television.

Stellings was dressed in what he imagines to be a non-homicidal-maniac-inciting outfit of blue jeans, stone windcheater and open-necked plaid shirt with a nasty little polo pony on the breast pocket.

He's very butch about being normal and makes a thing of saying hello to anyone he remembers from previous visits. 'Hi, Frank!' he calls with a wave to creepy Frank Usborne, who, I told Stellings, had killed three rent boys and kept bits of them in the freezer compartment of his fridge.

This is completely untrue. I've no idea what crime Frank committed, but by far his worst offence inside is that he always gets to the Sudoku puzzle in the newspaper before anyone else and completes it before breakfast. If above the grid it gives the rating 'Difficult', Frank puts a little left-out sign and adds 'Not Very' in ballpoint next to it.

This is really annoying.

At the age of 52, Stellings has retired from Oswald Payne. He renounced his equity partnership to give some of the younger bloods a shot, but in fact he had little choice in the matter as fifty is considered the end of the line in his world.

'Some of these young guys, they're just animals, Mike. There's a twenty-eight-year-old called Sean Busby I'm afraid I was responsible for hiring. Normally our partners work on a lockstep arrangement, but Busby wouldn't stay unless he worked on an 'eat what you kill' basis.'

'Couldn't you have done that in your day, Stellings?'

'No. I was very much for lockstep, it's more collegiate, it encourages people to pool their resources and work as a team. I'd hate to be on an eat-what-you-kill basis. That way, everyone's just working for themselves.' He puffed out his cheeks. 'Though I suppose I wouldn't have minded eating what Sean Busby killed.'

'Or Frank Usborne.'

'For Christ's sake, Mike.'

I don't think Stellings likes coming to Longdale with its barbed-wire walls and silly

450

regulations. 'Toiletries. Patients can only receive these if they are in plastic bottles. NOT glass or aerosols. Items should be new and in the original wrapping. Any seals must not be broken.' Christ knows what Clarissa and her smart friends with their personal trainers make of his visits. He can't bring food or sweets in case he's tampered with them; he can't even bring cigarettes for fear that he's replaced the tobacco with a bit of Glynn Powers's finest.

The only reason Stellings comes to see me is because entirely by chance, one evening almost thirty-five years ago, he found himself sitting next to me at dinner in a candlelit hall in our first week in college.

Everything else — every single thing in the intervening thirty-five years — is down to politeness.

★ ★ ★

I've been in here since March 1989, so that makes seventeen years. And I'm managing. I'll come up for review again in 2008, apparently, and by then society or the *Daily Mail* may feel I've done enough, even though in theory I haven't been punished at all, I've only been treated. It is a weird thing with us guys who are not 'mentally ill'. There was a schizophrenic who in a moment of early mania cut off his mother's head and baked it in a pie. His father killed himself from grief. The son did seven years in a Special Hospital, got better, and was released. People like me, on the other hand, are for ever

451

defined by what we did; we can't really get 'better' in that way. But don't let's go there again, or I'll get as 'vexed' as Dr Turner.

I often sit on a bench in a part of the grounds known as the Verandah — in fact a sort of raised grass embankment that gives long views down over Rookley, towards Chatfield. I have thoughts there. I remember.

Once I saw a mother in a supermarket in Paddington — an obese, poor woman with bare legs and a small child who was making a noise. She swore at him and slapped him in the face, which only made him howl more. It wasn't her fault really; she was clearly exhausted, broke and stretched to snapping point. But I knew that when she got the child home she'd beat him more, and if there was a father (a bit unlikely) he too would hit him.

And that child would slowly ascend towards full awareness in a world whose sky was violence and whose horizons were fear. And however resourceful he was, however patient and fortunate in the events of his life that followed, he was like a creature in a nest of imprisoning boxes who could never really break free. That was his world and any attempt to persuade him that it was merely a 'subjective' or 'individual' experience could never convince him.

And all of us, I think, are like him. We may think as we grow older that we know more, but in truth no one has an overarching view, no one can see in the round. We are like cards in a pack, and the king of spades is a better thing to be than the two of diamonds; but none of us is a dealer or a player with free will and power to dispose; none of us can see or understand the value of the entire deck, let alone the rules of the game in which it's employed. Even the best of us is no more than an inert piece of card with some markings.

All of us — Julie and Jennifer and me and creepy Frank Usborne and even Dr Turner — are like that child because we are so severely limited by the operation of our consciousness — the faculty that Unamuno called a 'curse', that made us lower than the jackass or the crab.

In much of my childhood and adolescence I never knew how unhappy I was. I accepted everything as being the norm because I knew no different. How could I? I had nothing with which to compare it, and all my impulses were towards normalisation on the 'constancy principle' (Freud surely did get that bit right). Only now can I see with a little more perspective how damaging that degree of misery was to me. Not because (and here the psychoanalysts are mistaken) I pressed into service the mysterious hypothetical mechanisms of 'repression' to put it to one side, away from the normal processes of mind, so that it festered and grew toxic until such time as it was ready to wreak havoc on my entire metabolism. No; but just because that much pure, continuing unhappiness is bad for you. It burns away your gentler impulses. It corrodes the soul.

When I look at Gerry and Mark and I think of poor Jennifer and all the people that I've met and talked about in these pages, they seem to me all in their way like that little boy in the Tesco aisle. They seem part of a great biological accident: viz., that the defining human faculty — that of self-awareness — is a faulty one, at best partial and frustrating, at worst utterly misleading.

It's as though we discovered that hawks' famous eyesight didn't really work or that all hounds secretly have a duff sense of smell. The failure of any other faculty we could bear with patience, even with humour, but not the failure of the one that distinguished us from all previous species. That is beyond irony, beyond cruelty.

What I fear most of all is that when I die, my consciousness won't be extinguished but will survive to be reborn in a small boy in a striplit supermarket; and I will have to go home with that exhausted violent mother, and will go through this struggle of life all again, caught in an eternal loop of return.

Scientists now believe that my sense of self is an illusion generated by the chemical activity of the brain; that there is no such thing as 'mind', that there is only matter, but that over the successful *Homo sapiens* years the idea of self has become a 'necessary fiction'. We think that some small grey bits of brain, following a random inaccuracy in cell duplication many years ago, began in one individual and his offspring to generate an illusion of mind; and that, in history, the chance mutation that allowed them this chimera had side effects so helpful to the species that its possessors were naturally selected, to the extent that we are all now descended from them — mutants every one of us, whose key mutation is a fib.

If that current thinking is right and consequently there is no self, then my consciousness is so biochemically similar to that of the small boy in the supermarket as to be functionally indistinguishable. Therefore 'I', since I am not an individual entity, cannot cease to be, but am doomed to exist for ever — until or unless some new freak mutation finds favour with the powers of natural selection, and human consciousness, like the bat's blind eye, falls back into disuse, deselected, along with the other hopeful monsters — back into the welcoming void whence it came.

★   ★   ★

Naturally, I try not to think about *that* too much.

There are things to do here that keep your mind off it. I used to go to 'group therapy', which was of limited use since many of the group were mad. Some of them were at least coherent and wanted to talk about their crimes; they wondered what had made them rape small children or set fire to their own houses. A lot of them sat staring straight ahead, stunned by drugs or anomie.

Few of them had the smallest interest in the remainder of the group, though I remember the otherwise silent Benny Frost perking up one day when it transpired that one of the others had cancer. Benny sat forward and took a close interest. Was this person going to die? What were his chances? Benny is very frightened of death, so frightened that he killed three men, very slowly, hoping to learn something self-protective from their experience of dying.

For a while, I used to go to church. There is a fine Victorian chapel, rather like the one in Jennifer's old college where Anne made her impassioned address from the pulpit. I liked the stories from the Bible, but the music was unendurable, particularly Frank Usborne on the tambourine. After some bell, book and candle ritual, the chapel briefly went interfaith to accommodate the Muslims, of whom we have a growing number. Now they have their own miniature mosque, a former punishment room outside which you sometimes see a row of laceless shoes. Inside, it's done up like the carpet shop at Harrods.

There is no synagogue because Jews don't do murder. What about Cain? you're thinking. But he wasn't a Jew because the Jews didn't start till Abraham, and if the Garden of Eden was where we think it was, Cain, like his parents, was probably from Mesopotamia, which was on the site of modern Iraq. And on the sixth day, God created . . . an Iraqi. Of course, the children of Abraham did then do a lot of killing on their own account, but the modern British Jew doesn't. When Jennifer Turner first told me this, it made my head spin for days. Nature-nurture, culture, religion, genes, schizo, psycho . . . In the end, I gave up; my thoughts seemed no more conclusive than those provoked by the 'modern' painting

456

in Stellings's drawing room all those years ago.

For years I also did a course in 'social skills'. Much of this focussed on how to approach the opposite sex, and for this purpose we were allowed to mix with women patients. There was a good deal of 'role play', much of it taped on video for our later delight. Somewhere in the archive is a film of me pretending to be queuing outside a cinema and 'striking up a conversation' with Lizzie 'the Hatchet' Rockwell that culminates in me asking her if she would like to join me for a drink later. In the rushes I saw, it doesn't, to be honest, look as though my heart is really in it.

And then of course there was teaching. There are paid instructors in any number of crafts and trades, from tinsmith to bookbinder, but some men also wanted to do school work. When I arrived, this was under the supervision of a patient with a degree from Oxford in Classics, though he always referred to it as 'Greats'. Under prompting from Dr Turner, I eventually volunteered to help. I was paid for my work, and it secured my ownership of the envied parole card that gives me freedom to roam. I had a class of half a dozen for GCSE Maths and Physics, three for History and English, while one year I taught Geography A level by keeping one step ahead in the book. I didn't give it much of a socialist slant, as my old moral tutor Dr Townsend might have done, but my candidate secured a B-grade in the exam and I believe it helped him get released back into the world. Such are the consolations we teachers cling to.

I stuck at the pedagoguery for several years, though not as long as Mug Benson, who, the *Chatfield Year Book* — yes, the bastards tracked me down again, or perhaps they just bicycle a copy up the slope — informs me is still grinding out irregular verbs in the valley. Our exam results kept on improving. Johnnie Johnston, who to my certain knowledge, couldn't count from one to five without ten minutes' hard digital labour, applied to do Maths GCSE one year. It was uphill work for him, me and the rest of the class, but he was adamant that the transmitter signals from Redruth were giving him the all-clear. In August, he brought me a piece of paper that reported he had scored an A-star. The thrill rather went out of it for me after that.

★　★　★

I don't do much these days, but I find listening to music helps distract me. I'm allowed a radio and CD player in my room and I've been hearing one or two of the old records I used to like at university. What I'm looking for is songs that buy into the human illusion in a really simple way, but have just a touch of comfort in them. Old Dylan, for instance:

It ain't no use a-turnin' on your light, babe,
The light I never knowed;
It ain't no use turnin' on your light, babe,
I'm on the dark side of the road.

He just tells the girl she wasted his 'precious time', but it doesn't really matter, so, 'Don't think twice, it's all right.' That's a good attitude, there's something noble about it and outside its time; I guess that's what's good about folk music: when it's good it can have an eternal ring.

'Girl From the North Country' makes me think of Jennifer, sitting in the firelit circle in Ireland.

> If you go when snowflakes storm,
> When rivers freeze and summer ends,
> Please see she has a coat so warm
> To keep her from the howling winds.

It's the simplicity of the old folk tune he adapted overnight from 'Scarborough Fair' that makes it almost intolerably poignant to listen to. That, and the use of 'storm' as an intransitive verb.

We're not allowed to download anything from the Internet, so I have to get Stellings to send me CDs ('Only original recordings in the original packings will be accepted'). You're only meant to use the computer for ten minutes, under supervision, and because it's a PC with a Bill Gates programme it spends most of that time freezing and crashing. Stellings sent me a copy of *Grand Hotel* by Procol Harum. I lay awake all night with that song going round my head: 'I'm thinking of renting a villa in France;/ A French girl has offered to give me a chance./Or maybe I'll take an excursion to Spain,/Buy a revolver and blow out my brain.'

Not that I go along with people who try to

make out the musicians of my generation were Great Artists. I read in the paper the other day that some professor at a university — Redcar, or Stoke, I think — has written a book arguing that Dylan is not only the Columbia recording artist who touched millions, but that he is the greatest *poet* since Yeats. Or possibly Keats.

But then again maybe the prof has special insight; perhaps he knows something I never knowed.

★ ★ ★

I had a consultation with little Dr Vidushi Sen this morning. I was feeling rather reflective and — though I tried to curb the feeling in myself — quite fond of her. She's so young! She's also a product of modern (i.e. post-*trahison des clercs*) British schooling, so has almost no general knowledge, and no familiarity with: grammar, foreign languages, myth, art and history — ancient or modern. Poor child, she has a job on her hands.

The consulting area is being redecorated, so we were in a small room in the old wing, which still has the Victorian shutters and bars from when it was a padded cell. Now it has piles of papers and folders and unread reports with daunting titles and two NHS 'comfortable' chairs, madmen for the use of, and a filing cabinet on which is a circular metal tray with unwashed coffee cups and an old carton of milk. A male nurse hovered outside.

I began the *causerie*, as is expected.

'If you were God, why would you absent yourself from earth?'

No answer.

'I mean, what is the point in divine terms of being *not* here? What purpose does that serve?'

Still no answer.

'Traditionally,' I went on, 'it's explained as a 'test of faith'. But if God was evident, then you wouldn't need faith, would you? So it's a circular argument. It looks like it's also an *ex post facto* one, doesn't it?'

'What do you think?' said Dr Sen.

'I don't think that a wise God would conclude that the advantages of being absent outweigh those of being present.'

'And?'

'The consequence of being absent is that you place a heavy premium on blind 'faith'. You leave belief open to human credulity. You make religion open to perversion by politics and fanaticism.'

'So?'

'Better to turn up, I would have thought.'

Silence.

'I mean, if Woody Allen knew that ninety per cent of success comes from showing up, you'd think the Almighty could have figured it out too.'

Longer silence. By looking fierce yet staying silent, I tried to make her speak.

'Do you have religious belief?' she said eventually.

'Does it sound like it? I see the people nodding their heads at the Wailing Wall and I think God needs us more than we need him. It's

461

all about absence, isn't it?'

The eyebrow.

'They say that someone is most intensely present just after they have left.'

'Someone you love?' said Dr Sen.

'Not a word I use.'

'Ever?' Despite herself. 'Have you never loved someone?'

'From what I understand, love is something that ceases to exist if you stop feeling it.'

The eyebrow again.

' 'My love died.' You've heard people say that, haven't you? With sincerity and self-regard. 'Love' is a force or value by which most people would claim to regulate their lives. Yet if you stop feeling it, then it no longer exists.'

'And?'

'It's like fear or envy. One day you feel jealous of someone else; another day, for no discernible reason, you just don't. Sometimes you're frightened in a car; other times with the same driver, you aren't. 'Love' is like that. You feel it, you don't feel it. Nothing wrong with that. But surely that makes it too unstable to be given a privileged position in life — let alone used as a foundation.'

'To what have you given a privileged position in your life?'

This was quite a good question.

'Accuracy,' I said.

'What?'

'Integrity of fact.'

'Is that all?'

I smiled. 'You're thinking that sounds a little

462

'cold'? Well, I certainly don't think you could say in retrospect that my life has been . . . What's a phrase you might enjoy? I know, I know. You couldn't say that I've been 'on the side of life'.'

Dr Sen didn't answer.

'No one would describe my story as 'life-affirming', would they?'

I laughed, but she didn't.

'No. And I suppose if I haven't been on the 'side of life' I must have been on the other side.'

'And what's that?'

The side of death, obviously. I didn't say that, though, because I didn't want to freak her out. But I thought about it after the consultation was over. I haven't really been on any 'side' in my life, and maybe that's part of the difficulty. Perhaps I should just pick a cause, as people pick a football team, not because it 'is' the best, but just because it gives them something to believe in, like a dummy or an idol.

On the other hand, to do such a thing knowingly, to admit to the self-deception, would be like giving up on any idea of integrity.

★   ★   ★

In the dining room, my heart lifted when I saw Mark sitting alone by the window. I grabbed a tray full of death-swill and went to join him.

'Ah, Wilson,' he said. 'Pull up a chair.'

Mike, Toilet, Groucho, Irish Mike, Mike (!), Prufrock, Michèle, M.K. Watson . . . Wilson!

Mark has this fantasy in which the people in Longdale are characters from *Dad's Army*, which often seems to be showing on television. Johnnie Johnston is dotty Corporal Jones. Dr Vidushi Sen is Private Pike ('stupid boy . . . ') Creepy Frank Usborne is the vicar. Gerry, really just because he looks a bit like him, has to be Mr Mainwaring. Mark himself is the verger and is always annoying Frank Usborne by calling him 'your reverence'. And Mark cast me, to my great delight, as fey, superior Sergeant Wilson.

It has been Mark's obsession, brewed now for nine months or more, to contrive a set of circumstances in which Dr Sen (Pike) is compelled to refer to me as 'Uncle Arthur'. He has gone so far as to write a one-act play for Christmas, currently being scrutinised by the 'entertainments committee' (sounds like Stalag Luft II, I know), in which the line is uttered. I've agreed to play 'Arthur' and he's done everything he can to make it inevitable that the part of Lakshmi, the 32-year-old Indian heroine, can be taken only by Dr Sen.

We await the outcome of the committee's deliberations with intense excitement.

★   ★   ★

One thing I ought perhaps to clear up. Am I in fact homosexual? I remember hearing the American sage Gore Vidal on the radio. In his humorous bass baritone he assured his listeners: 'There are no such things as homosexual or heterosexual people, only homosexual or heterosexual acts.'

It sounded wise. By that criterion, I must be straight, since I've never known any homosexual 'acts'. Though to be frank, I suppose I haven't seen much girl action either.

And Jennifer? What was sexually going on there? There's a belief you find in some biographers of the upmarket kind that knowing whether two people once spent the night together is the Rosetta Stone for understanding their 'characters'. If Lytton Strachey's semen once found its way onto Maynard Keynes's waistcoat, their belief runs, then the stories of literature and economics are altered. I think not.

From the evidence of her diary, Jennifer was having some difficulty with Robin Wilson over what she called 'sex, lack of'. My guess is that she had had a physical affair with him but was trying to move it on to more of a 'good friends' thing. Girls were always doing this at that age, because they found themselves out of their depth and wanted to get back to safety. Or perhaps she just went off him.

And who was this mysterious 'Simon' from whom ('sob') there was no letter in her pigeonhole? We'll never know, and my guess is that if Jen were alive today she might not even remember. And what of the boy from Downing and the boy from King's quoted in the newspaper as having been her lovers? Maybe one did, perhaps both, maybe neither. Most likely is that the newspaper reporter made it up. Any quotation in any paper in which the speaker is not named is valueless (because it *could* be made up without legal repercussions); and in the tabloids these unattributed 'quotes' are generally just invented.

It certainly doesn't matter whether Jennifer slept with one boy or many or none unless those actions had a significant bearing on her life, development or happiness. Clearly they didn't.

With the passage of time, all such actions or lack of them, appear less significant. And anyway, since the cells in our body die and are renewed, replaced by different ones, we do in a literal sense become different individuals. The connection I have to the boy I once was is now so fragile that it requires an act of conscious 'faith' to maintain that we are in any significant sense the same person.

At a certain remove, when passion and circumstance have died or altered beyond recall, our past selves are no more than characters in a fictional tale, like dead, half-forgotten Emmy and Anna and Lucy and all the other girls in Dr Freud's short stories.

In that light you can now perhaps see how hard I'm struggling to keep Jennifer alive.

*　*　*

There are some days in Longdale when I see it as the reincarnation of the old men's poorhouse that I used to see as a child in Reading — with its teatime gaslamps, stone corridors and dripping windows occasionally washed by the bending headlamps of passing Humbers and Wolseleys in the evening rain. I know that my infant foreboding has been fulfilled and that I will be housed forever in an English institution that has escaped the release of time passing or of death.

On other days, it is merely an extension of Chatfield, and I encounter McCain in the toilets, Batley in the gardens and Francis on his way to the assault course. Hello, Francis, you again. No, I never did escape, and I see that you didn't either.

Yet if I try hard enough I can remember another institution, too: the old men's almshouses by the stream. The men wore caps and collarless striped shirts with woollen waistcoats; they all had Woodbines stuck, unburning, to the lower lip. The flowerbeds were a fire of wallflowers and dahlias. When the men hoed them, the metal made a distinctive sound as it struck a stone or scraped over the dry earth. I remember one called Ted, a veteran of Passchendaele, who leaned on his hoe and talked to me. He smelt of tobacco and breadcrumbs and old man's sweat. His face was crossed with small lines, deep in the brown skin, and many of his teeth were missing. He took me into his almshouse, the front room dark and cold despite the summer outside. His wireless was playing a Test Match commentary by Rex Alston and John Arlott, only names to me, but probably something more to him. He gave me lemon squash in a dirty glass and a Custard Cream biscuit. On the kitchen shelf he had rows of empty jam jars and topless fish tins in which were screws, nails and bits of cut string. He had a tabby cat called Susan who dozed in his chair beneath the antimacassar. The almshouses were single-storey brick with leaded windows and tile roofs. I remember thinking that there must be many places like this in England and I envied him his small house. I thought I'd like to be old, like Ted, and pass my days hoeing the beds, smoking Woodbine and listening to the cricket on the wireless. It was something to do with him and his past, that I felt we'd lost somewhere, when I was on the main street of Lymington all those years ago. Can you ever know what it's like to be another man, what we've missed or what died with them?

★ ★ ★

Don't feel sorry for me. Whatever you do, don't feel sorry for me.

I don't, so why should you?

I do not need your pity. I showed that girl none when I killed her.

Please, whatever you do, don't 'forgive' me. Don't ask for 'closure' or 'release' for me because it's not really me you'd be asking for, but yourselves: granting me forgiveness would free you from your own anguish at what I did; it would be a way of putting me out of your mind.

And what would I do with such phoney gestures? What good would they do me?

Jen's mother didn't forgive me. On the contrary, she wrote to me in the harshest terms expressing a wish that I would 'rot in hell'. Perhaps we're already there — not just me, but all of us, stuck in this absurd existence with its non sequitur, shaggy-dog death ending.

These days I doubt whether I'm the creature Julian Exley described (though of course I remain grateful for the diagnosis that steered me to Longdale not Strangeways). For one thing, he said I had no empathy or feeling for other people, but that isn't really true, is it? I tried to imagine the lives of those girls in their remote Victorian college, having tea. I took an interest in my father's war and in Julie, rather less in Mum. And when I went to Jen's house, I really worked at picturing the thoughts and feelings of her mother. And Margaret, Charlotte, Stellings, Dr Turner, Dr Sen a little bit, Gerry, Mark, Jeffrey Archer, Ralph Richardson, Julian Exley himself . . . I've felt something for all of them.

And even in the damaged person Exley described there was a consistency of character and behaviour that I failed to recognise. It wasn't just that it wasn't me; it was that it wasn't feasibly human. It was an intricate and enjoyable piece of reasoning, like a Freudian case history, and about as scientific.

I enjoyed reading it. He nailed the moment I killed Jennifer and fully explained it. Defended narcissism in the face of intolerable threat to the self. His explanation was logical, all right; its problem was that it wasn't true.

My own diagnosis of my problem is a simpler one. It's that I share 50 per cent of my genome with a banana and 98 per cent with a chimpanzee. Bananas don't do psychological consistency. And the tiny part of us that's different — the special *Homo sapiens* bit — is faulty. It doesn't work. Sorry about that.

★ ★ ★

Last Friday I was given a quite exceptional treat, and one that, if news of it reached the newspapers, would cause an outrage. So don't tell.

I was allowed out of the hospital grounds. Yes, Schizo Scribbler, Fen Beast was At Large. Two nurses, Tony, an elderly Lancastrian with spectacles, and a burly charge nurse called John, walked me down into the village of Upper Rookley.

To begin with, I was alarmed by the cars and the people. I held tight to Tony's arm. He talked to me in a soothing way, 'Don't worry, Mike. We'll make sure you come to no harm. Steady now.'

It was the first time I'd seen a pavement or a shop for more than eighteen years. I looked at the sane people going about their business like termites in a mound.

We went into a shop so that John could buy some cigarettes. I somehow expected that I'd know the man behind the counter, but he was a stranger and I wondered what he was doing there.

There were cars parked all along the side of the street as well as going up and down the road. Upper Rookley was slightly bigger than I remembered, but I suppose when I was fifteen I had only looked at the pavement. What was I thinking in those days? At what brute level of awareness was I functioning?

After a time, I became more confident and let

470

go of Tony's arm. I asked if I could walk ahead without them flanking me like gaolers, and Tony said yes. They knew me well enough.

I threw back my head and breathed in normal life: the chemist, the electrical goods shop, the gabled pub with a sort of white blackboard, if you see what I mean, advertising Thai food.

'Are there many Thai families in Rookley nowadays?' I asked Tony, and he explained, suppressing a smile, that it was just a pub fad.

We passed the back gate into Chatfield and walked on up the high street. We went past the tobacconist's whose supplier's van I used to rob and came to where I thought the record shop had been, where I had spent my saved or stolen money.

'Was there a record shop here?' I asked Tony.

'Yes. It's still here,' he said. 'Just a bit further on.'

And so it was. It still sold records, too, a few anyway, though mostly CDs, videos and computer games.

We went inside and I sniffed a bit, to reorientate myself after all these years. I turned by instinct to the side wall where the deep wooden bins had been, where I spent so many hours flipping through the sleeves, stopping now and then to pull one out and flick it over. *A Song for Me* by Family with Roger Chapman on vocals and John 'Poli' Palmer on vibes; *Split* by the Groundhogs; *Stonedhenge* by Ten Years After; *Songs for a Tailor* by Jack Bruce.

Time was pressing very hard on me. Things

before my eyes were there and not there. I asked to leave.

We went to the top of the street and into a café, where they bought tea and cake. It was clear to me that Tony and John wanted to prolong their outing as long as possible. They chatted and smoked and drank tea in a natural, friendly way.

Eventually, I couldn't stand it any more and I said, 'Do you mind if we go back?'

★ ★ ★

Last night I lay in my room at the top of one of the old Victorian buildings. These days I have a good, long view down the hill and over the village to the school and the woods beyond. I can almost see the playing fields from which Baynes was returning late that afternoon.

In between, in the foreground as I look down, is the tall perimeter wall of Longdale with grey brick and rolled barbed wire.

And as I lie here in the dusk, I suppose that I am evidently (and I have chosen that word carefully, for its denotation, connotations and all the ripples in between) bonkers.

I have a world in my mind, in the inexhaustible repertoire of my memory. I can recall at will, note-perfect, from the reams I have stored there.

As the electrical self-deceit of human consciousness ebbs and fires at random through my brain, there are long hours when I don't know if I'm alive or not.

472

Sometimes I see myself as one of those magi of the guitar — Rory Gallagher, D. Gilmour, Jeff Beck or Jan Akkerman. I stand in the spotlight and take a solo.

I build the choruses and sequences in any order I choose.

I improvise; I make the familiar seem new; I reinvent, recast and bring to life.

So where's it coming from, this feeling, this funny low euphoria? A little bit from the town, I think. I do love the dirty brick of the miniature terraces and the mist from the river and the cold mornings, even now in May. And then the sudden huge vista of a great courtyard of King's or Trin or Queens', when everything that's been pinched, and puritanical and cold and grudging and sixpence-in-the-gas-meter is suddenly swept away by the power and scale of those buildings, with their towers and crenellations and squandered empty spaces, built by men who knew that they'd calculated the mechanical laws of time and distance and there was therefore no need whatever to build small.

It's teatime on Friday in November. The road is lit by the lamps of bicycles; cars pass at their peril, slowly, because the pedalling girls, some frizzy and stout, some slight and eager, the girls with their lights front and rear, are the queens of the highway.

Back from games, the girls are flushed; their faces are red from the Ural wind. Red Russian wind from communist mountains, from the giant Soviet factories. Jennifer is running down the corridor, lively with the sense of her good fortune. They're having tea now in Anne's room, which has a gas ring. Molly comes in with cake she bought in town: a sponge cake with cherries. They sit on chairs and floors and beds. There isn't much room, but there's music on Anne's cheap record player: a balladeer, a minstrel, shock-haired with a guitar — afternoon songs for girls in jeans with coloured silk scarves knotted or held with silver woggles from Morocco.

There's a tortoiseshell cat who lives opposite and he's half adopted us. I pull back the curtain and see him on the roof, stretching in the thin early sun. I love the jumble of small slate roofs on the brick terraced cottages. I lie watching for a few minutes while an 'inane disc jockey' (Dad) babbles on the radio. Then I put on socks, slippers, sweater and coat and go down to the kitchen, and, while the kettle's on, open the back door to the cat and call him in. He tumbles off the roof of the shed and comes shyly to the step where (if lucky) he gets a saucer of milk and a stroke.

Jennifer sat back against the wooden settle in a slightly defensive posture; she wore a floral print skirt. I could see her bare legs. She had a sharp patella that gave a fetching inverted-triangle shape to the knee. She was smoking a cigarette and trying not to laugh, but her eyes looked

474

concerned and vulnerable as Robin's low voice went urgently on.

She is alive, God damn it, she is alive. She looks so poised, with that womanly concern beginning to override the girlish humour. I will always remember that balanced woman/girl expression in her face. She was twenty-one.

They left. She was so absorbed by what Robin was saying that she forgot to say goodbye either to me or to her friend Malini who was at the other end of the room. She went through the door, hoisting her brown leather shoulder bag up, the hem of the skirt fluttering for a second as she tripped down the step onto the cobbles.

I cut down Pembroke Street and Silver Street and over the river and I think of all the people who've gone before me — the men in the Cavendish Labs and the Nobel prize-winners and Milton and Darwin and Wordsworth, of course, but mostly of the generations of young men and women who weren't famous but were so relieved to be here at last and meet people like themselves, and didn't mind the freezing cold and no money for the meter and the greasy college breakfast. I think of the men in their tweed jackets with the elbow patches and the bluestockinged women in their clunky shoes and I feel glad for them still. Feel v lucky and not that cold. Goodnight, Dad. Thank you for everything. Sleep well back in Lym. x

As Hannah came into the sodium light of the street lamp, I recognised the navy blue coat, a replica of Jen's own that had presumably vanished with her. She also wore a grey sweater, the polo neck that wasn't quite, blue flared jeans and boots.

She walked down the grey pavement, going away from us; her step was light and confident, and you felt all that Jenniferish excitement about being alive and it *was* her in all but fact: it was her again, you could smell her hair, her skin, and sense how much she was looking forward to the bump of the lit gas fire and the ski socks, as she quickened slightly in the cold, thinking of the cat tumbling from the roof in the morning and the day ahead.

She walked, this girl, with that slow stride suppressing gaiety, her love of living, the slight sway of her narrow hips as she moved onwards, away from us, turned right at the end of the street and vanished in the Fenland mist.

Well, maybe the love generated between people who behave well and kindly adds somehow to the available pool of existing good feeling in the world, and lives on after them. (Now sound like drippy hippy, but actually it's true and easy to prove.) Without good example such as preserved in literature, there would be nothing to live up to, no sense of transcendence or of our lives beyond the Hobbesian. So these feelings do endure and I believe they also survive through memory, orally and in families as much as in written word. So while living may have no <u>meaning</u> in any teleological sense, it does have practical purpose in the way that how we live can improve the experience of others alive and yet to be born; and thus, a bit more contentiously (because harder to define scale on which it's measured), it also has value. This seems so obvious to me as to be almost axiomatic.

We knew nothing of drugs. I wondered how many of the brighteyed boys — their parents' treasures, the comets of their hope — were now in Fulbourn and Park Prewett, fat and trembling on the side effects of chlorpromazine: an entire life, fifty indistinguishable years, in the airless urine wards of mental institutions because one fine May morning in the high spirits and skinny health of their twentieth year they'd taken a pill they didn't understand, for fun.

What will happen to all these people? Previous generations did great things in politics, diplomacy, medicine, industry, 'the arts' — became great and good as though by natural progression, birthright.

All people I know resolute that they will do no such thing. No one will have 'nine to five' job. Can't imagine anyone I know here appearing on television in twenty years' time to offer expert view on — anything. Just not cut out for it.

I wonder why. Drugs? Partly, but we're not all out of it all the time. A generation thing, I suppose. We are a lost gen. (Rather

477

than lost Jen, ha, ha.) Before us, the hippies; after us, perhaps keen people in suit and tie who will go straight to work in Con Party research and American banks. Poor us, lost souls.

She walked, this girl, with that slow stride suppressing gaiety, her love of living, the slight sway of her narrow hips as she moved onwards, away from us, turned right at the end of the street and vanished in the Fenland mist . . .

★ ★ ★

There are some things in the past that may have happened and some that may not have happened. But the reality of their happening or not happening *then* has no weight *now*.

Until we can navigate in time, I'm not sure we can prove that what happened is real.

★ ★ ★

Yes, up here in the spotlight, I can do anything. Anything at all. Listen.

16 FEBRUARY, 1974
Last night went to party at Pete and Vicky's in Malcolm Street. Typical student bash, though in unusually nice house. Charlie from Emma there, a bit freaked out.

Danced a lot to good selection of records, mostly Tamla, and drank perhaps rather too freely of Pete's Algerian red. Irish Mike turned up with two bottles, also v welcome.

Had intense conversation with Philippa from Newnham about historical perspectives and whether historiography <u>necessarily</u> political, naive to pretend otherwise etc. Slight sense that she trying to get things clear in her own mind before finals, esp re Foucault (And I'd always thought F was a physicist — rotation of earth etc . . .)

Also v amusing talk with Charlie about why men look so good in mascara! He amused that I find this annoying. 'But, Jen, since women have abandoned make-up, why shouldn't we use it? Someone has to.' Did not let on that I was actually wearing panstick (nasty small spot on side of chin; 'Harold' due shortly) as well as artfully applied eyeshadow . . .

V good fun, though. Smoked some of Vicky's Afghan black and felt pretty good though somewhat heavy in the feet and rather indiscriminately affectionate. Thought better to leave while still on top (if I was) and went out into b. freezing night, dreading long walk home sans bike. Bloody hell.

Then on Jesus Lane got lift from Mike. What piece of luck. Up Vic Rd, round one-way system and down to our house.

Felt I had to ask him in as it was still not very late and least I could do was offer him tea. Lit gas fire in sitting room and put on *Bryter Later* by Nick Drake.

Sat on floor by fire and let amazing melancholy music flood room. Mike visibly moved and rather poured out his heart to me about his home and family and so on.

I got more dope from my room and made some more tea. Nick was at Hannah's, Molly had gone to her parents' and no sign of Anne.

On doubtless very ill-advised whim, put my arm round Mike in sisterly way and he rested head on my bosom. Music played. All very innocent. Eventually wanted to go to bed. He said he now incapable of driving because stoned, and could he stay. I felt so full of warmth and dope that said all right, but no funny business and he swore not.

Kept on knickers and ski socks as well as old-lady nightie so hardly much of a lure, I imagine. Lent him tee shirt and after kiss on cheek, turned away for night. Duvet cover and sheet clean that morning. Fell asleep at once.

Somehow in course of night found 'things' happening. He v sweet and pleading. V cold outside. What could I do? Relented in magnanimous hippie way. Silly girl, but surely no harm done.

Woke up appalled. No hangover, but just appalled. Went down and made tea, brought it back to room. Mike asleep and snoring slightly with half-smile on his face. I felt an utter fool but couldn't help laughing a little bit. Pulled back curtains. Pissing with rain. Couldn't face bikeless trek to Sidgwick. Then remembered: Saturday anyway.

Closed curtains again. Finished tea. Put J. Mitchell *Ladies of the Canyon* very softly on my small record player, got into bed, put arm round Mike and fell asleep again at once, hearing the rain beat down outside.

For some reason dreamed of sparkling Greek sea, Aegean blue, with wooden boats, their white sails filled with love.

We do hope that you have enjoyed reading this large print book.

Did you know that all of our titles are available for purchase?

We publish a wide range of high quality large print books including:
Romances, Mysteries, Classics
General Fiction
Non Fiction and Westerns

Special interest titles available in large print are:
The Little Oxford Dictionary
Music Book
Song Book
Hymn Book
Service Book

Also available from us courtesy of Oxford University Press:
Young Readers' Dictionary
(large print edition)
Young Readers' Thesaurus
(large print edition)

For further information or a free brochure, please contact us at:
Ulverscroft Large Print Books Ltd.,
The Green, Bradgate Road, Anstey,
Leicester, LE7 7FU, England.
Tel: (00 44) 0116 236 4325
Fax: (00 44) 0116 234 0205

Other titles published by
The House of Ulverscroft:

ON GREEN DOLPHIN STREET

Sebastian Faulks

America, 1959: With two young children she adores, loving parents back in London, and an admired husband, Charlie, working at the British Embassy in Washington, the world seems an effervescent place of parties, jazz and family happiness to Mary van der Linden. But the Eisenhower years are ending, and 1960 brings the presidential battle between two ambitious senators: John Kennedy and Richard Nixon. An American newspaper reporter called Frank Renzo dramatically enters the van der Lindens' lives, and through him Mary is forced to confront the terror of the Cold War that is the dark background of their carefree existence.

CHARLOTTE GRAY

Sebastian Faulks

It is 1942. London is blacked out, but France is under a greater darkness, as the Vichy regime clings ever closer to the Nazi occupier. From Edinburgh, Charlotte Gray, a volatile but determined young woman, travels south. In London she conceives a dangerous passion for an English airman. Charlotte goes to France on an errand for a British organisation helping the Resistance, and for her own private purposes. Unknown to her, she is also being manipulated by people with no regard for her safety. As the weeks go by, Charlotte finds that the struggle for France's soul is intimately linked to her battle to take control of her own life.

Getting into

Law

Emily Lucas

14th edition

trotman | **t**

Getting into guides

Getting into Art & Design Courses, 12th edition
Getting into Business & Economics Courses, 14th edition
Getting into Dental School, 12th edition
Getting into Engineering Courses, 6th edition
Getting into Law, 14th edition
Getting into Medical School 2023 Entry, 27th edition
Getting into Oxford & Cambridge 2023 Entry, 25th edition
Getting into Pharmacy and Pharmacology Courses, 2nd edition
Getting into Physiotherapy Courses, 10th edition
Getting into Psychology Courses, 14th edition
Getting into Veterinary School, 12th edition
How to Complete Your UCAS Application 2023 Entry, 34th edition

Getting into Law

This 14th edition published in 2022 by Trotman Education, an imprint of Trotman Indigo Publishing Ltd, 21d Charles Street, Bath BA1 1HX.

© Trotman Indigo Publishing Ltd 2022

Author: Emily Lucas

12th–13th edns: Emily Lucas
11th edn: Steven Boyes and Melanie Allen

British Library Cataloguing in Publication Data
A catalogue record for this book is available from the British Library.

ISBN 978 1 912943 58 6

Printed and bound by Severn in Gloucester, UK

Contents

Preface

Law has always been a sought-after profession for students, and now, perhaps more than ever before, aspiring lawyers face tough competition at virtually every stage of their route to qualification, from securing a place on one of the 'best' university law degree courses to finding a job at the end of it all.

During the course of MPW's work advising students on their choice of university course and subsequent career path, we have gathered together a huge amount of information on law courses and the legal profession. With the encouragement of Trotman Indigo Publishing, that information has been brought together in this guide.

This edition has been substantially revised and updated. We hope that this guide will be useful to anyone considering a career in law.

About the author

Emily Lucas read medical science at the University of Birmingham before joining MPW Birmingham to teach biology in 2013. She completed her master's in genomic medicine at Queen Mary, University of London in 2019, and is now completing her PhD in developmental biology. She has worked as the University Support Officer and Head of Careers at MPW, and helps students with their applications as well as supporting students with preparation for university entrance examinations.

Acknowledgements

I would like to thank MPW and Trotman Education for giving me the opportunity to produce this edition of *Getting into Law*. Many thanks are due to all those who have written previous editions.

I would like to thank all of the individuals who have contributed to the book, especially John, Daniel, Jinder, Reanna, Edward, Sam, Martin, Nina, Jessica, Henry, Stewart, Andrew, Robert, Julia, Cameron, Jade and Alesha for their insights into applying to law courses, as well as studying and working in the field of law. In addition, I would like to thank Roly, Shivinder and Jade for allowing me to reproduce their personal statements here as successful examples; I am extremely grateful that these individuals were willing to take time out of their busy schedules to contribute.

I would like to thank those at the Law Society, the Solicitors Regulation Authority, the Bar Council of England and Wales and the Bar Standards Board, as well as the university admissions departments, law firms and barristers' chambers who have responded to my endless pestering regarding statistics and advice.

Finally, I would like to thank all of the students who I have worked with on their university applications over the last few years. Supporting students with their university applications is among my favourite aspects of my job, and much of the insight offered here was developed through these experiences.

About this book

This book is written for anyone considering a career in law. Law is a perennial favourite as a career choice: it offers intellectual stimulation, ancient customs, a morally satisfying focus on justice and fairness, and potentially great financial rewards.

However, with popularity comes competition: now, more than ever before, competition for places to read law at university, for solicitors' training contract places and barristers' pupillages is intense. You will therefore need to do your research and be as fully prepared as possible. I hope that this book will go some way towards arming you with the necessary information to help you to succeed.

The book will start with an introduction to the legal profession, an overview of the UK's legal systems, and a discussion of what lawyers do.

The next two chapters will then outline how to qualify as a lawyer, including the different qualification routes, and then consider the importance of work experience.

The remaining chapters will guide you through the university application process, including choosing the right university law (or other) course, completing the UCAS form (including the all-important personal statement), preparing for an interview if necessary and what to do on results day. There is then a chapter outlining the arrangements for fees and funding for university degree courses.

At the end of the book there is a glossary of terms, relating to the study of law, applying to university and qualifying as a lawyer.

Of course, you will still have to show lots of ability and drive to impress university law admissions tutors and your potential future employers. You should make sure that you:

- revise thoroughly for your exams and get the best grades you possibly can, giving you the widest choice of degree options.
- become a legal eagle and do your own research. Talk to your teachers, family, friends, lawyers and anyone else who knows something about the legal profession. Consider carefully what type of degree course is appropriate for you, or, indeed, whether you should even study law and become a lawyer in the first place. There is also a huge amount of information and guidance online, which the references in this book will help you find, so make sure that you use it!

1 | An introduction to the legal profession

Most people's first impressions of the legal profession come from the glamorous world of film and television. Legal dramas paint a picture of lawyers striding heroically across the courtroom, standing up for truth and justice. But what are lawyers and what do they actually do?

The term 'lawyer' is a loose one that covers barristers, solicitors, judges, legal executives, paralegals, in-house legal advisors, some civil servants and academic lawyers. In England and Wales, the crucial distinction to make is between the two main branches of the profession: solicitors and barristers. The legal professions in Scotland and Northern Ireland have a similar distinction and are outlined at the end of Chapter 3. The essential difference between solicitors and barristers relates to their respective rights to advocate on behalf of a client in court: traditionally only barristers were permitted to undertake advocacy on behalf of a client in the highest courts. This distinction means that law is sometimes referred to as a 'split' profession – but the split is increasingly becoming blurred, due to modern reforms that permit solicitors to undertake further training and then represent clients in the higher courts.

> **Solicitors** work on all aspects of the law, but do not normally present their clients' cases in court.
>
> **Barristers** are instructed by solicitors to represent their clients in the courtroom or give opinions on specific points of law.

The main focus of this book is on the solicitors' and barristers' professions, but there are many other careers within the legal field that can also be pursued, and also many non-legal careers for which a law degree might provide a good foundation.

Solicitors

Solicitors are often described as being like medical general practitioners (GPs). They deal directly with their clients and often have an ongoing professional and/or business relationship with them. Solicitors in private practices group together in law firm partnerships, with the senior solicitors being partners and the more junior solicitors being employed assistants. Most solicitors now deal with specific areas of the law, for example employment or family law or, in the City, specialist areas such as syndicated loans, bonds or takeovers and mergers. In this respect they differ from GPs, who are usually generalists.

However, in most cases, law firms cover a wide area of legal practice; this means that in smaller firms solicitors may be required to cover a broader range of areas, whereas the larger law firms will have specialists in very narrow areas of law.

Historically, solicitors could only appear in lower courts, such as the magistrates' and county courts. These days, however, solicitors who obtain higher rights of audience can appear in the higher courts, including the Supreme Court, and may even apply to become QCs (Queen's Counsel), although this is still rare.

The Law Society is the body that represents and supports solicitors in England and Wales. The Solicitors Regulation Authority is the independent regulator of solicitors and law firms in England and Wales, and deals with all regulatory and disciplinary matters, including:

- setting the standards for qualifying as a solicitor
- administering the roll (register) of solicitors
- drafting the rules of professional conduct
- monitoring solicitors and their firms to make sure that they are complying with the rules.

Barristers

Barristers have traditionally been described as more like medical consultants. They are 'self-employed referral professionals' who are often, although not exclusively, trial lawyers – meaning that they appear robed and wigged in court on behalf of their clients. Clients are usually referred to them by a professional advisor, often a solicitor – although modern reforms allow barristers to see the public directly where the Bar Council has agreed that no referral is necessary (for example in relation to tax advice when referred by an accountant).

It is usual for barristers (often called counsel) to specialise in certain areas of law, such as criminal law, company law or tax law and so on. Barristers in private practice group together in chambers, sharing overheads and office support, but remaining self-employed professionals.

Barristers in England and Wales are represented by the Bar Council, which promotes barristers' services and upholds ethical standards in the profession. The Bar Standards Board performs a similar function to the Solicitors Regulation Authority, and is responsible for regulating barristers in the public interest. Its functions include:

- setting the education and training requirements for becoming a barrister
- setting the standards of conduct for barristers
- monitoring the service provided by barristers.

Legal executives

Legal executives are lawyers who have not undertaken the professional training required to become a solicitor or barrister, but have qualified instead with the Chartered Institute of Legal Executives (CILEX, www.ciles.org.uk). CILEX is a professional association and governing body for those training to become lawyers, legal executives, paralegals and other legal professionals.

Historically, the modern legal executive role evolved from the role of law clerks, who used to help solicitors with their cases. In the 1960s, the legal executives' profession was created in order to offer a recognised career path.

The Legal Services Act 2007 made chartered legal executives 'authorised persons' who are able to undertake 'reserved legal activities' alongside solicitors and barristers. Qualified chartered legal executives can now do much of the same work that solicitors do, but are trained to work in one or two areas of the law rather than having a broader, more general role. Typical day-to-day tasks of legal executives might include preparing contracts, advising clients on legal matters, contacting professionals on their behalf or representing them in court.

From June 2021, all former CILEX training routes were replaced by the CILEX Professional Qualification (CPQ), which provides a more flexible and affordable pathway to becoming a CILEX lawyer, advanced paralegal or paralegal.

By studying the CILEX CPQ, students will cover core legal knowledge, ethics and professional responsibility, practice and skills and professional experience. The professional experience component is acquired through legal employment. There are three stages to the CPQ – Foundation, Advanced and Professional – which allow individuals to enter at a level that reflects their prior experience and qualifications, as determined by the training provider. Along with the reform to their qualifications, CILEX have also introduced new titles for their graduates: CILEX Lawyer (who will have practice rights), CILEX Paralegal and CILEX Advanced Paralegal – for those completing the Professional, Foundation and Advanced stages respectively. CILEX Lawyers have parity with solicitors as a consequence of them holding practice rights in their specialist area.

Further Information about the CILEX CPQ

There are a number of pathways available with the CPQ, including:

- immigration
- probate
- family law
- business and employment law
- conveyancing
- criminal law and litigation
- dispute resolution.

In total, there are 22 modules across the CPQ.

- The CPQ Foundation stage comprises five mandatory modules.
- The CPQ Advanced stage comprises four mandatory modules and one optional module (from a selection of three).
- The CPQ Professional stage comprises one mandatory module and one optional module (from a selection of nine).

Trainees who wish to practise in dispute resolution, family litigation or criminal litigation will also need to take CILEX's advocacy course.

Other lawyers

The Legal Services Act 2007 also defined various other groups of lawyers as being entitled to undertake reserved legal activities. These lawyers are trained and qualified in particular specialist areas of law and often work in law firms alongside solicitors. They are notaries (www.thenotariessociety.org.uk), licensed conveyancers (www.clc-uk.org), law costs draftsmen (www.associationofcostslawyers.co.uk), trademark attorneys (www.itma.org.uk) and patent attorneys (www.cipa.org.uk).

Case study

Prior to becoming a patent attorney, John had his sights set on becoming a research scientist. It was while studying for his biochemistry degree at the University of Oxford that he had his eyes opened to the prospect of a career in law instead.

'Throughout my biochemistry degree, I had always assumed that I would want to work in research after graduation. The intellectual stimulation that research presents was always appealing to me. However, during my fourth year, I undertook a research project in the field of pharmacology and stumbled across patents in action.

I was intrigued by the legal processes involved in patenting and contacted some UK companies to undertake work experience in that field. After a few short weeks, I decided this was the career path that I wanted to embark on.

'Following graduation, I commenced a role as a patent attorney in training in the field of life sciences. After four years of working in the role, I successfully completed all of my qualifying Patent Examination Board and European Patent Office examinations and, as such, qualified as a UK and European patent attorney. I opted to move to the Munich branch of the company that I was working for to work in their life sciences department.

'The work that I do ranges from supporting companies with employee inventions, advising on product marketing in the field of health care, regulatory issues with clinical trials, production and distribution, and licence agreements for research and development cooperations. A typical day might involve meeting with clients and advising whether something is patentable, filing applications and advising on how to use a patent. On occasion, I might also need to defend a client in a patent challenge, or challenge patents that infringe upon those of my clients.'

Size and make-up of the legal profession (England and Wales)

Solicitors

The solicitors' profession in England and Wales is the largest branch of the legal profession. In July 2019, the Law Society (www.lawsociety.org.uk), which acts as the governing body for solicitors, reported that there were 195,821 registered solicitors, and 146,953 of these held a practising certificate. To qualify as a solicitor, you would normally be expected to complete a training contract period of employment that lasts two years. In July 2019, the Law Society reported that there were 6,344 trainee registrations.

The solicitors' profession is divided between solicitors who work in private practice for law firms and those who work 'in-house' (i.e. for companies, government legal departments and so on). In 2019, there were 9,339 private law firms employing 95,028 solicitors, meaning that 65% of all practising solicitors were working in private practice. The number of solicitors employed outside private practice amounted to 33,652. In 2019, almost 40.9% of practising solicitors were located in London, with 20.6% working in City firms.

Of all the practising solicitors in 2019, 75,764 were women, meaning that women now account for 51.6% of all solicitors on roll. Close to two-thirds of new trainees were women. The proportion of practising solicitors who are from minority ethnic groups was around 14% in 2019.

Barristers

The barristers' profession, known as the Bar, is much smaller than the solicitors' profession. According to the Bar Standards Board (www.barstandardsboard.org.uk), there were a total of 17,078 barristers in practice in 2020, of whom 38% were women and 14% described themselves as belonging to an ethnic minority. Most practising barristers (13,502 in 2020) are self-employed. A further 3,044 barristers are in employed practice.

	Number	% women (approx)	% in London (approx)
Solicitors	146,953	51.6%	40.9%
– private practice	– 95,028		
– in-house	– 33,652		
Barristers	17,078	38%	64%
– self-employed	– 13,502		
– employed	– 3,044		
– dual capacity	– 532		

Table 1: Solicitors and barristers in practice (England and Wales), most recent statistics available

Legal executives and other lawyers

The much younger profession of legal executives is smaller still: the Chartered Institute of Legal Executives (www.cilex.org.uk) reported in 2015 that there were around 7,500 qualified chartered legal executives, of whom 250 were partners in law firms. The total number of members of the Institute (including paralegals and other legal professionals) was around 20,000, of whom 74% were women. More than a third of their new members are of an ethnic minority.

The other groups of lawyers mentioned above (notaries, licensed conveyancers, law costs draftsmen, trademark attorneys and patent attorneys) are also much smaller in number than solicitors or barristers. This book will therefore focus on the two main branches of the legal profession: solicitors and barristers.

Gender balance

It is difficult to imagine that less than 100 years ago the legal profession was the preserve of men. Things have changed and are still changing.

The Law Society reports that just over 60% of training contracts were issued to women in 2019. Some 51.6% of practising solicitors are female, and, in July 2019, there were nearly 8,708 female partners in law firms. Around 60% of practising solicitors under the age of 35 are now women. The Law Society's most recent report suggests that the number of women practising as solicitors exceeds the number of men working in the profession, and this has been the case for a number of years.

There has been a feeling within the solicitors' profession in the past that not enough female solicitors make it to partnership in some of the very large law firms, and there is still a substantial difference between the representation of men and women at partner level, with women currently representing 33% of partners. In larger firms with more than 50 partners, there is an even smaller percentage of female partners: 27%, with a 35% representation in smaller firms (typically two to five partners). However, the gap has been narrowing over recent years. The percentage of women solicitors working outside private practice, i.e. in-house, is higher.

Some 38% of practising barristers are women, with 39% of new entrants undertaking pupillage being female. Whereas in the past it was difficult for women to break down the traditional barriers, today the profession is increasingly open to all. This is evident in the fact that in 2019–20 just over 52.4% of barristers called to the Bar were women.

However, there is still progress to be made by women in terms of judicial appointments. In 2021 only 34% of court judges were female, though there was greater representation among tribunal judges, of which 50% were women. Over the last few years, the number of women in these roles has increased, but this trend has not been reflected in senior court appointments; only 29% of judges in the High Court and above are women. Only three women have made it to the most senior judicial appointment of the Supreme Court; in 2017, Lady Hale became the first female president of the Supreme Court since its creation. Lady Hale was open in her criticism of the lack of female representation in the Supreme Court and about the importance of diversity in a body that must make decisions that represent society. Following the retirement of Lady Hale and Lady Black, Lady Justice Rose was appointed as a second female justice in the UK's highest court. However, significant concerns remain around the lack of diversity in the all-white panel. Efforts are being made to increase the number of female judges and the number is increasing every year. It will, however, take time before parity can be reached.

Do I need a law degree?

The legal profession in England and Wales is virtually unique in not requiring all entrants to have a law degree. In fact, many non-law graduates enter the profession through the full-time Graduate Diploma in Law programme, which is an intensive one-year postgraduate course for non-law graduates covering the essential foundation subjects taught as part of a law degree. A substantial percentage of non-law graduates are direct entrants into the solicitors' profession, and many UK-domiciled students enrolled on the Bar Professional Training Course (BPTC) have a non-law related undergraduate background. This demonstrates that the skills acquired on many non-law degrees are often highly sought after by legal recruiters. For example, language skills or scientific/technical skills may be particularly useful in certain areas of law, and humanities degrees teach and test many of the skills that are essential for a lawyer, such as the ability to research information and analyse and present it in a clear and concise way. It is therefore important to bear in mind that you do not need a law degree to become a lawyer and many employers positively welcome applications from non-law graduates who can offer broader skills in other areas. There are, however, cost implications due to the extra year of postgraduate study that will be required (see Chapter 4, page 51 for more details).

It is also important to be aware that not every law degree is recognised by the professional bodies as a qualifying law degree (QLD) that will satisfy the requirements for the academic stage of training. It depends on the subjects that are studied on the course. This means that, if you do decide to do a law degree, you must be careful when choosing your course. The Solicitors Regulation Authority (SRA) and the Bar Standards Board (BSB) keep registers of which degrees are approved QLDs and these are available on their respective websites. They are also discussed further in Chapter 6.

Similarly, many students graduate with degrees in law and then, for whatever reason, do not go on to qualify as a solicitor or barrister. The number of law graduates compared with the number of professional training places available is very telling: according to the most recent figures from the Law Society, in 2019, 16,499 students graduated with law degrees from universities in England and Wales, which was 2.8% higher than in 2014. This number continues to rise each year. These figures only include those with 'straight' law degrees and not those with joint honours degrees that include law, so the total number of law graduates is likely to be considerably higher.

However, the limited number of training places available means that many undergraduate law students do not carry on to qualify as solicitors or barristers. The number of solicitors' training contracts registered annually has, according to the Law Society, increased slightly from around 5,000 in 2009–10 to around 7,000 in 2018–19. In the legal year 2019–20, only 404 aspiring barristers obtained their first six months' pupillage, which is the first part of the mandatory 12-month training stage for those who want to practise as a barrister. Some law graduates will also enter the legal profession via the graduate fast-track diploma to become legal executives, but there are still considerably more law graduates than entrants to the legal professions. Therefore, the link between taking a law degree and becoming a qualified lawyer is not nearly as clear-cut as many people believe, and one definitely does not imply the other.

What if I don't want to go into the law after my degree?

As well as those who, unfortunately, do not manage to get into one of the legal professions after taking a law degree, there are also some students who study law with no intention of becoming a professional lawyer. The legal knowledge and additional skills gained from a law degree are highly prized and can be applied to a number of jobs.

But what else can a law graduate do other than law? Many public figures have degrees in law that have led them in all sorts of different directions, from politicians to comedians. Some of the careers that a law degree can lead to are listed below.

- **Accountancy.** Many aspects of accountancy relate to those found in legal practice, such as analysing large amounts of technical material, writing reports and advising clients. Law graduates are often particularly attracted by tax consultancy.
- **Civil service.** If you are interested in policy making and implementation, then you might think about a career in the civil service. Administrators such as civil servants need a methodical and precise approach, as well as good writing and communication skills – all skills that are developed and honed on a law degree course. Some government departments, such as the Home Office, HM Revenue & Customs, the Ministry of Justice and the Foreign, Commonwealth and Development Office, have particular legal responsibilities and might be especially attractive to law graduates. Local government and the health services are also possibilities for public sector careers in administration.
- **Commerce and industry.** The skills you learn from a law degree will also be invaluable in the world of commerce and industry, where there are career opportunities in general business management.
- **Banking and finance.** A number of law graduates are lured into the highly paid world of banking and finance, where a legal background can certainly be useful.

Law graduates also go into many other areas, such as legal publishing, the media, journalism (legal or otherwise), the police service, teaching, human resources and more.

Some law graduates choose not to pursue the training to become either a solicitor or a barrister, or, indeed a legal executive, but would still like to do something in the legal field. They will often move into areas such as paralegal or clerking work. Paralegals research cases, scan and collate documents and generally assist qualified lawyers in their work. Clerks undertake duties such as taking witness statements on behalf of solicitors' clients and conducting legal research for solicitors, barristers and others plus any administrative work that is required.

Case study

Dan completed his undergraduate degree in law at the University of Warwick, and used the skillset that he had acquired to pursue a career in accountancy.

'I was always drawn towards the study of law because of the academic challenges that it presented. I thought I wanted to pursue a career in the field, ideally as a barrister, but while I enjoyed the study of law, it wasn't something I could see myself doing for the rest of my life. This was confirmed for me when I undertook work experience during the course of my undergraduate study.

'After graduating, I knew I would miss the challenge of academic study and so I decided to pursue a role in an accounting firm. I worked as an accounts payable clerk for several years, which allowed me to get to grips with what the field of accounting was like. In this role, I mainly undertook clerical tasks, such as processing invoices and tracking payments. After deciding I wanted to work in accounting, I started studying for the ACCA exams and qualified over a period of four years, during which time I worked in a number of slightly different roles with varying companies, including junior accountant and assistant accountant. After qualifying, I took on a management accountant role which allowed me to work towards my current position as a finance manager. In this role, I work with companies on financial planning, financial analysis and looking into finance operations.

'I was able to pursue a career in accounting because of the strong skillset that I developed through studying law, which is a very challenging subject that stretches you intellectually and instils resilience. Law also allows you to get a better understanding of broader industry sectors. In the interview process, I was able to draw on my experiences in working with law firms – having an understanding of how different sectors overlap. As an accountant, my law degree has given me a better understanding of how the law influences accounting practices. Having a law degree from a good university is viewed as a strong platform for graduate positions, and I think this helped enormously in getting me to where I am now.'

2 | The UK's legal systems

This chapter looks predominantly at the legal system in England and Wales, with the Scottish and Northern Irish legal systems briefly outlined at the end of the chapter. Welsh and English law are really one and the same, with a few important differences, such as the the Wales-only laws passed (pertaining to devolved matters only) by the Senedd. And the Welsh Language Act 1993 puts the Welsh language on an equal footing with English in the conduct of public business and the administration of justice in Wales. See www.assemblywales.org for more information.

The English legal system

English law comes from two main sources: statute law made by Parliament (also known as 'Acts of Parliament' or 'legislation') and case law made by judges (also known as 'common law'). The UK's membership of the European Union significantly impacted on the English legal system historically, and following the execution of Brexit in January 2020, changes are now underway on the system again. These sources are summarised below, together with a description of the court structure.

Statute law

Parliament is the supreme law-making body in the English legal system, and is made up of the House of Commons and the House of Lords. The House of Commons is made up of 650 democratically elected Members of Parliament (MPs) from various political parties, and it is the political party that has the majority of MPs elected to the House of Commons that will form a government. It is worth noting that in 2017, there was a two-thirds vote for a snap election. Despite winning a majority in 2015, the Conservative Party failed to do so in 2017, so entered into an informal coalition with the Democratic Unionist Party (DUP), whereby the DUP aimed to support governmental bills and display confidence in the government. In 2019 the government's ability to maintain a majority in Parliament became even more precarious, with MPs defecting (formally changing the political party they represent in the commons) and losing the party whip (having their status as an MP for a given party revoked) over Brexit and Boris Johnson's suspension of Parliament. The smaller the majority a government has, the harder it can be for them to pass laws. However, in December 2019 another snap election was held in an attempt to break the deadlock on Brexit. This time, Johnson's Conservative party won with a considerable majority of 365 seats, thus strengthening their ability to pass laws.

The House of Lords is made up of the most senior bishops in the Church of England and life peers who are nominated by the Prime Minister and then appointed by the Monarch. There are also currently 92 hereditary peers (people who have inherited their seats in the Lords) – these are eventually being phased out due to concerns about their appointment being unmeritocratic. Since the 1990s, there have been calls for reform of the House of Lords, including the suggestion that a proportion of the members be democratically elected. In May 2011, the government published detailed proposals for reform of the House of Lords, but the plans were dropped in August 2012. Instead, the House of Lords Reform Act 2014 introduced much more minor reforms, including allowing Lords to retire or be disqualified for non-attendance. Recently, Baron Lloyd Webber retired from the House of Lords, which is something he would have been unable to do prior to these reforms. Despite these changes, the Lords as a body is often criticised, largely due to the fact that the individuals are unelected and to the phenomenon of silent peers: an estimated 300 Lords have never spoken in a debate since their appointment.

In addition to concerns about how politically inactive some peers are, there are criticisms about the appointments system which can be subject to misuse. In 2006, the Cash for Honours scandal highlighted the association between political loans and the award of life peerages. The investigation by Scotland Yard was initiated when several large undisclosed loans to the Labour Party were followed by those giving the loans being nominated for peerages. Ultimately, no one was charged due to a lack of evidence, but the political fallout was damaging to the Labour Party and Labour Prime Minister Tony Blair. More recently, the appointments system was called into question by domestic abuse charity workers when Geoffrey Boycott, an ex-cricketer who was convicted for domestic abuse, was awarded a knighthood in Theresa May's resignation honours list. Many felt that it sent out the wrong message to survivors of domestic abuse.

A report published in October 2017 by the speaker of the Lords, Norman Fowler, stated that in order to maintain confidence in the Chamber, it should be reduced in size to no more than 600 members, with new peers being limited to 15-year terms. While the majority of appointed members are able to make valuable and significant contributions, many know very little about what the role can entail. Introducing an element of screening to the process would prevent any new influx from 'diluting' the quality of the Lords.

Despite concerns about its composition and unelected status, the Lords can provide a useful democratic function in that they are able to effectively scrutinise government and parliamentary decisions without fear of electoral recriminations; this can make them bolder. In some instances, the Lords have used their position to defeat controversial government bills or amend them to ensure human rights are protected. This can be seen by the Dubs amendment to the Immigration Bill (2016) which forced the government to arrange the relocation of a determined number of child refugees that come to the UK.

What else have the Lords changed?

- Ensured that protections are in place for low-paid workers before cuts to tax credits were actioned.
- Put in place safeguards for vulnerable people, including pregnant women, in immigration detention.
- Banned smoking in vehicles carrying children.
- Introduced a client money protection scheme for property agents to protect the money of landlords and tenants.
- Ensured that children with special educational needs are given the same legal support in academies as in other mainstream schools.

At interview, you might be asked to comment on proposed House of Lords reforms, such as those mentioned above, and discuss the role of this unelected chamber within a parliamentary democracy. See Chapter 8 for further considerations for interview preparations.

New laws are mostly put forward by the government, and these are known as public bills. However, not all bills come from government – backbencher MPs and opposition parties can propose private member bills, which have the potential to be transformative. Both the fox hunting ban and the smoking ban originated from private members' bills.

Following its proposal to Parliament, draft legislation has to go through several stages of debates and votes in both the House of Commons and the House of Lords prior to its passage. In the vast majority of cases, the draft legislation has to be approved by both Houses in order for it to become law. On occasion, bills are passed back and forth between the Houses in a process known as 'parliamentary ping pong' – the Investigatory Powers Act (2016) went back and forth four times prior to its passage. The final stage in the legislative process is Royal Assent, which is where the Monarch gives approval to the draft legislation and at this point it becomes an Act of Parliament. This is merely a formality and the last time that a monarch refused assent was in 1707.

Typically, Acts of Parliament cannot be challenged by the courts, and can only be changed by a subsequent piece of legislation. Acts of Parliament are also known as 'primary legislation' because they are made by Parliament, the supreme law-making body. Parliament can delegate its law-making power to other bodies, including government departments and local authorities, and law made by such bodies is known as delegated legislation or secondary legislation. Delegated legislation is subject to the control of Parliament and can be challenged in the courts.

Common law

Although Parliament is the supreme law-making body, and judges are simply supposed to apply the laws made by Parliament in cases, the doctrine of judicial precedent and the rules of statutory interpretation mean that in practice judges also make law through decided cases. This is known as 'case law' or 'common law' and is a major source of law in the English legal system.

The doctrine of judicial precedent is based on the Latin maxim 'stare decisis' which means 'stand by what has been decided', so, very simply, when a judge makes a decision in a case, this should be followed in future cases that are similar. The system of precedent operates through the court hierarchy, so that only certain (higher) courts create binding precedents (precedents that must be followed in future cases). Precedents are created when a new situation or point of law comes up in a case that is not provided for in legislation and has not been decided in a previous case, so the judge has to decide the case by looking at situations that are similar and use reasoning by analogy.

When judges are applying legislation to cases before them, it is not always possible to simply take the words of the statute and decide the case, because words can have more than one meaning. In addition, new technology and changes in society can mean that it is not clear whether the legislation applies in some cases. This is where the rules of statutory interpretation come in. Some judges take a 'literal approach' of applying the ordinary meaning of the words in the legislation even if this leads to an absurd result, whereas other judges take a 'purposive approach' and decide the case based on what they think Parliament wanted to achieve through the legislation. When a judge makes an interpretation in a case, this can create a precedent so that future cases must follow this interpretation.

Cases to consider

In the USA, the Supreme Court (comprising the nine most senior judges and appointed by the President) uses the Constitution to determine the outcomes of cases. There are two strands of judicial outlook – strict constructionist (originalist) and loose constructionist (right to privacy).

In its ruling, **Roe v. Wade (1973)** led to the legalisation of nation-wide abortion in the United States and is viewed as a seminal ruling. It has since been used to keep abortion legal, despite the plethora of pro-life groups and pro-life politicians in existence in the United States. However, this case also raises questions surrounding the Supreme Court's power – some believe that this ruling involved the judges going beyond their jurisdiction and that the US

Supreme Court justices should simply guard the constitution. Other cases related to reproductive rights that you might choose to read include:

- Planned Parenthood v. Casey
- Gonzales v. Carhart.

Common law as a source of law only works because of the system of law reporting in England and Wales; an accurate record of decided cases is kept so that it can be referred to by judges and lawyers in future cases. It is mostly decisions of the higher courts in the English legal system that are reported, and all High Court, Court of Appeal and Supreme Court cases are now available on the internet, for example from the British and Irish Legal Information Institute (www.bailii.org).

European Union law

Following the UK joining the European Economic Community (EEC) in 1973, its legal system became closely aligned with the European Union (EU) and many of the legislative and legal changes that happened in the UK in the years that followed had links to EU law. Despite the fact that Brexit has weakened the ties between UK and European law, a knowledge of European Union law is still required of any student wishing to study law, especially given that some elements of European law have been retained post-Brexit.

The EEC was established in 1957 by Germany, France, Italy, Belgium, the Netherlands and Luxembourg. In 1993, the EEC became the EU. Over the years European law has had an increasing impact on the legal systems of member states. There are now 27 member states.

The European Union produces its own primary and secondary legislation, and has its own court, the European Court of Justice. Case law has confirmed that European law is supreme over the national laws of member states, and that national law must be interpreted in accordance with European law. The principle of supremacy of EU law no longer applies to any UK laws made or passed after 31 January 2020, meaning that, in theory, national laws that contradict EU law could be introduced. This is, however, unlikely to happen. While the UK can no longer take cases to the European Court of Justice, it is unlikely that we will be entirely beyond their reach, as trading with the EU means that the UK will have to comply with EU standards, which are governed by the European Court of Justice.

The EU Withdrawal Act 2018 repeals the European Communities Act 1972, which affects the enforceability of EU law and the supremacy of EU law in the UK. However, it also ensures that much EU law is retained as part of UK law. As such, the UK does not look too dissimilar to EU member states in terms of its national laws.

Further information about the European Union (Withdrawal) Act 2018 and the EU Exit Arrangements can be found at www.legislation.gov.uk.

Cases to consider

In the **R (Factortame Ltd) v. Secretary of State for Transport (1989)** case, a group of Spanish fishermen claimed that the United Kingdom was in breach of European Union law regarding fishing boat ownership. This was the first time that the European Court of Justice restrained and overturned an Act of Parliament for contradicting European law.

The highest court of appeal in the UK is the Supreme Court, but individuals could also take cases to the European Court of Human Rights. This was particularly useful if cases related to the UK government contravening its citizens' human rights. For instance, in a case entitled Hurst v. United Kingdom in 2005, the UK was called to account under the convention for not allowing prisoners the right to vote. The European Court of Human Rights ruled this a breach of the convention on human rights. There was some concern that Brexit may prevent individuals from holding the UK to account for actions that are deemed contrary to the European Convention on Human Rights through appealing to the European Court of Human Rights. However, the UK will maintain its commitment to the convention, with recent amendments to the legislation following the Independent Human Rights Act Review in 2021 highlighting that the Supreme Court will have the power to interpret human rights law in a UK context.

Human Rights Act 1998

The Human Rights Act 1998 officially incorporated the European Convention on Human Rights into the English legal system. The Convention sets out certain fundamental rights of the citizens of Europe, including the right to life, the right to a fair trial and the right to respect for private and family life. Prior to the Human Rights Act 1998, English citizens who believed that their human rights had been infringed had to take their case to the European Court of Human Rights in Strasbourg. The Human Rights Act 1998 means that such cases can now be dealt with in the courts of the English legal system.

The Human Rights Act 1998 has affected the English legal system in several other ways, including the obligation that our courts must take into account any decision of the European Court of Human Rights, and, so far as it is possible to do so, interpret national legislation so that it is compatible with the European Convention on Human Rights. All draft legislation must also state whether or not it is compatible with the Convention. This is intended to encourage the government and civil service to consider the human rights implications of proposed legislation before it is introduced.

In 2015, the Conservative government proposed replacing the Human Rights Act with a British Bill of Rights. The Human Rights Act has been deemed by some as controversial, as it has been used as a means to protect individuals such as the Muslim cleric Abu Qatada, who was accused of having links to terrorist organisations, from extradition.

Cases to consider

The **Othman (Abu Qatada) v. United Kingdom (2012)** case is an interesting case to consider in the context of human rights. Abu Qatada, a Jordanian national, required refugee status in the United Kingdom. Qatada having been convicted in absentia by Jordan on the grounds of terrorism, the United Kingdom planned to deport him. Under Article 6 of the European Convention on Human Rights, the European Court of Human Rights ruled that Qatada could not be lawfully deported owing to the risk of torture upon his return.

Qatada was ultimately deported to Jordan on the basis that he would be tried fairly by the Jordanian State Security Court and would not be subject to torture, but the case made for considerable debate.

Other interesting cases to consider regarding the controversial elements of human rights include those associated with:

- the killers of James Bulger (1993)
- the Libyan soldiers convicted of sex attacks in the UK (2015).

Upon leaving the European Union, the UK was still committed to the European Convention on Human Rights. However, the finalised agreement was vague and left scope for future changes. In December 2020, the UK Government announced its plans to review the Human Rights Act in the UK, to consider how it is operating and whether any changes might be required to make it directly applicable to the UK. The Independent Human Rights Act Review sets out to explore how the domestic courts and the European Court of Human Rights work together, and the relationship between the judiciary and the legislature as a result of the impact of the Human Rights Act. In December 2021, the outcome of the Independent Human Rights Act Review was published, with Dominic Raab, the UK's Justice Secretary, claiming that the proposed new legislation will counter 'wokery and political correctness' following the decision to tighten laws surrounding deportation. The vast majority of successful human rights cases in the UK are foreign nationals appealing deportation, usually citing a right to family life as outlined in Article 8 of the Human Rights Act. The new legislation will allow the Supreme Court to operate in a UK context rather than taking into account any relevant cases that have been decided by the European Court of Human Rights. The proposed changes have received some criticism from opposing parties and from the Law Society, who argue that they do not address the most significant failings of the justice system in the UK and who have encouraged the government to act on evidence rather than political rhetoric respectively.

Further information about the Independent Human Rights Act Review can be found at www.gov.uk/guidance/independent-human-rights-act-review.

Court structure

The court structure in England is divided into two systems: those courts with civil jurisdiction and those with criminal jurisdiction. Civil cases are private disputes between individuals or companies. There are many different types of civil law, including family law, employment law, the law of contract, the law of tort and commercial law. Criminal cases are where the state prosecutes people for breaking laws, even though there is usually a victim.

Most civil cases are heard, in the first instance, by the county courts, but in cases where large amounts of money are in dispute, they will initially be heard in the High Court. Appeals from both the county courts and the High Court can be made upwards through the court hierarchy.

All minor criminal matters are dealt with by the magistrates' court. Serious cases are referred to the crown court. Here, the case will be decided upon by a lay jury, a fundamental part of the criminal justice system. Cases can be appealed from the magistrates' court to the crown court and from there to the Court of Appeal (Criminal Division).

The highest court in the land is now the UK Supreme Court, which is the final court of appeal for civil cases throughout the UK, and for criminal cases from England, Wales and Northern Ireland. The Supreme Court replaced the Appellate Committee of the House of Lords in 2009. It only considers appeals that concern points of law of general public or constitutional importance. Each case is normally heard by five Justices of the Supreme Court.

When a court is considering a point of European law it may refer to the European Court of Justice in Luxembourg for interpretation. It's worth noting that the UK government had intended to end ties with the

European Court of Justice on the completion of the withdrawal agreement in December 2020, but discussions are still ongoing. Some argue that this will allow the location of sovereignty to be returned to the UK, meaning that we have the utmost power regarding judicial decisions and that European Court of Justice rulings will have no bearing on us. The European Court of Justice has been something of a political hot potato in recent months, with the UK government's stance varying but ultimately stating that they are maintaining the position of ending the role of the European Court of Justice in resolving UK–EU disputes.

The Judicial Committee of the Privy Council is the court of final appeal for many current and former Commonwealth countries, UK overseas territories and Crown dependencies. During 2020 the Privy Council heard 37 appeals. By far the most contentious work relates to appeals against the death penalty.

Cases to consider

The really interesting UK Supreme Court Case of **AM (Zimbabwe) (Appellant) v. Secretary of State for the Home Department (Respondent) (2019)** reflects the complexity of the cases that make their way to the Supreme Court, and is a good example when considering the rights of people who have been convicted of offences.

In this case:

- The Supreme Court was asked to consider whether the return of AM to Zimbabwe would violate his right (under Article 3 of the European Convention on Human Rights) to not be subjected to inhumane treatment by reason of his medical condition (following the decision of the European Court of Human Rights in Paposhvili v. Belgium in 2017).
- AM is a national of Zimbabwe who arrived in the UK aged 13 in 2000 to join his mother.
- In 2004, AM was granted indefinite leave to remain in the UK.
- In 2006, AM was convicted for possession of a firearm and supply of heroin.
- After a sentencing of nine years in jail, the Secretary of State sought to deport AM.
- However, AM is HIV-positive and is currently receiving Eviplera, an antiretroviral drug not available in Zimbabwe.
- AM appealed his deportation on medical grounds and the impact it would have on his wife and child.
- First-Tier Tribunal, Upper Tribunal and the Court of Appeal dismissed the appeal based on Article 3 and Article 8 of the European Convention on Human Rights.
- The Supreme Court unanimously allowed the appeal.

Judges

In contrast with many other European countries, the judiciary in England and Wales is not a separate career. Judges are appointed from both main branches of the legal profession. Chartered legal executives can also now become judges.

Judges in the Supreme Court are known as Justices of the Supreme Court (formerly Law Lords in the House of Lords) and judges in the Court of Appeal are known as Lord or Lady Justices of Appeal. In the High Court, there are High Court judges and also masters and regis-trars, who hear certain types of applications.

Circuit judges, recorders and district judges are the remaining three types of judges. Circuit judges sit either in the crown court (to try crim-inal cases) or in the county courts (to hear civil cases). Recorders are part-time circuit judges, and district judges sit in the magistrates' courts and county courts.

Alternatively, a panel of lay magistrates can try criminal cases in the magistrates' court. They are not legally qualified or paid but are respected members of the community who sit as magistrates on a part-time basis.

New members of the judiciary are selected by the Judicial Appointments Commission, an independent body that was created specifically for this purpose following the Constitutional Reform Act 2005. The aim was to provide a fair and transparent selection process. Once appointed, judges are completely independent of both the legislature and the exec-utive, and so are free to administer justice without fear of political interference. Justices of the Supreme Court are not selected by the Judicial Appointments Commission, but are instead selected by a special Supreme Court Selection Commission.

Case study

His Honour Judge Jinder Singh Boora is a circuit judge who, some-what unusually, works in three different courts – Leicester, Northampton and Stoke-on-Trent – on primarily weighty criminal cases.

'As a circuit judge, I sit on serious criminal cases such as terrorism, robbery, fraud and rape. I also undertake money claims involving private individuals and companies. Working in three different courts allows me to undertake a rich variety of work and meet many different people.

'My typical day involves conducting trials, in which people give evidence and juries decide whether an accused person is guilty.

If an accused is found guilty or pleads guilty, I will sentence them. This is not necessarily imprisonment; I have other powers: for example, to direct a person to undertake work in the community, attend a drug rehabilitation course or pay a fine. The longest prison sentence I have passed so far is 20 years.

'Being a judge is different from most other professions because it can only be a second career. A judge first qualifies as a solicitor or barrister. Then, if they are successful in their career as a lawyer, they can apply to become a judge. This is usually after about 20 years in practice.

'My first career was as a barrister. I entered this profession because I had watched so many films and TV programmes about the drama of courtrooms and famous trial advocates. I was spell-bound by the romantic notion of a brilliant advocate securing the acquittal of an innocent person wrongly accused.

'I did a law degree at university. While there, I undertook work experience in a solicitors' office and in barristers' chambers. This work gave me invaluable experience and fortified my view that I was destined for the bar.

'After university, I undertook the bar vocational course, which is the barristers' professional course. After that, I did pupillage, which is practical training through shadowing an experienced barrister.

'After 15 years as a barrister, I decided to apply to become a part-time judge. I was successful, and for 12 years I practised as a barrister, with occasional part-time sittings as a judge.

'Becoming a judge is a highly competitive process. The part-time judicial sittings helped lift my profile and eventually, after a number of unsuccessful applications, I became a full-time judge. Success in the interview to become a circuit judge really came from being confident in my capabilities, which involved careful reflection on my successes in the courtroom as a barrister.

'Aspiring judges should work closely with a senior lawyer or another judge on their application form. They will need to use a lot of examples to demonstrate the appropriate skills, and it is useful to find someone more senior to help you identify your strongest examples.

'Throughout your career – from work experience at undergraduate level to work as a lawyer – you should note down each time you have successfully achieved something on the job, such as communicating effectively with someone from a disadvantaged background. By doing so, preparation for interviews will be much easier!'

Tribunals

A system of tribunals operates alongside the court system. Each type of tribunal specialises in a particular area of law. For example, Employment Tribunals handle workplace disputes between employers and employees, such as disputed deductions from wages, unfair dismissal, redundancy and discrimination. A tribunal is a more informal setting than a court. There are no judges; tribunals are chaired by a legally qualified tribunal judge, who will often sit with specialist non-legal members who have particular experience in the subject matter of the tribunal. There is no standard form of procedure. Nonetheless, they operate in a similar way to court proceedings, with witnesses usually giving evidence on oath.

Reform

The English legal system is constantly changing, so it is very important you keep up to date with current affairs in the legal field if you are thinking about a legal career. Essential preparation for a legal career includes reading a good quality newspaper such as *The Times*. You can also look at professional journals such as *The Law Society Gazette* and *The Lawyer*, which are both available online. Further details and website addresses are contained in Chapter 12.

The Scottish legal system

Scotland has its own legal system, with significant differences from those of the other constituent nations of the United Kingdom. The two fundamental differences are the role of the Scottish Parliament in formulating legislation, and the basis of Scottish jurisprudence in a mixed system of uncodified civil law and common law.

Since 1999, the Scottish Parliament has been responsible for legislating on a wide range of domestic matters relating to Scotland, but there are certain policy areas reserved for the UK Parliament at Westminster. Notably, these include constitutional matters, defence and national security policy, foreign policy, and fiscal and economic policy. Scotland's legal system and court structure is separate and autonomous from that of England and Wales and Northern Ireland. Historically, it has its basis in Roman law, with some English common law influence since the Act of Union of 1707. Recent developments in Scottish law have seen the strong influence of English (and other jurisdictions') common law, as well as the influence and incorporation of European Union law.

While some areas of law are similar to that of England, Scotland has its own system of criminal law and procedure, of civil procedure, and of certain areas of private law (such as land law). The court system reflects these differences, with its own system of separate criminal and civil courts. By way of illustration, the Court of Session is Scotland's supreme court for civil cases and the High Court of Justiciary is Scotland's supreme court for criminal cases. Decisions of the High Court of Justiciary are not generally subject to review by the UK Supreme Court, which reflects Scotland's distinctive tradition of criminal law and procedure. Most cases in Scotland are dealt with in either the Sheriff Court, which deals with the majority of civil cases and more serious criminal offences, or the Justice of the Peace Court, which deals with less serious criminal offences. Tribunals also sit in Scotland. The legal profession in Scotland is outlined in Chapter 3.

For more information see: www.scotcourts.gov.uk/about-the-scottish-court-service.

The Northern Irish legal system

Like Scotland, Northern Ireland (NI) has a legal system separate from that of England and Wales. Unlike Scotland, NI's legal system to a large extent mirrors that of England and Wales, with the following differences.

In terms of legislation, the Northern Ireland Assembly (which gained legislative powers in 1999 following the Good Friday Agreement) has the power to make laws for NI on all transferred matters, which are generally in the economic and social field. The Westminster Parliament retains responsibility for matters of national importance, such as the constitution, national security, defence and foreign policy. The Assembly operates under a unique power-sharing arrangement between the two main political communities in Northern Ireland.

NI has its own judicial system (the Northern Ireland Courts and Tribunals Service), which parallels that of England and Wales. It includes the Court of Appeal, the High Court of Justice in Northern Ireland, the crown court, magistrates' courts and county courts. The highest court of appeal for both criminal and civil matters, as in England and Wales, is the UK Supreme Court. Judicial law in NI partially derives from English common law and is based on the doctrine of judicial precedent. It has developed along very similar lines to that of English common law. English precedent from the higher courts is not, however, binding, but is deemed to be persuasive. The higher Northern Irish courts also pay attention to important decisions made in the Republic of Ireland (ROI), the major Commonwealth nations and even the USA. The legal profession in Northern Ireland is outlined in Chapter 3.

For more information please see www.niassembly.gov.uk, www.gov.uk/guidance/devolution-settlement-northern-ireland and www.nidirect.gov.uk/information-and-services/crime-justice-and-law.

3 | What do lawyers do?

The legal profession in England and Wales is divided into two main branches: solicitors and barristers. This chapter will run through the working practices of each of the branches of the profession in more detail, as well as providing an overview of the legal profession in Scotland and Northern Ireland.

Solicitors

Solicitors' work is as diverse as life itself – they will be behind the scenes offering legal advice to their clients on everything from corporate takeovers to individual personal injury claims. The day-to-day tasks of a solicitor vary enormously depending on where they work. About 65% of all practising solicitors work in private practice for law firms: the rest work in-house either for companies or for government agencies. Even for those working in law firms, the work will be completely different depending on the type of firm. For example, in a large firm it is not unusual to be working as part of a team of lawyers on one large case for several months, whereas in a small firm you may have 20 or more cases on the go at one time and be solely responsible for dealing with these.

This section offers a brief overview of the different types of law firms and the sort of work that the solicitors who work in them undertake.

Large corporate firms

The largest law firms by turnover tend to be the big corporate law firms specialising in corporate and finance law, which usually have their head-quarters in the City of London. Most of them also have large international operations. Data on these firms is collected and published regularly by the legal press and shows information such as turnover, number of lawyers employed and profits per partner.

There are broad categories into which these law firms are placed. There is a certain amount of debate about which firms should be in which category, and the precise picture changes annually, as some firms will grow faster than others, and the profitability of each firm will clearly vary year on year. There are also fairly frequent mergers between law firms. Therefore, all the categories in this chapter are broadbrush generalisations, and the lists of law firms within them should be viewed as illustrative examples only.

The Lawyer newspaper, which is available online, publishes a report in October every year on the top 200 law firms. The Legal 500 also publishes a directory of law firm profiles and this is also available online (www.legal500.com/books/l500/directory). The general picture at the time of writing is as follows:

Magic Circle

There is a 'Magic Circle' of the most prestigious large international corporate firms which are based in London. The generally accepted view at the moment is that the Magic Circle firms are:

- Allen & Overy (964 UK lawyers)
- Clifford Chance (871 UK lawyers)
- Freshfields Bruckhaus Deringer
- Linklaters (1,100 UK lawyers)
- Slaughter and May (797 UK lawyers).

The figures in brackets are the number of UK fee earners in each firm (comprising partners, assistants, trainees and legal executives) and are taken from The Legal 500 at the date of writing where available, or confirmed directly by the company.

These firms can offer great rewards, with high salaries and high profits per partner. However, the work often involves working long hours in a high-pressure environment. The first four firms have an extensive network of international offices, whereas Slaughter and May instead has strong links with selected overseas firms for international work. In general, many major London law firms have expanded considerably internationally.

Silver Circle

The term 'Silver Circle' was coined by *The Lawyer* in 2005, and refers to a group of elite law firms that are ranked just below the Magic Circle in terms of turnover, but still have considerably higher profits per partner and revenue per lawyer than other firms, together with a premium client base. These firms are also based in London, but most also have an international network of overseas offices.

The Silver Circle is a less settled group than the Magic Circle, but, at the time of writing, the firms within it are generally considered to be:

- Macfarlanes (450 UK lawyers)
- Travers Smith (344 UK lawyers).

In previous years, the firms Ashurst, Berwin Leighton Paisner and Herbert Smith Freehills were members of the Silver Circle, but have since followed international expansion strategies that prevented them from maintaining membership. Slaughter and May, Mischon de Reya and CMS have also been considered members of the Silver Circle in the past.

Although each of these firms falls within the top 50 for total revenue, they are quite spread out in terms of total revenue and are not simply the next biggest firms after the Magic Circle. The size and the number of international offices for each firm also differ. Macfarlanes and Travers Smith each have two offices abroad, while Mishcon de Reya has just one. It is important to consider that a global workforce will allow for trainees to experience potential overseas work.

Each of the firms within the Silver Circle has its own set of specialisms, but individual practices still span a wide range of jurisdictions.

American firms

The trend for large leading US law firms to open branches in London has continued apace and the largest US firms are now firmly entrenched in the UK legal market.

The US law firms with significant London branches include:

- Baker & McKenzie (424 UK lawyers)
- Kirkland & Ellis (375 UK lawyers)
- Latham & Watkins (250 UK lawyers)
- Reed Smith (313 UK lawyers)
- Shearman & Sterling (161 UK lawyers)
- Skadden, Arps, Slate, Meagher & Flom (152 UK lawyers)
- Squire Patton Boggs (314 UK lawyers)
- Weil, Gotshal & Manges (197 UK lawyers)
- White & Case (387 UK lawyers).

Other major City firms

In addition to the Magic Circle and Silver Circle, some other large, well-respected City firms are:

- Ashurst (272 UK lawyers)
- Clyde & Co. (246 UK lawyers in London and 362 across all UK regions)
- CMS (1,072 UK lawyers)
- Dentons (520 UK lawyers)
- Herbert Smith Freehills (783 UK lawyers)
- Hogan Lovells (462 UK lawyers)
- Norton Rose Fulbright (516 UK lawyers).

Major national and regional firms

If London is not for you, then there are some very large national and regional law firms with a major presence in large cities outside London. They offer the chance to do top-quality work with high-profile clients outside of London. Some of these firms have branches all over the country and many also have offices abroad, or associate offices abroad. These major national and regional law firms include:

- DAC Beachcroft (743 UK lawyers)
- DLA Piper (546 UK lawyers)
- Eversheds (1,055 UK lawyers)
- Irwin Mitchell (1,105 UK lawyers)
- Pinsent Masons (642 UK lawyers).

What is the work like?

Large law firms tend to offer a comprehensive service to corporate clients, covering areas such as:

- company law
- mergers and acquisitions
- banking/finance law
- capital markets
- commercial litigation
- commercial property law
- competition law
- employment and pensions law
- financial regulatory law
- intellectual property law (i.e. copyright, trademarks and patents).

Work is often undertaken by teams, and the most junior members of the team may have little or no direct contact with the client. A typical area of work for a trainee involves conducting practical legal research or undertaking document checking work known as 'due diligence'.

Large corporate law firms tend to demand extremely high standards from their lawyers, who are well known for working long hours. In exchange, however, these firms offer excellent training and high salaries. They also usually offer good benefits, such as gym memberships, and also in-house catering services, possibly to avoid you ever having to leave your desk!

Most of the larger law firms will sponsor students that they have given training contracts to by paying their course fees for the Legal Practice Course (LPC) and Graduate Diploma in Law (GDL) (the postgraduate qualifications necessary to become a solicitor – see Chapter 4 for more details). In most cases, they also offer a maintenance grant to help with living costs. The grants vary considerably depending on firm and geographic location, and can fall between £6,000 and £11,000, though on average they tend to be around £7,000. For more information on the sponsorship and maintenance grants offered by solicitors' firms, visit https://targetjobs.co.uk/career-sectors/law-solicitors.

Starting salaries for trainees in City firms tend to be high, with typical training contract salaries for major law firms in London between £38,000 and £55,000 per annum and many firms offering between £50,000 and

£133,000 on qualification. However, for smaller firms outside of London the figures are not as high.

Usually, the larger law firms recruit two to three years ahead of when they expect the trainee to start work, and most will have a vacation placement scheme which typically takes place twice yearly, during the Easter and summer periods. As you can imagine, the large law firms tend to be massively over-subscribed. It is not unusual for a lawyer to leave a large law firm once qualified and move to a smaller firm for what is regarded as a better quality of life, due to shorter working hours.

Case study

After submitting a competitive application, Reanna secured a place to study medicine at the University of Liverpool. She gained entry onto the course having obtained outstanding grades in biology, chemistry, physics and French. However, after accepting the place, Reanna realised that medicine wasn't for her, and made the switch to law.

'From a young age, I was very good at science at school and I was always encouraged to become a doctor as a result. This made sense to me throughout my education: it was a well-established and well-respected career that combined my enthusiasm for science with my desire to work in a person-centred role. I was always very academic, and my interests were wide-ranging, but it hadn't really occurred to me that my interest in politics and law could amount to anything until I started university and met other students that had chosen to study law at degree level. Out of interest, I attended some mooting competitions and I loved it. I started to research law as a career and after a few months of trying to decide whether to pursue medicine or be brave and jump into law, I opted for the latter. My main reasoning for this was the wide range of skills it would allow me to develop, and the way in which it combined so many of my academic interests.

'I completed my first year at medical school before reapplying to university and accepting a place to study law at King's College, London. After careful consideration, I opted to pursue a career as a solicitor because of the greater scope of the work, being able to work as part of a team, and the close working relationships that are developed when working with clients. Being in London really allowed me to immerse myself into City firms, and I worked extremely hard to obtain places on vacation schemes with three large firms. These schemes were a huge wake up call, and alerted me to the fact that qualifying as a solicitor would be incredibly tough, but I found the work extremely rewarding and knew it would be worth the investment.

'I applied for numerous training contracts and received offers from two. I decided on a firm with a large international impact as I was excited at the prospect of the wide range of work that I would be faced with. My current work is predominantly corporate, and working with clients directly has proven to be really interesting – I really enjoy the research and preparatory work that goes into building cases. While my introduction to these roles has been gentle, I have been tasked with a number of other roles as a trainee, which predominantly involve research.

'I would encourage any prospective lawyers to fully immerse themselves in the experience and make the most of any opportunities that come their way. They can be exhausting, but the potential for learning is never ending!'

Case study

Edward always knew that he wanted to pursue a career in the field of law, and had his sights set on being a solicitor. As he knew what he was working towards, he took meticulous steps to ensure that he could stay on track.

'I studied Politics, Economics, History and Law at A level. I had read that A level Law may be frowned upon by universities when applying to study it at degree level, but as I was already taking three other A levels, I felt it would be worth it in order to have a grounding in what I would be studying for three years afterwards. However, it didn't present any problems with my university application, and it actually led me to wider reading that I might not have undertaken otherwise. While my other A levels were not directly linked to law, I was always keen to try and identify where there was an overlap. By the time I came to apply for university, I felt I could discuss law in a number of different contexts by staying up to date with what was going on in the legal world. I hadn't been able to get any work experience before applying, but reading and visiting law courts certainly helped to fill in gaps. If you find yourself in a similar position, I would encourage you to access whatever you can online about the world of law and to speak to people working in the profession where possible.

'I ultimately chose to study LLB Law at the University of Sheffield. In the first year, we covered a broad range of content, including private, public, property, contract, tort and criminal law, as well as learning in depth about the English legal system and developing practical skills. In the following two years, there were core training and modules that were taken alongside a smaller number of optional modules. I chose to specialise in contract law, as it was an area that I felt drawn to and could see myself working in. The degree involved a great deal of independent reading. Some people can find this extremely tedious, but it can be fascinating. I also participated in law society activities that involved debates and mock trials. They can be daunting and uncomfortable at first, especially if you're naturally more introverted, but that makes it all the more important. Getting used to putting yourself out there can be invaluable later in your career.

'I was very fortunate to be in a position after graduating from my undergraduate degree with a 2.i to self-fund the LPC. I knew that I wanted to work for a big firm, and I didn't feel that my CV was strong enough at that point to apply for training contracts. I still applied that year in order to get experience of the application process, but opted to stick with my original plan of completing the LPC. I knew that the LPC was intense, so I wanted to make sure I could focus my efforts on that. At the same time, I also used that period to apply for a number of placements and schemes that could help me to develop my exposure, skills and experience. I was able to do a lot of wider reading about the world where law operates. I was able to fully immerse myself in the study of law, and while I knew having completed the LPC wouldn't necessarily put me in a stronger position for applying for training contracts, I felt more confident and worldly.

'After many applications, I was able to secure a training contract with a relatively large firm in Birmingham. The application process was tough and it can be really difficult to take the rejections at times. I also found it very frustrating when I didn't get feedback after a rejection, but I appreciate now that there would have been vast numbers of candidates to sift through. My advice is that if you get rejected at this stage, don't be disheartened – keep going! The interview process was extremely thorough and I think having the extra time to study and read and keep up to date with legal events put me in a much stronger position, even though my hands-on experience was probably limited compared to other applicants.

'Throughout my training period, I gained exposure to a number of different areas of law, including government, employment, contract, commercial and corporate. All of these areas had their advantages (and disadvantages), but there was something that drew me towards commercial law. I really enjoyed the ability to link my knowledge of law to the workings of a business, especially as the latter changes so often. It was an area that I found intellectually challenging, interesting and exciting, and I also enjoyed the pros-

'pect of a relatively stable career. On a day-to-day basis, I work with numerous clients with differing demands, and sometimes it can be just that – demanding – but I always find that the job satisfaction outweighs the complexities and long working hours. Being part of a big firm means that, with each year, I am becoming more specialised in what I offer.'

Smaller law firms

These make up the largest number of law firms, and range in size from one solicitor (sole practitioner) to firms with over 50 lawyers. They tend to specialise in areas more relevant to individuals than companies, or have smaller company clients. For example, on most high streets or in smaller town centres you will find at least one small firm dealing with:

- civil litigation (disputes between individuals)
- conveyancing (sale and purchase of property)
- wills, probate and trusts
- employment law
- family law
- criminal law.

Due to the location of their offices, these firms tend to be categorised as high-street firms – but remember that small firms can still offer high-quality corporate work if they have the clients, and every high street is surrounded by small businesses! Do not forget that most large cities will have many small commercial firms dealing with good commercial work, as well as true high-street firms which concentrate more on individuals. Larger firms may take half a dozen trainees a year, whereas the smallest firms may recruit trainees only occasionally as the need arises.

Typically a trainee solicitor in a small firm will have much more client contact from an early stage. You may still be working as part of a team, but normally you will work closely with the supervisor and, upon qualification, you will work autonomously. It is not unusual to have a high degree of responsibility, and even partnership, cast upon you early on.

The financial rewards might not be as high as those in the larger law firms, but smaller law firms tend to offer a different quality of life (such as shorter working hours) and work that is more related to everyday life. The SRA's minimum required salary for trainees was scrapped in 2014 although employers must pay at least the national minimum wage. Typical trainee starting salaries outside of London are between £23,500 and £50,000, depending on location.

Usually small firms do not offer any support with course fees or maintenance, though there are an increasing number of exceptions. Most people who secure a training contract at a smaller firm will rely on scholarships and bursaries (such as hardship funds and the Law Society Diversity Access Scheme for those who qualify), loans (such as career and professional development loans), part-time work and family support to finance their studies. The support offered varies significantly between firms. It is also worth considering that at some institutions, the LPC and the GDL can be studied part-time over a two-year course, allowing more scope for part-time work and, ultimately, funding

Case study

When faced with the decision of choosing a course to study at university, Sam decided to pursue the academic area that he found the most interesting – politics – as he was unsure about what he wanted to do as a career. It wasn't until after he graduated that he considered venturing into the field of law.

'My interest in politics had led me to consider a number of career paths, including law, though it wasn't until I had graduated that I really gave it any serious consideration. Having obtained a first class degree in Politics from the University of Warwick, I undertook a part-time administrative role at a small law firm in order to save up some money for postgraduate study, and give myself some time to think about what I actually wanted to do.

'It was while working at the law firm that my interests started to drift towards working in law. Given the small nature of the firm, I was able to get a great insight into what it was that solicitors did on a daily basis, and the close attention to detail of the work and the academic rigour of the tasks really piqued my interest. After a year of working there and having had some incredibly helpful conversations with the partners, I opted to go ahead and complete a Graduate Diploma in Law at university while working full time. It was an intense year but I thoroughly enjoyed developing the foundation of knowledge required to practise.

'I had heard it was incredibly difficult to secure a training contract, but hadn't anticipated *quite* how competitive it would be. As I hadn't always been focussed on this particular career path, I didn't have a great deal of experience, and this worked against me. However, I knew it was what I wanted to do and so I took it in my stride. My previous employers welcomed me back and allowed me to work as a paralegal which considerably enhanced my exposure to legal work.

'Unfortunately, the small firm that I worked for weren't in a position to offer me a training contract, but after a year of paralegal and voluntary work, I was really lucky to secure a training contract with another smaller firm. I opted for smaller firms because of the smaller trainee intake, allowing me to practise in a more focussed setting with a greater deal of support, as well as the wider range of cases that I would be able to work on.

'Though I have only been working at the firm for a short period of time, I have already been able to work with clients directly and I don't think I would have had this experience at a larger firm. The work is tough and it is a steep learning curve, but I really enjoy the intellectual stimulation and how each client requires a different kind of support. I especially enjoy working with clients and discussing the legal components in a more broad manner. At the moment, I am just enjoying working through cases as they come, but I am hoping to become a partner of the firm in the future.

'Although my route into law wasn't typical, I was able to get where I wanted to be with a few years of hard work. My advice to aspiring lawyers who know what they want to do in advance would be to make sure that you get as much experience as you can, and target firms of particular interest to you early on in the process.'

Office-based or in the courtroom?

Traditionally, the work of a solicitor has been predominantly office-based, with some undertaking advocacy work in the lower courts, such as criminal work in the magistrates' court. This is still mainly the case as, in practice, solicitors can earn more money working in the office than they can waiting around at court for cases to be heard. In addition, the typical hourly charge-out rates for solicitors far exceed the average charge-out rates of barristers (for example, it is not uncommon for a junior barrister to earn £450 per day for an appearance, whereas trainee solicitors, on average, can earn up to £186 per hour!) – so it is often more economical for the client to instruct a barrister to undertake court work.

Solicitors have been able to obtain the same right to be heard in the higher courts as barristers, known as the higher rights of audience. Once a solicitor has obtained experience of advocacy in the lower courts, they can undertake an additional training course and, upon successful completion of it, take up the higher rights of audience. A number of solicitors have taken this path and 7,179 practising solicitors are now able to represent their clients in court.

What makes a good solicitor?

Because solicitors deal directly with clients, perhaps the most important attribute required to make a good solicitor is excellent communication skills. Solicitors need to bridge the divide between the academic letter of the law and the practicalities of what the client is trying to achieve.

The law needs to be explained to the client in terms they can appreciate and understand. Clearly, the demands placed on a solicitor in a large corporate City firm are very different from those placed on a solicitor in a high-street practice dealing with individuals, but all solicitors, wherever they work, will need:

- excellent communication skills
- the ability to cope with time pressure
- attention to detail
- good academic ability
- to be well organised
- the ability to work as a team.

Barristers

One of the complaints about the English legal system is that lawyers are like buses: as soon as one appears, another two or three turn up as well. This impression comes from the fact that solicitors can often employ barristers to give specialist advice or to represent the client in court – so, instead of hiring only one lawyer, the client now has at least two on their hands. This section will outline what barristers do and how their work differs from that of a solicitor.

What is the work like?

Barristers are specialist legal advisors and courtroom advocates: they are lawyers whom other lawyers consult on a specific issue, whether for advice or to make use of their advocacy skills. As suggested in Chapter 1, their work compares to that of consultants or surgeons in the medical profession, whereas the work of a solicitor compares more to that of a GP.

Just as the usual route to a consultant is through a referral from a GP, so the usual route to a barrister is through a solicitor (although there are a few exceptions to this): the Bar is a referral profession, so members of the public cannot generally directly engage a barrister. Solicitors will have good working relationships with barristers and are likely to know or be able to find out the most suitable barrister to deal with a particular case.

Barristers work as individual practitioners: most are self-employed and are responsible for their own caseload. They do, however, form groups, known as chambers, or sets, in which a number of barristers have their offices in the same building and share the administrative expenses of clerks and facilities – but these are not firms. Every chamber has an experienced barrister at its head; there will be a number of other members of varying seniority – permanent members of a set of chambers are known as tenants and temporary members are known as squatters.

Barristers are independent and objective, and will advise a client on the strengths and weaknesses of the case. Unlike solicitors, they automatically have rights of audience (the right to appear and present a case) in any court in the land. When a barrister qualifies, it is said that they have been 'called to the Bar', which refers to the bar or rail which used to divide the area of the courtroom used by the judge from the area used by the general public: only barristers were allowed to approach the bar to plead their clients' cases. The term 'barrister' is derived from this usage of bar. Barristers' seniority is measured in terms of their 'years of call', or how many years it has been since they were called to the Bar.

There are two types of barrister: senior counsel and junior counsel. Senior counsel are those senior barristers who have been made Queen's Counsel (QC) as a mark of outstanding ability. This is also known as 'taking silk', which refers to the silk gowns they traditionally wear – thus a senior barrister is often referred to as a silk. A QC is therefore a senior barrister who is normally instructed in serious or complex cases, and would usually appear only in the higher courts. Most senior judges once practised as QCs. Junior counsel is the term used to describe all other barristers who have not been made QCs.

Barristers tend to specialise in particular areas of law, for example civil law, family law, criminal law or immigration law. The work of a civil barrister may be divided into two types: contentious and non-contentious. Contentious work involves cases where litigation is contemplated or a real possibility. Non-contentious work involves advising on matters which have arisen not from a dispute between parties but often from a desire to avoid litigation in the future (for example the drafting of a will, the creation of a trust or advising on the terms of a contract).

Why engage a barrister?

A solicitor might want to engage a barrister for two main reasons. First, to gain an opinion on a matter of law from a person who is an expert or specialist in a particular field; second, to represent the client in court where the solicitor is not allowed to or would prefer a specialist advocate to take on the task. A well-argued case will impress a judge: good cross-examination will impress a jury. A barrister's specialist advocacy skills could make a difference to the outcome of a case.

When a solicitor asks for a barrister's view on a legal point it is known as seeking 'counsel's opinion'; where the barrister is asked to undertake litigation work (for example, disputes between individuals) in court it is known as 'instructing or briefing counsel', though the two expressions are often used loosely today. If an opinion is sought the barrister will be sent the relevant paperwork and will research the area of law and consider the issues before expressing a view as to the merits of the case or what steps to take next. In many cases, barristers are able to give advice on a case simply by looking at the papers. In more complex cases, and certainly cases which go to court, it will usually be necessary to have a conference or consultation with the barrister, typically at the barrister's chambers. If counsel is instructed to act, then the barrister will begin to prepare his or her arguments that will later be used in court. Thus most of a barrister's work will typically be centred on legal disputes. The barrister acts like the old medieval champion: stepping in to fight in the place of the client.

What makes a good barrister?

'You need to have utter confidence in what you are doing – or at least appear to,' says one young barrister. 'You are absolutely vulnerable to the whims of the solicitor. You need to be flexible and robust.' A key skill for a barrister is to persuade, so strong communication skills are high on the list. You also need to be interested in people and business, and to be commercially aware (you will, after all, effectively be running your own small business). Below is a list of skills and qualities you might need:

- strong written and verbal communication skills
- confidence
- energy and drive
- the ability to think on your feet
- flexibility and adaptability
- excellent academic ability
- independence
- interpersonal skills
- meticulousness and ability to master detail
- computer skills
- commercial awareness.

Indeed, the website of the Bar Standards Board (BSB) contains a health warning about the difficulties of getting into the barristers' profession (www.barstandardsboard.org.uk). This warning sets out the qualities that the BSB believes are required of a barrister, which are:

- have a high level of intellectual ability
- are highly articulate in written and spoken English
- can think and communicate under pressure
- have determination and stamina and are emotionally robust.

Who works where?

There are over 13,502 barristers in self-employed independent practice in England and Wales. Although some do a wide variety of legal work, many focus on particular aspects of litigation and the law, specialising in areas such as construction, property, company law, crime, employment, personal injury, taxation, intellectual property and many other areas.

Barristers also work for the Crown Prosecution Service (CPS), the Government Legal Service and magistrates' courts. Some barristers may hardly ever appear in court but spend their time writing opinions and giving advice on complex and difficult areas of law. Most barristers practise from London but many are based in other cities and towns, including Birmingham, Bristol, Cardiff, Leeds, Manchester and Nottingham. All barristers who practise in England and Wales are members of one of the six legal circuits (geographical areas) into which the two countries are divided. The circuits are the areas around which the High Court judges travel to hear the most important cases.

Case study

Before pursuing a career in law, Martin studied Politics, Philosophy and Economics at the University of Oxford. After speaking to barristers working in the profession and getting the opportunity to shadow some of them, he felt that the Bar would offer him the fulfilling career he was looking for.

'As a teenager, I wasn't sure what I wanted to do career-wise. Coming from a working-class background, I knew I wanted to pursue a career that was stable with a good income, but I also wanted to make sure that it was intellectually challenging and stimulating. Studying at Oxford, I met people from many walks of life with differing backgrounds, and I used this to my advantage. I got in touch with relatives of friends to speak about their career paths, and in doing so met with barristers and gained an insight into their everyday lives. This might sound daunting, but if you know someone who knows someone who might be able to help, it's always worth reaching out as it may well alter the trajectory of your life!

'I spent my summer breaks shadowing people working in different areas of law, but the barristers' chambers was the most illuminating. It really came down to the fact that you have to be good with people to excel as a barrister, and I knew this wasn't something I would have difficulty with. After graduating, I went on to complete a law conversion course before studying the BPTC. While I lapped up the opportunity for further study, the pupillage applications really took their toll. I was one of the lucky few who was successful first time around, but I was fully prepared to fail. It is an especially challenging process and the interviews push you to your limits.

'The first half of my one-year pupillage was thoroughly enjoyable. I shadowed my superiors and put my newly developed knowledge of law to the test by drafting documents and carrying out research. The second half of the year was terrifying! I was thrown into the deep end with my own hearings. I ultimately got to grips with this, and even started to enjoy them. I had made a good impression and was offered a permanent role, which I still hold.

'For the most part, I love working as a barrister. Every day presents a new set of challenges and the unpredictability really keeps me on my toes. There are difficulties though, and these are mainly associated with getting everything done in good time and maintaining a strict work–life balance. However, I didn't pursue the role expecting an easy life, and the rewards overshadow the negatives.

'My advice to any aspiring barristers would be, don't give up! It's a tough nut to crack, but it's all worth it in the end.'

Legal executives, paralegals and legal secretaries

Working alongside solicitors in firms are various other legal and support staff who are not fully qualified solicitors, but depending on the level of qualifications they hold may be able to carry out similar work to solicitors.

Legal executives will carry out many of the same tasks as solicitors, usually concentrating on one particular area of the law. They will therefore advise clients, carry out legal research and draft documents.

Paralegals (who may also be known as legal assistants) will work in law firms carrying out more routine legal tasks, including collating documents (for example putting together trial bundles), drafting more straightforward documents and carrying out legal research. Paralegals will often be law graduates who have not moved on to the vocational and professional stages of training. Working as a paralegal can often provide a route into becoming a qualified solicitor. The paralegal profession is currently not formally regulated, which means that it is not necessary to have any formal qualifications to become a paralegal. Nevertheless, paralegals working in law firms are employed by solicitors and therefore regulated by the SRA, although in practice, the SRA usually holds the solicitors responsible if any problems occur with paralegals, as they are meant to be supervised by solicitors at all times. However, owing to the hectic nature of a solicitor's job, increasingly intricate tasks are being delegated to paralegals who are seeing cases through from beginning to end at a much higher frequency. This is especially true of areas where the work involved is fairly repetitive and similar in all cases. The Institute of Paralegals, the leading representative body for paralegals in the UK, publishes a code of conduct, which is a code of best practice. It also administers qualifications for paralegals. For more information see www.theiop.org.

Legal secretaries are basically secretaries who work in law firms – they give administrative support to solicitors. This will include taking telephone calls from clients, typing up documents and letters to clients, invoicing clients, and preparing and filing legal documents. There are no formal qualifications required to become a legal secretary, but good typing, communication and IT skills are the qualities that any firm employing a legal secretary would look for. There are several bodies offering various training courses for legal secretaries, including the Institute of Legal Secretaries and PAs (www.institutelegalsecretaries.com).

More paralegals are being recruited to do routine work. This is often seen as a way in for law students hoping to find training contracts.

Case study

After securing excellent A level grades in Law, Government and Politics and Business Studies, Ethan took up his place at Aston University to study Law, where he obtained a first-class honours degree. Since graduating, Ethan has taken on a number of roles and is now working as a paralegal for a large multinational law firm.

'I always knew that I wanted to study and practise law, and my A level choices helped confirm this decision. I chose Aston because of the outstanding reputation of its business school and the quality of working links that were promised. I enjoyed studying all of the modules covered, but especially equity and trust law, commercial law and intellectual property law. While I was at university, I was able to put my newly acquired skills into practice when advising students in the engineering department of their intellectual property rights, and I became heavily involved in a number of law-related societies, as well as making the most of guest lectures and networking events.

'After graduating, I knew I wanted to work in the legal sector, but I knew I still had a lot to learn before I would be able to make a final decision about the specific career path I wanted to pursue. The first role I took on as a graduate was as a legal assistant for a commercial company, and this involved supporting departments with clerical work that involved legal terminology and fact checking. I was also able to get stuck into contractual work by redesigning some of the contracts with international partner businesses and supporting staff with contractual arrangements with new clients. With the new GDPR laws being set out in recent years, I was also given the opportunity to work in a new role alongside the data protection officer at the company to redact personal and business sensitive data, conduct research into data protection topics to support the legal team and proposing alterations to existing contracts with business partners.

'I then decided to take on the role of a paralegal for a large law firm with many offices in the UK and abroad. I decided to target the paralegal role to continue to expose myself to a wide range of legal work, and the firm was an added bonus as their work is wide ranging, both in terms of their international impact and the multijurisdictional nature of the projects. In the short time that I have been working at the firm, I have had the opportunity to work with clients directly under the close supervision of a solicitor to build, maintain and develop helplines and billing processes; conduct research and analysis to generate metric reports and present them to clients during monthly meetings; and work with advisory bodies globally to ensure that international clients were working maximally to minimise the risk of disputes.

'At this moment in time, I am still unsure where my career will take me, but I am constantly seeking opportunities to enhance my exposure and develop my knowledge and skills.

'With a legal career, it is important to remember that things won't always go to plan – and it doesn't matter if you don't really have a plan! It is more important to be open minded when it comes to new roles and learning new things, as you never know where they might take you.'

The legal profession in Scotland

The main difference in the composition of the legal profession in Scotland is that instead of there being the two separate professions of solicitors and barristers, in Scotland there are solicitors and advocates.

Solicitors

As in England and Wales, solicitors in Scotland give advice on a wide variety of areas of law, with individual solicitors specialising in particular areas. Solicitors in Scotland can represent clients in the Justice of the Peace and Sheriff courts.

Solicitors in Scotland are both represented and regulated by the Law Society of Scotland, which sets standards for the profession, including education and training requirements, and disciplines solicitors where necessary.

Solicitor advocates

Solicitor advocates are experienced solicitors who have extended rights of audience and can also appear in the High Court of Justiciary and the

Court of Session. They are members of the Law Society of Scotland and are regulated by that body.

Advocates

Advocates (sometimes referred to as 'counsel') are lawyers that are specifically trained in advocacy, so can represent clients in any Scottish court. They are equivalent to barristers in England and Wales, and the relationship between solicitors and advocates works the same as that between solicitors and barristers in England and Wales, in that advocates are usually instructed through a solicitor instead of being instructed directly by individuals.

Advocates are members of the Scottish Bar, and are regulated and represented by the Faculty of Advocates, which carries out similar functions as the Law Society of Scotland does for Scottish solicitors.

Reform of the legal profession in Scotland

The Legal Services (Scotland) Act 2010 made various changes to the operation of the legal profession in Scotland. It aimed to reduce the restrictions on solicitors entering into business relationships with non-solicitors, as the Legal Service Act 2007 has allowed solicitors, barristers and non-lawyers to work together in England and Wales. However, the introduction of so-called alternative business structures in Scotland has been long delayed due to a failure to introduce an appropriate regulatory structure.

> For more information on the legal profession in Scotland see www.lawscot.org.uk and www.advocates.org.uk/about-advocates.

Case study

Nina's career in law is extremely wide and varied, and highlights that after qualifying, you don't have to stay in one lane.

'I completed my undergraduate degree in law at the University of Edinburgh, and, at the time, I was determined to work as a barrister. As such, I doggedly pursued this path and jumped through the hoops and over the hurdles that the path presents. After being called to the Bar, I worked successfully as a barrister for five years. I enjoyed the work – it was rewarding, demanding and rigorous, kept me on my toes and allowed me to carve out a name for myself. I loved law, though, and something told me I was missing out on something by not exposing myself to the work of a solicitor, so I decided to undertake the Qualified Lawyer Transfer Test (QLTT) to qualify as a solicitor.

'My main justification for doing this was that I wanted to use my skillset more broadly. I went on to work in the legal departments of a number of businesses, providing legal counsel and also contributing to sales roles because of my work approach. By developing my legal and commercial awareness in these roles, I was able to provide legal counsel for a number of company acquisitions worth billions of dollars, which took my negotiations global. In these roles, I was responsible for resolving all legal issues that arose globally through the acquisitions.

'I have since held the titles Head of Legal and Chief Legal Officer, helping to establish new companies, broaden their international impact and developing legal, marketing and public affairs teams. As with any legal role, no day is the same and the work is tough, but it is enormously exciting.'

The legal profession in Northern Ireland

As in England and Wales, the legal profession in Northern Ireland is divided into the two distinct branches of solicitors and barristers, and these professions have the same roles as in England and Wales. Solicitors in Northern Ireland are represented and regulated by the Law Society of Northern Ireland, and barristers are regulated by the General Council of the Bar of Northern Ireland.

For more information please see: www.lawsoc-ni.org/about-us and www.barofni.com.

4| How to qualify as a lawyer

So now we come to the crucial matter: how do you start on the long road to becoming a lawyer? As there are two distinct branches of the legal profession, there are different training routes for each branch. This chapter will start by looking at how to qualify as a solicitor in England and Wales, followed by an overview of how to qualify as a solicitor in Scotland and Northern Ireland, and will then move on to qualifying as a barrister in each of the three jurisdictions.

Solicitors: England and Wales

There are a number of different routes to qualifying as a solicitor. Most of these are set out in the diagram on page 47 and then described in more detail in the text that follows.

Before university

A levels

A wide range of A levels provide an acceptable grounding for a law degree and there are no specific subject entry requirements to be able to study law at university. The traditional essay-based subjects such as history and English have an obvious appeal: they involve assimilating and analysing information, and a significant amount of writing, which will all be required on a law degree course. Languages may also prove to be very attractive to employers, particularly if you end up working for a firm with offices overseas, and sciences will develop logical thought and application, which are key skills for any lawyer. Many universities do not accept either General Studies or Critical Thinking A levels at all for any of their courses.

The website Informed Choices (www.informedchoices.ac.uk) outlines the subjects that might be required or be most useful for a chosen course, as well offering general guidance to those unsure about their future career paths. It states that there are no specific subjects that must be studied to gain access onto undergraduate law courses, giving A level students free rein in their choices. While it is encouraged that students choose subjects that they enjoy, the website suggests that 'essay-based subjects may be useful'. Aspiring lawyers should be aware that studying for a law degree involves a considerable amount of reading and research, requiring a high degree of literacy. Students who choose to study all maths and science A levels would not be penalised for their subject choices, but the volume and intensity of more essay-based subjects should not be underestimated; it may be advisable to practise these skills as much as possible in other areas, such as in the completion of the Extended Project Qualification (EPQ) or other extra-curricular activities.

The EPQ is an additional qualification, which requires you to undertake a self-directed period of research, which is then usually written up in a dissertation-style essay. This can be related either to one of your current A level subjects or to your future career, and could be a really useful way of demonstrating your passion for law.

Whether or not an aspiring lawyer should choose A level Law has, historically, caused some controversy. The obvious advantage of taking law at A level is that it will provide you with an introduction to the subject and give you some idea of what studying law is like and whether or not it appeals to you before you have to commit to studying it at university. Historically, it was rumoured that studying A level Law could be held against undergraduate applicants, but this is not the case. Much of the discussion surrounding A level Law is based on its lack of rigour when compared to undergraduate study and, in this way, potentially being misleading. As with many A level subjects, the content covered within A level Law is brief and introductory, with students often finding the jump considerable. However, as long as you are prepared for the intellectual rigours of undergraduate study, choosing law as an A level subject should not be a hindrance.

With all of your A level choices, it is important to choose subjects because you think you will enjoy them and they will play to your strengths. To be on the safe side, you should also take the following steps:

- if you already have a university in mind, check with the admissions section of its website to determine its specific entry requirements; and, if you wish to take law, whether or not it will be considered
- if you are already studying for your A levels but have not yet chosen which universities you would like to apply to, then do your research before applying so that you know which universities will accept your combination of A level subjects.

UCAS advises that subjects such as physical education, dance, art and photography may not be considered as a suitable subject for one of the three A levels. At the time of writing, no UK universities stipulate specific A level requirements, but it is always worth checking before an application is submitted.

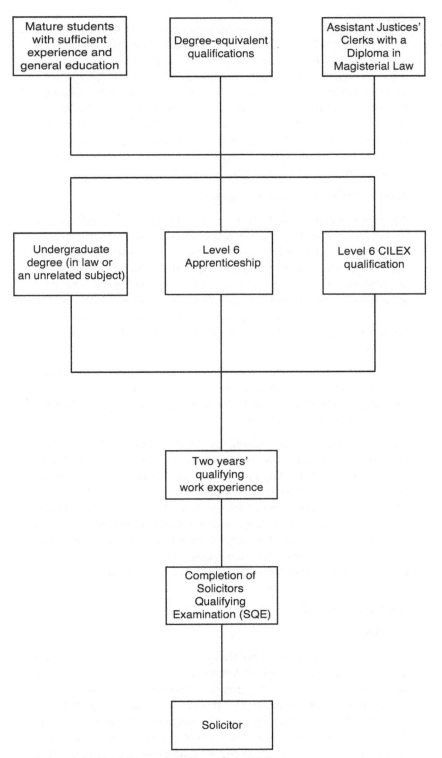

Figure 1: Qualification route for solicitors from 2021

T levels

In September 2020, the government rolled out a new qualification in the form of T levels. A T level is a two-year course that follows GCSEs and is the equivalent of studying three A levels. The demands differ in that T levels combine classroom learning with a 315-hour industry placement in one of a number of subject areas, including legal. At the time of writing, there is no set start date for legal T levels, but for those interested in pursuing this route, it would be worth keeping an eye on the government website for updates (www.gov.uk/government/publications/introduction-of-t-levels/introduction-of-t-levels).

Access to Higher Education courses

If you are a mature student who missed out on completing your secondary education, and cannot satisfy university entry requirements, Access to Higher Education (HE) courses are designed to help you move into higher education and on to degree-level studies. Most Access courses are delivered in further education colleges (although some are available at certain universities) and are available across England and Wales. The courses can be taken in a range of different subjects and lead to the Access to Higher Education Diploma, which is widely recognised by universities.

To find out more about Access to HE courses, visit the Access to Higher Education website (www.accesstohe.ac.uk), which contains further information on the Diploma and a link to a database of further education colleges offering Access courses.

Some employers will particularly welcome applicants who have had some 'life experience' in other fields before starting their legal career and the skills and qualities that more mature applicants offer can be much valued. This will be the case more for some employers than others (the civil service and teaching profession are good examples), although all employers must disregard age in their recruitment decisions to avoid breaking anti-age-discrimination laws. However, you should research the legal career you are interested in carefully before embarking on the expensive and time-consuming training to becoming a lawyer.

Degree-level study

Law degree

The most common route for qualifying as a solicitor is to pursue it as a graduate. Many people with an interest in law choose to study law at university, but this is not a requirement, and your first degree can be in any subject. Due to the recent changes in the pathway for qualifying as a solicitor, however, studying law at undergraduate level is a sensible option. The reason for this is that successful completion of the Solicitors Qualifying Exam (SQE) will require a good knowledge of law. It is also thought that many law degree providers will incorporate SQE preparation elements into their courses in the coming years.

Many universities offer law degrees, and these vary to some extent in style and content – for example:

- some are more traditional and 'academic' in approach
- some are slightly more vocational in outlook
- some enable you to obtain a joint degree (e.g. law and languages, law and politics, law and accountancy).

This variety gives you the opportunity to choose the degree that best suits your skills and interests. When identifying which universities to apply to, it is important to look at the specific modules and content that will be covered, as these can vary between providers, though there are some fundamental modules that tend to be covered by all. Further details regarding the types of law degree that are available are covered in Chapter 6.

Up until September 2021, there was an option to study a Qualifying Law Degree (QLD), as recognised by the Solicitors Regulation Authority (SRA). Having a QLD means that you have studied the subjects that the SRA considers to be the core foundation subjects for any lawyer. It is likely that many providers will still ensure that the core foundation subjects are covered within their law degrees, as these will help to prepare aspiring solicitors for the SQE, which is discussed in detail later in this chapter.

The core foundation subjects are:

- criminal law
- equity and the law of trusts
- law of the European Union
- obligations (including contract, restitution and tort law)
- property law
- public law (including constitutional law, administrative law and human rights law).

The SRA maintains a list of institutions and the degrees they offer that are recognised as QLDs, so if you want to pursue a degree historically considered as a QLD, you can check the list by visiting the SRA website (www.sra.org.uk/become-solicitor/courses/qualifying-law-degree-providers).

Once you complete your degree and enter the world of work, you will discover that many firms will expect you to have either a First or Upper Second class degree. You will need to work hard right from the outset of your degree to maximise your chances of getting a role with the firm of your choice.

Non-law degree

As previously mentioned, there is no requirement for your undergraduate degree to be in law, and you can pursue a career in law from a variety of backgrounds. Given that the SQE requires a thorough understanding of law, you may choose to undertake a postgraduate qualification in law, although this is not a requirement.

Historically, non-law graduates qualified as lawyers by completing the Graduate Diploma in Law (GDL) – although some universities and colleges (and indeed the SRA) still refer to it by its former name: the Common Professional Examination (CPE). This qualification is accepted by both the Bar Council and the SRA, so you could start the GDL without having decided whether you eventually intend to qualify as a solicitor or as a barrister, and then make your decision during the course of your studies.

The GDL is a condensed programme of study, usually comprising a one-year full-time course offered at around 50 universities and law schools across England and Wales. Many of the same institutions offer the GDL on a part-time basis over two years for added flexibility. Part-time online distance learning programmes are also available through some institutions, allowing students to work while studying. The SRA maintains a list of all institutions that offer the GDL (available at www.sra.org.uk/become-solicitor/courses/cpe-gdl-course-providers).

Application for a full-time GDL course is made via the Central Applications Board (the CAB), which runs an online system similar to UCAS, acting as a hub for all full-time applications for the GDL and LPC. Up to three different institutions can be applied to at once. There are no application deadlines for the CAB, which simply recommends that candidates should apply at their 'earliest convenience', but it does advise you to check on the individual course providers' websites for application closing dates as they may not accept late applications. Applications for part-time or distance learning GDL courses are made direct to the institution(s) of your choice. Applicants must register on their website (www.lawcabs.ac.uk) and there is a £25 registration fee.

The current cost of a full-time GDL ranges from around £6,000 to around £11,000. You should check what the course fee includes – for example, some providers will include the cost of all books and materials within their fees, whereas others will expect you to pay for these direct. You should also investigate the amount of contact time offered by the different course providers. Remember that you often get what you pay for, so do not necessarily opt for the most inexpensive course. Try to talk to some students who are currently studying or have previously studied at the institution you are interested in to find out whether they were happy with the course. You should also consider where you would like to undertake your work experience for the vocational part of the training, or which law firms you would like to work at in the future, as certain law firms favour specific law schools. For more information on funding the GDL, please see page 151.

Given that the GDL is no longer a requirement, a number of other post-graduate qualifications and training courses are also available that might provide a suitable basis of education for SQE preparation. Conversion courses such as the GDL are especially useful as they allow individuals considering a career in law who are unsure about whether to qualify as a barrister or solicitor to learn the knowledge and skills required for both pathways. Alternative qualifications range from postgraduate diploma level (PgDL) courses to master's level (MA Law) courses, of which there are many variations. Some courses will also incorporate SQE preparation, so if this is an important factor in your decision you should check the course content carefully. Other significant factors that might influence your decision include location of the provider, course content, course duration, flexibility and delivery type (i.e. self-study options and options for part-time study).

Case study

Jess didn't know what she wanted to pursue as a career, so opted to pursue a non-law undergraduate degree before undertaking a conversion course. She now works as a solicitor in employment law for a large firm.

'At sixth form, the prospect of choosing a degree to determine my future career was terrifying. I was interested in law as a possible option, but as I hadn't had any exposure to it at that point in my life, I was unsure about committing to it. At A level I studied English Literature, English Language, Geography and German. I also under-took an EPQ in a law-related area, and independently researched whether capital punishment should be reintroduced in the UK. English Literature was my favourite subject by far, so I decided to study that at the University of Bristol. I knew it would develop my skills in reading, writing and critical analysis, which would help to prepare me for a potential career in law if I decided to pursue it.

'While I was at university, I tried to make the most of the options available to me – I joined societies and attended lectures and work-shops on a wide range of career options, but I especially enjoyed the law-related ones. I joined the Law Society, which allowed me to gain an insight into the law course, participate in mock debates, attend talks from law firm representatives and develop an all-round better understanding of what a career in law would entail, as well as what I'd need to do to pursue one. I also attended workshops on commercial awareness, leadership, negotiation and public speaking. The people I met through these activities led to several work experience placements with both small and large law firms over the course of my undergraduate studies, and three vacation schemes between my second and third year.

'I enjoyed these experiences so much that I knew the GDL was my next logical step. I maintained my attendance at Law Society events and got involved with any competitions that were taking place. I also provided voluntary legal aid for an employment rights service, which was invaluable experience, and piqued my interest in employment law. My undergraduate and postgraduate studies were an intense period, but it was well worth it and I enjoyed every minute.

'I was fortunate enough to gain a training contract with a law firm who offered financial support for the next stage of my training, the LPC. I studied the LPC with the University of Law over the course of one year. Once my training contract began, I rotated through four seats with a private client and then in commercial litigation, employment law and public law. Upon qualifying, I pursued a role in employment law, which means that I help clients with all legal matters that relate to employees in the workplace, such as dispute resolutions, contracting and managing relations.

'On a day-to-day basis, what you do can vary dramatically. Recently I advised a client on discrimination allegations, policy reviews in light of Brexit and an employee dismissal on the same day. You have to work with the facts, which requires a lot of skill that comes from legal training but ultimately, it all boils down to being good with people and having a high degree of emotional intelligence. When you are working with people, the same facts and laws can lead to very different outcomes, just because of how different people react. The other thing that I really enjoy is that employment law is always changing, which means that you're always learning to stay on top of the developments.'

Alternative routes into law

Non-graduate route

If you do not possess a degree, there are still a number of options available to you. You may apply to the SRA for a certificate of academic standing which will allow you to apply for the GDL course. This is granted by the SRA if it is satisfied that you hold other academic or vocational qualifications that it considers to be equivalent to a degree. Briefly, the situations where this may be possible include the following.

- **Mature students** – if you have a considerable amount of experience (normally at least 10 years) or have shown exceptional ability in an academic, professional, business or administrative field and have been educated to at least A level standard, and have a good command of both spoken and written English, the SRA may issue a certificate to allow you to take up a place on the GDL course.
- **Assistant Justices' Clerks** – clerks who have gained a Diploma in Magisterial Law are usually eligible to take the GDL, and may even be granted exemptions from some of the papers.
- **Chartered legal executives** – those already working in the legal sector, for example as a paralegal, could take the Chartered Institute of Legal Executives examinations during a period of qualifying employment. These qualifications are recognised by the SRA as being equivalent to a law degree and therefore enable you to progress to the next stage of training, the LPC (see below) without obtaining a degree.
- **Degree-level qualifications** – these may include professional accountants' or surveyors' qualifications.

More information on the non-graduate route to qualification is contained in the Academic Stage Handbook, which is available on the SRA website. If in any doubt, you should contact the SRA, whose staff will be able to give you advice on your particular circumstances.

Law apprenticeships

Aligned with the government's flagship campaign to promote apprenticeships, legal apprenticeships have increased in recent years. These pathways allow those who do not necessarily want to study at university – preferring to get stuck into the working side of the field – to pursue a career in law. There are four levels of law apprenticeship – legal administration, paralegal, chartered legal executive or solicitor – which can be completed as standalone apprenticeships, or can be studied consecutively to allow progression. The legal apprenticeships currently available include:

- CILEX Level 2 Diploma for Legal Secretaries: An introductory apprenticeship to secretarial work in a legal setting, which can be followed by Level 3 Legal Administrator Apprenticeship studies. These apprenticeships typically take around 18 months to complete. Generally, the study content will be determined by the firm offering the apprenticeship, but will include broad themes such as legal text processing, principles of criminal liability, conveyancing, family law, communication skills, proofreading, minute taking and providing reception services.
- Level 3 Paralegal Apprenticeship: A two-year introduction to the background required for studying law, how this knowledge can be used in practice, how to conduct legal research and how to work with clients. It provides a solid grounding to allow progression onto

the Level 3 Diploma in Law and Practice, or the Level 6 Chartered Legal Executive Apprenticeship. Day-to-day tasks might include the management of data and client records, the production of legal documentation, recording client correspondence, conducting research into the legal field for specific cases and communicating directly with clients.

- Level 6 Chartered Legal Executive Apprenticeship: A five-year programme that covers all of the qualifications required to work as a chartered legal executive. This pathway is only available to those who have a background in the field, either through completion of the Level 3 Paralegal Apprenticeship or Level 3 CILEX qualifications.
- Level 7 Solicitor Apprenticeship: A six-year Degree Apprenticeship that allows apprentices to obtain an undergraduate law degree and master's degree (LLM) with City, University of London or Northumbria University, as well as covering the content of the legal practice course (LPC). This particular route is aimed at those who have completed A level study (obtaining grades BBB or above), or are currently working as paralegals or chartered legal executives. The overall study time is reduced for those who have completed the Level 6 Chartered Legal Executive Apprenticeship. After completing the Level 7 Apprenticeship, apprentices will sit the Solicitors Regulation Authority's centralised assessment and, upon passing, will qualify as a solicitor. For solicitor apprentices, managing your own cases is not uncommon, and this will involve research, interviews, advising clients, developing working relationships, producing legal documents, advocacy and negotiation.

These apprenticeships offer an incredibly exciting opportunity for school leavers to qualify as lawyers without having to study at university full time. A wide range of UK law firms offer these apprenticeships, which allow people to carry out paid employment in a legal environment while studying to acquire professional qualifications. While all apprentices are guaranteed the national minimum wage, many firms will offer considerably better pay, but this varies from firm to firm.

As well as the routes listed above, a number of other legal-related apprenticeships are available, including for training in occupations such as actuarial technicians, conveyancing technicians, financial advisers, insurance professionals, internal audit practitioners, investment operations specialists, paraplanners, probate technicians and taxation technicians. Similarly, as well as undertaking a Degree Apprenticeship to become a solicitor, wider Degree Apprenticeships are available in areas such as accountancy and taxation, actuarial work, financial services, internal auditing, licensed conveyancing, economics, banking management, senior compliance and risk, senior insurance, senior investment and commercial banking. While these are not specifically legal apprenticeships, there are strong law elements to each of them that may be worth considering. The UCAS website is an excellent source of up-to-date subject-specific information on apprenticeships and Degree Apprenticeships related to law (www.ucas.com/explore/subjects/law).

There is fierce competition for a relatively small number of legal apprenticeships. There is no centralised route for applications; firms must be contacted and applied to on an individual basis. For students studying A levels and looking to apply for Level 7 Solicitor Apprenticeships, it would be a good idea to research the available options in the summer between years 12 and 13, before applying in year 13. There are no fixed deadlines with apprenticeship applications and application requirements will vary depending on the firms that are advertising them.

Solicitors Qualifying Examination (SQE)

In 2021 the Solicitors Qualifying Examination (SQE) was rolled out and changed the way in which solicitors in England and Wales qualify.

The SQE is a series of examinations that provide a centralised assessment route and eradicate the variable and inconsistent pass rates of the LPC due to differences between providers. The SQE will now start to replace the LPC, but for those who have already commenced training to become a lawyer, a transition period is in place to give them the option to pursue the LPC route if they so desire. The SQE is considerably cheaper, with the exams totalling £3,980 (independent of any postgraduate or SQE courses).

Summary of the new qualification route

- Undertake first degree or equivalent qualification (such as a Degree Apprenticeship)
- If required, take an SQE Stage 1 preparation course (i.e. for non-law graduates)
- Complete Stage 1 of the SQE
- Complete Stage 2 of the SQE
- Undertake two years' worth of legal work experience
- Meet the suitability and character requirements of the SRA
- Qualify as a solicitor

In order to commence the SQE route, a first degree or an equivalent qualification (such as a Level 6 apprenticeship or a Level 6 CILEX qualification) must be held. This condition can also be met through equivalent experience as determined by the SRA, and might be suitable for those who have been working in the legal profession in an alternative role, such as a paralegal, for a considerable period of time. For non-law university graduates, undertaking a postgraduate law qualification is advised to ensure that they have the thorough theoretical legal ground-ing required for success in the exams.

It is thought that, as the SQE rolls out, both undergraduate and post-graduate providers of law courses will start to deliver SQE-specific training. Many providers of law courses have also started to offer courses specifically for SQE preparation. For example, the University of Law have adapted their LLM Legal Practice programme to cover both SQE stages (SQE1 and SQE2), while their PGDL and MA programmes have incorporated SQE1 preparation. They are also offering SQE-spe-cific courses, including SQE Law Online Essentials and SQE1 Preparation Courses (see www.law.ac.uk/study/postgraduate/sqe/courses). The SRA has also published a list of training providers (see www.lawsociety.org.uk/career-advice/becoming-a-solicitor/solicitors-qualifying-examination-sqe/preparatory-courses), although it is important to note that they are not accredited or regulated by the SRA in any way. While these courses are available, the SRA states that preparatory courses are not a requirement, and that a candidate's edu-cation and training should be sufficient to provide them with the skills and knowledge that they require to pass the formal assessments.

The SQE is divided into two main components: Stage 1 (SQE1) and Stage 2 (SQE2), which are summarised in Table 2 below. Stage 1 should be completed before undertaking work-based experience, with Stage 2 being completed following the conclusion of work-based experience, though this is flexible providing that SQE1 is passed in advance of SQE2. There are two sittings per calendar year for each assessment (in spring and autumn). Assessment specifications for both SQE1 and SQE2, as well as sample questions, have been published on the SRA website (see https://sqe.sra.org.uk/exam-arrangements/assessment-information). Candidates have a six-year window to complete the assessments, with three resit attempts allowed within that period.

SQE1	SQE2
Two functioning legal knowledge (FKL) assessments comprising 180 multiple-choice questions, covering:	Divided into two parts, which are then combined to give one overall pass mark:
• Business law and practice; dispute resolution; contract; tort; legal system of England and Wales; constitutional and administrative law and EU law • Property practice; wills and the administration of estates; solicitors' accounts; land law; trusts; criminal law and practice Ethics and professional conduct will also be assessed throughout the exams.	• SQE2 Oral: interview and atten-dance note/legal analysis and advocacy; assessed in four oral assessments over two days • SQE2 Written: case and matter analysis, legal research, legal writing and legal drafting, assessed in 12 written assessments over three days.

Table 2: Solicitors Qualifying Examination (SQE) stages

As well as passing SQE stages 1 and 2, aspiring solicitors must also undertake two years of qualifying work experience. Appropriate work-based training could be obtained in a variety of ways, including formal training contracts, working in a law clinic, undertaking an apprentice-ship, working as a paralegal, or through a placement as part of a sandwich degree. A maximum of four organisations can be used to obtain this experience. In each instance, a supervising solicitor would be required to sign a declaration that the student had the opportunity to develop the competencies in the Statement of Solicitor Competence. The work-based training component is designed to offer more flexibility for solicitors, which is an exciting step given the difficulty in obtaining formal training contracts, though some larger firms have indicated that they are likely to maintain the traditional training contract format. A detailed summary of what constitutes qualifying work experience and the competencies that should be developed can be found on the Law Society website (www.lawsociety.org.uk/career-advice/becoming-a-solicitor/solicitors-qualifying-examination-sqe/qualifying-work-experience-qwe).

The final SQE hurdle is satisfying the SRA's character and suitability requirements, which involves an assessment by the SRA to ensure that those wishing to work as solicitors are suitable to do so. The SRA will look at criminal records, any involvement with the police, any evidence of cheating in an educational context or significant financial difficulties. An initial screening process is required, which costs £39, before a deci-sion is made.

These changes are unlikely to affect aspiring solicitors who are begin-ning their law degree or LPC before September 2021, with 11 years to qualify under the traditional route (before 2032). The LPC will no longer exist beyond the 2025/2026 academic year, leaving the SQE as the only qualification route.

The most up-to-date information regarding the SQE is available from the SRA website www.sra.org.uk/become-solicitor/sqe.

Transitional Arrangements

Following the introduction of the SQE route of qualification in Septem-ber 2021, the SRA put in place transitional arrangements for candidates who have already commenced their qualification to become a solicitor beyond this date, including anyone enrolled on a QLD, GLD or LPC.

For these candidates, rather than completing the SQE, they must first complete the academic stage of training through either a QLD, exempt-ing law degree (ELD, see page 58) or GDL (if they have studied a non-law degree at undergraduate level) before completing the Legal Practice Course (LPC) and obtaining a training contract. Details of these stages are outlined below.

Legal Practice Course (LPC)

Following completion of the academic stage of training, aspiring solicitors can choose, instead of the SQE, to complete an LPC at one of around 35 universities and law schools across England and Wales. The LPC can be completed over one year full-time or two years part-time (in a variety of formats including day, evening or weekend study patterns). The current cost ranges from around £10,500 to around £17,00 for the full-time course. The yearly fees are less for the part-time courses.

The LPC is made up of a combination of compulsory and elective modules. The compulsory modules cover the subjects and skills in the core practice areas, including business law and practice, property law and practice as well as litigation, and these must be covered irrespective of where the LPC is studied. You will also take three elective modules which you will be able to choose from the range offered by your chosen course provider. Different institutions offer different elective subjects, so when you apply for the LPC, you should make sure that you choose courses that offer the elective modules that you are interested in studying and pursuing as a career.

The larger solicitors' firms that offer help with fees for the LPC often only do so if you study for it at one of their preferred course providers and take the optional modules that are most relevant to their areas of practice. For example, if you intend to work in the City as a corporate lawyer, you will need to take commercial law options. BPP University has strong ties to the leading firms in the City and is the exclusive course provider for trainees from over 50 leading law firms. The University of Law is the preferred training provider for over 30 more law firms. You need to make sure that you take the LPC at the institution preferred by the law firm at which you would like to work.

The LPC is very different from the academic stage of training: it is based on legal practice rather than theory, and you will spend a lot more time in small groups with other students. The skills content of the course means you will experience much more 'learning by doing'.

As with the GDL, applications for a full-time LPC course must be made via the Central Applications Board (www.lawcabs.ac.uk). Again, the CAB does not have application deadlines for the LPC, but you should check with the institutions individually to see whether they have their own application deadlines. Applications for part-time courses are made direct to the institution(s) of your choice.

Exempting degree

The idea behind the exempting degree is to combine the academic and vocational stages of training. At the time of writing, only seven exempting law degrees are on offer. The universities that offer these are:

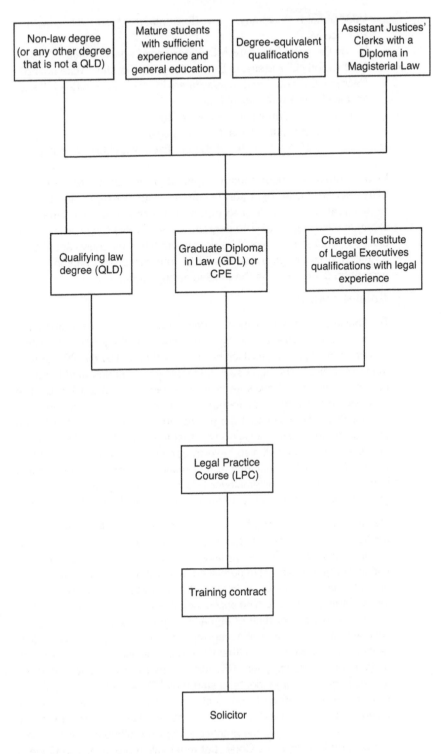

Figure 2: Qualification route for solicitors pre-2021 or via the transitional route

- Huddersfield University, Law (Exempting) Master of Law and Practice MLP
- Leeds Beckett University, MLaw: Law and Legal Practice
- Northumbria University, LLB Law Hons with Master's (Exempting)
- Pearson College London (validated by the University of Kent), M. Law Legal Professional Practice
- University of Central Lancashire, M. Law
- University of South Wales, M. Law, Legal Practice
- University of Westminster, Solicitors Exempting LLB Honours.

More information about exempting law degrees can be found on the SRA website (www.sra.org.uk/become-solicitor/legal-practice-course-route/qualifying-law-degree-common-professional-examination/exempting-law-degrees). The degrees are four years long and, on completion of your studies, you'll be deemed to have the equivalent of both a qualifying law degree and the LPC. The obvious attraction of the exempting degree can be the funding arrangements.

Training contract

The final stage of the traditional route to qualification as a solicitor is the training contract. This is (usually) two years of on-the-job training with a firm or other organisation which has been authorised by the SRA to take trainee solicitors. The purpose is to enable you to understand the practical implications of the law as well as developing your legal skills. The SRA requires you to gain experience in at least three distinct areas of law during your training contract and to further develop your legal skills while doing so. You should spend at least three months working in each of these areas. You will also have to complete the Professional Skills Course (PSC), which includes further training and some assessment in legal skills. Your firm or employer is expected to support you through this process and must pay your fees and reasonable travel expenses.

Depending on the sort of firm you want to go to for your training contract, you may need to apply up to three years in advance of your possible start date. This is certainly the case with the large City and national corporate and commercial firms, which will be recruiting as you are entering either the penultimate or the final year of your degree studies or starting your GDL. The application deadlines vary from firm to firm – some recruit earlier than others and some only have relatively short windows in which they will accept applications in any one year. Most recommend applying early. Other firms and organisations will recruit you as you are completing your LPC, with a view to an immediate start, so it is also common for students to start their LPC without knowing if they have a training contract to go to at the end of the course. There is a voluntary Code of Good Conduct for the recruitment of trainee solicitors, which represents good practice in legal recruitment. Law firms are not obliged to follow this Code, but most will in practice. The Code is available on the Law Society's website and specifies, among other things, that the opening date for training contract applications must not be earlier than the penultimate year of your undergraduate study. You cannot accept or decline any offers before 15 September in your final undergraduate year.

You can complete your training contract on a part-time basis and also combine your training contract with attendance on a part-time LPC. If you have considerable previous work experience in a legal environment, then you may be eligible for a reduction in the length of your training contract of up to six months, but this will depend on whether your employer supports your request. Any application has to be made to the SRA.

Competition for training contracts is fierce. Following the advice in this book should put you in the best possible position to obtain a training contract. You should also consider your A level choices carefully and obtain the best grades you can, as well as considering your choice of university carefully – there is some evidence that the top firms still look to what they perceive as the 'good' universities for their trainees. Finally, enrol on some vacation schemes and try hard to obtain some relevant work experience (see Chapter 5 for more details).

Students enrolling on the LPC (2015/2016)	5,952
New training contracts started (2015/2016)	5,728

Table 3: Competition for solicitors' training contracts

Funding your qualification

Qualifying as a solicitor can be an expensive business, and there is no funding available for preparation courses at the time of writing. The Law Society is currently lobbying for a source of funding for those in financial need.

For those undertaking postgraduate study or who are qualifying through the LPC route, some potential sources of funding are outlined below

Sponsorship

Most of the larger firms will sponsor you through the LPC, and possibly the GDL, if you have secured your training contract before commencing the course. The sponsorship will cover the cost of the GDL/LPC course fees and usually a contribution towards your living expenses as well. You'll need to check whether the firms that interest you would offer sponsorship of this kind. Firms providing sponsorship deals often do so on the proviso that you take your LPC at their preferred university or college. This is so that they can make sure that you study the subjects that they will need you to know about once you start working for them.

While there is now a postgraduate loan available of £10,906 to those who do not hold any postgraduate qualifications, these are typically not available for the GDL or LPC (the GDL is a diploma and the LPC is a certificate). However, some LPCs now include a master's qualification, which qualifies them for the loan.

There are some private student loan providers, such as Future Finance loans, and graduate bank loans that can also be explored.

Law Society Diversity Access Scheme

The Law Society has a Diversity Access Scheme (DAS), which is aimed at students from disadvantaged backgrounds or those who face exceptional obstacles to qualification. Applicants must meet several of the listed criteria, which include aspects such as:

- no access to familial loans or financial gifts
- no access to more than £5,000 in savings accounts, current accounts or ISAs
- attended a non-fee paying school
- part of the first generation of the family to have attended higher education
- recipient of free school meals during compulsory-aged education
- exceptional circumstances relating to gender, ethnicity, sexual orientation, health, disability, educational or other personal obstacles.

Its purpose is to increase social diversity in the legal profession. The DAS offers payment of LPC course fees, plus the provision of work experience and a professional mentor.

The scheme is, however, extremely limited: in 2021, the Law Society received 277 applications, shortlisted 34 applications, and offered 15 DAS awards. The scheme also guarantees a training contract at a national law centre. Applications are typically accepted between February and April each year, and students are required to reflect on their financial situation, their desire to become a solicitor, the contributions they could make, current affairs and their work experience to date. Competition for awards is keen and applicants must have a confirmed place on the LPC.

More details are available on the Law Society's website (www.law society.org.uk/law-careers/diversity-access-scheme).

Career development loans

Once you get to the LPC stage of training, you may be eligible for a career development loan up to the value of £10,000. These are deferred repayment loans offered by certain banks to fund vocational training courses. The government pays the interest on the loan while you are studying and you repay the loan once you start working. For more information see www.gov.uk/career-development-loans.

Access funds and scholarships

These are available at some universities offering the LPC. Access funds may be available at publicly funded colleges and are discretionary awards aimed at assisting with your living costs if you are experiencing financial hardship. Scholarships may be awarded by any of the universities or colleges offering the LPC to students with particularly good academic backgrounds. Details are available direct from your institution of study.

Payment by instalments

Some institutions where you can take the LPC course offer the option to pay by instalments. You should check the institutions' individual websites for details.

Charities and grant-making trusts

Some grant-making trusts and charities may offer financial assistance to those seeking to qualify as a lawyer. You should search online to see whether you meet their criteria for an award, as these can be very specific.

Study part-time

More and more students are completing their professional training part-time, mostly due to the lack of financial support. This will enable you to work part-time to help support yourself. You should, however, make sure that you allow yourself enough time to study so that you pass the course.

Funding: conclusion

When you are looking for sources of funding, remember:

- do your research
- plan ahead
- read the criteria for any grant/award you are applying for very carefully and make sure you can demonstrate that you meet them
- don't be put off – you're hoping to train to be a solicitor so try to come up with a good case for yourself
- be realistic.

Case study

Henry grew up in the care system, and attending university was always something that seemed out of reach. After graduating from university, the DAS award allowed him to embark on the path to becoming a solicitor.

'Throughout my childhood, I was constantly moving schools as I moved between foster families. This made education challenging

---

for me, and it wasn't something I enjoyed. However, I was fortunate that through my final years of secondary school and sixth form, I was able to stay with a supportive family. It was at this time that I realised how much I loved learning, and I got my head down and performed very well in my GCSEs and A levels. I was unsure of what to do after my A levels as studying at university was a daunting prospect. My foster care was coming to an end and heading to university rather than working full time felt like a huge gamble. Thankfully, my school was very supportive in helping me apply for all available funding and scholarships, which made university possible. I wasn't sure what I wanted to pursue as a career, but as I'd enjoyed studying Chemistry at A level, I decided to run with that.

'After graduating, I started working in medical sales but quickly realised that it wasn't for me. I considered chemistry-specific options but none of them felt right. Around my work, I also carried out a lot of voluntary work, providing support for homeless people in my area and for refugees. I ultimately took a role with a refugee charity that involved giving practical support with finding work and accommodation, as well as completing legal paperwork for their citizenship. It was through this role that I met a number of lawyers working in immigration and public law and realised that this was what I wanted to do with my life.

'I researched law conversion courses and identified universities that offered scholarships for which I qualified. I was successful in gaining a place at the University of Exeter on their Graduate LLB course, which I was able to afford by securing a number of scholarships and bursaries and accessing available loans. The course was very intense and intellectually demanding, but the academic challenge and the end goal was very motivating. I was also working to pay my way and put some money aside for the inevitable enormous costs of the LPC, and balancing both was hard and meant I didn't have much time to undertake meaningful work experience, which I feared may be detrimental to any future applications.

'I came across the DAS award without really having much hope, although I knew it was realistically my only chance of a seamless transition into the LPC. It was incredibly competitive, but I threw everything into the application and was successful. It is an exceptional scheme that provides financial support for the LPC as well as excellent work experience opportunities. You get access to networking events and a professional mentor, both of which were transformational as I wasn't well connected at the outset.

'I was able to secure a training contract, which meant I could study for the LPC part time and work full time. Despite having financial support for the LPC, this option felt the most secure, although it is very tough. If you're in the fortunate position to be able to study for the LPC full time, it may be a smoother ride. Getting the award felt like some of the hardships I had faced had been acknowledged, and I felt proud to have achieved everything I had despite the bad start I had in life. I'm very grateful that I am working towards a career where I can help others in vulnerable situations.'

Solicitors: Scotland

The legal system in Scotland differs from that of England and Wales and Northern Ireland, and so does the qualification route. This section aims to summarise the process of qualifying as a solicitor in Scotland.

Briefly, the route to qualification involves studying for a four-year law degree at a Scottish university and then proceeding to the vocational training stage. There is no equivalent of the GDL in Scotland, so it is slightly more difficult to become a lawyer if your degree is in a subject other than law, as this necessitates taking a two-year accelerated law degree after your first degree. Further details on qualifying in Scotland are available on the Law Society of Scotland's website (www.lawscot. org.uk/members/business-support/recruitment-guidance/overview-of-the-route-to-qualification).

Academic stage

Law degree

It is possible to study a Bachelor of Law degree (LLB) at the following Scottish universities:

- University of Aberdeen
- University of Abertay
- University of Dundee
- University of Edinburgh
- Edinburgh Napier University
- Glasgow Caledonian University
- University of Glasgow
- Robert Gordon University
- University of Stirling
- University of Strathclyde.

More detailed information about the content of the courses can be obtained from the universities' websites.

A law degree from an English university will not be accepted as a QLD in Scotland, and vice versa. However, if you have qualified in England, Wales, Northern Ireland or the European Union, there are transfer tests available in order to requalify in Scotland.

In November 2019, the Law Society of Scotland introduced the Qualified Lawyers Assessment (QLA), which is a universal set of exams that allows solicitors who qualified outside of Scotland to work there. Depending on prior training, there may be some exemptions from the 11 subjects that must be assessed through the exams. Potential candidates must first apply for the QLA to determine whether they are eligible. Further information about the exams can be found on www.lawscot.org.uk.

The non-graduate route

Alternatively, there is a non-degree route where someone who has been working as a full-time pre-Diploma trainee with a qualified solicitor in Scotland for three years can take the Law Society of Scotland's examinations and then proceed to the vocational stage of training in the same way as a law graduate. This route is known as the Pre-PEAT Training Contract and LSS exams, and, according to the Law Society of Scotland, is followed by between 10 and 20 people each year. For more information please see www.lawscot.org.uk/members/business-support/recruitment-guidance/overview-of-the-route-to-qualification.

Vocational stage

Diploma

After completion of the LLB degree all aspiring Scottish solicitors are required to take the Diploma in Professional Legal Practice (DPLP) which is also known as the Professional Education and Training Stage 1 (PEAT 1). It is usually taught full-time over one academic year, though some two-year part-time courses are also available. These can be studied at:

- University of Aberdeen
- University of Dundee
- University of Edinburgh
- University of Glasgow
- Robert Gordon University
- University of Strathclyde.

The DPLP is the equivalent of the LPC in England and Wales, in that the course has been designed to teach the practical knowledge and skills necessary for the working life of a solicitor. The focus is highly practical and skills-based. To obtain a place on the diploma course, applicants would need to have passed all of the Law Society of Scotland's 'professional subjects' in their LLB (or Law Society examinations). Applications are made through UCAS between February and April each year.

At each institution, the content will be similar but the compulsory and elective modules on offer may vary, so research ahead of the application is advised to ensure that the most appropriate courses are selected. The Law Society of Scotland runs a Virtual Diploma Fair each year in January or February to allow providers to be compared.

Training contract

After successful completion of the degree (or non-graduate route) and diploma, you need to serve a two-year post-diploma training contract (Professional Education and Training Stage 2, or PEAT 2) with a practising solicitor in Scotland. This can be served with solicitors in private practice, the Crown Office, or local authorities and certain public bodies. The training contract is very similar to that in England and Wales, giving trainees the chance to put into practice what they have learnt at university. At the end of the two years, if the training contract has been successful then the trainee is qualified and can apply for a full practising certificate. As in England and Wales, competition for training contracts is intense and there are now fewer trainee roles available for a similar number of students passing the DPLP. A good academic profile is therefore important and the benefits of having obtained some work experience, particularly in the legal sector, cannot be over-estimated.

Case study

Stewart works as a solicitor in Scotland at an accident and injury claims firm. His route into law was long-winded and undoubtedly tough, but his perseverance paid off!

'I grew up in quite a rough part of Edinburgh, the kind of area where aspirations are thin on the ground and very few prosper due to lack of hope, money and opportunity. In short, I left school with no qualifications. I was told by my teachers at a very early age that I would not amount to much in life and I believed them. I eventually left school with nothing to show for my time there and a paper round that yielded £7 per week. I later took up a part-time job in a local music store but despite my best efforts, no full-time roles became available for me. I had a friend who worked in a solicitors' firm as an Office Junior and one day, he mentioned that there was a position available. I applied but was once again met with rejection, until I eventually received my stroke of luck – the person who had taken the position initially left after just a few weeks, so the job was mine!

'The solicitors' firm was a small trade union firm where I worked as an Office Junior in the Filing Department. I loved it – one of the perks of working for a small firm is that it feels as though you are working with a big family! From filing I moved onto data processing, before eventually being promoted to the role of Executive in Information Technology, which was a position I maintained for a number of years. To earn some extra money, I took on a part-time job as a barman. It was while working in the bar after a day at the office that I had a bit of an epiphany – I was working with the next generation of lawyers who were not much smarter than me. I decided to go for broke and see whether I could qualify as a lawyer myself.

'I contacted the Law Society to find out what was required and it was contingent on a lot of things coming together: primarily, consent from my employers, attending night school to get higher academic grades, then passing nine exams before applying to do the diploma. I then approached one of the partners to gauge his views and, like many other times in my life, he told me he didn't think I was up to it. I was deflated somewhat but not deterred, and instead approached the most senior partner in the firm. To my surprise, he completely supported my decision and told me to return after I'd completed my exams so that I could talk to the partners. He was true to his word, and the company then supported me through the Law Society exams while allowing me to work as a pre-diploma trainee.

'This was a tough undertaking and I had to give up a lot – football, seeing my friends and family – as it meant long working hours, seven days a week, for four years. I was handed a syllabus but, other than that, no direction at all – there were no lectures or tutors, just huge piles of books! One of the stipulations from the Law Society was that all exams had to be passed within four sittings. By the end of the fifth year of studying, I had passed every exam other than the nemesis of taxation, in which I was about to undertake my fourth attempt at the exam. Having done so, I received a call to say I had failed. I was heartbroken and the Law Society bluntly told me I was out of options. I contacted directly each of the universities offering the diploma, but despite my pleas, they all closed the door. A glimmer of hope came from Alan Barr at the University of Edinburgh, who suggested I sit the taxation exam at undergraduate level the following term and, if I passed, he would allow me to study the diploma. I took him up on his offer and really couldn't believe how easy the exam was – the lecturers were incredibly helpful and I passed the exam, allowing me to ultimately qualify as a solicitor.'

Solicitors: Northern Ireland

The system for qualifying as a solicitor in Northern Ireland is different again from those in England, Wales and Scotland. Below is a brief summary, but further details can be obtained from the Law Society of Northern Ireland's website (www.lawsoc-ni.org/becoming-a-solicitor).

Academic stage

The usual route to qualification as a solicitor in Northern Ireland begins with a law degree. This must be considered by the Law Society of Northern Ireland to be a 'recognised law degree', and must contain eight core subjects. These are:

- law of evidence
- land law
- European law
- equity
- constitutional law
- law of tort
- law of contract
- criminal law.

Further details of what constitutes a recognised law degree, and a list of recognised law degrees and the universities offering them, are available on the website of the Institute of Professional Legal Studies, part of Queen's University Belfast (the 'Institute'). This list of recognised law degrees contains many from English and Welsh universities, as well as some in the Republic of Ireland, so this part of the route to qualification does not have to be taken in Northern Ireland. Degrees in Scottish law are not, however, recognised.

Students with non-law degrees can also qualify as a solicitor by first taking the master's in Law at Queen's University Belfast. This is an accelerated, fast-track programme that lasts two years when studied full time.

There is also an alternative, non-degree route available. Typically, these individuals must have qualifications that render them suitable for consideration (i.e. the same as those required for a place at Queen's University Belfast), and would usually be over 30 years of age. Please visit the website of the Law Society of Northern Ireland (www.lawsoc-ni.org/becoming-a-solicitor) for further details.

Vocational stage and apprenticeship

The vocational training to become a solicitor in Northern Ireland (the Postgraduate Diploma in Legal Practice) is undertaken at the Institute. All applicants applying for the diploma must sit an entrance exam in the

December before they wish to commence the course (known colloqui-ally as the 'Institute exam'). Applications must be submitted to the Institute by 15 November in the relevant year. The main difference from the system in England and Wales is that applicants must have already found a master (a solicitor with whom the applicant proposes to serve his/her on-the-job training, known as the apprenticeship) by the time they apply for the vocational course. The vocational course is then com-bined with the apprenticeship. Finding a master can be a difficult and competitive process.

The apprenticeship is similar to a training contract in England and Wales, in that it will last for two years for trainees who completed the traditional qualification route. However, in order to combine it with the vocational training, each year is structured as follows.

- September to December: spent in-office.
- January to December: spent at the Institute of Professional Legal Studies (but returning to master's office during vacations).
- January to August: spent in-office.

Once a trainee has passed all the relevant examinations and completed their apprenticeship, they can apply to be enrolled as a solicitor of the Court of Judicature in Northern Ireland and apply for a Practising Certificate. A restricted practising certificate is issued for the first two or three years, meaning that newly qualified solicitors can only practise as employees within a firm of solicitors and cannot set up their own practice.

For more information on qualifying as a solicitor in Northern Ireland, please see www.lawsoc-ni.org/becoming-a-solicitor.

Case study

Andrew is a solicitor at the Law Society of Northern Ireland. He followed a relatively straightforward route into law and has amassed a range of experience in different areas of law.

'At the age of 17, I took on a month-long placement at my family's solicitors' firm in my home town of Coleraine. It was a typical small country practice with three solicitors dealing with all different types of work. I experienced a variety of cases including criminal, con-veyancing, personal injury, Children Order, family and administration of estates. It also gave me the opportunity to sit in on police inter-views, court hearings and meet the local judge in chambers. This was my first real introduction into the field of law.

'Shortly afterwards, I commenced my A level studies in economics, maths and politics, securing grades ABB. This was sufficient to get me into Queen's University Belfast, to study law. I decided upon a law degree because I thought it was a good general degree to have. I did not have any burning desire to do anything in particular so was essentially trying to cover my bases! I knew I would pick up a wealth of transferable skills that would be beneficial regardless of what I decided to do after graduating.

'The degree was very much the traditional three-year law degree that covered each of the core areas. While I was academically capable, I found the course quite dry and still hadn't really pinned down what I wanted to do with my life. At the end of my degree, I worked for a summer in an accountants' firm while also putting in my application to the Institute of Professional Legal Studies (IPLS) in Belfast. The IPLS works on the basis that you must obtain a master's degree, so I got a place in a solicitors' firm in Belfast. The term commenced with a full-time placement in the office followed by lessons at the IPLS. The course itself was a mixture of lectures and small group study sessions. It also incorporated practical exercises, such as mock bail applications and client interviews. This course offered a much more practical introduction to the day-to-day work of a solicitor than the undergraduate degree course.

'I worked in corporate and commercial law for nine months after qualifying. I did not particularly enjoy this type of work so I moved to another firm to do property and private client work. This work was much more to my liking and I stayed there for several years until I joined the Law Society. During my time at the property firm, I became a member of the Society of Trust and Estate Practitioners.

'My experience in private practice was challenging, particularly on the property side. With the property crash from July 2007, there were a number of rounds of redundancies which I thankfully managed to avoid, mostly due to being the only solicitor in the firm who did private client work. I acted for a large number of property developers, some of whom went bust during those years so there was very little work around. My private client work basically supported my property work during this time. The commercial realities of life in private practice were reinforced at this time. Billing, outstanding costs and cashflow became even more vital than previously.

'I moved to the Law Society to deal with all non-contentious work. I am secretary to the Conveyancing & Property Committee, Non-Contentious Business Committee and the Human Rights & Equality Committee, among other duties. The work is challenging but interesting. In particular, I am currently dealing with the review of the Home Charter Scheme (the Northern Irish equivalent of the QCS which has been in place since 1994); this means servicing four additional sub-committees and dealing with all the technical drafting that is produced. The most difficult but most interesting part of this is the review of the General Conditions of Sale (the NI standard property contract). I also give seminars to our members on a variety of subjects. I will have done 15 seminars this year around the province. The job is not like any other, but I find it interesting and it has certainly given me a much wider understanding of the issues facing the legal system in Northern Ireland, including regulatory issues and statutory issues.'

Barristers: England and Wales

Academic stage

The academic stage of training required to become a barrister is the same as that to become a solicitor. It is only once a student reaches the vocational stage of training that the qualification routes for solicitors and barristers diverge. A good academic background is even more important for aspiring barristers than it is for solicitors: it will be very difficult to obtain a pupillage unless you achieve at least an Upper Second class degree.

Vocational stage

New pathways to qualifying

To become a barrister entitled to practise, the Bar Council requires you to have completed a stage of academic training, followed by vocational training and then the completion of a pupillage. Historically, the vocational stage of training involved completing the Bar Professional Training Course (BPTC), which is still an option, but the Bar Standards Board have recently outlined alternative pathways to qualifying. These include:

- **Three-step pathway.** This involves an academic component, followed by a vocational component and, finally, a pupillage or work-based component.
- **Four-step pathway.** This involves an academic component, followed by a vocational component in two parts, and then a pupillage or work-based component.
- **Integrated academic and vocational pathway.** This combines academic and vocational components, which are then followed by a pupillage or work-based component.
- **Apprenticeship pathway.** This combines academic, vocational and pupillage components.

The BPTC option is the most long-standing and, therefore, well-established three-step pathway, which many aspiring barristers will continue to pursue. However, it is important to note that alternative options are

becoming available and these are likely to become more widely accessible in the coming years.

The Authorised Education and Training Organisations (AETOs) and the
Bar training that they have been authorised by the Bar Standards Board
to deliver from September 2020 are summarised in the table below. At
the time of writing, there are no established providers of the apprenticeship pathway, but AETOs have been invited to submit proposals. As such,
apprenticeships for barristers may be an option in the coming years.

Bar training provider	Components delivered
BPP University	Vocational component of the three-step pathway Vocational component of the four-step pathway (delivered in two parts) Academic and vocational components of the integrated pathway
Cardiff University	Vocational component of the three-step pathway
Manchester Metropolitan University	Vocational component of the three-step pathway
Northumbria University	Vocational component of the three-step pathway Vocational component of the four-step pathway (delivered in two parts) Vocational and academic components of the integrated pathway
Nottingham Trent University	Vocational component of the three-step pathway
City Law School, City, University of London	Vocational component of the three-step pathway Vocational component of the four-step pathway (delivered in two parts)
Inns of Court College of Advocacy	Vocational component of the four-step pathway (delivered in two parts)
University of Law	Vocational component of the three-step pathway
University of the West of England	Vocational component of the three-step pathway Vocational component of the four-step pathway (delivered in two parts)

Table 4: Bar training provided by AETOs

Bar Professional Training Course

To become a barrister entitled to practise, the Bar Council requires you
to take the one-year (full-time) or two-year (part-time) Bar Professional
Training Course (BPTC), previously known as the Bar Vocational
Course (BVC). A partial distance learning course is also available.
Before registering on the BPTC you will need to be admitted to one of
the four Inns of Court: Gray's Inn, Inner Temple, Lincoln's Inn, or Middle
Temple (all based in central London). These Inns provide support for
barristers and student members, advocacy training and other continuing
professional development opportunities, lunching and dining facilities

and access to common rooms and gardens. The Inns are also responsible for Calling barristers to the Bar, which is the mechanism by which students become barristers once they have completed the BPTC and pupillage (see below).

The BPTC aims to help you gain the knowledge of procedure and evidence and skills of advocacy, conference skills, drafting, legal research, negotiation and opinion writing to prepare you for the practical stage of training on the job, the one year of pupillage. The BPTC is available at eight different teaching institutions in 16 locations across the country:

- BPP University (Birmingham, Bristol, Leeds, London and Manchester)
- The University of Law (Birmingham, Leeds, London, Manchester and Nottingham)
- Cardiff Law School
- City Law School
- Manchester Metropolitan University
- Nottingham Law School, Nottingham Trent University
- University of the West of England, Bristol
- University of Northumbria, Newcastle.

The BPTC costs between £12,000 and £18,500 depending on the chosen institution. Applications must be made directly to the institutions.

Bar Course Aptitude Test (BCAT)

The Bar Standards Board introduced the Bar Course Aptitude Test (BCAT) which applicants for the BPTC have to pass before their offer of a place on the BPTC can be confirmed. The purpose of the BCAT is to test applicants' critical thinking and reasoning, which are considered to be the core skills required for the BPTC. The idea is to make sure that students starting the BPTC have the necessary skills to pass it.

The test comprises 60 multiple-choice questions that must be completed in 55 minutes. The test is computerised and must be sat at a Pearson VUE centre. The fee for taking the test is £150 if it is taken in UK and EU test centres and £170 for non-EU test centres.

BCAT registration tends to open in February, with the deadline for booking and completing the exam in September, but early sittings are advised as retake examinations are permitted if the scores required are not obtained. The BCAT must be passed prior to commencing the BPTC in September. Once passed, the BCAT is valid for five years.

For more information on the BCAT, including a practice test so that you can familiarise yourself with the type of questions asked, visit www.talentlens.com/uk/about/the-bar-course-aptitude-test-bcat.html.

Pupillage

Pupillage is the final stage to qualifying as a barrister and is hard work. The first six months of pupillage (known as the 'first six') are non-practising and involve training with a senior barrister (your 'pupil supervisor') at work for six months. During the first six months you will be expected to undertake legal research, draft opinions, and read your pupil supervisor's paperwork.

Once you have completed the first six months, you will spend the second six months (the 'second six') practising and be able to appear in court as an advocate. This is when you start to build your own reputation and have your own cases. Pupils must be paid a minimum salary of £16,601 per annum (or £18,960 in London), plus reasonable travel expenses where applicable.

Those of you eager to become a barrister are in for a tough time. Competition for places is very high. The Bar Standards Board website even includes a health warning about the intense competition for pupillages. In 2019/20, it reported that 1,685 students enrolled on the bar course, whereas the number of pupillages for 2020/21 was only 435. To make things even tougher, students are allowed to try to find a pupillage for up to five years after completing the bar course, so in any one year, there could be over 3,000 people applying for pupillages. Some barristers' chambers report having over a hundred applicants for each pupillage placement. Even if you are successful in obtaining a pupillage, there is no guarantee of work after completing it – in every year, there are usually fewer tenancies available at chambers than there are students completing their pupillages, and the opportunities for employed barristers are few and far between. The Bar Standards Board recommends undertaking thorough research to find out if a career at the Bar is really for you, and this includes making a realistic assessment of whether you have the capacity to become a good barrister.

Student enrolments on BPTC in 2019/2020	1,685
Pupillages available in 2020/2021	435

Table 5: Competition for barristers' pupillages

Applications for pupillage are made through an online pupillage application system, called 'Pupillage Gateway', which is operated by the Bar Council. The system allows applicants to search and apply for pupillage vacancies. All pupillage providers must advertise all pupillage vacancies on the Gateway. There is a common timetable for the application process, which is typically as follows:

- November: Gateway pupillages are listed for browsing and a practice application form becomes available
- January: submission window opens

- February: submission window closes
- February to April: interview period
- May: offers made.

No charge is made to applicants. For more information and specific dates for the application process for a particular year, visit www.pupillage gateway.com.

Before applying, you should find out as much as possible about your preferred set of chambers. You should study the chambers' website carefully and look at online bar directories. You should also try to attend a pupillage fair. These are held every so often to enable students who wish to pursue a career at the Bar to meet different sets of chambers.

Case study

Rob is a well-established barrister with over 20 years' experience in a wide range of areas, encompassing international, immigration, public and serious fraud law. His expertise in human rights has gained him several visiting lectureships.

'A huge part of being a barrister is just being approachable, being able to think hard and consistently, and having a very strong work ethic. All of those elements are required for success as a barrister. It's a challenging role, and there are times when your work-life balance suffers as a consequence of the workload. It's certainly never boring! You have to work hard to keep up to date with the law, which is my favourite aspect of being a barrister – the constant challenge and learning – though at times it can be exhausting!

'When I embarked on my pupillage, I rotated through various areas on mini pupillages to narrow down the areas that I was interested in pursuing. I now focus on extradition, immigration and international crime. This means I have to stay up to date on other countries' legal systems to do the best work for my clients. Recently, Brexit has caused significant ripples in the legal system, and it has been very interesting working in immigration in this context.

'Before pursuing law, I studied economics with history at university, and qualified as a barrister following the completion of the law conversion course (PGDL), then the Bar vocational course. After completing the academic qualifications, I worked as a paralegal for a year to gain experience in a legal setting before starting work as a barrister the following year. Getting a pupillage was difficult, even back then, which is why the year of work was invaluable, but in today's climate, it is even more so. My advice to aspiring lawyers would be to take every opportunity of experience that presents itself, as it might just be that extra something that sets you apart from everyone else.

'As well as working as a barrister, I also deliver lectures on human rights in a UK university, and I try to incorporate as many of my own cases as possible to illustrate these. Of course, it adds to the workload, but lecturing is also a very nice privilege for those deemed experts in a field.'

Funding your qualification

The average cost of completing the vocational stage of training is estimated at over £20,000 if living expenses are taken into account. The fees for the BPTC for 2020/2021 were between £10,500 and £17,450 for the year. Only a limited number of awards, grants and scholarships are available for the vocational stage of Bar training. The Inns of Court offer a range of scholarships and some chambers give awards towards the BPTC. However, the majority of students have to depend on bank loans or other forms of support. Please refer to the individual chambers' websites or the Bar Council website for further details.

Advocates: Scotland

The academic and vocational stages are the same as qualifying as a solicitor in Scotland (see the section on qualifying as a solicitor in Scotland on page 65). The intending advocate in Scotland needs to take a law degree followed by the postgraduate Diploma in Professional Legal Practice plus a minimum of 21 months' training in a Scottish solicitor's office.

This is followed by nine months' further unpaid practical training called 'devilling', or work-shadowing. Initially, this involves a Foundation course where the pupils' oral and written advocacy skills are developed through intensive workshops and seminars. There are further compulsory skills courses that must be completed. Pupils will also work for an experienced advocate who has been practising for more than seven years (a 'devilmaster'), to gain experience of civil practice and the criminal courts. Passing the Diploma in Professional Legal Practice culminates in the completion of the Faculty of Advocates' written examinations. The Faculty does not charge for the training and scholarships are available to support with living costs.

Please visit the Faculty of Advocates website for more information: www.advocates.org.uk/about-advocates/becoming-an-advocate.

Barristers: Northern Ireland

Details on how to qualify as a barrister in Northern Ireland are available on the website of the Bar of Northern Ireland (www.barofni.com/page/becoming-a-barrister). The academic stage is the same as for qualifying as a solicitor; students must have completed a recognised law degree (see page 69). For the vocational stage of training, students must complete the one year full-time Bar Postgraduate Diploma in Professional Legal Studies at the Institute of Professional Legal Studies, Queen's University Belfast (the IPLS). After graduating from the Institute when they have passed the Bar course, students are called to the Bar of Northern Ireland. Bar trainees must then undertake a pupillage with a master for a period of 12 months.

Case study

Niall works as a self-employed barrister in Northern Ireland, and is a visiting lecturer at several universities.

'I had visions of working in accounting and finance as a youngster, and for this reason I studied finance at Queen's University Belfast for my undergraduate degree. After graduating, I started to work in an accounting firm, but was more drawn to the legal proceedings. After talking to the legal team there and shadowing some of their work, I decided to study a law conversion course with BPP Law School and immediately followed this up with the Postgraduate Diploma in Professional Legal Studies (Bar).

'The academic training component for law was very rigorous, with lots of reading and cases to work through. For the most part, I found the work very interesting, but there were also some incredibly dull elements. When studying law, don't be put off if you find some areas dull – you will naturally find yourself more drawn to some areas and you can pursue those. I especially enjoyed constitutional and public law, which are the areas I focus on in my work now, both as a lawyer and a lecturer. After being called to the Bar, I undertook a 12-month pupillage. This was a steep learning curve, but I enjoyed being able to put everything into practice and seeing it in action. Taking my own cases was daunting at first, but thorough preparation is key to settling the nerves.'

5 | Getting work experience

Getting work experience is crucial in terms of helping you secure a training contract or pupillage in today's extremely competitive climate. It is not enough to be purely a brilliant academic. The more relevant experience you have, the better the chance of succeeding.

You can apply for work experience at any stage in the qualification process, whether it be during A levels, during a law (or other) degree, or even at a later stage if you are having trouble obtaining a training contract or pupillage. There are many types of vacation schemes run by the larger firms of solicitors, and chambers also offer mini pupillages; these are invaluable ways of gaining experience and getting a foot in the door. You will be much more attractive to potential employers if you can show that you have relevant work experience. Most of these work experience schemes are only available to undergraduates.

However, having some work experience is also very useful in applying to university for a law degree. You are less likely to be able to find a place on a formal work experience programme while you are still at school, but you should still look for some sort of experience just to get you into a legal environment and see what lawyers actually do. This will support your application for a law degree and help you write the personal statement on your UCAS form. Most importantly, though, it will allow you to see whether a career in law is really for you.

What can you gain from work experience?

When considering a career in any field, work experience is an excellent way of gaining an invaluable insight into the profession. Work placements within a legal setting will enable you to see whether a career in law is for you. You should endeavour to organise placements in the specific field of law in which you are interested. If you are unsure, try and obtain experience in various settings to enhance your knowledge of the different areas within the legal field. Work experience would be beneficial for a number of reasons, including the following.

- It will give you a real insight into the profession. You will be able to observe the day-to-day duties of legal professionals and identify the skills that their roles command. It will also give you an excellent opportunity to weigh up the pros and cons of becoming a lawyer. This can be further explored by discussing the profession with the individuals that you are working with, as they will be able to give you honest answers to your questions. Finally, you will be able to see whether being a barrister or a solicitor is for you, and if it is the latter, the type of law firm in which you would prefer to work.

- By observing legal professionals in practice and reflecting on their duties, you will be much more informed when discussing your interests and aptitude in your personal statement when applying for a law degree at university, and in your applications for legal jobs. Undertaking these placements will demonstrate your commitment to a career in law, and prove that you have given it some real thought.
- Working with legal professionals will allow you to build those all-important contacts that will be beneficial in an extremely competitive environment. Providing that you are able to demonstrate your enthusiasm and willingness to learn, you should be able to secure some strong references, as well as the possibility of acquiring further placements at a later stage.
- By developing your knowledge of what a particular role entails and getting a feel for the pace and demands of the job, work experience will help you to make the transition into full-time work once you have completed the academic component of qualification.

However, it is not that easy getting legal work experience, and can in itself be a competitive process. Most universities and employers recognise this and do not stipulate that work experience is essential, although it is preferred and you should put some considerable effort into obtaining some. This will allow you to reflect on the skill set commanded and demonstrate that you are conscious of the skills that need to be developed. If you cannot get experience in a firm of solicitors or chambers, any work experience that demonstrates use of the skills they are interested in will be valuable. Skills such as communication, determination and business awareness can all be developed in many other sectors of business and commerce. Even just showing that you can get up every day and present yourself for work at 9 o'clock in the morning is of some use.

There are also other ways of gaining relevant legal experience while you are at school or university, for example, participating in a debating society or in mooting or mock trials will help hone your advocacy skills. Some university students hoping to enter the legal profession volunteer at their university law centre or law clinic.

Generally, universities state that if you are able to undertake work experience, it will undoubtedly benefit your understanding of what the role entails and therefore support your application. However, being unable to do so will not put applicants at a disadvantage. In essence, any way in which you can demonstrate that you have made the effort to develop your understanding of what a career in law involves will be viewed as being beneficial. This could be demonstrated through wider reading, extra-curricular activities and visits to law courts, for example. Academic attainment is the main reason behind offers being made, though if an offer is narrowly missed, a strong overall application based on a competent knowledge of what the course and career entail could allow for some leniency on results day.

Similarly, employers understand that securing mini pupillages or placements on vacation schemes is tough owing to the extremely competitive climate. While it is inevitable that the knowledge and skills obtained on these placements will be invaluable in your development as a lawyer, the same skills can be developed elsewhere, such as mooting experience, voluntary work and alternative work experience placements. Mini pupillages and vacation schemes are designed to be enjoyable and useful, but they are not a prerequisite for securing a pupillage or a training contract.

If you look through the case studies contained in this book, it is noticeable that all the young lawyers did a variety of work experience while at school and university, and they all think it played an important part in landing them a job at the end of their studies.

Things to consider during work experience

Work experience placements provide you with excellent opportunities to cultivate knowledge of the field and an understanding of the career. As a result, it is crucial that you are aware of what is going on around you so that you can develop your insight.

Making a good impression

In general, you should aim to maintain a high level of professionalism throughout the duration of your placement. Remember, the legal professionals that you work with at this point could play a crucial role in the development of your career at a later stage. With this in mind, always try to adopt the following attitudes.

- **Maintain a formal appearance:** dress smartly and present yourself appropriately. If you are unsure of how to dress, it is always better to wear more formal attire.
- **Be polite:** offer to help with routine tasks where sensible and aim to show your interest by asking questions. In general, people will be quite flattered when you show an interest in their role and how they reached that point in their career, so don't be afraid to demonstrate your curiosity! If you show that you are friendly and reliable, there is a greater chance of you acquiring more opportunities.

- **Be organised:** make sure that you are on time and plan your commute accordingly. Punctuality makes a lasting impression! You should also make sure that you take anything with you that might be required, such as a pen, a notebook and any formal documentation that may have been requested, such as proof of identity. Similarly, make sure that you organise your time effectively so that you can complete set tasks, and note down the times of meetings or hearings that you have been invited to attend.
- **Be enthusiastic:** demonstrate your competence by completing all tasks that you are set, and don't shy away from responsibility. No one is expecting you to get everything right – work experience is a learning curve, so get stuck in! If you think you have something valuable to say, raise it. Regardless of whether your suggestion is taken up, it will give employers a chance to see that you are really interested.

Doing all of these things will get you on the right track for making the most of your work experience placement. It is also worth considering the following aspects.

The qualities possessed by lawyers

Depending on whether a lawyer is practising as a barrister or a solicitor, they will need to possess and consistently exhibit a range of skills that allow them to carry out their roles successfully. During your placement, it is important to keep a keen eye on the characteristics that the lawyer demonstrates when carrying out their everyday duties. Being able to reflect on these qualities will be an important part of your qualification process; in written applications it will show your knowledge about the skills required to excel in the field, and provide useful aspects to discuss at interview. It will also allow you to identify traits that you need to develop yourself.

Day-to-day tasks

A work experience placement will give you a really thorough insight into a typical day for a solicitor or a barrister. Though it can be argued that there is no 'typical day' and tasks can be quite varied, it should give you a strong indication of what is expected. From this, you should be able to determine whether a career as a solicitor or a barrister is for you.

Solicitors tend to work with clients more closely, typically as part of a larger team. As such, solicitors must hone their communication skills to effectively convey legal positions in layman's terms. This contrasts heavily with the independent work of a barrister, who must then present cases in court following instruction from a client or solicitor. Therefore, the daily tasks for each job could differ significantly, and work experience should allow you to see which elements appeal to you and which do not.

The roles of other legal professionals

Through your time in a legal practice, it is important to consider the roles of staff other than solicitors or barristers. For example, legal secretaries, paralegals and legal executives will all work alongside and for solicitors, and it is essential to acquire an understanding of how these individuals work together to form a functional team. Make sure that you take the time to speak to as many people in different roles as possible, showing an interest in the specific tasks that they undertake.

Working as a lawyer

There is no denying that qualifying as a lawyer is tough, with high demands and long hours. It is for this reason that it is so important that you ask questions about these aspects: find out which areas of the job lawyers find rewarding, and which areas they dislike.

Keeping a work experience diary

Your work experience will likely be fundamental when looking to develop your career. With this in mind, it is worth you making notes of any interesting observations so that you have a full record to review in preparation for university applications, job applications and interviews.

It is advisable to lay out a formal diary in which you list your daily activities, noting down any key observations regarding specific tasks that were undertaken by lawyers and the skills that they used to conduct them effectively. Keeping a notebook with you will also allow you to jot down any questions that you may have, as well as the answers given to those questions.

Where to apply for work experience

Law firms' vacation schemes for aspiring solicitors

The big corporate law firms offer a range of different vacation schemes, and if you are at all interested in this type of law, you should apply for some of these while studying law at undergraduate level. If you are interested in commercial law, but do not necessarily want to train at one of the biggest firms, it is still useful to have done one of these vacation schemes as it will impress any smaller commercial firm that you may apply to for a training contract by showing that you have done your research into working as a commercial solicitor. Even if you are not sure what type of law you are really interested in (or, indeed, whether you would like to become a solicitor or barrister) it is worth applying for some of these schemes as it may help you make up your mind.

There are different sorts of schemes depending on what stage of your education you are at and whether or not you are studying law at university. Many firms offer shorter 'taster' schemes for first year undergraduates, followed by slightly longer schemes (of two, three or four weeks) for students in their penultimate year of university. The same schemes may be open to those taking a non-law degree, or different schemes may be available. Most take place during the summer, but some are available during other university holiday periods. To research these vacation schemes, you need to look at the websites of all the big law firms. There are often strict application timetables that require you to apply up to a year in advance (so, for example, in the first term of the academic year for a placement the following summer).

Generally, vacation schemes pay a small amount of money to cover your expenses while you are there. Many of these big firms link their vacation schemes to their training contracts. You may not necessarily have to do a vacation scheme to be offered a training contract, but it will certainly help, and some firms use vacation schemes as a way of finding suitable candidates to offer training contracts to. Some firms recruit trainees almost exclusively from their vacation schemes. They will also give you a genuine insight into the culture of the different firms and help you decide where you would like to work. One junior solicitor commented that she only applied to firms that she had done a vacation scheme with as she knew much more about what they were like and whether she would enjoy working there.

Mini pupillages at chambers

Similarly, many barristers' chambers offer mini pupillages, which allow you to shadow a practising barrister for up to two weeks to find out what working as a barrister is really like. If you think that there is any possibility that you might like to become a barrister, then it is crucial to try hard to undertake a mini pupillage. You can search online for barristers' chambers that offer mini pupillages and there are also online search tools available, such as at www.lawcareers.net.

'Informal' placements

Work experience can also take place on less of a formal basis than a vacation scheme or mini pupillage through shadowing court officers or a barristers' clerk. Such work experience would be invaluable for a university application.

As vacation schemes are incredibly competitive and only offered by a small subset of practices, you can take a speculative approach to applying by contacting law firms directly. This could involve a phone call, email or face-to-face discussion initially, but is usually followed up by sending in a CV and covering letter for consideration. An excellent time to procure such placements would be during summer and Easter breaks. Both the Law Society and the Legal 500 list UK law firms with contact details and provide a useful source of information when making speculative applications.

In the same way, you can also approach sets of chambers that do not offer formal mini pupillage schemes. The Chambers and Partners directory provides the names and addresses of UK chambers.

Voluntary work

Some legal work can be undertaken on a voluntary basis and, for several reasons, conducting such work would prove to be invaluable in terms of developing the necessary skills to succeed in the field of law.

Perhaps the most useful voluntary work that can be undertaken to enhance your legal skills is voluntary work at a law clinic, which is accessible to undergraduate students. A variety of roles can be undertaken, and all of these will allow you to witness first-hand the range of queries that arise and the manner in which they are dealt.

The Citizens Advice Bureau and the Free Representation Unit also provide volunteer opportunities with a legal basis, giving you the opportunity to gain experience in dealing with several legal issues such as housing and welfare law. It will also allow you to develop your understanding of how to appropriately advise clients.

However, voluntary work does not necessarily have to have a legal basis for it to be useful. Volunteer work in any field presents a wide range of opportunities to engage with people from different backgrounds and age groups, and gain new or develop existing skills as well as confidence. Maintaining a long-term voluntary position demonstrates an individual's commitment to helping society and developing their skills in communication. It will also give you the chance to enhance your understanding of the wider world.

As most charitable organisations are enthusiastic about recruiting volunteers, securing a placement should not be too difficult. Examples of areas that could be considered include:

- **charity work:** typically involves working in a charity shop or supporting the fundraising efforts of a charitable organisation
- **care work:** provides the opportunity to develop your communication skills when working with vulnerable people
- **humanitarian work:** will improve your understanding of wider international issues, potentially presenting you with the opportunity to overcome obstacles in communication such as language barriers
- **educational work:** supporting students in schools or voluntary teaching roles, e.g. teaching English to refugees.

Information on voluntary positions can be found on a number of websites, including:

- Do-It (https://do-it.org)
- Volunteering Matters (https://volunteeringmatters.org.uk)
- NCVO (www.ncvo.org.uk/ncvo-volunteering/i-want-to-volunteer)
- Volunteer Scotland (www.volunteerscotland.net)
- Volunteer Wales (www.volunteering-wales.net).

Other potential sources of useful experience

Outside of work experience and voluntary placements, additional valuable experience could be obtained elsewhere.

- Internships within the legal sector, which typically last several months and take place during the summer holidays.
- Joining an Inn provides opportunities in mentorship, marshalling with a judge (i.e. shadowing and sitting with a judge in court), and in-house societies for aspiring barristers.
- Extra-curricular activities, such as involvement in law societies at university, participating in debating societies and mooting competitions. Similarly, joining finance-related societies could prove to be beneficial if you are considering a career in the commercial sector.
- Courts allow the public to observe lawyers in action, making this an easy way to observe court activity.

Looking through the case studies (and example personal statements) contained in this book will also give you some ideas.

Try as many ways of getting work experience as you can think of and be creative in the process. Here are a few suggestions.

- Ask your teachers at school/college if they have any contacts in the legal profession.
- Use your careers service and speak to your careers officer.
- Talk to your family and friends and ask them if they can suggest anyone to contact.
- Make sure everyone you know is aware you are looking for work experience.
- You can also approach sets of chambers that do not offer formal mini pupillage schemes. The Chambers and Partners directory will also give you names and addresses of chambers.

While you are trying to get work experience, you should make sure that you keep up to date with current affairs relating to the legal world and the legal profession by reading a quality newspaper and looking at specialist journals such as *The Law Society Gazette* and *The Lawyer*, which should both be available from large public libraries and are also online (see Chapter 12, page 157 for details).

You should ask to go in for one or two weeks' work experience during the holidays or even just ask for one day's work-shadowing to get an insight into what the working environment is like. Anything that anyone is prepared to give you will be useful. Whichever route you take will almost certainly be unpaid unless you have specific skills to offer, such as good office and keyboard skills. If you can touch-type, you could try to get some paid work with a firm of solicitors during the summer or register with an employment agency.

Virtual Work Experience

As Covid-19 continues to disrupt our daily lives at the time of writing, there is no doubt that this will also impact a student's ability to acquire work experience. Work experience providers across all sectors have been quick to adapt, and online or 'virtual' work experience opportunities have become readily accessible and widely acknowledged by universities. These virtual placements can give you an excellent insight into what the career entails, and will highlight to admissions tutors that you are well-informed about the study and practice of law. It should also help you to decide whether it is an area you definitely want to pursue.

Online work experience opportunities

There are many virtual work experience opportunities, but online placements that ran in 2021 and are due to continue include:

- Pinsent Masons Virtual Work Experience: Pinsent Masons have designed this online platform to allow aspiring solicitors to see behind the scenes at their firm, assist with helping a hypothetical client and gain practical skills. As it is quite a challenging course, it is targeted at degree-level students, but may also be useful for A level students considering their options. The course can be found at www.pinsentmasons.com/careers/graduate/work-experience/virtual.
- Bright Network Internship Experience: Bright Network partnered with different firms to run sessions covering the remit of commercial law. It is suitable for A level students, undergraduate students and graduates. Information can be found at www.brightnetwork.co.uk/internship-experience-uk/law.
- Clifford Chance Virtual Internship: Through the Forage platform, Clifford Chance are offering a number of virtual internships that are self-paced. They cover business and human rights, climate change and cyber security. These courses can be accessed from www.theforage.com.

As well as online work experience placements, there are a variety of online courses, sometimes known as MOOCs (massive open online courses), that may also be valuable in improving your knowledge of law and developing your applications. The FutureLearn platform is an excellent, free resource with hundreds of law-related courses that are led by leading universities. These range from introducing law as an area of undergraduate study to detailed reviews of specific areas of law, such as human rights and commercial law.

Some courses that may be of particular interest to aspiring lawyers include:

- Exploring Law: Studying Law at University – University of Cambridge (www.futurelearn.com/courses/exploring-law-studying-law-at-university)
- Introduction to Studying Law – The University of Law (www.future learn.com/courses/international-foundation-programme-in-law-the-first-step-towards-your-future-successful-career)
- How to Become a Lawyer – The University of Law (www.future learn.com/courses/how-do-i-become-a-lawyer).

Additional law-related courses can be found on the Law Courses section on the FutureLearn website (www.futurelearn.com/subjects/law-courses).

How to apply

CV

Many formal vacation schemes and mini pupillages will require you to apply online using an application form. For anything else, you will probably need to put together a CV to support your application. This is a summary of what you have done in your life to date. If you have hardly any work experience then one page on good-quality A4 paper will be sufficient. If you are a mature student with a lot of jobs behind you there is sometimes a case for going on to a second page. So what should go into your CV? Here are the main headings:

- name
- contact details
- education and qualifications
- previous work experience.

There is no standard CV but there is a sample on page 90. Make sure to include the following points. You should ensure that you don't leave any gaps and account for all your time. Also, if something such as illness prevented you from reaching your potential in your exams, point this out in the covering letter (see below). Lawyers have excellent attention to detail, so make sure your spelling and grammar are perfect!

Education

Start with your present school, college or university and work back to the beginning of secondary school. No primary schools please! List the qualifications with grades you already have and the ones you intend to sit.

Work experience

Start with the most recent. Don't worry if you've only had a Saturday job at the local shop or a paper round. Put it all down and focus on drawing out any relevant skills that you have gained from it. Employers like to see that you are able to carefully consider your experiences.

Skills

List those such as computer skills, software packages used, languages and driving licence.

Interests and positions of responsibility

What do you like to do in your spare time? If you are or have been captain of a sports team, been a committee member or even head boy or head girl at school, put it all down.

Referees

Usually two: an academic referee such as a teacher or head of your school plus someone who knows you well personally, who is not a relative, such as someone for whom you have worked.

Covering letter

Every CV or application form should always be accompanied by a covering letter. The letter is important because it is usually the first thing a potential employer reads.

Here are some tips.

- The letter should be on the same A4 plain paper as your CV and should look like a professional document. It should be no longer than one side of A4.
- Employers accept typed letters, unless they specifically request one to be handwritten.
- Find out the name of the person to whom you should send your letter and CV. It makes a great difference to the reader if you can personalise your application. If you start the letter 'Dear Mr Brown', remember you should finish it 'Yours sincerely'.
- The first paragraph should tell the reader why you are contacting them and what stage of your education you are at.
- The second paragraph should give them some brief information to make them interested in you, e.g. highlighting your interest in law, along with some specific IT skills.
- Thirdly, explain why you are applying to them, for example interest in their line of work, desire to experience work in a small/large firm/set, etc. Mention anything you already know about the firm/chambers and make sure that it is correct. Look carefully at their website and make sure you know what area of the law they practise in!
- Check very carefully for spelling and grammatical mistakes.

A sample CV

PERSONAL DETAILS
Patrick Jones
17 Bloomsbury Road
Leeds LS1 1XJ
01234 567890
patrickjones@btinternet.com

EDUCATION & QUALIFICATIONS
2020–present: Law LLB, University of Leeds
Year 1 Modules included Foundations in Law, Contract Law,
Constitutional Law and Criminal Law
2012–2019: Leeds High School
A levels: Government & Politics (A), Biology (A), Physics (A)
GCSEs: English language (A*/8), English Literature (A/7), Maths
(A*/8), Geography (A/7), German (A/7), Latin (A*/8), Physical
Education (B/6), Science (B/6), Additional Science (B/6)

WORK EXPERIENCE
Citizens Advice Bureau, September 2020–present: Shadowing
legal volunteers providing advice regarding employment law to
develop my knowledge of the cases requiring legal support and
assisting with legal research and drafting.
Leeds Tuition Centre, July 2019–present: Paid role tutoring young
people in maths and English, which has allowed me to develop my
skills in communication and build my confidence in a person-
centred role.
Call Centre Operative, February 2017–July 2019: Providing
customer support by using my initiative to handle complaints for
a commercial company while developing my skills in verbal and
written communication.

SKILLS
Computing: competent in Microsoft Word, Excel and PowerPoint.

POSITIONS OF RESPONSIBILITY
Secretary of the University of Leeds Law Society: Organising
memberships, handling law society emails and acting as the inter-
face between the society and its members.

INTERESTS
Rugby and Spanish.

REFERENCES

Mrs B Greene	Mr A Jones
Personal Tutor at University of Leeds	Legal Volunteer at Leeds
b.a.greene@leeds.ac.uk	Citizens Advice Bureau
	a.jones@cab.org

A sample covering letter is shown below.

Dear Mr Cooper,

I am an aspiring solicitor currently in my second year of the undergraduate law course at the University of Leeds. In order to enhance my exposure to legal work and learn more about the profession, I am interested in securing a work experience placement, and wondered whether SPM LLP would have any opportunities available.

I am extremely interested in the field of land law, and can see from your website that SPM LLP has an outstanding reputation in this area both nationally and internationally.

I am currently undertaking an independent research project under supervision into this field, in preparation for the upcoming land law module on the course, which has cemented my interest in this area. I have volunteered alongside trained solicitors at the Citizens Advice Bureau to develop my insight into legal work and to practise the skills required, such as research and both written and verbal communication.

Please do not hesitate to contact me if you require any further information or would like to meet me in person.

Yours sincerely,

Patrick Jones

Case study

Alesha is currently in her third year of a law degree at the University of Warwick.

'Prior to starting my law degree, I had not obtained any legal work experience as it is difficult to obtain. However, I had always been interested in law as an academic subject and learning about its operation in society. Attending the Crown Court and sitting in on cases allowed me to explore my interest and helped me to decide that it was a career that I could really see myself following in the future. I also attended lectures given by barristers and scholars of law. While providing a great opportunity to learn more about my chosen field, this was also a really good way to network and speak to legal professionals, which allowed me to learn about the way that law is practised and implemented.

'I studied humanities-based subjects at A level, including English literature, politics, history and classics. These provided a really good foundation for developing my essay writing skills and pre-pared me for the vast amount of reading required for studying law at undergraduate level! Getting the A level grades required is by far the most important aspect of your application, especially when aiming to secure a place at a top university, and this will also impact your employability later in life. I would advise getting involved with extra-curricular activities such as debating, as this will help to make your application stand out and provide examples where you can demonstrate your advocacy skills.

'When trying to identify the right university for you, it is important to look at the modules taught in each of the years and its assess-ment methods. At Warwick, I have really enjoyed learning about how law relates directly to society as a whole. Global intellectual property law and international law have been the modules that I have found the most interesting and are the fields that I am considering as a career. It is also well worth investigating the department's links to solicitors' firms and chambers, as these will be crucial in helping you secure placements and experience in the future.

'Most universities will provide law-specific societies and I would encourage getting involved as much as possible, as applying for graduate positions is extremely competitive so you will need to stand out! I have been involved in a number of activities, including:

- participating in first year CMS mooting competition
- participating in Warwick witness examination competition
- attending a "Day in the City" event which involved visiting Chambers in London and the Royal Courts of Justice
- getting involved with societies and becoming Vice President of the Warwick Bar Society for aspiring barristers (where I was also able to develop important skills in organising the Law Ball)
- an internship at the Houses of Parliament
- participating in an international venture – Warwick Finance Societies in Dubai
- attending insight days at Dubai Islamic Bank, PwC, The Boston Consulting Group, AL Tamimi & Company, Freshfields Bruck-haus Deringer, Linklaters, Francis Taylor Building and Quadrant Chambers
- mini pupillages at St Ives Chambers and 2 Bedford Row
- being Campus Representative for The University of Law.

'Undertaking all of these additional elements has been time consuming, and some of them have been difficult to secure, but they have been invaluable in allowing me to learn new skills, gain hands-on experience that I can use to demonstrate those skills and identify what exactly I want to pursue as a career.

'I hope to become a barrister following graduation. At the moment, I am applying for the BPTC and trying to secure funding through an Inns of Court Scholarship. I will then undertake a pupillage as a training year before eventually being called to the Bar.'

6 | Choosing your university law course

This chapter focuses on how to go about choosing a law degree. The aim is to produce a shortlist of degree courses you are interested in and from that to choose the top five courses to put down in your UCAS application.

As previous chapters have made clear, you do not need a law degree to enter the legal profession. Equally, a law degree can be an excellent springboard into a wide range of other careers. Employers are generally impressed by a good-calibre law graduate, since law is known to be a challenging discipline requiring skills such as research, analysis, application, clarity, advocacy and effective written communication. These are relevant in many other careers as well as those in the legal professions.

If you do not wish to read law at university, most of the advice in this chapter will still be relevant to choosing your degree course, but for more general advice on choosing degree courses, please refer to some of the guides mentioned in Chapter 12.

Things to consider

The basic criteria for choosing your degree course are:

- the type of law course you are interested in
- your academic ability
- where you want to study.

Most of the information you need to know about universities and the courses available at them is available online either through:

- UCAS (www.ucas.com)
- universities' own websites. Most universities have their prospectuses available to download online (although you can request a paper copy to be sent through the post if you prefer) and there should also be information on who to contact if you have a specific question.
- university comparison guides and league tables such as the Complete University Guide (www.thecompleteuniversityguide.co.uk) and the Guardian University Guide (www.theguardian.com/

education/ng-interactive/2021/sep/11/the-best-uk-universities-2022-rankings). There are also books providing similar information, such as *The Times and Sunday Times Good University Guide*. Make sure you use the most up-to-date edition.

Going to university is an investment, particularly with the rise in tuition fees in recent years, so the choice of what to study and where to apply to must be given careful thought. You will also spend three years of your life there, so you will want to make sure that you will be somewhere you will enjoy living. There are many institutions offering law courses and you will need to look at ways of narrowing down your options.

Types of law degree

Many law degree courses are offered by many different institutions across the country and the choice may at first appear daunting. However, the range of options can quickly be narrowed down once you know what you are looking for. The important thing is to choose the right course for you. The key points to consider are:

- if you intend to qualify as a solicitor or a barrister in the future, the degree must be a qualifying law degree (QLD) if you wish to go straight on to the LPC afterwards
- whether you should choose an LLB or a BA (and whether it matters)
- should you choose a single or joint honours degree?

Note on qualifying law degrees

Qualifying law degrees (QLDs) were recognised by the Solicitors Regulation Authority (SRA) up until September 2021, when the new qualification route for solicitors began. Having a QLD means that you have studied the subjects which the SRA consider to be the core foundation subjects for any lawyer, including criminal law, equity and the law of trusts, law of the European Union, obligations (including contract, restitution and tort law), property law and public law (including constitutional law, administrative law and human rights law). These are areas that must be studied in order to commence the LPC, and so the QLD description is likely to remain throughout the transitional period for the new route of qualification.

LLB or BA?

Some law degrees are classified as LLBs, whereas others are BAs. As a broad generalisation, LLB degrees will involve spending all of your time studying law, whereas a BA or BSc degree may involve spending some time studying non-law modules. For historical reasons, the universities of Oxford and Cambridge do not award LLBs at all and their law degrees are BAs. If you are interested in studying non-law modules as part of your law degree (for example, foreign languages), then the increased breadth of a BA of BSc degree may well be preferable for you and also welcomed by future employers.

Single or joint honours?

Law can be taken on its own (a single honours degree) or mixed with one or more other subjects (a joint honours degree).

A single honours degree will allow you to focus on studying law, although some courses will also permit you to take individual modules from other subject areas, even from completely different disciplines. As well as the core subjects, you will also be able to choose optional subjects (particularly in second and later years). Some institutions can offer only a limited selection of options, while others provide a much greater variety. If there is a particular area of law you are interested in, for example intellectual property law, then you may want to apply to a university that offers this as an option.

A joint honours degree will allow you to divide your time between law and one or more other disciplines. Usually, where two subjects in a degree title are joined by the word 'and', this indicates that the course will involve a 50/50 split between the two subjects, whereas the word 'with' suggest a two-thirds/one-third split. However, this is a broad generalisation and you should always check the details of any particular course on the university's website. A popular combination is to study law with a European language, although you should note that these courses often specify that candidates must have an A level or at the very least a GCSE in the relevant language.

Approaches to teaching law

It is interesting to note that there are broadly three different approaches to teaching law, but you should not base your selection on this criterion since few institutions adhere to one kind. Most places are likely to opt for a mixture (sometimes even within an individual unit, especially if it is taught by several different tutors). However, the emphasis of different law schools may be different. The approaches are as follows.

- *Pure academic approach*. This approach focuses on the core legal subjects and doesn't look much beyond statutes and law reports for its sources of law. It provides a thorough grounding in the relevant legal system and its laws.
- *Contextual approach*. Law can also be examined in context; that is to say, law, its role and its effectiveness are looked at in relation to society (past and present), politics and the economy. This approach may include elements of critical legal theory. Students are expected

to analyse the problems (for example, loopholes, contradictions, injustices and so on) within the law. This can make for some heated and controversial seminars.

- *Vocational approach.* This stresses professional training and skills such as negotiating, interviewing, counselling, drafting, research, analysis, clear expression and the ability to read through vast amounts of material, sift out the legally relevant points and present a logical argument. These skills are mainly covered during the vocational stage of training to become a solicitor or barrister, but may also be looked at in a law degree. Extra-curricular activities such as mooting (a mock courtroom trial), debating and law clinics, in which students get the opportunity to help out with a real-life case from start to finish, also help develop these skills at university.

Academic requirements

Entry requirements for law degrees vary greatly, both in terms of the standard that they expect students to have achieved and also in how they are expressed. You will need to research which degrees at which universities your likely A levels, Scottish Highers, IB or BTEC qualifications will enable you to access. It is important to be realistic about the grades you are likely to achieve: don't be too pessimistic, but make sure that the entry requirements for the courses you choose include some safer options. Talk to your teachers for an accurate picture of your predicted results as this will allow you to target universities accordingly. Don't forget that you need to select one or two universities with lower grade requirements than your predictions as 'insurance' choices.

Most of the top universities require applicants to have three A levels (or their equivalent) and the most selective universities, such as Cambridge, now regularly include an A* grade in their offers. Information on the entry requirements for law degrees at different universities is available through UCAS or the websites of the universities themselves.

Less academically selective universities often express their entry requirements as a target number of UCAS Tariff points. The UCAS Tariff system allocates points to the different qualifications taken by students before they access higher education. It therefore allows students with different qualifications to access the same undergraduate degree courses, and allows universities to compare applicants with different qualifications.

Your A level subject choices may also have a bearing on which universities you can realistically expect to receive an offer from. Few courses specify subjects they want you to have studied (with the exception of most language joint degrees), although qualifications in traditional academic subjects are preferred at the more selective universities and are welcomed everywhere. Some universities won't accept A levels such as General Studies or Critical Thinking. No institutions require A level Law from potential students. You should always check carefully on the websites of all the universities that you are interested in to confirm their specific requirements.

If your predicted A level results (or chosen A level subjects) effectively prevent you from taking a law degree, then it's time for a rethink. If you wanted to take a law degree with a view to entering the profession, then you could opt for the non-law degree entry route instead. Most employers stress that a large number of trainee solicitors and pupil barristers have a non-law degree. Remember that if you read a subject other than law, you will still need a thorough knowledge of law for the SQE, so you may need to consider a postgraduate qualification in law or standalone SQE preparation courses. The disadvantage is that the route might be longer and therefore more expensive (if sponsorship cannot be found).

Choosing a university

Once you have made a realistic assessment of your likely A level grades (or other qualifications) you can think about choosing specific institutions. Remember, university life isn't going to be solely about academic study. It is truly a growing experience – educationally, socially and culturally – and besides, three or four years can really drag if you're not happy outside the lecture theatre. Here is an assortment of factors which might help you to choose where you would like to study. Some of these will be more important to you than others, so you should use the paragraphs below to think carefully about the things that matter most to you.

Warning: different legal systems

If you're hoping to practise law, then you must be sure where you intend to work within the UK (i.e. England or Wales, Scotland or Northern Ireland). Since the legal systems differ throughout the UK, you must qualify in the part of the UK you intend to practise in. If you did subsequently decide to move, then it is usually possible to convert qualifications from a different country (e.g. if you qualified in England but want to practise in Scotland). To work in England or Wales having qualified elsewhere, lawyers will have to undertake the Solictors Qualifying Examination (SQE). More information can be found by visiting the websites of the Law Societies and Bar Councils for each country, mentioned in Chapter 3. More detail on the differences between the professions in each of the UK countries can be found in Chapters 2 and 3.

Open days

If you get the opportunity, attend the open days for the universities where you are interested in studying. Visit the law departments and talk to former or current students and course lecturers and tutors. Doing so should give you an idea of what life on campus at that particular university is like, and this will allow you to determine whether you would enjoy your time there. If you cannot attend any open days, there are often campus tours available, or you can make an independent visit. Try to go on a taster course for law at any university if possible. This does not need to be a university to which you are actually thinking of applying – even if it is not, it will still give you an idea of what to look for in universities in general and will also give you something to mention in your personal statement.

Virtual open days

In light of the coronavirus pandemic, many universities have converted their open days into virtual events that are conducted wholly online, in order to protect the health of prospective students. Even as restrictions continue to lift, it is highly likely that virtual open days will continue. A virtual open day is different to visiting a campus in person, but it is still an excellent opportunity to see what a university has to offer and get an insight into a place where you might choose to study.

As you won't have to factor in travelling to the universities, you can attend more open days than you might have initially intended. This might open up more doors for you in terms of your university options.

Virtual open days have differing formats depending on the university, but typically provide an opportunity to look at virtual tours, attend online webinars and talk to current students, lecturers and admissions officers, allowing you to ask any questions that you might have.

Types of university or college

There are a number of ways of categorising universities and higher education colleges, but there are two broad categorisations by which these institutions are often sorted:

Old or new?

Almost all law degrees are taught by universities and these can be categorised as 'old' or 'new'. A few other colleges of higher education also offer law degrees:

1. 'Old' universities. Traditionally the more academic universities with higher admission requirements. They are well established, with good libraries and research facilities, and are well respected by employers and provide an academically rigorous training.

2. 'New' universities. Pre-1992, most of these were polytechnics or institutes of higher education and these generally still hold true to the original polytechnic doctrine of vocational courses and strong ties with industry, typically through placements and work experience. Their approach to teaching law may generally be slightly more vocational in nature. They can still be looked down upon by some employers because of their generally lower academic entry requirements, but many of the new universities have a good name for flexible admissions and learning and modern approaches to their degree teaching. There are also some private universities, such as BPP University, the University of Law and Buckingham University. These universities can offer even greater flexibility in the way your degree course is structured. Some private universities now offer the chance to take a degree that would normally take three years in only two years of full-time study, which can be really helpful if you want to qualify as quickly as possible, and possibly of particular interest to mature or overseas students. You will simply forgo the long holidays usually associated with university degree courses. Private universities tend to be more vocational in their approach. They receive no state funding, so are not subject to the government's cap on tuition fees, but may not necessarily be more expensive, especially if you choose the two-year degree option. Some institutions offer part-time degree courses.

3. Colleges of higher education. Usually specialist institutions and therefore provide good facilities in their chosen fields. They are sometimes affiliated to universities, which means the college buys the right to teach the degree, which the university will award, provided that the course meets the standards set by the university.

4. The Open University, which is a very well-established provider of part-time distance-learning degree courses, offers an LLB degree.

City or campus?

Universities are also often divided into campus or city universities. So, when looking at which university to choose you need to consider whether you would prefer to live on a university campus, surrounded by your fellow students and the university's facilities, or whether you would prefer to be more integrated into town or city life. The choice is slightly more sophisticated than this broad division, since many universities offer something of a mix between these two extremes. For example, there are campuses in the middle of, or right on the edge of, cities or towns. Other campuses are practically surrounded by open fields and the nearest town or city is a bus ride away. Some city universities are largely contained in one area, whereas others are spread throughout the city.

The town or city where the university is based, particularly its size, can also have a big effect on the 'feel' of the place. Some city universities have a largely separate university area, but are close to the centre of a large city, such as Leeds. Others are more integrated into the city, such as Sheffield. Some have a largely self-contained campus, but are still in a big city, such as Nottingham. Universities more often thought of as campus universities may be more likely to be near a smaller town than a big city, such as Lancaster and Warwick.

Other factors to consider

Attractiveness to employers

Few employers will openly admit to giving preference to graduates from particular universities. Most are looking for high-quality degrees as an indication of strong academic ability. But since students with higher A level grades tend to go to the older and more prestigious universities, it is unsurprising that a large proportion of successful lawyers come from these universities. Employers are often so swamped with applications that they use university background as an easy way to filter applicants, reckoning that the better universities will have picked the higher-calibre students and therefore have done part of their job for them. It therefore makes sense to be aware of the reputations of the different universities, which can often be gleaned from their position in the league tables, and factor this into your decision. You must obviously choose to go somewhere that you will enjoy, but since (at least part of) the object of the exercise is to find a good job at the end of your university studies, it is foolhardy to ignore how potential employers will view your degree.

Quality of teaching

This is difficult to establish without the benefit of an open day, and even then you will only have the opportunity to meet one or two of the teaching staff and speak to one or two students. However, league tables of universities for each subject are published by several organisations, such as the *Guardian*, the *Times and Sunday Times* and The Complete University Guide. The *Guardian's* 'The best UK universities 2022 – rankings' for law is available online at www.theguardian.com/education/ng-interactive/2021/sep/11/the-best-uk-universities-2022-rankings and the Complete University Guide 2022 Law league table is at www.thecompleteuniversityguide.co.uk/league-tables/rankings/law. *The Times/Sunday Times Guide* is published annually.

The National Student Survey is conducted each year to get feedback from students who have studied at university, and is more focused on overall student satisfaction. Scores are given for many factors, including the quality of teaching and how good teachers are at providing feedback to students. The results of the survey can be seen online, through www.officeforstudents.org.uk/advice-and-guidance/student-information-and-data/national-student-survey-nss. Since the raising of tuition fees, students have become a lot more interested in issues such as teaching quality and 'contact time' – i.e. how much face-to-face teaching you will actually get, and it makes sense to investigate this as much as you can.

Teaching quality may suffer if seminar or tutorial groups are too large, so try to also compare group sizes for the same courses at different institutions.

Educational facilities

Most universities should have a well-stocked and up-to-date law library. They should also have good-quality IT resources and fast broadband internet connections. More vocational courses might also use mock courtrooms with video and audio equipment. The facilities available will depend on the budget of an institution, and obviously how they choose to spend it. You may want to look at the law department at the university. Is it in the new, shiny, state-of-the-art building or a dilapidated 1960s monstrosity hidden from view? At the end of the day, university is about more than just buildings – academically, the quality of teaching is more important and non-academic factors will also make a big difference to whether or not you enjoy your time there. However, if you are concerned about the environment in which you study, you should investigate the building housing the law department.

Non-academic considerations

- **Finances.** The cost of living differs substantially throughout the UK, so will you be able to reach deeper into your pockets for rent or other fundamentals and entertainment if you are living in a major city or in the south? If you are living in London, you will need particularly deep pockets.
- **Distance from home.** Do you want to get away from your family and friends or stay as close to them as possible? While there can be advantages, financially at least, to living at home if you go to your local university, you may prefer the challenge of looking after yourself and the opportunity to be completely independent. You should also think about whether you want to be able to go home at weekends without spending half a day (or more) on a train.
- **Accommodation.** What sort of accommodation is on offer? Do you want to live on campus or in halls of residence with other students, or in private housing that you may need to organise yourself that could be a considerable distance from college? Most universities provide accommodation for first year students at least, but how far this is from the teaching areas of the university will vary. You may simply be able to roll out of bed and totter next door for your 9am lectures, or you may be looking at a half-hour bus journey in rush hour. Some universities offer accommodation beyond the first year, which will save you having to live in private housing.
- **Catering.** Would you prefer to go somewhere where you can have your meals cooked for you, or are you keen to unleash your inner chef and cater for yourself?

- **Interests.** Will the university allow you to pursue your interests? Are you going to be spending much time in, for example, the sports centre, the theatre or student bars? How about university societies: is there one that allows you to indulge your existing hobbies or the ones you've always dreamt of trying? Most universities have a huge choice of extra-curricular activities and entertainments and very good facilities. However, you should think about exactly what is provided, the standard of participants and whether all abilities are catered for (are you a county squash player or simply keen to have a go?) and how far the facilities that you will want to use are from the accommodation or teaching areas. Some universities have particular reputations for particular extra-curricular activities – for example, Loughborough for sport.

Studying overseas and work placements

The opportunity to study overseas and/or complete a work placement could also be factors affecting your degree selection. Some universities will allow you to go to an overseas university with which they have an arrangement for one year of your studies. Others will allow you to spend a year in the middle of your degree on a work placement. You do not need to be a linguist to study abroad, since you can study or work overseas in English in, for example, North America, the Netherlands or Malaysia.

Prior to Brexit, the Erasmus scheme allowed students from the UK to undertake placements in the EU and vice versa as part of their studies. The Turing scheme has now replaced Erasmus and it provides funding for students who want to undertake study periods or training internationally. UK universities classed as hosting organisations can send students to non-UK higher education providers or non-UK public or private organisations active in the labour market or in the fields of education and training. The scheme is open to undergraduate students and graduates who have received their degrees within the last 12 months. Opportunities to study or work abroad are an exceptional opportunity to develop new skills, gain exposure to new cultures and enhance your employability. Further information can be found on the Turing Scheme website (www.turing-scheme.org.uk), which also has a detailed programme guide that covers eligibility and funding information.

If you are planning to study law at university, these opportunities may be more limited, as law is a very jurisdiction-specific subject.

Similarly, few law degree courses offer work placements during your degree. You will usually need to arrange this for during university holidays (see Chapter 5, page 79).

7 | The UCAS application and the LNAT

So you have chosen a few universities that you would like to apply to for a law degree; now what? This chapter will guide you through the UCAS application process for a law degree, and then give you some advice if you are applying to any universities that require the LNAT entrance exam.

Suggested application timescale

Below is a suggested timeline that you could follow throughout your time at sixth form or college to ensure that you are thoroughly prepared for your application.

Lower Sixth

September–December

- If you already know that you want to study law at university, or you think it could be a serious possibility, the beginning of your A levels is a good time to explore academic options available to you, such as the EPQ if your school or college runs this. Doing so will allow you to start identifying your academic interests within the field of law, and whether or not it might be an area you want to pursue further.

January onwards

- Research degree courses, considering the kind of course you might want to study and where you might want to study.

Take note of any entry requirements, including GCSE grades, predicted A level grades, and whether or not they require you to sit the LNAT entrance exam.

- Book onto taster courses at universities.
- Discuss your plans with teachers, family and friends, to see whether they have any contacts or insight into the profession.
- Update your CV and start enquiring about work experience placements, writing to any firms or companies that may be able to support you in providing a placement.

April onwards

- Find out when university open days are being held and book onto any of interest to you. A useful tool is www.opendays. com. Always check to see whether the Law department has any specific talks, and book onto them where required to get a good idea of what studying there would be like and to give you the opportunity to ask any questions you might have.

June/July

- Attend any open days that are available and look at university department websites and prospectuses to narrow down your choices.
- Register on UCAS with your school and complete as much of the form as possible with background information and academic exam results to date.

July/August

- Make a shortlist of your courses. Try to do as much research as possible over the summer holidays. This is particularly important for applicants to Oxford and Cambridge.
- Undertake work experience and wider reading (see suggestions in Chapter 12).
- Start writing your personal statement.
- If applicable, review your courses shortlist when you receive your summer exam results.

Upper Sixth

September onwards

 Finalise your personal statement and UCAS form, then complete your application and send it off to UCAS.

 Register and book a place to sit the LNAT if you are applying to a university that uses it (see below).

October

 15 October (6pm UK time): Deadline for submitting your UCAS application if you are applying for places at Oxford or Cambridge.

 20 October: Deadline for sitting the LNAT if you are applying to Oxford.

November

 If you have applied to Oxford or Cambridge, start preparing for the interview stage so that you are ready when the invite arrives!

December

 Interviews for Oxford and Cambridge.

January

 Last Friday in January (6pm UK time): Deadline for submitting your application to UCAS. While UCAS will process late applications, all universities may not accept them.

February–April

- Decisions (and hopefully, offers!) should arrive during this time. Universities are encouraged to respond by 31 March, but don't worry if you haven't heard back from all of them by this point, especially if your application is late.
- If you have received all your university/college decisions by 31 March, you must tell UCAS which offer you have accepted firmly and which one is your insurance choice by a date yet to be determined by UCAS in May.
- Once you have received decisions from all five of your choices, and were either rejected or have declined the offer you received from all of them, you can enter UCAS Extra, a scheme that allows you to apply to other universities, one at a time. See the UCAS website (www.ucas.com) for details.

May–June

- Sit your exams!

August

- On the third Thursday of August, A level results are available.
- If you got the grades, well done! UCAS will send you confirmation of your place.
- If you missed your grades, don't be too disappointed. Clearing starts straight away so don't waste any time – get hold of a list of unfilled places and contact the universities directly. You will be sent instructions on Clearing automatically.
- UCAS also runs a scheme called Adjustment which allows students who have performed significantly better than they had expected a short period of time to approach universities that require higher grades than the offer they were holding. See Chapter 10 for more information on your options on results day.

The UCAS form

The online UCAS form is accessed through the UCAS website (www. ucas.com). For applications for 2022 entry and beyond, applicants will need to generate an account on the UCAS Hub. The UCAS Hub is a free tool that allows you to conduct research into your options beyond sixth form and store it all in an accessible way, as well as providing useful resources to help with personal statement and CV writing. Previously, the UCAS Hub and UCAS Apply registrations were separate with different login information, so UCAS has combined the two to eliminate confusion. While it is encouraged that you utilise the UCAS Hub, as it is an excellent resource that combines all of the information you will need for your application, you can just use it to create an account for your application.

Upon generating an account, you will be asked for the year of entry, the level of study that you are interested in, the country that you are from, your contact preferences and subject areas of interest. These answers will tailor the information presented to you on the UCAS Hub. Most applicants register through their school or college using their buzzword, but it is possible to register independently. Once the account has been created, you can access the UCAS form through the applications section. The application sections are summarised below.

1. **Personal details:** Upon creating an account you will be asked to fill in your personal details, including funding and sponsorship options, residential status, any special needs or disabilities, details of any criminal convictions, and the individual selected as your nominated access (someone who can talk to UCAS on your behalf if required).
2. **Additional information:** This section includes providing information about your ethnic origin, national identity, summer schools and taster sessions that you have attended, care background, parental education and occupational background. This section is used by UCAS to gather information for statistics, so any information you provide here will not be used in the selection process. Only UK applicants are required to fill in this section.
3. **Student finance:** If you are a UK applicant and have selected that you will be using student finance in the personal details section, you can fill in this section. UCAS is not linked to student finance directly, but you can consent to them passing your details on to speed up the application process for getting a loan.
4. **Course choices:** In this section, you can add in up to five university or college choices. If you are applying to Oxford or Cambridge, remember that you can only apply to one of them and you can specify a particular college. If you are applying for deferred entry, you can choose this option here.

5. **Education history:** For this section, you will need to add in any qualifications that you hold with the grade obtained, or with qualifications you are currently studying, the grade must be left as 'pending'.

6. **Employment history:** You can add in the details of up to five paid jobs in this section.

7. **Personal statement:** You will need to write a personal statement that outlines your motivation for studying the course that you have applied for, with a limit of 4,000 characters and 47 lines. This will be reviewed by admissions tutors.

8. **Reference:** Once you have completed your application, click send. If you are applying through your school or college, the application will first be sent to someone who can check your application and provide a reference. If you are applying independently, you will be asked for the details of a referee, who will be contacted by email and asked to upload their details before you are able to send your application to UCAS. Your reference is usually provided by a teacher, or someone who knows your professionally.

> General advice on filling in your UCAS application is given in *How to Complete Your UCAS Application* (Trotman Education).

Your personal statement

The personal statement is the most important part of your UCAS application and is your opportunity to demonstrate that you are fully committed to studying law and have the right motivation and personal qualities to do so successfully. It is therefore vital that you think very carefully about how to complete it so that it shows you in the best possible light. You need to sell yourself to the law admissions tutors. It will take time and effort to get it right, so you must allow yourself plenty of time and not attempt to rush it. Expect to go through many drafts before you come up with the final version that you are happy with.

There can often be over 20 applicants per place at some universities offering law degrees, so applying for a law degree is very competitive. A good personal statement can help you to stand out from the crowd and persuade an admissions tutor to give you an offer rather than one of the other equally well-qualified applicants.

Obviously, there are as many ways of writing a personal statement as there are candidates. There are no rules as such, but you should try and adhere to the following advice.

The personal statement should cover three key areas.

1. Why you want to study the course for which you are applying.
2. Why you would be good at the course and are well qualified to embark on it.
3. What other interests you have and (if possible) what transferable skills they give you which would be relevant for the course.

Section 3 should make up no more than 25% of the personal statement (or even less for the most academically competitive universities, such as Oxford, Cambridge and LSE). The focus should be on your academic interest in the courses applied for, and why you are a good candidate, and in most cases this should account for around 75% of the statement.

Some key points to remember.

- The personal statement must be no longer than 4,000 characters (including spaces). This is a strict limit, so you need to ensure that you do not exceed the character count.
- Write in your own words. The statement must be honest and personal and it must sound like you. After all, it is a *personal* statement, and admissions tutors will be using it to gain an insight into you as a potential student.
- Use evidence. Don't make broad-brush statements, but focus on what you have **actually done** and what you have learnt from it. Focus on how what you have done has helped you to decide a law degree is for you or to become a good candidate for a law degree.
- Check and re-check the statement for spelling, punctuation and grammar. Even better, ask a parent, teacher or family friend to do this for you.
- Do not over-use superlatives ('most passionate' etc.) although you should sound enthusiastic and committed.

Why you want to study law

The first part of the statement should show why you wish to study for a law degree. You can do this by providing answers to some of the following questions.

- Why do you wish to study law? Money, status or family traditions are not good reasons. Refer to evidence and the things that helped you reach your decision. For example: 'I am particularly interested in pursuing a career at the Bar. My enthusiasm was initially sparked by my active participation in the debating society at school, of which I am president. I found that I thoroughly enjoyed the challenge of putting across my point of view and trying to counteract the opposing argument.'
- What precisely is it about the law that interests you? Give details and examples, referring to recent cases and debates.
- Which particular area of law interests you most and, again, why?

- What related material have you recently read and why did you appreciate it? (See below for further guidance.)
- What legal cases have you followed and what recent judgements have you admired and why?
- What legal controversies have excited you? Are you up to date with current affairs and can you demonstrate your knowledge and understanding?

Well-chosen references to books you have read, including specific information you have gleaned from them, are very helpful. Some suggested reading for aspiring law students is contained in Chapter 12. Be careful not to just reel off a list of books – be specific about what interested you about them and what you learnt from them. You should also refer to any law taster courses you have attended but, again, don't just mention them – spell out what you gained from going to them and how they helped you decide that you would like to study law. You should also refer to any current legal issues appearing in the press and what you think of them or have learnt from them.

Work experience is very useful as it demonstrates a commitment to the subject outside the classroom, so mention any experience, paid or voluntary. Explain concisely what your job entailed and what you got out of the whole experience. Even if you haven't been able to get legal work experience, if you have spoken to anyone in the legal profession about their job, then it is worth mentioning as it all builds up a picture of someone who is keen and has done some research. Wanting to be like the characters in legal dramas on television is not enough, and neither is wanting to follow in a parent's footsteps!

Future plans, if any, should also be included on your form. Do not mention a desire to make a lot of money, since this is unlikely to impress admissions tutors who may well have shunned lucrative career opportunities in order to pursue an academic career.

Why you are a good candidate

You should also set out what makes you a good candidate for a law degree. If you have already explained why you wish to be a lawyer and how you made that decision, you will already have gone a long way towards demonstrating that you will be a committed student of the law. However, you should also briefly explain how your current school subjects (usually A levels) prepare you for studying a law degree. What skills have they allowed you to develop? If you have taken only maths and science A levels, you will need to describe how you are prepared for the more literary aspects of a law degree – i.e. reading and assimilating lots of information and preparing longer pieces of written work. You will also need to show that you can write an essay, so it would be a good idea to discuss any work you have carried out beyond your A levels, such as completion of the EPQ.

Extra-curricular activities and transferable skills

The last part of the statement should set out your extra-curricular activities, with a particular emphasis on what key transferable skills they have given you – for example, teamwork, self-motivation or leadership skills. If possible, you could try to link these in with the skills that will be necessary when studying for a law degree. If you are a school prefect, or team captain, then mention it here.

If you are planning to do so, state your reasons for applying for deferred entry and outline what you intend to do during your gap year. For example, you might be planning to find some relevant work experience in a firm of solicitors, and then spend some time overseas to brush up your language skills.

General advice

It is imperative that the focus of your personal statement is on the course of study that you wish to follow. Make sure that for each point you make, whether that be which A levels you are studying or the work experience that you have done, you are relating it back to the course.

Many universities now publish detailed advice about what they are looking for in a personal statement on their websites. You should carefully check the websites of all the universities you wish to apply to and make sure that you follow their advice. Most of it will simply be along the lines of the advice given above, but you should make sure you address any specific requirements or suggestions from the universities you are particularly interested in. You should also bear in mind the way that the universities describe the courses you are interested in on their websites. For example, if they emphasise the need for a practical approach, then it makes sense to highlight how you demonstrate an ability to be practical.

Finally, you should try to avoid some common pitfalls when writing your statement.

- Avoid cheesy clichés (e.g. 'for as long as I can remember') and over-use of quotations. One short quotation is acceptable if it is relevant and you comment on it.
- Do not include unsupported statements (e.g. 'I am hard-working'), which lack credibility. Instead, give evidence to support statements (e.g. things you have done which proved your capacity for hard work).
- Do not refer to specific courses as the same statement will go to all five of your university choices. You will not be able to write a convincing statement if you are applying to a variety of different courses (see below).

- Do not lie or exaggerate. You must be prepared to be asked on anything you mention in your statement if you are called for interview.
- Do not try to be funny. Humour is very personal and can easily be misinterpreted or backfire.
- Do not be tempted to get someone else (a friend, teacher, parent or one of the many internet sites that offer 'help') to write your personal statement. It has to sound like you, which is why it is called a personal statement.

Caution!

Never, ever, copy and paste any part of your statement from any other sources (whether from a friend or the examples in this book or somewhere online). UCAS runs all applications through anti-plagiarism software. If you do this, you will be caught out and your application will be void.

Make sure you print out a copy of your personal statement when you have finished it so that you can refer to it again and remind yourself of the points that you raised, should you be called for interview.

As emphasised in Chapter 1, it is not necessary to study law at university in order to become a lawyer (although it saves you a year of study). This chapter focuses on applying to university to study law, but if you are applying for a non-law degree, exactly the same issues arise. Your personal statement should focus on why you wish to study your particular subject at university and why you are a good candidate.

Warning: mixing courses and joint honours courses

You will write only one personal statement, which is read by admissions staff at the five courses for which you are applying, so you must make sure that it is suitable for all five courses. Each university sees only its name and course code on the form that UCAS sends to it: your other choices are not revealed. So, if you are applying to read psychology at one university (remember, you do not have to read law at university to become a lawyer), management at another, history at a third, and so on, then you cannot possibly write a personal statement that will satisfy the criteria for all of the courses. The psychology admissions tutor will wonder why you have written about history, and so on. The likelihood is that you will be rejected by all of your choices.

If you apply for a joint honours course such as law and French, your form will be seen by admissions tutors from both departments, each of whom will want to see that you are a serious candidate for his/her course. You must therefore cover both subjects in your statement.

Tips from admissions tutors

The following advice has all been given by law admissions tutors at leading university law schools over the last few years.

Admissions tutors want to see that you have a genuine reason for wanting to study law and have made your decision to apply for a law degree based on thorough research. You must show that you have thought carefully about why you want to study for a law degree and have properly researched the degree programmes you are applying for. Do not list your achievements without explaining their applicability to a law degree. You should also have an idea of the different areas of law you can work in, although it is perfectly acceptable not to have made up your mind yet about which area you would prefer.

You also need to show that you have a firm grasp of current affairs and regularly read a quality newspaper. An up-to-date understanding of the legal profession is also important. Some admissions tutors consider an awareness of current issues to be more important than reading law texts.

You should include any relevant work experience in your statement, although admissions tutors are very sensitive to the fact that not all students will have had the opportunity to get high-quality legal work experience. The general agenda to widen access to universities means that admissions tutors will make sure they avoid discriminating against applicants because of their background and the opportunities available to them. However, you still need to show what you have managed to do in the way of work experience and what you have learnt from it, even if it is not directly law related.

One important consideration for admissions tutors is the breadth of the application. In recent years, admissions tutors have commented on the fact that many applicants lack culture. While they may be committed to their studies or have undertaken a wealth of work experience, they don't often show their readiness to expand their knowledge, for example, by learning a new skill such as a language.

You should also:

- focus your personal statement on the course you are applying for
- make your personal statement sound like you
- apply early
- check carefully for spelling and grammatical errors.

Some sample personal statements for law degrees are shown below. Use these to get some ideas but **do not copy** any part of them into your own personal statement.

First sample personal statement *(3,938 characters)*

My desire to study law was initiated by my A level tutor whose passion was infectious. Since she had practised law as a barrister, she brought her experience within the courts to the theory of the A level curriculum. I became fascinated by tort law, in particular negligence. I was intrigued by the incremental developments in law and how it is often based on concerns surrounding public policy. The constant progression of the legal field attracts me.

I have taken the opportunity this year to study religious studies in an intensive one-year A level programme. This subject complements law due to the analytical and critical thinking skills it develops. I am particularly enjoying *Philosophy of Religion*, such as the cosmological argument, and look forward to studying natural moral law and ethics.

Retaking English Literature with a new board and entirely different texts is also preparing me well for undergraduate law; in the dystopian unit, Orwell's *1984* and Atwood's *The Handmaid's Tale* have encouraged me to question whether a state should remove the rights of an individual for the benefit of the regime, particularly one imposed; while *Hamlet* explores whether revenge for murder can ever be justified. Discussing characters facing ethical and legal dilemmas has provided different insights into the relationship between our personal and public lives that I hope to explore further at university.

Within my A level study of law, I was encouraged to consider different perspectives on claimant and defendants' rights and the potential injustices that may arise. For example, in the case of Collins v. Wilcock it was declared that a battery would be any intentional touching of another outside of the scope of what would be regarded as being normally acceptable. This was reinforced in the obiter comment in the case of R v. Chief Constable of Devon and Cornwall of 'even an unwanted kiss can be a battery'. These cases proved to me how developments in the law have the potential for a retrograde effect, as although the rights of the claimant were protected, it could lead to injustice for the defendant and the possibility of opening the floodgates with many new claims. The opportunity to debate broader implications of any act or judgement and the extent to which the legal system can bring about social justice appeals to me.

To gain insight into the legal profession, I have embarked on a year-long internship with a family law barrister, where I learn more about court proceedings. As further work experience I shadowed a QC judge in Derby Crown Court, where I gained experience by engaging with legal teams and judges and found myself within the dramatic proceedings of a criminal law trial. This taught me the necessity for precision and accuracy within the legal system.

Further work experience was gained in Nottingham and Coventry Magistrates' court, where I had the opportunity to achieve a mini pupillage. I was able to observe the court's procedures and the vast amount of organisation and strict preparation that is carried out every day throughout the works of a barrister.

Through LAMDA speech and drama qualifications, I developed confidence in public speaking and a high level of emotional intelligence, both key to professional success in the legal field. I showed commitment to a dance team for 10 years, participating in national competitions and utilising skills in tactical thinking and teamwork. Work experience at the BBC London enabled me to learn how the media handled stories with wider legal implications. I wrote a double-page article for my local newspaper regarding a charity cycling event that I organised, which was supported by over 200 cyclists and raised £30,000 for pancreatic cancer research.

I am genuinely excited at the prospect of starting university and studying a subject that I not only find enthralling but will enhance all the opportunities and experiences that university life may offer.

Second sample personal statement *(3,982 characters)*

Primarily my interest in studying undergraduate law began with my natural inquisitiveness into how the world works, particularly how laws are created and used to govern a society effectively. I have been exposed to legal affairs by sorting out my own tenancy agreement and ensuring that the contract's terms and agreements were correct. The implications of Brexit on society and our laws fascinates me greatly, especially as I am studying A level Politics. I am determined to increase my awareness of what's occurring in the world presently and historically as I believe this knowledge will benefit myself and the people I work with in the future.

I have a passionate interest in legal systems around the world, seeking to understand their effect on society. Taking A level Politics has allowed me to gain further insight into how laws are established in the US and the UK, but has also spurred further research into current political and legal affairs.

Discovering that the justification for the imprisonment of Nazanin Zaghari-Ratcliffe in Iran was spreading propaganda shocked me.

From my research, I recognised the ambiguity of her accusation and wondered why her trial wasn't as clear cut as it should have been. Furthermore, it is a breach of her right to free speech and under the Iranian constitution free speech is a fundamental law. It made me wonder to what extent laws are influenced by religious and cultural beliefs, since laws are made for humans to abide by and yet in some regimes they are disregarded. This gave me insight into Catch 22s in which the laws in Iran must also abide by the principles of Islam, creating a paradoxical situation. Even in the text that I am studying in A level English Literature, *The Handmaid's Tale*, the ability of the theocratic government to override laws in the name of religion, despite violating fundamental human rights speaks volumes to me as I can see it happening in the world today.

Politics has also introduced me to the different powers of the judicial system in the US. The use of judicial review particularly interests me as it allows for reinterpretation of the Constitution. I realise that this can be considered as a positive aspect as the amendment process is especially difficult, but I also wonder if the Supreme Court is truly as unbiased as it is meant to be.

Even taking biology has enhanced my interest in legal cases due to discussion of ethical and legal implications of genetic modification, for example the Nuffield Council of Bioethics has green-lit that changing the DNA in a human embryo is 'morally permissible'. Biology has also improved my analytical skills and taught me the importance of precision in experiments.

A level English Literature has taken these evaluative skills even further, especially through studying *Hamlet* as I began to question the morality of revenge and the right to take law into our own hands. When given vast amounts of critical interpretations about the play, I have learned how to pick out necessary information efficiently and effectively for my upcoming exam and this will help me in the future when examining cases. In particular, the study of *1984* by George Orwell provided me with insight into different ideologies on how governments 'should' be run and how certain methods are detrimental to society. Although the focus was very much political, I contemplated how a legal system would come into play but there was obviously no such system in place. In this way, I recognised the importance of the legal system in protecting democracy.

Beyond the classroom, I have performed Bollywood dancing for charities that seek to educate about the importance of diversity. I learned how to communicate with people from diverse backgrounds and cultures. I believe the point of the legal system is to provide justice for individuals fairly and justly and look forward to exploring the precedents for this as part of a degree in law.

Third sample personal statement *(3,978 characters)*

My interest in the legal system stemmed from volunteering for three weeks at a women and children's refuge centre. Working with the centre's residents allowed a first-hand insight into specific situations that result in having to seek refuge, such as domestic violence and fleeing from countries where the jurisprudence still allows for practices such as FGM. The rapport I forged at the centre inspired me to research the UK's justice system, human rights and family courts, and I realised that I wanted to do something that would help the most vulnerable in society and ensure they have a voice. Law is intrinsic to maintaining a civilised country where individuals are able to enforce their rights, if they can have access to legal advice and representation, hence why the study of law is vital. Pursuing law will enable me to develop an expansive skillset while delving into many aspects of human life and, ultimately, undertaking a career that will be enormously fulfilling.

Studying biology and chemistry were both vital for development of skills, such as being able to learn and recall a large amount of detailed content, as well as having to analyse complex information. Religious studies enhanced my essay-writing skills and ability to construct arguments based on evidence and theories. The debating aspect of the subject was what I enjoyed most; I was able to develop as a critical thinker through discussion of philosophical arguments and ethical dilemmas. Ethics involved learning about the laws surrounding topics such as embryo research, abortion and voluntary euthanasia; this led to my interest in medical law.

In preparation to study law I have read *Letters to a Law Student*, which has provided a solid basis for what the course will entail and require and given me the important starting knowledge needed to be able to succeed at undergraduate level. I also read *The Secret Barrister* which allowed me to reflect on how a career in law isn't always plain sailing. It provided an eye-opener into the imperfections within parts of the system, however reinforced the need to retain my own moral integrity and uphold the values of our legal system.

I worked for Quest as a tutor for young children for over a year. During this time, I worked closely with children from various schools and backgrounds, which allowed me to develop my communication skills and work within a team. Through this experience I learnt to adapt to situations quickly and gained problem-solving skills, often having to change my teaching approach based on the age group or figure out new methods in order to explain concepts. National Citizen Service furthered my communication and interpersonal skills by working in a team to organise a sports day event for adults with learning difficulties. As the project manager, I had to liaise with the team of employees at the adults' day centre and make sure that the event being planned would cater for the needs of all the participants.

After much deliberation around subject choice, I began studying psychology at undergraduate level at the beginning of this academic year, with a view to broadening my intellect and pursuing law at postgraduate level. However, the course was not as intellectually stimulating as I had hoped, and I decided to leave to pursue law, as it had always been what I eventually wanted to do. I have organised work experience at a criminal and property law firm, so that I can gain first-hand experience in the workings of a law firm. I am also planning to get a job in retail so that I can gain more skills in a business-related field.

In my free time, I enjoy kickboxing and Bhangra dancing, and I will be keen to join similar societies and be an active member of university life. While I realise that this is an academically rigorous course that will be intellectually demanding, the challenge of it and a strong work ethic is what drives me.

The LNAT

The LNAT is the National Admissions Test for Law. It is an externally set test which is used by a number of universities to help them select suitable candidates either for interview or for conditional offers. It does not test legal knowledge, but instead tests your aptitude for the skills required to study law, in particular:

- verbal reasoning
- ability to understand and interpret information
- ability to analyse information and draw conclusions
- deductive and inductive reasoning abilities.

The test lasts two-and-a-quarter hours and is in two sections – a multiple-choice section and an essay.

The multiple-choice section (95 minutes) is computer based and consists of 42 questions, based on passages of text setting out fictional scenarios. The score for this section is known as your LNAT score.

The essay section (40 minutes) tests your ability to construct logical, structured and clear arguments by writing one essay chosen from a list of essay questions. The essay is not actually marked by LNAT but is passed on to the participating universities with your LNAT score.

The best way to prepare yourself for the LNAT is to do several practice tests. The LNAT website (www.lnat.ac.uk) contains further details and also plenty of specimen questions and practice papers. There is also a practice test simulator that you can download. This is an on-screen simulation of the LNAT and includes a tutorial and two live practice tests. These will allow you to familiarise yourself with the format of the test and the skills it requires.

The multiple-choice section is based on fairly substantial passages of text, and examples of this section can be found on the LNAT website. However, below are some examples of the sort of essay questions you might be asked, with more examples available on the LNAT website.

1. In what circumstances should abortion be permitted and why?
2. Would you agree that travel and tourism exploit poorer nations and benefit only the richer ones?
3. Wearing a burkha in Western countries is just as offensive as wearing a bikini in Arab countries. Do you agree?

The LNAT is used by the following universities at the time of writing:

- University of Bristol
- Durham University
- University of Glasgow
- King's College London
- London School of Economics and Political Science (LSE)
- University of Nottingham
- University of Oxford
- SOAS, University of London
- University College London (UCL).

(See below for details about the University of Cambridge.)

In 2021, registration for the LNAT opened on 2 August, with testing beginning on 1 September. The deadline for registering and booking the LNAT was 15 January 2022, and the test had to be sat by 20 January 2022 (or 15 October 2021 for the University of Oxford). Current details can be found at www.lnat.ac.uk.

Other key points associated with the LNAT:

- The test is sat at an external test centre.
- The current cost of the test is £75 at UK and EU test centres, and £120 for other centres. The fee is payable online by credit or debit card at the time of booking.
- You can sit the test only once in any application cycle. If you sit it a second time, the later result will not count.

- If you reapply to universities that require the LNAT in subsequent years, you will have to sit the LNAT again.
- Candidates who may need extra time (for example, students with dyslexia) or need special arrangements (for example, students with sight or mobility problems) should register for the LNAT online, but should not book their test online. Documentary evidence must be supplied. Further information can be found on the LNAT website.

University of Cambridge

The University of Cambridge stopped using the LNAT test in 2010. It has replaced it with the Cambridge Law Test, which is used by nearly all Cambridge colleges. It consists of a one-hour paper that is normally sat when you attend for your interview. The questions do not require any prior knowledge of the law. The test is designed to ascertain a candidate's skills in comprehension and expression. Assessors will be looking to see how well the candidate engages with the question, the clarity of their written communication, logical presentation and a convincing argument. Details can be found on the University of Cambridge website (www.ba.law.cam.ac.uk/applying/cambridge-law-test).

Case study

After securing three A* grades at A level, Julia accepted a place at the University of Southampton to study LLB Law. She has recently commenced her first year of the course, having deferred her place for a year.

'The academic rigour of studying law was very appealing to me. I find the scope of law fascinating and chose the University of Southampton for its reputation for academic research; it has unique ties with the Institute of Maritime Law and the Stefan Cross Centre for Women, Equality and Law, both of which we have the option to engage with over the duration of the course. Although it is early days for me, I intend to work in the law clinic that the university runs and utilise the marshalling schemes that will give me first-hand exposure to the work of barristers and judges. I am also keen to engage with outreach programmes to educate people on their rights in specific areas.

'As well as having a nice campus, the strength of the contacts at Southampton, as well as its relative proximity to my hometown, ultimately led me to choosing it. I had initially wanted to study at a London university, but decided that the high costs could be a hindrance.

'I want to try and use my summer breaks to get work experience and vacation schemes with big firms or chambers. In order to be considered, I had to study for the LNAT, which was very time consuming, but the wider reading and practice that I did helped to develop my critical thinking skills and my broader knowledge of how law impacts daily life. The LNAT website recommends some books to read and provides plenty of resources – and these worked for me. They also advise against going on LNAT courses and having any formal training, as it really isn't needed.

'Even before the pandemic, I had decided to take a gap year, and had planned to do voluntary work in Calais. I was fortunate enough to spend some time there before commencing my studies, but not being able to travel as planned actually worked out in my favour, as I was able to get a paid job in a law firm as a junior legal assistant in residential conveyancing. My tasks on a day-to-day basis involved maintaining filing systems and taking phonecalls, but I was able to liaise with many people working in the profession and gain a strong insight into what the role of a solicitor entails.

'At this point, I don't know what I want to do in terms of my career after my law degree. There are so many options and I don't yet feel I have seen enough to have made a decision. I intend to get a lot more experience and perhaps even undertake postgraduate study before committing.'

8 | Succeeding at interview

Outside Oxford and Cambridge, formal interviews are rarely part of the admissions process for law degrees. Most universities, even those in the highly respected Russell Group of top universities, do not interview candidates for law degrees at all, other than those with unusual qualifications or mature students. In these cases, the universities interview because they need more information to help them make a decision. One notable exception at the time of writing is the University of York Law School, which does interview applicants – as much of their programme delivery is through problem-based learning, York uses the interview as an opportunity to assess the relevant skills that cannot be demonstrated on the UCAS form. Oxford and Cambridge also interview all applicants. If you are invited to attend an academic interview, this chapter contains some guidance on what to expect at the interview and how you might be able to prepare.

You may also be invited to an interview for work experience at a firm of solicitors or set of barristers' chambers. Much of the advice in this chapter is equally relevant to this situation and the same recommendations also apply. A few additional tips that apply particularly to interviews for work experience are given near the end of the chapter.

Oxbridge and York examples

Guides to interviews, including sample questions and video examples, are available on the websites of Oxbridge and York universities.

- www.ox.ac.uk/admissions/undergraduate/applying-to-oxford/guide/interviews
- www.undergraduate.study.cam.ac.uk/applying/interviews
- www.york.ac.uk/law/undergraduate/interview

What to expect at the interview

The purpose of an interview is to test your:

- motivation to study law
- logical reasoning ability
- effective communication skills.

The university is not seeking to test your prior knowledge of the law.

You are likely to be asked questions on the following:

- why you wish to study law
- why you wish to go to that particular university
- your academic qualifications
- the personal statement in your UCAS form
- some questions on legal issues which are designed to assess your logical reasoning and communication skills.

You will also be asked whether there is anything you would like to ask your interviewer.

Interviews need not be daunting. They are designed to help those asking the questions to find out as much about you as they can. Interviewers are more interested in what you know than in what you do not.

The interview is a chance for you to demonstrate your commitment to and enthusiasm for the law. Interviewers clearly wish to know your reasons for wanting to study law and, possibly above all, they will be looking to see whether you have a mind capable of developing logical arguments and the ability to articulate such arguments powerfully nd coherently. You should view an interview as a chance to put yourself across well rather than as an obstacle course designed to catch you out.

Preparation for a law interview

Once you have been asked to attend an interview, it is sensible to prepare thoroughly. You should take the time to think through your answers to some of the questions you are likely to be asked. You should also be very well informed about the course you are applying for and any current legal issues which you might be asked about. Try to arrange some mock interviews, carried out by a teacher at school, careers advisor, family friend, or anyone else you can persuade to help. These can be very useful. Reeling off pre-prepared answers to questions is obviously not going to impress an interviewer, but thinking in advance about what you are likely to be asked about can help you get your thoughts in order and sound confident and prepared at the interview.

Re-read your personal statement

You are very likely to be asked questions about your personal statement, so read it through well before the interview and make sure you can remember and speak coherently about any books you mentioned having read. If you have followed the advice contained in Chapter 7 of this book, you will not have included anything in your statement that you are not prepared to speak about at interview. Take a copy of the statement with you to the interview and read it through again shortly beforehand.

Why do you want to study law?

This is an obvious question and you should think about your reasons carefully before the interview. Reasons for wishing to study law vary. A passion for television courtroom drama series is not enough. You need to think about the everyday practice of the law in this country and it is very useful to spend time talking with lawyers of all kinds and learning what is involved. You may well be asked whether you have spoken to any lawyers about their work or visited any courts.

In terms of answering the question at interview, it is crucial that you convey a genuine interest in studying law. Often, your response will be in line with your personal statement. There are several possible aspects that you could cover when answering this question.

- An interest in law that has stemmed from a genuine interest in political affairs and the legal system. You might have followed some cases closely that you found particularly interesting, or read a book that piqued your interest. You need to be prepared to provide specifics here, and to answer questions on the things that you mention as evidence to support your answers.
- An event that occurred may have motivated you to pursue a degree or a career in law. This could be witnessing a lawyer represent someone you know, or perhaps even observing a perversion of the course of justice that you want to help overcome. It is important that these narratives are true, as you will need to be able to convey your resulting enthusiasm convincingly and be able to answer any related questions that an interviewer might have.
- It may have been a work experience placement or a conversation with a lawyer that stimulated your interest. You should consider exactly what it was that got your attention – a specific element of the work a lawyer was conducting that you found interesting, or a role that you were allowed to support with that you enjoyed. Lawyers can carry out a wide range of tasks, so reflect carefully on all elements of the job and the kind of environment in which they work.
- You may want to study law for the academic challenge that it represents as opposed to the career prospects. If this is the real motivator, then you should consider the ways in which the course will stretch your capabilities and the skills that it will allow you to develop. Highlight any modules of particular interest, and explain why they interest you.
- The skills that you have may lend themselves well to the study of law, and reflecting on them at this point could strengthen your case. It is important to be modest, though – resist the urge to exaggerate!

It is important to be aware of the many types of law that lawyers practise – criminal, contract, family, taxation, etc. – and be clear about the differences between them. You may be asked what areas of law you are particularly interested in or whether you hope to become a barrister or solicitor (although you would not be expected to have come to any firm decisions at this stage). You should be clear in your mind about the difference between them.

Never talk about how much you expect to earn, or demonstrate any passivity about your decision to study law. Your parents making the suggestion for you to do so, following a family tradition or watching TV shows are unlikely to make a good case for obtaining an offer.

Many interviewers will also expect you to answer a question along the lines of 'Why should we offer you a place?' These questions often arise towards the end of an interview, and therefore provide a useful opportunity for you to summarise the key points that you have covered in your interview, highlighting the reasons why you want to study law, your skills, what you have to offer and reasons for choosing that particular university. It is also worth discussing how you might be able to contribute to other aspects of university life, including extra-curricular activities such as sports and music. It might also be useful to discuss any ways in which you have contributed to your school community, such as organising charity events or participating in clubs and societies.

Make sure you know all about the course and the university

Read through all the information on the university's website relevant to the course you have chosen and also read any brochures or other written information you may have been given at any open day you attended.

A common question early on in an interview is why you chose to apply for that particular university. It is important to look carefully at the information available on the course. If there is a particular element of the course that differs from others, reflect on it. For example, a university may have a very well-established research department if you are interested in academia, while others may have a particular emphasis on work experience and provide good links to assist students in securing placements. Or there might be a specific module on offer, delivered by a specialist in the area, in which you have a particular interest.

The reputation of the department will typically be a determining factor in choosing a university, but it is also worth investigating the approach to teaching. Some of the more academic universities expect a greater degree of independent work, while others offer more support. Some universities deliver sessions using problem-based learning, which can be an excellent way of developing your skills, but it is not suitable for everyone.

necessity of a low-carbon future are prominent themes at present. Concerns about the environment and air quality have intersected with the legal sphere, as seen by the multiple cases brought forward against the government by organisations such as ClientEarth. Some possible aspects to consider include the following.

- The culpability of governments with regard to air quality. You should consider whether or not you believe the government can be held liable.
- Issues associated with green crime and environmental laws and the challenges involved in deciding culpability and accountability.
- Whether the ClientEarth cases set a new legal precedent and what can be done in cases where there is no direct or clear victim.
- Cases brought against those who have protested using direct action, such as the Heathrow 13 or anti-fracking protesters.

The judicial branch in the USA

When appointed as 45th President of the United States, one of the first things that Donald Trump was able to do was appoint a member to the Supreme Court. This is a power that all US Presidents have held, yet their ability to use it depends entirely on a vacancy occurring as a result of either death, retirement or gross misconduct resulting in impeachment as Supreme Court justices are granted tenure for life. The life tenure raises concerns that the court could potentially serve as an echo chamber for presidential views, which could be indicative of the President having too much power.

Given that this differs significantly from the UK judicial system, it is certainly worth researching.

White-collar crime

Another area of interest is crime committed by the wealthy. These crimes are often corporate in nature and the term 'white-collar crime' can be applied.

As with green crimes, white-collar crimes are often difficult to prove as they tend to have no direct victim, and often there is very little delineation between legal and illegal behaviours. Take for instance the concepts of tax avoidance and tax evasion – one of them is completely legal, while the other is not.

There is a great degree of interest about how the wealthy and elite within society move their money, often as a means to avoid taxation. The widespread nature of such practices came to light in the Panama Papers in 2015 and, more recently, in the Paradise Papers in 2017. It is well worth considering the legal implications of both these papers.

While exploring the low conviction rates for white-collar crime, it is worth considering the concerns that exist regarding the disproportionate number of working-class people within the prison population, and

Mentioning aspects such as the local excellent nightlife is not recommended, even if it did influence your decision initially! Law is an incredibly demanding course, and interviewers and admissions officers won't want to hear about potential distractions.

Practise getting the right body language

This is not as obvious as it seems, so a small amount of practice will make all the difference. Use mock interviews to give you some practice of walking into a room, looking your interviewer in the eyes, smiling, saying hello and shaking their hand. The handshake should be firm and confident – but without crushing their fingers. Sit down upright in your seat and do not slouch or lean back too far. You want to look interested and engaged and also relaxed, but not overly casual.

Be informed about current affairs

Reading a quality daily newspaper will keep you up to date with current legal issues and how they are reported in the media. Issues relating to politics, the police, sentencing and prison reform are possible interview topics.

Quality newspapers, such as the *Independent*, *The Times* and the *Guardian* all report on current legal issues and give you insight into important legal cases. You could also read *The Law Society Gazette* or *The Lawyer*, which are published weekly in print format and are also available online. *The Law Society Gazette* contains reviews of current legal issues and matters affecting the legal profession. *The Lawyer* tends to focus more on news and comment about comings and goings in the legal profession (such as mergers between law firms); it also has an online litigation tracker which holds over 9,000 cases with data points including counsel, law firms, judges, clients and sectors that are all fully searchable, which can be incredibly useful when researching current affairs.

Many current issues discussed on radio and television have legal implications. Watching or listening to *Question Time*, *Newsnight* and certain *Panorama*-style documentaries and Radio 4's *Today* programme, *The World This Weekend* and *Today in Parliament* will enable you to develop a thorough knowledge of current affairs. You could also visit the legal websites mentioned in the 'Further information' chapter at the end of the book.

In preparing for an interview, you should consider wider questions such as:

- What do you think should be happening in the prison system at the moment?
- What reforms would you like to see implemented in the running of the police force?

To be confident in presenting your opinions, it is helpful to discuss such issues with friends or family and then practise answering the questions at mock interviews.

In addition to discussing specific cases and legal reforms, it is highly likely that recent political events will form part of the interview. Politics can change rapidly – no one predicted a General Election in 2017, for example – so it is vital that you stay well informed.

Outlined below are themes prominent in the political and legal sphere at the time of writing. Remember, this is just a rough guide as opposed to an exhaustive list – it is up to you to stay abreast of current affairs.

Brexit

The legal implications of the UK's departure from the EU on 31 January 2020 should be closely followed by any prospective lawyer. You may be asked to discuss the impact of Brexit on parliamentary sovereignty and also on the UK's legal system. Aspects to consider include:

- the impact of the UK's decision to leave the EU on parliamentary sovereignty and the power of the judiciary
- the Miller cases (2017 and 2019) and the implications these have for parliamentary sovereignty, governmental authority and the legal landscape.

Not only has Brexit resulted in unprecedented levels of political uncertainty, it has seen legal channels being used to hold the government to account in a way that has arguably shifted public perception of the UK's Supreme Court. Three key cases are explored below.

Cases to consider

R (Miller) v. the Secretary of State for Exiting the European Union (2017) is a legal case where the UK government was taken to court over its handling of Brexit. The premise of the case was that the Cabinet were neglecting the principle of parliamentary sovereignty as they made the decision to trigger Article 50 without a parliamentary vote. As a result of the court case, the UK's Supreme Court ruled there must be a vote within both chambers prior to triggering Article 50.

Cherry and others (Respondents) v. Advocate General for Scotland (Appellant) (Scotland) and R (on the application of Miller) (Appellant) v. The Prime Minister (Respondent) are both cases that attracted a great deal of attention regarding Brexit negotiations. Following Boris Johnson's decision to prorogue (suspend) Parliament, two cases were brought to the Supreme Court, first in Scotland and then in England.

This was due to questions surrounding the legality of John[ ] decision to prorogue Parliament – while prorogation is a ro[ ] event, the issue with this request was that it was for an exte[ ] period of time, which limited the time available to MPs to d[ ] and give their input on EU withdrawal arrangements, as w[ ] preventing decisions being made regarding the way in whic[ ] UK would exit the EU. Many saw the decision to pror[ ] Parliament and prevent MPs from sitting in a crucial period i[ ] run up to the Brexit deadline as a way for Johnson to exit wi[ ] a deal. In addition, many felt that the Prime Minister had m[ ] vised the Queen, but it is important to note that the monarch[ ] not have a discretion, and the system is premised on the [ ] Minister honestly advising the Queen in the country's best inte[ ] As such, there was a huge amount of political opposition surr[ ] ing the decision from both opposing parties and MPs withi[ ] Conservative Party. In Cherry v. Advocate General for Sco[ ] the court found that the Prime Minister had not been acting u[ ] fully in suspending Parliament. Conversely, in R v. The [ ] Minister, it was found that prorogation was unlawful and [ ] Parliament should reconvene immediately. This shows tha[ ] given situation can be open to an element of interpretatic[ ] judges, especially when they are acting in such an unprecede[ ] context.

When reflecting on the above cases, it is important to consi[ ] implications of utilising legal frameworks to hold a governn[ ] account. You should consider the arguments for and against t[ ] sion of the plaintiff to launch the case.

It is also worth considering the media coverage of these case[ ] the 2017 Miller case the tabloid *Daily Mail* dubbed the Suprem[ ] judges that came to the decision 'the enemies of the people'.[ ] some interesting perceptions about the legal profession. Som[ ] potentially view such judges as acting 'ultra vires', or beyon[ ] power. You should consider whether unelected individuals shou[ ] the power to hold a government to account or not.

Although the Brexit date is now well in the past, there still remain[ ] uncertainty about how certain sectors will be affected, with ma[ ] still to be reviewed in Parliament. It is important to keep a close[ ] the news to follow updates as they occur.

Environmentalism

The Paris Accord (2014) established legal expectations re[ ] emissions reductions which all signatories must abide by. With th[ ] fourth carbon budget fast approaching, environmentalism a[ ] the ability of the middle classes to get away with criminal activity. Exploring this area could be augmented through researching the works of the theorists Snider and Chambliss.

Aspects to consider include:

- the administration of fair justice
- the issue of diversity in the legal profession. Since law is the profession with the highest proportion of privately educated individuals, you could consider whether this may cause barriers to other individuals accessing the legal profession, as well as whether this lack of diversity has an impact on conviction rates.

Terrorism and anti-terror legislation

Concerns about the compatibility of the Human Rights Act with anti-terrorism legislation focus on how a major terrorist threat can be used to restrict people's civil rights and liberties. Consider whether you believe that human rights should be suspended or limited in the face of a terrorist threat and how this interacts with the notion of judicial precedents. If contexts are constantly changing, is it better for the judiciary to consider things on a case-by-case basis?

Covid-19

The coronavirus pandemic and subsequent lockdowns has affected practically every sector since the outbreak started in the UK in early 2020. From a legal perspective, devolution in the UK has had a significant impact on the management of Covid-19, as different countries have taken different approaches. The most notable comparison is the slow response in England, which still faces criticism to this day, compared to the more strict approaches put in place in Scotland. The government's response and its overall power in crisis situations has been called into question many times since the outbreak began, and is certainly worth considering in preparation for a law interview. In addition, it is also worth considering the impacts of Covid-19 in different sectors, including hospitality, aviation and retail.

Current affairs

Current affairs are constantly changing, which is why it is so important to stay up to date. Other aspects that are in the media at present include:

- cases pertaining to historic sex abuse (including rape victims having to hand over their mobile phones or risk having their cases dropped)
- prison riots and deaths in custody
- the effectiveness of different methods of administering justice: rehabilitative, retributive, punitive and restorative
- LGBTQ+ rights, parental rights and gender
- No-fault divorce (Owens v. Owens case).

It is recommended that you add to this list as and when new topics present themselves in the news.

In addition to keeping a close eye on current affairs, compile a list of five to ten cases that you can discuss in both your personal statement and at interview. It would be a good idea to group these in themes. For example, the transformative power of the law regarding civil rights would be likely to include cases such as Brown v. Board of Education (1954); whereas cases regarding the rights of African Americans with Affirmative Action cases might include the recent case of Fisher v. University of Texas. Whichever cases you choose, ensure you know the facts and are able to express an informed opinion.

Joint degree subjects

If you have chosen a joint or combined honours course, then obviously you will have to prepare yourself for questions on the other subject you are hoping to study alongside law as well as questions on law.

Questions on legal issues

Knowledge of the structure of the legal and judicial systems is vital. Read Chapter 2 of this book to give you a basic understanding of the legal system. You should know who the Lord Chief Justice is, who the Director of Public Prosecutions is and what he or she does. You should be aware of recent controversial legal decisions, who took them and what their consequences are or could be. Who is the Home Secretary and why is he or she important?

Interviewers will ask questions with a view to being in a position to form an opinion about the quality of your thought and your ability to argue a particular case. You may be presented with a real or supposed set of circumstances and then be asked to comment on the legal implications of them. Is euthanasia wrong? What is the purpose of prison?

At the end of this chapter there are some sample questions, which show the type of legal questions you may be asked. Questions may be straightforward and specific, but can also involve more convoluted scenarios for you to think through. Remember that there are no right or wrong answers – you simply need to show that you can think through the issues in a logical and reasoned way and communicate your arguments and conclusions effectively.

On the day: practicalities and general advice

Arrive early

Make sure you know where you are going and leave plenty of time to get there. Allow for trains and buses to be delayed. Print off a map before you leave home and make sure you take the telephone number of the admissions office so that if, despite your best efforts, you are still late, you can phone and let them know. Remember to re-read your personal statement just before the interview.

Dress carefully

Dress comfortably, but show that you are taking the interview seriously: wear smart, clean clothes. Do not wear anything too revealing. You should also clean your shoes and make sure your hair is neat.

Be calm

Take a few deep breaths before the interview and, if you are nervous, try to calm and relax yourself. Listen to a favourite piece of music or something that you know will make you feel more relaxed. Remember you wouldn't have been invited for interview unless you were a serious candidate for a place, so be confident and let your talents shine through!

Demeanour during the interview

- Be yourself.
- Be enthusiastic and show a strong commitment to your subject.
- Maintain good eye contact with your interviewer(s) and confident body language.
- Listen carefully to the questions you are asked and make sure you understand what you are being asked before you answer. Don't be afraid to ask questions if you are unsure of what the interviewer wants.
- Be concise and logical – put forward your answer and use examples and factual knowledge to reinforce your points.
- If you are asked a question you don't know the answer to, say so. To waffle simply wastes time and lets you down. To lie, of course, is even worse – especially for aspiring lawyers!
- Be willing to consider new ideas, if your interview involves discussion of legal or other current issues. An ability to see the opposite point of view while maintaining your own will mark you out as strong law degree material.
- Show a willingness to learn and be prepared to admit defeat if you put forward an argument that is demolished by your interviewer. A touch of humility will not hurt.

An ability to think on your feet is vital – another prerequisite for a good lawyer. Although you will (hopefully) have thought through answers to some of the questions you are likely to be asked, you do not want to sound as though you are reeling off a pre-learned answer as this will sound false and will not impress anyone.

Much of the practice of law in this country rests on an adversarial system, so don't be surprised if you receive an adversarial interview.

Remember to keep calm and think clearly!

Think of some questions to ask your interviewer(s)

At the end of the interview, you will almost certainly be given the chance to ask if you have any questions. It is sensible to have one or two questions of a serious kind – to do with the course, the tuition and so on – up your sleeve. It is not wise, obviously, to ask them anything that you could and should have found out from the prospectus. If there is nothing, then say that your interview has covered all that you had thought of.

Above all, end on a positive note and remember to smile!

The interview for work experience

Most of the advice in this chapter will equally apply if you are going for an interview for work experience to a firm of solicitors or a set of chambers. However, in addition you should do the following.

- Research the firm/chambers thoroughly before interview. Look at their brochure and website.
- Plan in advance what you think your key selling points are to the employer and make sure you find an opportunity in the interview to get your points across.
- Prepare a few questions about the firm to ask your interviewer at the end. You can demonstrate your preparation here by asking them about something you have read about the firm/chambers recently, if appropriate.
- Dress smartly and appropriately. Lawyers tend to look quite formal, so a suit is probably appropriate in this situation.

Sample interview questions on legal issues

Here are a few sample legal questions which show the type of thing you may be asked.

1. Should cannabis be legalised?
2. What are the pros and cons of fusing the two branches of the legal profession?
3. Should the police in this country be armed?
4. If you were in a position of power, would you change the current civil legal aid situation?
5. Should the police spend their time enforcing the laws concerned with begging?

6. What do you think of recent law reforms?
7. What are your views on the right to silence?
8. How can you quantify compensation for victims of crime?
9. Should criminals be allowed to sell their stories as 'exclusives'?
10. How does the law affect your daily life?
11. What would happen if there were no law?
12. Is it necessary for the law to be entrenched in archaic tradition, ritual and jargon?
13. How are law and morality related?
14. Do you believe that all people have equal access to justice?
15. What is justice?
16. Why do we send criminals to prison? What are the alternatives?
17. Should the media be more careful with the way in which they report real crime?
18. Do you think the press should be allowed to report the names of celebrities when unproven allegations of sexual abuse have been made against them?
19. Is law the best way to handle situations such as domestic violence/child abuse/rape?
20. What causes crime rates to increase?
21. Is trial by jury a good idea? Should anyone be allowed to serve on a jury?
22. Do you think capital punishment should be reinstated?
23. Should the law permit suspected terrorists to be held indefinitely without trial?
24. If shoplifting were punishable by death, and therefore nobody did it, would that be a just and effective law?
25. You are driving along a busy road with the window down when a swarm of bees flies into your car. You panic and lose control of the car, causing a huge pile-up. Are you legally responsible?
26. A blind person, travelling by train, gets out at his/her destination. Unfortunately the platform is shorter than the train, and the blind person falls to the ground, sustaining several injuries. Who, if anyone, should compensate him/her?
27. A cyclist rides the wrong way down a one-way street and a chimney falls on him. What legal proceedings should he take? What if he is riding down a private drive signed 'no trespassing'?

9| Non-standard applications

Not all of those who become lawyers decide on that career at an early age. Many successful lawyers are people who started out on a completely different career path. Equally, a number of successful lawyers in the UK come from overseas. Law firms and chambers welcome applicants from a wide range of backgrounds, and often have diversity initiatives in place. This chapter offers a brief overview of non-standard applications. For more information, please check with individual universities or the professional representative bodies for solicitors and barristers – i.e. the Law Societies of England and Wales, Scotland and Northern Ireland or, for aspiring barristers, the Bar Council of England and Wales, the Faculty of Advocates in Scotland or the Bar of Northern Ireland. Website addresses for all these institutions are given in Chapter 12.

Graduates with degrees other than law

Many lawyers, particularly in England and Wales, have obtained a degree in a subject other than law. As is explained more fully in the relevant sections of Chapter 4, this simply necessitates taking a further postgraduate qualification in law in order to cover the material that would usually be studied during a law degree. This qualification is the GDL in England and Wales, a two-year accelerated law degree in Scotland and a Master's in Law in Northern Ireland. The additional qualification is taken before moving on to the vocational stage of training. Please see the relevant sections of Chapter 4 for more information. Many employers positively welcome applications from non-law graduates, with the different range of skills that they bring. There are, however, financial implications as the additional years of study will need to be funded.

Mature students

Many law firms and sets of chambers positively welcome new recruits who are embarking on law as a second career. Experience or knowledge of particular business or industry sectors which form a law firm's client base can be especially welcomed. For example, former medical practitioners have the knowledge and experience to become excellent medical negligence lawyers. Many lawyers have not gone straight from school and university to the legal profession.

The possible routes for mature students to enter the legal profession depend on their level of academic qualifications.

Mature students who have a degree in a subject other than law are in the same position as other non-law graduates and are eligible to take the SQE, or its equivalent outside England and Wales.

Mature students who do not have a degree can, if they can satisfy the entry requirements (i.e. they have A level or equivalent qualifications), contact the SRA to determine whether they would be eligible to take the SQE. While there is no specific requirements to have a law degree, it would be a good idea to undertake some formal study in law in preparation for qualifying, as a thorough understanding will be required to pass the SQE.

Mature students without A levels (or equivalent qualifications) would need to take an Access to Higher Education course at a local further education college before applying to university. Each year around 20,000 Access to HE students apply for a degree course at a UK university to study subjects including law. In Scotland, a different system, called the Scottish Wider Access Programme, operates and Northern Irish universities have their own arrangements for access courses. More details are available at www.accesstohe.ac.uk.

Some universities offer law degrees with a Foundation year. These courses are designed to allow prospective lawyers without formal qualifications to gain access onto the course. The requirements for entry vary between universities, but applications tend to be considered from those who have completed the Access to Higher Education course, mature learners with no formal qualifications and young learners who have not undertaken post-16 qualifications. A list of providers and their entry requirements can be found on the UCAS website.

Alternatively, there are non-graduate routes to becoming a lawyer (see Chapter 4). For example, the solicitors' profession in England and Wales offers a unified route with the roll-out of the SQE. Non-graduate routes to qualifying are also available in Scotland (see page 66) and Northern Ireland (see page 70).

Overseas students

Overseas students who already have a degree in their own country may apply to either the Solicitors Regulation Authority (for aspiring solicitors) or the Bar Standards Board (for barristers) for a certificate of academic standing, which will then allow them to take the SQE in England and Wales, possibly following a period of postgraduate legal training or taking a standalone SQE preparation course, in the same way as non-law graduates (see above).

Solicitors who have trained in a different country and wish to practise in England or Wales will need to undertake the SQE, which replaces the Qualified Lawyers Transfer Scheme (QLTS).

Alternatively, overseas students might wish to start their training to become a UK lawyer by applying to study for their degree at a UK university. If you are in this situation, then the advice and guidance contained in Chapters 6 and 7 applies equally to you. However, the statistics show that overseas students are a lot less successful than UK students in gaining places at UK universities to read law, as the Law Society's figures for 2019 entry show:

Applicants' nationality	Number of applicants	Places	% Success
UK	27,950	19,820	71%
Overseas	9,130	4,755	52%

Table 6: Nationality and success rate for university law degree courses

This section therefore includes particular advice for overseas applicants on applying to a UK university to read law.

The process of applying as an international student is similar to that used by UK students: you use the same online UCAS form, provide the same information, and have the same deadlines. The differences are likely to be these:

- the examinations you have taken and/or will be taking may not appear in the drop-down menus on the UCAS form
- the fee codes and support arrangements will be different
- your school may not have registered with UCAS and so you may have to apply as a private individual rather than through an institution.

Detailed advice about how to fill in the UCAS form, and to deal with these issues, can be found in the 'Apply' section of the UCAS website (www.ucas.com). This section of the UCAS website contains special advice for international students for each section of the UCAS form. There is also a summary of tips for international students (www. ucas.com/undergraduate/applying-university/ucas-undergraduate-international-and-eu-students).

However, many well-qualified, serious and motivated international students are unsuccessful in their applications because they or their referees (or both) are unfamiliar with what the university selectors are looking for in two particular sections of the application form:

1. the personal statement
2. the reference.

The personal statement

Students who have applied for universities outside of the UK may be familiar with the idea of writing a statement about themselves to support their applications. These can often take the form of a 'hard sell', in which the student extols his or her personal qualities, achievements, hopes and dreams. This format is not suitable for a UCAS personal statement, which needs to focus on the course itself, and what the student has done to investigate it. The advice given in Chapter 7 is equally applicable to international students, and you should read it carefully. The UCAS website also recommends that you should specifically mention in your personal statement why you want to study in the UK, your English language skills (and any tests or courses you have taken) and why you do not want to study in your own country.

The reference

Often, a promising application is rejected because the person providing the reference is unfamiliar with what is required, and the selectors have no choice other than to reject because they are not given enough information. UCAS references need to focus on the following:

- the student's suitability for the course and level of study
- an assessment of the student's academic performance to date (including the student's level of English if this is not his or her first language)
- how the student will adapt to studying in the UK
- the student's personal qualities.

If you are unsure as to whether the person who will write your reference fully understands what is required, show them the section on the UCAS website called 'How to write UCAS undergraduate references': www.ucas.com/advisers/references/how-write-ucas-undergraduate-references.

LNAT

Some universities require candidates to sit the Law National Admissions Test (LNAT) in addition to gaining academic qualifications. This online test can be sat outside of the UK. See Chapter 7, pages 119–21 for more details.

Academic qualifications

The UCAS website (www.ucas.com) gives details of the acceptable non-UK qualifications. The international sections on individual university websites will provide further details. International students whose local qualifications are not acceptable to UK universities will need to study A levels or the equivalent either at an international school in their own country or at a school or college in the UK, or possibly follow a one-year university Foundation course. Details of providers of UK qualifications can be found on the British Council website (www.educationuk.org/global/articles/further-education-institutions).

Case study

Cameron grew up and studied in Perth, Western Australia. He is currently studying for his QLTS in order to transfer his qualifications and be admitted as a solicitor in England and Wales.

'Out of high school, I wasn't clear on the career I wanted to pursue, and was drawn to the various legal and non-legal options that a law degree can offer. I was also drawn to learning about writing and drafting, government and politics and how businesses operate generally.

'Out of university, I was interested more in the commercial side of things, and worked in logistics and procurement. It took some time before I decided to pursue a career in law, and to complete practical legal studies in order to be admitted as a solicitor in Western Australia. A few years ago, I moved from Australia to the UK, and have been working as an in-house legal advisor since arriving. I am now studying for the QLTS in order to transfer my qualifications and be admitted as a solicitor in England and Wales.

'My current role involves working closely with business stakeholders to negotiate client and supplier contracts, as well as reviewing and implementing internal policies and procedures to ensure regulatory and procedural compliance. In addition, my role also involves protecting the business from risk.

'To be successful in law, it is really important to identify the areas that you find most interesting. Getting involved is the best way of moving forward in that field as gaining hands-on experience will allow you to develop your knowledge of the area and to gain practical skills at the same time.'

10 | Results day

A level results day is arguably one of the most important days of your life, but don't panic: this chapter will provide you with some calm and practical advice on what to do on the day, whatever your results are.

The A level results will arrive at your school on the third Thursday in August. The universities will have received them a few days earlier. It is much better for you to go into school in person on the day the results are published, so do not arrange to be away on holiday then. Do not wait for the results slip to be posted to you. Try to get hold of your results as soon as possible on the day – if you need to act to secure your place or go through Clearing, then time is of the essence as you will be competing with other students in the same situation.

If you live overseas and are unable to go into school, make sure that you get hold of your results in some other way as soon as possible on results day.

Hopefully, you will need to do nothing other than celebrate! If you have a conditional offer and your grades equal or exceed that offer, then you can relax and wait for your chosen university to send you joining instructions. To check that all is in order, you can log on to the 'Track' facility on the UCAS website to make sure that your place has been confirmed.

> **Caution!**
>
> You cannot assume that equivalent grades such as A*AB will satisfy an AAA offer. Always check with your chosen university.

If your results are not as good as you had expected, or better than you expected, or you did not receive an offer from any of your chosen universities, then there are a number of options.

What to do if your grades are significantly better than anticipated

You may have significantly beaten the terms of your firm offer and now think that you might like to go somewhere 'better'. UCAS now uses a scheme called Adjustment, which is aimed at applicants who achieved better grades than predicted. It is primarily designed for students who might have been predicted low grades and therefore applied to universities that would accept them rather than those where they would really like to study. The Adjustment system allows you to put your existing firm offer on hold for a short period of time (five days) while contacting other universities where the standard offers are higher to see whether they will offer you a place with your higher grades. If you do not secure a new offer within this time period, or if you do not like what else is available, your original firm offer still stands and can still be accepted. Full details can be found on the UCAS website.

Alternatively, you may choose to withdraw from UCAS and reapply the following year with your higher grades.

What to do if you hold an offer but miss the grades

If you have only narrowly missed the required grades (either for your 'firm' or 'insurance' choice), it is important that you contact the university as soon as possible on results day, because you may be able to persuade the university to consider you.

If you miss the grades for your firm choice, but meet the grades for your insurance choice, you will automatically be accepted onto the insurance place. You can still contact your first-choice institution, or an alternative, preferred institution, to see whether or not they have spaces and may be able to accept you. A lot changes on results day, and those that are offered places may decline or defer them, meaning that though the likelihood of receiving your first-choice place is slim, it is worth a try. You will have the option to release yourself into Clearing on results day via UCAS Track if your preferred university is able to make you an offer that you are unable to take up due to being bound by the insurance offer.

If you do not achieve the grades required for either your firm or insurance choice, and you are unable to persuade either university still to accept you, then you are eligible to enter Clearing. This is a list of places that are still available on various courses at all of the universities. The list is published on the UCAS website. Places on law degrees available through Clearing will be few and far between, but if there is a place available at a university you would be interested in going to, then you must contact the university by telephone as quickly as possible on results day, because you will be competing with other students in the same position. Clearing is a stressful system, but it is important to contact universities that you would consider studying at in a logical and calm manner. You can acquire a number of verbal offers which will later appear on your UCAS page, which gives you some time to consider your options. You must make your decision carefully and in a measured way despite the time pressure. There is no point in accepting a place at a university where you do not realistically want to study.

In reality, due to the popularity of law as a degree, you should not pin your hopes on obtaining an offer of a place through Clearing. You may find that despite your best efforts, there simply are not any places available on law courses at universities where you would want to study. If you are unable to obtain a suitable place through Clearing, your best option would be to withdraw from UCAS altogether and then wait and reapply in the next academic year to courses for which you meet the entry requirements, with the benefit of your A level results to support your application. Given what has been said about the importance of choosing your university law course in Chapter 6, you do not want to settle for any university just because it has a place available, but hold out for a place at a university you are actually really enthusiastic about attending. In the meantime, you can use the time constructively by getting some work experience to build up your CV. You may also want to consider retaking some or all of your A levels in order to improve your chances of getting into a university you are really interested in going to.

What to do if you have no offer

If you did not receive any offers, you may have managed to find an offer through UCAS Extra. This scheme allows you to apply to other universities, either for law or for other courses. You will automatically be sent details by UCAS. UCAS Extra starts at the end of February and usually ends in July. If UCAS Extra does not provide you with an offer, you can enter Clearing in August once you have your results.

However, if you did not receive any offers when you applied, perhaps because your predicted results were not particularly strong, but you have ended up with better A level results than expected, then you need to make universities aware of this. Try to get in touch with them as early as possible on results day to see if they will reconsider their decision in the light of your results. The best way to do this is by telephone and email, and your UCAS referee may be able to help you in this respect. Try to persuade your referee to ring the admissions officers on your behalf – they will find it easier to get through than you will – or to email universities a note in support of your application; while many universities will not talk to your referee on your behalf on the day, this support can be recognised by universities in some circumstances.

Retaking your A levels

This may be a sensible option for students who know they are capable of achieving better grades than they did first time round. However, you should be aware that the grade requirements for retake candidates are often higher than for first-timers. You should investigate the particular universities you are interested in to find out what they require from retake students, as this due diligence will undoubtedly pay off. While there are some universities that rarely consider retake applications (except in the case of mitigating circumstances), many universities welcome applications from students who are so driven to study at their university that they are retaking their A levels to do so.

Extenuating circumstances

If your grades were below those that were predicted or expected because of extenuating circumstances, such as illness or family problems during exam time, make sure that you have written confirmation of this (such as a letter from a doctor, solicitor or someone at your school or college) and send this to the admissions department for your chosen course, as well as asking the exams officer at your school to pass this information on to the examining boards. The extenuating circumstances should be serious enough to merit special consideration and not just minor irritations.

Ideally, if something does go wrong at the time you are sitting your exams, you or your school/college should inform the universities immediately, warning them that you might not achieve the grades. It is more likely that they can make concessions then rather than when they have already made decisions about who to accept when the results are issued. For extenuating circumstances to be considered, universities often expect evidence to have been submitted to the relevant exam board for the affected exam.

If you are retaking your A levels or reapplying to university because of extenuating circumstances, it is good practice to email the admissions department outlining your academic profile and the circumstances that prevented you from securing the grades that you required, asking them whether they would be happy to consider your application. Generally, universities are transparent with their answer, and this is extremely useful when selecting which universities to put down on your UCAS form.

Case study

Initially, Jade was unsure about what to pursue as a career. She ultimately decided that law would be the best fit after completing an extremely worthwhile work experience placement.

'I chose to study law once I realised I wanted to become a solicitor, which was confirmed after my work experience in a law firm. I also knew that law was a degree that a number of different avenues could flow from due to the many different transferable skills it teaches, and this was appealing to me.

'At A level I studied Biology, Chemistry and Religious Studies. I originally applied to do dentistry, which I missed out on the grades for. During my year of resits, I decided I no longer wanted to do dentistry and instead applied to do psychology. After one semester, I quickly realised that psychology was not the right fit for me and I decided to look to law as it had always been a field I'd been interested in but had never pursued.

'I undertook three weeks' work experience at a local law firm who specialised in criminal, property and family law. I was able to attend the Magistrates' Court alongside a criminal lawyer and watch a number of various cases, mostly involving driving offences, which allowed me a brief insight into the court system. In addition, I was able to read criminal case files and I had the opportunity to discuss these cases with senior solicitors, which was really interesting and enabled me to see the ethical dilemmas some criminal lawyers face and how they deal with it. The majority of the work I carried out at the law firm was in the conveyancing department, and I was fortunate enough to be offered a job as a legal assistant in this department prior to starting my degree. During this time, I gained a lot of experience writing letters to clients and emails to other solicitor's firms, as well as answering client phone calls. I also learnt how to draft contracts involving the sale and purchases of property, as well as organising files for property transactions. My work experience really gave me an insight into the workings of a local law firm and how the life of a solicitor plays out in reality. The experience I had here assured me that law was definitely what I wanted to study.

'Overall, my experience of studying law so far has been a positive one. My first year was during the pandemic, which meant that all learning was online. This was quite daunting as the only interaction I had with my peers and the law school faculty was through Zoom. However, being back on campus for second year is great. Studying law involves a lot of reading, a common preconception that is actually true. Once you get to grips for what you are looking for within a case and key concepts, this becomes much easier. At first, I found that I was spending hours combing through information but with practice this has become something I find interesting and actually enjoy.

'The modules studied are fairly diverse, and alongside studying the better-known modules of criminal law, land law, etc., we study modules such as Law in Action and Decolonising Legal Concepts; these give us free rein to research a topic and are thought provoking. Our week is composed of about 10 hours of lectures plus seminars; lectures allow us to have a briefer explanation of legal concepts, whereas seminars are where an in-depth discussion of these topics occurs and where you get a chance to speak with peers and your seminar leader so that a better understanding forms. The exams and assignments so far have been essay- or problem question-based. Problem questions have become my favourite form of exam – you are given scenarios and get the opportunity to put on a "lawyer hat" and advise the parties in the scenario by applying the concepts we have learnt in that particular module.

'The heavy workload is something that was first hard to get to grips with, and you will end up spending most of your time independently studying. It is the work that is done outside of lectures that counts, which includes preparing for seminars, reading cases, working through assignments. This is manageable, but it can take a number of weeks to get used to a routine and structure.

'Making sure you are organised is a big tip for anyone studying law, as with a routine you can still get everything done and have down time as well. I usually study from 9am–5pm, and then I have the rest of the day to enjoy university life. Getting involved with extra-curricular activities is also important, universities often have pro-bono groups or law societies you can join, and this is really important when it comes to applying for vacation schemes. It is good to start interacting early with any extracurricular activities your law school may offer. A good aspect of the course at my university is a scheme run for students that provides talks around future plans post-graduation. Actually doing the reading that is set, whether that be legal journal articles, cases, textbooks, etc., is critical, because this is what amplifies your knowledge and enables higher grades. Maybe before starting Law School read a case or a legal journal to get a feel of the type of thing you'll be expected to read. Keeping up to date with happenings in the legal field will also help to build up legal awareness, and I recommend *Legal Cheek* as a good, easy read for potential law students.

'An important thing for me when picking a course was that I wanted to be learning something I not only found interesting but would also be able to use in future life. This is something I really feel you get from studying law. In 10 years' time, I hope to be a solicitor working in commercial law.'

Students with disabilities and special educational needs

For the most part, universities are able to accommodate students with a wide range of disabilities and special educational needs. As such, they are encouraged to apply to study law. On the UCAS form, there is a section that allows students to disclose such information, and it is recommended that a full description of the disabilities or special educational needs are provided, as well as the support required. All institutions are committed to supporting students with such considerations, but it is always worth contacting each institution and, where possible, the specific department, to determine how much support they will be able to offer. Most institutions will have a dedicated team of equality and diversity advisors employed solely to provide guidance and support.

When you receive an offer from a university, they should follow up with you directly regarding the disabilities outlined on your UCAS form. It is vital that you ensure there is complete transparency at this stage, as a lack of coherence or failure to reveal a full picture may result in complications in securing appropriate accommodation and could even result in withdrawal from the course.

It is also worth considering how accessible a career in law is for someone with a disability. The Equality Act (2010) has ensured that workplaces put the appropriate measures in place, as much as possible, to allow disabled people to thrive in the workplace. In theory, there is no barrier to working as a lawyer with a physical disability, though it is evident that not all workplaces will be suitable. Large solicitors' firms, for example, are likely to comprise appropriate disability measures such as lifts and adapted entrances and exits, whereas smaller firms may not have the means to adjust.

Students with special educational needs who require support in the form of additional time in exams, for example, will need to provide the appropriate supporting documentation. As long as this can be provided, there should be no issues in securing these arrangements.

11 | Fees and funding

Seeking to qualify as a lawyer is expensive: first you have to fund a university degree and then you need to fund the SQE (possibly preceded by a postgraduate qualification in law, such as the GDL in England and Wales, if your degree was not in law). This chapter looks at the fees for the university degree stage of qualification and how those fees are funded. The fees and funding arrangements for postgraduate studies in law and the vocational stage of training depend on whether you wish to qualify as a solicitor or barrister, the qualification route you choose, and the jurisdiction within which you live. The fees and funding arrangements for these courses are therefore discussed in Chapter 4 under the relevant headings for the different qualifications. This chapter briefly outlines the current fee structure for UK universities and the way in which the governments of the constituent countries of the UK help students fund their university studies. More information can be found at www.gov.uk/student-finance.

UK students

Universities in the UK can charge students up to £9,250 a year in tuition fees, and most of the higher-ranked universities in England charge the maximum amount. Private colleges and universities are not subject to the £9,250 maximum, so can charge more. In most cases, these fees are not actually charged directly to students as the vast majority of students take out a student loan, which is repayable only after graduation and only once certain salary thresholds are reached (see below). There are different fee structures and different types and levels of financial assistance available, depending on which part of the UK you are from and where you choose to study. These are briefly summarised below, but you should check the websites of individual universities for specific fees and visit the recommended government websites below for more information about student finance.

English residents

English students will pay tuition fees of up to £9,250 wherever they study in the UK for the 2021/22 academic year, and though this has been frozen for several years, it could increase with inflation for the

2022/2023 cycle. A tuition fee loan is available to cover these fees in their entirety, and can be accessed through Student Finance for UK students.

Maintenance loans are available to cover your living expenses while you are at university. The amount of maintenance loan is income-assessed. The guaranteed portion of the loan (which is less than half) is available to all students, but those from lower-income households are able to borrow higher amounts on a sliding scale up to the maximum loan available (which is £7,987 for students living at home, £9,488 for those studying outside London and £12,382 for those studying in London for 2021/2022).

The tuition fee loan and the maintenance loan are repayable via the income tax system only after you have graduated and only if and when you are earning more than £27,295. Once your income exceeds this value, you will pay 9% of anything that you earn above £27,295. The repayments are a fixed part of your income and therefore depend on your future earnings and not on the size of your loan. All remaining debt is wiped after 30 years if it has not been fully repaid by then.

Student loan applications are made through the government's Student Finance website: www.gov.uk/apply-online-for-student-finance. You apply for student finance for the 2022/2023 academic year in 2022. The deadline for applying is nine months after the start of the academic year.

Welsh residents

Welsh students will also be charged up to £9,250 wherever they study in the UK. The Welsh government offers means-tested maintenance grants which will only be paid to families with a combined household income of below £59,200. These students will receive up to £11,920 per year if they are studying in London, and £9,350 a year for the rest of the UK. Irrespective of household income, all students will receive a minimum grant of £1,000.

The Welsh government also runs a partial cancellation scheme, whereby upon their first repayment students get up to £1,500 towards reducing their maintenance loan.

For more information on fees and student finance available in Wales visit www.studentfinancewales.co.uk.

Northern Ireland residents

Northern Irish students will pay up to £9,250 per year tuition fees if they study in England, Wales or Scotland, but will pay a reduced fee (£4,530 for 2021 starters) if they study in Northern Ireland. For more information on fees and student finance available in Northern Ireland visit www.studentfinanceni.co.uk.

Scottish residents

Scottish students will not pay any tuition fees if they go to a Scottish university, but they will pay up to £9,250 if they study anywhere else in the UK. The rules for help with funding living expenses differ from those in England and there are some living-costs grants available for students from lower-income households. For more information on fees and student finance available in Scotland visit the website of the Student Awards Agency Scotland: www.saas.gov.uk.

EU and non-EU international students

In an announcement in June 2020, the Universities Minister in England stated that, from August 2021, EU, other EEA and Swiss nationals will no longer qualify for home fee status for degree-level study, and they will no longer be able to access financial support from Student Finance England. Instead, universities will set their own fees for EU students, with many of these being in line with the fees for non-EU international students. The respective governments in Northern Ireland, Scotland and Wales later confirmed that the same changes to EU fee status would be applied as in England from 2021.

The fees for international students do not have an upper limit, and will depend on the course and the university. International students should contact individual universities for information on the fees they will be charging non-EU students. For more information visit the website of the UK Council for International Student Affairs, which also has advice on student visa applications (www.ukcisa.org.uk).

Bursaries and scholarships

UK universities now offer a wide range of bursaries and scholarships to support some of their students. In order to charge the maximum permitted tuition fees of £9,250, universities must prove that they are awarding bursaries to poorer students. These are contributions towards the cost of going to university that do not have to be repaid. The terms of these will vary between the universities and you should check the universities' websites carefully to see whether you may be able to apply for any financial help. Usually, bursaries are completely dependent on your household income, whereas scholarships are at least partly dependent on academic or extra-curricular (e.g. sporting) ability.

The Law Society details a number of opportunities available for funding your studies, which can be accessed via their website (www.lawsociety. org.uk/career-advice/becoming-a-solicitor/funding-and-support-during-your-studies-internships-scholarships-and-sponsors).

Funding the SQE

From 2021, the SQE was introduced as a new pathway of qualifying to become a solicitor. SQE1 costs £1,558 and SQE2 costs £2,422 (totalling £3,980). At present, there are no funding options for the SQE itself or for standalone SQE preparation courses, though the Law Society is working to establish a source of funding for those who need it.

Funding the GDL, LPC and BPTC

Though the qualification route for solicitors and barristers in England and Wales is changing, here are existing funding options available for these pathways, which are set out below.

GDL

The GDL is an expensive but unavoidable way of qualifying as a lawyer for graduates without QLDs before the complete introduction of the SQE. Unfortunately, postgraduate funding is not an option for covering GDL fees, but there are a number of ways of obtaining financial support. Often, GDL students will need to combine a number of sources of funding to pay the fees and support themselves for the duration. Some providers recognise the cost implications and now offer part-time courses and instalment payment plans, so research the stance of the provider on this when applying.

Perhaps the most obvious way to secure funding is to determine whether the GDL provider offers any scholarships or bursaries. You need to be on the ball with these, as they tend to be competitive with early deadlines. Many law firms will offer to cover the fees of the GDL if a training contract is secured early, with some even providing a maintenance grant to support with living costs. Some will even pay retrospectively if a training contract is secured mid-GDL, but the stance of law firms doing so is highly variable, so research carefully and check with them directly. The Law Society also offers a bursary scheme and these are awarded on the applicant's merit.

Graduate loans are also available through high street banks. These are not always ideal as repayments often start immediately, so be sure to exhaust all other options first.

LPC

As with the GDL, the LPC is a costly but crucial element of qualifying as a solicitor. Many of the funding options are the same as with the GDL, with the option of part-time study being popular as it allows students to work part-time, too. Scholarships and bursaries will be available from course providers and the Law Society, including the DAS scheme (as outlined in Chapter 4), and law firms will often fund your training once you have secured a training contract. In addition, studying the LPC qualifies for a Professional Career and Development Loan of up to £10,000, with repayments beginning one month after completion.

Though Student Finance Postgraduate Loans do not cover a standard LPC, the University of Law has now started offering master's degrees in law with integrated LPCs, thereby qualifying the training for this source of funding. This will mean that your fees are covered, and you will complete both the LPC and a master's degree simultaneously, so it is certainly worth consideration!

BPTC

Scholarships for the BPTC can be accessed through the Inns of Court, and these are the most significant sources of funding for this particular stage of training. Some chambers offer pupillage awards if a pupillage is secured prior to the commencement of the BPTC, but this is quite rare. The BPTC can also be funded using a Professional Career and Development Loan, though it is recommended that all scholarship options be researched first.

12| Further information

Useful websites

Legal professions

Solicitors
- The Law Society (of England and Wales): www.lawsociety.org.uk; www.lawsociety.org.uk/en/topics/research/annual-statistics-report-2019
- The Law Society of Northern Ireland: www.lawsoc-ni.org
- The Law Society of Scotland: www.lawscot.org.uk
- Solicitors Regulation Authority: www.sra.org.uk

Barristers
- The Bar Council of England and Wales: www.barcouncil.org.uk
- The Bar Standards Board: www.barstandardsboard.org.uk; www.barstandardsboard.org.uk/news-publications/research-and-statistics/statistics-about-the-bar.html
- The Faculty of Advocates in Scotland: www.advocates.org.uk
- Gray's Inn: www.graysinn.org.uk
- The Inner Temple: www.innertemple.org.uk
- Lincoln's Inn: www.lincolnsinn.org.uk
- The Middle Temple: www.middletemple.org.uk
- Northern Ireland Bar: www.barofni.com

Other legal professions
- Law costs draftsmen: www.associationofcostslawyers.co.uk
- Legal executives: www.cilex.org.uk
- Legal secretaries: www.institutelegalsecretaries.com
- Licensed conveyancers: www.clc-uk.org
- Notaries: www.thenotariessociety.org.uk
- Paralegals: www.theiop.org
- Patent attorneys: www.cipa.org.uk
- Trademark attorneys: www.citma.org.uk/home

Legal profession: directories

- Chambers UK and Chambers UK Bar Guide: www.chambersandpartners.com; Chambers publishes comprehensive online directories, containing ranking tables and commentary, of firms of solicitors and barristers' chambers. They are also published annually in print format.
- Legal 500: www.legal500.com; an in-depth survey of the UK legal profession, also published annually in print format.
- TARGETjobs: https://targetjobs.co.uk/careers-products; TARGETjobs publishes online graduate careers guides and directories for various professions including law:
  - TARGETjobs: Law
  - TARGETjobs: Law vacation schemes & Mini pupillages
  - TARGETjobs: Law Pupillages Handbook.
- Law firm gossip: www.rollonfriday.com

Legal systems

- Ministry of Justice: www.justice.gov.uk
- Northern Ireland:
  - www.niassembly.gov.uk
  - www.gov.uk/guidance/devolution-settlement-northern-ireland
  - www.nidirect.gov.uk/information-and-services/crime-justice-and-law
- Scotland: www.scotcourts.gov.uk/about-the-scottish-court-service
- Wales: www.assemblywales.org

Other legal organisations

- Crown Prosecution Service: www.cps.gov.uk
- Legal Action Group: www.lag.org.uk

Education and training

A levels

- Access to Higher Education courses: www.accesstohe.ac.uk
- Russell Group: www.russellgroup.ac.uk
- UK qualification providers overseas: https://study-uk.britishcouncil.org

University applications

- LNAT: www.lnat.ac.uk
- UCAS: www.ucas.com
- UCAS Parent Guide (information about the UCAS undergraduate application process): www.ucas.com/undergraduate/applying-university/ucas-undergraduate-advice-parents-and-guardians
- UCAS reference: www.ucas.com/advisers/references

- University guides:
    www.thecompleteuniversityguide.co.uk
    www.theguardian.com/education/ng-interactive/2021/
    sep/11/the-best-uk-universities-2022-rankings
- University of Cambridge law: www.law.cam.ac.uk
- University open days: www.opendays.com

Law interviews
- Cambridge: www.undergraduate.study.cam.ac.uk/applying/
  interviews
- Oxford:
    www.ox.ac.uk/admissions/undergraduate/applying-to-oxford/
    guide/interviews/interview-timetable
    www.ox.ac.uk/admissions/undergraduate/applying-to-oxford/
    guide/interviews
- York: www.york.ac.uk/law/undergraduate/interview

Fees and funding
- England: www.gov.uk/student-finance
- Northern Ireland: www.studentfinanceni.co.uk
- Overseas students: www.ukcisa.org.uk
- Scotland: www.saas.gov.uk
- Wales: www.studentfinancewales.co.uk

Vocational training
- Bar Course Aptitude Test (BCAT): www.barstandardsboard.org.uk/
  training-qualification/bar-qualification-manual/part-2-for-students-
  pupils--transferring-lawyers/b3-the-bar-course-aptitude-test-bcat.
  html
- Bar Standards Board (Becoming a barrister): www.barstandards-
  board.org.uk/training-qualification/becoming-a-barrister.html
- Bar Student Application Service (for BPTC): www.barsas.com
- Central Applications Board (for GDL and LPC): www.lawcabs.ac.uk
- GDL course providers: www.sra.org.uk/become-solicitor/courses/
  cpe-gdl-course-providers
- Pupillage Gateway: www.pupillagegateway.com

SQE
- Law Society – Solicitors Qualifying Exam (SQE): www.lawsociety.
  org.uk/career-advice/becoming-a-solicitor/solicitors-qualifying-
  examination-sqe
- Solicitors' Regulation Authority – Solicitors Qualifying Examination
  (SQE) route: www.sra.org.uk/become-solicitor/sqe

Funding training
- Career development loans: www.gov.uk/career-development-
  loans/overview

- Diversity Access Scheme: www.lawsociety.org.uk/campaigns/diversity-access-scheme
- Postgraduate loans: www.gov.uk/postgraduate-loan
- Sponsorship: TARGET jobs: https://targetjobs.co.uk/careers-advice/law/which-law-firms-will-fund-your-lpc-and-gdl-course-fees-and-pay

Careers

- www.lawcareers.net
- www.simplylawjobs.com

Law reports

- www.bailii.org

Useful books

University entrance

Getting into Oxford & Cambridge 2023 Entry, Trotman Education, 2022.
HEAP 2023: University Degree Course Offers, Brian Heap, Trotman Education, 2022.
How to Complete Your UCAS Application 2023 Entry, Ray Le Tarouilly, Trotman Education, 2022.
How to Write a Winning Personal Statement, Ian Stannard, Trotman Education, 2016.
The Times Good University Guide 2022, Times Books, 2021.
The University Choice Journal, Barbara Bassot, Trotman Education, 2017.
University Interviews, Ian Stannard and Godfrey Cooper, Trotman Education, 2017.

LNAT

Mastering the National Admissions Test for Law, M Shepherd, Routledge, 2013.
Passing the LNAT, R Hutton and G Hutton, Learning Matters, 2011.

Studying law

Glanville Williams: Learning the Law, A T H Smith, Sweet & Maxwell, 2010. (This book, first published in 1945, is a very popular introductory book containing lots of useful information on studying law.)
Is Eating People Wrong? Great Legal Cases and How They Shaped the World, A Hutchinson, Cambridge University Press, 2010.

Learning Legal Rules: A Students' Guide to Legal Method and Reasoning, 8th edition, J A Holland and J S Webb, OUP, 2013.
Letters to a Law Student: A Guide to Studying Law at University, Nicholas J McBride, Pearson, 2013.
What about Law? Studying Law at University, 2nd edition, C Barnard, J O'Sullivan and G J Virgo, Hart Publishing, 2011.

The English legal system

The Discipline of Law, Lord Denning, OUP, 2005.
The English Legal System, Jacqueline Martin, Hodder Education, 2013.
Introduction to the English Legal System 2019-2020, M Partington, OUP, 2019.
The Law Machine, Marcel Berlins and Clare Dyer, Penguin, 2000.
The Law (Theory and Practice in British Politics), J Waldron, Routledge, 1990.
Legal Method, Palgrave Macmillan Law Masters, 2013.
Politics of the Judiciary, J A G Griffith, Fontana, 2010.

The criminal justice system and miscarriages of justice

Blind Justice: Miscarriages of Justice in Twentieth Century Britain, John Eddleston, ABC-CLIO, 2000.
The Juryman's Tale, T Grove, Bloomsbury, 2000.
The Magistrate's Tale, T Grove, Bloomsbury, 2003.
A Matter of Justice, M Zander, OUP, 1989.
Memoirs of a Radical Lawyer, Michael Mansfield, Bloomsbury, 2010.
Miscarriages of Justice: A Review of 'Justice in Error', C Walker and K Starmer (eds), OUP, 1999.
Standing Accused, M McConville et al, OUP, 1994.

Careers

Is Law for You?: Deciding If You Want to Study Law, Christopher Stoakes, Christopher Stoakes Ltd, 2013.
Tomorrow's Lawyers: An Introduction to Your Future, Richard Susskind, OUP, 2013.

Professional journals

The Law Society Gazette
www.lawgazette.co.uk
(Publication for solicitors in England and Wales.)

The Lawyer
www.thelawyer.com
(A website for the legal professions containing news, analysis and comment.)

Legal Action
www.lag.org.uk/magazine
(Monthly magazine of the Legal Action Group, the access to justice charity.)

Legal Business
www.legalbusiness.co.uk
(Monthly magazine for legal professionals.)

Glossary

Administrative law
Law governing the duties and operations of the government and public authorities. A branch of public law, usually studied with constitutional law. One of the core subjects.

Advocate
A person who represents someone in court, arguing the case on their behalf. Barristers are the traditional advocates in the English legal system, but solicitors can also now conduct advocacy in certain cases. Advocates in Scotland are the equivalent of English barristers.

Bar
Collective term for the barristers' profession. Aspiring barristers are 'called to the Bar'. The Bar Council is the representative body for barristers.

Bar Professional Training Course (BPTC)
Vocational training course (of one year if studied full-time) for future barristers, taken after completing a law degree (or non-law degree followed by the Graduate Diploma in Law).

Black-letter law
A well-established law that is no longer in dispute.

Brexit
The withdrawal of the UK from the European Union on 31 January 2020.

Chambers
Offices occupied by a group of barristers. The term also describes a group of barristers practising from a set of chambers.

Civil law
Can mean either:
- private law, as opposed to criminal, administrative, military and church law; or
- the system of law that grew from Roman law as opposed to the English system of common law.

Common law
Law derived from case law: that is, law created by judges and developed on a case-by-case basis, rather than laws enacted by Parliament.

Constitutional law

The rules and practices determining how the state is governed, defining the functions of the different entities within a state – i.e. the executive (government), the legislature (Parliament) and the judiciary, and regulating the relationship between the individual and the state. The constitution of the UK remains largely unwritten, unlike most other states. It is usually studied with administrative law and is one of the core subjects.

Contract law (law of contract)

The law governing contracts, i.e. legally binding agreements (written, verbal or even implied) between two or more parties. Contracts arise as a result of offer and acceptance, although there are several other criteria that must be satisfied for an agreement to be legally binding. One of the core subjects.

Core subjects

The foundation subjects that must be studied during a degree if the degree is a Qualifying Law Degree, which satisfies the academic stage of training requirements to qualify as a lawyer. Currently these are constitutional and administrative law; contract law; tort; criminal law; equity and trusts; European Union law and property/land law.

Criminal law

The law defining those acts that are deemed to be public wrongs and are therefore punishable by the state in criminal proceedings. Most crimes are made up of two elements – the act itself (*actus reus*) and the thinking behind it (*mens rea*), both of which must be proved 'beyond reasonable doubt' in court to establish guilt. Criminal law is one of the core subjects.

Crown Prosecution Service (CPS)

The CPS, headed by the Director of Public Prosecutions (DPP), is responsible for virtually all the criminal proceedings brought by the police in England and Wales.

Delict (law of delict)

The Scottish name for tort.

Equity

The part of English law originally developed by the Lord Chancellor (and later by the Court of Chancery) to do justice where the common law remedies were limited in scope and flexibility and would lead to an unfair result: equity was more concerned with a fair result than the rigid principles of the law. Even now, equity prevails over the rules of law, but the system of equity is no longer as arbitrary as before. The main areas of equity now cover trusts, property and remedies (e.g. injunctions). 'Anton Piller' orders are a more recent example of equity at work. Equity is studied with trusts as one of the core subjects.

European Union law
The laws of the European Union and how they impact on the English legal system. One of the core subjects.

Evidence
Something that proves the existence or non-existence of a fact. The law of evidence refers to the rules governing the presentation of facts and proof in court, including whether or not evidence is admissible.

Graduate Diploma in Law (GDL)
Also known as the Common Professional Examination (CPE). The one-year (full-time) course that non-law graduates can take to satisfy the academic stage of training to become a lawyer. It covers the seven core subjects that would be studied in a qualifying law degree.

Jurisprudence
The philosophy and theories of law.

Jury
Group of (usually 12) people who are selected at random to give a verdict in court.

Land law (property law)
The law of rights in different types of property and how these rights may be established or transferred. It covers subjects such as mortgages, property trusts, landlord and tenant, leases, easements and covenants. One of the core subjects.

Law school
A law department within a university.

Legal Practice Course (LPC)
The vocational one-year (full-time) training course taken after graduation with a qualifying degree, or after taking the GDL, and prior to the two-year training contract, designed for intending solicitors.

Moot
A mock courtroom trial of a hypothetical case organised as an extra-curricular/optional activity to help develop legal skills of presenting a clear, logical argument and questioning a witness.

Obligations (law of obligations)
Another name for the laws of tort and contract.

Private law
The parts of the law that deal with the relationships between individuals that are of no direct concern to the state. It includes property law, trusts, contract, tort and family law.

Property law
See land law.

Public law

Law dealing with the constitution and functions of the organs of government, the relationship between individuals and the state and the relationships between individuals that are of direct concern to the state. It includes constitutional law, administrative law, tax law and criminal law.

Pupillage

The final stage of training to become a barrister, involving shadowing a qualified barrister for two six-month periods.

Qualified Lawyers Transfer Scheme (QLTS)

A series of assessments set by Kaplan to allow qualified lawyers from Solicitors Regulation Authority recognised jurisdictions or barristers who have qualified in England and Wales to practise as solicitors in England and Wales.

Solicitors Qualifying Examination (SQE)

A series of assessments set by Kaplan that must be passed by all aspiring solicitors after 2021 in order to qualify. This will ultimately replace GDLs and the LPC.

Statute

A law passed by Parliament.

Statute book

All statutes that are currently in force.

Tort

A wrongful act or omission for which the person who has been wronged can obtain damages (i.e. compensation) in a civil court. The definition does not include breaches of contract. Most torts involve personal injury or damage to property caused by negligence. Other torts are defamation, nuisance, etc. The law of tort is one of the core subjects.

Training contract

The two-year period of on-the-job training undertaken by all future solicitors after the LPC in order to complete the vocational stage of training.

Trusts

A legal arrangement whereby one or more trustees hold property for the benefit of one or more beneficiaries. The property is said to be held 'on trust'. Studied with equity as one of the core subjects.